SERGEANT JOE AND
ON MOTHER BROWN'S DOORSTEP

Also by Mary Jane Staples

MARY JANE STAPLES

SERGEANT JOE AND
ON MOTHER BROWN'S DOORSTEP

LONDON   NEW YORK   SYDNEY   TORONTO

This omnibus edition published 1992
by BCA
by arrangement with Bantam Press Ltd.

Sergeant Joe © 1992 Mary Jane Staples
On Mother Brown's Doorstep © 1992 Mary Jane Staples

CN 6996

Printed in England by Clays Ltd, St Ives plc

Contents

SERGEANT JOE

CHAPTER ONE

The thick yellow fog, rolling up from the river, blanketed London, blotting out its parks, its streets and its buildings. The capital of the Empire lay as mute as a suffocated corpse wrapped in an impenetrable shroud. The fog smothered every street lamp, reducing each light to a vague blur, and it made shapeless ghosts of every human being abroad. No man could see another unless they blundered into each other. Horse-drawn traffic had given up long ago. So had belching omnibuses and electric trams.

Wisely, old men sat by their firesides and dreamt of the sunshine of their yesterdays, while the smoke from their coal fires issued from their chimneys to thicken the fog. In the East End, mothers brought their broods in off the streets and bolted their doors, for on a night like this the Ripper's ghost itself might be lurking outside. Fancy women sought the cosy comfort of pubs, from where men looked out into the fog, ordered another glass of ale and stayed where they were for the time being. The doxies rubbed elbows invitingly with them.

It was March, 1911, the year that was to see a royal unveiling of the Queen Victoria Memorial and the coronation of King George V and Queen Mary.

In a house in Newington Butts, Walworth, ex-Sergeant Joe Foster was actually preparing to brave the fog. Late of the 2nd Dragoon Guards, known as the Queen's Bays, he limped from his bedroom to his living-room on the first floor. He limped because a wounded knee-cap had left the joint permanently stiff. It had also earned him his discharge at the age of twenty-seven. He was twenty-nine now, a stalwart veteran of the Boer War and campaigns in India, with the long legs and handsome dark brown moustache of a dragoon.

A navy blue jersey and trousers clothed him. He picked his jacket off the back of his fireside armchair and stood for a moment watching the burning coals of the compact stove, which had an oven to it. Twelve-year-old Linda Beavis, daughter of his landlady, came running up the stairs and showed herself at his open door. Her red hair glinted in the light of the gas mantle.

'Sergeant Joe, can I shine yer shoes for a penny? Well, I don't mind an 'a'penny, if yer like, only I can do more spit for a penny.'

'Come in, Carrots,' he said. Every boy or girl who had red hair was called either Carrots or Ginger in Walworth. He smiled as she skipped in, her white belted pinafore frock with a short skirt worn over a calf-length frock of dark grey. Her black woollen stockings were slightly wrinkled, and a button was loose on one of her ankle boots. Her round face was a little smudged, and her bright eyes regarded him hopefully. 'Right, a penny or a ha'penny, is it? Let's see now, stand to attention, Private Carrots.'

Linda did her best, although with a bit of a giggle.

'Is that all right, Sergeant Joe?' she asked. Nearly everyone called him that, because he'd been a sergeant in the Army, and because he had square shoulders, a straight back and a military moustache. The wind, the sand and the sun of the African deserts had burned him to a deep brown, and he still looked tanned. 'Is me feet doin' it proper?'

'I'd say so,' said Sergeant Joe. 'Yes, so I would. Not bad at all, Private Carrots. In return for which, a penny it is for a shoe-shine. Wait a moment, though, let's have a look at your spit.'

'I fink I've got lots of really good spit,' said Linda. She

10

rolled some around, then opened her mouth and showed him her wet pink tongue.

'Spit passed A1,' said Sergeant Joe. 'Get to work, little lady, I'll be going out in five minutes.'

'Crikey, in the fog?' said Linda.

'I'll fight it,' he said, and she got to work. She knew where everything was. Sergeant Joe watched her with good humour written all over him. He liked kids. He liked his landlady's kids and he liked all the other kids who ran around the streets adjacent the Elephant and Castle. Good kids, saucy kids, adventurous kids, ragamuffins, scally-wags and young varmints, they all meant the country was alive and well. They'd grow up to be the backbone of old England. Never mind that their families were poor, that the multitude of pawnshops in Southwark were laden with family articles waiting to be redeemed. The people were tough. Some went to the wall by way of drink, but the majority fought the good fight, and if some cheated a bit or thieved a bit, it was the law that rebuked them, not their neighbours. London's cockneys were cynical and earthy in all they said about their Government and their politicians, but what kept them going year in and year out was neighbourliness and close family union. Sergeant Joe, making what he could of his own life, considered the taking ways of some cockneys simply an extension of their determination not to let conditions beat them. He was Chatham-born himself, but he liked cockney London, even if he did not intend to spend all his years in lodgings there. Already he had useful savings.

Young Linda, seated on the fireside rug, treated one polished shoe to more spit, then rubbed vigorously with a soft leather cloth. She regarded the resultant shine proudly.

'I done an 'a'porth, Sergeant Joe,' she said.

'Right, top of the class,' he said. Up came his landlady, fat and jolly Mrs Bessie Beavis, her grey blouse putting up its usual doughty fight to contain her bosom, and her long

11

black skirt sweeping the floor. She was as rosy-faced as a farmer's wife. She'd seen a farm once, and she'd seen its cows too. She'd seen them lumbering towards her, and she'd picked up her skirts and fled shrieking. Big as elephants they were, she told her mum, and decided she'd stick to London for ever.

Joe greeted her arrival with a smile.

'Evening, Bessie,' he said.

'And 'ow's yerself, Sergeant Joe? I've come up to see if that gel of mine's makin' a nuisance of 'erself. What's she doin' down there?'

'Spitting and polishing,' said Joe.

'Oh, doin' one of 'er shoe-shine jobs, is she?' said Mrs Beavis fondly. 'Still, don't let 'er be a nuisance, nor come up askin' for pennies.'

'No nuisance, Bessie,' said Joe. 'She's a first-class shoe-shiner, aren't you, Carrots? Good clean spit as well. And A1 as a private.'

'Yes, and I can stand to attention proper, can't I, Sergeant Joe?' said Linda, busy on the second shoe.

Mrs Beavis laughed, and her jolly bosom went up and down.

'Sergeant Joe, you'll 'ave us all in the Army one day,' she said.

'Need an army, Bessie,' he said. He was pretty certain that in a few years' time a war would be on its way. Germany had been rattling its sabre for ages, and its bombastic Emperor liked the sound. He'd be over later this year to attend the unveiling of the memorial to his late grandmother, Queen Victoria. He'd be bound to show off his flashiest uniforms and to drop large-sized hints about the German Army being the most powerful in the world. One day his generals would try to persuade him to let their hordes go into action. Pity that Queen Victoria wasn't still alive, she'd chop his head off. She'd been the only person able to put Kaiser Bill in his place.

'Look, I done 'em both now, Sergeant Joe,' said Linda, holding up the shoes for his inspection. 'Are they shiny enough?'

'Top of the class again, Private Carrots. Right, on your feet.' Up came Linda from the rug. 'Stand at ease. Good. Hold out your hand.' Linda held out a slightly grubby pink palm. A penny dropped into it, and her happy fingers closed around the copper coin. 'Right, well done. Dismiss.'

'Can't I stay a bit till me cocoa?' asked Linda.

'Not tonight, Josephine.'

'Who's Josephine? She ain't me,' said Linda.

'Just as well, young copperknob, or Napoleon would be after you. Point is, I'm going out, remember?'

'Oh, 'elp,' Mum, 'e's goin' out in all that fog,' said Linda.

'I don't know you should be doin' that, Sergeant Joe,' said Mrs Beavis, 'Charlie says you can't see yer own nose even.' Charlie was her husband. ''E says 'e don't know 'ow 'e managed to get 'ome from 'is work, 'e says 'e first finished up in Yard Row, in Mrs Scott's 'ouse.'

'Lucky old Charlie,' said Joe, putting his jacket on.

'Trust 'im to land up on a widow woman's doorstep,' said Mrs Beavis, and laughed again. 'Now don't you go gettin' yerself lost like 'e did; that widow woman might take it into her 'ead to keep you for good.'

'Oh, lor',' breathed Linda, 'I just 'ope Jesus looks after yer, Sergeant Joe, it 'ud be 'orrible for yer to be kept by Mrs Scott. Me mum wouldn't let none of us go out in a fog as fick as this, nor me dad, neither. 'E'd give us a beltin'. Not me, though, 'e don't take 'is belt to me, 'e says I'm 'is little plum duff wiv jam on. I likes me dad, don't you, Sergeant Joe?'

'I've got likings and mislikings,' said Joe, pulling his blue peaked cap on, 'and your dad is one of my likings. So's your mum. And so are you, Private Plum Duff with jam on.'

Linda giggled, her mum smiled. They went down the stairs with Sergeant Joe. In his cap and overcoat he looked well equipped to brave the wintry fog. The gaslit passage itself seemed misty with creeping yellow. Mrs Beavis returned to her warm kitchen. Linda saw Sergeant Joe to the door.

'Yer won't get lorst, will yer?' she said anxiously, not liking the thought of the widow woman pulling him into her house and keeping him.

'Wouldn't do to get myself lost, Carrots,' he said. 'Right, go and show yourself to your dad, we don't want him thinking you've disappeared up my chimney.'

Linda giggled again and skipped away to the kitchen. The front door closed behind Sergeant Joe and he went limping on his way through the thick fog of the March evening. He was carrying an old carpet-bag.

CHAPTER TWO

'There you are, then, that's your new commission, my
friend,' said Mr George Singleton, portly form comfortably ensconced in a leather-padded wall seat. Sergeant Joe
sat next to him. They were in Hennessey's in the Strand
and tucked into a corner. Their conversation was dis-
creetly quiet. The place, with its bright gas lamps, shut
out the fog. Sergeant Joe tucked papers into cardboard
folders and put the folders into his carpet-bag, together
with a square-shaped bottle of special ink. 'Lord Byron, of
course, has a romantic appeal.'

'Byron it is,' said Sergeant Joe.

'And Shelley. And their ladies.' Mr Singleton chuckled.
'All sailing on a sea of Italian misadventures.'

'End of Shelley, poor devil.'

'You've read some of his poetry?' enquired Mr Singleton, sipping his whisky.

'None.'

'Byron's?'

'None. Not my style, poetry.'

'Yet you have your own artistic gift.'

'Is that what you call it?' Sergeant Joe smiled. 'Most
people would say it's a gift for forgery.'

Mr Singleton looked pained. Another sip of whisky
cleared his brow and restored his prevailing expression of
geniality. He was, outwardly, a happy friend to the whole
world.

'Come, Sergeant, never think the copying of handwriting equates with the forging of banknotes. A talent
that results in giving exquisite pleasure to collectors of
memorabilia is to be admired, not deprecated.'

15

'It's still forgery,' said Sergeant Joe, although it amused him rather than troubled him, this gainful exercise of his talents. His cockney friends would have called it honest endeavour in a dishonest world. They were broadminded. So was he. A moderate scholar at his Chatham school, he had nevertheless amazed his teachers by his ability to write copperplate script at the age of eleven. At fourteen he found he could also copy perfectly any handwriting placed in front of him. But he had always had a wish to join the Army, and at sixteen he enlisted as a drummer boy. That led to Africa and to Kitchener's campaigns. And to a wounded knee-cap.

He had met Mr George Singleton two years ago in Petticoat Lane, at a stall that sold knick-knacks, bits and pieces, and other oddments that appealed to people with a passion for collecting things, particularly things that had belonged – or might have belonged – to a figure of history. A hat, a locket, a snippet of hair curled inside a little velvet-lined comfit box, an ornament, a bill, a letter. Yes, a letter was always prized. Every collector prized letters above all. Except that one had reservations about what was genuine on a Petticoat Lane stall. That was where Mr Singleton came in. He had a shop in Charing Cross Road. He sold second-hand books and rare first editions. He could never get enough of the latter. He could get items that had once been owned by this author or that author, and there was a market for these, particularly for letters. He and Sergeant Joe, having met in Petticoat Lane and having talked, repaired to a pub and had a long and very friendly conversation. They both had principles. They could both stretch them.

Mr Singleton knew other talented people, among them an extremely obliging fellow who could treat a sheet of notepaper to give it the feel and appearance of age, and could also produce ink of a quality used in the past. Could Sergeant Joe use a quill pen? 'Don't make me laugh,' said Sergeant Joe. 'Apologies, my dear fellow,' said Mr Singleton, 'momentarily I failed to appreciate I was talking to an artist.'

The outcome of the conversation was another meeting three days later. A third followed after two more days, when Sergeant Joe visited Mr Singleton in his shop in Charing Cross Road and produced two letters ostensibly written by the Duke of Wellington on the eve of Waterloo. To ladies of his acquaintance. Mr Singleton sold them for two pounds each. He split the proceeds with Sergeant Joe, down the middle. That to Sergeant Joe was money for old rope.

Subsequently, such authors as the Brontë sisters, Jane Austen, Oliver Goldsmith, Jonathan Swift and others of great renown were the apparent signatories of letters placed in the care of Mr Singleton and sold by him by way of his bookshop or through the hands of trusted business friends who ran seemingly dowdy or seedy little second-hand enterprises in shops dark and dusty. It was in such shops, however, that questing collectors often seized upon priceless memorabilia. And there was also the Petticoat Lane stall and its owner, a shrewd East End cockney who knew Mr Singleton well. There began to appear on his stall the occasional letter, its edges artfully worn, its folds artfully aged. Sometimes there was even an envelope, particularly when it was plain from the contents of the letter that it had been delivered by hand. Or so it appeared. Mr Singleton advised Sergeant Joe at the beginning to be careful about envelopes. They were relatively recent.

'You should not speak too bluntly of forgery, my dear fellow,' said Mr Singleton, delicately imbibing more whisky. 'You are an artist, as I have said many times. A genius even. Your efforts are of a harmless kind. They hurt no-one. They merely induce wealthy collectors to dip into their pockets. If they mistake the origin of a letter of

17

yours, it's neither your fault nor mine. I never give guarantees. If what I say leads a buyer to believe he's acquiring an original, that, I assure you, is mainly because it's what he wishes to believe.'

'One day,' said Sergeant Joe, 'one of them will come back with proof that you've sold him a forgery.'

'I shall defend myself with all the eloquence at my command,' said Mr Singleton unworriedly. 'Nor would I ever mention your name.'

'Wouldn't you?'

'Sergeant, I like you too much.'

'Fetch up there, George.'

'It's true, my friend. You are the last one I'd throw from a lifeboat.'

Sergeant Joe laughed. It was a deep and pleasant sound. It made Mr Singleton smile. His smile gave a beam to his plump face, and he looked like Mr Pickwick in the flesh.

'I'll give this business one more year,' said Sergeant Joe. 'I'd be a fool, and so would you, to risk longer.'

'Ah, I must mention that the sun is shining,' said Mr Singleton. 'Forget the fog. Think of Italy, for that is where the many letters you are about to produce will end up. Italian romanticists have a great fondness for Byron and Shelley. Allowing for commission and certain expenses, the sales in Italy will modestly enrich us. And the risks you have in mind will not exist there. Nor shall I stay longer than I need.'

'You're taking the letters yourself?' Sergeant Joe regarded his business partner with gravity. But he knew his man. There was never a note of distrust in any of their transactions. 'Understood.'

'Trust me.'

'If I didn't, I'd come to Italy with you. Now I'll be on my way. I've got another walk to make through the fog. Back home.' Sergeant Joe finished his warming whisky,

18

shook hands with Mr Singleton, took hold of his carpet-bag, and limped out of the cosy, club-like atmosphere of Hennessey's.

A good fellow, a fine soldier, thought Mr Singleton. And an artist to boot.

Sergeant Joe paused for a moment on the pavement. He turned up his coat collar and gave his eyes time to adjust to the thickness of the night fog. The Strand was buried in rolling dirty-yellow clouds. Traffic had long left the streets. Hansom cabs had returned to their mews. All sound was suffocated, and the light from street lamps was all but smothered. However, he began his walk back to Newington Butts. It took him over Waterloo Bridge. Faintly he heard the sound of a hooting tug. The fog lay upon the river and swirled over the bridge. He seemed alone in one of London's infamous pea-soupers. He passed no-one. He was silent in his limping walk, his footwear rubber-soled. He thought about hob-nailed Army boots and the crisp sounds of infantrymen drilling on the square. It reminded him of the vigorousness of Army life. But he had not missed it as much as he'd thought he might. He had realized early on that social life in the Army was painfully restricted, especially when serving abroad. As a civilian, his horizons were far broader. On the other hand, more than a few civilians were sloppy and needed to smarten up a bit. Most women had straighter backs than most men. Well, women were carriers. They carried their offspring and they carried shopping bags. Carriers always walked upright. Men who walked with their hands in their pockets slouched along. Not good, that. Made them look old before their time.

A lone horse and cart approached, coming at a snail's pace from the direction of the Elephant and Castle. It was invisible in the fog except for the faint blur of its lamp. But he heard its turning wheels and the slow clop of the horse. What a night. He entered London Road, feeling his way

19

by keeping close to buildings on his right. Midway down, the muffled sounds of running feet suddenly reached his ears. Whoever it was had to be desperate to be running through fog as thick as this. A street lamp threw faint light and out of it came a young woman. She ran straight into him. The collision staggered her and she fell. A little gasp of pain escaped her, then some hissed words. He made sense of none of them, but thought she was probably swearing at him.

He dropped his carpet-bag, stooped and helped her to her feet. She winced, clutched him for support as she eased her right foot off the ground, and a shabby handbag touched his chest.

'Fetch up there,' he said, 'what's your hurry on a night like this?'

She drew a breath.

'They're after me – quick, 'elp me, won't yer?' she begged in a whisper.

He heard other footsteps then, and the shouting voice of a man.

'Stop! We'll get yer, yer thievin' 'aybag!'

Joe's thoughts flashed. What was one more thief in Southwark, and what was there for some of its people except snatching and pickpocketing? Even more, what was there for some of its women except that or selling themselves?

A man, panting and cursing, emerged at a run from the small patch of light. He glimpsed two figures and pulled up. He laid a fast hand on the woman's wrist and twisted her arm.

'Gotcher!'

'Hold your horses,' said Joe, 'the lady's with me.'

The man, burly, and with a flat cap on his head, said, 'That she ain't, mister, and I ain't lettin' go of 'er. Shove off.'

Another man arrived. He wore a trim bowler hat and an

20

overcoat. The overcoat was unbuttoned. He said nothing for the moment. He was breathing hard, and Joe thought he was even sweating. Which meant he was either out of condition or in a state of agitation.

He spoke then. To the young woman.

'So,' he said. Just that.

'So nothing,' said Joe, 'she's with me.'

'So's me Aunt Fanny,' said the burly man. 'Listen, cock, suppose you mind yer own bleedin' business, eh? This thievin' cow's snaffled this 'ere gent's wallet. Didn't I see 'er with me own eyes, down in the Rockingham?' The Rockingham was a public house by the Elephant and Castle. 'Didn't I offer to go after 'er on be'alf of the gent? And now I got 'er, ain't I?'

'Oh, yer rotten liar,' breathed the young woman, a shabby black straw hat on her head, 'I never snaffled no gent's wallet in all me born days.'

'Not so,' said the bowler-hatted gentleman, who also sported a neat black beard. 'You have taken mine.' His English was accented. 'You are one filthy thief. Give.' He put out a gloved hand. 'Give it back.'

'Me?' protested the young woman. ''Ow can I when I ain't got it? I just got an 'urt foot, that's all.'

'Divvy up, yer bitch,' said the burly man, 'or yer'll 'urt all over. I got a reward comin' from this gent for coppin' yer. So let's 'ave 'is wallet, an' quick.'

'I ain't got it, I tell yer!'

'A lie,' said the foreign gentleman. He looked at Sergeant Joe. 'You are her accomplice, I think.'

'I'm just standing here listening,' said Joe.

'Search her,' said the gentleman to the bruiser. 'Strike her if she resists.'

'Don't like the sound of that, mister,' said Joe. 'Don't advise it, either.'

'You are not the one who has been robbed,' said the gentleman. 'Search her,' he repeated to the bruiser.

''Ere, no yer don't,' said the young woman, suffering the pain of a wrenched ankle. 'No-one's goin' to search me, it ain't decent, I'm a respectable girl and nor ain't I a thief – oh!' She gasped as the bruiser's hand struck her mouth.

'Pity you did that,' said Joe, and put the bruiser on his back with an iron right-hander to his jaw. 'Can't have it. Don't like it. It's uncivilized. And what's more, I'm against it.'

'Stand back.' The bearded gentleman was steely. The pervading fog enclosed the group, and the world outside seemed at a silent standstill. Not a single vehicle moved on the road, nor a footstep. 'Stand back, I command you.' For all that they were wrapped in fog, the revolver that had appeared in a gloved hand was all too visible to Sergeant Joe. It was pointed at his stomach. 'Believe me, I will shoot you if you move again, and I will then have this filthy woman carried away. You understand?'

'I understand all right,' said Joe, 'but I still don't like it.'

'Oh, me dear gawd,' gasped the young woman, 'I've never seen the like of that, it's a gun.'

'Take your clothes off and empty your handbag,' said the gentleman, who was no gentleman.

'Take me clothes off? 'Ere, what d'yer think I am?'

'A thief. You have my wallet. Do as I say.'

Sergeant Joe thought the man ferociously determined. The bruiser was back on his feet, shaking his head dizzily.

'I bleedin' owe you for that one,' he growled at Joe.

'Not now,' rapped the icily ferocious man. 'Search that filthy woman. Her handbag first, then her clothes. Strip her if necessary.' His cold rage thickened his accent, but the revolver in his hand remained steady. Joe watched him. The bruiser went to work, wrenching the young woman's handbag from her. He opened it and plunged his hand in.

'Oh, yer swine,' breathed the young woman as he flung the handbag to the ground. He stooped. Her skirts tossed and swirled. She uttered gasps and protests. And she winced again.

'Bleedin' 'ell,' growled the searching bruiser, 'where's she put it?'

'Break her arm. She will tell us where it is then, or her other arm will be broken.'

''Ere, 'old on, guv,' said the bruiser, 'I dunno I go along with that. It ain't too clever, yer know, breakin' 'er arms on account of a wallet. A bleedin' good 'iding, that'll make her divvy up.'

'Strip her.'

'I'll scream the 'ouses down!' shouted the young woman.

'And I'll lose my temper,' said Joe.

'Shut up!' hissed the bearded man, and pushed the barrel of the revolver hard into Joe's stomach. The fog was an impenetrable yellow wall around them, and it favoured the opposition.

''Ere, guv, what's that?' asked the bruiser. He had spotted the carpet-bag. It was still on the pavement, close to Sergeant Joe's left foot, and faintly visible. ''Ere, that's where yer wallet is, I'll lay to it. That's where she put it.'

'Search it.'

'Now yer talkin'. We don't want no bleedin' bullets flyin' about, guv, if yer don't mind, it'll bring the rozzers down on us like a ton of bricks, even in this fog. I brought yer the letter, and I offered to catch this thievin' 'aybag for yer, but I ain't partial to firearms—'

'Quiet, you fool. Earn your twenty pounds. Search that bag.'

Twenty pounds? Sergeant Joe silently whistled. He was watching the man with the revolver, watching and waiting. His thoughts took a new turn. Twenty pounds was a small fortune to most cockneys. The missing wallet must be stuffed with banknotes.

The bruiser took up the carpet-bag, at which point every ear caught the sounds of slow, measured footsteps and a man's voice. The bruiser, opening the bag, jerked his head up. He swung round.

'Guv, it's the bleedin' rozzers on their beat!' he whispered.

'What? What?'

'Police, guv, on their beat – I'm off.'

'Give me that bag!' hissed Blackbeard, but Sergeant Joe was quicker by far. He wrenched the bag from the bruiser. An obscene oath in a foreign language escaped Blackbeard's furious lips. Then he was gone, with the bruiser, back the way he had come.

Did it on himself, thought Joe. Could have stayed and reported the theft of his wallet to the police if he hadn't produced that revolver. The police might have nicked the young woman. They'd have certainly nicked him.

They loomed up, two uniformed constables. Since the murderous excursions of Jack the Ripper in London's East End some years ago, the patrolling of streets on both sides of the river had been strictly enforced, particularly on foggy nights.

The constables halted. The young woman had picked up her handbag, but hadn't moved apart from that. Her right ankle wouldn't let her.

'Evening,' said Joe, the carpet-bag out of sight behind him.

''Ello, ain't it an 'orrible night?' said the young woman.

'Not the kind to hang about in,' said one constable.

'What're you up to, anyway?' asked the second.

'Up to? 'Ere, you bein' cheeky to a respectable girl?'

'Highly respectable,' said Joe.

'Looks like it,' said the first constable.

'Prime case of solicitin', if you ask me,' said the second.

'Not by a long shot,' said Joe.

'Oh, I never been more insulted,' said the young woman. ''E's me best friend.'

'Well, get your best friend to take you home,' said the first constable, 'or we might have to take you down to the station for the good of your health.'

''Ere, that ain't funny, yer know,' said the young woman.

'Serious, I'd say,' said the second constable, but they both had grins on their faces as they resumed their beat.

'You're well out of that,' said Joe to the young woman.

'Don't I know it? You've been a real sport, mister, standin' up for me like you did, and fetchin' that brute a lovely wallop. Only what am I goin' to do now? Me ankle hurts every time I put me foot to the ground. I'm near crippled. You can chuck me in the river, if you like, for all the good I am to meself. It ain't far.'

'I'm not keen on that idea,' said Joe.

'All right, I'll chuck meself in,' she said.

'Don't like that, either,' said Joe. 'Where'd you live?'

'Oh, it's all right, I—' She stopped and did her best to get a really good look at him through the fog. She did a bit of thinking. 'Well, I don't like sayin' so, mister, but I don't even 'ave the price of a night's lodging. I got thrown out of me previous room this morning, on account of owings.'

'Hard luck,' said Joe. 'Well, we can't leave you to the wolves. Hold my bag.' He placed it in her arms and she clutched it to her bosom, with her handbag, the toe of her right foot gingerly touching ground. He stooped and lifted her. She gasped.

'Here, excuse me, what d'you think you're doin'?' she demanded, as he began to walk.

'I'm carrying you,' he said.

'I didn't say you could – crikey, what a liberty. You're takin' advantage just because I'm near crippled. Where you takin' me to?'

'My lodgings. Then I'll have a look at your ankle.' He peered into the fog, proceeding slowly with his warm-bodied burden. 'Then I'll find a bed for you.'

'Whose bed?'

'Mine, probably.'

'Here, what d'you think I am? You're not draggin' me into your bed, I'll scream the place down.'

'Don't get funny ideas,' said Joe.

'Me? I like that. I'm respectable, I am. Did you see that rotten perisher, searchin' me clothes? I nearly died of blushin' all over.'

'Report on what happened to the wallet,' said Joe, thinking he needed to watch out in case Blackbeard and the bruiser were still around.

'What wallet?' she asked.

'The wallet. What did you do with it?'

'That's it, go on, insult me.'

'Was there any money in it, or haven't you looked yet?'

'Mister, you're givin' me a hard time, you are, and just when I'm thinking I've met a real gent for a change. Mind, I hardly know how to get a proper look at you in all this fog.' But snug in his arms and very close to him, she could at least see his looks weren't villainous. She sighed. 'I'm honest but unlucky, mister.'

'Are you?' said Joe. The dark bulk of buildings on his right gave way to emptiness, and he knew he'd reached Princess Street. He came to a stop to feel for the kerb. Finding it, he crossed the entrance to the street and then he was on the pavement again, with buildings again his guide. The fog was dense, a killer to old people with bronchitis.

'Mister, are you a gent?'

'Can't answer a question like that,' said Joe, 'can't make sense of it.'

'No, but you've got a gent's moustache, I can see that,'

26

she said. 'Here, d'you 'ave a funny ankle too? Only you're limpin', ain't you?'

'Stiff knee,' he said, watching for obstacles he might only know about by walking into them. He reached the Elephant and Castle, a busy junction by night as well as by day, but it was a silent yellow emptiness tonight. The time was past ten, kids were wrapped up in their beds, and parents were probably about to retire themselves. Most mums and dads in Walworth had to get up early.

He turned right into Newington Butts, the young woman no great weight in his arms, although he was sure she wasn't skinny.

'You sure I'm not too much for you, mister?' she asked. 'I mean, your limp and all.'

'Exercise is good for it,' he said, the familiarity of the Butts lost in the fog and making it necessary for him to still proceed carefully. He kept listening for sounds that would tell him Blackbeard and his henchman were in the vicinity. 'I'll beat my stiff knee one day. One day it'll start bending again. If not, I'll take a hammer to it.'

'Don't do that, mister, I begs you,' she said. 'It'll give you an 'orrible pain and do your knee in for good.'

'We'll see,' said Joe. There was not far to go now. But he thought then that there was someone behind him, he thought for a moment that he heard footsteps. He stopped and listened. The young woman peered at him from under the brim of her ancient straw hat. Hearing nothing, he went on. Someone, perhaps, had turned into a house.

'What did you stop for?' she asked.

'I thought someone was coming up behind us.'

'Fog plays funny tricks, mister, don't you think so? It makes you feel old Nick is about. Where'd you hurt your knee?'

'Playing soldiers,' said Joe.

'Help, 'ave you been in a war?' she asked.

'Not the same kind you have,' said Joe.

27

'Here, when we get to your lodgings, you ain't really going to take advantage of me, are you?' she asked.

'Don't fancy that,' said Joe. 'Wait till you've been tidied up. Then we'll see what you look like.'

'What a sauce,' she said. 'I ain't going to be tidied up and looked at so's you can make up your mind about fancying me. Oh, help, me blood keeps running cold about that bloke havin' a gun. Him and his wallet, what a carry-on.'

The wallet must have been fat, thought Joe. The bruiser wouldn't have been promised a reward of twenty quid otherwise. And Blackbeard wouldn't have threatened to start shooting.

'Here we are,' he said, stopping outside the right house. 'Pull the latchcord for me, would you?'

'What?' she said.

'The latchcord.'

'Oh, lor',' she said, 'it's like come into me parlour, said the spider to the fly.' She leaned in his arms, groped for the latchcord dangling from the letter-box, and pulled it. The door opened and he carried her in. He closed the door with the heel of his right foot. 'Oh, help,' she said in the lamplit passage.

After all, she didn't know him, and a fate worse than death might just be awaiting her.

CHAPTER THREE

As soon as he closed the door, Joe knew the Beavises were all in bed. There were no sounds or vibrations. Mr and Mrs Beavis, their three daughters and two sons were all larger than life, except for young Linda. They could make the house shake when they were in full flow, the vibrations spreading from the kitchen. They attacked life, they didn't sit quietly around waiting for it to flatten them. It would have a job flattening that boisterous family, thought Joe as he carried the young woman through the passage and up the flight of stairs to the first floor. He had no option now but to speak to his landlady in the morning about letting this homeless female have his bed for the night.

He set her down on the landing and she stood on one foot, using the wall for support while he opened his living-room door. He went in, struck a match and applied the flame to the gas mantle. It sprang into bright white light and he covered it with its glass globe. He returned to the young woman and carried her in, sitting her down in the fireside armchair. If her ankle was painful, she wasn't making a fuss about it. That was in her favour, and if she did happen to be a female tea leaf, well, he was the last person entitled to throw stones. He relieved her of the carpet-bag, and she looked around, her eyes quick and observant. The fire in the compact range was burning slowly, and the room was warm and cosy. On the hob plate stood an iron kettle. A square-topped mahogany table was covered with green baize, and there were two upright chairs, a small dresser, a larder and a tallboy. On the tallboy was an inkstand with four wells, a squat bottle of

29

ink in each. Nibbed pens lay in the groove. Old velvet curtains of dark red draped the window.

Joe took a good look at the young woman. What a mess. Her black straw hat, secured by a beaded hatpin, had seen its best days long ago. So had her dark blue jacket, white blouse and black skirt. Over the jacket she wore the inveterate shawl of cockney women. But at least she didn't look starving or thin. Nor could he say she had no colour and no bosom to speak of. On the other hand, her grey eyes were big, and that was usually a sign of hunger. But she had quite good looks, and beneath her hat a loop of luxuriant dark auburn hair was showing.

'All right,' she said, making a face at him, 'I know I ain't much to look at, but I've had some blokes fancy me.'

'Have I said something, then?' he asked, taking off his cap and overcoat and hanging them on the door peg.

'No, you've just been lookin',' she said. 'Lookin' and saying nothing, well, a girl knows what that means. It's not fair.'

'What isn't?' he asked, lifting the kettle, removing the hob plate and putting the kettle in its place. He raked the fire with a poker, pulled out the damper, and the fire began to glow. 'What isn't fair?'

'Being looked at by a bloke that's saying nothing.'

'What's not fair about that?'

'It's the way you're lookin',' she said. 'Can I help it if I ain't an oil painting? It's bein' poor and 'omeless that does it. Mister, I suppose you wouldn't have a bite of food to spare, would you?'

'I'll find you something, but let's look at your ankle first,' said Joe. She regarded him suspiciously, but couldn't find anything shifty about him. His eyes were frank, his features regular and his expression quite friendly. His thick moustache, neatly trimmed, gave him a handsome look. 'Sit on the table,' he said, 'and oblige me by not being sorry for yourself.'

'Mister, I ain't complaining about me lot, honest, I'm just saying, that's all. All right, I'll sit on the table, you've been good to me, savin' me from those blokes that came after me for nothing.' She got up. 'Could you believe your eyes when you saw that gun? Mad, that's what he was – oh—' Her ankle gave way as she moved, shooting pain, and he caught her as she fainted. He carried her to the bedroom then, and in the darkness placed her gently down on the bed. He lit the gas mantle and light beamed. He looked down at her. An empty stomach and the pain of her ankle had been too much for her. Further, the thug had been rough with her. It couldn't be helped if she was a pickpocket. Something had to be done for her.

He leaned over her, removed her cheap hatpin and her old straw hat. A little grin parted his mouth. There was the wallet. Clever girl. She had hidden it under her hat, in her wealth of hair. But it was out now. It was made of expensive brown leather, but it wasn't fat, it was thin. He opened it. All it contained were four white English banknotes and an envelope. The banknotes were fivers. Four amounted to twenty quid, the sum offered to the bruiser. Odd, that. If Blackbeard was carrying only that amount, what was the point of offering it all? Why so much fury? Why the threat to use his revolver? Didn't make sense. Unless it wasn't the money, but the envelope, which obviously contained a letter.

There was no name on it. He mused over it, thinking about Blackbeard's sweat and his icy rage. It had to be the letter that was important. He'd forfeited the money in advance.

Joe smiled and slipped the letter into his pocket. He placed the wallet on the bedside table. The young woman opened her eyes and stared vaguely up at him, her hair a spilling mass of deep auburn.

'There you are,' he said, 'hold on a tick.' He disappeared. She lay frowning until her mind cleared. Then she sat up. Galahad reappeared, with a glass containing a small amount of brandy. 'Drink this,' he said, 'it'll give you a lift.'

'I fainted,' she said, looking disgusted with herself. 'I've never fainted before. Here, what's in the glass?'

'Brandy,' said Joe.

'Mister, don't you try gettin' me one over the eight. Not a drop of gin or brandy ever touched me lips in all me born days. I ain't goin' to let it now, either; I ain't goin' to be taken advantage of.'

'Stop fussing,' said Joe, 'I don't go in for that sort of thing. Come on, drink it, all at one go.'

She took the glass. She rolled her eyes at him, put the glass to her lips and drank the brandy, a small nip. She didn't cough. It all went down and it immediately flooded her with warmth.

'Help,' she breathed, 'it's burning me alive.'

'Good,' said Joe.

'What's good about burning alive?' she said. 'Why couldn't you give me a nice drop of port?'

'Don't have any,' said Joe. 'Right, don't let's take all night seeing to your ankle. I'll get you some food in a few minutes, but first let's have your shoe and stocking off.'

'Oh, all right.' She put the glass back into his hand, fumbled under her skirts and pushed a black lisle stocking down over her right leg. He placed the glass on the bedside table, leaned over her and unbuttoned her weary-looking ankle-boot. He removed it quite gently and drew her stocking off. Her foot was clean. He inspected her ankle. It was swollen and tinted with blue. He hoped that didn't mean a fracture. Gently again, he turned her foot. She winced.

'Painful?' he asked.

'Well, hurtful, like.'

'Yell if this is really painful,' he said, and slowly turned her foot the other way. She didn't yell, she just winced again. 'No sharp pain?' he asked.

'No, it just aches a lot,' she said. 'Hurtfully, like.'

'Well, we've got a sprain,' said Joe.

'Oh, we 'ave, 'ave we?' she said with typical cockney pertness. 'I thought it was just me.'

He gave her a smile then, a kind of comradely one, as if her sprain and his stiff knee meant they had something in common.

'Hold on,' he said, and disappeared again. He returned with a basin of cold water, a flannel and a towel. He placed the towel on the bed under her bare foot. He dipped the flannel in the water and bathed the swollen joint not once but many times, leaving the flannel wrapped around it for long seconds each time. Water dripped on to the towel, and the cold wet flannel soothed the ache. Eventually, he left it fully wrapped and fastened with a safety-pin.

'Mister, that's done wonders,' she said.

'Hot tea and something to eat next,' he said, and was gone yet again, taking the basin and towel with him. She lay musing, eyes on the ceiling. She was cross with herself, and she was also very hungry, she'd had nothing much all day. That bruiser. She'd followed him into the Rockingham public house by the Elephant and Castle. The pub had drawn her out of the cold and fog into warmth. The publican had looked at her several times as she offered little posies of limp flowers to customers for a penny a time. There were no takers. The bruiser had just given her a growling look. She found a penny and two ha'pennies in her purse, and the publican had served her a little port in exchange, which she sipped close to the blazing fire. The bruiser sat by himself, drinking a hot toddy, and he hardly moved except to bring the glass to his lips. Then a bearded man in a bowler hat and overcoat came in, looked around and found himself a seat in a corner. The burly bruiser got up, carried his toddy over and sat down opposite the bearded man, who listened to him muttering, then gave him a silver coin. The bruiser got up again and bought a large measure of whisky, which he gave to the bearded man, who made short work of it. Two swallows and it was gone. Then the bruiser produced a letter, the bearded man gave him a bit of a stony look, but took it and put it in his wallet. Then he said something in a very low voice, while gesturing at the bruiser with the wallet. She moved then, swaying a bit as if she was drunk. She lurched, reached out a hand and plucked the wallet clean from the bearded man's grasp. The bruiser bawled at her, but she was out of the door in a flash. She ran into the fog and through the fog, its thickness a blessing now, although she was risking a fall and broken bones. But the bruiser was after her, and the click-clack of her heels over the pavement kept him from losing her. While running, she took off her hat, placed the wallet inside it and put it on again, thrusting in the pin and nearly falling while doing so, handbag swinging from her arm. She kept going, blindly, and with both men chasing her. Then some way along London Road she'd run straight into a man. It knocked her off her feet and wrenched her ankle. That was when everything could have got really ugly if the man hadn't sided with her.

Now here she was, in his lodgings and on his bed, and out of action because of her ankle.

Oh, her hat!

She sat up again, looking around.

She saw the wallet on the bedside table.

That's done it, she thought.

Joe brought tea and sandwiches on a tin tray that was decorated with a colourful imprint of Queen Victoria. The tray was a little battered, and so was the likeness of the late Queen. It was nothing personal, just the result of usage.

'Here we are,' he said. The patient was sitting up.

'Oh, ain't you kind to a poor girl?' she said. 'I don't know I've ever met anyone more kind.' He placed the tray

34

on her lap. The tea was hot, and the sandwiches, filled with sliced ham, were made of crusty bread, fresh that day. She sipped the tea, cradling the cup in both hands. 'Mister, 'ave you been a soldier?'

'I have,' said Joe.

''Ave you got medals?'

'One or two.'

'Well, you ought to 'ave another one, for savin' a homeless girl from them 'orrible geezers and all the cold and fog.' She gulped the hot tea, put the cup down, took hold of a sandwich and sank hungry white teeth into it. Joe sat down on the edge of the bed, taking note of the wallet. It was still there, but not as he had left it. It had been moved. Her eyes, following his, alighted on the item of contention. 'Oh, help, look at that,' she said.

'The wallet?' said Joe. 'Had you forgotten about it?'

'What wallet? Oh, that one. Is it yours, mister?'

'Not mine, no.'

'How did it get there, then?' she asked.

'You'd better smarten up, my girl, or it'll be seven days general fatigues for you when you're back on your feet. All right, so you lifted the bearded geezer's wallet, but never mind that for the moment. What's your name?'

'Dolly,' she said, casting him a cautious look.

'Dolly? Dolly what?'

'Dolly Nobody, I suppose,' she said, drinking more tea. 'Well, I was brought up in that orphanage in Dalston, and that's what they called me there. Just Dolly. I don't know who me mum and dad were. Ain't Dolly a soppy name? No wonder you're laughin'.'

'I'm not,' said Joe.

'Oh, ain't you kind? I run away when I was fifteen and got a job as a skivvy with a fam'ly up on Brixton 'Ill.' She finished the sandwich and started on the second, eating hungrily. 'They didn't pay me no wages, not real wages, they just gave me a bob now and again, and me board and

35

lodgin', and some clothes. I run away again when I was eighteen. Well, the woman's 'usband started to fancy me, but I wasn't 'aving that, I'm not that kind of a girl, I never 'ave been. I've been doin' all sorts of jobs since then, and livin' in all sorts of lodgings, and now I've been chucked out of me last place because I didn't 'ave any job or any money. I've never had any luck, I was born under an unlucky star, mister.'

'No such thing,' said Joe, 'it's all in the mind. Look, what you've got at the present moment, Private Nobody, is a badly sprained ankle. Right, you can stay here till it's better. I'll speak to my landlady in the morning. And while you're here, let's see if we can get you straightened out. You can start by chucking all that hard luck stuff out of the window.'

'Honest, mister, I'm the 'ardest luck case I ever 'eard of,' she said, halfway through the second sandwich.

'Can't have you talking like that,' said Joe, 'don't like that kind of attitude. Won't stand for it. Get yourself a good night's sleep, and first thing tomorrow morning I'll put you into a hot bath. Then—'

'Here, 'old on,' said Dolly, 'I ain't five years old, y'know, I'm twenty-one, and I ain't lettin' you put me into a bath with no clothes on, it ain't first thing decent. What about me honour and virtue? I've still got them, y'know, and I ain't losin' them in any bath.'

'You'll take a bath, Private Nobody, first thing in the morning, and all by yourself. I'll boil a saucepan of water for you. Then we'll get you to square your shoulders and liven yourself up. Once you're back on your feet, I want a straight back, polished footwear and buttons done up. Also, a clean face and no swinging the lead or nicking wallets. Then I'll see if I can find you a job and some decent lodgings. In return, I don't want any more hard luck stories or any answering back. Have you got that, Private Nobody?'

36

Dolly blinked.

'Here, what's your game?' she asked. 'I ain't simple, mister, I bet you'll want something more than no answering back. It ain't fair, bein' kind to me and gettin' me obligated. It makes it 'ard for a girl to say no when she's obligated.'

'Stop thinking about things I'm not thinking about,' said Joe. 'All I'm after is getting you to stand up straight so that you can look people in the eye without feeling you need to pinch their wallets.'

'Me? Pinch wallets?' Dolly looked indignant. 'I don't know what you mean. Crikey, what an insult. Still, as long as you're not thinking about makin' me your fancy piece, I'll do me best to stand up brave to the world.'

'You'd better,' said Joe, who thought it wiser to help her get up and fight her hard luck than to harp on it.

'Mister, you 'aven't told me your own name.'

'I'm Joe Foster. You can call me Sergeant. That—' He stopped as a sudden little laugh escaped her. It had something of a giggle to it. He looked at her. She put her face straight. 'That'll get us on the right footing,' he said, 'and no arguments. You can get yourself into bed now. Reveille's at seven for you, and that's when I'll have the bathtub ready.'

'Mister, you lettin' me sleep in here, in your bed?' Dolly eyed him disbelievingly.

'You need to be comfortable with that ankle of yours,' said Joe, picking up the tray. He glanced again at the wallet. 'I'll take charge of this,' he said, and placed it on the tray.

'Don't look at me,' said Dolly, 'I don't know where it came from. What's in it?'

'Banknotes and a letter.'

'But—' Dolly checked.

'But what?'

'Well, I don't know, do I?' she said. 'It's nothing to do

with me. Look, can I wash me hands before I get into bed?'

'Of course,' said Joe. He put the tray down, lifted her and carried her to the WC on the landing. It had the extra amenity of a handbasin. He set her down on her good foot. 'Hopping job now,' he said, opening the door for her.

'Ain't you kind?' she said. To her, the house was quiet. To Joe, it was a quiet with underlying vibrations, the vibrations of the Beavis family rumbling in their sleep. Mr and Mrs Beavis slept downstairs, their sons and daughters on the second floor of the three-storeyed house. 'I think I'll be able to 'op back to the bedroom by meself,' said Dolly. 'Where are you goin' to sleep?'

'In the other room.'

'Oh, it don't seem right, me takin' your bed.'

'Get a good night's sleep,' said Joe, and left her to it. In his living-room, he examined the envelope again after collecting the tray from the bedroom, and after noting that the fivers were still in the wallet. It reawakened his curiosity, the fact that Blackbeard had been willing to hand them all over for getting back a wallet that otherwise contained only a letter. Dolly, of course, had played the innocent for the moment and had left the money untouched.

Had he been a man of no imagination and of totally strict principles, Joe would never have considered steaming the letter open. During his time in the Army he had been exemplary as far as conduct in battle and general discipline were concerned, but he would not have been as traditional a British soldier as he was if he hadn't stretched a principle or two during life in barracks. And his return to civilian life soon made him realize that almost every principle needed to be a little elastic.

It didn't hurt his conscience too much, therefore, to spend time steaming the envelope open and letting curiosity prevail. He took the letter out and unfolded it.

There was no address, and the writing was in a foreign language. It was all Greek to him. He put the letter back in the envelope, but did not reseal it.

He tidied up, damped the fire down, undressed down to his underwear, took a cushion from the armchair to use as a pillow, used his overcoat to cover himself and went to sleep on the rug beside the hearth. He had no difficulty in dropping off. Ex-Sergeant Joe Foster could sleep anywhere.

Dolly also slept soundly, with nothing on her conscience and her ankle at blissful rest.

CHAPTER FOUR

'Private Nobody?'

Dolly woke up. There he was, standing beside the bed in grey trousers and a black jersey, and looking disgustingly wide-awake.

'What's the time?' she asked.

'It's gone seven. Did you get a good sleep?'

''Eavenly,' said Dolly, digging herself deep under the bedclothes because she was naked.

'Report on the state of your ankle.'

'Report? Look, I'm not in your Army, y'know.'

'Do you good,' said Joe. 'Report state of ankle.'

'It's a bit better,' she said. 'Well, it feels a bit better.'

'Right, we'll have you on sick parade after your bath and give it an inspection. For now, let's have you out of your cot.'

'I ain't gettin' out while you're here, what d'you think I am?'

'I'll bring the bath.' He went to the lavatory, lifted a large tin bath off its wall hook, took it into the bedroom and placed it on the floor. 'Hot water next.' Out he went again and back he came, carrying a huge saucepan of boiling water. He emptied it into the bath, and a cloud of steam rose. Dolly watched him, bedclothes up to her chin. He fetched cold water in the saucepan, adding it to the hot water. Testing the mixture of hot and cold, he said, 'Right, that'll do. Soap, towel and scrubbing brush next.' Out he went once more, and back he came again with soap, towel and scrubbing brush.

'Here, give over,' said Dolly, 'I don't need no scrubbin'

brush, I went in the public baths two weeks ago. I keep meself clean, I do.'

'Give you half a minute to get in or be chucked in,' said Joe. He spotted her clothes hanging over the bottom rail of the iron bedstead. A white petticoat, black stockings and white drawers lay over outer clothes. The underwear was not only surprisingly clean, it was also pretty with ribbons and bows. 'Damn my eyes,' he said.

Dolly blushed.

'That ain't nice, lookin',' she said. 'Anyway, I nicked 'em from a shop. Me own stuff was all ragged and I thought I might as well nick something decent, it 'elps a girl, knowing she's dressed decent.'

'Can't say I like all this nicking, Private Nobody. It's got to stop. Right, proceed with your ablutions, but mind your ankle.'

He left, closing the door.

Dolly took her bath. She used the soap, but not the scrubbing brush. That man, what a funny character, did he treat everyone as if they were in the Army? What had he done with that wallet? What a nerve, taking it away. It was hers more than his. He'd nicked a letter that was in it. You just couldn't trust some people.

She winced then as she stubbed her right foot on the side of the tin bathtub.

Joe went downstairs to have a word with the Beavis family, to let them know he had a young woman upstairs and why. It was seven-fifteen and they were all in the kitchen having breakfast. It was a large Victorian family kitchen, and looked so when it was empty or when only Mrs Beavis was there. But when they were all present, its size seemed reduced. Big of heart, they were also big of body, except for young Linda. Mrs Beavis looked plumply overflowing at the table. Mr Beavis looked mountainous. Well, he was five feet ten tall and five feet wide, or thereabouts. His sons Albert and Alfred, sixteen and nineteen respectively, were as full-girthed as the famous Fat Boy of Peckham, or almost. His elder daughters, seventeen-year-old Nancy and fourteen-year-old Ella, were round all over. Twelve-year-old Linda looked like a happy accident. Mr Beavis was a navvy, and his sons worked at the Bermondsey shunting yards of the railway. Nancy had a job in a leather factory. Accordingly, father, sons and one daughter all brought wages home, and on top of that they had seven and sixpence a week from their lodger. So the whole family ate handsomely and with a great amount of hearty relish. They were a cheerful and noisy lot at meal times. Food was a joy to them, and they had no sooner finished one meal than they were enthusiastically discussing the next.

At this moment they were enjoying a sustaining breakfast of sausages, bacon, eggs and fried bread. Knowing that not many Southwark families sat down to a breakfast like that, the Beavises blessed their luck and addressed the world with beaming gratitude. They all beamed at Sergeant Joe as he knocked and put his head round the door.

'Well, 'ello, 'ello,' said Mr Beavis in his fruity voice.

'Come in, come in,' cried Mrs Beavis happily.

''Ave a fried egg,' invited Albert.

''Ave a banger,' said Alfred.

''Ave a kiss,' offered Nancy.

'Sergeant Joe,' said Linda, 'you can 'ave me last bit of fried bread, if yer like.'

''E can't 'ave mine, I just ate it,' said Ella, 'but I got 'alf a sausage left.'

'Appreciate all offers,' said Joe, 'but I'll be having my own breakfast in a little while.'

'We're 'aving Irish stew an' suet dumplings for supper tonight,' informed Ella.

'An' spotted dog for afters,' said Nancy.

'With custard,' said Albert.

'An' sugar,' said Linda.

'What can we do for yer, Sergeant Joe?' asked Mr Beavis.

'Give 'im a kiss,' said Nancy, plump mouth pursing.

'That gel's gettin' forward,' said Mrs Beavis fondly.

'Sergeant Joe ain't gettin' no kiss from me,' grinned Albert.

'Much obliged for that, Albert,' said Joe, and explained that he'd got a guest and how it came about, although he said nothing about the wallet or the men.

'Crumbs, she bumped yer in the fog?' said Ella.

'An' done 'er ankle in?' said Alfred.

'An' she ain't got no 'ome?' said Linda.

'Poor thing,' said Mrs Beavis.

'I wouldn't mind bumpin' yer in the fog, Sergeant Joe,' said Nancy.

'Ain't that 'eart-warmin', Bessie?' said Mr Beavis. 'Bringing the poor gel 'ome an' givin' 'er 'is bed.'

'I don't like you not 'aving no bed for a bit, Sergeant Joe,' said Mrs Beavis, 'I'll air the one in the spare room for yer.' There was a third room, a large one, on the first floor, and it was empty. A previous lodger had departed on receipt of a message that the rozzers were after him on account of a jeweller's broken window.

'No need, Bessie,' said Joe.

'Course there's need,' said Mrs Beavis, 'and it won't be no bother, nor no charge.'

'Ain't it romantic?' said Nancy. 'I wouldn't mind bein' carried 'ome by Sergeant Joe to 'is bed, it 'ud be worth sprainin' me ankle for.'

'It 'ud sprain 'im all over,' said Linda.

'Cheeky,' said Nancy. 'Oh, me gawd, look at the time, I'll 'ave to run all the way to me work if I don't get goin'.'

There was a general rush then. The kitchen overflowed with large bodies, plump bodies and colliding bodies as

Mr Beavis, his sons and his elder daughter all prepared to leave the house. There were shouts, yells and happy Bedlam, with Mrs Beavis doling out huge brown paper packets of sandwiches to be eaten at work at midday. Out of the kitchen they bounded, father, sons and daughter.

'Look after yer 'omeless bit of stuff, Sergeant Joe,' called Alfred, 'get 'er some steak-an'-kidney pudden.'

'And a nice bit of jam roly-poly,' called Albert.

'Nourishin' stews, that'll do the trick!' bawled Mr Beavis from the passage.

'An' some lovin' cuddles,' sang Nancy, and shrieked with laughter.

Out of the house they went, into a morning magically clear. The kitchen ceased vibrating, and its walls relaxed.

'Am I still on my feet?' asked Sergeant Joe.

'Course you are,' said Linda. She and Ella had plenty of time before they needed to set off for school.

'Can't think why, Carrots, I've just been steamrollered.'

The girls giggled. Mrs Beavis laughed.

'I got a rumbustious lot,' she said cheerfully, 'like an 'erd of noisy elephants sometimes. Still, no-one can say they ain't 'ealthy. Now don't you worry about that young woman that's upstairs, Sergeant Joe, except of course I wouldn't want no talk goin' on.'

'No grounds for it, Bessie,' said Joe. 'Just thought I ought to let you know about her.'

'Well, I know you'll treat 'er proper an' get 'er on 'er feet again,' said Mrs Beavis, 'you ain't one for 'anky-panky, that you ain't. I'd trust all me gels with yer. I'll come up when I've got a bit of time, I'll come an' cheer her up.'

'Take 'er some of the jam tart, Mum,' said Ella.

'I'll do that,' said Mrs Beavis.

'I'll come up this evenin',' said Linda, 'and if 'er shoes want a polish, I fink I could find some spit for 'er, I expect I could easy find a penn'orth.'

'Little monkey you are, Linda,' said Mrs Beavis, beaming proudly.

'Top monkey in the class,' said Joe. 'Right, behave yourselves at school, girls.' Returning to his living-room, he mixed some porridge oats with milk and water and put the saucepan on the open hob. He used a wooden spoon to stir the mixture, whistling softly.

Dolly looked up at a knock on the door.

'You can come in,' she called, and in he came, carrying a bowl of cold water. Dressed, except for one stocking, she was sitting on the edge of the bed. Her long hair was gathered and twisted into a topknot, much like the style affected by the acrobatic cancan dancers of Paris. She looked clean of face but shabby of clothes. 'I've 'ad me bath,' she said, 'd'you like me looks better now, mister?'

'You'll do,' he said, eyeing her. Quite good-looking on the whole. No reason why she should be homeless, jobless and hungry all her life. A decent blouse and skirt, or an attractive frock, either outfit worn with a clean straw boater, and she ought to be able to get a job in a store. Something needed to be done to stop her picking pockets and nicking underwear. While he was in no position to read her the Riot Act, it was plain commonsense to discourage her from her present ways. She should be able to do far better for herself than that. 'Right, expose injured ankle, Private Nobody.'

That Dolly had never met anyone quite like Sergeant Joe was obvious. For all that she was twenty-one, she had a hard job to smother giggles as hysterical as a schoolgirl's.

'You don't 'alf talk funny,' she said. She hitched her skirts. A white petticoat danced as she lifted her bare right leg. Her ankle was swollen and blue. No, no fracture, he thought. She'd have known by now if there had been, and the blue would have been dark and ugly. 'Oh, look at that,' she said, 'what a lump of an ankle.'

'Is it very painful?' asked Joe.

'Tender, more like, and achin',' said Dolly. Joe placed the bowl of water on the linoleum floor, took the discarded flannel from the bedside table and went down on one knee to apply treatment. 'I 'ope it's not damaged permanent,' she said, 'I don't know what I'd do if I 'ad more 'ard luck and found I couldn't ever walk again.'

'Chuck yourself in the river off one leg, I suppose,' said Joe, dipping the flannel.

'Here, that's not a nice thing to say,' protested Dolly, eyes on his bent head as he began to apply cold compresses. He had a good head of dark brown hair, and it looked as if he knew a decent barber. And he knew how to treat her ankle, he was doing another soothing job on it. 'Mister, 'ave you got a crust or two for me breakfast?'

'Hot porridge,' said Joe. He applied the flannel repeatedly, then wound it around her tender joint and fastened it again with the safety-pin. 'Then a boiled egg with some bread and butter.'

'Butter? Did you say butter?' asked Dolly.

'I can run to butter sometimes,' said Joe, getting to his feet.

'Blimey, are you rich, then? Or 'ave you just come into a bit of money?'

'Money out of that wallet?' said Joe.

'What wallet? Oh, that one.'

'Yes, it fell out of your hat,' said Joe.

'Now don't make me laugh,' she said. 'How could it 'ave jumped out of that geezer's pocket into me hat?'

'Listen, Private Nobody, don't try to teach me how to suck eggs, let's get you to your porridge.'

But Dolly insisted on testing her ankle first. It protested at once, so she let him carry her to the living-room. He sat her down at the table, where she could feel the warmth of the fire after her bath. They breakfasted on sugared porridge, boiled eggs, bread and butter, and a pot of tea.

Dolly ate with the enjoyment of a healthy young woman, and said he was useful considering he was a man. So-so, he said. Well, yes, said Dolly, so-so was about right for a man. Mind, that didn't mean he wasn't a kind bloke, he'd been very kind to her. Call me a port in a storm, said Joe. I don't know about port in a storm, said Dolly, more like an Army parade ground. Not that she was complaining. Pleased to hear it, said Joe.

'Are you the only lodger?' she asked.

'I am at the moment,' said Joe. 'The other room on this landing is empty. It might do for you when you get a job. By the way, I've let my landlady and her family know about you.'

'Oh, help,' said Dolly, 'I suppose that gave 'er ideas.'

'What ideas?'

'You'll 'ave to tell her I'm not that kind of a girl.'

'What kind?'

'The wrong kind,' said Dolly.

'She'd chuck you out if you were, and me as well for bringing you here,' said Joe. 'Anyway, you can stay until your ankle's better and something's been sorted out for you.'

'Mister, I don't know 'ow to thank you, honest I don't, you've got more human kindness than a bishop. D'you 'ave to go off to your work soon? I don't mind being left alone.'

'I work here,' said Joe.

'Here? In your lodgings?' Dolly didn't seem to think much of that. Wants to look around for the wallet while I'm not here, thought Joe. 'What sort of work?' she asked.

'Writing letters for businessmen,' said Joe.

'That don't sound like a man's work,' said Dolly.

'What's a man's work, then?' asked Joe, smiling.

'Well, being a sergeant in the Army, for a start,' said Dolly, 'and fightin' for your king and country. I bet you've been a sergeant, I bet you 'ave.'

'Most people call me Sergeant Joe.'

'Well, I ain't goin' to,' said Dolly, 'I'd feel daft.'

'Nothing daft about a bit of discipline,' said Joe. 'Let's get it clear, if I'm going to knock you into shape, you'll obey orders, answer up smartly when you're spoken to, and be alert at all times. Got that, Private Nobody?'

'Here, I'm not an orphanage kid any more,' said Dolly, 'I've come of age, I 'ave.'

'Yes, and you're on the downward path,' said Joe. 'Can't have any more of that. Right, breakfast over, now let's get you back on the bed. Your ankle needs to be rested all day.'

'Am I goin' to be by meself?' asked Dolly in disgust. 'I won't 'ave anyone to talk to.'

'I thought you said you didn't mind being alone.'

'Only if you 'ad to go to work,' said Dolly.

'I'll find you a book,' said Joe, who needed to keep his living-room to himself when he was doing his specialized work. He got up, lifted her and carried her back to the bedroom despite her threats to do him a fatal injury if he didn't stop carting her about like a sack of old cabbages. He placed her on the bed and looked down at her. She made a face. 'Can you read?' he asked.

'Well, what a cheek! Course I can read,' she said. 'I 'ad schooling at the orphanage, didn't I?'

'Good,' said Joe. 'Right, a book it is, then.' He stooped and lifted the tin bath. It was weighty with water now cold, but he limped to the lavatory with it, emptied it, cleaned it and put it back on its hook. Then he found a book for her, one of a dozen given to him by George Singleton from a clear-out of Victorian titles. 'Here you are, this should be just right for you,' he said. Dolly took it and opened it. She read the title and inscription.

USEFUL HINTS FOR YOUNG WORKING LADIES. Being a Detailed Summary of Rules, Requirements and Virtues Concerning Young Ladies Desirous of

Working in Shops, Stores, Hotels and Business Houses.

'Here, what's this?' asked Dolly in disgust. 'It ain't my kind of book, it ain't even a proper book.'

'Yes, it is. Digest it,' said Joe, 'and it'll teach you how to go after a job in a store or a ladies' dress shop, how to get the job and how to keep it. Start from the beginning.'

'You've got a hope,' said Dolly, 'I'll bore meself silly readin' this stuff, and I'll get an 'eadache as well. Look, don't you 'ave a nice romantic book, one that's called a novel? I read a nice one once, all about a poor girl who was found in the snow with a lost memory by a young and 'andsome squire that took her home to 'is castle and—'

'Fetch up there, Private Nobody, squires don't live in castles.'

'Well, it was something like a castle, and he 'ad tons of servants and a butler as well, and a sister who was secretly a witch and tried to make the poor girl worship Satan, but—'

'But the squire found out and chopped his sister's head off, which made her change into a baby rabbit. Yes, good stuff, but make do with what I've given you. It'll be more help to you than a novel.'

'You don't 'alf order a girl about,' said Dolly. 'Anyone can see you've been a sergeant. Mind, I'm not complaining.'

'Pleased to hear it,' said Joe. 'I've got some work to do now.'

'Wait a tick,' said Dolly, 'where's that wallet? I'll split the money with you, if you like, and wasn't there a letter in it as well?'

'Was there?'

'I'm only askin',' said Dolly. 'It's funny 'ow it managed to get under me hat. I suppose that bearded bloke must 'ave dropped it, I suppose I must 'ave picked it up without thinking and that I went off with it in an absent-minded way. I must 'ave been light-headed with starvation. But we can't give it back to 'im, can we, not knowing who 'e is or where 'e lives.'

'His name and address might be in it,' said Joe.

'What?' Dolly looked startled. 'Is it, then?'

'I'll have a good look.'

'Oh, blow that,' she said, 'he don't deserve to 'ave it back, anyway, and it's really mine now. Well, I was the one who found it.'

'Found it?'

'Yes, I suppose it was on the floor somewhere, in a pub where I was tryin' to sell some violets to save meself from real starvation. And it's finders keepers, y'know. You let me 'ave it back and what was in it, and I'll split with you. That's fair, mister, ain't it?'

'Read the book,' said Joe.

'Oh, blow you,' said Dolly.

'Relax,' said Joe, and left her. He washed up and tidied up, and put the baize cover back on the table. He opened the larder, which he kept locked whenever he was out, and picked up his carpet-bag from the stone floor. Sitting down, he extracted folders and studied some of the contents, including photographs of letters written by Byron, Shelley, Claire Clairmont, Byron's mistress, and Shelley's wife Mary, author of *Frankenstein*. Joe never forged letters that were known to exist. Far too risky. George Singleton, a dab hand at composing missives purporting to have originated under the pens of famous people of the past, supplied pencilled drafts of same. Joe's task was to write these out in the forged handwriting of the deceased.

He studied a letter written by Lord Byron to his sister, Mrs Leigh, on 29 August 1816. It was about Claire Clairmont, madly in love with him.

Now don't scold me, but what could I do? A foolish girl, in spite of all I could say or do, would come after me, or rather

50

went before – for I found her here – and I have had all the
plague possible to persuade her to go back again but at last
she went.

And so on for several more lines, and all to say he meant
to finish with Claire, even though she was expecting his
child. Joe thought Lord Byron, at that stage of his life,
needed frog-marching around Horse Guards Parade for a
week, with ragamuffin boys allowed to chuck rotten
vegetables at him. He began to execute some sample
specimens of the poet's handwriting. Satisfying himself
after a while, he commenced to write a follow-up letter,
composed by George and dated 31 August. His quill pen
scratched away on a sheet of treated notepaper, creating a
little masterpiece of querulous complaint about a mistress
Byron was tired of.

'Mister, here!' Dolly was calling. He put the quill down
and went to see what she wanted. She was still resting on
the bed. That was something in her favour. 'Look,' she
said, 'I told you this wasn't a real book. It's daft, it says a
girl's always got to wear grey if she works behind a counter
or in a business 'ouse or as an 'otel clerk. I ain't dyin' to
wear grey all me life, y'know.'

'You need a job,' said Joe, 'so never mind what you have
to wear, as long as it's not fig leaves. Keep reading, find
out the best way to apply for a job and how to keep it.'

'You've already said that,' sighed Dolly. 'I wouldn't like
to think a kind bloke like you can be 'ard-'earted, makin'
me stay here all alone and with a daft book like this. A girl
likes to 'ave someone to talk to now and again, it's all right
for men, they ain't as sociable as we are. Can't you come
and talk to me for a bit? I could tell you lots about me
orphanage days. Here, there was a boy there who wasn't
'alf a saucebox, he was always trying to get a look at me
legs and drawers—'

'Stop,' said Joe.

'What for?' asked Dolly.

'Can't have you talking like that, Private Nobody, don't want to hear about your legs and drawers. It won't do, won't make a lady of you, and you have to be some kind of a lady to get a decent job in a decent ladies' shop. All the same, I think I know how you feel. You want someone to talk to. Right, hold on.'

He went down to see his landlady again. Mrs Beavis was existing in an atmosphere of relative quiet, the boisterous echoes of her rumbustious family having long since died away. She at once offered Joe a cup of hot morning Bovril and a warm sausage roll, if he'd like. She'd made all the beds and done her cleaning, and was feeling like some Bovril herself. Joe said he liked the sound of that, and could she bring her Bovril up and drink it while having a chat with the young woman who was resting her sprained ankle on his bed? Said young woman was dying for female talk, and he was busy himself, anyway.

'Well, you got a nice way with you, Sergeant Joe,' said Mrs Beavis, 'and I don't suppose many women would find it easy to say no to you, whatever you wanted.'

'Steady, Bessie,' said Joe, who didn't intend to ask the ultimate of any woman until he'd acquired enough savings to put an end to his career as a forger. The ultimate meant marriage in his book.

'Well, you're a manly feller, Joe, that you are,' beamed Mrs Beavis. 'I'll go up to that poor gel and 'ave a nice chat with 'er. I'll take some Bovril up for 'er too, and some sausage rolls, we all 'ave to keep body an' soul together. I'll bring yours up the same time, in a few minutes.'

'Much obliged, Bessie,' said Joe, 'you'd make a fine corporal. Can't say fairer than that.'

Dolly lay numb.

'Then there was me sister's weddin' eighteen years ago,' said Mrs Beavis, seated on the bedside chair. 'What a day

52

that was for 'er, it nearly give 'er permanent 'ysterics, though she's been all right lately, except for 'er chilblains. Lovely bride, she was, she 'ad apple blossom in 'er weddin' bokey. 'Er weddin' dress 'ad been run up for 'er by Mrs Stuart that 'ad only just give up 'er job workin' for a dressmaker in Shoreditch. Well, she was gone sixty by then, an' they give 'er ten yards of pink silk an' five pounds on 'er retirement day, and I asked 'er if she fancied makin' me sister's weddin' dress to keep 'er 'and in a bit – 'ere, you ain't ate your other sausage roll yet. You all right, love? It's a shame you ain't got no 'ome nor fam'ly, but I don't like to see someone not eatin' when they're laid up, you need a bit of food then. Anyway, the weddin' day come along, but would yer believe it, that Arthur Goodwin, the bridegroom, didn't turn up. Well, not at the time 'e didn't, nor 'is best man, not for nearly an hour. That Arthur 'ad stopped at a pub on 'is way to the church, 'e said 'e needed fortifyin', and 'im and 'is best man both went in the pub an' stayed there a lot longer than they should of. At the church, me poor sister was near to swoonin', our mum 'ad to give 'er smellin'-salts, with 'is reverend the vicar sayin' 'e'd 'ave to cancel the ceremony. Well, that Arthur turned up at last and the vicar married them, but afterwards me sister let Arthur know just 'ow she felt, she chucked the whole weddin' cake at 'im, then 'er bokey an' then a full bottle of port. She might easy 'ave murdered 'im if our dad 'adn't pulled 'er off. You sure you don't want that other sausage roll, love?'

'I ain't got the strength,' said Dolly faintly.

'I'll eat it for yer,' said Mrs Beavis with cheerful understanding, 'it don't do to let good food lie about not eaten.' She took a large and happy bite. 'I must say you've 'ad an 'ard time, not 'aving no job or anything, but you're in good 'ands, love. Sergeant Joe'll see yer sprain don't get worse, 'e'll get the doctor in if it does. 'E's got a warm 'eart, 'e'll call the doctor in if 'e thinks yer leg's broke.

Doctor Watts, near the Elephant an' Castle. Mrs Baldwin's been under 'im just recent, poor woman, with a leg ulcer. 'E treated our Nancy when she 'ad w'oopin' cough, but 'e told Mrs Walker that 'er varicose veins is provin' obstinate. Well, when varicose veins catch up with yer—'

'Is that Sergeant Joe goin' out?' asked Dolly, exhausted from the flow of words pouring relentlessly into her ears.

'Is that you goin' out, Sergeant Joe?' called Mrs Beavis.

'Right first time, Bessie. To get a paper.' Joe descended the stairs, a grin on his face. He knew all about his landlady's ability to talk the hind-leg off a cockney donkey.

''E usually goes out an' gets a daily paper about this time,' Mrs Beavis informed Dolly, 'and an evening paper later. And a bit of shoppin' quite reg'lar. 'E don't like sittin' too long at 'is work. Well, it's what you might call clerkin' work, writin' letters for business firms at 'ome, which don't come too welcome to an active man like 'im, so 'e likes to get out as much as 'e can to give 'is gammy leg a walk. Mind, it don't make sense to me, an 'andsome feller like 'im not 'aving no wife. Our Nancy might be only seventeen, but she's already a full-growed woman to look at, and I know she'd be pleased to be 'is wife, 'e'd only 'ave to ask 'er, except 'e did say once that 'e's waitin' a while before 'e gets married. All me three gels is fond of 'im . . .' On and on the happy landlady went.

I'll murder her in a minute, thought Dolly.

And him as well.

CHAPTER FIVE

Mrs Beavis had gone at last. Joe reappeared, a copy of the late edition of the *Westminster Gazette* in his hand. Dolly, from the bed, ground her teeth at him.

'You rotten swine,' she said.

'Is that a complaint, Private Nobody?'

'Stop callin' me that, it's daft. I suppose you realize I'm nearly dead from suffocation?'

'State your complaint in full,' said Joe.

'I wish I could, but I'm all wore out,' said Dolly bitterly.

'From having someone to talk to?'

'Don't make me laugh,' said Dolly, 'your landlady's not just someone, she's a bloomin' steamroller. You did it on me, gettin' her to come up and talk to me, and don't think I don't know you're laughin' about it. You ought to be stood up against a wall, you ought. It ain't funny, y'know, gettin' a steamroller to come up and suffocate me, and me in an unwell condition. I thought at first you was a kind bloke, I didn't think you was goin' to help put me in me grave.'

'Cheer up, you're not dead yet,' said Joe. 'I think an improvement's setting in.'

'All right, I forgive you,' said Dolly. 'What's in the paper?'

'Usual kind of news. Thought you might like to read it. For a bit of light relief, except that there's been a murder.'

'A murder?'

'Some unlucky bloke was found late last night in Houndsditch, with his throat cut from ear to ear,' said Joe.

'That's it, cheer me up,' said Dolly, 'it's just what I need. Are you always the life and soul of the party?'

'Not always,' he said. 'Here.' He placed the newspaper on her lap. She picked it up. In the Stop Press column on the front page were details of the murder. She read a few lines, then made a face. 'Poor bloke,' she said soberly, and read on, her expression registering distaste. 'Awful,' she said.

'Don't like it much myself,' said Joe. 'Are you thinking about the fact that we might have been murdered ourselves last night?'

'Oh, blimey,' she said, and bit her lip. 'Don't talk about it, I'll 'ave bad dreams.'

'The peculiar thing is that Blackbeard seemed ready to murder us for a wallet with a few fivers in it, all of which he was going to give to his bruiser, anyway. Makes no sense, does it?'

'Don't ask me,' said Dolly, 'I ain't educated enough to work out Chinese puzzles.' She didn't, he noticed, ask him how many fivers. She knew, of course. She cast him a glance. 'How many's a few fivers?' she asked.

Joe smiled.

'Two,' he said.

'What?'

'Four.'

'That's more like it,' said Dolly. 'Well, I mean, all the fuss 'e made.'

'Yes, but what about exactly? Four fivers make twenty quid, and he was going to give that amount to his bruiser. I just pointed that out.'

'Well, I suppose – well, didn't you say last night there was a letter as well?'

'You think that was what he was really worked up about?' said Joe.

'I don't know, do I? I'm only an 'omeless girl out of an orphanage; you're the clever one. Still, you shouldn't worry about it, mister, I'll take it off your 'ands, you just keep ten quid of the money. Well, you deserve that, standin' by me like you did and givin' me your bed when I 'adn't got a farthing to call me own. We'll split the money down the middle, shall we?'

'Can't encourage splitting the proceeds of thievery,' said Joe, and went back to his work.

In frustration, Dolly read the newspaper. Yet she couldn't help thinking he was a bit of a giggle. Well, he was slightly off his rocker to start with. He couldn't forget he'd been an Army sergeant, he talked like one and acted as if he was still on a parade ground or something.

There was a report in the paper about the coronation and the unveiling of the memorial to Queen Victoria two days before the coronation, and about the many crowned heads of Europe who were going to be present, including the German Emperor, the late Queen's grandson. The safety of all these august personages must be assured. Certain European monarchs were constantly troubled by agitators, anarchists and pro-republican factions. Bombs that were thrown at monarchist gatherings in Europe must not be thrown in London. The Home Office was willingly cooperating with other authorities to ensure the events passed off peacefully and with due respect.

Dolly made a face, then rustled the newspaper irritably.

'Oi, mister!' she called.

Joe failed to respond this time. He was busy forging a letter in the handwriting of Claire Clairmont. To Byron, concerning their child Allegra.

I have this day received a letter from Dearest Mary about that which has so distressed me, your unbelievable decision to place Allegra in a convent—

'Oi, mister!'

Resignedly he put his quill down and went to the bedroom.

'Now what?' he asked.

57

'Oh, hello,' said Dolly.

'What's your problem?'

'Me foot 'urts,' she said, sitting up.

'Badly?'

'Well, it ain't good,' she said.

'Can't have that, can we, Private Nobody?' said Joe. 'Sick-list cases are a liability. Right, let's have a look at you.'

'You and your Private Nobody,' said Dolly, and pulled her skirt up, saucily unveiling her white petticoat with its foamy lace and pink ribbons. Joe gave her a questioning glance. Dolly responded with a sweet smile.

'Yes, all right, I can see,' he said. 'Very pretty.'

'Well, when a girl's sufferin' desperate times, she might as well nick something nice,' said Dolly. 'I told you that before.'

'Well, I'm now telling you that if you go nicking again, you'll get seven days' hard labour scrubbing this house out. Present injured foot that's hurting.'

She drew her petticoat up. Her left leg was clad in one of her black lisle stockings. Her right leg was bare. It looked smooth, shapely and healthy. Around her ankle was the pinned flannel. He undid it and drew it off. The swelling was still very evident, but the blue tint was no worse.

'Oh, lor', look at that,' she said, 'ain't it 'orrible? Who'd have a leg like that? You wouldn't think I'd been complimented on them, would you, but when I 'appened to show them accidental to a gentleman once, he said I ought to go on the stage and wear tights and a little frou-frou skirt – here, where you goin'?'

'To get some cold water.'

He brought some in the basin, and treated her ankle as before. Dolly, still sitting up, watched him.

'You're a nice bloke really,' she said, 'I'm not 'olding it against you that you're keepin' the wallet and all that money to yourself, even if it is rightly mine, like I said. Well, it is.'

'Yes, in a thieving kind of way,' said Joe.

'I'll get the rats in a minute,' said Dolly. 'You shouldn't say things like that to a girl who's had my kind of 'ard luck. D'you really think me legs are pretty?'

'I said your petticoat was.' Joe fastened the wet flannel around her ankle again. 'I'll get you some food now,' he said.

'I'll come out and 'ave it with you, shall I?'

'I'll bring yours in,' said Joe.

'Don't you care that I'm all bored?'

'I'll bring a pack of cards as well,' said Joe on his way out. 'You can play Patience.'

'Think you're funny, don't you?' she called after him.

'Not much,' called Joe.

He took food to her ten minutes later. Cold ham, pickle and a plateful of crusty bread and butter.

'Thanks ever so,' said Dolly gratefully, 'you're a nice bloke mostly.'

'Midday rations,' said Joe, 'hot supper this evening.' He placed the tray on her lap.

Dolly, healthily peckish, said, 'I don't know how you can be so good to me, nursin' me ankle, givin' me your bed, and feedin' me as well, and me a girl that's done pinchin' and nickin'.'

'It's all out of the goodness of my hard heart,' said Joe.

'Oh, you're not so bad most times,' said Dolly. 'You goin' to come in and talk to me after you've eaten?'

'Sorry, I'm busy. I've got a full day's work to do.'

'Oh, you're mean, you are,' said Dolly.

Joe made a sandwich for himself. Having eaten it, he brewed some tea and took her a cup. She fell over herself in a spasm of new gratitude, only to give him an earful because he wouldn't bring his own tea in and talk to her. It all bounced off him. It was Dolly's first encounter with the

59

imperturbable nature of a British Army sergeant, and it made her want to spit.

He drank his own tea while getting on with his work, work that demanded care and concentration. Each forgery had to be faultless, and each took time. He was allowed forty minutes of peace before the patient made herself heard again.

'Mister? Mister, you there?'

He ignored the summons.

'Oh, me foot, I've fell off the bed!'

He appeared. She was on the bed.

'Report on what happened, Private Nobody.'

'Me?' said Dolly.

'You fell off the bed, then what?'

'Me? Oh, that. Well, I nearly fell off, that's all, and it gave me foot a bit of a twinge. Still, it's all right now. Here, ain't you an 'andsome bloke? 'Ave you got a lady friend? I bet you 'ave, I bet she's a treat and wears posh hats. Your landlady said you wasn't married, that you was waiting for a while. Does your lady friend mind? I wish I was some 'andsome gent's lady friend, but I don't 'ave the looks really, I've just got a sort of orphanage face – here, what's goin' on? Oh, you brute!'

Dexterously, Joe turned her on to her stomach, then slapped her bottom. Dolly didn't think much of that. For one thing, she was unprepared for it. For another, it wasn't decent. True, it was only one slap, but even that was one too many. She yelled.

'Punishment applied for playing up, Private Nobody,' said Joe. 'Slate's clean now. Behave yourself.'

Dolly, still lying face down, breathed, 'Oh, you ain't decent. You wait, I'll 'ave the police on you for assault and battery. You've bruised me, you have.'

'Well, if it gets painful, let me know,' said Joe, 'and I'll bathe it. With warm water.'

'Oh, I never 'eard the like,' said Dolly, 'that's downright

indecent. I don't know 'ow you can talk like that to a girl that's twenty-one.'

'Well, be your age,' said Joe, and returned to his work. Dolly quivered all over and buried her face in the pillows to smother her shrieks of laughter. But she stopped playing up. It tried her patience, but she left him alone. He reappeared at four o'clock, when she was just about dead from boredom.

'Anything to report?' he asked.

'I ain't talkin' to you,' said Dolly, perking up.

'Ankle feeling better? Bottom up to scratch?'

'Oh, you cheeky cuss,' she said, 'I might be poor and 'omeless, but I'm respectable, I am, and I ain't goin' to listen to you talkin' about my bottom, you ought to be locked up for even mentioning it.'

'That's the spirit,' said Joe, 'I like to hear a girl standing up for herself. I'll treat your ankle again now, then I'm going to the shops. D'you like fish? How about plaice? Right, I'll get a couple and we'll have them with mashed cream potatoes. Fancy that? Good, we'll have that, then.'

Dolly tried to say it would be nice if he'd give her the chance to tell him what she liked, but he was away again. He came back with the basin of cold water and put more cold compresses on her ankle. She said she was grateful that he could be a real gent when he tried.

'So-so,' said Joe. 'I'm off to the shops next, I'll bring you a cup of tea on my way.'

He brought her a cup, and with it a small cardboard packet.

'What's this?' she asked.

'Pack of cards. For playing Patience.'

Dolly chucked the pack at him.

Mrs Beavis, busy preparing a large supper for her family, answered a knock on her front door. Archie Cousins stood on her doorstep. He let a neighbourly grin slide over his

61

foxy face. Thin, quick and elusive, he was never where he was expected to be. He was also workshy, and no-one could remember when he last had a regular job, but most people could recall when he'd last tried to touch them for the loan of a bob. Yesterday, usually. His habitual dress was a long black jacket with undone buttons, baggy grey trousers, a woollen scarf and an ancient brown bowler.

''Ello, Bessie me old sweet'eart,' he said, ''ow yer keepin'?'

'I ain't yer old sweet'eart,' said Mrs Beavis, whose naturally sunny beam did not always shine for everyone, 'and I 'appen to be keepin' me hands to meself.'

Archie, accepting this reference to his pickpocketing activities on occasions such as the Derby, put a finger against the side of his nose and winked.

'All in a day's work, Bessie me love,' he said.

'What day's work?' asked the large lovable landlady.

'Well, as I'm always sayin' to me old Dutch, what the eyes don't see the 'eart don't grieve about, and a bloke's got to make a livin' some'ow. 'Ere, what did I come for? I know – is Sergeant Joe in?'

'Not just now,' said Mrs Beavis, ''e 'appens to 'ave just gone out.'

'That ain't too inconvenient to me,' said Archie, 'I'll go up an' wait, I don't suppose 'e'll be long, will 'e?'

''E didn't say, but 'e won't want you nosin' around 'is room – 'ere, come back 'ere.'

Archie had sidled adroitly past her.

'Save me callin' again, me old darling,' he said, making for the stairs.

'You ain't to go up there,' said Mrs Beavis, 'there's a – oh, 'ello, me loves.'

Ella and Linda bounced in through the open front door. At least, Ella did. Her plumpness never restricted her movements. She bounded through life. Into the house she came like an Indiarubber ball, Linda skipping in behind her.

'Watcher, Mum,' said Ella, 'is there a slice of cake?'

'Course there is, pet,' said Mrs Beavis, and Archie, moving fast and silently, ghosted up the stairs to the landing.

A few minutes later, Linda, a slice of cake in her hand, slipped out of the kitchen and ran up the stairs, thinking to ask Sergeant Joe if the poor young woman with a sprain wanted her shoes polished, although at the moment the eating of the cake was interfering with her spit. The living-room door was ajar. She pushed it open and put her head in.

'Sergeant Joe – oh, what you doin' of, Mr Cousins?'

Archie had already been through every drawer in the tallboy. He had in his hurry left one drawer just a little open, and was now delving into the carpet-bag, which he'd found at the bottom of the shelved larder. His rummaging hand hastily withdrew.

'Well, 'ello, Linda me pretty, 'ow yer doin'?' he said. The carpet-bag was on the table. 'Just 'ome from school, eh? Bet you're the teachers' fav'rite.'

'What you doin' of?' persisted Linda. She knew Archie Cousins was a loafer whose sharp nose pointed him at everything except honest toil. His slippery feet could take him in and out of a West End emporium in two shakes of a fox's tail, but what he collected on his way through was as much as six pairs of hands could manage. 'What you got that bag out for? It ain't yours, it's Sergeant Joe's, and it's private.'

'Oh, I was just waitin' for 'im,' said Archie easily. ''E won't be long, yer mum said. I just 'appened on 'is bag, it was near to fallin' off the table. Anyway, don't you worry yer pretty little 'ead, Linda, I'll tell 'im you come up to say 'ello.'

'I ain't goin' downstairs,' said Linda, 'I bet you was goin' to pinch things from that bag. I'll tell Sergeant Joe—'

'Here, who's that out there, what's goin' on?' Dolly suddenly made herself heard from the bedroom.

'Now you've done it,' accused Linda, 'you've woke up a poor young woman Sergeant Joe's been lookin' after.'

'Well, ain't that a coincidence?' said Archie. 'I just 'eard about 'er.'

'Who is that?' Dolly made herself heard again, having swung herself off the bed to hop to the door of the bedroom. 'Come on, what's goin' on?'

'Miss, it's a bloke from down the street,' called Linda, determined not to leave the living-room while the fly Archie Cousins was still there. ''E's been lookin' in Sergeant Joe's private bag.'

'What?' Dolly thought about the wallet. 'He's doin' what?'

'Now, Linda me cherry blossom, yer don't need to say nothing, yer know,' said Archie. ''Ere, would yer like a new penny? I might just 'ave one on me.' He fished around in his pockets.

'I don't want no money from you,' said Linda, 'I don't trust yer, Mr Cousins, I bet yer up 'ere to do thievin'.'

'Me?' said Archie, a classic study of injured innocence.

Dolly hopped to the open door of the living-room. She saw the girl and the man.

'That's 'im, miss,' said Linda, 'an' that's Sergeant Joe's bag.'

''Ello,' said Archie amiably, 'got an 'urt leg, 'ave yer? I 'ad one once. Well, there was this runaway 'orse—'

'How d'you know I've got an 'urt leg?' asked Dolly suspiciously, holding on to the door frame for support.

'Oh, I 'eard, yer know,' said Archie, 'and I can see you're standin' on yer good 'un, aincher, ducky? Tell yer what, I'll pop off 'ome and get yer me bottle of embrocation, seein' I can't wait no longer for Sergeant Joe, anyway. I got a bloke to see about some business.'

'Oh, no you don't,' said Dolly, 'I want to know what you're doin' 'ere.'

'Me?' Archie looked positively pained. 'Me? I just popped up to see Sergeant Joe, didn't I? 'E's a mate of mine. I don't tell no lie, I was goin' to ask 'im for the loan of a bob so's I could get to see this bloke that might be puttin' a bit of business in me way. Well, 'e 'angs out in Barnet market, and I ain't got enough to cover me train fare. Sergeant Joe wouldn't want me to walk all the way, 'e'd see me straight with a bob.'

'Sergeant Joe ain't your mate,' said Linda. ''E ain't 'is mate,' she said to Dolly for good measure.

'He looks more like someone's bad luck, if you ask me,' said Dolly.

'I like a joke,' said Archie, 'but I've got to be off, if yer'll excuse me. Not that it ain't been nice talkin' to yer. You too, Linda me sweet'eart.'

'You're lyin',' said Dolly. 'Come on, what've you been lookin' for?'

'Me?' said Archie. 'I – 'ere, what's that?' He turned his head to look at the mantelpiece. Dolly and Linda followed his gaze. He was out in a flash, going past Dolly like a fox slipping the hounds. He whisked down the stairs at speed.

'Blow that,' said Dolly, 'he's dished us.'

'Oh, me dad always says 'e's 'ere today an' gone today,' said Linda.

'Are you one of the landlady's girls?' asked Dolly.

'I'm Linda, I'm fav'rite with Sergeant Joe. 'E calls me Private Carrots. I bet 'e won't like Mr Cousins lookin' in 'is carpet-bag.'

'We'd better 'ave a look in it ourselves,' said Dolly, 'in case he's taken anything.'

'Oh, d'you fink we'd better?' asked Linda.

'Yes, let's 'ave a look,' said Dolly, and hopped to the table. She pulled the carpet-bag open wide and saw cardboard folders. Downstairs the front door opened and closed. Dolly felt between the folders in a quick hopeful search for the wallet.

'What's this?' asked Sergeant Joe from the landing, and came in. Dolly leaned on the table to help keep her right foot off the floor.

'Someone's been up 'ere,' she said.

'Yes, it was Mr Cousins,' said Linda. 'I fink 'e was after pinchin' somefing from yer bag, Sergeant Joe, only I come up an' caught him openin' it.'

'He mentioned he was a friend of yours,' said Dolly. 'I wouldn't want 'im as a friend of mine.'

'Yes, we fought we'd better see if 'e'd pinched anyfing,' said Linda.

'Can't think why Archie Cousins should pick on me,' said Joe, eyeing his carpet-bag frowningly. He'd made an unusual mistake in not locking the larder. 'Not his style to try his luck on his close neighbours.'

From the passage downstairs came the sound of the landlady's singing voice.

'Linda, you up there worryin' Sergeant Joe again?'

Linda, going out to the landing, called down, 'Yes, I'm up 'ere, Mum, but I ain't a worry to Sergeant Joe.'

'Young pickle, that's what you are. Come down 'ere now, there's a love, Sergeant Joe's got things to do.'

'Oh, all right,' said Linda, and went down to tell her mum about catching Archie Cousins rummaging around. Her mum said Sergeant Joe would take care of that Flash Harry, but if he didn't she'd have a go herself, she'd bash Archie's bowler so hard over his head he'd never get it off again, he'd have to go about like a man with no eyeballs. Linda thought that good for a giggle. So did Ella. They watched their mum making suet dumplings for the stew which, in the iron cauldron on the hob above the glowing range fire, was already giving off an aroma that was a delight to anyone's nose on a winter evening.

Upstairs, Sergeant Joe noticed the partly open drawer in

his tallboy. He pulled it farther open and saw that a bunch of quill pens in an elastic band had been moved. He examined other drawers. The contents of each had been disturbed. Dolly watched him.

'What was he lookin' for?' she asked.

'No idea,' said Joe, placing his carpet-bag on the tallboy.

'Money?'

'Probably. I'll go round and see him this evening.'

''Ave you got money lyin' about, then?' asked Dolly.

'I don't let money lie around,' said Joe. 'Right, I'll start doing something about supper now, but I'll carry you back to bed first.'

'Oh, don't be rotten,' said Dolly, 'I'll go mad if I 'ave to lie on that bed any more today. I can sit down in 'ere a bit, can't I?'

'Sounds reasonable,' said Joe. 'Yes, you can sit and peel the potatoes.'

'Me do what?'

'Peel the potatoes.'

'I 'ate peelin' potatoes,' said Dolly.

'Don't we all. You can sit at the table and do them. Idle hands equal lazy brains. Not good for either of us. Smarten up, Private Nobody, do your bit.'

'Do me bit?' said Dolly. 'I ain't an Army skivvy, mister.' But she let him help her into a chair. However, when he placed a bowl of potatoes on the table in front of her, and gave her a peeling knife, she wasn't at all pleased. 'Me peel all them?' she protested.

'Glad to have your help,' said Joe. He poured some water into the bowl and brought a saucepan containing more water to the table. The baize cover was off, revealing an oil-cloth cover beneath. 'The saucepan's for the peeled spuds,' he said.

'Oh, lor',' muttered Dolly, and went to work with gritted teeth and the knife. Joe began to prepare the plaice, using a thin and very sharp knife to fillet them. He paused in his work to stare at what Dolly was doing to her first potato. The skin was coming off in chunks.

'Fetch up, Dolly, don't chop it to pieces. Peel it.'

'I am, ain't I?'

'Perishing punkah wallahs,' said Joe, looking at the finished potato. Dolly had reduced it to the size of an irregular-sided marble. 'That's a peeled spud?'

'Yes, and I can play the mouth-organ as well,' said Dolly.

'Didn't they teach you how to peel potatoes at the orphanage?'

'I never let 'em,' said Dolly, 'I told you, I 'ate peelin' potatoes.'

'Right, it's kitchen fatigues for you when you're on your feet again,' said Joe, 'and that'll include teaching you how to do a fair job of work on spuds. Got that, Private Nobody?'

'You don't half keep on at a girl,' said Dolly.

'Leave the rest of the spuds,' said Joe, 'I'll do them. But at least you're sitting up straight. You've got a good back. Keep at it and I might let you have a couple of those fivers.'

'Now you're talkin',' said Dolly. 'I don't mind you 'aving the others. Here, I think I could get a bit for the wallet, it's pigskin, did you notice?'

'I noticed.'

'Could you let me 'ave it back, then?'

'Not yet,' said Joe, wondering exactly what Archie Cousins had been after, and why.

'Oh, blow you,' said Dolly.

68

CHAPTER SIX

Mrs Connie Cousins, a long-suffering woman of forty, opened her front door and found Sergeant Joe smiling at her. The evening was cold and misty, the fog beginning to creep up the Thames and to sneak into the alleyways on either side of the river. Still, a woman could forget that when a nice upstanding chap like Sergeant Joe called on her.

''Ow'd yer do, old soldier?' she said.

'All the better for seeing you, Connie.'

''Ello, 'ave yer come for a cuddle, then?'

'Not if Archie's around. Is he?'

''E is, if 'e ain't slipped me.'

'I'd like to see him,' said Joe.

'That's right, be a disappointment to me,' said Mrs Cousins, warmly clad in a dark brown woollen dress with huge leg-of-mutton sleeves now going out of fashion. Well, the dress was five years old, and there was little chance of affording a new one unless Archie finally backed a Derby winner. 'You sure you want to see Archie an' not me?'

'Well, you're better-looking, Connie, but it's Archie I'd like to have a word with,' said Joe.

'What's 'e been up to this time?' asked the put-upon wife. 'I don't know if that shifty old man of mine is ever goin' to be a credit to 'is fam'ly; I don't know there's any man that can spend more time doin' nothing than Archie can. Come in, Sergeant Joe, don't stand out there in the cold, I'll get Archie for yer – 'ere, no yer don't, yer crafty fly-be-night.' She turned to catch Archie in the act of trying to vanish upstairs. 'You come down 'ere now,

69

Sergeant Joe wants a word with yer, and if it means 'e's goin' to knock yer 'ead off, I'll give 'im an 'and.'

'Me? What've I done?' asked Archie, sidling sideways up the stairs in the hope of reaching the lavatory and locking himself in.

'Come 'ere,' said his trouble-and-strife, whisking along the passage. She reached and grabbed the tail of his long jacket, and she hauled him back down the stairs. Joe entered the passage and closed the door. 'Would yer be wantin' to speak to 'im in private, Joe?'

'In your parlour, Connie, if that's all right with you.'

'Yes, I don't want 'im bein' shown up in front of 'is fam'ly in the kitchen,' said Mrs Cousins. ''E gives me enough embarrassment as it is by what 'e gets up to. In yer go, Archie.'

'Now look, Connie me pet, it's bleedin' cold in the parlour,' complained Archie, 'and, anyway, I got to see a bloke about a job.'

'Don't come the old acid with me,' said his better half, 'you ain't seen any bloke about a job since Noah built the Ark, and if anyone offered you one you'd fall down dead. In the parlour you go, me lad, or I'll crown yer with me kitchen poker.'

'Stone me Aunt Fanny,' said Archie, 'I ain't got nothing to talk to Sergeant Joe about – oh, all right.' He flitted into the parlour as his wife made a threatening gesture.

'There y'are, Sergeant Joe,' she said, ''e can't slip yer now, only watch 'e don't wriggle out through the keyhole. Mind, I ain't sayin' 'e don't 'ave 'is good points, nor that 'e don't come up with a cuddle and a present sometimes. Except,' she added regretfully, 'the presents usually turn out to be nicked. 'E give me a lovely pair of stays once with satin panels. Just what I wanted at the time, to 'elp me keep me figure tidy. I could've sworn they was new, but what d'yer think I found out? That 'e'd nicked them off a woman's washing-line in Brixton. I chased 'im all the way up the Butts with me stew saucepan, and a bobby 'ad to come an' save 'im from 'aving 'is brains bashed in. Well, you can go an' talk to 'im now. You shouldn't need no 'elp, but if 'e gives yer any lip, just call me.'

'I'll manage, Connie,' said Joe.

'Know yer will, me old soldier,' said Mrs Cousins, and departed to her kitchen.

Joe entered the parlour. It was in darkness.

'Light the gas, Archie,' he said.

'No, I can see yer all right—'

'Light the gas.'

Archie muttered, but struck a match. He lit one of the gas mantles above the fireplace. Sergeant Joe made a thoughtful study of him. Archie tried a friendly grin.

'Look, me old mate—'

'What were you after in my lodgings, Archie?'

'Me? In yer lodgings?'

'You heard.'

'Oh, yer lodgings.' Archie blinked. 'See what yer mean, Joe, me neighbourly visit. Well, I 'eard – well, someone told me you was lookin' after some poor tart that 'ad 'urt 'er leg, an' young Linda said so. I popped in on yer to see if I could do anything for yer, like did yer want a medical bandage that I could get cheap. She was there all right, standin' on one leg – 'ere, yer done yerself proud, Joe, findin' a nice-looking bit of stuff like 'er. That's all, me old mate, been nice talkin' to yer—'

'Cut the fairy stories,' said Joe. Somehow, his mind was still on the wallet and the letter, discounting the money. He could not forget that Blackbeard had arrived on the scene sweating and then become coldly murderous in his need to get the wallet back. 'What were you after, Archie? I want to know.'

'Course yer do, Joe,' said Archie, 'course yer do. Well, I ain't one not to be frank, so I'll tell yer. I got to admit I didn't pop over just to offer yer some neighbourly 'elp, it was on me mind while I was there to touch you for the loan of a bob. I'm a bit skint at the moment.'

'Won't do, Archie,' said Joe, 'won't stand up.' Guesswork made him flight an arrow. 'Who sent you?'

'Eh?' Archie's face fell apart. 'What d'yer mean, who sent me?'

Joe was remembering how he thought he heard someone behind him when he was carrying Dolly through Newington Butts. It occurred to him now that Blackbeard had got on his tracks in the fog. It was in keeping with the determination of the man, and he'd probably only held off because those bobbies had to be somewhere in the vicinity. But he'd made sure he knew where the quarry lived. And today he'd made enquiries, of course, and had found it easy to be put in touch with someone who would sniff around in search of the wallet, someone like Archie.

'I mean what I say, Archie. Who sent you, and for what?'

'I ain't quite observant of your meanin', if you get me drift,' said Archie.

'Don't play about,' said Joe. 'Answer up, or I'll tread on your foot. It'll put you in hospital.'

''Ere, that ain't neighbourly, talkin' like that,' said Archie in alarm. 'I'm surprised at yer, mate, I never reckoned you was that kind of bloke. I've said more'n once to Bessie Beavis what a credit you was to the human race.'

'Give you thirty seconds, Archie, to spill the beans,' said Joe, who was still guessing. But he had a feeling it wasn't a bad guess. Walworth was hardly the place where families had money lying about, except perhaps a few pennies in a cocoa tin for feeding gas meters. Archie had turned the living-room over not in search of money, but in search of the wallet. In which case, someone had sent him to do just that. Blackbeard. 'Thirty seconds, Archie.'

''Ere, and then what?' protested Archie.

'I'll cut your hamstrings, you bugger, and you'll never walk again.'

'Oh, yer bleedin' terror, yer mean it.'

Sergeant Joe didn't quite, but he looked as if he did, his eyes like gimlets, his mouth a hard line beneath his moustache.

'Cough up,' he said.

'All right,' said Archie, 'only for gawd's sake don't say I did. I was walkin' 'ome to me Connie this afternoon, and a bloke stopped me an' spoke to me. Asked me who lived in yer lodgings. Well, the 'ouse. 'E pointed it out. I told 'im. Well, 'e give me 'alf-a-crown, so I 'ad to pay me dues in the way of informin' 'im. 'E asked me to describe yer, which I did, thinkin' maybe 'e was goin' to tell yer you'd come into some money, but 'e said you'd taken in a young woman, that the pair of you 'ad nicked 'is wallet an' made off with it. When I said why didn't 'e go an' get it back 'isself, 'e said don't ask questions. 'E asked me if I'd go an' look for it, and 'e gave me a quid. Well, I put it to yer, Joe, a quid for just 'aving a look around, you can't 'old that against a mate like me. Mind, it was the surprise of me life to 'ear you'd teamed up with a fly female pickpocket, I didn't know you was one of the lads.'

'It's a long story,' said Joe, 'with a different ending from yours. What was the bloke like?'

'Funny geezer, but dressed dapper, yer know. Smart overcoat an' bowler.'

'Funny?'

'Foreigner, like,' said Archie, forthcoming on account of the fact that Sergeant Joe still looked ready to do him grievous bodily harm. 'Can't say much about 'is looks, 'e 'ad a scarf wrapped around 'is neck an' face; you could only see 'is hooter an' mince pies. I 'ad to meet 'im after I'd 'ad me look around. Course, I 'ad to 'ang about a bit until I saw yer go out, and afterwards I met 'im at the Elephant an' Castle. 'E didn't 'alf spit when I told 'im no luck. 'E said I'd got to give it another go. 'E said if you didn't 'ave the wallet, then yer female accomplice did. I was to get at 'er in the bedroom, 'e said. Use a knife on 'er, 'e said. Tell 'er you'll cut 'er throat if she don't come up with it. I said I wasn't cuttin' no-one's throat, I didn't go in for it. Well, a bloke can't, can 'e, unless 'e don't mind the 'igh jump. Blimey, 'is eyes bulged at that, 'e looked blue murder at me. 'E's got funny blue eyes, they stare at yer all the time. I tell yer, Joe, I ain't too partial to that cove, and nor ain't I 'appy that 'e knows where I live. What's more, 'e's callin' on me late tonight to find out if I've 'ad another go and if I've earned the quid.'

'Right,' said Joe.

'What's bleedin' right about it?' asked Archie.

'Pop over in an hour,' said Joe, 'and I'll give you the wallet. You can tell him you showed the girl a knife, that you got into her room and that she handed the wallet over. Right?'

'Always knew you were one of me mates,' said Archie, highly gratified that things had suddenly been made easy for him. 'Only I been sufferin' 'orrible suspicions about endin' up gettin' me own throat cut.'

Sergeant Joe looked long and hard at the fox of Newington Butts. Archie shuffled his feet and looked as if he'd like to vanish up his parlour chimney. But Joe wasn't thinking about Archie's throat, or Dolly's. He was thinking, suddenly, about the stop press report on a man who had suffered that fate in Houndsditch late last night. Now why should that enter his mind? He had no answer to his unspoken question.

'Pop over in an hour, Archie,' he said again.

'What a pal,' said Archie. 'And what's more, yer me friend as well.'

Dolly hopped back to the bedroom just in time, for a moment later up came Linda and Ella to say that as

Sergeant Joe was out, their mum had asked them to keep her company for a bit.

'She told us yer like bein' talked to,' said Ella, as round as Humpty Dumpty.

'Yes, she told us you couldn't do much 'cos of yer sprain,' said Linda. 'She told us to come up an' do yer a nice kindness by talkin' to yer.'

'I'm overcome,' said Dolly, resigning herself. She wasn't having the best of luck lately. She'd hopped into the living-room a few minutes after Sergeant Joe had gone out to have a few words with Archie Cousins. She'd searched and searched for the wallet. She had a feeling it was in that carpet-bag, but couldn't get at the bag. The larder door was locked.

'We all do talkin',' said Ella. She thought. 'It's like Bedlam in our kitchen sometimes,' she added proudly.

'Ain't you lucky?' said Dolly.

'We're awful sorry you ain't got no fam'ly, nor no 'ome,' said Linda.

'Still, yer got nice looks,' said Ella.

'Well, thanks,' said Dolly.

Linda saw ankle-boots beside the bed.

'Oh, would yer like me to shine yer boots?' she asked. 'I'll do 'em for a penny, if yer like, I got lots of spit.'

'A penny?' said Dolly, who couldn't help smiling.

'I does Sergeant Joe's gent's shoes for a penny,' said Linda.

'That's not much,' said Dolly, 'you can do mine for tuppence, we'll ask 'im to pay as I'm a bit 'ard-up me-self.'

'Oh, d'yer fink 'e'll pay tuppence?' asked Linda.

'I'll talk to 'im if 'e argues,' said Dolly.

'I'll go an' get the box,' said Linda, 'and I'll get me best spit ready.' She fetched the box containing the polish, brushes and velvet polishers. She sat down on the floor and went to work.

''Ere, miss, we 'ad stew an' dumplings for supper,' said Ella, face still shiny from her large meal.

'Stew an' dumplings?' said Dolly. 'Crikey, what a spread.'

'Ella 'ad seconds,' said Linda.

'We all did,' said Ella, residing plumply on the edge of the bed.

'I didn't,' said Linda.

'Mum says you'll get poorly not 'aving seconds,' accused Ella.

'You 'ad dumpling seconds,' said Linda.

'Well, Dad told us dumplings keep yer body and soul together,' said Ella. She looked at Dolly, resting on the bed. Dolly was visibly slim. 'Don't you 'ave dumplings?' she asked.

'I ain't 'ad much chance,' said Dolly.

'Oh, course, you ain't got no job nor 'ome, 'ave yer?' said Ella sympathetically. 'There was two dumplings over from our supper. Would you like 'em? I'll go an' bring them up, if yer like, with some gravy.'

'How kind,' said Dolly, 'only I ain't long had fried plaice an' mash.'

Linda, doing some good spit and polish work, said, 'I fink Sergeant Joe's comin' up the stairs.'

'Us is in 'ere, Sergeant Joe,' called Ella, 'Mum told us to come up and talk to yer lady friend.'

Joe entered the bedroom.

'Well, who's doing the talking, then?' he asked.

'We all are,' said Ella.

'I ain't,' said Linda. 'Well, not much, I'm cleanin' Dolly's boots for 'er. She said tuppence for doin' them, Sergeant Joe.'

'Tuppence? That much?'

'She said you'd give it to me, Sergeant Joe.'

'Well,' said Ella, 'she ain't got no job, yer see, an' she's 'ard-up.'

76

'Got her head screwed on the right way, though,' said Joe.

'I 'ope you ain't goin' to be mean,' said Dolly.

'All right, here's tuppence, Carrots.' Joe fished out the coppers and handed them to Linda.

'Oh, yer swell,' she said. 'Are yer goin' to sit an' talk wiv us?'

'Sounds exciting,' said Joe. Dolly put her tongue out. 'But I've got a little job to do. You carry on, just as you are. Or what about your mum, Ella, think she might like to come up and join the hen party?'

Dolly expelled a hiss. Joe departed for his living-room, another grin on his face. He left Ella asking Dolly if she should go down and get her mum. He knew what the answer to that would be.

He studied again the letter he had found in the wallet, then got to work making a careful copy of it. He had to take care because the language was foreign. Not French, though. Nor German. He would have recognized French or German, without being able to speak either language. Some of the letters were very odd.

Finishing, he put the original back into its envelope, applied the merest smear of thin gum to the flap and stuck it down. Satisfied, he returned the envelope to the wallet. The fivers were still there. He gave them some thought, then extracted two and stowed them in his hip pocket. At that moment he heard Mrs Beavis call up to her girls.

'Come an' 'ave yer 'ot cocoa, loveys.'

Down the stairs the girls went seconds later. Ella sounded as if she was bouncing down, with Linda skipping after her. He smiled. The whole family liked to be heard, as if they wanted people to know they were alive in a world where young and old alike were here one day and gone the next.

For the next ten minutes the house was quiet except for the perceptible hum of healthy life from the kitchen. Then Dolly made herself heard.

77

'Here, you there, Napoleon?'

Dolly, in fact, was fed-up. She didn't like immobility, she didn't like being on her own, and she didn't like the fact that the wallet still hadn't been given back to her, not when she'd nicked it at great personal risk.

Joe appeared, looking as if he'd just finished knocking the Army into shape, and the Navy as well.

'State your requirements,' he said.

'State my what? Look, stop talkin' like that,' she said.

'Feeling poorly, are we?'

'It's all me frustrations,' said Dolly from the bed. 'Still, I don't like to keep botherin' you.'

'No bother,' said Joe, observing that her pretty petticoat was showing.

'It don't seem right, though, askin' for things when you've been such a kind bloke to me, and doctored me as well.'

'Can't remember doctoring you,' said Joe. 'Isn't that something to do with—'

'Oh, help,' she said hastily, 'me tongue fell over me feet. I meant – well, if you must know I wouldn't 'alf like a cup of tea.'

'Good. I'll get you one. Won't take more than—' Joe was interrupted by a double knock on the front door. 'I think I know who that is,' he said. 'Won't be a minute.'

It was Archie, of course.

'I'm 'ere, mate,' he announced. Behind him the fog was rolling. ''Ave yer got it?'

'Here,' said Joe, producing the wallet. Archie was bound to nose around in it, but wouldn't interfere with the contents. He had the wind up. 'Hand it to your funny friend just as it is. Understand?'

'You bet I do,' said Archie, receiving the wallet with gratitude. 'I tell yer, Joe old cock, my bleedin' trouble is that I'm misunderstood meself, I been sufferin' misunderstandin' all me life. All I want now is to get this 'ere wallet into the mitts of that geezer I don't like the look of.'

'You can let me know tomorrow morning if he cuts your throat,' said Joe.

'Eh? 'Ere, that ain't much of a joke,' said Archie.

'Well, who's laughing?' asked Joe.

'I ain't,' said Archie. 'Anyway, ta, Joe, yer a pal.' Off he went, and the fog wrapped itself around him.

Joe climbed the stairs again, exercising his stiff knee in his persevering way.

'You back again?' called Dolly.

'I'll bring you some tea in a few minutes,' he said.

Dolly perked up when he brought it, because the tray contained two cups, together with the pot itself.

'Oh, you goin' to be sociable?' she said, sitting up.

'Don't see why not.' Joe placed the tray on the bedside table and poured the tea.

'You're a good bloke,' said Dolly, receiving her cup. Joe sat down. 'Would you like to hear about me orphanage days? You can tell me about the Army after. You don't mind talkin' a bit with me, do you?'

'I'm not much good at parlour talk,' said Joe.

'Don't make me split me sides,' said Dolly, 'you can talk all right, don't I know it. It's me that's not much good at it. At the orphanage I was complimented on me English composition, but I've always been a bit shy about speakin' up for meself.'

'Have I noticed that?' asked Joe.

'Yes, I thought you 'ad,' said Dolly. 'Of course, you talk more than I do because you've 'ad more education than me.'

'Not much,' said Joe.

'If I'd been educated proper, I expect I'd be able to talk more,' said Dolly, 'specially if I 'ad good looks and not just a sort of orphanage face. Mind you, when I was skivvying for that Brixton fam'ly, the head of the fam'ly didn't 'alf take a fancy to me.'

79

'Probably had a funny kind of weakness for a sort of orphanage face,' said Joe.

'Yes, that's what it was, I expect,' said Dolly. 'Did I tell you I 'ad to run away in the end because he got to fancy me too much? Well, not being that kind of a girl, I wasn't goin' to stay there with me virtue in danger.'

Joe let her talk. Usually, he took a walk in the evenings, going down Kennington Park Road as far as the Oval, and dropping into a pub on the way back for an ale and a chat with any friends or acquaintances he found there. His knee stood up well to any excursion. He repeatedly told himself he'd beat the stiffness out of it one day.

Dolly Nobody or Whatever was coming along. Her ankle had had a full day's rest, and it shouldn't take long for her to be on her feet again. What she'd need then would be some fresh clothes. In fact, that was what she needed now. Her present outfit was a mess. Well, as soon as she was up and about she could buy some new stuff. She had ten quid coming to her. In the meantime, perhaps he could get her a blouse and skirt from somewhere.

'Have to find you a change of clothes,' he said.

'Here, ain't you listening?' she asked. 'I've just been tellin' you how Mr Winterburn chased me all over the house when 'is fam'ly was at church one Sunday. He was set on sweepin' me off me feet and doin' me wrong. I 'ad to hit him with an ornament, and when his fam'ly got back from church 'is wife asked him what 'ad happened to his face. He said he walked accidental into a door – here, who's that?'

Someone was coming up the stairs, treading quickly and lightly.

'It's Linda,' said Joe.

It was. She wanted to know if Sergeant Joe would like her dad's evening paper, if he hadn't bought one for himself. Joe said no, he hadn't today, and that he'd like a look at her dad's.

'I brought it up,' said Linda, and gave it to him. 'My, ain't you 'aving a nice rest,' she said to Dolly, 'an' wiv Sergeant Joe sittin' by yer bedside.' She giggled at a sudden thought. 'I best not tell Nancy, or she might come up and 'ave a jealous fit all over the room. Well, Sergeant Joe ain't ever sat by 'er bedside.'

'Yes, keep it dark, Private Carrots,' said Joe, and Linda departed with more giggles. Joe took a look at the front page of the paper. There was a headline about the murder in Houndsditch, together with a photograph of the victim. He was wearing a flat cap, a suit and a choker, and there were dock gates in the background. He looked a tough and burly man, and Joe thought he was vaguely familiar. It made him think about last night's events. No, he was imagining things, he hadn't seen the man all that clearly in the fog.

'What's up?' asked Dolly.

'Take a look,' said Joe, and handed her the paper. The photograph sprang to her eyes and startled her.

'Oh, Lord,' she breathed. She knew she had seen this man not just in the fog, but in the Rockingham public house. She had seen him hand a letter to the man with a black beard. 'Joe, that's him, that's the bloke you knocked down!'

'Can't say I like the look of this,' said Joe, frowning.

CHAPTER SEVEN

The murdered man's name was Dan Pearson. He was a docker, living in Artillery Lane off Bishopsgate, not far from Houndsditch. The police were making enquiries and would be pleased to hear from any person who had seen the victim on the night he was murdered.

'That means us,' said Dolly.

'And a few others, I suppose,' said Joe, who had closed the bedroom door.

'What're we goin' to do?' asked Dolly.

'I'm not going to do anything, except wait and see how the police get on,' said Joe, 'and I don't know what you can do except tell the police that you got acquainted with the unfortunate bloke when he came after you for nicking that wallet from Blackbeard. That would put you right in the soup. Can't have that, can we, not on top of all your other hard luck. You need taking care of. I wonder why Dan Pearson was murdered?'

'He didn't deserve that,' said Dolly. 'I mean, he was a bruiser all right, but he didn't like the idea of Blackbeard doin' you and me in.'

'Yes, think about Blackbeard and what a cold-blooded character he is, and a foreign one at that. He was sweating on getting that wallet back. What's he doing in London? What's the betting he's up to no good, and that he felt Dan Pearson got to know too much about him and needed to be silenced?'

'Oh, crikey, d'you think so?' asked Dolly.

'Where was it you first saw them?'

'In that pub by the Elephant and Castle, the Rockingham,' said Dolly. 'I was cold and starvin', so I went in. I'd found some bunches of violets that weren't much good, but I thought I might sell them in the pub, or that some kind gent might treat me to a sandwich. They do mouth-waterin' ham sandwiches in the Rockingham. Well, I saw Blackbeard there. This other bloke came in and joined 'im. They talked a bit in whispers, then the other bloke, Dan Pearson, gave Blackbeard a letter, which he put in his wallet. Well, as no-one 'ad bought any of me violets or treated me to a sandwich, and me near dyin' of starvation, with no job and no lodgings, well, I was so desperate I went up and grabbed the wallet, which Blackbeard was wavin' about at Dan Pearson. Then I just rushed out of the pub and started runnin', then you got in me way and knocked me over and sprained me ankle.'

'Pardon?' said Joe.

'Well, good as,' said Dolly. 'Still, I liked you for standin' up for me like you did. You don't 'old it against me for pinchin' the wallet, do you?'

'You need an uncle,' said Joe. 'You sure you're twenty-one?'

'Of course I am.'

'Where's your birth certificate?'

'I don't know that I ever 'ad one, the orphanage never said I did, but they did say me birthday was December the second, and that I was born in 1889.'

'Well, you don't need an uncle, after all, not at that age,' said Joe, 'you need a sergeant-major. I'll have to promote myself and tidy your life up for you.'

'You're bossy, you are,' said Dolly. 'But look, what about this murder, d'you really think Blackbeard did it?'

'He looked capable of murdering us,' said Joe.

'Oh, help, you're right, he did,' breathed Dolly. 'He'll come after us now, seein' he was desperate to get 'is wallet back.'

'He's probably got it back by now.'

'What?' Dolly stiffened.

'Didn't I tell you about it?' asked Joe.

'Tell me?' Dolly fumed. 'You don't hardly pass the time of day with me, this is the first time you've sat and talked to me. How could Blackbeard 'ave got his wallet back, go on, tell me.'

'Slippery Archie's the go-between,' said Joe, and explained. Dolly looked as if she wanted to spit.

'Oh, you daft loony,' she said, 'call yourself a sergeant?'

'Watch your mouth, Private Nobody.'

'But lettin' him 'ave it all back, the money and letter as well,' said Dolly bitterly. 'Don't you see, there could 'ave been five 'undred quid in fifty-quid notes in that letter, which was why he was spittin' blue murder.'

'No, there was no money,' said Joe, 'just a letter.'

'How d'you know?'

'I steamed it open.'

'You did what?' Dolly stared suspiciously at him.

'Steamed it open. I was curious. Couldn't understand it, though, it was in a foreign language. What d'you think, Dolly, might it have been details of a plan to rob the Bank of England?'

'Well, if it was, what a daft thing to do, lettin' him 'ave it back,' fumed Dolly. 'We could 'ave kept it and blackmailed him.'

'Pardon?' said Joe.

'Well, so we could,' said Dolly.

'You go in for blackmail as well, Private Nobody?'

'No, course not,' said Dolly. 'Well, not much.'

'It's going to be harder work than I thought, tidying your life up.'

'It's all right for you,' said Dolly, 'you ain't never been a poor orphan girl.'

'Point taken,' said Joe, 'so in view of all your hard luck, I kept two of the fivers.' He drew them from his hip pocket. 'I think Blackbeard owes you this much. Here we are, ten quid. When you're back on your feet, you'll be able to buy yourself some new duds.'

Dolly, taking the fivers, stared at them.

'You left the other two in the wallet?' she asked.

'Yes, to let Blackbeard know we only charged him fifty per cent for returning it.'

'Oh, you're a soft touch, you are,' said Dolly.

'Think so?' said Joe. 'But now he doesn't have to come after us. You felt he would. Don't want that, do we, young Dolly?' Neither of them could afford to get mixed up in something that might involve the police.

'Oh, blow it,' said Dolly, 'and fancy you not takin' the other ten quid for yourself. You can't get paid much for writin' out business letters.'

'Well, it's done now,' said Joe. Dolly made a fidgety gesture. 'Cheer up, Blackbeard's off our backs now. Right, let's have one more go at your ankle before we both turn in.'

Dolly let him get on with it in the usual way. The swelling was still very perceptible, and so was the bruised look. He asked how it felt.

'Better,' she said. 'I'll be able to get up and go out tomorrow.'

'You can forget that,' said Joe. 'You're not getting up and you're not going out.'

'Who says so?'

'I do,' said Joe, busy with the wet flannel.

'Here, mind yourself,' said Dolly, 'you're not me keeper, y'know.'

'You're confined to barracks for the time being, Private Nobody.'

'I'll hit you if you keep callin' me that daft name,' said Dolly. 'And d'you mind not playin' about with me petticoat? It 'appens to be private.'

'Not touching it,' said Joe, 'and stop trying to kick me. I'll see if I can get you some clothes tomorrow. Can't have you wearing that grubby skirt and blouse much longer.'

'Well, thanks very much,' said Dolly, 'and why don't you try and get me a spare face as well, seein' you don't like the one I've got?'

'Why shouldn't I like it? It's quite a nice face.'

'Honest? You don't think all me days of starvation 'ave ruined it?'

'Hardly at all,' said Joe. 'It strikes me that in new clothes you could be highly presentable. If we can get you a job in a store, we might later on get you married to one of the floorwalkers. Would you like that?'

'Can't wait, can I?' said Dolly, and Joe fastened the cold compress.

'Good night, Dolly,' he said, and was smiling as he went out.

It left Dolly fretful.

She had a job getting to sleep later.

He took breakfast to her the following morning. She woke up, her eyes dreamy.

'Morning,' said Joe. 'Breakfast. Toast and tea. Sit up.'

'What?' She came to. 'Not likely,' she said. She had nothing on.

'Understood,' said Joe. 'I'll leave it here.' He placed the tray on the bedside table. 'I'll be going out when I've had mine. Don't try going out yourself or you'll catch it. I'll bring a daily paper in for you.'

'I'm goin' to be all by meself again?' asked Dolly, her hair flooding the pillow with auburn.

'Only for an hour or so,' said Joe. 'Shall I ask Mrs Beavis to bring you up some knitting?'

'What a joke,' said Dolly, 'don't you know any funny ones?'

The morning was fine. It was the last day of March, and overnight the belated wind had arrived to clear every vestige of fog from the brick and stone of London. The sun was out, the air bright and crisp, the traffic busy. Office and factory girls were hurrying to their work, some boarding trams and some walking. Straw boaters sat perkily on the heads of office girls, and the hems of their long skirts swirled around their ankles. Saucy hats were favoured by the factory girls, and saucy lights danced in their eyes as van drivers or cart drivers whistled at them.

'Oi, Gertie, what yer doin' tonight?'

'Mind yer business, 'Oratio, I ain't doin' it with you.'

Over Waterloo Bridge, the horse traffic was a slow-moving procession, and pedestrians, streaming along to their places of work in the West End or the City, passed rumbling drays and laden carts as if these horse-drawn vehicles were standing still. Men and women, seated on the open top decks of newfangled motorized omnibuses, had elevated views of what the bright morning sun was doing to the muddy Thames. It was coating the flowing brown surface with shimmering, sparkling gold. Along the north bank, the crisp light was sharpening the noble outlines of majestic buildings, although it could do very little for stone blackened by the soot of ages.

Joe, limping along amid the flow of workers and enjoying the exercise and the clear air, saw barges cleaving the sunlit surface of the river, a crowded passenger boat in their wake.

It was good to be out. It was always good, the more so because he spent a great deal of time trapped indoors by his choice of work, a choice governed by his wish to acquire a useful little nest-egg in a relatively short time. He would have preferred an outdoor job. With horses, perhaps. He knew about horses from his years as a dragoon. Well, he could look around in time. As for marriage, yes, he fancied that. A wife and some kids, a family. What men didn't have that urge? Some, of course, but he wasn't one of them. Ivy Williams, a shopkeeper's daughter, twenty years old, was a very nice girl. So was Alice Dodds, who lived with her family at the far end of the Butts. He knew them both quite well. Not that he supposed either of them would jump at him, since neither was short of admirers. And he had no intention of getting seriously involved while he was executing dubious commissions for George. All that would have to go before he took up with any woman. He was giving forgery another year. George accepted that. Then he would put his quill pens aside and consider an honest job of work. And marriage.

He turned into the Strand. It was a bustle of traffic and workers. In this popular thoroughfare, restaurants and theatres existed side by side with shops and offices. The time was coming up to nine o'clock, and shopkeepers were making ready to open their doors. Romano's, the restaurant haunt of fashionable people, was closed, but would be open for lunch. Dignified City men in top hats, using rolled umbrellas like walking-sticks, advanced unhurriedly towards Fleet Street, Chancery Lane and other City venues. Their clerks, mostly in straw boaters, hurried along. So did shop girls and office girls. To be late would earn a reprimand and possibly a warning from those who stood above them.

Joe crossed the Strand to St Martin's Place, and from there entered Charing Cross Road. He passed theatres sleepy with morning, and walked on to Singleton's bookshop, noted for its excellent array of new books and old books, and for its service to customers looking for something special in the way of rare editions. The shop was open and George was there but still yawning. He came fully awake, however, when Joe walked in.

'Ye gods, at this time of the day, my friend?' he said, his portly form draped by a dark grey suit comfortable enough to give his portliness room to live and breathe.

'Won't keep you long,' said Joe.

'Never say so, my dear fellow,' said George. 'My hope with some people is that they don't stay any longer than they need to. Not so with you. You are a natural gentleman, Joe. A natural gentleman is a man who serves his friends honourably and doesn't bore them.'

'Have you had a good breakfast?' asked Joe.

'I fancy you could say so,' said George, 'yes, I fancy you could.'

'Thought so. Can you do me a small favour?'

'Why not a large one?'

'Don't need a large one,' said Joe. 'Can you get someone to translate this for me?' He produced the folded sheet of notepaper on which he'd copied down Blackbeard's letter. He unfolded it and handed it to George. 'Any idea of the language?'

'Russian,' said George immediately. 'What's it all about?'

'Don't know, can't say, haven't the foggiest,' said Joe. 'I'm curious, that's all. You can't translate it yourself, I suppose? I'll wait if you can.'

'I can recognize it's in Russian, but no, I can't translate it myself, old chap,' said George. 'Never mind, leave it with me. I know two or three people, any of whom will do it.'

Something made Joe say, 'Someone you can trust. It's confidential.'

'Now I'm curious myself.'

'Yes, we're all a bit nosy, aren't we?' Joe smiled.

'Call again in a couple of days,' said George. 'Meanwhile, allow me to give you glad tidings. I'm promised by our very reliable agent that we'll receive the excessively handsome sum of fifty guineas, in the form of a draft from Paris, for the two letters from Molière to his lady love.'

'Fifty guineas?' Joe whistled. 'Dangerous amount, George.'

'Worthy, old fellow, worthy. Your genius for copying

89

the handwriting of the noble, the illustrious, the famous and the infamous is remarkable. Your letters in French, particularly the French of Molière, are incredibly so, for you don't speak the language. I envisage a mountain of guineas from France. Capital, Joe, capital, and we're safer selling abroad.'

'Yes, less chance of being found out,' said Joe.

'Well, my friend, it's a happy fact that not every collector would wish to advertise the fact that he's been fooled. They'd rather settle for a return of their money, if it came to that. But yes, abroad lies our final year of partnership, although I've been toying with the idea of alighting upon a play by Shakespeare hitherto unknown, unseen and unenacted.'

'What did you have for your breakfast, a bottle of brandy?' asked Joe.

'I rarely shake hands with Bacchus, Joe, until the sun goes down,' said George. 'Or Eros, for that matter. I'm quite sober, although elated by the thought of an unknown play by Shakespeare coming to light.'

'You're off your rocker,' said Joe. 'Who'd write it?'

'As a scholar and a Shakespearian, I would. I fancy my acquaintance with the Bard's works and my gift for scribbling would inspire me to produce a dramatic masterpiece. And your own exceptional gifts would help us to confound critics, experts and scoffers. What d'you say to that as a triumphant finale to our partnership, old man?'

'Off your rocker,' repeated Joe.

'Alas,' sighed George, 'have you so little faith in our collective talents?'

'We'd be on a hiding to nothing,' said Joe, 'and that would probably include being shot at dawn. I'll see you in a couple of days, then, and with a packet of some finished stuff.'

'Byron and his associates are coming along?' enquired George in pleasure.

'I'm satisfied with what I've done so far,' said Joe, 'but what a scoundrel.'

'Magnificent poet,' said George, 'and who's perfect?'

'Good point,' said Joe. 'So long, George.'

'So long, my friend.'

On his way back, Joe called in at the local pawnbroker's shop, run by 'Uncle' Jeremiah Baldwin and his daughter Annie. 'Uncle' wasn't around, but Annie was. Annie was a cheerful, tireless and obliging young lady who had a young man, a dowry in an old sock, and a helpful welcome for customers who were not only hard-up but a bit embarrassed. Joe had a job to get through to the counter, for the pawnshop was overflowing with articles awaiting redemption. Suits, coats, dresses, boots, shoes, bicycles, tools, furniture, companion sets, china, ornaments, pictures, stuffed parrots, music-boxes and linen were only some of the things that caught the eye and sometimes an elbow. There was even a piano. There was also a section where goods not redeemed within the allotted time were for sale.

Joe, shouldering his way through, called, 'Come out from wherever you are, Annie, I know you're there somewhere, I've just seen your knees. But don't faint, it was only your knees.'

A little shriek escaped a startled mouth, and Annie popped out from behind a bamboo table containing a large potted aspidistra.

'Oh, yer cheeky cuss, Sergeant Joe, it would be you to catch me fixin' me stocking garter.'

'Well, sometimes a bloke's lucky, sometimes not,' said Joe.

Annie laughed. In a high-collared striped blouse of blue and white, and a dark blue skirt, she looked attractively neat. Just right for size, thought Joe, just about the same measurements as Dolly.

91

'What can I do yer for?' asked Annie. 'You ain't come to put yerself in pawn, 'ave you? Don't know where I could put you, except in me bedroom, only if I did it might send me young man potty. Here, I heard you'd got a young lady stayin' with yer.'

'She's a lodger of mine,' said Joe.

'A likely story, you're a lodger yerself,' said Annie.

'I've sub-let,' said Joe. 'Well, she's got a damaged ankle, no home and no family. I found her in the fog. Didn't want her to chuck herself off a bridge, so I've let her have one of my rooms.'

'Sounds as if she needs an 'elping hand,' said Annie. 'I suppose she's broke as well, is she? 'Ave you come to pawn something of hers?'

'No, I've come to see if you can fix her up with a couple of skirts and blouses, Annie, from your unredeemed stuff. Nothing tarty, something respectable.'

'Tarty? Like yer sauce,' said Annie. 'Still, we've got skirts and blouses.'

'Yes, she needs a change of clothes until she's on her feet and can do her own shopping,' said Joe. 'She's only got the stuff she's wearing.'

'That's hard on a girl,' said Annie, and kept her face straight as she asked, 'What about a change of other things?'

'I'm not answering that,' said Joe.

'You can confide in me,' said Annie, 'it's what I'm 'ere for, to be a help to customers. I mean, we've got bloomers and things.'

'I'm not listening,' said Joe, at which point a middle-aged woman came in, found her way through the maze and reached the counter. She'd come, she said, to redeem her husband's watch and chain. Joe stood aside.

'That's quick, Mrs Goodbody,' said Annie, 'it's only been a couple of days.'

'I know,' said Mrs Goodbody. She handed over the

pawn ticket. 'But me old man says 'e never knows what the time is.'

'Don't you 'ave a mantelpiece clock, then?' asked Annie.

'Oh, 'e don't believe in tin clocks, only in 'is pocket watch,' said Mrs Goodbody. 'It come to 'im from 'is dad; 'e says 'e feels undressed without it an' don't know whether it's 'alf-past five or ten to eight when 'e gets up, or if it's teatime or dinnertime. So I better 'ave it out, Annie, that's if I can pawn me lace tablecloth for one an' six, same as you gave me on the watch.' She took the tablecloth, wrapped in brown paper, from her shopping-bag. Annie unwrapped it and inspected it. It was a domestic treasure.

'One an' six, Mrs Goodbody? Two bob, if yer like.'

'Yer a good sort, Annie, so's yer dad. I'll take two bob, then, and you can take the one an' six an' the penny interest out of it. I'll come in on Saturday and 'ave the tablecloth back for Sunday tea, seein' me sister and 'er old man's coming to 'ave shrimps an' winkles with us. Me sister's 'aving terrible trouble with 'er eldest daughter. She wants to do bareback ridin' in a circus and show 'er legs like all them circus girls do. Me sister never showed 'er legs in all 'er life, nor me, neither. I don't know what girls are comin' to. Ain't it shockin', mister?' she said to Joe.

'Queen Mary won't like it,' said Joe.

'Oh, lor', nor she won't,' said Mrs Goodbody, 'I just 'ope she don't get to hear about it. I read she's partic'lar about be'aviour. I wouldn't iike me niece's be'aviour to spoil the coronation. Oh, ta, Annie.' She received the watch and chain from the pawnbroker's daughter, together with the new pawn ticket and fivepence, and went off in a pleasured state over the transaction, although a little worried that Queen Mary might find out that her naughty niece wanted to show her legs riding bareback on a circus horse.

'Now, Sergeant Joe,' said Annie, 'let's see about your wants. What size you after for the skirts and blouses?'

'Your size,' said Joe.

'Oh, you've measured yer sub-let lodger, 'ave you?' said Annie. 'I don't recollect you measurin' me.'

'I'm relying on my eyesight,' said Joe.

'Cheeky. All right, let's see what me dad's emporium can offer.'

Annie was a great help after finding out from Joe what the young lady's colouring was. She sold him something simple, one skirt of navy blue, one which she said was autumn brown, and two white blouses. She also persuaded him to buy a hip-length jacket to help the suffering young lady keep warm if she was only sitting around nursing her ankle. The lot cost Joe only a few bob.

'What's that?' he asked, pointing.

'A lady's straw boater,' said Annie.

'Thought so. Try it on.'

'I should think she needs other things more than a boater,' said Annie.

'I'm having nothing to do with things,' said Joe, 'so stop your tickling. Be a good girl and try that boater on.'

'Well, me dad always says we've got to be obligin'.' Annie put the boater on, tilting it. It fitted and gave her a perky look. 'Mind, it might not fit 'er.'

'I'll chance it,' said Joe, and paid for the boater.

'Tell you what, Joe,' said Annie, 'you 'aven't got new stuff there, but you 'aven't got rubbish, either, and you've 'ad me best attention as well. On top of which, I'll put everything in a cardboard box for you free and for nothing.'

'Go top of the class, Annie, especially as I've had a look at your knees,' said Joe. 'Strikes me you'd look a treat yourself riding bareback at a circus.'

'Saucy this mornin', are we?' said Annie. 'You'd better

'oppit now or me young man might get to 'ear I've been dilly-dallying with you.'

'Don't like the sound of that,' said Joe, 'it could mean I might get damaged and laid up myself. So long, Annie, and good luck.' He departed, cardboard box under his arm, his back straight and his limp brisk.

CHAPTER EIGHT

On his return, Joe took the *Westminster Gazette* in to Dolly.

'How's the patient?' he asked.

'Nearly dead,' she said, lying flat out on the bed. 'Mrs Beavis came up again, and with Bovril and a cheese roll. You can laugh. She's only just gone down, after givin' me her life story and what 'appened at her granddad's funeral when a wheel came off the 'earse. Thank 'eavens you're back – oh, the swine, he's gone again.'

But he came back, this time with a cardboard box.

'Have you read the paper?' he asked.

''Course I 'aven't, you've only been gone a minute.'

'There's nothing in it about the murder, except the police are continuing with their enquiries,' said Joe, 'but it'll help you pass the time. By the way, what name did you answer to in your jobs? Not Nobody, that's just a lark.'

'It ain't a lark to a girl that's got no 'ome, no fam'ly—'

'Answer up,' said Joe.

'Well, it was Smith, of course,' said Dolly.

'Understood,' said Joe, feeling that all her years of hard luck hadn't wrecked her spirit.

'What's in that box?'

'Clothes,' said Joe. 'I mentioned I'd try to get hold of some for you. There you are.' He placed the box on the bed. 'Skirts and blouses.'

'You 'aving me on?' said Dolly.

'You need a change of clothes,' said Joe.

'Where'd you get them from?' asked Dolly, sitting up.

'Local pawnshop,' said Joe.

'What? Here, I ain't wearin' clothes from a pawnshop.'

'Yes, you are, and they're quite clean. Don't let's have any fireworks, Private Smith. Get changed.'

'You're as bossy as a copper, you are,' said Dolly.

'Would you like bacon and eggs at midday?' asked Joe.

'Oh, you lovely feller, not 'alf I wouldn't,' said Dolly, 'I was too weak to eat the cheese roll, so Bessie ate it for me.'

'Bessie?'

'Well, she's not so bad really,' said Dolly, 'she's just a bit overflowin', that's all.'

'Well, there's a lot of her,' said Joe, making another exit.

'What?' asked Dolly. 'Oh, what's the use, he's gone again.' She called him a little later. 'Here, mister, would you like to see what you've been and done to me?'

Joe came to take a look. She was wearing the navy blue skirt and one of the white blouses, with a frilled front. The boater was on her head and she was looking at herself, her bare right foot touching the floor lightly.

'Not bad, not bad at all,' said Joe.

'What, me in these pawnshop leftovers?' she said, turning. The blouse shaped her very nicely, he thought. Actually, both garments fitted her very well, and the boater gave her the same kind of perky look it had given Annie. 'Ain't you ashamed, makin' me wear things out of a pawnshop?'

'No, not much,' he said.

'Still, the blouse and skirt don't look too bad, d'you think?'

'You look very nice, Dolly.'

'Like to take me out, would you?'

'Not yet,' said Joe, 'your ankle wouldn't stand for it.' He picked up the garments she'd taken off. He picked up the old shawl and straw hat too. 'I'll chuck this lot in the dustbin.'

'What for?' she asked.

'Best place for them, the dustbin.'

'Oh, don't mind me,' said Dolly, 'I'm only – here, where you goin' again? You're like a bloomin' jack-in-the-box, you are.' She hopped to the open door to make sure her voice followed him. 'You're drivin' me dizzy, you ain't no sooner in here than you're out again.' He was descending the stairs now. 'Can't you stay still for five minutes? I don't know, chuckin' me clothes in the dustbin, I suppose you'd like to chuck me in as well. You listening, mister?'

'Yes.' His voice floated up to her. 'I'll see you in a couple of minutes, Private Smith.'

'What for?'

'To chuck you in the dustbin for unbecoming bawling and shouting.'

Dolly limped to the bed and flung herself down on it, stifling hysteria. That man, he didn't know what a comedian he was. All that funny Army stuff. Not that he was dotty all the time. She'd never seen anyone move as fast as he did when he put poor old Dan Pearson on his back. And he'd done the right thing in getting that wallet back to Blackbeard, because Blackbeard was horribly evil and would have come after them if Joe hadn't been sensible. And he'd given her two fivers first. All the same, she owed him one for slapping her bottom. No-one had ever done that to her before. Even so, what other man would have helped her like he had and given her his bed as well? But bringing her clothes from a pawnshop, oh, help.

Dolly had to stifle more hysteria.

She heard him coming back up the stairs, she knew his limping step now. He came into the bedroom. She turned over on the bed and sat up.

'I'm for the dustbin now?' she said.

'Not this time,' he said, 'I'll bathe your ankle with warm water in a moment, and put some liniment on it.'

'Ain't you kind? And thanks ever so much for the

clothes, honest. You're a real help to someone like me. Were me other clothes startin' to smell a bit?'

'Not that I noticed,' said Joe. 'But there were one or two fleas.'

'Oh, you rotten beast, I've never 'ad fleas in all me born days.'

'Don't worry,' said Joe, 'what you collected recently are in the dustbin now, saying hello to a pair of old boots. Right, I'll bring some warm water in, with the liniment.'

'Well, you'd better make your will out before you come in again,' said Dolly, 'because I'm goin' to do you in as soon as you put your face round the door.'

But she didn't, of course. She let him treat her ankle and put liniment on it. The swelling was beginning to subside.

'It's coming along,' said Joe.

'Well, you've got a nice touch, Joe, honest you 'ave,' she said. 'Can I come and sit at the table with you when the eggs and bacon are ready?'

'All right, I'll come and carry you in,' said Joe. 'Don't want you limping about too much, not now your ankle's on the mend.'

'You're a good bloke really,' said Dolly.

A tall gentleman, a diplomatic courier with a permanently diplomatic expression of kindness, was sitting in a private room in Collins Coffee House in the City. A person was with him. The gentleman thought of him only as a person, no more than one step up from a peasant. But he was extremely useful at times. That was what made him a person. The gentleman, however, being a diplomat, spoke to him as an equal.

'You are sure the letter had been opened?'

The person, who had a pointed black beard, a large nose, bushy eyebrows and deep-set blue eyes, nodded.

'I'm positive,' he said.

'It was opened by this man and woman?'

'Of that I'm even more positive.'

'Unfortunate. Very. But might not the woman be a mere pickpocket and the man her accomplice, as you first thought?'

'No, I tell you. Only half the money had been taken. That was to mock me. And a mere pickpocket would not have taken the trouble to steam the envelope open.'

'Perhaps they had already spent half the money, perhaps they returned the rest in a gesture to placate you. After all,' said the kind-looking gentleman in his pleasant voice, 'they were aware by then that you knew where they lived, and that there was a chance you'd have them arrested.'

'By the police?' said Blackbeard. 'I am not here to make myself known to the police. No, I believe them to be spies working for a rival power aware of my presence in London and suspicious of my intentions. The steaming open of the letter convinces me.'

'Well,' said the courier, 'you and your confederates must accomplish what you came to do. You have plenty of time to perfect arrangements. But first you'll have to deal with this man and woman to satisfy yourself one way or the other about them. Even if they are what you think they are, rival agents, how could they have known you were expecting a letter, and how could they have known you were expecting it on that particular night?'

'Name of a fox,' said Blackbeard between his teeth, 'the woman was in the place and saw it handed to me. Does that mean it was what she expected? I suspect she'd been following that fool of a carrier.'

'In such a fog as that?'

'We, Your Excellency, are not the only ones who make sure we don't lose the quarry once we have him in our sights. But the handing over of the letter was not something she necessarily expected, it was simply something

100

she saw. What fool picked the carrier, who was an idiot and an inquisitive one?'

'One who knew him, I assume.'

'We are committed, myself and the woman,' said Blackbeard. 'I object to having idiots used as go-betweens. I am always at risk in the things I do for the Motherland, but idiots create the kind of additional risks one cannot always allow for.'

'Well,' said the kind-faced courier, 'you have dealt with this idiot and his inquisitiveness.'

'A greedy inquisitiveness,' said Blackbeard. 'So, now I have to deal with this man and woman.'

'If your assumption that they are the agents of another power is correct, you may be too late. They may have already informed their masters of the contents of the letter.'

'I shall find out,' said Blackbeard. 'What is to be accomplished means too much to the Tsar—'

'Be warned.' The courier's kind expression became slightly reproving. 'His Imperial Highness is not to be mentioned. He knows nothing. You are quite aware the venture is the brainchild of certain senior officers.'

'Nevertheless—'

'Nevertheless has no place in this conversation.'

'My lips, Excellency, are sealed,' said Blackbeard, but his blue eyes hardened a little. He considered himself to be his own master, and deference to this aristocratic head of Russian Intelligence, Count Zhinsky, did not come easily to him.

'The meeting with your colleague will take place when?'

'This afternoon.'

'There must be few meetings between you while you're in London. Make sure you aren't followed, for if it's known you're here you must avoid being seen together.'

Blackbeard was inclined to curl his fleshy lip. Was he an idiot himself? He was not.

'I should not be alive today if I had ever been guilty of complacency or carelessness,' he said.

'We value your gifts,' said the courier. 'Might I suggest you leave now? I will do so a little later.'

What a fool, he's trying to teach me how to suck eggs, thought Blackbeard. Except, of course, he was not a fool. He was the brains of Russian Intelligence. Which was why Blackbeard accepted directives from him, even if he felt that he did not need them.

Over the eggs and bacon, eaten with bread and butter, Dolly said, 'Like you told me, there wasn't anything in the paper about the murder except the police are still workin' on it. But they didn't say there'd be an arrest soon.'

'It's only been a couple of days,' said Joe.

'It's worryin', though, ain't it?'

'Who for?'

'Well, for us. I mean, Blackbeard must know we could 'ave recognized the man from the newspaper photograph, and that we might go to the police about it.'

'Pass the salt, Dolly, would you?'

'Blow the salt, I'm talkin' to you,' said Dolly.

'Yes, I'm listening,' said Joe. 'If we went to the police, we'd have to explain in detail. They'd nick you for lifting the wallet, and me as well probably, for helping you. Pass the salt, please.'

Dolly pushed the cruet across.

'But don't you see that Blackbeard might come after us?' she asked.

'To murder us because he murdered the man we saw him with? It's a point, I suppose. I'd better think about getting you out of here. I'll ask around and see if there's a room vacant somewhere.'

'Me, why just me?' asked Dolly.

'Because you're a young lady, and because you've

102

already had your share of hard luck,' said Joe. 'I'll find you a room—'

'I ain't goin',' said Dolly.

'Now look—'

'I'll scream the place down, I'll tell Bessie you tried to ruin me virtue, I'll tear some of me clothes to prove it.'

'Stop waving your knife about,' said Joe.

'Well, stop upsettin' me, then,' said Dolly. 'Mister, you wouldn't really get rid of a poor girl who's got no 'ome or fam'ly, would you? Oh, me foot, it's all painful suddenly, I think it's 'ad a relapse – that's it, go on, laugh.'

Joe straightened his face.

'I'll have another look at it,' he said.

'Oh, all right,' said Dolly blithely, 'I don't mind you, you like lookin' at me legs, I can tell. Well, I do 'appen to 'ave good legs, and I've been complimented on me knees too.'

'What have we got here?' asked Joe of the salt cellar. 'Another bareback circus rider in white tights?'

'Now what're you talkin' about?' asked Dolly.

'Legs,' said Joe.

'Don't be vulgar,' said Dolly. 'No, but you've got to be serious, Joe, you've got to watch out for Blackbeard. I mean, if it really was him that done the murder, he won't like it if he thinks we've got suspicions. You've got to take care.'

'I think I'll go and see Archie,' said Joe.

'Yes, find out what Blackbeard said to 'im last night.'

'Yes, Archie's in,' said Mrs Connie Cousins. 'I don't know what you said to 'im last evenin', but 'e 'ad a bloke call later and done a bit of a business deal with 'im that earned a fiver, would yer believe. 'E took me out this mornin' an' bought me a new dress. I couldn't 'ardly credit it. Still, it showed 'e's got 'is good points, an' that I don't 'ave to clip 'is ear every day.' She turned in the passage and called. 'Archie, Sergeant Joe wants to see yer.'

103

'In the parlour,' said Joe.

''Elp yerself, love,' said Mrs Cousins, and Joe went in. Archie joined him a few seconds later, closing the door behind him.

''Ello, mate.'

'Well?' said Joe.

'I'm fine, 'ow's yerself?'

'Don't come it,' said Joe. 'What happened?'

'Eh? Oh, see what yer mean, about the funny geezer. Well, 'e called, like 'e said 'e would, all wrapped up still, and I brought 'im in and 'e stood just where you're standin'. 'E wasn't 'alf lookin' at me. Mind, when I give 'im the wallet and 'e looked inside it, 'e was a mite more pleasant, even if I couldn't see nothing but 'is mince pies and 'is 'ooter. 'E shook me 'and then, an' said I was to forget all about 'im. Pleasure, I said. Well, 'e ain't the kind of bloke I want to remember. I reckon 'e's ate new-born babies in 'is time, so I was 'ighly relieved that we parted on friendly terms, as yer might say.'

'After he'd given you how much?' asked Joe.

'Eh?' said Archie.

'You were supposed to report this morning.'

'Report?'

'To me.'

'Was I?' said Archie, beginning to shift his feet about.

'Ruddy black mark, Archie,' said Joe, 'ought to tread on your foot, you bugger. I suppose you thought I'd ask for my share.'

'Search me, Joe, I dunno what you're on about,' said Archie. 'Share of what?'

'Don't make me cross,' said Joe, 'or I'll march you off to Wellington Barracks and drill you till you've got no legs left.'

''Ere, Joe, what's eatin' yer?' protested Archie. 'Didn't you say I'd only got to come an' see yer if the geezer got awkward?'

'No, I didn't say that.'

'Funny, I could've sworn you did,' said Archie. 'Still, me ears ain't as good as they was. Anyway, I didn't get no trouble from the bloke, 'e plonked a couple of quid into me mitt just before 'e said cheerio.'

'Just two quid, was it, Archie?'

'That's it, Joe, for gettin' 'is wallet back an' mindin' me own business now and in the future, like. 'Ere, if yer a bit short of the ready at the moment, I can let yer 'ave five bob without askin' for it back.'

'Keep it,' said Joe. 'Listen, did the bloke ask any questions about me and my lady lodger?'

'Not a dicky bird,' said Archie.

'Good enough,' said Joe, 'and don't spill any dicky birds yourself.'

'Not me, Joe me old pal. What's it to me if you and yer lady friend are goin' in for liftin'? It ain't custom'ry, yer know, to let on who's one of the lads and who ain't. You got my best wishes, Joe. Just keep yer mince pies peeled for the rozzers when yer doin' yer lucky dips.'

'Don't get demented,' said Joe.

'Nuff said, eh, me old cock?'

'So long, Archie.'

'See yer around, Joe.'

Joe went back and advised Dolly that Blackbeard, having received his wallet, had rewarded Archie and asked no questions.

'I still ain't happy,' said Dolly.

'Well, let's hope he is, now that he's got that letter back,' said Joe. 'Now I've got work to do and you've got to stay on that bed. Your ankle's improving, so keep it that way.'

'Oh, all right,' said Dolly, 'I suppose I'll get a good hidin' if I start runnin' about.'

'I'll think about it,' said Joe.

'That's it, take advantage of a weak defenceless girl,' said Dolly.

'You're safe at the moment, Private Smith. Have you finished that book on how to get yourself a respectable job?'

'No, I ain't,' said Dolly.

'Well, finish it this afternoon.'

'All of it?'

'Yes, good idea,' said Joe.

'I might as well be dead, I might,' said Dolly.

'Wait till you're ninety,' said Joe, 'that's the best time to go.'

'Oh, what a kind thought,' said Dolly.

'Think nothing of it,' said Joe. 'I'll bring you a cup of tea in an hour.'

'You're good to me,' said Dolly.

The man and woman met by arrangement at Waterloo Station, although they did not appear to. That is, they did not acknowledge each other, but each bought a first-class railway return ticket to Clapham Junction. She had actually bought hers before he arrived.

They knew each other. They had been brought together in St Petersburg two months ago. She knew him to be Alexander Rokovssky, the dark tool of autocratic monarchs and a fanatical servant of Tsarism, a man who could slit another's throat or shoot him at point-blank range without any change of expression. He was the scourge of socialists and revolutionaries, and had carried out numerous assassinations for monarchist factions of the Balkan countries. It was said that if the Tsarists of Russia asked him to, he would even despatch his own mother. Black Wolf he was called, and there was nothing he would not do to make the Russian Empire the greatest the world had ever known. Or so it was said. His one weakness was the lack of patience he showed with people he considered idiots.

He knew the woman to be a protégée of Count Zhinsky,

head of Russian Intelligence, and the man he had met in Collins Coffee House. She was also the Count's mistress. She was clever, capable and resourceful as an agent, and acceptable to Rokovssky as his confederate on this mission of assassination. She was using a French passport and the name Marcelle Fayette.

She boarded the train in advance of him. As it was early afternoon there were no madding crowds, and she secured a first-class compartment to herself. He entered a second-class compartment moments before the guard waved his flag and blew his whistle. He went through to the corridor, and as the train began to move he sauntered along to the first-class coach. The train's wheels were churning, the engine rattling over points and spouting clouds of steam. The service was non-stop to Clapham Junction, ensuring an absence of interruption. Reaching the compartment occupied by Marcelle Fayette, he entered and sat down opposite her.

'Your telegram was late,' she said.

'My reading of the letter was delayed,' he responded. They spoke in French, the pre-eminent language of St Petersburg.

'Why?' asked Marcelle.

'Because the carrier was a fool,' said Rokovssky. 'He handed it to me as if it was no more than offering me an apple in a market-place. I told him to wait until we left, but no, he put it into my hand with a pleased grin on his stupid face. I put it into my wallet, and my wallet was snatched.'

'Ah,' said Marcelle softly, 'perhaps he did not understand what you said. I have found one must speak slowly to people who live in the back streets of London. If one does not, then they say, "Eh? Eh?" So, your pocket was picked by a thief and you lost the wallet containing the report from our student friends?'

'It was lost for a while.' Rokovssky explained in detail,

and Marcelle, after a moment's thought, agreed with his conclusion that the man and woman in question had to be agents of a rival power.

'They are only a nuisance, they have only inconvenienced you,' said Marcelle, 'and the letter will tell them very little.'

'It will tell them enough to alert them if they're working for the British Government.'

'And if the British know enough about you, as they probably do, they will begin to police you. Good.'

'Good?' Alexander Rokovssky reflected. 'Yes, in some ways,' he said.

'You are a perfect red herring,' she said. 'Let them police you.'

'The British have a law which allows them to deport people whom they consider to be undesirable aliens.'

'Undesirable aliens?' Marcelle, looking through the window from her corner seat, wrinkled her sensitive nose at the grimy roofs and façades of houses and buildings, the train steaming towards Clapham at a steady speed. 'Who but the English could put together two such unwelcome words and make such an appropriate term of them? You are an undesirable alien, my friend, because of your reputation?'

'The English are all old women and reputations frighten them,' said Rokovssky. 'I have not come here to be deported. I must find out exactly who the man and woman are.'

'Very well,' she said, 'but I hope there will be no more fatalities. One assassination is enough for the time being.'

'He was the kind of man who would have sold his suspicions for money.'

'His unfortunate death has agitated the police,' said Marcelle.

'It has given them work to do,' said Rokovssky.

'Shall we discuss our commission, and exactly how we

108

are going to execute it?' she asked. 'I know what was decided in St Petersburg. Now I must know what you have decided in regard to precise details. When is our final meeting to be?'

'The day before the ceremony. Let us say eleven in the morning at the London Zoo,' said Rokovssky. 'We must have that final meeting. Now, let me talk to you about how we shall do what is required of us.'

He told her at length of what he would do and what she would do. At Clapham Junction, he alighted from the train and crossed by the footbridge to the platform from which to catch a train back. She alighted after him, and she crossed the footbridge too, but delayed stepping on to the platform until the train for Waterloo came in. He found an empty first-class compartment, and she reached it by way of the corridor after the train had pulled out.

During the journey back to Waterloo they continued their discussion. The plan was basically simple, but they went over the details again and again until mutual satisfaction prevailed. Then Rokovssky went back to the subject of the man and woman who lived in Newington Butts. Marcelle promised her help if he required it.

At Waterloo, he was again the first to leave the train. He departed from the station on foot. She took a hansom cab, and left knowing he would send her a signal if he definitely required her help in the matter of a man and woman presently residing in a house in a place called Newington Butts.

CHAPTER NINE

A frisky April breeze, dancing around the houses and backyards of Walworth in search of inlets, found a partly open window and darted through the gap. Joe was responsible for the gap. You need some fresh air, he said to Dolly when he brought her a cup of tea, and he pulled the top window frame down a little. Since when he'd left her alone again, and Dolly was having to put up with the April breeze. Fresh spring air was quite popular in Walworth after the fogs of winter, but Dolly had her reservations about it at the moment. It was like a succession of cold draughts, and it was making her fed-up again. Well, she was generally fed-up, knowing she had to keep resting her ankle if she was to be up and about as soon as possible. She was desperate to get out, but each time she tested her sprain it told her not yet.

Why couldn't Joe let her sit in the fireside armchair in the living-room so that she'd at least have company? Why did he always have to work alone? What was so private about writing letters for business people, who ought to have clerks for doing it?

Another draught of air entered and rushed about. Not the most patient young lady in the world, Dolly sat up and swung her legs over the edge of the bed. She raised her voice.

'Help!'

There was no response. But someone was climbing the stairs. That someone reached the landing and appeared at the open door of the bedroom.

'Was that you callin', ducky?' asked Mrs Beavis, her apron doing its best to fit itself around her plumpness, and

110

a plate containing a large segment of sausage and onion pie in her hand. 'What d'yer want, a bit of 'elp to get to the lav? Is yer poor foot still cripplin' yer?'

'It's not me foot,' said Dolly, 'it's me soul that's sufferin'.' She coughed loudly and said loudly, 'And I'm gettin' frozen up in all these draughts.' And she added, even more loudly, 'He's a hard man, did you know that, Bessie?'

'What, our Sergeant Joe?' said Mrs Beavis.

'He won't let me get up or go out, or even sit in the armchair for a bit,' said Dolly. 'I'm not sayin' he 'asn't been a good Samaritan, but I never thought he'd beat me black and blue just for arguin' with him.'

'Well, I never did,' said Mrs Beavis in astonishment, 'I can't 'ardly credit Sergeant Joe doin' a thing like that. And I don't like 'im doin' it in my 'ouse. I'll 'ave to talk to 'im.'

She took her full-bodied self to the door of Joe's living-room and knocked.

'You there, Sergeant Joe?'

There was silence for a moment, then the living-room door opened and Dolly heard him say, 'What's up, Bessie?'

'I'll give you what's up,' said Mrs Beavis, and Dolly, boredom lifted, listened in delight to what she herself had provoked.

'Well, what *is* up?' asked Joe, work on the table and body guarding the doorway.

'I can't believe what I just 'eard,' said Mrs Beavis. 'I come up with some of me 'ome-made sausage and onion pie fresh out of me oven. I thought you an' Dolly might like it for yer supper tonight, but what 'appened? The shock of me life. I'm downright flabbergasted to know you're treatin' Dolly so unkind an' beatin' 'er as well. I'm sure I don't know why you took 'er in if yer didn't mean to treat 'er kindly. What's come over you?'

'Can't say,' said Joe, 'I'm speechless.'

'Now, Sergeant Joe, you ain't ever been speechless before,' said Mrs Beavis. 'I'm sure you've got something to say about why you're treatin' that poor gel so shameful.'

'It wouldn't be fit for your ears, Bessie. She's having you on.'

'Eh?' said Mrs Beavis.

'She's making it all up,' said Joe, 'but she can't help it, she's had no family life and it's held her brain back a bit. She hasn't grown up yet.'

'Here, I heard that!' shouted Dolly.

'Must make allowances for her, Bessie,' said Joe.

'Well, I never, what a monkey,' said Mrs Beavis. 'Not that I mind 'er pullin' me leg, I'm just thankful you ain't beatin' 'er black an' blue, it upset me when—' The landlady stopped. A shriek of laughter had come from the bedroom. 'Well, listen to that, and after she near 'ad me cryin' me eyes out for 'er. Saucy gel.' Mrs Beavis tried to look offended. It was beyond her. Her happy outlook always prevailed. She smiled at Joe. 'Well, would yer like this piece of pie?'

'You bet. You're a rattling good sort, Bessie, and a first-class cook as well.' Joe took the plate, transferred the pie to a dish, and returned the plate. 'Thanks, Bessie old girl, bless you.'

'I'll leave you to talk to yer monkey,' said Mrs Beavis.

'I'll start with a beating,' said Joe.

'Oh, yer don't mean you 'ave been doin' that, do yer?'

'No, I'm starting now,' said Joe.

'Now it's you that's 'aving me on,' said the landlady, and went down to her kitchen with a smile. She guessed what it was all about. Dolly, like any young lady, wanted attention.

Joe entered the bedroom. Dolly was lying on the bed.

'Oh, hello, Joe, nice you've come to see me,' she said, 'how's your dear old dad?'

'Still bringing wages home to me dear old mum,' said

112

Joe, who spent the occasional weekend with his parents in their Chatham home and was always there at Christmas. 'Private Smith, you're playing up again.'

'Me?' said Dolly.

'I beat you black and blue, do I?'

'No, not all the time,' said Dolly, 'just once so far.'

'Like some more, would you?'

'You'll be lucky. Here, be a sport, could you close that window? It's not fresh air that's comin' in, it's freezin' draughts.'

Joe closed the window.

'Like another cup of tea?' he asked.

'Oh, would I, not 'alf I wouldn't.'

'Right, tea and a couple of biscuits now, and supper later.'

'You do treat a girl swell, Joe. What's for supper?'

'I'm having fresh sausage and onion pie with fried potatoes and a green vegetable,' said Joe. 'You're having dry bread and water.'

'Could I 'ave just a scrape of marge with me bread? And could I come and 'ave it with you at the table?'

'Permission granted, Private Smith.'

But there was no bread and water for her, of course. He shared the pie with her. Afterwards, he made her go and rest again, much to her disgust and outrage. She said she might as well chuck herself out of the window. He said do it quietly, make sure you don't land on the backyard dustbin. The noise would upset the hard-working neighbours. Dolly said his jokes still weren't very funny. No joke, he said, upset neighbours could get very ratty.

He went out for an evening walk, and that really got Dolly's goat. When he came back she said she'd go out herself tomorrow, and if he tried to stop her she'd smash up all his crockery. She also said she'd poison all the food in his larder, only the larder was locked. Why did he keep it locked?

'To stop you poisoning the food,' said Joe. 'I'll make some coffee now, if you don't mind Camp.'

'Ain't you lovely to me sometimes?' said Dolly.

He laughed. She was a character. He could imagine her fighting to hold her own in the orphanage instead of letting herself become meek and mousy. The orphanage was where she'd developed her pert tongue, no doubt about it. If all her rough times had turned her into a pickpocket, at least they hadn't defeated her. All she needed to put herself right was a decent job. George might be able to help there.

When he brought the coffee in, he also brought a rolled bandage, purchased during his morning excursion. Her ankle needed support and could take a bandage now, he said.

'Oh, good,' said Dolly, 'I'll be able to start waggin' me foot about, will I?'

'Let's have it,' said Joe. Dolly drew her skirts up. 'Just your foot, I meant, Private Smith, not your legs.'

'I hope you ain't complainin',' said Dolly. 'I met a gentleman once who said me legs were worth 'alf-a-crown a look.'

'I'm not complaining, but I'm not handing over any half-crowns,' said Joe. He wound the bandage around her ankle, making sure it was firmly supportive but not constrictive. He secured it with the safety-pin. 'How's that?'

'A treat, honest,' said Dolly, flexing her foot. 'Thanks ever so much, Joe.'

They drank coffee together, sitting companionably on the edge of the bed.

'You might be able to go for a short walk in a couple of days,' said Joe.

'What, two more whole rotten days?' said Dolly. 'I'll die, I will.'

'Can't have that kind of talk,' said Joe. 'I've told you

114

before, it won't do. Let's have some fighting talk.'

'All right, then,' said Dolly, 'let me tell you that if I 'ave to spend two more rotten days just kickin' me heels, I'll smash the place up.'

'That's better,' said Joe, 'in that kind of mood I could put you on a horse and let you join in the charge of the Light Brigade.'

'Honoured, I'm sure,' said Dolly. 'Did you go out this evening to meet your lady friend? I bet you've got one round the corner somewhere.'

'I've got several.'

'Go on, 'ave you? Where?'

'Round the corner somewhere,' said Joe.

'Think I'm simple, do you?' said Dolly.

'No such thing as a simple woman,' said Joe, 'they're all too clever by half.'

'Oh, 'ave you been done down by one, Joe?'

'Not yet,' said Joe, and grinned. And Dolly wondered why he wasn't married or even engaged.

Later, just before they both retired, he brought her another book.

'What's this?' she asked.

'Some better bedtime reading for you, which you can enjoy now and over the next two days.'

She looked at the title. *The Indian Mutiny*.

'Oh, you daft loony!' she yelled and threw it at him. Too late. He was already out of the room. The book hit the door.

She laughed. She stood up and tested her ankle. Firmly bandaged, it hardly protested at all.

Newington Butts had the dark, deserted look of night far advanced. The sky was inky with cloudless black velvet studded by a million diamonds. It was nearly two o'clock in the morning.

Question. Was the door bolted or not? It was said that

115

the working people of London had no need to bolt their doors at any time.

Alexander Rokovssky carefully inserted a skeleton key, and slowly turned it. It met a little resistance, then the lock yielded. He pushed the door open. He stood for a moment, looking up and down the dark street before quietly entering the passage. He paused for thought. Yes, leave the door slightly open to ensure that if necessary he could leave at speed. He waited, adjusting his eyes to the darkness of the house. He had a picture in his mind of the layout of passage, stairs and landing, a picture unwittingly painted for him by the man who had retrieved his wallet.

He moved forward, hand against the wall of the passage. It guided him to the stairs, which were straight ahead. He climbed them, slowly and cautiously.

Dolly jerked awake to find a brutal hand clapped over her mouth and to feel a slight pricking sensation in her throat.

'Do not move, filthy woman, do not scream,' whispered a voice with a foreign accent. Dolly recognized it immediately. Its menace and her memory of the cold cruelty of the man, together with the realization that it was the point of a knife pricking her neck, made her shudder. 'You will speak only when I ask questions, and you will speak very softly. If you shout or scream, you will die. Do you understand?'

With the hard hand so tight over her mouth, Dolly did her best to nod.

'Take care, then, if you wish to remain alive.' The hand lifted a fraction, and she sucked in air. The voice hissed at her. 'Why did you open the letter?'

Her blood surged, her body tensed.

'What letter?' she breathed, and the point of the knife pricked deeper.

116

'You think me a fool, woman? The letter was steamed open. Why?'

Dolly, quick-witted, didn't take longer than a second to come up with an answer, and one that didn't incriminate Joe.

'Well, there wasn't much money in your wallet, not for a gent like you, so I thought there must be a bit in the letter.'

'Filthy liar. Pickpockets do not steam open envelopes.' The sibilance of his whispering voice and the recollection that a certain man had been found with his throat cut, turned Dolly rigid in the bed. 'Nor do they return a wallet with money still in it.'

'No, I 'ad to give half of it back,' breathed Dolly. 'I knew you'd tracked me down, so I thought if I only took some of it you wouldn't put the cops on me. You've got to believe me, mister, I'm only a workin' girl without a job.'

'You are lying. You attempted to delude me. It was the letter you wanted, not the money. You read it.'

'No, I was just lookin' for a bit more money, honest,' gasped Dolly, the knife a hideous threat. Again her quick wits worked for her. 'I just thought there might be a fifty-quid banknote in that envelope, but there was only a letter, which I couldn't read, anyway, it was in a foreign language. I don't know any foreign languages, I'm an orphanage girl.'

'Lies. What country are you working for?' hissed Rokovssky. Outside, the April breeze travelled friskily through the Butts. The front door, ajar, sighingly opened wider.

'What d'you mean, what country?' Dolly was cold all over, icy tremors running down her back. 'I don't work for nobody, I ain't got a job, honest.'

'Your accomplice, then. You work for him. He had a bag, yes? The wallet was in it. Yes?'

Paralysed though she was, not for anything was Dolly

117

going to drop Sergeant Joe in the cart, not for anything would she even admit he was in the house.

'Honest, I'd never seen 'im before, I just bumped into 'im in the fog and it made me sprain me ankle. He carried me here, he knows the fam'ly, and they took me in. He wasn't interested in any letter—'

'You are an agent. So is he.' Another question. Should he kill them or not? First, in any case, he must find out if they had yet informed others of the contents of the letter. 'I will give you a minute, no more, to tell me if you are working for the British Government or another. Which is the one that has been informed of the letter? Give me the truth or I will slit your throat, then go to him and slit his too. I know he is here, which room he is in. You have a minute to decide.'

Dolly wanted to scream, to raise the roof and to wake Joe. As it was, she had to think of something to say that would satisfy a man who was so evil he should never have been born. What could she say? Suppose she said she was an agent? Then what else could she say?

Outside, the night breeze strengthened. It gusted around chimneys and roofs, and it gusted through Newington Butts. It blew and it plucked. The open front door of the Beavis house closed with a thunderous crash.

Rokovssky, for all his tried and tested ability to react to the unexpected, was startled into losing his concentration. He jerked up. Dolly was out of the bed in a flash, on its other side. Sergeant Joe was awake, so were members of the Beavis family. Dolly screamed.

'Ruddy bananas,' said Mr Beavis, sitting up in his bed, 'what the 'ell was that, Bessie?'

Rokovssky was out on the landing. He went down the stairs like a flying shadow, and rushed through the passage. He pulled the front door open, and out he went. He ran at speed.

Everyone was awake. Someone struck a match at the

118

open door of the landing bedroom. In the light of its little flame, Dolly saw the face of Sergeant Joe.

'Oh, come in, won't you?' she gasped.

Down from the top floor bounced the offspring of Mr and Mrs Beavis, the girls in nightdresses, the boys in nightshirts. Up from the ground floor, a lighted candle in his hand, rumbled Mr Beavis. Everyone was heading for the bedroom from which had come the screams. Fulsome bodies filled the landing.

'What's 'appening?'

'What's goin' on?'

'What was them screams for?'

'Who done 'em?'

'Who's 'urt?'

'Who fell down the stairs, did anyone fall down the stairs?'

'What went crash? Who done it?'

'Is the 'ouse on fire? Can yer smell smoke?'

Those in the van of the invasion were jammed in the doorway. Dolly, sitting on the floor against the wall on the farther side of the bed, reached and tugged a blanket free. Hastily, she covered herself up. Joe had lit a gas mantle. From the passage below, Mrs Beavis called.

'What's 'appened up there?'

Joe saw Dolly, blanket-wrapped, tumbled hair touching her bare shoulders. Her eyes looked enormous.

'What happened?' he asked.

'Thunder an' bleedin' lightning, that's what it sounded like,' said Albert.

Dolly found her voice.

'A burglar got in,' she said.

'What?' said Joe.

'Ain't no burglars round 'ere,' said Alfred.

'Well, there's one or two that live 'ereabouts,' said Mr Beavis, 'but they do their burglin' elsewhere.'

'They'd get done in if they did it 'ere,' said Nancy,

using her healthy roundness to expel herself from the jammed-up doorway. She shot into the bedroom like a released balloon. She saw Joe. Joe, who hadn't stopped to put anything on, was wearing only his long pants, his chest and feet bare.

''Elp, look at you, Sergeant Joe,' she said. Then she saw Dolly. 'Crikey, what yer doin' down there?' she asked.

'It was better for me 'ealth down 'ere,' said Dolly, the bedroom getting smaller as more of the family spilled in.

'Did I 'ear someone mention burglars?' Mrs Beavis was in the doorway.

Dolly said one had got in, that he threatened to do her in if she didn't tell him where all the valuables were. Who he was she couldn't say, because the room was too dark, but he must have left the front door open and the wind must have caught it and made it shut with a crash. That startled him and she fell out of bed to get out of his way. Then he hopped it quick.

'I suppose 'e got in by usin' the latchcord,' she said. Rokovssky, of course, knowing nothing about the use of latchcords in Walworth, hadn't even looked for one.

'What a bleedin' cheek, we ain't got no valuables,' said Mr Beavis, ''e didn't treat yer rough, did 'e?'

Dolly said she was more aggravated than bruised.

'Oh, yer poor young dear,' said Mrs Beavis, 'life ain't treatin' you a bit nice.'

'Fancy a burglar gettin' in our 'ouse,' said Linda.

'Don't make sense to me,' said Mr Beavis, a bulging man in his nightshirt. 'Mind, 'e might 'ave been after all me little gels, they bein' 'ighly valuable.'

'Wasn't it lucky you 'ad Sergeant Joe down 'ere with you, Dolly?' said Ella.

'I'm near faintin',' said Nancy, 'can't I 'ave Sergeant Joe upstairs with me?'

'Gettin' saucier all the time, you are, Nancy,' said Mrs

Beavis. 'Charlie, yer best call in at the police station on yer way to work tomorrer mornin'.'

'Now, Bessie, yer know people round 'ere don't interfere with coppers' work,' said Mr Beavis. 'You all right, love?' he said to Dolly.

'I am now,' said Dolly.

'That's good.'

'Ain't me Sergeant Joe 'andsome?' said Nancy.

''Ere, leave orf,' said Ella, 'Sergeant Joe ain't yours, 'e's all of ours.'

'I ain't makin' any claims,' said Alfred.

'Nor me,' said Albert, 'you girls keep 'im to yerselves.'

'Listen, Dolly,' said Mrs Beavis, 'would yer like a nice cup of 'ot tea and a slice of apple pie to 'elp yer get over the 'orrors?'

'Thanks,' said Dolly, 'but if you don't mind I'd just like to go back to bed.'

'Would yer like me to fetch our mum's smellin'-salts?' offered Linda.

'Oh, it's kind of you, but no thanks,' said Dolly, still keeping to the floor and the protection of the blanket.

'Come on, out you all go,' said Mr Beavis, and with a rustle of nightwear and a bustle of bodies, his brood rolled out of the room, all talking at once about how could any burglar be daft enough to try burgling them. Linda said perhaps he was a hungry burglar who'd come after their mum's apple pie and fruit cake. More like Nancy's dumplings, said Alfred, and received a bash from his eldest sister for being personal. Mrs Beavis shooed them all back to their beds, and Mr Beavis said to Joe, 'Well, we'll leave yer to tuck Dolly in, eh? Good night to both of yer.'

Alone with Joe, Dolly said, 'I suppose you know you ain't decent, standin' there in your reach-me-downs.'

'Never mind that,' said Joe, and closed the door.

'Here, what's that for?' she asked in alarm.

'You can get up now,' said Joe.

'I dare say I can, but I ain't goin' to,' said Dolly, 'the blanket might fall off.'

'Like that, is it?' said Joe. 'I suppose I should have got hold of a nightdress for you. Anyway, let's get down to business. Who was it?'

'The burglar?' said Dolly. 'Look, would you mind turnin' your back?' Joe put his back to her and she got up and scrambled into the bed. Then in sober vein she said, 'It was him.'

'Blackbeard?'

'I couldn't see him properly, not in the dark, but it was him all right. I told you he'd come after us. He 'ad a knife and said he'd do me in if I didn't tell him why we steamed the letter open. You've landed us in it, doin' that. You sure you don't know what language it was? You must know foreign languages, you've been all over with the Army, 'aven't you?'

'Africa and India,' said Joe, 'and the letter was in Russian.'

'Here, you said you didn't know before.'

'Well, I know now,' said Joe.

'It's made 'im mad,' said Dolly, 'he said we'd read it.'

Why, thought Joe, should Blackbeard think either of them could read Russian? Exactly what was the letter all about? Something pretty important to Blackbeard. Well, George was going to come up with a translation. Dolly had stirred up a hornets' nest when she pinched the wallet, and he hadn't made it any better by steaming the letter open. Despite the careful way he'd re-sealed it, Blackbeard had spotted it.

'Frightened you badly, did he, Dolly?'

'I thought me last moments 'ad come,' she said.

'Well, I don't think he'll come back again, he'll know we're not going to be caught napping a second time. We'll get Charlie Beavis to bolt the front door at night. Can't

122

have a character like Blackbeard popping in and out just as he likes.'

'I've got a surprise for you,' said Dolly, 'he thinks you're a spy.'

'A what?'

'A man that does spyin' for his country.'

'Off his rocker,' said Joe.

'Still, you keep yourself very private,' said Dolly. 'I mean, sittin' in your room writin' all day. You don't write spy messages, do you?'

'They'd be more interesting than business letters, I'll give you that,' said Joe, 'but no, that's not me. It's food for thought, though. Point is, what's Blackbeard up to that he doesn't want to be spied on?'

'Don't ask me,' said Dolly, 'I'm just 'ere by accident.'

'And for nicking the wallet,' said Joe. 'Anyway, get back to sleep and tomorrow perhaps we'd better think seriously about getting you away from here, after all.'

'I ain't goin',' said Dolly, 'I already told you so.'

'Why, exactly?'

'Because nobody's goin' to treat me as kind as you do.'

'Except, of course, when I beat you black and blue.'

'Oh, a grateful girl like me can put up with a few bruises,' said Dolly, sheet and blankets up to her chin.

'Pleased to hear it,' said Joe. 'Good night.'

'More like good morning, if you ask me,' said Dolly. 'What a life.'

Rokovssky, at this moment a man of curses and oaths, knew he had to send a telegram to Marcelle Fayette in the morning. It was work for her now, dealing with the bitch and the male accomplice in Newington Butts.

CHAPTER TEN

Dolly slept late. Joe did not disturb her, he went out and bought a paper, interesting himself in its report on the progress of the murder investigation. The police, having interviewed working colleagues of the victim at the London Docks, had elicited information to the effect that at the end of his shift he met two men outside the gates and said he was going for a drink with them. He earned a bit on the side, did Dan Pearson. The fog had not set in at that time, late afternoon, and the dockers were able to describe the men as respectable-looking young gents in peaked caps. The police were now making enquiries in all the neighbouring pubs.

Joe began to wonder if he should go to the police. But that would land Dolly in trouble. And the police had a lead now. They'd do a thorough follow-up job. Give them enough time and they'd catch up with Blackbeard, if Blackbeard really was the killer.

Joe took a walk along the Walworth Road, going as briskly as his stiff knee would allow. Horse-drawn buses and electric trams were only partly full, most people being at their places of work by now. Night-shift workers were probably in their beds, and late day-shift workers probably having a lie-in. Many London factories worked a twenty-four-hour day, and their chimneys only stopped belching smoke on Sundays. What a contribution they made to winter fogs, thought Joe.

It occurred to him then that Dolly might be under greater threat than he was because she could describe Blackbeard more accurately. He had seen him only in the dense fog. She had seen him, and the murdered man, in

124

the Rockingham pub. Joe had a feeling it wasn't too clever, leaving Dolly alone. He'd better get back. He turned and retraced his steps. Arriving at his lodgings he found she was missing. Hell, he thought, has she bunked?

No, she'd left him a reassuring note.

'My ankle's better, so I'm going shopping, behave yourself while I'm out.'

The monkey. Her ankle still needed another full day's rest. He went down to see his landlady, who told him Dolly had gone out just about ten minutes ago. She was dressed quite nice, did she have spare clothes, after all? Joe said he'd got them from the pawnshop.

There was nothing for him to do except settle down to some work. He turned to Mary Shelley. George had drafted a letter in her name concerning her thoughts on her novel *Frankenstein*. It was a first-class concoction.

By the middle of the afternoon, Dolly was still not back, and he was worrying about her. Either something had happened to her or those two fivers had gone to her head and she was on a day-long spree.

'Now who can that be?' asked Mrs Beavis of herself when the front door knocker went. Couldn't be the rent man, he'd come yesterday and been paid. Couldn't be a neighbour, either. A neighbour would have opened the door by the latchcord and called out to ask if anyone was in. Couldn't be a tally man, either, because the family didn't have owings. Wiping her floury hands, Mrs Beavis answered the knock. A dark and lovely young woman smiled at her from the doorstep. She was dressed quite nice, thought Mrs Beavis, but not overpowering, in a three-quarter-length coat and ankle-length dress, and a flat-brimmed hat sort of quietly decorative on top. You could see outfits like that on shop manageresses.

The young woman, suitcase resting on the doorstep, said, 'Good afternoon.'

'Same to you, I'm sure,' said Mrs Beavis.

'I am so sorry not to have made an appointment.'

'Pardon?' said Mrs Beavis.

'To see you.' The young woman sounded as if she wasn't English. 'To ask if it is true you have a room that can be rented. I have not the money to pay for any hotel room – ah, how expensive London hotels are, isn't it so?' Her smile put warm light into her dark brown eyes. 'A most kind person told me you might accommodate me.'

'Well, bless me soul,' said Mrs Beavis.

'Pardon? Excuse me? My English is not very good? You do not comprehend?'

'There, I thought you wasn't English,' said Mrs Beavis. 'I said to meself, Bessie, I said, this young lady ain't English. D'yer mind tellin' me where yer come from?'

'France. You do not mind people from France, I hope? I am here to work in a London drama academy, to teach – ah, yes – deportment. You know?'

'What's deportment?' asked Mrs Beavis in good-natured enquiry.

'I have not said it right? Deportment?' The lovely young woman, with thick lashes an inch long, offered another appealing smile. 'It is how to walk most elegant, madam. It is most important for young ladies wishing to become actresses.'

'Deportment, well, bless me,' said Mrs Beavis in happy understanding. 'But I ain't usually called madam, I'm Mrs Bessie Beavis, and I do 'ave a room for rent. Not that I'm desp'rate, mind, me fam'ly not bein' in want. Still, I must say I'm taken with yer nice manners and everything.'

'I have asked at houses near the academy, but to rent a room there – yes, it is most embarrassing to say I cannot afford what is asked, and I shall not be earning until I begin my work in two weeks. But I have come to London early to make myself familiar with it, you see. Ah, the boat and the Channel this morning, I thought I would die

126

of sickness. Do you say, madam, that I may rent the room?'

''Ere, you best come in,' beamed Mrs Beavis, having made up her mind. 'I never 'ad a French lady lodger before – mind, it's four shillings a week, being a nice large front room with a comfortin' bed and an 'andsome fireplace.'

'Four shillings?' The young woman lifted her suitcase and stepped in. Mrs Beavis closed the door. 'Four shillings? Ah, that is most kind and not at all expensive. Thank you, madam.'

'It's Mrs Beavis.'

'Thank you, Mrs Beavis.'

'I'll show you the room, which if you like it you can rent with pleasure. Could I 'ave yer name, love?'

'I am Mademoiselle Marcelle Fayette of Dieppe. Please, yes, I should like to see the room.'

Mrs Beavis took her up to the first-floor landing. She led the way past Sergeant Joe's bedroom to the front room. It could not be faulted in respect of how clean and tidy she kept it. Its bed and furniture were entirely homely, however, and perhaps not as dainty as the elegant young French lady might like, but it did have a nice view of the hustle and bustle of Newington Butts, and Mrs Beavis always reckoned that if you could see life going on from your window, you couldn't grumble too much about not having dainty furniture.

'It's a nice size, don't yer think?' said the affable landlady.

'Ah, perfect, yes, perfect,' said Mademoiselle Fayette. 'I will take it, if you please. From now, you agree? See, I have all my things in this case. I am to commence paying this moment? Willingly, Mrs Beavis.'

'Well, I think I'd best fill some of the 'ot water bottles an' put them in the bed right away,' said Mrs Beavis, 'just in case there's a bit of cold about the sheets. Mind, all the

127

bed linen's clean, and we don't have no bugs or fleas, I wouldn't 'ave anything like that in any 'ouse I lived in.'

'Oh, I am sure,' said Mademoiselle Fayette. She took a purse from her coat pocket, found two silver florins and handed them to the landlady, who said she'd get her a rent book. 'Do you have other tenants, madam?'

'Tenants? Oh, yer mean lodgers.' Mrs Beavis nodded. 'Well, there's just Mr Foster, 'e's got the other two rooms on this landin'. He's a nice upright gent that people like, and all me gels is very fond of 'im, specially young Linda.'

'Then I must introduce myself to him, yes? We have to share amenities, perhaps?'

'Well, there's the lav and the 'andbasin that's on the landin',' said Mrs Beavis, 'but you got your own gas ring in the corner there. Would yer like to meet Mr Foster now?'

'He is not at work?'

'Oh, 'e does 'is work in 'is livin'-room,' said Mrs Beavis. 'I'll take yer to 'im, you might as well meet each other now.' She led her new lodger to the closed door of Joe's living-room and knocked. 'You there, Sergeant Joe?' There was the sound of a chair being pushed back over the floor linoleum. 'Everyone calls 'im Sergeant Joe, 'e's been in the Army, yer see.'

The door opened. Mademoiselle Fayette saw a man straight of back, broad of shoulders and handsomely moustached. And she saw a soldier's face, permanently browned and weathered by sun and wind. He wore a black jersey and grey trousers, and his dark brown hair was slightly ruffled. Joe saw a dark-eyed young woman, modestly dressed, with the lush looks of – an Italian, perhaps? He judged her worthy of finer clothes, for what she did have on she wore with an air. Her colouring was vivid.

'Hello, Bessie, who's floated in?' he asked.

'Well, it's – what did yer say yer name was, miss?'

'Marcelle Fayette.'

'There y'ar, Sergeant Joe,' beamed Mrs Beavis, 'this young lady's our new lodger, she's just took the front room, she's just come over from France. She thought she'd best meet you, would yer like to shake 'ands with 'er?'

Joe shook hands.

'Welcome,' he said. 'What's brought you to London?'

'Work, you see,' said Mademoiselle Fayette. 'Yes. I am to teach at a London drama academy. I am most happy to live in the room here, this lady has been so kind in accommodating me. Ah, your own room looks nice. Cosy, yes, and with a fire.' She could not see much of the room because of how he filled most of the doorway, but she saw the glow of the fire and a glimpse of a baize-covered table on which were papers.

'I'd invite you in for a chat,' said Joe, 'but I'm just about to go out. Never mind, we'll see each other. I'm Joe, of course.'

'Joe? Yes? How nice. Then I am Marcelle.' Her smile was very warm. She seemed delighted to have met him, and to have found there was no need to be formal.

'Well, I'm that pleased you've met each other,' said Mrs Beavis. 'Would yer like a nice hot cup of tea, Miss Fate?' What a funny name, she thought, and the young lady pronounced it funny, too. 'I'm just goin' to make one for meself.'

'How kind.' Marcelle Fayette hated tea, but one could not say so under present circumstances.

'You can come down for a nice sit in me kitchen,' said Mrs Beavis. 'I expect you'd like a bit of rest while you drink yer tea. Then I'll see about doin' the 'ot water bottles for yer.' Despite her weightiness, Mrs Beavis got about her house like a two-year-old. She liked being on the go. 'No good askin' you to come down an' join us, Sergeant Joe, if yer goin' out, I suppose.'

'Thanks all the same, Bessie,' said Joe.

'I will unpack and then come down,' said Marcelle.

'Yes, you do that, love,' said Mrs Beavis, and down she went to her kitchen. Marcelle smiled at Joe and went to her room, closing the door. Joe cleared his table, put his carpet-bag in the larder, locked the door and went out for some fresh air and to get an evening paper, afternoon edition.

Marcelle entered his room seconds after she saw him cross the street from her window. And she unlocked his larder door with ease. She pulled out the carpet-bag. Methodically, she went through its contents. It took her no more than four minutes to elucidate what kind of work he did in his lodgings. Name of a magnificent name, he was a forger and a beautiful one. Such a man, with this talent and his frank and fearless looks, was made for espionage. Rokovssky was right. This Englishman, who had once served in the British Army, had steamed that letter open with all the careful deliberation of an espionage agent. And this was how many such agents lived, in rooms in the back streets of cities. Where was his confederate, the girl who had stolen Rokovssky's wallet in such daring fashion?

'Miss Fate?' Mrs Beavis was calling. 'Tea's ready to be poured, and there's a nice slice of cake to keep yer goin'. Miss Fate?'

Marcelle was quietly negotiating the landing. Not until she reached the door of her room did she respond to Mrs Beavis.

'Ah, I will come down in one minute, madam. One minute.'

When she came down, all Sergeant Joe's files of papers were back in his carpet-bag, and the bag had been restored to the larder. And the larder was locked again.

She ate the slice of her landlady's home-made fruit cake, which she thought delicious, and she drank the tea that had milk in it, and which she thought only fit for the uncivilized.

Not long after they arrived home from school, Linda and Ella went up to see Sergeant Joe. Linda skipped up, Ella bounced up. Linda put her head round the door.

'Sergeant Joe, Mum says as yer didn't let 'er treat yer earlier, would yer like a cup of tea and a slice of cake now?'

'Can't say no to that, Private Carrots,' said Joe, sliding his quill pen into hiding. While he was careful not to give the impression to the Beavis family that his work was anything out of the ordinary, he nevertheless made sure it was not open to even the most casual glance. Normally, he only had the Beavises to worry about, and they were typically friendly and unsuspicious cockneys.

'We're 'aving some too,' said Ella. 'Mum says it's to keep our bodies an' souls together till suppertime. Can we bring ours up and 'ave it with you?'

'Right, let's have ten minutes of tea and cake for three,' said Joe. He shuffled papers, bringing them together and placing them to one side, face downwards.

'I'll go down an' bring it all up,' said Ella, whose energy kept her plumpness active.

'No, I will,' said Linda, 'you bump cups of tea up an' down, and it goes in the saucers. Mum says you'll bump yerself up an' down one day till yer 'ead comes orf.'

Down she went and came back with the cups of tea and slices of cake on a tray.

'Good carrying job, Carrots,' said Joe.

'That's your cup,' said Linda, 'it's wivout sugar, like you like it. Mum says we can stay the ten minutes as long as we ain't a nuisance.'

'You're not nuisances,' said Joe, 'you're good for me.'

'Mum says we got a new lodger, a nice French lady,' said Linda.

'Yes, fancy French,' said Ella, and filled her healthy

mouth with fruit cake. A few crumbs flew as she added, 'Mum says she's ever so romantic-lookin'.'

''Ave yer fell for 'er, Sergeant Joe?' asked Linda.

'Not yet,' said Joe. 'I don't think I'll have time to yet, not till we get Dolly fixed up with a job and lodgings of her own.'

'She ain't goin' to like that,' said Linda.

'Pardon?' said Joe.

'Well, I don't fink she will,' said Linda. 'Where's she gone?'

'Shopping,' said Joe.

'Is 'er wounded leg all right?' asked Ella.

'It had better be,' said Joe grimly. 'How was school today?'

'The teachers told us it was Victoria and Albert lessons today,' said Ella through her last mouthful of cake. 'They all told us that, didn't they, Linda?'

'Yes,' said Linda. ''Ere, you went and ate the biggest bit of cake. Mum said that bit was for Sergeant Joe.'

'What, that small bit?' said Ella.

'You're always takin' the biggest bits,' accused Linda.

'We're goin' to do a Victoria and Albert pageant at school on Empire Day,' said Ella. 'Sergeant Joe, fancy Dolly not bein' back yet.'

'I'll clap her in the guardhouse when she does arrive,' said Joe.

The girls giggled.

'Now, you gels!' Mrs Beavis made herself heard from below. 'Down you come, the pair of you, I want yer both in the scullery bath before yer dad and brothers get 'ome from their work.'

'Mum, I don't want no bath,' called Ella.

'It ain't what you don't want, lovey, it's what yer goin' to get. Come on down now, both of you.'

'Oh, blow,' said Linda, but she and Ella went down. The stairs sang to Ella's boisterous descent. Then the house vibrated to a yell, a thump and a crash. Sergeant Joe went out to the landing in haste, and Marcelle also appeared, her skirts rustling.

'Heavens, what has happened?' she asked.

Linda's voice supplied the answer to that.

'Oh, yer clumsy elephant, Ella, yer sittin' on top of me, an' yer've broke the cups an' saucers. Mum, could yer get 'er orf, she's squashin' me.'

'Dear oh lor',' said Mrs Beavis, 'why don't yer just walk down the stairs, Ella, instead of fallin' down them? An' look what you done to the china. Well, can't be 'elped. Pick all the pieces up, then come and 'ave yer baths. There's boiled beef an' carrots for supper when yer dad an' the boys get in.' Mrs Beavis glanced up and saw her new lady lodger and Sergeant Joe looking over the banisters. 'Lor', I'm sorry, Miss Fate, Ella makin' all that 'ullabaloo. Still, she don't do it every day.'

'Please do not worry, madam, it is nothing except a little accident,' said Marcelle. 'I do hope no-one is hurt.'

'I am,' said Linda, 'I been squashed all over and I ain't got no breath left. Me sister Ella's like an elephant when she falls on yer.'

'This is me daughter Linda, and that's Ella,' said Mrs Beavis.

'Ah, such happy girls, yes?' said Marcelle.

'I 'ope it won't disturb yer if they're a bit rackety at times,' said Mrs Beavis, her girls collecting the pieces of smashed china.

'Rackety?' enquired Marcelle.

'Noisy,' said Joe.

'I shall not mind, no, no,' smiled Marcelle.

The pieces all on the tray, the girls looked up at their new lodger.

''Ello,' said Ella.

''Ello,' said Linda.

'Hello, yes? Hello,' said Marcelle.

133

'Shoo,' said Mrs Beavis to her girls, and the passage emptied.

'One can always forgive the young,' said Marcelle.

'When I was in the Army I sometimes wondered if the young could forgive the grown-ups,' said Joe, thinking the new lodger a beauty.

'For what?' she smiled.

'For trying to kill each other every once in a while,' said Joe.

Her eyes opened wide.

'You are looking at me, Joe?' she said. 'But I am not a soldier.'

'Oh, it's not only soldiers, mademoiselle.'

She laughed.

'Pooh to mademoiselle, did I not say I am Marcelle?'

'So you did.'

'Would you like some coffee?' she asked.

'Coffee?' said Joe.

'I have a little percolator and some ground coffee. Yes, it is true. My parents, you see, said ah, in England they will only give you tea. Do you like coffee? There is a gas ring in my room and the percolator is bubbling. And I have found cups and saucers in a little cupboard. Please come.'

'You're on,' said Joe.

'Excuse me?'

'Yes, I'll join you,' said Joe. 'Sounds friendly.'

'Good, we should be friendly together,' said Marcelle.

CHAPTER ELEVEN

Dolly tried to keep her weight off her right foot as she climbed the stairs. Her ankle, despite the supportive bandage, was aching. He'd be bound to notice, to give her a look and say black mark, Private Smith. Reaching the landing, she heard the murmur of voices. From that spare room, the front one. She looked into the living-room. Empty. So was the bedroom. Funny. Was he in that other room with someone, then? She listened. A woman's voice. Yes, and his. What was he doing in there with a woman? Mrs Beavis had said he could use the bed at nights, if he wanted, but he'd said no, he didn't want three rooms to look after, he wasn't as domesticated as that.

Dolly, not one to hold back her curiosity, knocked on the door of the front room. It was opened by Marcelle. Her dark green dress with a flounced skirt was of a pleasant and conventional kind, such as respectable young women wore. But she didn't have modest looks. That is, her face wasn't as ordinary as her dress. Dolly had to admit she was lovely, with striking dark brown eyes and long thick lashes. And her jet black hair was magnificent.

'Yes?' she said, her smile enquiring.

'Excuse me,' said Dolly, 'but who are you?'

'I am new here,' said Marcelle, and Joe appeared beside her.

''Ere, what's goin' on?' asked Dolly.

'So you're back, are you?' said Joe.

That's it, thought Dolly, here comes the look.

'Oh, dearie me, sorry to interrupt,' she said and went into his bedroom.

'Ah, a friend?' said Marcelle to Joe. She had had a

135

wickedly subtle conversation with him, a very enquiring one, but he hadn't given a thing away. Behind that frank countenance of his lay a man who could fence with the best of them, she thought. 'A close friend, Joe?'

'Oh, I found her in the fog with a sprained ankle and no home or family,' said Joe, 'so I brought her here to help her get on her feet in all ways. You can't pass every hard-luck case by.'

'Some might,' said Marcelle. What a facile man he was. The young woman was his confederate, of course. 'Now I know exactly what is meant by an English gentleman. Poor unfortunate creature. Such dreadful clothes.'

Joe showed a little grin.

'Not as dreadful as what she was wearing when I first found her,' he said. 'Well, thanks for the coffee, Marcelle, now I'd better go and talk to her.'

'Of course. It is not enough to find a woman. One must also talk to her. Myself, I have much enjoyed having you talk to me.'

'Pleasure,' said Joe, and crossed to his bedroom. Entering, he was immediately attacked by Dolly. If the Victorian era was over, the example set by Queen Victoria during her long reign was still fresh in the mind, and all women who had the right amount of sense and spirit knew that attack was the best form of defence when dealing with men who liked to lay down the law.

'D'you mind tellin' me what you've been up to all day?' demanded Dolly. 'I just go out for a bit, just for an hour or two, and when I come back you ain't even got the kettle on. When I think of me days of pain and sufferin' here, and how I've kept cheerful and 'elpful so as not to be a burden, as well as givin' you the benefit of me company so that you could 'ave someone to talk to, well, it's a shock to me to find you lazin' about with a gypsy woman on your lap. Well, as good as, I should think. Still, I might 'ave known. I suppose I'll 'ave to get the supper while you go

136

back and comb the nits out of her hair. Of course, it ain't my business who she is and what she's doin' here, you probably found her in a gypsy caravan outside Spurgeon's Tabernacle and brought her here while me back was turned. I don't know what's goin' to 'appen to my respect for you. I said to Mrs Beavis this morning, I said Sergeant Joe's a hard man, but I've still got respect for him.'

'Finished?' said Joe, standing with his back to the closed door.

'No, I ain't,' said Dolly. 'I suppose you know gypsy women do vulgar dancing that's a disgrace? I suppose she's just done one for you, no wonder you can't look me in the face.'

Joe, in fact, was looking her straight in the eye.

'Finished now, Private Smith?' he asked.

'Yes, I've said me piece,' declared Dolly. 'It was me Christian duty to. Oh, I bought some new clothes today, I 'ope you like them. There's a flounced skirt with a matchin' jacket in russet brown, and a mushroom-coloured blouse with a lace collar and front. Oh, and a little velvet 'at with a feather. Well, I thought I'd spend some of that ten quid. They're all in these boxes.' She began to unpack them.

Joe looked at the clothes she was wearing, the clothes he'd bought her. Marcelle thought them dreadful, but Marcelle was French, and even if she was attired soberly, she would still think no-one outside France could dress at all.

'You monkey,' he said.

'I beg your pardon?' said Dolly haughtily.

'Stand to attention and explain yourself,' said Joe. Her prolonged absence had affected his concentration, and he'd made a hash of the signature of Percy Bysshe Shelley. The letter in question would have to be written all over again. No woman had ever caused him to make that kind of mistake before. Can't have that sort of thing happening to me, he thought. Looking after a young woman with a sprained ankle, no job and no family was one thing. Letting her become a worry to him was another. Won't do, Joe. 'Private Smith, answer up.'

'I ain't standin' to attention,' said Dolly, 'I'm not soft in the head.'

'You've been absent without leave. Can't have that, and especially can't have it while you're still on the sick list. You're confined to barracks for twenty-four hours, and on half-rations. Right, that over, report on what you've been up to and the condition of your ankle.'

'Don't make me spit,' said Dolly. 'What's that cross-eyed gypsy woman doin' here?'

'She's French,' said Joe, 'with a job in some academy, teaching deportment. She's a new lodger. She gave me a cup of French coffee and we had a chat.'

'Tell me another,' said Dolly. 'And what d'you mean, what 'ave I been up to? I just went shoppin', that's all; I took an 'ansom cab at the Elephant and Castle to save wear and tear on me ankle, and went up West in it. It didn't 'alf make me feel posh. I didn't do a lot of walkin', except round the shops, and I treated meself to another 'ansom cab to bring me back. I mean, fancy an 'ard-up orphanage girl like me 'aving all that money in me purse. D'you like what I bought?'

'Very nice,' said Joe, eyeing the purchases she'd set out on the bed, 'but explain why it's taken you all day.'

'Excuse me,' said Dolly, 'but a girl don't buy a new outfit in five minutes. A day's about right, you ask any woman. You sure you like mine?'

'Should make you look like a lady,' said Joe.

'Honest? Imagine you bein' complimentary like that. Mind, you wouldn't believe some of the prices they charge up West, talk about daylight robbery. The people who run them shops ought to be tried at the Old Bailey and given years of 'ard labour. Some of them wanted to charge as

138

much as twelve and six just for a skirt. Can't believe it, can you? Nor could I. Did you miss not 'aving me to talk to? It wasn't any good askin' you if I could go, I knew you'd 'ave one of your hard-hearted turns. But my ankle's fine, it just aches a bit, that's all.'

'It had better be fine,' said Joe, 'or you'll cop it.'

'Yes, all right,' said Dolly, 'I'll go and stand in the corner in a minute.' She sat down instead. 'Oh, I bought a new coat as well, it's in that other box. Would you mind if I asked what's for supper, only I'm starvin'.'

'Chops and two veg,' said Joe. 'The chops are in the oven.'

'Ain't you a love?' said Dolly. 'Oh, I bought something for you too.' She leaned and opened up a flat box. 'I 'ope you like it, Joe, it's for being me best friend ever.'

Joe looked. Inside the box, resting on tissue paper, was a folded royal blue cashmere jersey.

'Well, I'm jiggered,' he said. He took the jersey out. It must have cost her over a quid.

'It's a 44,' said Dolly, 'you 'aving a manly chest, like. And you like jerseys. They're 'andsome on you.'

'What a gift,' said Joe, 'I'm lost for words. You sure I deserve this?'

'You been kind to me, Joe.'

'With a bit of an effort, I suppose. I said to Mrs Beavis this morning, Bessie, I said, I'm a hard man, but—'

'Oh, you clown,' said Dolly.

'Many thanks, Dolly, it's a very generous gift.'

'Oh, just a little something,' said Dolly.

They met on the Embankment this time, Alexander Rokovssky and the gentleman known as a diplomatic courier. He was actually Count Zhinsky, anonymous head of Russian Intelligence. His kind-looking face concealed a steely dedication to duty and the Motherland.

In the dusk, the street lamps illuminated the long

riverside walk, and patches of light danced on the Thames in the clearness of the evening. April's inheritance of the winds of March had cleansed the air of London. Count Zhinsky carried a walking-stick, Rokovssky had his hands in his overcoat pockets.

'I'm not sure you should have made such an attempt,' said the Count.

'It was necessary.'

'Your audacity is remarkable.'

'Necessity is always a spur,' said Rokovssky.

'Indeed. But I prefer your alternative and the sensibility of its prearrangement.'

'I telegraphed the command to proceed.'

'Excellent,' said the Count, but wondered if his protégée liked to be commanded. She was as individualistic as Rokovssky, as much in love with her own competence as he was with his. 'So, she is there now, sitting on the tails of our suspect foxes?'

'I am confident she is,' said Rokovssky.

'Good,' said the Count, who was in London himself because of the importance of the venture and the advisability of maintaining direct contact with his operatives. He would, however, as a self-protective precaution, be back in St Petersburg on the day the assassination took place. 'I'm happy to inform you, by the way, that there is no agitation inside Scotland Yard.'

'That comes from our contact?'

'It does. I can say positively that the contents of the letter have not come to the notice of the British. Otherwise the men of Scotland Yard would be moving in all directions. So, whoever this man and woman are working for, it is not the British.'

'Another power, then,' said Rokovssky.

'That is not unlikely. But they aren't in a position to harass you as the British on their home ground would be. I commend you, by the way, for insisting on arriving early,

140

for as the set time approaches they will tighten their surveillance at their ports of entry. They will take very seriously their responsibility for the protection of crowned heads and deport all known anarchists, as well as people they consider suspect. You are keeping strictly apart from the decoys?'

'I promoted this arrangement, Excellency, and don't intend to break it now. I'm in touch, however, and have warned them not to make use of other idiots. As their letter informed me, it's enough that they know they're being watched.'

'Deportation may follow, of course,' said the Count.

'I think not,' said Rokovssky. 'I think they're being watched in the hope that they'll give something away. That was the idea.'

'It appears to be working.'

'It's a small diversion,' said Rokovssky, peering at the dancing lights on the moving surface of the dark Thames.

Knowing his man, the Count said, 'I won't argue that. Simply advise me when you have finalized everything. You are keeping no company?'

'I'm treading a solitary path for the Motherland.'

'You have my sympathy, admiration and best wishes,' said the Count, and parted from him a minute later.

Dolly viewed her mutton chop, mashed potatoes and spring greens, then cast her eyes over the table, spread with a plain white cloth.

'I don't want to be awkward,' she said, 'but ain't there no mint sauce?'

'Should be, shouldn't there?' said Joe, who'd put his new jersey on and given himself an expensive look. 'I'll never get to be a good cook. Hold on.' He got up, put the plates of food in the range oven to keep them hot, then went down to see if Mrs Beavis could help. She was at supper with her family. All seven of them at table together

141

had shrunk the kitchen, and they were in noisy, exuberant enjoyment of boiled beef and carrots. Visibly, faces were turning red and shiny. Feminine plumpness was expanding, masculine girths straining at belts.

''Ello, 'ello,' said Albert.

'Nice to 'ave yer pop down,' said Mr Beavis.

'Come over 'ere and I'll give yer a kiss when I've finished me mouthful,' said Nancy juicily.

'Bless the cheeky gel,' smiled Mrs Beavis. 'What can we do for yer, Sergeant Joe?'

'Sorry to interrupt your supper,' said Joe, 'but I'm on the cadge. Got any mint?'

'In me larder,' said Mrs Beavis, showing herself beamingly happy to be able to oblige. 'It's in a jam jar, dried mint that's already chopped up. 'Elp yerself, love.'

'P'raps 'e might like me too,' said Nancy. 'Not 'ere, though, somewhere private, an' when I've 'ad me afters.'

Ella exploded into shrieks, and her brothers roared with laughter. Mr Beavis chortled.

'That Nancy,' said Linda, 'I don't fink much of 'er as me sister.'

'The sauce she's got,' said Mrs Beavis, as Joe took the jam jar of dried mint from the larder.

'I'll do some talkin' to 'er, Bessie,' said Mr Beavis. 'Not 'ere, though, somewhere private, an' when I've 'ad me afters.'

'Use yer belt, Dad,' said Alfred.

'Well, I tell yer, Alfred, it'll be a relief to get it orf after me afters,' said Mr Beavis.

'Thanks for the mint, Bessie,' said Joe amid the yells of laughter.

'Pleasure, love,' said Mrs Beavis.

In the gaslit passage, Joe saw the new lady lodger coming down the stairs, her hat and coat on. She descended with a natural elegance.

'Ah, how nice, it is you again, Joe,' she said. 'Please to

tell me why the house is rumbling and shaking.'

'Our landlady, Mrs Beavis, is having supper with her family in their kitchen,' said Joe. 'There are seven of them, and they're all talkers. And they're all healthy. You're going out?'

'To the West End, to find a little restaurant that is not expensive,' said Marcelle, smiling. 'You would like to come with me, perhaps?'

'Not this evening,' said Joe, 'I'm just about to have my meal.'

'Ah, so? Never mind. Perhaps tomorrow you will take me to the National Gallery? Would you be so kind? I am anxious to see its treasures.'

Her smile was winning, her charm delightful. Joe couldn't see any good reason for not obliging her.

'Well, it so happens I'm going to town in the morning,' he said. 'I'll meet you at the National Gallery at ten o'clock.'

'I am thrilled,' said Marcelle, 'I did not think it would be as easy as this to make friends with an English gentleman.'

'You're out of luck there,' said Joe, 'I'm no gentleman. Excuse me now, must get upstairs.'

Dolly gave him a suspicious look when he entered with the mint.

'Well, it's nice you're back,' she said.

'I got delayed,' said Joe, mixing some of the chopped mint with vinegar in a gravy boat.

'Yes, I heard you bein' delayed, by that French gypsy woman. Did she do one of 'er gypsy dances for you?'

'Not that I noticed. There we are.' Joe returned the warm plates of food to the table, and Dolly helped herself to the mint sauce.

'I don't want to worry about you gettin' yourself mixed up with gypsies.'

'Good,' said Joe.

'You're a nice bloke mostly.'

'Good.'

'And you've done a nice supper.'

'Good.'

'Will you stop sayin' good?' Dolly shook her fork at him.

'Eat your rations,' said Joe.

'Well, I am. Fancy you bein' able to cook chops as tasty as this. Did you learn cookin' in the Army?'

'No, I learned how to ride a horse and look after it.'

'Oh, can you ride a horse, Joe?'

'All dragoons ride horses.'

'What's a dragoon?'

'Heavy cavalry able to dismount and fight on foot.'

''Ave you done much fightin'?'

'Here and there.'

'Crikey,' said Dolly, 'no wonder you're tall and 'andsome and brave-lookin'.'

'Yes, no wonder,' said Joe, grinning.

'I'll stay in here with you after supper, shall I?' said Dolly. 'We can sit and talk.'

'I ought to do some work,' said Joe, who felt events were causing him to fall behind with his current commission.

'You're just sayin' that. Can I 'elp it if I like talkin' with you? Besides, people are supposed to 'ave conversation with each other. Tell me what it was like in the Army.'

'Well, for one thing,' said Joe, 'we didn't have to have conversations with little old ladies carrying on about talking.'

'Here, I ain't a little old lady,' said Dolly, enjoying her juicy chop.

'No, not yet, just give yourself time,' said Joe. 'But all right,' he said sociably, 'were there days at the orphanage that were better than others?'

'Well, there was that boy who saw me legs when I fell

over one day,' said Dolly. 'He didn't 'alf like them, he said he'd give me a penny every time I showed them. I asked him where he was goin' to get the pennies from, and he said he'd nick them from the superintendent's gas money. Well, none of us ever 'ad money, so I said all right, a penny each time I showed 'im my legs. And what d'you think? When I run away twelve months later I took two 'undred and nineteen pennies with me, which meant I'd showed him me legs two 'undred and nineteen times in a year. Here, are you laughin'?'

'Not much.'

'I don't see it was anything to laugh about,' said Dolly huffily. 'How would you like to 'ave to show your legs in an orphanage just because you 'adn't got a farthing to your name?'

'Can't think you'd pay a penny to see mine,' said Joe. 'Then what happened?'

'What, after I'd run away?' Dolly picked up the chop bone and nibbled at it with sharp teeth. 'Well, I thought I'd best get as far from Dalston as I could, so I came this side of London Bridge and looked for lodgings. Well, I had all those pennies, didn't I?'

'Eighteen and thruppence,' said Joe.

'As much as that? Fancy me legs earnin' that amount. Here, Joe, you should 'ave seen some of the rooms I was offered, they wasn't fit to keep cats in even. I 'ad to pay three bob for a decent one. Then I 'ad to get a job; that's when I saw a notice in a shop window about a Brixton fam'ly wantin' a maid, so I went after it. I got it all right, but like I told you, it wasn't a maid's job. I was just a skivvy. After I run away again, I 'ad real hard times and was nearly starvin' the night you walked into me and did me ankle in. Oh, lor', that Blackbeard, he's nearly been our doom. Still, I think you're right, I don't suppose he'll come back again. Excuse me, but is there any afters?'

'Treacle tart from the baker's do you?' offered Joe.

'Treacle tart?' Dolly looked delighted. 'Oh, you really do treat a girl swell.' Joe fetched the tart from the larder and cut her a large portion. 'I met a parson once that was good to me, but he never gave me any treacle tart, just a kind message of 'ope. I've been thinking that if I ever meet the kind of young lady who'd make you a nice wife, I'll get her to come round and introduce 'erself.'

'That's your idea of friendship?' said Joe.

'Well, you deserve a nice wife, Joe, honest you do. Only if you don't mind me sayin' so, it'll be best if you don't treat her like a private in the Army.'

'I'll bear that in mind,' said Joe, giving up any thoughts of work. Dolly was obviously set on being sociable for the whole evening. 'Tell me how you came to take up a life of crime.'

'I'm ignorin' that uncalled-for remark,' said Dolly.

Joe smiled. In one way, he and Dolly were two of a kind.

CHAPTER TWELVE

Dolly burned the breakfast toast the next morning. Joe gave her the toasting fork with a slice of bread on the end of it, and pointed her at the glowing coals of the fire. She muttered a bit, but knelt on the rug and applied the slice of bread to the heat, while Joe laid the table and made the tea. The slice of bread turned black. Dolly looked at the smoking wreck and gulped. Joe said black mark, Private Smith, and put a fresh slice on the fork for her. She not only managed to burn that as well, the slice went up in flames.

'Mother O'Grady,' said Joe.

'Wasn't my fault,' said Dolly, 'the fire's too hot.'

'One more slice,' said Joe, 'and if you burn that, I'll have you court-martialled.'

'Oh, you and your daft Army,' said Dolly, 'you wait.' Gritting her teeth, she made her third attempt. Joe, a grin on his face, watched her. Her face turned rosy from the heat of the fire. She produced a perfect slice of toast and stared at it in rapture. 'Crikey, look at that,' she breathed, 'I did it.'

'What a triumph at the age of twenty-one,' said Joe, and put another slice on the end of the fork.

'Yes, ain't I a clever girl?' said Dolly, and repeated her success three times. They breakfasted on two slices each, with butter and marmalade, and Dolly said she'd like to go to the East Street market some time.

'You'll get mobbed,' said Joe. She was wearing her new outfit and looked astonishingly the young lady. Her dark auburn hair was full of burnished glints. She'd used his hairbrush. Her face was lightly made-up, her lips tinted

147

with pink. Her grey eyes accepted his regard demurely.

'You really like me in me new clothes?' she said.

'You look like the West End,' he said. 'However, state condition of your ankle after gallivanting about all day yesterday.'

'It's better all the time.'

'Sure?'

'The swelling's nearly gone right down.'

'All the same, rest it today,' said Joe. 'I'll be going out after breakfast, and while I'm out, massage your ankle, put a little liniment on, and then the bandage. Make sure it's firm but not too tight.'

'Yes, me lord,' said Dolly.

'I'll be back about one, when I'll get us something to eat.'

'That's it, don't mind me, you go out and enjoy yourself,' said Dolly, teeth crunching her last piece of toast. 'I'll just twiddle me thumbs. Of course, if I 'ad a decent book to read—'

'I think there's an old copy of *Alice in Wonderland* floating about somewhere,' said Joe.

'I read that when I was ten,' said Dolly. 'What are you goin' out all morning for?'

'To see a businessman.'

'One you write letters for?'

'That's it,' said Joe. 'Then I'm going to the National Gallery.'

'National Gallery?' said Dolly. 'I didn't know you was arty.'

'I'm not sure if paintings of fat women are arty or not,' said Joe, 'but I promised to go round the place with our French lodger.'

'What, that gypsy tart?' said Dolly.

'Couldn't refuse her, seeing she's a visitor from abroad. And she's got a funny idea that I'm a gentleman.'

'Well, you are a bit of a gent, Joe, honest you are,' said

Dolly, 'but 'ave you got it that bad already? Fancy you wantin' to go and look at paintings just to please that 'umpbacked woman.'

'Humpbacked?' said Joe. 'I didn't notice that.'

'It must 'ave been that ugly dress of hers, I suppose,' said Dolly. 'I'm really sorry for you, Joe, you must be nearly blind to fancy her. We're both unfortunate, ain't we? I mean, me with all me 'ard luck and you nearly blind. Is that why you left the Army, because you couldn't see who was friend and who was foe?'

'Something like that,' said Joe. 'Glad to see you're perky; you'll be fighting fit by the weekend. Then we'll see about finding you a job and some decent lodgings. I've a friend who might help.'

'Here, don't talk like that,' said Dolly. 'I wouldn't 'ave the 'eart to leave you alone with that French gypsy woman. After all you've done for me, I couldn't go off and leave you 'elpless, I'd never forgive meself. I bet a woman like that would eat you, she'd drag you into her bed as soon as me back was turned.'

A broad grin on his face, Joe said, 'Say that again.'

'It wouldn't be right, a kind bloke like you meetin' a fate worse than death,' said Dolly. 'You might shoot yourself afterwards out of bein' ashamed at lettin' it 'appen. 'Aving been a soldier, you're bound to 'ave a lot of pride.'

'Not a good thing, shooting myself, Dolly,' said Joe. 'Don't worry, I think I could fight my way out of her armchair. Now, if you've got anything that needs taking to the local laundry, I'll take it with mine tomorrow.'

'Yes, I've got things,' said Dolly, 'and I bought more yesterday. They're private.'

'Understood,' said Joe. 'Right, if your ankle's up to it, I'll let you go out tomorrow and you can take them yourself, with some stuff of mine. A short walk there and back should be just right for you.'

149

'How kind,' said Dolly.

'Don't mention it,' said Joe.

'You'll be back at one, you said?'

'That's it.'

'Well, I 'ope you won't come in all wore out,' said Dolly. 'I like gypsies gen'rally, and their caravans, but I don't trust ones like her that come from France. You just mind yourself.'

'All right,' said Joe, 'if she asks me for a dance in Trafalgar Square, I'll point out I've got a stiff leg. How's that?'

'Sounds like another one of your jokes that ain't funny,' said Dolly, eyeing him critically. He was wearing the new cashmere jersey. Her critical look gave way to a smile. 'That jersey's swell on you, Joe.'

'Feels fine,' said Joe. 'Bless you, Private Smith.'

He went out fifteen minutes later, to walk all the way to Charing Cross Road again. He wore a jacket over the jersey. He didn't like high stiff collars and choking ties, they made him feel like a City clerk. Somehow, when it became necessary, he'd have to get an outdoor job.

Left alone, Dolly waited ten minutes, then put her little velvet hat on and went out herself.

George Singleton had the translation ready, and looked on intrigued as Joe read it.

There was no address, and no date. But there was a name, and there were signatures.

Our dear Boris,

Our visit here is of all things satisfying and educational. Alexandra Petrovna has arrived, and we have gained other company. They have been with us since we landed, and they are keen in their pursuits and keep us on our toes. This is what you led us to expect, so we are very happy about it and would not be without their company.

150

We are not neglecting our studies. We go out to buy food and to look at the sights of London. Our portfolios contain some excellent pencil sketches of St Paul's Cathedral, Buckingham Palace, Tower Bridge, which is new and fascinating, and other notable attractions. You could not fault our diligence. Our lodgings are cheap and comfortable, and there are some very friendly people next door. The friend recommended to us has promised to supply us with personal requirements very reasonably, with delivery at the right time guaranteed, which is more than one can expect at home.

We are finding English people very friendly and uninterfering, and our close companions keep us here every evening, which ensures we have no option but to write up our notes on which we will each base our thesis.

We trust we shall earn good marks from our professor!

We hope your own studies are going well, and understand it is unlikely you will be able to visit us because of your commitments. We are sending this letter by hand in case the post here is as dilatory as it is at home.

Our blessings, Ivan and Igor.

Joe rubbed his chin and fingered his moustache.

'What's it all about, old chap?' asked George.

'Haven't the foggiest,' said Joe.

'Hate to say so,' observed George mildly, 'but I think it smells a little. It's a peculiar letter for you to have, isn't it?'

'It fell accidentally into my lap.'

'Glad to hear it,' said George. 'Something tells me it's fishy. Try letting it fall purposely into the hands of the police. It's written in Russian by Russians, and Russia is breeding anarchists by the score. Dilatory post my foot. What's urgent about a letter like this unless it's clogged with hidden meanings?'

'Don't like the sound of anarchists,' said Joe thoughtfully.

151

'Don't like the sound of them in London,' said George.

'I'll do something about it,' said Joe. 'Meanwhile, here's part of the present commission.' He handed a file to George. 'You'll get the rest later.'

'I know,' said George. 'You're an exceptionally reliable friend. By the way, half-a-crown for the translation. Fairly steep, I agree, but the professor's on his beam ends and won't say a word to mother.'

'That's fair,' said Joe, handing over the silver coin.

'Where would civilization be, old man, if all fairness flew out of the window?'

'In the dark, I should think,' said Joe.

Marcelle Fayette arrived outside the National Gallery at five minutes to ten. She stood to survey Trafalgar Square, the morning fresh but bright. Her maroon jacket and skirt, and her sheer white blouse, were faultless in style and cut, her elegance undeniable. Her flat-brimmed spring hat was tipped forward to shade her forehead.

She observed the people. The breeze was playing tricks with ladies, plucking at their skirts and ruffling the feathers in their hats. Long skirts and hidden feet gave the impression that some ladies were sailing along without using their legs. Men sauntered or strode briskly. Top hats, bowler hats or straw boaters were worn with individualistic style. Most top hats sat importantly, bowlers sturdily and straw boaters raffishly. Ah, the Englishmen and their hats, they wore them in their own way, as if they were masters of the world. Perhaps they thought they were. What a thing it was, to let one's hat speak for a whole nation.

A flower girl in a battered boater, an extraordinary amount of clothing, and a shawl as well, walked the pavement with the curving handle of her basket over her arm. She stopped and turned the basket towards Marcelle.

'Buy me sweet vi'lets, lady?' she asked with a smile.

'I do not buy flowers for myself,' said Marcelle.

'Oh, come on, lady, be a sport.' The flower girl lifted a posy. 'There y'ar, a nosegay for yer button'ole, bring yer luck, it will. Only thruppence. Well, tuppence if yer want to push me.'

A shadow fell across her.

'Let's have a look,' said Joe, and the flower girl glanced up at him.

'Oh, yer'll buy, won't yer, sir? See, fresh as mornin' dew they are.'

The posy did look fresh, the blooms velvety. Marcelle watched with a slight smile on her face as Joe inspected them. He was very natural, she thought, in his approach to people. Not everyone would be able to keep their secrets from him.

'I'll take six,' he said.

'Six bunches? Oh, ain't yer a toff?' said the flower girl. 'They're grown under winter glass, these are, sir, so I can't sell 'em for a penny. But I won't charge yer thruppence as yer buyin' six. Are they for yer lady friend?'

'Two are for this lady,' said Joe, nodding at Marcelle, who smiled sweetly.

'Lummy, she's yer one and only, sir?' whispered the flower girl.

'Can't tell a lie, Daisy, she's just an acquaintance.'

'Still, I wish yer luck, sir. 'Ow did yer know me name was Daisy?'

'You're all called Daisy,' said Joe, as she gathered six posies together.

'I'm always 'ere in Trafalgar Square,' she said.

'Are you? Do me a favour, then. Hang on to my order and I'll pick the lot up from you later. We're going into the National Gallery for a while. All right?'

'It's me pleasure, sir, but yer won't forget, will yer?'

'No, I won't forget.' He dug into his pocket and brought out a florin. 'There you are, Daisy, keep the change.'

'Oh, ain't you a sport, sir?' said Daisy, eyes bright. 'And I likes yer as well. I'll be lookin' out for yer when you've finished lookin' at the paintings.'

'Hope they're not all of ladies of the bath,' said Joe, 'hope there's some of the Duke of Wellington at Waterloo.'

Daisy laughed and went singing on her way.

Marcelle, closing in on Joe, said, 'Do you always flirt with flower girls?'

'No, not much,' said Joe, 'I don't see enough of them. Don't often buy flowers. What's happened to you, by the way?'

In the great open quadrangle of Trafalgar Square, the light enhanced her elegance and her colouring.

'Excuse me?' she said.

'You look rich today,' said Joe.

'Ah, but yesterday, you see, it was necessary to look as if I could only afford cheap lodgings. Otherwise, madam the landlady would have asked far more for the room.'

'I can't make sense of that,' said Joe, 'but it's your own business.'

'Yes, isn't it so?' she said, a little purr to her voice.

Joe looked around. Busy street cleaners with their little handcarts had their work cut out to deal with horse-drawn traffic. Westminster City Council prided itself on keeping the West End presentable, especially around Trafalgar Square, the meeting-place at lunchtime of young men and their young ladies, the rendezvous of visitors from the suburbs, and the confluence of the streams of traffic which poured into it from a host of thoroughfares. Hansom cabs by the score, delivery vans, private carriages and motor-ized omnibuses all provided a never-ending spectacle of colour and movement.

'Shall we go in?' he suggested. The National Gallery offered a release from hustle, bustle and noise.

They went in. Admission was free. The grandeur of the gallery had been inspired by eminent Victorians who felt great works of art should be brought to the eyes of the people at no cost to them. Marcelle seemed impressed. Joe just hoped that not too many of the great works would also be great with flesh. He knew that even sweet cherubs were always painted as if the artists saw them as chubby mounds of fat dumplings. He bought a catalogue at Marcelle's insistence. She examined it during their progress through the halls, casting amused glances at him the while. Perhaps he was only interested in horses. Horses and armies went together. The informative catalogue enabled her to begin torturing him, to lead him to an exhibition of Italian masters. Joe found himself surrounded by paintings of ladies abundant with flesh.

'Don't believe it,' he said, 'can't be true.'

'Shush,' said Marcelle, 'you must examine with reverence. Ah, such magnificence, such colour, such life.'

'Can't see it myself,' said Joe.

'Come, what do you really think?' asked Marcelle.

'Can't think,' said Joe, 'can't even look.'

'But you must look, it is only fair to the artist. There, at least look at Salome. She has cast all her veils. Look at the colours, look at King Herod and his court, and how they are regarding Salome.'

'They all look numb to me. I'm not surprised. I feel the same way.'

'Have you no soul, Joe?' asked Marcelle.

'I'm fonder of horses.'

She laughed. Yesterday's impulse had led to this, a light interlude of pleasure amid the deadly seriousness of her mission. A landowner's daughter, spoiled and capricious, she had felt her life had little purpose until she met Count Zhinsky during a visit by her family to St Petersburg. She became his mistress, his confidante and his most subtle operative. She had few scruples about the part she played in the destruction of people who plotted against the established order.

This man, this ex-sergeant of the British Army, a nuisance and a worrying irritation to Rokovssky, was a game to her. While keeping an eye on him, perhaps she might amuse herself with him.

She smiled, she lingered. It was *most* amusing, making him linger with her amid the depictions of abundant flesh.

A hansom cab stood on the corner of Leyden Street, a stone's throw from Middlesex Street in the East End. It was not exactly a salubrious area. Poverty in many of its debilitating effects existed here. It was seen in the drab look of some of the dwellings, and in the ragged attire and peaky faces of street kids. Even so, there were worse places in the East End. Queen Victoria had deplored the fact that in the heart of the Empire's capital there was the eyesore of slums. Nor had she liked knowing that none of her governments had ever found the resources or the will to improve the lot of people direly poor.

In the cab sat a woman and a man. The man was in his forties, a tubby and alert character. She was much younger, and although she had never been called a quiet person, she was very calm and composed at the moment. She was leaning forward, and with the aid of a little hand mirror and the cab window, she was watching a house in Bell Lane, which ran at right angles to Leyden Street. She had been watching it for some time. The tubby gentleman was sitting back, effacing himself. Outside and behind them, the cabbie was in a relaxed attitude in the driving seat, smoking a clay pipe. His horse stood patiently.

'Did yer say they always went out about the same time?' asked Tubby.

'No, I didn't,' said the young woman, Henrietta Downes, 'and they don't.'

'Ruddy inconvenient of 'em.'

'Very. But one learns to wait.'

'Don't I know it. D'yer use a cab often?'

'Seldom,' said Miss Downes.

'So I should 'ope,' said Tubby. 'Do they sometimes not go out at all?'

'Not to my knowledge. Be patient, Tubby. I can at least tell you that when they do go out, it's always in the mornings.'

'I'm gratified I ain't goin' to 'ave to wait all day. I can't say their lodgings is choice. Couldn't they 'ave afforded Bloomsbury?'

'How do I know?' said Miss Downes. 'I imagine they've a good reason for choosing this hole. Sit back, Tubby, and wait.'

They had to wait only a few more minutes. Then the mirror reflected the movement of a door opening. Miss Downes tensed slightly.

''Ello, they're comin'?' whispered Tubby.

'Yes. They're out of the house. Now it's up to you, now you can take over. But wait, not yet, they'll see you. They're going towards Wentworth Street. Now, now you may get out. I hope that at last they'll do something more telling than looking at the Houses of Parliament or the Tower of London, and making sketches. Off you go.'

Tubby, alighting, murmured, 'You're sure they've never met anyone?'

'They picked up a man once, the one who had a fatal accident. Go on now.'

Dressed in nondescript fashion, Tubby closed the cab door quietly and walked to the street corner. There he turned right into Bell Lane. Some way ahead were two young men. Both walked with self-assurance, both wore high blue student caps with shiny peaks, and both were laughing at the antics of street kids playing truant. Each carried a stiff cardboard portfolio, the kind used by art students.

'So there you are,' said Marcelle, smiling.

157

Joe turned. He had to admit she was a creature of exceptional good looks. She fitted easily into this setting of art and culture. He could take or leave picture galleries himself, although he liked a landscape or a depiction of a hunt in full cry. The National Gallery was right for Marcelle Fayette. He was not sure, however, that he wholly trusted her or her instant friendship. Accordingly, he was slightly on his guard. Women like her were new to him. She was hardly typical of a Walworth lodger. She was up to something. Well, most women were most of the time.

'Yes, here I am, Marcelle. I managed to slip you in that crowd around Diana at her bath. Did you notice her bottom? Big as a balloon. She could never have put all of that on a horse.'

Marcelle could not help laughing. She glanced at the canvases he preferred. She laughed again.

'Yes, I might have guessed,' she said. Battle scenes adorned the walls. 'Swords and cannon and horses. Alas, Joe, you are still playing soldiers.'

'Can't find Wellington at Waterloo,' said Joe. 'Can't be helped, and it's time to go, anyway. It's twelve-fifteen.'

'Very well,' said Marcelle, 'where shall we have luncheon?'

'Luncheon?' said Joe. He'd never come across luncheon in Chatham or Walworth, although he'd encountered tiffin in India.

'Yes, where shall we eat?' asked Marcelle. 'I had only coffee for breakfast.'

'Back to the lodgings for food,' said Joe.

'Are you serious?' asked Marcelle, as they made their way out.

'Yes. D'you fancy a kipper?'

'Kipper? Kipper?'

'How about poached eggs on toast, then?'

'For luncheon?' said Marcelle. 'How disgusting.' They

158

emerged into sunlight and the brisk breeze tugged at her skirt. 'We are here, but you wish to eat in the lodgings?'

'Sounds right for a hard-up young French lady,' said Joe.

'What a wretch,' said Marcelle, 'you are turning down the privilege of taking me to a restaurant.'

'The fact is,' said Joe, 'I promised to get back and eat with Dolly.'

'Ah, the poor creature you found in that very dreadful fog, yes. I should not dream of coming between you. I shall stay and find a little restaurant.'

'Soho's the place for little restaurants and Continental food,' said Joe. 'I'll see you back at the house some time. So long.'

'*Au 'voir*, Joe.' She watched him go on his way. He had a limping walk. She supposed that was to do with his time as a soldier. But he was very upright. He limped, yes, but was still soldierly. He was also handsome. Rokovssky was grotesque and arrogant. Count Zhinsky had pleasing looks and a deceptive kindness of manner.

Joe headed towards Daisy, the flower girl. She saw him coming and hurried to meet him. Marcelle was still watching.

'I still got yer vi'lets, sir,' said Daisy, 'I kept you the best.'

'Thought you would,' said Joe, 'thought you'd be a pal.'

Her bright eyes sparkled.

'Pleasure, sir,' she said. He wasn't a toff. Toffs didn't wear jerseys and caps. They were dandified and talked as if they'd got plums in their mouths. This man was just nice. She handed him the posies, which she had wrapped in brown paper, and the open top showed a clustering circle of the velvety blooms. 'Oh, yer did bring me luck, sir, I'm all sold out. I've met two kind gents lately, an' you're one of 'em.'

'Then could I ask you to do me a favour?' said Joe.

'Would you go and tell that lady that I'm taking her posies with me to save her carrying them about?'

'Shall I give 'er yer love as well, sir?' asked Daisy with a saucy smile.

'Why not? Good idea, and can't do any harm. By the way, I often come to Charing Cross Road. I'll look out for you and your flowers in future, Daisy. Good luck.'

'You too, sir,' said Daisy, and carried the message to Marcelle, who listened to it with a smile, and then a raised eyebrow.

'Excuse me?' she said.

'Yes, that's right, lady, 'e sent yer 'is love as well,' said Daisy.

'How reckless of him, he will find himself having to fight a duel with my husband,' said Marcelle, and sailed away. Well, Rokovssky has come up against an intriguing man, she thought, one who is hiding his talents and his secrets in a lodging house, and pretending to be as ordinary as all the people around him. But he is far from ordinary, he played a little game with me in the National Gallery, professing himself unsympathetic to masterpieces. Somewhere in his room, perhaps, she might find that which would tell her from whom he received his orders. How strange that he had made himself so pleasant to that flower girl, for Rokovssky had already done so. He bought flowers from her every other day, so he had said. He had plans for her.

CHAPTER THIRTEEN

Joe, reaching the landing, immediately caught the smell of smoke. The door to his living-room was ajar, and little tendrils were issuing through the gap. He pushed the door open hurriedly. On the hob, above a fire glowing with heat, stood his frying-pan, sizzling. Black smoke was rising and filling the room. Dolly, one hand to her mouth and coughing, had a tea towel wrapped around her other hand and was trying to take hold of the frying-pan.

'Leave it,' said Joe, putting aside the violets and some groceries.

'Oh, help,' gasped Dolly.

'You open the window,' said Joe, 'I'll see to the pan.' He stooped in the smoke, picked the coal glove from the scuttle, put it on and lifted the frying-pan off the hob. Dolly jerked the window open and breezy April rushed joyfully in. Joe carried the smoking pan downstairs and out through the back door next to the kitchen. He placed the pan on the ground beside the dustbin and went back upstairs. Dolly was fanning herself at the open window, the incoming air cooling her flushed face.

'Here, that frying-pan of yours is downright dangerous,' she said, 'look what it's done to me and your lodgings.'

'Stand to attention,' said Joe.

'Me do what?'

'Burnt toast, burnt frying-pan, what kind of a private are you, Private Smith? You'll get drummed out with all your buttons stripped off if you carry on like this.'

'Here, leave off,' said Dolly, 'how was I to know that pan was goin' to turn nasty?'

'What was in it?' asked Joe.

'Half a pound of cultivated mushrooms—'

'What?'

'Don't they call them that? Cultivated? That was what the bloke said who sold them to me. And there was half a pound of kidneys as well.'

'Mushrooms? Kidneys?' said Joe.

'Oh, I 'ad to go down the market for them,' said Dolly. 'The bloke said they're from a mushroom farm in Kent.'

'Never heard of it,' said Joe.

'Well, fancy that,' said Dolly, gratefully taking in fresh air. 'Well,' she said to the open window, 'did you 'ear that? Fancy me findin' out that Sergeant Joe don't know everything. One up to you, Dolly. Take a bow. Yes, all right, I will. Pleasured, I'm sure.' She turned to Joe, her face marked with faint smuts. 'I thought I'd give you a treat and 'ave the mushrooms and kidneys all cooked and ready for when you came in, except when I put the frying-pan on the hob they all went up in smoke while I was powderin' me nose. It's no good you givin' me looks, that frying-pan of yours ought to be chucked in the river for ruinin' me lovely mushrooms and kidneys. No wonder you're ashamed of it.'

'I'm not,' said Joe. 'Did you put any dripping in the pan?'

'Drippin'?' said Dolly cautiously.

'Stand to attention.'

'Don't you holler at me, Joe Foster.'

'I'm not.'

'No, but you're goin' to, I can see you are, and how did I know about any drippin'?'

'Jesus give me strength,' said Joe. 'Don't you know you can't fry anything in a dry pan?'

'Never mind that, I ain't standin' to attention,' said Dolly. 'I told you before, it's daft.'

'I've got a sorry feeling, Private Smith, that you've been dodging the column while you've been growing up. You can't peel spuds and you're not much of a cook, either.'

'I 'ope you're not goin' to be a trial to me, mister; I learned cookin' at the orphanage, I'll 'ave you know. I could 'ave got a certificate from the superintendent if I 'adn't run away. I did 'im a birthday cake once and he said he'd never tasted anything like it in all his born days.'

'I'll pass on that one,' said Joe. 'Listen, there's a little basin of first-class beef dripping in the larder.'

'Well, bloomin' hooray,' said Dolly, 'the larder 'appens to be locked.'

'That's a point,' said Joe.

'Yes, and why d'you keep it locked?' asked Dolly. 'You never said.'

'My work's in there,' said Joe, who'd always known that if he let a woman get close to him she'd be bound to ask questions. 'The businessmen I work for expect it to be kept private.'

'Oh, beg your pardon, I'm sure,' said Dolly.

'Private Smith, you owe headquarters for three slices of burnt toast and one frying-pan. You were also absent without leave again this morning. What've you got to say for yourself?'

'Of all the daft questions,' said Dolly, 'you ought to see a doctor, you ought.'

'Further,' said Joe, 'your face is all sooty.'

'Oh, help!' Dolly wailed and limped fast to the bedroom, to the mirror and to the pitcher of water on the washstand.

Joe called from the landing.

'I'm going down to borrow our landlady's frying-pan. Eggs and bacon suit you again?'

'I ain't listening,' gasped Dolly, 'I've fainted.'

Joe went down with a grin on his face. Bessie Beavis was out, so he helped himself, knowing she wouldn't mind. He made use of it while Dolly did a prolonged repair job on her face and morale, and gave her hair and clothes a sustained brushing. Then she reappeared and sat down to eggs and bacon with him.

'Good as new,' said Joe, and that earned him a haughty look.

'I'm not talkin' to you,' she said.

'Chin up, Dolly.'

'I'll give you chin up,' said Dolly. 'All that smoke and sizzlin', I thought me last moments 'ad come. It's your fault; it wouldn't 'ave happened if you 'adn't been out gallivantin' with Fanny Bonbon or whatever her name is. I don't know what you see in an ugly woman like her. You must be weak in the head. Oh, you've done the bacon nice, Joe.'

'Yes, pretty good,' said Joe.

'I suppose you got off with her, did you?'

'Fanny Bonbon? Bit of a struggle to survive, as a matter of fact. She tried to surround me with fat women all twice as big as Bessie Beavis. Lucky for me they were only pictures on a wall or I'd have been flattened. But I did have an interesting time reading a translation of that letter from Blackbeard's wallet.'

'What?' asked Dolly, sitting up very straight.

'Yes, I made a copy of it before I put it back in the wallet,' said Joe.

'You copied Russian?' said Dolly.

'As best I could,' said Joe. 'One of my businessmen who runs a bookshop got it translated for me. I was curious.'

Dolly stared at him.

'You're a deep one, you are, Joe,' she said. 'What's it say? Show me.'

The meal finished, Joe said, 'I'll take a look at your ankle first. You've been punishing it. Then I'll show you the translation and talk to you about it. I've got an idea we're sitting on a red-hot brick.'

He cleared away and washed up, using a bowl of hot water on the table, with soda crystals in it. Dolly dried up,

164

using a clean tea towel. She cast him repeated glances. She was all agog, but he seemed just thoughtful. With everything tidy again, she sat down in the fireside armchair and drew her skirts up. She was wearing new stockings.

'I think me ankle's all right really,' she said.

'Stocking down,' said Joe.

She released it under cover of her skirts and rolled it down. Joe unwound the bandage. The swelling was much reduced, but it still looked tender.

'Told you it was all right,' said Dolly.

'It's better, but not all right,' said Joe, and applied some liniment from a bottle. He massaged gently. Dolly sighed. 'It doesn't hurt, does it?' he asked.

'It's gone farther up me leg,' said Dolly.

'What has, your ankle? It seems in its right place to me.'

'I mean the ache's gone farther up,' she said, and he massaged her calf as well as her ankle. 'Here, wait a bit, you sure that's decent?'

'Helpful, I hope,' said Joe, and looked up at her.

'Now you've caught me blushin',' she said.

'Why?'

'Why? Why? Well, I'm a respectable girl and I'm shy about me legs, ain't I?'

'I don't know, are you?' said Joe. 'Two hundred and nineteen times for a boy at a penny a look?'

'Agony it was,' said Dolly, and Joe rewound the bandage in competent style. Rolling her stocking back on, she said, 'Here, what's all them violets doin' out there in the washbasin?'

'Well, two posies are for Mrs Beavis, two for our French lodger and two for you, Dolly.'

'Well, I don't know, you're a proper ladies' man, Joe. Thanks ever so much for mine, I'll put them in that little vase in the bedroom. Can I see that translation now?'

'Here,' said Joe, and produced it. Dolly took it and slowly scanned it.

'What a funny letter,' she said. 'Would that be Blackbeard's name? Boris?'

'Might be, but more likely not.'

'What about Ivan and Igor?'

'Search me,' said Joe.

'What's it all mean?'

'Not much to me, but a lot to Blackbeard, I should think.'

'I bet he's Russian all right,' said Dolly. 'They're all shockers, don't you think? They chuck bombs, and look what 'appened to me, nearly murdered in me own bed.'

'My bed.'

'Yes, you're ever so kind to let me 'ave it,' said Dolly. 'You'll 'ave to do something, you'll 'ave to write to the police. Yes, best to write. We don't want to go to a police station, they might not let us out. You don't 'ave to give your name when you write, or your address, and you can put the translation in with it. Well, you don't want to leave it lying around, and I expect the police 'ave got experts who can find out what it means.'

'Anything else?' asked Joe drily.

'Yes, you don't want to use your own 'andwriting,' said Dolly, 'it's best to disguise it, just in case. Only we ought to 'elp the police get hold of Blackbeard. I'm sure he did the murder and they 'aven't caught anyone yet, 'ave they?'

'Not according to today's paper,' said Joe. 'Yes, it's time we did our bit for them, time we gave them some useful information. I'll get you a pencil and a sheet of paper, and you can write down a description of Blackbeard. You saw him in the pub, I only saw him in the fog. Can you remember exactly what he looked like?'

'I'll 'ave a go,' said Dolly.

'Good,' said Joe, 'and while you're doing that, I'll write the anonymous letter.'

'The what?'

'Anonymous letter.'

'Crikey, I wish I could use words like that,' said Dolly, 'but I only 'ad an orphanage education.'

They got down to it at the table, Dolly thinking hard while sucking the pencil, and inscribing words in spasms. Joe wrote with a little smile on his face as he composed the letter in disguised handwriting.

Sir. Let it be known that the unfortunate man recently found murdered in Houndsditch and named as Mr Dan Pearson was seen on the evening of his murder in the Rockingham public house by the Elephant and Castle, in company with a man whose description is as follows.

Joe looked up from his writing and said, 'Finished, Dolly?'

'Here,' said Dolly, and passed her effort over to him. She had put down that the man was about five feet ten with big shoulders, oblong face, black beard, beeky nose, blue eyes, and wearing dark grey overcoat with black fur collar and black bowler, spoke forren English, had a pistol and was about forty.

'That'll do,' said Joe. 'Your spelling's a bit weak, though.'

'Well, excuse me, I'm sure,' said Dolly, 'but I didn't 'appen to go to Eton and Harrer.'

Joe continued the letter.

About forty, five feet ten, broad shoulders, black pointed beard. He was wearing a dark grey overcoat with black fur collar and a black bowler. His eyes are blue, he has a foreign accent and is almost certainly Russian. He carried a revolver on his person, and has a large nose. This information is sent to you by a citizen wishing to do his duty. Enclosed for your further interest is a translation of a letter received by this man, the original being in Russian.

He passed the completed letter to Dolly, who read it.

'Oh, what a good letter, Joe,' she said, 'you're clever, you are.'

'Not very,' said Joe, 'or I wouldn't be living in lodgings, would I?'

'No, you're really clever, writing a letter like that. 'Ave you ever thought about being clever enough to marry a rich girl?'

'I thought about the Colonel's daughter once,' said Joe. 'Then she told me to hold her horse. I went off her.'

'What a shame,' said Dolly. 'Still, serve her right. Who you goin' to post the letter to?'

'To the Police Commissioner, Scotland Yard.' Joe addressed an envelope, folded the letter, inserted it with the translation and sealed the envelope. 'I'll pop out, buy a stamp and post it. Then I've some work to get on with.'

'All right, I can take a hint,' said Dolly. 'Here, I'll post it for you, you said I could 'ave a walk to the laundry.'

'That ankle of yours is tender,' said Joe.

'Oh, come on, let me go out for a bit while you're workin',' said Dolly. 'Look, after I've been to the laundry with our things, I'll get an 'ansom cab at the Elephant and go for a ride over Waterloo Bridge. Then I can post the letter in the Strand. We don't want to post it round 'ere, Joe, the postmark might bring the coppers nosin' about to see if they can find who sent the letter. I mean, they're bound to think you're a valuable witness. I'll come back in another cab, I've still got plenty of that money left to pay the cabbies.'

'Good point about posting the letter in the Strand,' said Joe. 'All right, have your cab rides, but no running around the shops and doing your ankle in. Understood?'

168

'Don't I always do what you tell me?' said Dolly.
'Not often,' said Joe.

'Sergeant Joe?' Mrs Beavis called from the foot of the stairs and Joe came out to the landing.

'What can I do for you, Bessie?'

'Well, I'm doin' steak-and-kidney puddin' for me fam'ly tonight, a big one in me cauldron. I don't know as you'll ever do yer own self a steak-and-kidney puddin' up there, so seein' as you once said it was a fav'rite of yours, I'm pleasured to invite yer to join us this evenin'. An' that poor girl Dolly as well. Me gels like 'er. So do me boys. An' there's stewed plums an' custard for afters.'

'Can't say no to that, Bessie, can't say anything except bless your cotton socks.'

'Pleasure to 'ave yer both, Sergeant Joe.'

'That reminds me, hold on a tick.' Joe took two posies out of the water in the handbasin and carried them down to his landlady, who beamed all over.

'Well, ain't that a kind thought?' she said.

'So's the steak-and-kidney pudding,' said Joe.

'Come down about quarter-past six.'

'Right. Um – put an extra leaf in the table, eh?'

'Yes, I think I'll 'ave to,' said Mrs Beavis. 'Did I 'ear Dolly go out?'

'Just for some fresh air.'

'Well, I never,' said the surprised landlady, 'that's the first time I ever 'eard there was fresh air round 'ere.'

Dolly returned after a couple of hours. She'd had lovely cab rides, she said, they'd made her feel she was coming up in the world. She'd bought a stamp for the letter and posted it in the Strand, and Scotland Yard would probably get it before the day was out. And she'd found a nice chemist's shop where she'd bought one or two things and where she'd had a sit down, and the chemist had said what

169

a nice hat she was wearing, and his lady assistant came and looked at it, and she'd said it was nice too.

'I can't remember you sayin' it was nice, Joe.'

'I said everything made you look like a lady.' Joe conceded that when she was in funds, she knew how to dress herself very attractively.

'Yes, but me hat, do you like it?'

The little velvet hat with its feather sat quite enchantingly on her dark auburn hair.

'It's got a cheeky look today,' said Joe. 'Yes, I like it.'

'Well, you ought to say, y'know,' said Dolly, 'it gives a girl a lift to be complimented. I 'ad a bloke in the Strand tryin' to get off with me, a bloke in a top hat, would you believe. I said I'd call a copper if he didn't push off. I know what them kind of blokes are after. 'Ave you ever got off with a girl in the Strand, Joe?'

Joe, from his chair at the table, looked up at her. She smiled sweetly.

'Not lately,' he said.

'Why don't you go out with girls?' she asked.

'Can't afford it,' said Joe, who could but wasn't bothering for the time being.

'Well, I ain't expensive,' said Dolly, 'you can take me out when me foot's really better. Of course, I know I'm only an—'

'Don't say it.'

'I 'ope you're not goin' to turn into an old stick-in-the-mud,' said Dolly. 'I mean, a bloke like you – here, that's a quill pen on the table. What d'you use a quill pen for?'

'I like quill pens,' said Joe, who had his work turned face down. 'By the way, public baths tomorrow.'

'Eh?'

'It's Saturday tomorrow. I always go Saturday mornings. I'll take you with me.'

'Well, of all the nerve,' said Dolly, 'I ain't gettin' into any public bath with you, what d'you think I am?'

'You're due for a proper bath,' said Joe, 'there's a ladies' section.'

'I ain't goin',' said Dolly.

'Now listen here, Private Smith, in all those new duds of yours you look like the cat's whiskers. Can't have the cat's whiskers not taking proper baths. Won't allow it. Have you got that?'

'You don't 'alf order a girl about.'

'Discipline's the name of it, discipline. And remember, I'm the sergeant here, you're only the private.'

'Oh, you cuss,' said Dolly, 'will you stop talkin' daft all the time?'

'This evening,' said Joe, 'we've been invited to join our landlady and her family in a steak-and-kidney-pudding supper.'

'Steak-and-kidney pudding?' said Dolly. 'I don't know I ever 'ad that before. I know I didn't at the orphanage.'

'Well, you're having some this evening,' said Joe. 'You'll enter paradise.'

'Be a change for a poor girl, that will,' said Dolly, making for the bedroom. 'Here,' she called, 'there's still some violets in the handbasin.'

'Yes, they're for Marcelle,' said Joe. Marcelle was still out.

'Oh, you've got it bad all right,' called Dolly. 'Oh, you poor old soldier, I pities you from the bottom of me heart.'

Joe smiled, got up, closed the door and resumed his work.

At Buckingham Palace, at the Home Office, Metropolitan Police headquarters and military barracks, important people and their assistants were engaged in processing arrangements relating to the coronation of King George V and Queen Mary, and to a royal unveiling of the Queen Victoria Memorial.

CHAPTER FOURTEEN

'No go, guv,' said the man nicknamed Tubby. It was close to seven in the evening, and he was in an office in Whitehall, addressing himself to Sir Hubert Wilkins. Sir Hubert, distinguished-looking with his iron-grey hair, his trim beard and his immaculate black frock-coat, was seated at his desk. Beside him stood a uniformed Army officer, an interested listener. 'They're back in their lodgings now, and the relief's taken over. It's been a long walkin' day for me, I can tell yer. All they did was look at old buildings and draw sketches, except when they ate bread an' cheese in a park. They did a bit of shoppin' on their way back to Bell Lane, in their local grocer's, but all day they didn't speak to no-one except a copper at Ludgate Circus, when it looked to me as if they were just askin' their way to somewhere. Well, nothing gained is all in a day's work, guv, that's the way it goes, and I'll take me 'ard-earned dibs now, if yer'd be so kind, then toddle off to me supper. I ain't 'ad a bite to eat since me breakfast.'

'Dibs?' said Sir Hubert, who was in his late forties. 'Ah, yes, I see.'

'Course yer do, guv. I didn't bring me observational gifts out of the Queen's Navy for nothing, as yer know. It's daily pay, as 'eretofore agreed, every time you use me special services, which ain't exactly every day, more's the pity.'

'Quite so, Mr Sharp,' said Sir Hubert. 'You shall have your pay for today. You've given us excellent service many times, and are well worth the retainer you receive from us.'

172

'Fair dues, the retainer, guv,' said Tubby Sharp, 'but not exactly real oof, if yer'll pardon me sayin' so.'

'An increment may be considered, Mr Sharp.'

'Pleased to 'ear it,' said Tubby who, having been in the Navy, knew what an increment was.

'I'm now going to ask you to alter your brief,' said Sir Hubert. 'Certain new information has convinced us that daytime watches will bring no results, that during the day the two suspect students pursue an entirely innocuous course designed, no doubt, to make monkeys of us.'

'Innocuous, guv?' said Tubby, cap off as a mark of respect to this Government gentleman. 'Never 'eard of that before. Could yer kindly speak English?'

'It means harmless, Mr Sharp,' said Sir Hubert, while the Army officer merely nodded.

''Armless, eh?' said Tubby. 'See what yer mean. Up to their 'orrible deeds at night, I suppose. So yer want me on night duty?'

'We do.'

'But you got blokes on night roster already, guv.'

'We want you to take over indefinitely, Mr Sharp. From dusk until two in the morning.'

'I'm sorrowed that you ain't brought me in on this before now,' said Tubby, 'it's 'urt me feelings.'

'We're guilty of an oversight,' said Sir Hubert.

'Well, I ain't too mollified, guv, I tell yer. Still, it'll be water under the bridge by tomorrow. Who is it I'm after?'

'A contact, probably. A woman. We believe she's lodging next door to the suspects. If not, we believe she comes and goes from it, and is the contact between them and the man we really want.'

'You reckon, guv?' said Tubby. 'You reckon she talks to the suspects through the dividin' wall of the houses? That don't make sense to me, she'd have to shout and holler, and so would they.'

173

'Perhaps, Mr Sharp, they enter the other house by the back door, by climbing the wall dividing the yards. The yards back on to those of the houses in Toynbee Street.'

'Is that a fact, guv?' said Tubby. 'Well, I need one of yer reg'lars, and some 'ard oof to pay for the use of a back room in one of the houses in Toynbee Street, one that's in the right position. Can't give up watchin' the front door, of course. But we've got to watch the door to the yard as well. Which I'll do, seein' that might be a more lively caper. So there's got to be two of us. And respectfully, guv, I'll take charge. Now, if I've got it right, it's a woman we're after and who she'll lead us to, which might be what we could call the principal delinquent.'

'Quite right, Mr Sharp,' said Sir Hubert.

''As the lady been spotted by day?'

'A lady might have been spotted. So might others, as long as they came from or went into the house lodging the suspects. But none would have been followed. Only the suspects have concerned us until now.'

'Supposin' the principal himself turns up?' enquired Tubby.

'You'll know him. He has a black beard. We'd like to know where he's living. So don't lose him.'

'Beg yer pardon, guv?' said Tubby in a pained way, and a little smile appeared on the Army officer's face.

'My apologies, Mr Sharp,' said Sir Hubert, who was well acquainted with the talents of this ex-petty officer of the Royal Navy. He was an invaluable bloodhound, a man whose homely looks and cockney speech gave no indication of his shrewdness and tenacity. 'I think you have the distinction of never having lost a quarry.'

'It's me nose, guv, it's a professional nose, come by naturally. You and me, both bein' experienced subjects of His Majesty, know it ain't wise to employ amateur noses. Which makes me so bold as to say, if yer don't

174

mind, that it won't do for that young amateur lady of yours to get mixed up with the kind of characters that's often a bother to you and His Majesty. Such characters 'ave been known to turn nasty.'

'The young lady, mmm,' said Sir Hubert.

'Miss 'Enrietta Downes as is, guv.'

'An exceptional young lady, Mr Sharp.'

'Well, guv, I don't know any young ladies meself that ain't exceptional,' said Tubby, who always liked to know what was taking place in the dark corners of Sir Hubert's department. 'They all talk an exceptional nineteen to the dozen, and give a bloke an exceptional goin'-over if he displeasures them a trifle.'

'Occasionally,' said Sir Hubert, 'an exceptionally exceptional young lady can be used by us.'

'I wouldn't occasionally use any of 'em meself, guv. Respectfully, it ain't what they're for, nor what they're born to. Specially at night. At night, if yer don't mind me sayin' so, all ladies ought to be sittin' at home doin' needlework or makin' themselves likewise useful.'

The Army officer coughed. Sir Hubert said, 'Unfortunately, Mr Sharp, some ladies are contrary.'

'Don't I know it, guv,' said Tubby, shaking his head. 'Me daughter Ivy is as contrary as a mule. What I'd like to point out, well, it wasn't 'ighly professional of Miss Downes to use an 'ansom cab this mornin'. Waitin' cabs in that kind of street stick out like sore thumbs on 'arpists.'

'I note that, Mr Sharp,' said Sir Hubert.

'It ain't like you, guv, to employ unprofessional bodies,' said Tubby. 'If I might ask, who is the young lady?'

'My niece,' said Sir Hubert.

'Lord forgive yer, guv, it ain't fair on 'er. I'd recommend 'er dad to lock 'er up. Now, d'yer want me on watch tonight?'

'Could you manage that after the hours you've put in today?'

'No 'ardship,' said Tubby. 'I'll join me relief an' see about rentin' the use of an overlookin' back room. The right kind of oof is required, guv. Mind, I'll 'ave to ask a bit extra on me pay, if yer don't mind, on account of me old Dutch not likin' me out on night work and accordingly 'aving to be sweetened.'

When Tubby left, he had all the necessary money in his pocket and time to enjoy a hearty meal before going back to Bell Lane.

Alone with Sir Hubert, the Army officer said, 'Damned important to catch Rokovssky before the police track him down and hold him on a murder charge. Damned important for us to know exactly what's afoot and who are in it with him, and before police custody gives him the protective benefit of a solicitor.'

'Precisely,' said Sir Hubert. 'It's preferable to have him in our hands for a while.'

'Who the hell let him in?'

'Some unsuspecting port official. But it's Rokovssky right enough. The description fits him to a T.'

'And look here,' said the Army officer, 'what's Henrietta playing at?'

'Exercising her adaptability.'

'Good God, why can't she take up painting trees?'

'Her governess tried that when she was younger. She threw the lot into the river, easel, canvas, paints and brushes as well. The governess escaped.'

'Keep her out of Russia, Hubert.'

'Why?'

'She'll start a revolution.'

The kitchen walls seemed to be closing in on the large table, the family of seven, their two guests and the huge helpings of steak-and-kidney pudding with mounds of vegetables. Dolly sat between Albert and Alfred, and Nancy and Ella had contrived to have Sergeant Joe

176

between them, much to Linda's disgust. The meal was a cockney banquet, the Beavis family consuming it with enormous relish. Cockney quips brought forth yells of laughter. Around the table, with an extra leaf in, plumpness seemed to visibly spread. Dolly looked as if she might be reduced to a mere streak by the increasing largeness of Albert and Alfred, and Joe, for all the resilience of his body, looked as if he was fighting a losing battle against the overflowing abundance of Nancy and Ella.

Linda was making bitter protests about it.

'Squashed to 'is death, that's what me Sergeant Joe'll be,' she muttered.

'Did yer say something, Linda?' asked Mr Beavis, growing red and shiny.

'Yes, I'm sayin' it ain't fair.'

'What ain't, lovey?' asked affable Mrs Beavis.

'Well, 'e can't even breave proper,' said Linda.

'Who can't?' asked Albert.

'Sergeant Joe can't,' said Linda.

'Course 'e can,' said Alfred. ''E'd be turnin' all red if 'e couldn't.'

''E's lovely, ain't yer, Sergeant Joe?' said Nancy.

'We won't be able to see what 'e's like in a minute,' said Linda darkly, ''e'll be all squashed to nuffink.'

The family hooted with laughter. Dolly, quite sure it was like a train running through the house, blinked.

'Ain't our Linda a wag?' said Mr Beavis proudly.

'Ain't she a pet?' said her jolly mum. 'But don't you worry, Linda ducky, Nancy and Ella's just keepin' Sergeant Joe nice table company. Did yer see the bunches of vi'lets 'e kindly give me?'

'Yes, I seen 'em,' said Linda, 'but I can't see 'im. Crikey, Mum, 'e's disappearin'.'

Nancy gurgled and Ella giggled.

'Yer like it, don't yer, Sergeant Joe?' said Nancy.

'Do yer?' asked Ella.

'Well, as long as my elbows aren't bothering you,' said Joe.

''Olly'ock between two 'aystacks, if you ask me,' said Albert. 'I 'ope me own elbow ain't botherin' you, Dolly.'

'Nor mine,' said Alfred.

'Pleasure to be 'ere, I'm sure,' said Dolly, unable to look at Sergeant Joe and the overflowing sisters without wanting to shriek with laughter. He could hardly use his knife and fork decently, not when those bosoms were in the way of his elbows.

''Ow's yer steak-an'-kidney puddin', Dolly?' asked Mrs Beavis.

'Lovely,' said Dolly, even if she was making hard work of her minor mountain.

''Ere, did anyone 'ear the story about the cannibal chief what come to London an' saw 'is first steak-an'-kidney puddin'?' asked Mr Beavis.

'No, go on, tell us, Dad,' said Ella.

'Well, 'e said, "Ah, 'ead of number one wife, 'ow did that get 'ere?"'

The family, erupting, grew larger. Dolly laughed and Joe roared.

'What 'appened next, Dad?' asked Linda, when tumultuous expansion had receded.

'Well, 'e ate it, of course,' said Mr Beavis. 'Then 'e smacked 'is lips an' said, "Number one wife's 'ead plenty good, bring on number two wife's loaf."'

It was some time before the kitchen walls stopped shaking. Then Mrs Beavis asked who wanted seconds. There were takers, although Dolly, Linda and Joe excused themselves. Dolly, in fact, just couldn't finish her first helping. When the seconds had been demolished in healthy fashion, Mrs Beavis brought the afters to the table, a huge dish of stewed prunes, dark blue, and a huge basin of custard. The prunes and custard were hot. Cold afters, except for jellies and blancmanges, would have been chucked at the cook.

'Mum, what's them?' asked Linda.

'Stewed plums, lovey.'

'They don't 'alf look like prunes,' said Linda.

'Well, same thing, ducky,' said Mrs Beavis.

''Ere, what yer givin' us prunes for?' asked Albert suspiciously.

'Now you know they're good for yer, Albert.'

'I like plums best,' said Ella.

'Same thing sort of, Ella me pet, like I just told Linda,' said Mrs Beavis.

'I'm lookin' at you, Bessie,' said Mr Beavis, grinning.

'Yes, they're good for you as well, Charlie,' said Mrs Beavis, and began serving the prunes and custard, starting with her lady guest, as was only polite. Dolly asked to be excused the afters, but the expansive landlady said you must have some, ducky, you need building up. Joe asked if she was sure prunes were for building up. Well, said Mrs Beavis, she'd been talking to Mrs Livermore only yesterday, Mrs Livermore having been to the doctor about a remedy for her children. Nancy asked remedy for what? Well, for their health, said Mrs Beavis. Mr Beavis said he'd never heard of a remedy for anyone's health, only for someone's complaint. Mrs Beavis said it was for their general health, and the doctor told Mrs Livermore prunes three times a week. General health was important, the doctor had told Mrs Livermore so, and charged her a shilling. Albert said what, a shilling just for saying prunes and general health? Well, doctors have got to earn their living, said Mrs Beavis. Nancy said she couldn't see why the family had to have prunes, there wasn't anything wrong with their general health, nor Sergeant Joe's, come to that.

'Yes, there is,' said Linda, persistent about the table seating, 'you and Ella's squashin' all 'is gen'ral 'ealth to death.'

179

'We're just keepin' 'im nice company, like Mum said,' declared Ella.

'Anyway,' said Mr Beavis, 'it's nice to know that your gen'ral 'ealth's improved, Dolly, yer lookin' a treat. Sergeant Joe done a good job nursin' yer ankle, 'as 'e?'

'He's looked after it like it was his own,' said Dolly. 'Mind, he could've kept me a bit more company than he has. Is he a bit shy, d'you know?'

'Eh?' asked Albert.

'Eh?' asked Alfred.

''E ain't shy with me,' said Mrs Beavis happily.

'Nor me,' said Nancy.

''E give us all kisses at Christmas,' said Ella.

'Not me 'e didn't,' said Alfred.

'Nor me,' said Albert.

''E give me four kisses,' said Linda proudly, 'and a story book.'

'There y'are, Dolly,' grinned Mr Beavis, 'Sergeant Joe might get to you next. Mind, I suppose yer'll be up and away soon as yer properly on your feet.'

'Yes, a job and some lodgings of her own, that's the next step,' said Joe.

'Can't wait, can I?' said Dolly.

'Now, who wants seconds of the afters?' asked Mrs Beavis.

'Shame to leave any, even if they is prunes,' said Mr Beavis.

'Mum, don't give Nancy and Ella no more,' begged Linda, 'you don't want Sergeant Joe to breave 'is last in our own kitchen, do yer?'

The house shook to its foundations.

After a long evening with the hospitable and uproarious family, Dolly and Joe retired upstairs. Marcelle met them on the landing.

'Heavens,' she breathed, rolling her eyes, 'are the

180

earthquakes over? You have both been down there and you are still alive? Never have I heard earthquakes in a house before. Ah, you poor one,' she said to Dolly, 'it is no wonder you look so pale and unwell.'

'Beg your pardon?' said Dolly.

'No, no, it is not your fault,' said Marcelle, finding the situation diverting, 'it's the fault of this man Joe for taking you into all that noise. Such a family. Boom boom, zoom zoom, bang bang. The ceiling trembles and my room shakes. It has made you ill? What was it all about?'

'Just steak-and-kidney pudding and prunes,' said Joe.

'Pudding? Pudding and prunes?' Marcelle rolled her expressive eyes again. 'I am to believe something so disgusting?'

'I met some garlic sausage once,' said Joe. 'I couldn't believe that, either.'

'Excuse me, Miss Whatsit,' said Dolly belligerently, 'but I ain't ill or pale. I was once admired for me looks and figure by an artist gentleman who wanted to paint me.'

'Yes?' Marcelle smiled. 'Ah, I know the kind, they do not mind if a girl has bags under her eyes as long as she will undress for them.'

'Oh, 'ave you done a lot of that?' asked Dolly.

'Come, do not be upset,' said Marcelle, finding it wickedly engaging to tease the confederate of this clever man. 'To be lost in the fog and to hurt your ankle, and then to suffer earthquakes and pudding, that is enough to make anyone look ill. See, you will recover and get your looks back, I am sure, yes?'

'Oh, I expect you know about these things, being a lot older than me,' said Dolly.

'Glad you two are getting on so well,' said Joe, 'it makes for peaceful lodging.'

'Yes, she is sweet,' smiled Marcelle. 'Now I must go to my bed and hope that the walls of the house do not fall down.'

'I'll give you your violets,' said Joe.

'Oh, I have them,' said Marcelle, 'I saw them and now they are in my room. How kind, thank you, Joe. Good night to both of you.'

She disappeared. Dolly, following Joe into his living-room, said loudly, 'What a funny woman, I 'ope I'm not like that when I'm as old as she is.'

'You're all the same to me, young or old,' said Joe.

'What d'you mean, all the same?'

'You're all Chinese puzzles.'

'Flattered, I'm sure,' said Dolly. 'But I still don't know how you can fancy someone like her. It's that weak head of yours. You need protectin' from it. I expect Mrs Beavis would 'elp; you can see she's fond of you, she'd protect you all right if you married Nancy. Nancy's a nice big girl, she and her mum would both save you from Fanny Bonbon. Did you hear her patronizin' talk about me being lost in the fog?'

'Yes, I heard,' said Joe, and was reminded of Marcelle referring to that after they had left the National Gallery. *Ah, the poor one you found in that very dreadful fog.* Now how did she know it was a real pea-souper on that particular night if she'd only come over from France on the day she found lodgings with Bessie Beavis? It might have been a guess, of course, except that pea-soupers didn't often happen when April was just round the corner.

'What's up, what're you thinkin' about?' asked Dolly.

'Public baths tomorrow, Dolly.'

'Blow that for a lark,' said Dolly.

In her bed, Marcelle thought of the search she'd made of Joe's rooms while he was downstairs. She had found nothing that told her who his masters were.

'Hello, missus, 'ow'd yer do?' Tubby had put this greeting to the blowsy woman who opened the door to him just

182

before nine. The house was in Toynbee Street, and backed on to the one in which the suspects were living.

'What you after?' asked the woman.

'I'd like to rent yer upstairs back for a bit,' said Tubby.

'You what?'

'As you can see, I'm 'ighly respectable and can get references, if yer like,' said Tubby.

'I don't see it's 'ighly respectable knockin' on me door at this time of night,' said the woman.

'No 'arm intended, missus, and I can offer yer fair goodwill in the shape of a financial advance.'

In the light of a street lamp, the woman looked him up and down. Tubby smiled ingratiatingly. She'd seen plenty of that in her time. Usually from characters who'd pinch the shirt off anyone's back. Still, you had to live and let live, and you minded your own business as well, as long as they didn't come it personally.

'Listen, mister, we've got five kids, me 'usband an' me.'

'I envy yer, missus, I ain't 'ad the luck to 'ave any, bein' a bachelor, y'see, and 'aving been at sea nearly all me life. I'd like some kids now I'm back on land.'

'Well, you ain't 'aving none of mine, and nor ain't you 'aving me upstairs back, nor the front. Nor nothing. This 'ouse is full up with us an' the kids.'

'Well, it ain't as if I need the room for long, not more than six or seven weeks,' said Tubby. 'And me goodwill is such that I can offer yer two bob a night.'

''Ow much?' The woman gaped.

'Two bob a night, lady, which is fourteen bob a week. And in advance, of course.'

'Fourteen bob a week?' The woman went dizzy. Four bob would have been handsome enough, if she was looking for a lodger. Fourteen bob was mouthwatering under any circumstances. She shook herself. ''Ere,' she said, 'you ain't bringin' swag in, are yer, you ain't askin' to use that room for unlawful purposes, are yer?'

183

'Cross me 'eart, missus,' said Tubby. 'It just 'appens this street an' your upstairs back specially suit me at this point in me life. And what I say is, ask no questions an' there won't be any lies. All honest and above board, missus. Cross me 'eart.'

'I believe yer, thousands wouldn't,' said the woman. 'But yer can't 'ave the room tonight, me two youngest is in bed. I can put 'em on floor mattresses from tomorrer, though. You sure you got that much goodwill to offer in advance?'

Tubby produced a wallet, extracted a pound note and showed it to her.

'That's ten nights in advance, missus, and yer welcome to it. You can 'ave it now if I've got yer word I can start usin' the room tomorrow.'

'I ain't done no-one down in all me life.'

'Nor me,' said Tubby, 'which makes it a fair start, eh?'

'All right,' said the woman, and took the pound note. 'Could I 'ave yer name?'

'Henry Oliver Sharp.'

'Pleased to know yer, then. I'm Mrs Ethel Bailey. 'Ere, you'd best come in an' meet me old man. 'Ere, 'alf a mo, you ain't got a ten-bob note an' ten bob's-worth of silver, 'ave yer?'

'Suit yer better, would it?' asked Tubby with a knowing grin. He made the exchange, and Mrs Bailey took him through to the kitchen to meet her husband, a brawny man in shirt, braces and trousers. Tubby had no difficulty in turning the man into a receptive acquaintance, and Mrs Bailey had even less difficulty in making him believe she was getting as much as seven bob a week for the room, plus a bob for using the gas. And she thereupon gave Mr Bailey two bob for himself, thus proving a simple cockney housewife could put one over on her old man with the greatest of ease. Except that none of them were simple.

* * *

Dolly still didn't seem too keen on going to the public baths on Saturday morning. But she had to go. Joe was adamant. You're overbearing, you are, she said. Just looking after your welfare, he said, just making sure you can take pride in yourself. Chin up, he said, when they were on their way. You wait, said Dolly, I'll take that grin off your mug one day.

She thought the public baths primitive when she was finally caged in a cubicle and a great steaming bath was awaiting her.

By arrangement, Rokovssky arrived at Paddington Station on the stroke of eleven. Marcelle was already there. They did not approach each other. She left the station immediately, her clothes looking fairly commonplace. He followed. She took a hansom cab to Regent's Park. He hired another and asked to be taken to the Zoo. They met in the park. They walked and talked. It was entirely necessary to keep up-to-date with what was happening to each other, primarily in respect of being sure that neither had fallen foul of British Intelligence. It was also necessary to come to a final decision on what each would do on the chosen day.

It having been established that neither of them had come to the attention of British law and order, Rokovssky asked what, if anything, Marcelle had found out about the man and woman in Newington Butts.

'Now that I'm living in the same house,' said Marcelle, 'I've found out that the man, Joe Foster, gives nothing away, although he has offered the opinion that the models used by the world's greatest artists were far too fat.'

'What?' said Rokovssky, his lack of a sense of humour always evident. 'Explain yourself, woman.'

What a pig, thought Marcelle.

'It means he has unimaginative ideas about art,' she said. 'Or it might mean that is what he would like people to think, for he's an artist himself, an exquisite forger. I have also found that out.'

'That,' said Rokovssky, 'could be a great asset to him as an agent.'

'I've found nothing that could associate him with whoever he works for,' said Marcelle. 'He's very much a soldier, with a limp caused by a wounded knee, and can't easily be caught off guard. He's also handsome, charming and companionable.' Which you are not, she thought.

'Spare me trivial details,' said Rokovssky.

'Being handsome, charming and companionable is not in the least trivial in an agent,' said Marcelle.

'So,' said Rokovssky with heavy sarcasm, 'here is a clever agent who is handsome, charming and companionable, and also an exquisite forger. A paragon in his profession, but you haven't yet found out who he's working for.'

'Are miracles expected of me? Give me time. We have weeks yet. There must be something in his rooms that will tell us.'

'Which will also tell us to whom he communicated the contents of the letter. Before we leave, you will have to kill him, of course. He knows too much about us.'

'About you,' said Marcelle.

'So does the filthy woman, his confederate. Are they lovers?'

'She is a peasant,' said Marcelle, 'and dresses like one. True, she has suddenly found something smart, but she's still a peasant. He's not a man who would make a lover of a peasant.'

'He's to be finished when the time is right,' said Rokovssky. 'Now, are we sure at this stage of exactly what each of us will do?'

'I have first to collect the weapon,' said Marcelle, 'and will do so as soon as Ivan and Igor inform me it's ready. Then, when the time comes for me to use it, I will be

186

where we can see each other. I will wait for you to create the harmless diversion. That is, harmless for you. You can assure me you have this in hand?'

'I have the flower girl in hand,' said Rokovssky.

'Good,' said Marcelle, and smiled at the memory of Joe buying violets from the girl in question.

CHAPTER FIFTEEN

By Sunday morning Dolly's ankle was still inclined to protest, but not by any means would she admit it. She knew Joe was quite capable of making her spend all day lying on the bed, even if it meant dumping her on it. He didn't seem to realize a new age had arrived, the age of King George and Queen Mary and that the bustle was dead and buried. He probably thought the Boer War was still going on and that it was his job, as an old soldier, to get everyone into shape for it.

Over breakfast of porridge and toast, he announced he was taking her and Linda to St John's Church in Larcom Street, off the Walworth Road.

'What?' she said.

'Just a five-minute walk round the back doubles,' said Joe. 'Just far enough for you.'

'I don't care if it's just ten seconds round the corner,' said Dolly, 'I ain't goin' to any church. I've never been in all me born days, except at the orphanage, and that was all doom and gloom, that was. The Holy Trinity's never done much for me.'

'Hello, suffering a bit of the old Nick this morning, are we?' said Joe.

'Lucky for you I've eaten me porridge,' said Dolly, 'or I'd pour it over your head. You don't want to go to church with me, I'm as good as heathen.'

'That's got to be changed,' said Joe.

'Oh, lor', you ain't religious, are you?' asked Dolly.

'No, I just go to church now and again with Linda,' said Joe, 'and it's not harmful. Fall in for church parade at ten-forty-five with Linda.'

'You've got a hope,' said Dolly. She could never resist having this kind of conversation with him, and she didn't mind a bit that all her slings and arrows bounced off him. She didn't think much of ordinary talk, she liked it to fizz a bit, and Joe made her fizz more than anybody. 'I'm not fallin' in for any church parade, and 'aving you march me there.' She would fall in, of course, but it wasn't much of a lark just saying all right. 'Me ankle feels a bit—' She checked. Too late.

'Right, on the bed with you after breakfast, Private Smith.'

'Oh, help, I'll come to church, then.'

Someone knocked on the door.

'Come in,' said Joe.

Marcelle entered. Oh, the wicked hussy, thought Dolly. Marcelle, her jet black hair in loose soft loops, was wearing a pink silk negligée over what Dolly was sure was very little else.

'*Bonjour*,' she said with a smile. 'Ah, how charming, how sweet.'

'Yes, ain't we cosy?' said Dolly, who had never at any time shown the slightest worry about what people might think of her presence in Joe's lodgings.

Marcelle made the obvious point. 'What a dreadful man you are, Joe, to have no regard for this poor young lady's reputation. She has a reputation, I am sure.'

'Where's the bread knife?' demanded Dolly, and reached for it. Joe put it in the table drawer.

'Not now, Dolly,' he said.

'Such a sweet girl, Joe,' murmured Marcelle. 'You are giving her some breakfast? Good, she is much in need of food, I think. It is not healthy to be so thin.'

'Thin? Me?' said Dolly, the light of battle showing. Marcelle's negligée softly draped her rounded bosom, and Dolly eyed it challengingly. 'I'm near to perfection, I am, and I never did want to be fat. I can see you don't mind. I

189

expect it's because you're mature, like our landlady.'

'I am happy with my age and my figure,' smiled Marcelle. 'Now, if you please, Joe, I would like to see you this afternoon. Please knock on my door at three.'

'You can see me now,' said Joe.

'No, no, it is private,' said Marcelle. 'At three, yes? Good. I shall be out until early afternoon, and again this evening. How nice the weather is. Spring has come to London, I think.'

'Looks like it,' said Joe, and added casually, 'There'll be no more fogs as thick as the one in which Dolly and I met with a bump.'

'Yes, such a dreadful fog, so terribly thick,' said Marcelle. '*Au 'voir*, Joe, take care of your hungry one.' She eased herself out and the door closed behind her. Dolly looked at Joe. Joe winked. Dolly burst into laughter.

'Can't believe her, can you?' she said.

'No, not much,' said Joe.

'I wonder what she wants to see you about?'

'No idea.'

'You can't really be gone on her.'

'Can't say she's not an eyeful,' said Joe.

'That's done it,' said Dolly, 'when we get to church I'll 'ave to do some prayin' for your weak head and funny eyesight.'

Actually, she surprised him in church by singing the hymns clearly and musically. But in between the hymns she kept asking for instruction in whispers.

Now what do I do? Sit. *What comes next?* You kneel again. *Now what?* Stand up. *What do I do now?* Kneel. *What, more kneeling? You sure?*

He didn't kneel himself, she noticed. His gammy knee wouldn't let him. He just sat forward on the edge of the pew, his right leg straight.

190

Young Linda behaved herself admirably, sitting on the other side of Joe. She liked going to church with him.

When the service was over and they were outside, Dolly said, 'Do I look a bit more holy?'

'No, you just look nice,' said Linda ingenuously.

'You're a pet, you are,' said Dolly.

'I'm Sergeant Joe's fav'rite,' said Linda. Some of her friends came charging up and pulled her aside.

''Ere, Linda, 'as yer Sergeant Joe got hisself a young lady?'

'Course not,' said Linda, ''e's just got me.'

''Oo is she, then?'

'Oh, she's a poor young lady that ain't got no fam'ly nor no 'ome,' said Linda, 'and Sergeant Joe's lookin' after 'er till 'e can find 'er a job. She's quite nice, so I let 'er come to church wiv us, but I don't let 'er shine 'is shoes. Well, she don't 'ave lots of spit like I do. 'Ere, what yer doin' of, Percy Potter?'

'Just givin' yer a cuddle, Linda.'

'Well, take that,' said Linda, and pushed his nose in.

'Oh, me bleedin' 'ooter,' said Percy, nursing it.

'Serves yer right,' said Linda, and walked proudly off with Joe and Dolly. Up through Larcom Street they went, then across the Walworth Road into Amelia Street, where Joe asked Linda why she'd squashed Percy's nose. ''E give me a cheeky cuddle, that's why,' said Linda.

'Well, good for Percy,' said Joe, 'you should be given a cuddle once in a while, Private Carrots. Pretty girl like you.'

'Listen to who's talkin',' said Dolly. 'I suppose you've noticed, Linda, that Sergeant Joe 'ands out cuddles like a man with no arms. You'd think he'd give your mum one now and again, and Nancy and Ella as well.'

''E give me a big cuddle at Christmas,' said Linda loyally.

'Oh, what a noble bloke,' said Dolly, 'and with any

191

luck, Linda, you might get another one next Christmas.'

Linda, giggling, said, 'She's makin' fun of you, Sergeant Joe.'

'Duly noted, Private Carrots,' said Joe.

'What yer goin' to do to 'er?' asked Linda, dressed in her Sunday best.

'Smack her bottom,' said Joe.

'Oh, you can't 'it 'er,' said Linda, 'you can't 'it ladies, it ain't nice, me mum an' dad said so. Mum went an' bashed Mr Topliss once for givin' Mrs Topliss an 'eadache.'

'It won't be Private Smith's head that'll ache,' said Joe.

'You'll be lucky,' said Dolly, her bandaged ankle carrying her along with a slight limp beside Joe's more pronounced limp. Street kids were out and about, a Sunday aspect to their behaviour, and from open doors in every street issued the aroma of dinners on the go. Even the poorest parents did all they could on meagre incomes to provide a Sunday roast.

In Newington Butts the traffic was light. There wasn't a horse and cart in sight, but there was a bicycle or two. And from the direction of Clapham an open motorcar came belching along, the driver capped and goggled. Two young men and three young women were crowded into the car. They were laughing and exuberant. One young man caught sight of Dolly in her glad rags and her little velvet hat. He whooped as the car passed her on its way to the Elephant and Castle, turned in his seat to get a better look at her, then took off his cap, waved it at her and shouted an invitation.

'What a cheek,' said Linda, ''e's tryin' to get off wiv Dolly.'

'It's her titfer,' said Joe, watching as the young man leaned forward and touched the driver's shoulder. But the driver laughed and went on.

'Come on,' said Dolly, and they crossed the street. She

pulled on the latchcord of the Beavis's house and they went in.

'Well, who was talkin' big, then?' called Dolly from the bedroom five minutes later.

'We're busy,' called Linda from the living-room. 'I'm cleanin' Sergeant Joe's spare shoes, and 'e's seein' to yer dinner.'

'Yes, he's best off being busy.'

'No, 'e's forgive yer for bein' cheeky,' called Linda. ''Ere, would yer like me to shine yer ankle-boots for yer, Dolly? I'll only charge yer a penny. I'll come an' get 'em, shall I?'

Dolly unbuttoned them, slipped them off and Linda took them away. She showed them to Joe with a little giggle.

'Look, I got 'em,' she said.

'Full marks, Private Carrots. Now listen for the signal.'

'I'll come chargin' wiv the fevver duster,' said Linda, and Joe went to the bedroom. The signal arrived only a few seconds later, in the form of shrieks from Dolly. Linda charged in with the feather duster. Dolly was lying across the bed, right leg kicking, and Joe had his hand around her left ankle, her sound one, offering her stockinged foot to the feather duster.

'Here we are, Carrots, this is her good foot,' said Joe.

'Oh, I'll go barmy!' yelled Dolly.

'Carry on, Carrots,' said Joe, and Linda, in huge delight, tickled Dolly's foot with the feather duster.

Dolly was as good as her word.

She went barmy.

But she swore a fearful revenge.

Marcelle was back at twenty minutes to three. At three, Joe knocked on her door. The house was quiet. Sunday afternoon quiet was the unwritten rule in Walworth. Kids just faded away, leaving mums, dads, grandmums and granddads to enjoy an undisturbed forty winks.

'Come,' called Marcelle. Joe entered. She was at her gas ring, and her coffee percolator was bubbling. The aroma was fairly foreign to Walworth, but no-one could have said it was unpleasant. 'Please to close the door and to sit.'

Joe closed the door and sat down. Marcelle smiled at him. She might have departed in boredom from the house once she had discovered all she could about him. Indeed, she did not have to be lodging here in order to make him do what she had in mind for him. But he intrigued her, and there were no diversions for her in the London apartment she was renting. Count Zhinsky had ordered no diversions, and she was not sure he would have approved of her getting too close to this man who had once served with the British Army. But however deep her relationship with Zhinsky was, she always liked to feel she was more her own mistress than his.

Joe regarded her with curiosity. Her high-waisted Empire-line dress of fine green velveteen might have been quite out of keeping with Newington Butts, but that did not prevent it making her a picture of elegance, if a little exotic against the plainness of the room.

'You're looking like Sunday in Paris,' he said.

'You have been to Paris, Joe?'

'Never. I'm just using my imagination.'

He was lying, of course, she thought. Paris had come too easily to his lips. Perhaps, yes, perhaps the French were his masters. But the letter would be of no interest to them.

'You will have some coffee?'

'Thanks,' said Joe, although he would have preferred tea at this time of day. She poured. There was no sugar about. Joe thought there was no food, either, that Marcelle Fayette was not a woman who would enjoy eating plain food in a rented room. She handed him his coffee, and sat down quite close to him.

'Now, my friend,' she said, 'I want to know more about you.'

'Do you? Why?'

'I am interested in you,' she said. 'You are an interesting man. You have talents.'

'That's news to me,' said Joe. 'If I had talents I wouldn't be out of work.'

'But you aren't out of work,' smiled Marcelle, 'you have a very artistic occupation as a forger.'

Bugger that, thought Joe, it sounds as if my chickens have come home to roost. What was she, a collector who had discovered a purchased letter was a forgery?

'I'll have to ask you to explain that,' he said.

'Must I? Is there any need, my handsome friend? Come, there's a bookshop, yes? What is the name now, the name of the proprietor? Singleton? Yes, Singleton, I think. That is right?'

Well, damn old George, thought Joe, he's spilled the beans for some reason. No, not George. Never.

'Singleton? Never heard of him.'

'But his name and his shop are on papers you have,' said Marcelle.

'Don't like the sound of that,' said Joe, 'don't like to think you've been putting your nose where you shouldn't. Black mark, Marcelle.'

'Oh, I'm always naturally curious about interesting men,' she said. 'What delicious letters you've written in the names of your poets, Byron and Shelley.'

'Young Linda told me this morning that it's not nice to hit ladies,' said Joe, 'but you need thumping.'

Marcelle laughed in genuine amusement.

'Thumping? Joe, you are serious?'

'Do you good,' said Joe. 'I don't know what the world's coming to; there's an overdose of dishonesty about, as well as hell of a lot of people not minding their own business.'

'Heavens,' murmured Marcelle, 'you are complaining as a forger that I am dishonest?'

'I'm complaining that you can't mind your own business.'

'Yes, I am terrible, I think.' Marcelle laughed again. 'So, then, tell me more about yourself. I shall treat it as confidential.'

'I wouldn't bet on it,' said Joe, 'I wouldn't bet on any woman who pokes her nose into other people's affairs. You broke into my larder.'

'No, no, I simply unlocked it,' said Marcelle.

'Why? What were you after?'

'I told you, I'm naturally curious about interesting men, especially one who locks his larder.'

'Who wouldn't when there are women as curious as you about?' said Joe.

'Do you sell all your forgeries to this man Singleton?'

'None of your business.'

'But I'm on your side, Joe, I like what you do. A forger is a much more exciting man than a clerk. Do you sell these artistic forgeries to Singleton and more special ones to more special people?'

'More special people?' said Joe. 'What the hell are you talking about?'

'I am simply interested, yes?' Marcelle put on her most winning smile. 'You are a clever man, aren't you, my friend? Why does a clever man like you live a very ordinary life in this kind of place?'

'Because I'm not clever, because I'm ordinary myself—'

'Of course you aren't. Do you think I would be interested in an ordinary man? I think you must do exciting work, which you keep to yourself, yes?'

'Sorry to say so, Marcelle, but I fancy you're off your rocker.'

'Off my rocker? What does that mean?'

196

'Barmy,' said Joe.

'Barmy?'

'Crazy,' said Joe.

'Ah, crazy,' said Marcelle, and laughed. What did it matter what he did? It mattered to Rokovssky. Rokovssky was furious, of course, that Ivan and Igor had used the wrong kind of man to carry that letter to him, a man idiotic enough to pass it so openly to him. Rokovssky was the one who felt himself threatened by Joe. She did not feel threatened at all. Let Rokovssky sweat. In any case, she was still sure that somewhere in his two rooms Joe kept some papers that would identify him as an agent and who he worked for. But perhaps he was independent of masters and sold information to the highest bidder. He was that kind of man. 'You have secrets, Joe,' she said. 'I shall find them out. It's my curiosity, you see.'

'You're a baggage,' said Joe.

'A baggage? No-one has ever dared to call me that.' Marcelle pointed a finger at him. 'Boom,' she said.

'Missed,' said Joe, and left.

'Well?' said Dolly, who had been reading a Sunday paper in the living-room.

'What a conundrum,' said Joe.

'Is that someone who plays a drum in the Salvation Army?' asked Dolly.

'No, it's a Chinese puzzle, you muttonhead,' said Joe.

'Oh, pardon me for breathin', I'm sure,' said Dolly. 'Can I 'elp it if I'm ignorant? It's all right for you, you were brought up in the bosom of your fam'ly. I wasn't. Mind, I'm not surprised that Fanny Bonbon's a bit of a puzzle, I bet she don't know 'erself if she's comin' or goin'. It's her age, I expect, some people get like that when they're old. What did she want you for?'

'No idea. Just a lot of French chat. Couldn't make head or tail of it.'

197

'Come off it,' said Dolly, 'she's after you. Didn't I say so, didn't I tell you?'

'I thought you said I was after her.'

'Yes, you want your 'ead seein' to, you do,' said Dolly. 'I suppose you've been doin' things with 'er. No wonder you're lookin' all flushed.'

'Well,' said Joe, who wasn't looking all flushed, of course, 'I'll have to fight my feelings, won't I?'

'You'd better,' said Dolly. 'Fancy a bloke like you lettin' an old woman like her get you all flushed. Listen, Joe, there's nothing in this paper about the police makin' an arrest. Wouldn't you think your letter would 'ave 'elped them nab 'im?'

'They've still got to track him down,' said Joe. 'Now, about you. I'd say another week will do the trick, your foot should be A1 by then and you'll be able to cope with a job. I'll take you up to town to meet a friend of mine, and we'll see if he can help. He knows people.'

'Yes, well, I'm desperate for a job, ain't I?' said Dolly.

'You need one, that's a fact,' said Joe. 'A job and your own lodgings will give you a first-class chance to make a go of things, and I'll be able to have my bed back.'

'Oh, yes, of course.' Dolly bit her lip. 'I'm sorry, I clean forgot you've been sleepin' out 'ere on the floor.'

'No hardship,' said Joe. 'Let's see, I had something else on my mind – yes, hold on a tick.' He went downstairs to speak to Mrs Beavis. When he came back he had a thick book in his hand. 'Here we are, Dolly, you'll like this.'

'What is it, a novel?'

'No, it's Mrs Beeton's cookery book.'

'It's what?'

'Regret to say you're a duffer in the kitchen,' said Joe, 'and you need Mrs Beeton. Get your nose into her book and we'll spend some evenings next week trying you out.'

'What, me read a cookery book?' said Dolly.

'Yes, good idea,' said Joe.

'You're off your chump, you are,' said Dolly. 'It's Fanny Bonbon that's done it. What a shame.'

'No sauce, Private Smith,' said Joe, 'just get on with it.'

'Oh, blow you,' said Dolly. 'One thing I know, when I've got to be more of a lady I ain't ever goin' to go out with sergeants.'

'Sensible girl,' said Joe.

Dolly made a face at him.

The light had gone from the day when a concealed man saw a woman enter Bell Lane in the East End. The pale glow of a street lamp enabled him to watch her progress. She stopped at the door of a house. There was no latchcord and she used a key to open the door, which obviously made her either the landlady or a tenant. She entered the dark passage and closed the door. Mr Rodney Masters, attached to Sir Hubert Wilkinson's department, emerged from his concealment, crossed the street, passed the house in question and went on until he reached a narrow alley leading through to Toynbee Street. Such alleys were a feature of many East End streets. This one was littered with rubbish, and Rodney Masters stepped carefully. At the end, he turned into Toynbee Street and entered the house of the Bailey family by using the latchcord. Quietly he climbed the stairs in the light of a naked gas flame, opened the door of the upstairs back room and showed himself to Tubby Sharp, who was sitting at the window. The room was in darkness.

'Something on yer mind?' murmured Tubby.

Masters, closing the door, said, 'A woman's arrived.'

'I know,' said Tubby, 'there she is. She lit the gas lamp a couple of minutes ago.'

Immediately opposite, a similar upstairs back room was seen between looped curtains. A standing woman was visible.

'That's her,' said Masters.

'But is it the right her?' mused Tubby. 'We'll see. What's she doin', just standin'? My guess is she's waitin'. She was out of sight for a few secs.'

'There, look,' breathed Masters.

The light from various back windows made yards distinguishable. Somewhere, cats were fighting, spitting and yowling. Over a dividing wall came two men, one after the other, from one yard into the next. They moved without haste or noise, and entered the house by the scullery door. Moments later the standing woman in the upstairs back was greeting them, talking to them and gesticulating at them.

'Foreign female,' said Tubby laconically. 'They all wave their ruddy feelers about. That's her right enough, she's the contact. You stay 'ere, me young friend, and I'll take up the front-door watch. If she leaves, I'll follow. If she don't, then I'll stay a while.'

'How did the suspects know she'd arrived?' whispered Masters.

'You askin' serious?' said Tubby. 'She knocked on the wall, of course. That was when she was out of sight for a couple of secs. Now, them suspect coves'll go back when they've finished 'aving a chat with 'er about the weather, and after that you keep yer mince pies skinned for the light bein' turned off. That'll mean she's either goin' to bed or goin' out. You come round to Bell Lane then, and if I'm still there it'll mean she's gone to bed. If I ain't there it'll mean she's out and that I'm on 'er tail.'

'They're all sitting down now,' said Masters.

'That's what chairs are for,' said Tubby.

'Information noted,' said Masters.

'Don't give me any cheek, sonny,' said Tubby, and ghosted out of the room and out of the house.

It being Sunday night, the City was deserted, and not until

200

the woman reached the south side of London Bridge did she come upon a line of hansom cabs for hire, which was a relief to Tubby. If she'd picked up a lone cab somewhere, he'd have been sunk. As it was, he watched her being driven from the approach to London Bridge railway station and then he followed in a second cab, at a distance.

CHAPTER SIXTEEN

After breakfast on Monday, Joe settled down to a full morning's work. His Italian commission from George was an ambitious and extensive one. He confined Dolly to the bedroom, with Mrs Beeton for company. It put her in a paddy, but she decided not to smash anything up, she decided to obey orders and then ask if she could go out in the afternoon.

Marcelle went out at ten o'clock, and at half-past ten Joe took a cup of tea to Dolly. On the grounds that she was suffering a boring morning without complaint, she asked about an afternoon excursion. Joe recommended a tram ride to Clapham Common. Dolly said all the sights to be seen from here to Clapham would be a lot more lively than Mrs Beeton's cookery book.

'Have you come across any recipes that interest you?' asked Joe.

'I saw one for a fam'ly egg custard,' said Dolly. 'Take six dozen eggs, it said—'

'Six dozen?'

'Yes, it knocked me sideways too,' said Dolly. 'I mean, six dozen eggs and then ten pints of milk—'

'Ten?'

'Yes, can you credit it?' said Dolly. 'Mrs Beeton must be as potty as a pancake, she must 'ave thought that recipe up for the old woman who lived in a shoe and 'ad so many children she didn't know what to do. I bet Mrs Beeton must 'ave said to herself, "I'll give her something to do all right, it'll take her a week of Sundays to make an egg custard as big as this."'

'Recommend you just make a small one,' said Joe.

'Divide everything by twenty, and to the nearest egg.'

'I hate egg custard,' said Dolly.

'Try a blancmange, then,' said Joe.

'I'll think about it on me ride to Clapham Common,' said Dolly.

Mrs Beavis, making apple dumplings, heard the front-door knocker go. She could have been vexed at being interrupted, but wasn't. She took nearly everything in her stride, and besides, a knock on the door might mean one of her neighbours had come for a bit of a chat. Mrs Connie Cousins often popped over to inform her of the latest shortcomings of Archie.

Wiping her hands on the skirt of her apron, Mrs Beavis answered the door.

'Good mornin', madam, good mornin',' said Tubby Sharp. Wearing a bowler hat and a raincoat, and with an open notebook in his hand, he looked official.

'The weather ain't much, it keeps on rainin',' said Mrs Beavis. 'Still, me 'usband said first thing this mornin' that it'll 'elp bring 'is rhubarb on, specially as there's been 'orses passin' by very convenient lately.'

'No, is that a fact?' said Tubby. 'Rhubarb, eh? You 'aven't got a garden, 'ave you, madam?'

'No, but we got rhubarb comin' up in a large tub in our backyard,' said Mrs Beavis chattily. 'Well, it's the bottom 'alf of a beer barrel, actu'lly. Comes up year after year, the rhubarb does, an' graces me table when I serve it with 'ot custard for afters. Well, it's eatin' rhubarb, yer see, me 'ubby don't grow it for decoration. What can I do for yer?'

'I'm from the town 'all,' said Tubby, 'Mr Fred Purser. I've got a few enquiries to make concernin' the census.'

'Census? I've been 'earing about that. What's it for?'

'It's a count of the population,' said Tubby. 'It's the law, yer see. His Majesty the King 'as to know every ten years just 'ow many subjects 'e's got, and where they're livin'. You'll get an official form for fillin' in soon.'

'Me 'ubby ain't keen on forms. Still, if it's the law. But what's the King want to worry about that for when 'e's got all 'is relations comin' over for 'is and the Queen's coronation? I bet they'll be worry enough. That German Kaiser, I bet 'e's a worry all by himself. Still, they say 'e was fond of the old Queen, she bein' 'is grandma. Anyway, Mr Purser, it's kind of yer to let me know, and Mr Beavis'll fill the form in when it comes.'

'I need to take a few details in advance, madam. Such as 'ow many persons reside in the 'ouse.'

'Persons?' Mrs Beavis's plump affability took a bit of a knock. 'We don't 'ave no persons residin' in our 'ouse. I mean, me fam'ly ain't persons, and me lodgers is nice people.'

'D'you know, I took it upon meself once to point out to a Government department that people are people,' said Tubby, 'but they still print persons on official forms. Anyway, there's yer fam'ly, eh?' A pencil appeared, Tubby poising it at the ready above his notebook. 'Would yer mind advancin' me the details?'

'There's me, I'm Mrs Beavis, and there's Mr Beavis, 'e's me 'usband. Then there's me daughters Nancy, Ella an' Linda, an' me sons Albert and Alfred. 'Ow many's that?'

'Seven, I make it, madam,' said Tubby, scribbling.

'Yes, I think that's right,' said Mrs Beavis.

'And lodgers, you said?'

'There's me settled lodger, a lovely gent – oh, and a poor young gel that 'e's lookin' after for a bit. Then there's me new lodger as well.'

'Their names, Mrs Beavis, if you'd be so obligin'?' Tubby's manner was agreeably persuasive.

'Well, me settled lodger is Mr Joe Foster that come out of the Army two years ago, and yer couldn't find a nicer gent anywhere. It was just like 'im to be a kind 'elp to that poor young woman that 'adn't got no parents, nor 'ome, nor job. I don't know 'ow long she'll be stayin', but 'er name's Dolly Smith. An' me new lodger, she's only been 'ere a few days, she come over from France to take a job in London. I never 'ad a French lodger before, I must say she's very polite.'

'French?' said Tubby, looking up from his notebook.

'Yes, would yer believe?' Mrs Beavis looked proud and happy that she'd bagged a lodger from France. ''Er name's Marcelle Fayette.' The good lady pronounced it Fay-it. 'It's a funny name, but French, I suppose. She wrote it on the rent book I got for her, I 'ad to ask 'er as I didn't know 'ow to spell it meself, and I like to do things proper.' Mrs Beavis spelled the name out.

'Fayette, I got you, madam,' said Tubby, licking his pencil, then scribbling conscientiously. 'Looks French, would you say?'

'Yes, she's got that very black French 'air, an' she walks very elegant. She don't 'appen to be in at the moment, but will she 'ave to be counted in the census, bein' a foreigner?'

'Only as someone residin' in your house at the time,' said Tubby. He gave Mrs Beavis a smile. 'Wonder what the young men round 'ere think? I expect she's young, is she, an' likely to get some 'opefuls knockin' on 'er door?'

'Well, she's in 'er mid-twenties, I'd say.'

'I'd chance me own arm if I was ten years younger,' said Tubby, 'and if Mrs Purser would let me. Well, that's all, Mrs Beavis, many thanks, sorry to 'ave 'ad to bring you to the door – oh, just a tick, seein' she's foreign and you're 'er landlady, I suppose you've checked 'er passport, which is a Government regulation?'

'Yes, she showed it to me when she wrote 'er name in the rent book. I ain't never seen a passport before, it's like a notebook. Mind, it was all in French, but 'er name was clear, except I didn't know as a landlady that it was a regulation for me to see it. She give me a bit of a French smile when she showed it to me, like she thought I was a bit suspicious.'

'Well, that makes it all very tidy, Mrs Beavis,' said Tubby. 'Good mornin', and lots of luck to yer husband's rhubarb. I might try growin' some in a pot meself.'

'You need to 'ave 'orses passin' by,' said Mrs Beavis helpfully.

'We've got them all right,' said Tubby, and lifted his bowler to her before going on his way. He called at several other houses, just in case by dint of gossip it became known he had only interviewed Mrs Beavis.

Mr Rodney Masters, having come up from his home in Richmond to report to Sir Hubert Wilkins on last night's events in Bell Lane, delivered the details without embellishment. Then he and Sir Hubert waited for Tubby Sharp to arrive.

Tubby was late. He did not show up until gone eleven.

'Mornin', guv, mornin', Rodney,' he said breezily.

'Good morning, Mr Sharp,' said Sir Hubert, consulting his pocket watch.

'Checkin' the time, are yer, guv?'

'Having heard what Mr Masters had to say, I thought perhaps you'd be here early with your own report,' said Sir Hubert.

'Quite right, guv, and I would've been 'ere first thing, specially after a full night's sleep,' said Tubby, 'but I decided to do some more work on this mysterious female that came to our peepers last night. I expect Rodney 'ere 'as told yer I was conspicuous by me absence when 'e came off duty fairly early last night. Well, there wasn't much point in 'im stayin' on once 'e knew I was tailin' the lady and the suspects had climbed back over the wall, which I presume they did, Rodney?'

'You presume right,' said Masters.

'And you found me gone, of course. I follered the

aforesaid female, guv, to London Bridge railway station, where she took a cab an' so did I. 'Er cab dropped 'er off at a house in Newington Butts, and my cab kept goin', of course. Subsequent, as you might say, I returned on foot and noted the house was number twenty-one. I then proceeded 'ome to me better half and me bed.'

'Are you sure the woman went into the house?' questioned Sir Hubert.

'I see yer point there, guv,' said Tubby. 'It might've been a bluff, eh, stoppin' there? Or precautionary, like. She might've gone anywhere from there. No, she went in all right. I was some way be'ind 'er, keepin' me distance, and by the time me cab was passin' by she'd paid 'er cabbie and was steppin' in through the open door. So this mornin' I returned to Newington Butts to ask some questions.'

Tubby went on to explain how he had established the identity of the woman and obtained details of other people in the house. Most informative, the lady of the house had been, and seemed tickled that she'd got a French lodger. The other lodger, a man she said had been in the Army, might be worth a look. He'd picked a homeless girl up off the streets, apparently, but she might not have been homeless, and nor might her name be Dolly Smith. Come to that, the man might not have been born Joe Foster. All three of them might be feloniously hand-in-glove.

'You think so, Mr Sharp?' said Sir Hubert.

'No, not really, guv. Just examinin' the possibilities.'

'The woman is French? Does that make sense? Are you sure her passport document was French?'

'I don't see I can be sure, guv, not 'aving laid my personal peepers on it and only bein' informed of same by Mrs Beavis.'

'I doubt if she can read French,' said Masters. 'It's quite likely that if she was told it was French, she would have accepted it as such. On the other hand, the name –

207

Marcelle Fayette – is as French as it could be. Of course, if she were arrested on some charge or other—'

'That would put the cat among the pigeons,' said Sir Hubert, 'and we'd lose the chance of having her lead us to her principal. She'd put two and two together and lie low. All we can do at the moment is to watch her and also to maintain the watch on Bell Lane. That means more men. Mr Sharp, will you and Mr Masters share a day watch on our French lady, arranging your shifts to suit yourselves?' Sir Hubert always made his requests politely, and many such requests were another way of giving orders.

'Startin' today, guv?' said Tubby.

'I should think so, wouldn't you?'

'Makes sense to me, guv, considerin' the general feeling is that she's up to no good.'

'Then kindly proceed,' said Sir Hubert.

Mr Rodney Masters, loitering at the Elephant and Castle, a bustle of people and traffic, had a good view of Newington Butts and a trained eye. At twenty minutes past two, a hansom cab turned into the Butts and stopped a little way down.

The woman alighted and paid the cabbie, who touched his bowler and drove off.

Masters watched the woman commence a walk. She did not look like one of those beautiful spies favoured by authors of gripping yarns or by those who told of dewy-eyed Southern ladies who had wormed secrets from Northern generals during the American Civil War. She looked quite ordinary in appearance, except that she did walk with visible grace. And she was very recognizable as the woman he and Tubby Sharp had seen in the house in Bell Lane last night.

She stopped at the door of number twenty-one Newington Butts. She opened the door and entered.

She had not had the cabbie drive her to the door. In

daylight, she probably wouldn't. A lodger alighting outside her rented accommodation in Newington Butts would draw attention to herself.

There was nothing to do now but wait. If she came out again before Tubby relieved him, he must follow her.

Marcelle knocked on Sergeant Joe's door. He opened it after a few moments. She smiled.

'Ah, my good friend,' she said.

'I thought you'd started your job today,' said Joe.

'No, no, that isn't for a little while yet. I am sensibly taking my time to get used to London. I am going out and about and talking to people.'

'Well, go down and talk to Mrs Beavis. She likes a chat and it'll give your feet a rest.'

'Joe, that is not very friendly,' said Marcelle, 'I would much prefer to come in and talk to you.'

'Out of curiosity?' asked Joe.

'Is it forbidden to be interested in you?'

'It's inconvenient when I'm busy.'

Marcelle peeped. She saw papers on his table. She smiled again. He was holding the half-open door to keep her out, of course.

'You are forging?' she said.

'None of your business,' said Joe.

'Ah well, never mind,' she said, 'you can take me out this evening instead.'

'Pardon?' said Joe.

'I am telling no-one of your secret, Joe, so let us go out this evening, yes?'

'You baggage,' said Joe.

'It is agreed?' Marcelle was surprising herself in finding just how interested she was in him. He was becoming a diversion of the kind that was inadvisable, the kind Count Zhinsky would certainly not approve of and which she herself knew agents should avoid. 'It is best to be good friends, isn't it?'

What was she up to? Joe couldn't think it made sense for an obviously sophisticated Frenchwoman to be personally interested in him. Marcelle eyed him winningly. A little grin showed on his face.

'All right, I'll take you to a theatre,' he said, but he had a music hall in mind, one popular with the cockneys.

'Ah, how lovely, Joe.'

'Yes, I'm sure you'll like it. Mind if I get back to my work now?'

'Oh, I'm certain it's a work of art,' smiled Marcelle, and returned to her room.

Miss Henrietta Downes entered Sir Hubert's office. His smile of welcome was a little wry. Henrietta was a handful, a young lady with a mind of her own and her own way of behaving. She gave suitors a terrible time and had ideas about attaching herself permanently to his department, on the assumption that he would not say no to her. He could not dispute her intelligence, but he could dispute the wisdom of letting her risk herself when the opposition was dangerous.

'Good afternoon, Uncle Hubert,' said Henrietta.

'I thought we'd agreed you should take a holiday,' said Sir Hubert.

'You made a suggestion, but there was no agreement,' said Henrietta. 'And I'm too valuable to you to go on holiday. You know I am, or you wouldn't have taken me on in the first place.'

'We do not – ah – take people on,' said Sir Hubert. 'I concede, however, that in weak moments I've allowed you to undertake the occasional little task for us.'

'Weak moments, Uncle Hubert? Your best moments, you mean. Now, what has been happening in Bell Lane?'

'We've found the contact, a woman, and are hoping she'll lead us to the man we want.'

'If the police don't get to him first,' said Henrietta.

'That would help in one way, it would put him out of action, but it would prevent us from finding out exactly why he and other questionable Russians are in London.'

'You could deport the whole lot,' said Henrietta, 'then you'd have no need to worry about what they're up to.'

'That would leave loose ends,' said Sir Hubert, 'and among those loose ends there might be other conspirators.'

'Conspirators, what an exciting word,' said Henrietta. 'Who is watching the woman?'

'Mr Sharp and Mr Masters.'

'Who is Mr Masters?'

'A War Office filing clerk temporarily on loan to us,' said Sir Hubert.

'Filing clerk? Tell me another,' said Henrietta. 'Where are all your other men?'

'Most are on duty at ports of entry, and will be for some time.'

'I'll take over from Mr Masters,' said Henrietta. 'Having come to know Tubby, I'm attached to him. I'll work with him from next week.'

'You're referring, I presume, to Mr Sharp.'

'Don't be stuffy, Uncle Hubert,' said Henrietta, gazing at the Whitehall scene from a window. 'Tubby and I will make a jolly good team, he's a wily old sailor dog, and I'm a clever young lady. Is the woman living in Bell Lane?'

'She has a room there,' said Sir Hubert. 'She obviously uses it to make contact with the two suspects who are lodging next door. She herself appears to be lodging in a house south of the river.'

'Where exactly?' asked Henrietta.

'Mr Sharp has the address,' said Sir Hubert, knowing that if he disclosed it to Henrietta, his irrepressible niece would sneak off and add herself to the team. 'Henrietta, these people are dangerous, and I can't let you take more risks.'

'But I'm good at this sort of thing,' said Henrietta, rustling restlessly about.

'You're very fidgety today, aren't you?' said Sir Hubert. 'What are you getting up to in that Kensington apartment in which I was foolish enough to let you install yourself with two servants?'

'I'm not getting up to anything. You won't let me.' Henrietta seemed very put out. 'Do you want me to complain to Aunt Amelia that you're trying to wrap me in cotton-wool? You know she doesn't believe in that old-fashioned stuff, she's not the leader of Advance Britannia for nothing.'

Sir Hubert coughed.

'Advance Britannia, I'm afraid, is a collection of eccentric ladies who want to run the Government,' he said.

'Yes, aren't they sweet?' said Henrietta. 'But be warned, Uncle Hubert, Aunt Amelia told me weeks ago that Advance Britannia has high hopes of securing the patronage of Queen Mary.'

'Not if His Majesty gets to hear about it,' said Sir Hubert.

'Are you going to let me team up with Tubby or not?' asked Henrietta.

'My dear girl, you're in my care until you're twenty-five,' said Sir Hubert, 'and I've already let you off the reins as much as I dare.'

'Off the reins?' Henrietta regarded her uncle and guardian sorrowfully. 'Really, Uncle Hubert, I'm not a horse, you know.'

'Henrietta, you're delightful but headstrong, and the fact is, matters have taken a serious turn. It was expected that a few anarchists might attempt to slip into the country. Any important public event in certain of Europe's capitals could tempt some anarchist or other into throwing

212

a bomb, especially at royalty. As far as we're concerned, such hotheads can usually be detected at ports of entry and sent back. But now we're beginning to suspect there's a well-laid plot by an organized group of revolutionaries to create mayhem during the coronation celebrations.'

'You mean these Russians, of course,' said Henrietta.

'Yes, and I repeat, they're dangerous. One murder has already been committed. Remember, no civilized country requires or allows its young ladies to risk their lives.'

'Oh, dear, now you're trying to spoof me,' said Henrietta. 'Uncle Hubert, you know very well that women spies have been used since Hannibal crossed the Alps with his elephants. His lady spies went on in advance to deceive the Romans into believing Hannibal was bringing huge mice that would eat them out of house and home. That's why when some Romans saw their first elephants they couldn't believe them.'

'Nor can I believe the mice,' said Sir Hubert, smiling again. 'However, as you're so set on offering your services, which I confess are of admirable quality, you may share the daytime watch on Bell Lane.'

'But those two men never do anything except tour the sights of London,' protested Henrietta.

'It's a little different now we know they make contact with the woman. I'll arrange for you to share the watch with a colleague, five hours each from ten in the morning until eight in the evening. What I want is a note of comings and goings. Not only in respect of the house lodging our two suspects, but the house next door as well, the house on the left. We have three people in our sights at the moment, Henrietta, and hope to lay our eyes on a fourth, the man we think is the principal. But there may be others.'

'Are the two suspects still to be followed?' asked Henrietta.

'Yes, because however innocent their excursions have

been so far, there is always the chance that, since we know they have contact with the woman, they will one day make contact with the principal. If that happens, turn your attentions on him and leave the two suspects to go their own way.'

'That's better, Uncle Hubert,' said Henrietta, 'I really need something to do.'

'So I gather,' said Sir Hubert drily. 'By the way, what's happened to Cedric?'

'Oh, I sent him packing ages ago,' said Henrietta, 'he's very much like all the others. Hopeless.'

'I think you're determined not to fall in love, young lady.'

'Yes, I'm putting up a tenacious fight,' said Henrietta, and laughed. But she did not look all that amused.

Sir Hubert felt fairly satisfied. He had given her something to do, something not too dangerous. He had a feeling the two suspects living in Bell Lane would continue to act as red herrings. Their entry into England by the port of Harwich had been noted. There was nothing known about them, nothing to justify arrest and deportation. They were art students, Gregor Palovich and Peter Czernov, from St Petersburg, visiting London and wishing later on to be present at the coronation celebrations. So they said. Art students had arrived in March when the celebrations were not until 22 June? That and the fact of being Russian had made it worthwhile to keep an eye on them. Henrietta could spend time watching them again from next week. It would not do to tell her that Tubby Sharp considered her a young amateur lady.

CHAPTER SEVENTEEN

Linda and Ella, on their way home from school, turned into Newington Butts at the same time as Dolly crossed from the other corner. Mr Rodney Masters, strolling about in the vicinity, cast a casual look at the two schoolgirls and the young woman, then sauntered on.

Dolly, deep in thought, jumped a little as Ella spoke.

'Oh, you been out?'

'What? Oh, it's you two,' said Dolly, coming to.

'Yes, it's me and Ella,' said Linda, given to imparting information. She thought what a shame it was that Dolly had no home or family, because she was nice really. 'We're on our way 'ome from school. Ella's 'ungry. Well, she's always 'ungry after school. Me teacher wasn't 'alf pleased with me today because of me composition an' me spellin'. D'you know 'ow to spell omnibus?'

'Me? Wish I did,' said Dolly.

'Oh, it's easy, really,' said Linda, and spelt it for Dolly. An approaching boy took a look at Ella.

'Watcher, Fatty,' he said.

'Watcher, Skinny,' said Ella.

'Eat yer for breakfast,' said the boy, passing by.

'Bet yer couldn't eat the skin off a rice puddin',' called Ella.

They reached their house, the house Masters was watching. He saw them go in, his interest mild. Neither of the girls, nor the young woman, related to his watching brief.

Dolly, going upstairs, heard voices in the living-room. She put her head in. Joe was sitting at the table, and that bit of French stuff was talking to him.

'Oh, beg yer pardon, I'm sure,' said Dolly, 'I didn't know you were entertainin' someone from the workhouse, Joe.'

'Ah, here is your charming friend with her funny way of speaking English,' smiled Marcelle. 'But she is recovering quite well, I think. She isn't nearly so pale or thin.'

'Enjoy your tram ride, Dolly?' asked Joe.

'Oh, I saw the sights all right,' said Dolly. 'Mind, I didn't know I was goin' to see another one when I got back.'

'Well, that's life,' said Joe, 'it's full of surprises.'

The stairs creaked to a heavy tread, and the landing sighed as Mrs Beavis reached it.

'You there, Sergeant Joe? I 'eard you an' the young ladies talkin'.'

'Come in, Bessie love,' called Joe, and his beaming landlady came in with three cups of tea and a plate of home-made jam tarts on a tray.

'I just made a pot for meself and the gels,' she said, 'and I did some bakin' this afternoon, seein' as me fam'ly's always partial to same. 'Ow'd you do, Miss Fay-it, I 'ope you've got a likin' for jam tarts not long out of me oven.'

'Madam, how kind,' said Marcelle, 'I am enchanted.'

'Pleasure, I'm sure,' said Mrs Beavis happily, and placed the tray on the table. 'Well, I must say you all look as if you're enjoyin' bein' friends, and what I say is we all need friends we can turn to.'

'Some of us need landladies we can turn to for home-made jam tarts,' said Joe. 'There's a shortage of cooks up here.'

Dolly rolled her eyes.

'Well, I'd best get down for me own cuppa,' said Mrs Beavis. 'Oh, I just remembered, a man from the town 'all come knockin' this mornin', would yer believe. About the census.'

'Census?' said Dolly.

216

'Yes, the Government's got to count the population, it's to let the King know 'ow many subjects 'e's got. The man 'ad to ask about who lives 'ere'.

'Is that a fact?' asked Joe.

'Oh, 'e was very partic'lar about it,' said Mrs Beavis, 'so I told 'im who was in me fam'ly and who was lodgin'. I told 'im you'd come from France, Miss Fay-it, which 'e was interested in, but nothing to worry about, 'e said. 'E was a nice man, 'e liked 'earing about Charlie's rhubarb. Well, I must go down now, enjoy the tarts.' She bustled out.

'I don't trust censuses,' said Dolly, and she and Joe each sampled a jam tart. 'Crikey, it's 'eavenly.'

'First-class,' said Joe.

'Perfect confectionery, yes?' said Marcelle. 'Please to excuse me if I do not drink the tea, I have to go out for a little while. Now you have said the time, Joe, I will be ready at seven-thirty.'

She whisked out.

''Ere,' said Dolly, 'what did she mean, she'd be ready at seven-thirty?'

'I'm taking her out,' said Joe.

'Oh, 'elp yourself, I'm sure,' said Dolly, 'don't mind me, I like bein' on me own.'

'Well, you'll have Mrs Beeton to keep you company,' said Joe.

'That's it, make me fall over laughin',' said Dolly. 'You've got it bad, you 'ave, wantin' to take that French tart out. You always 'ad weak eyes and a soft 'ead?'

'Only lately,' said Joe.

They heard Marcelle go out a minute later. She walked along Newington Butts and enquired of a helpful woman the way to the town hall. Told it was in the Walworth Road and how to get there, she made no mistake in following the directions. Once inside the handsome building, she asked about the census. The clerk in

217

'Enquiries' advised her that it would be conducted in late April. She asked if that meant there were officials making enquiries of families. The clerk said not to his knowledge.

'You are not sending people out to ask questions?' she said.

'Pardon?'

'To knock on people's doors?'

'No, it's our responsibility to deliver the forms, that's all. We don't send anyone round to ask questions, although we'll give advice to people who aren't sure how to fill them in. But there's nothing going on yet.'

'Thank you,' said Marcelle and left.

Rodney Masters, who had followed her, watched her come out, waited until she was well on her way and, feeling sure she was going back to her lodgings, entered the town hall himself. He asked questions of his own of the 'Enquiries' clerk. Then he made straight for the Elephant and Castle, where Tubby had arrived to take over from him. Masters gave him details of what had transpired at the town hall.

'Well, I never, bless me big toe,' said Tubby, and took out an old briar pipe and stuck it into his mouth. He chewed on the stem, then said, 'Well, yer don't say, Rodney. Went and asked about the census, did she?'

'Found you out, you clever old coot,' said Masters.

'Got brains, that one 'as,' said Tubby. ''Er friendly landlady must've told 'er about me call. Reasonable, reasonable. But who'd go round to the town 'all about it except someone who was always 'aving to mind 'er Ps an' Qs? Always 'aving to keep one step ahead. Yes, asked 'erself what it was all about, better go an' make sure, just in case. Pity you didn't knock 'er over accidental and break 'er leg. That would 'ave taken 'er mind off the town 'all.'

'Lot of good that would have done, putting her in hospital,' said Masters.

218

'She might 'ave 'ad visitors,' said Tubby. 'The point is, sonny, is she goin' to scarper? Right, me young 'earty, pop down to the 'ouse, present yerself to the landlady as a plainclothes policeman and ask 'er if she's 'ad a man call about a census, and if so did she let 'im into the 'ouse and was anything nicked. Tell 'er the geezer was a Flash Harry, and the police want 'im for false pretences and for nickin' household goods. Ask for 'is description and so on. Marcelle Fayette needs to 'ave a reason not to scarper. She might just slip us. On top of which, we don't want 'er suspectin' we're on to 'er. Off yer go, sonny.'

'I'm on my way, Dad.'

'What's that?' asked Mrs Beavis of the presentable young man on her doorstep.

'Yes, I'm afraid this character has been going the rounds in areas south of the Thames posing as a census official,' said Masters, 'and as I said, madam, this gives him the opportunity to invite himself in and to pocket little items of value. I hope he didn't invite himself into your house.'

'No, I can't say 'e did,' said Mrs Beavis, 'but I might easy 'ave let 'im in, 'e was that cheerful an' friendly.'

'Be grateful you didn't,' said Masters, 'you'd have lost something for certain, and probably from right under your nose. He's as artful as a waggon-load of monkeys. Can you confirm his description for me?' Mrs Beavis gave a description. 'Thought so,' said Masters, 'that's the joker all right. Perhaps you'd warn your family and your lodgers. They need to know about him.'

'Oh, I'll tell everyone,' said Mrs Beavis. 'What a saucy devil.'

'You're right, madam, and thanks for your help.' Masters lifted his bowler to her, smiled and went to knock on the door of the next house. Mrs Beavis went straight upstairs to inform her lodgers of the antics of a crafty geezer who was going around saying he'd come about a census.

Her French lodger received the information with a smile.

'Such a nerve, yes. One can almost admire him.'

'I ain't been brought up meself to admire no-one that can worm 'is way into people's 'omes and make off with what don't belong to 'im,' said Mrs Beavis.

'But it is amusing in its way, yes?'

'Well, I suppose you can't 'elp laughin', can yer?'

Leaving Dolly as huffy as a broody hen whose cockerel was seeking French pastures, Joe took Marcelle to the Canterbury Music Hall in Westminster Bridge Road. She was dressed for a West End theatre, not for a Lambeth music hall popular with cockneys. She who had known the magnificence of the ballet and opera in the theatres of St Petersburg, could hardly believe what Joe had brought her to some while after the curtain had gone up. The bars on both sides of the auditorium were open, noisy men and women patronizing them, and the place was thickly hazy with smoke from cigarettes and pipes. The stage turns were ridiculous, knockabout comedians whose garbled patter was all Greek to her, gaudily costumed female singers who were terrible, and male singers who were even worse.

The whole audience was noisy. From the front stalls, they threw rotten apples at one unfortunate performer.

She kept looking at Joe. His little grin kept appearing.

'You swine,' she hissed.

'Pardon?'

'Someone should cut your throat.'

'Don't miss the next turn, Marcelle.'

A well-known comedian came on to yells of delight. He told a new joke. Well, fairly new. The audience roared with laughter. So did Joe. A drunken man stood up and fell down.

'I shall do it myself.' It was another hiss from Marcelle.

'Do what yourself?'

'Cut your throat.' Well, she thought, there was something genuinely amusing in that. Rokovssky had said she must kill him in the end. He was clever indeed, this one, bringing her to a place full of rowdy peasants to perhaps make her think he was one himself. Never. She looked at him through the creeping blue haze. He was the epitome of all she had heard about Englishmen. Handsome, with his moustache making him look distinguished, never disconcerted, never boastful or brash, and wearing with ease the air of belief that all Englishmen had in themselves and their Empire. For some reason, her blood tingled. And because of her sense of humour, she began to see the funny side of things. This place, these peasants, she dressed for the West End and he knowing it. So he had brought her here.

'Not your style, Marcelle, an English music hall?' he murmured.

'Who knows? Perhaps I'm enjoying myself immensely, after all.'

She wondered then how it was going to be possible for her to continue her diverting relationship with him. She must leave the house. The motives of the man who had asked Mrs Beavis about her family and her lodgers were very suspect. He had her name now. Well, the name she was using. What had brought him to the house? Not the census. Nor an act of petty thievery, as the second man had declared to Mrs Beavis. Marcelle's every instinct found this suspect. She thought about British Intelligence. Yes, she had to consider the possibility that both men had been British agents, even though she'd been sure the name Marcelle Fayette meant nothing to them.

She glanced at Joe again. The swine's expression gave nothing away, but could he have been responsible? Somehow, she did not think so. In the profession himself, he would have tried to make use of her.

They left when the final curtain came down. Joe had the audacity then to take her to a pub. That was thick with smoke too and full of more peasants. He found seats at a table in a corner of the saloon bar.

'This is a London pub,' he said.

'I know.'

'You'll get to like pubs.'

'I already hate this one.'

'I'll order you a sandwich. Ham, beef or pork?'

She was hungry.

'English beef?' she said.

'Of course. With mustard?'

'Thank you. With a glass of red wine, if you please.'

'No wine, not in pubs,' said Joe. 'Try a glass of old English ale. Perk you up.'

'Perk me up? What is that?'

'It'll make you feel better.'

'Never have I known such a terrible man as you.'

'You need watching yourself,' said Joe, and went to order.

She enjoyed the sandwich, and she even enjoyed the biting tang of the old ale. She began to tease him then. Joe just laughed and shook his head at her. He could not take her seriously. He could take Dolly seriously. Dolly had got herself into murky waters, and seriously needed to be pulled out. Couldn't have her going around nicking wallets while she was still young enough to make a name for herself, even if it meant smacking her bottom to get her on the straight and narrow path.

Tubby was still on duty when he spotted the woman – Marcelle Fayette – returning to her lodgings in company with the limping but upright gent she'd gone out with just after seven-thirty. It was eleven now. Well, thought Tubby, what's her next step? Is she going to fly the coop and lead us to our number one suspect? That'll depend,

Tubby me lad, on her suspicions. Have them there suspicions been laid to rest by her landlady's account of what young Rodney had said about a fly-by-night geezer, which was myself? And what, I wonder, is the upright gent to her? There they go, indoors, with her giving him what you might call an intimate look, if this here lamplight ain't deceiving my peepers. Intimate, eh? Have I got to ask myself if he's a suspect too, or an innocent party? Interesting, Tubby me lad, interesting. I'll stick around for a bit.

He stuck around until a little after midnight. Nothing had happened, so he went home.

Marcelle fooled him. She slipped out of the house at six in the morning, with her suitcase, and her eyes watching out for bobbies on the beat. She had found that bobbies on the beat proliferated in London, and could pop up even at six in the morning. She left the house very quietly, though not before sliding a note under Joe's living-room door.

Rodney Masters arrived at the Elephant and Castle just before eight to take up the morning watch. It was not too difficult to avoid looking like a sore thumb, for the junction was always a hustle and bustle of people and traffic. Wherever his feet took him, he was able to keep the house in sight. He saw the two schoolgirls emerge at fifteen minutes to nine, one slender and the other roundly plump, but there were no signs of the woman. That she was there, he did not doubt. Tubby would have sent a runner to Richmond to let him know if she'd scarpered.

CHAPTER EIGHTEEN

April was at its most typical. Clouds were rushing about all over the sky, some in dark and bad-tempered fashion, others running white and billowing on their heels. Heavy showers alternated with bursts of sunshine. Joe was due to take Dolly up West to meet George. Over breakfast, she asked if that French gypsy woman had had her way with him last night.

'Well, no, as a matter of fact,' said Joe. 'I took her to the Canterbury Music Hall, and then to a pub. Neither place was suitable.'

'No-one's ever took me to a music 'all and a pub,' said Dolly.

'Your time will come when you get yourself a decent bloke,' said Joe.

'Can't wait, can I?' said Dolly. 'You sure she didn't drag you into her bed when you got her back 'ere? I mean, you don't 'alf look worn out.'

'No, I don't.'

'Well, the light must be a bit funny this mornin', that's all I can say,' said Dolly.

'Marcelle's gone, by the way,' said Joe. He had found her note, which merely said she had urgent business elsewhere, but would be in touch with him.

'Gone?' said Dolly.

'She left me a note to say she'd been called away on urgent business.'

'Well, if she's gone for good,' said Dolly, 'you can count your blessings. You could 'ave met a fate worse than death, y'know. I bet 'er gypsy caravan was waitin' outside

224

for 'er when she woke up this mornin'. What a bit of luck for you, Joe.'

'Yes, narrow escape,' said Joe.

After breakfast, he went down to let his landlady know Marcelle had departed. Mrs Beavis was surprised, of course. Still, she said, Miss Fay-it hadn't left owing anything, she'd paid a week's rent in advance. What a funny woman, though. Never mind, there were nice ones like Dolly.

'Yes, I'm taking her up West this morning to meet a friend of mine, Bessie. I'm hoping he'll be able to put a job in her way.'

'That's good,' beamed Mrs Beavis, 'she'll like 'aving a job so's she can stand on 'er own feet. Mind you, Sergeant Joe, she'd be best off 'aving an 'usband.'

'I'll try to find her one,' said Joe.

'You're a nice bloke, Joe. I suppose you've 'ad yer breakfast, but I've got one or two sausages left over from ours if you'd like them.'

'Thanks for the offer, Bessie, but not now, thanks.'

He walked Dolly to the Elephant and Castle. She looked like a perky working girl in clothes he had bought for her, plus the straw boater. Joe carried an umbrella, and had already protected her from a shower.

'City blokes carry umbrellas, y'know,' she said.

'Yes, good idea on a rainy day,' said Joe.

'Joe, you don't 'alf say daft things sometimes.'

'What a coincidence, so do you.'

'What're we waitin' 'ere for, a tram?'

'No, a treat if a hansom cab turns up.'

'Honest?' she said. 'I'm beginnin' to like ridin' in 'ansom cabs. Are you well off lately?'

'Can't say I'm well off, Dolly, but can't say I'm broke, either. I walk most of the time. Good for my knee.' Joe looked around. Blackbeard was still on his mind at times, times when he felt Dolly would be better off out of the area. He had a feeling the man was lodged somewhere in Walworth. His presence in the Rockingham that night pointed to it.

The junction was busy, although the workers' rush hour was over. The usual traffic was building up. Shops were opening and near the corner of the New Kent Road two old ladies in black granny bonnets and black shawls were waiting for the shutters to go up on an old-fashioned little shop that sold cat's-meat among other things.

'Where did you say your business friend 'angs out?' asked Dolly.

'He runs a bookshop in Charing Cross Road.'

'Well, I hope 'e runs it respectable,' said Dolly. 'Some of them shops 'ave got dark corners that ain't a bit respectable. You never know what goes on in them, I bet it's not to do with books. Has your friend's shop got dark corners?'

'Several,' said Joe.

'Well, I ain't goin' in his shop, then; I ain't goin' to die a death in any of his dark corners.'

'I don't fancy the chances of any bloke who tries that on you, Dolly – hey!' Joe, spotting a cab trotting up to the junction from the New Kent Road, called and whistled. Dolly joined in.

'Oi! Cabbie!' She waved a hand. The cabbie acknowledged the summons with a gesture of his whip. He crossed the junction and pulled up.

'Top of the mornin' to yer, lady. Where to, might I ask?'

'Charin' Cross Road, if you don't mind,' said Dolly. Joe thought that if there was one thing certain about her, it was that she wasn't keen on playing second fiddle.

'Ah, Charin' Cross Road now,' said the cabbie, as spots of rain began to fall. 'Would yer be thinkin' of the beginnin', the end, the middle, or somewheres in between one or t'other?'

'Me gentleman friend will tell you,' said Dolly, 'but don't give 'im any lip or he'll spoil Christmas for you when it comes.'

'Singleton's Bookshop,' said Joe.

'Ah, somewheres about the middle,' said the cabbie. ''Op aboard, sir, you and yer young lady, and I'll take yer to the very door of selfsame.'

'How kind,' said Dolly. Joe opened the door, she hitched her skirt and stepped in, seating herself with a multitude of rustles. 'Excuse me petticoat,' she said, as he sat down beside her, 'but it's a bit loud sometimes.'

'So I've heard,' said Joe. The cab moved off, and the horse, frisky at this time of day, trotted to join the gathering stream of traffic in St George's Road.

'I'm grateful that you're takin' me to meet your friend who might get me a job,' said Dolly, 'but I 'ope I don't end up in a fact'ry makin' gooseberry jam. I hate gooseberries. I don't mind raspberry jam, but gooseberry, well, I'd 'ave to tell your friend no thanks.'

Joe wasn't listening. Through the offside cab window he'd spotted a broad-shouldered man in an overcoat and bowler hat. With a picture in his mind of the furious bearded man he'd seen in the fog, Joe felt the pedestrian fitted the picture, particularly as his walk looked solid and purposeful. As the cab passed the man, Joe craned his neck to get a good look at his features. He was dark right enough, and of the right build, but he had no beard.

'H'm,' he said, sitting back.

'What's up, what were you lookin' at?' asked Dolly.

'Thought I saw someone I knew,' said Joe, not wanting to worry her by any mention of Blackbeard. 'What was it you were saying, Dolly?'

'Just that I don't want to work in a gooseberry jam fact'ry,' said Dolly. 'Here, Joe, am I more of a credit to

227

you since I've been dressin' better? Did you feel proud of what you'd done for me when the cabbie called me a young lady? When you think what a ragbag I was, don't you feel pleased with yourself? Well, it's only right I should be a credit to you in front of your friend. It's a shame you had to let that Fanny Bonbon drag you round the National Gallery. I mean, she wasn't a credit to anyone with her tarty looks, and she must be near to forty.'

'Yes, I suppose anyone in the mid-twenties is very near forty,' said Joe.

'Well, you don't want to be seen goin' out with any woman who looks as old as Fanny Bonbon does, Joe, not when you're still fairly young yourself. If you don't mind me askin', how old are you?'

Joe, flexing his gammy leg, said, 'According to the way you work things out, I suppose you could say I'm near to fifty.'

'Are you really?' said Dolly. 'You don't look it, you're wearin' ever so well. No wonder they say older men 'ave got distinguished looks. I've never been out with an older distinguished bloke before.'

'And I've never been out with an old-fashioned sauce-box before,' said Joe.

'Well, you can't always be lucky,' said Dolly.

The cab took them over Westminster Bridge as another shower lifted, and they saw the rolling brown waters of Old Father Thames dappled with gold. On the north bank, the Houses of Parliament and Big Ben were outlined against the sky.

'Your foot all right?' asked Joe.

'Better all the time,' said Dolly. 'I like the river and the Houses of Parliament, don't you? It's goin' to be grand when the King and Queen 'ave their coronation. London's goin' to be decorated all over, and there'll be hundreds of kings and queens comin'. Well, the King's got hundreds of relatives. Of course, they're Queen Victoria's relatives mostly, they say she had more relatives than anyone ever 'ad before. I suppose she would have, she must 'ave been nearly a hundred years old when she died.'

'Nearly two hundred, probably,' said Joe, as they turned into Whitehall.

'What d'you mean, nearly two hundred?' said Dolly derisively, snuggling herself into the corner of the seat. 'How could anyone be as old as that?'

'They'd have to live a long time, I grant you,' said Joe.

'Joe, I feel sorry for you sometimes, you're so daft. No-one could live as long as two hundred years.'

'How about nearly two hundred? I did say nearly.'

'I'm not fallin' for that,' said Dolly, 'd'you think I'm simple or something?'

'No, not much,' said Joe.

'I can't understand a bloke like you just writin' letters for businessmen,' said Dolly. 'I bet you could build bridges and things like that. 'Ave you written lots of letters for your friend that's got the bookshop?'

'Well, I've not been writing them all my life,' said Joe, as traffic brought the cab to a temporary halt at the top of Whitehall. 'I spent my first year at my mother's bosom.'

'Well, fancy that. My, you do surprise me.'

'Then there was school, then the Army, then coming out of it two years ago. Now here I am.'

'And that's the story of your life? Joe, you're never goin' to get rich, are you?' Dolly eyed him sympathetically. The hansom moved on and the broad vista of Trafalgar Square presented itself to the nag. A twitch of the reins sent it trotting towards St Martin's Place. The cab tangled with other traffic. A horse shied. The cabbie's nag, reduced to an amble, skilfully extricated itself and pulled the hansom on. 'We could 'ave come on a bus,' said Dolly, 'you shouldn't chuck your money about on cabs. I only wish you knew a rich lady that wanted to marry you. Here, why

229

don't you get a job as some rich lady's footman and get her to fancy you?'

'Think I'd be up to that?'

'Joe, of course you would. You could take her bedtime cocoa in every night, and do a bit of come-into-the-garden stuff with 'er.'

'Can't think she'd want to be taken into the garden once she was in bed. Wouldn't she just prefer to drink her cocoa?'

'Joe, what's up with you?' Dolly gave him an exasperated look. 'Don't you know anything about ladies?'

'We're being serious, are we?' said Joe, keeping his face straight.

'You've got to think about your future,' said Dolly, 'and writin' letters for businessmen ain't much of a future for anyone. Look, some rich lady wouldn't bother about any cocoa if you were there tellin' her how much you liked her French nightdress and her fancy 'air curlers.'

'Would that get her into the garden with me?' asked Joe.

'Well, not in a flash exactly,' said Dolly, 'you'd 'ave to wait till she took her curlers out.'

'I've still got doubts,' said Joe.

'Well, I might 'ave made it sound a bit like the music hall,' said Dolly, 'but you know what I mean.'

'I see,' said Joe. 'Well, thanks, Dolly, I'll remember all that when the time comes for me to take a good look at my future.'

'Yes, you deserve a rich wife, honest,' said Dolly.

The cab pulled up and they alighted. Joe paid the cheerful cabbie, adding a tip, and he and Dolly entered Singleton's Bookshop just in time to dodge one more shower of rain. George, talking to a customer, looked up. Seeing Joe, he smiled. Seeing Dolly, perky in her boater, he blinked.

'Be with you in a moment,' he said.

Dolly, staying close to Joe, whispered, 'Help, I ain't ever seen so many books, not all at once I ain't. And here, look at that dark corner back there. I bet many a poor girl's found out she doesn't get fairy stories read to 'er there. Is Porky the bloke you write letters for?'

'That's Mr George Singleton, the proprietor.'

'He's still a Porky, he's got a paunch. He ain't got your handsome figure.'

'But he does have customers all over the country.'

'Sounds daft to me,' whispered Dolly. 'Why can't they go to country bookshops?'

'What they often want can usually only be found by a bookseller like George.'

'That's a promise, Mr Unwin,' said George to his customer, an elderly gentleman with a dried-up look. 'Within two weeks. I shan't disappoint you.'

'With index, with index,' said the elderly gent fussily.

'That edition, yes, you may rely on it, Mr Unwin,' said George reassuringly.

'I hope so, I hope so, good morning,' said the customer and left the shop. George advanced on Joe and Dolly.

'Hello, and who is this young lady, Sergeant Joe?' he asked, his portliness expansive with good fellowship.

'Meet Private Dolly Smith,' said Joe.

'Pardon?' said George.

'Private Smith, meet Mr George Singleton,' said Joe, and George smiled at her.

'Pleased to meet you, I'm sure,' said Dolly, 'but you'll 'ave to excuse him, he's always callin' me that, he'd like to get me in the Army and march me up and down all day. Mind, I do 'appen to be Dolly Smith, it's what they called me at the orphanage. Sergeant Joe bumped into me in the fog last Monday week and managed to sprain me ankle for me, and as I didn't 'ave a job or home, he took me to his lodgings. He's been lookin' after me and me ankle ever since, so I don't mind him bein' a bit funny in the 'ead.

Well, you can't mind, can you, when a bloke's as kind as that?'

George looked slightly overcome.

'My dear young lady, I'm not sure I quite caught all that,' he said.

'Just as well,' said Joe, 'you wouldn't be able to work it out. I feel the same most of the time. But I'll confirm she's down on her luck and needs a helping hand. All the same, she's got her chin up, as you can see, and all she requires to get her right on her feet is a job and some decent lodgings. You know a lot more likely people than I do. Any chance of a job with one of them? She's willing to have a go at anything, but I think she'd prefer to be a shop assistant or a lady's maid, or something like that.'

'Why not a gentleman's maid?' asked George.

'Here, I'm not 'aving any of those larks,' said Dolly. 'I've 'eard about gentlemen's maids and what gents get up to with them. I'm a respectable girl, mister.'

'I'm sure, I'm sure,' said George hastily. 'I was thinking of an elderly gentleman, a widower, one whose dwindling years could be made less irksome by a maid competent and caring. Indeed, I have in mind the gentleman who has just departed. He's not as crusty as he sounded, and he's in need of someone who'll brush the crumbs from his waistcoat and make sure he doesn't go out wearing odd socks.'

'Crikey, don't you talk posh?' said Dolly. 'All the same, I'm not goin' to be that kind of a maid, I don't want anything to do with an old gent's socks, or his crumbs. It's not dignified.'

'Ah, I see,' said George.

'Dolly isn't fussy, but she is particular,' said Joe.

'Well, I'll freely admit that old gents' socks can't be precisely appealing,' said George, and paused for thought. Dolly looked challengingly at him. Some people might have thought she was daring him to come up with any job at all. Joe brushed his moustache and left George to hold the baby. 'I have it,' said George, 'the Imperial.'

'Imperial what?' asked Dolly.

'Hotel,' said George. 'I know the manager. I know him well enough to feel sure he can use the services of another chambermaid.'

'That'll do,' said Joe, who knew as most people did that jobs were hard to come by, especially in the West End. For every vacancy there were fifty girls ready to apply.

'Me? Me a chambermaid?' said Dolly.

'It's a start,' said Joe.

'Here, you said a shop,' protested Dolly. 'You made me read a book about 'ow to be a shop assistant. It didn't say anything about chambermaids.'

'Just an oversight,' said Joe.

'The Imperial is an excellent hotel,' said George.

'And you'll still be serving the public, Dolly,' said Joe. 'Well done, George, much obliged to you.'

'Here, wait a minute,' said Dolly.

'I'll speak to the manager,' said George affably, 'I'll drop in on him on my way home and advise him you'll apply tomorrow.'

'There you are, Dolly,' said Joe. 'Now, lodgings next.'

'No need, old chap,' said George, 'there's staff accommodation on the top floor of the hotel. It's an admirable establishment, Miss Smith, and staff are taken good care of. One can't say that about every hotel.'

'I'll get ratty in a minute,' said Dolly. 'Being a chambermaid ain't the right job for a respectable young lady like me.'

'There'll be tips,' said George, 'handsome tips from some. The Imperial is used by the gentry and frequently by visitors from abroad. My word, yes, and in June it will be full of visitors interested in the coronation.'

'Can't fault it as a start, Dolly,' said Joe encouragingly. 'Job and lodgings together, and handsome tips.'

'It ain't dignified, being a chambermaid,' said Dolly.

'It's an honest job,' said Joe. 'Apply tomorrow.'

Dolly gave him a dark look.

'Well, I suppose I'd better,' she said, 'but they might not give me the job; I've not 'ad any experience of undignified work like chambermaidin'.' She paused as George coughed. 'What's he coughin' about, your book-shop friend, might I ask?'

'Can't say,' said Joe. A customer entered the shop, a young man of studious visage. He glanced at Dolly. Dolly stared him out.

'Er – good morning,' he said. 'Er – I—'

'May I help you, sir?' asked George.

'Oh – er – I've just remembered – I'll come back later – excuse me.' He departed in a nervous rush. George smiled.

'That young feller-me-lad probably wanted a copy of something slightly naughty,' he said.

'He didn't say so,' declared Dolly.

'Some young gentlemen don't if there's a lady present.'

'Well, he didn't 'ave to worry about me,' said Dolly a little bitterly. 'I'm just a chambermaid – at least, I nearly am.'

'Yes, quite,' said George, who thought he'd done quite well for the cockney girl. 'And a charming one, if I might say so. By the way, Joe my friend, I think if you've – ah—'

'Oh, if you want to talk private about his work for you,' said Dolly, 'I'll go and do a bit of shoppin', like buyin' a pail and a scrubbin' brush for me new job.'

'Not at all necessary, my dear,' said George. 'The hotel supplies all staff requirements.'

'Well, I'll go shoppin', anyway,' said Dolly. 'I think I'll do the rounds and get back to Newington Butts later, say about teatime.'

'You'd like to do that?' said Joe.

'Be a treat for me, now I'm up 'ere,' said Dolly.

'Enjoy yourself,' said Joe, 'but don't give your ankle a rough time.'

'See you later,' said Dolly. 'Goodbye, Mr Singleton, pleased to 'ave met you, and kind of you to 'elp me get a job. Crikey, me a chambermaid,' she said, as she left the shop.

'Extraordinary girl,' said George. 'Looks too good to be a chambermaid, by Jove. Ought to have had the benefit of a decent education.'

'She's a character,' smiled Joe, 'but I think I'll still have to keep an eye on her. Don't want her to run into more bad luck.' He thought, however, that at the Imperial, Dolly would be well out of Blackbeard's way.

'What a good fellow you are, old chap,' said George. 'I confess I'd find it agreeable myself to keep an eye on a lovely young lady like that. Byron, Shelley and their ladies are all very fascinating, but being dead – alas, poor Yorick – one could truthfully say they're also as dry as dust. Now, anything for me?'

'A little,' said Joe, and drew a brown envelope from his raincoat pocket. 'I've been short of working time these last few days, but I'll get the rest of the letters done by next week.'

'Quite understand, old man. Charming girl. Fresh, you know. Ah – are you sure you want to throw her to the wolves?'

'What're you talking about?' asked Joe.

'I've inferred, of course, that you've enjoyed a delightful week with her,' said George, 'and if it's meant you've had to put your work aside to disport with her, well, good luck to you, old chap. I'm a firm believer myself in the maxim that all work and no play isn't as good as a roll in the hay.'

'How would you like to be shot at dawn?' asked Joe.

'Frankly, Joe old man, I don't fancy that at all.'

'And I don't fancy the suggestion that—' Joe stopped as a thin man with stooping shoulders came in, nodded to

George and made his way to the second-hand volumes at the far end of the shop. 'Listen, George, Dolly's lived with bad luck all her life, but she's survived because she's never let bad luck knock holes in her. Don't like to feel you think I've taken advantage of her.'

'I stand in humble apology, old fellow,' said George, 'but I can't think why you're casting the dear girl out if you're set on still keeping an eye on her.'

'Don't fall off your horse, George, you'll hurt yourself. The point is, she needs a job and the chance to make a name for herself.'

'As a chambermaid?' said George, and looked over his shoulder. The customer was browsing. 'And why does she have to make a name for herself? My dear old chap, much the best way of keeping an eye on her is to marry her, don't you think? Not my business, of course—'

'Marry her?' said Joe.

'Might I inform you that marriage is an institution that's been going from the year dot? All my worldly goods and that kind of stuff. I entered the happy state ten years ago. I provide Ruth with reasonable security from the bailiffs, and she does everything else. If I told her to go out and make a name for herself, she'd ask our doctor to come and examine me.'

'Like to point out I can't have a wife looking over my shoulder to see what I'm up to,' said Joe.

'Ah,' said George, and looked thoughtfully at the envelope Joe had handed to him. 'Quite,' he said.

'Right,' said Joe.

'I'll see you next week?' said George.

'I'll complete the commission by then.'

'It's a privilege, old chap, to know you.'

Joe shook hands and departed. He walked down to Trafalgar Square, thinking about Dolly. What would she say if he suggested marriage? She probably wouldn't be able to make sense of it. No rosy hues coloured Dolly's

236

images, she saw things in black and white. She would see him as he was, a man living in lodgings and supposedly earning a few bob a week at writing letters for business-men. Not much in that for a young woman who, having been through the mill, would be entitled to ask for a bit more. On top of which, he'd have to give up this forgery lark before he took marriage on. It was the kind of thing that couldn't be hidden from a wife. As a pickpocket – ex-pickpocket, he hoped – Dolly might think it a bit of a giggle, but it stopped being any kind of a giggle when it was used to finance a marriage. He wondered how much Mrs Singleton knew of George's part in the matter. Nothing, probably. George was a wily old bird, with a little bit of the devil-may-care about him.

Joe had a feeling it was time to stop, time to look around for a less risky career. George might be a help again, he knew all kinds of people who ran honest businesses. Now if he also knew a landowner who needed a gamekeeper, he'd be a friend right at the top of the class. Yes, better to put forgery behind him and establish himself in some kind of a job before talking to Dolly about marriage, and even then there was no telling if she'd take it seriously. For one thing, she obviously didn't like cooking. But after years of having life throw things at her, she was as game as a fighting cock. True, Blackbeard had frightened her. But he'd frighten any woman.

Trafalgar Square. He stopped. Moody April clouds, taking a dislike to the sun, rushed to blot it out and to shower cold spiteful rain over buildings, traffic and people. Some people ran for shelter, others put their umbrellas up, and others just let themselves get wet. Joe, having let Dolly take his brolly, turned his raincoat collar up and thought of the heat of Africa and India, and the longing among soldiers for Britain's showery April.

The sun burst through again and a rainbow curved over Whitehall. The rain glittered in the sunlight for half a minute, then ceased, leaving Trafalgar Square wetly shining.

'Lookin' for me, sir?' enquired a bright voice as Joe was about to move off. '' Ere I am. Buy me fresh daffs, sir?'

Joe smiled down into the perky eyes of Daisy the flower girl. Her old boater was wet, her shawl a little damp, but she had the same kind of cockney spirit as Dolly. Bunches of golden-headed daffodils stood long-stemmed in her basket.

'Hello, Daisy, how's trade?' he asked.

'Oh, up an' down, in and out, but not bad really. Pleasure to see you again, sir.'

'Mutual,' said Joe, 'and it's daffs this time, is it?'

'Ain't they lovely?' said Daisy.

'Look a treat,' said Joe, 'I'll have a couple of bunches.'

'Yer a sport, sir. You don't mind they're fourpence a bunch?'

'Don't mind a bit,' said Joe, 'so give us three bunches for a bob.'

'Bless yer, sir,' said the delighted flower girl, 'you're me nicest gent. Me other one's ever such a good customer, but I like you best.' She wrapped the flowers, and Joe handed over a bob. 'You goin' to meet yer lady friend, sir?'

'Not now I've met you,' said Joe. 'Who could ask for more? Regards to your mum.'

Daisy laughed and Joe went on his way.

CHAPTER NINETEEN

Dolly, at supper with Joe, was having a serious think about her future. Joe asked what was on her mind.

'I've been thinking,' she said. 'You're right, that 'otel job would be a start for me, specially as I'll be livin' there as well. And seein' I've only worked as a skivvy and in fact'ries, I suppose a chambermaid's job is a bit of a step up. I'll start as soon as the manager says I can 'ave the job, so I'll be sayin' goodbye to you tomorrow mornin'.'

'What d'you mean, goodbye?' asked Joe.

'Well, it'll be nice for you, gettin' your bed back. You've been swell about that, you've 'ardly grumbled at all.'

'Never mind that,' said Joe, 'what's all this goodbye stuff? You're not going to Australia, just to a London hotel. I'll come and see you, if only to make sure there's no backsliding going on.'

'No, it's best to say goodbye,' said Dolly, pushing food around her plate.

'Now look here, Private Smith—'

'No, once I'm in work, you see, and can really hold me 'ead up, I can start seein' Angus again.'

'Who the hell's Angus?' asked Joe.

'Oh, I never told you about him, did I? Well, I couldn't. I mean, when a girl's starvin' and nearly in rags, she can't talk about 'er young man. I met Angus when I was doin' some part-time work at a Bermondsey fact'ry. He was a clerk in the office, and a really nice bloke. Angus Dodds. It's a funny name, Angus, but nice, though.'

'Scottish,' said Joe.

'Is it? I wish I'd 'ad an education like you, Joe, so that

I'd know about things. Anyway, Angus took a fancy to me – in a respectable way, mind – and we started goin' steady together. His fam'ly lived near Bermondsey, where I 'ad me lodgings. In Rotherhithe, that was where his 'ome was. Then me job packed up and me hard times began again. I could 'ardly keep body and soul together. I just couldn't get another job, and me landlady chucked me out for owin' rent. I pawned all me belongings and 'ad enough shillings to rent another room for a bit, but all me clothes were that shabby I 'ad fits every time I saw meself in a mirror. Angus offered to lend me some money to tide me over, but me pride wouldn't let me take it. I stopped goin' out with 'im, I said I'd go and try me luck elsewhere. Well, I knew his mum didn't want 'im goin' out with a girl as shabby as I was, although she'd never 'eld it against me that I'd come out of an orphanage and didn't 'ave any fam'ly. I got a room in Camberwell, I 'ad just enough money for a week's rent, but I still couldn't get a job, and when I was three weeks owin' with the rent, me new landlady, she chucked me out too and kept what belongings I 'ad left. That was the night when you bumped into me in the fog and knocked me over, and, well, you know the rest. But now I'm goin' to start work in that 'otel I can go and see Angus, specially as you've seen to it that I'm not shabby any more. I'm ever so grateful, Joe, honest I am, and I'll never forget 'ow kind you've been. But a girl my age 'as got to go back to a young man she's fond of.'

'I'm fond of you myself, Dolly,' said Joe wryly.

'Oh, I ain't the girl for you, Joe. Me and Angus are more suited, like, and you could get to marry a real lady, you could.'

I've got problems, thought Joe. I've got Dolly going off to cuddle up to some bloke called Angus, sod him, and I've got to get off this forgery lark. And it's time the police laid their mitts on Blackbeard, a walking menace to the population.

'Well, I'll still look you up sometimes, Dolly.'

'No, you'd best not, Joe,' said Dolly, and pushed her half-eaten meal aside. 'If Angus still feels the same about me, it wouldn't be fair on 'im to let another bloke call on me.'

'Don't like it, but I suppose I'll have to lump it,' said Joe. He had a sour feeling that he'd like to dump Angus in the river, nice bloke though he was.

At nine-thirty the next morning, Dolly and Joe were in the Beavises' kitchen, and Dolly was saying goodbye to Mrs Beavis.

'You've been ever so kind,' she said, 'you and Joe 'ave both helped me get on me feet again.'

'It's been a pleasure, ducky,' smiled the landlady, 'and it's more of a pleasure knowin' you're goin' to a job that's givin' you board and lodgin' as well as wages an' tips. Mind, it's Sergeant Joe you've got to thank more than me. Still, I did enjoy the nice chats we 'ad. You sure she's got all she needs, Sergeant Joe?'

'Well, she's fully dressed,' said Joe, 'and she's got the rest of her stuff in that case you found for her last night. And she's got her head on.'

'She'll need that all right,' said Mrs Beavis, 'I wouldn't want to start work up West meself without me own 'ead.'

'I'll manage,' said Dolly, who looked as if this wasn't one of her better days.

'Fancy you and Miss Fay-it both goin',' said Mrs Beavis. 'You could of knocked me down with a feather when Sergeant Joe come an' told me she'd gone.'

'She left 'im a note,' said Dolly.

'What a funny woman,' said Mrs Beavis. 'Still, Charlie says all the French is funny. 'Ere, would yer like to take something to eat with yer, Dolly? I could easy make yer an 'am sandwich or wrap up a slice of cake and an apple, if yer'd like. You don't want to get faint for lack of nourishment.'

'Thanks ever so, but I'll be all right,' said Dolly, 'and I'd best be on me way now. It's been really nice knowin' you. Give me regards to all your fam'ly.'

'Good luck, lovey, come an' see us sometimes,' said Mrs Beavis.

Joe saw Dolly to the front door.

'Sure you don't want me to come with you?' he asked.

'Thanks, but I can manage,' she said.

'Well, if you don't get the job, come back here,' said Joe. 'And if hard luck hits you again, don't forget where I live.'

'Yes. Yes, all right.' Dolly wouldn't look at him. 'You've been swell to me, Joe, I won't never forget. Goodbye.' She was out of the door quickly then, and Joe thought she was making sure he didn't get a chance to kiss her. He stepped outside and watched her hurrying up the Butts to the Elephant and Castle. Her foot was all right, she had no limp. And she had her cockney resilience. With a job and a young man, there'd be no need for her to go nicking wallets again.

A young man passed by on the other side of the street, whistling to himself. It was Rodney Masters, presently keeping an eye on the house. Joe, with Dolly nearing the junction, was about to step back into the passage when he spotted a man emerging from a shop. The man, in a coat and bowler hat, began to follow in Dolly's footsteps. Dolly turned the corner. So did he, moments later.

Joe ran. Rodney Masters glanced over his shoulder, watched the running lodger for a few seconds, then strolled on. A running lodger was no concern of his, unless of the female sex and answering a certain description.

Joe threw his gammy leg about as he hared towards the Elephant and Castle. People at the junction stared at him as he turned the corner. He saw Dolly entering the

London Road. The man, about eight yards behind her, followed on. Joe had to wait for a tram to grind into St George's Road before he could cross to the corner of London Road. The awkward gait of a man with a gammy leg going at a run drew more stares. Joe just kept on. Turning into London Road, he saw Dolly standing a few yards on the far side of the tram stop. She was waving to the driver of an oncoming hansom cab, which meant she was going to treat herself again instead of waiting for a tram.

Blackbeard was standing directly behind her, the width of the pavement between them. Joe recognized him at once. The man's eyes were fixed on Dolly's back. Joe, quite sure he was capable of shooting her in broad daylight and then losing himself in the maze of streets around the Elephant and Castle, still kept going, his stiff leg swinging. The hansom cab pulled up, and Blackbeard saw Joe then, coming straight at him. Either his instincts or his recognition of Joe activated him. He turned and ran, strongly and at speed. Joe went after him, and Blackbeard disappeared into Princess Street. Dolly, blissfully unaware, gave her destination to the cabbie and stepped up into the cab. She pulled the door to and away the cab went.

Joe pulled up at the entrance to Princess Street, watching Blackbeard crossing to the corner, still running strongly. He disappeared again, this time into St George's Road. Knowing he had no hope of catching him, Joe wheeled round in time to see the hansom cab already well past him, going north-west to the river.

There was some consolation, since whether or not Blackbeard had been thinking of shooting her – he had had his right hand in his overcoat pocket – he would certainly have followed her. Dolly was safe from all that now, she was out of the Butts for good, and Blackbeard had no hope of tracing her.

Joe limped back to his lodgings. He had done the right thing in helping Dolly find a job and a new abode. Yet he didn't feel all that damned happy about losing her. Especially not to another bloke, name of Angus Dodds. Well, he thought, I'm going to keep an eye on you, Dolly, in some way or other. You need keeping an eye on. You're a bit scatty and you can't even cook.

He worked all through the morning. He felt in a hurry now to complete this commission and get it over with.

Mrs Beavis went shopping. That made the house sound very quiet. Too quiet. There was no Dolly.

'Well?' said Tubby, when he arrived to relieve Rodney Masters in the afternoon.

'All I can say is that my feet are complaining.'

'Dear oh dear, me 'eart bleeds for yer,' said Tubby. 'Put castor oil in yer socks.'

'What kind of a tip is that?' asked Rodney. 'My socks will stink.'

'So will yer plates of meat,' said Tubby, 'but they'll feel a lot better. Aside from that bit of news of no importance, has Mademoiselle Fayette put 'er pretty nose out-of-doors today?'

'Not while I've been here,' said Rodney, 'she's kept it under cover all morning.'

'Still lyin' low, is she? All day yesterday, all day today. What does that tell yer, sonny?'

'That she hasn't scarpered.'

'Or that she's expectin' someone, that she ain't quite sure when he'll turn up, and so she's waitin'? And meanwhile she's playin' French noughts and crosses with the male lodger?'

'Did something happen last night to make you think that?'

'Not from where I was keepin' watch,' said Tubby, 'which wasn't on the doorstep. Let's see, the landlady said

244

the male lodger brought an 'omeless girl to his lodgings one night. Is he partial to the ladies, I wonder?'

'The girl's left,' said Rodney, 'and for good, I think. She came out of the house just after half-nine this morning, carrying a suitcase. He was at the door. He went after her. Probably forgot to kiss her. He was back after ten minutes.'

''Old on,' said Tubby, viewing the house from the vantage point. 'Carryin' a suitcase? You sure it wasn't French Marcy?'

'Quite sure. She's dark. The girl's auburn. She was wearing a boater. That's not French Marcy's style, I'd say.'

'So that leaves our mademoiselle lodgin' nice and cosy next to the bloke that was once in the Army, or so his landlady said.' Tubby shifted his cap about. 'I'm Navy meself.'

'Is that relevant?' asked Rodney, amused.

'Senior Service, sonny, is 'ighly relevant. Well, it makes sense, the young lady leaving. The landlady said the Army bloke was just lookin' after her for a bit. Still, it's interestin'. I'm beginnin' to think more serious about – let's see, what was 'is name? Foster, that's it, Joe Foster. What's his carry-on? Has he got a job? Or might he be a special friend of Marcy's? Come to think of it, was there a special reason why she came to lodge 'ere?'

'That's it, thicken the plot,' said Rodney. 'It's your own worry for the rest of the day. I'm off home to Richmond.'

'Don't fall in the river,' said Tubby, 'you'll upset the tiddlers.'

He took a stroll along the Butts, chancing his arm. If he met the landlady she'd jump on him for telling her fairy stories about a census – if she recognized him under a cap instead of a bowler. He passed number twenty-one, and went on to Dante Road. There he idled about on the corner, filling his pipe and lighting it. A kid came up.

''Ere, mister, you the bookie's runner?'

'Wish I was, me young cock sparrer, then I'd know a bit about the gee-gees. Yer dad wants to place a bet for tomorrer, does he?'

'Course 'e don't, me mum don't let 'im 'ave no money for bettin',' said the kid. 'I just wanted to know 'ow fast you can run.'

Tubby, not losing sight of number twenty-one, said, 'Faster than you, so watch what comes out of yer north-and-south.'

The kid chatted to him. It helped Tubby to pass the time and to make him look like the kid's uncle, perhaps.

Joe went down to the shops during the afternoon, to buy a paper and something for his supper, and to have a break. Tubby, still idling about by the corner of Dante Road, was lighting his pipe. The kid, absent from school because he'd had measles, was still with him. Tubby glanced at the limping figure of the lodger who'd been out one night with French Marcy, and again wondered if he had any connection with the lady's suspicious activities.

Further, exactly what was French Marcy doing? She seemed to have gone to ground with a vengeance, she hadn't shown herself for a couple of days. Highly frustrating, that was, considering the forces of law and order required her to lead them to number one suspect.

Patience, Tubby me lad, patience.

Miss Henrietta Downes, having spent the afternoon in company with a gentleman friend whose pressing attentions had finally become a pain in the neck to her, entered her apartment in Kensington Square. It was huge and beautifully furnished. Her two servants, Cissie and Nell, were there. Nell's duties included cooking, and she had something to say about her kitchen responsibilities.

'Well, I just don't know, Miss 'Enrietta, that I don't.

246

All these comings and goings, if you don't mind me respectfully mentioning them, they make it so that I don't know when I'm to do cookin' and when I'm not. It's turning me grey.'

'Am I as shameful as that, Nellie?' said Henrietta, who had her own easy and unconventional ways with servants. If it had resulted in their responses being just as unconventional, she didn't mind a bit. In any case, they were the products of Aunt Amelia's household, and Aunt Amelia was more unconventional than anybody. 'Never mind, I shan't want to eat until about eight. I'm not hungry, anyway.'

'Not hungry?' Nell, a stout woman of thirty, was cast in the same mould as motherly bodies like Mrs Beavis. She couldn't bear anyone she was close to suffering from a lack of nourishment. The white front worn over her dark blue servant's dress quivered. 'But you've got to eat, Miss 'Enrietta.'

'Not a banquet,' said Henrietta, taking off her hat and pushing at her hair in front of her bedroom mirror. Her two servants gazed worriedly at her from the doorway.

'Now, Miss 'Enrietta, you know I only serve up what's enough to keep you 'ealthy,' said Nell.

'You used to eat like a horse most times, Miss 'Enrietta,' said Cissie.

'It grieves me to say that most times these days, Miss 'Enrietta, you're hardly here to eat at all,' said Nell.

'Well, I am out of my cot now, Nell,' said Henrietta. 'I'm an out-and-about young lady. Anything will do for me this evening. A sandwich with some coffee, if you like.'

'A – a sandwich, Miss 'Enrietta?' said Cissie, the maid-of-all-work.

'I don't think I 'eard you right, Miss 'Enrietta,' said Nell.

'Ham sandwich,' said Henrietta, 'that'll do.'

'Excuse me,' said Nell, her white front beset by more quivers, 'but it don't behove me to cook ham sandwiches, Miss 'Enrietta.'

'You make ham sandwiches,' said Cissie, 'you don't cook them.'

'Kindly keep your place,' said Nell. 'I happen to be speakin' of my profession, which was taught me in Lady Amelia's household, and which I am engaged in for Miss 'Enrietta. I cook dinners of an evening. Ham sandwiches do not happen to be a cooked dinner, nor are they a proper evening meal for Miss 'Enrietta. What would people think if I served up ham sandwiches for a young lady of her standin'? Accordingly, I will do braised kidneys for her.'

'Must you, Nell?' asked Henrietta.

'Yes, I must, Miss 'Enrietta, with a sole fillet to start with and a fresh pineapple dessert to follow, although that hardly amounts to enough for a five year old.'

'Oh, Lord,' breathed Henrietta, and made a face at herself in the mirror.

'What was that, Miss 'Enrietta?' asked Nell.

'Nothing,' said Henrietta.

'"Will you be dressin' for dinner, Miss 'Enrietta?' asked Cissie.

'No, Cissie, I can't be bothered.'

'Well!' Nell looked at Cissie. They looked at each other. 'What's come over her, Cissie?'

'Miss 'Enrietta, you sure you're all right?' asked Cissie.

'I'm getting a headache,' said Henrietta.

'Oh, I'll mix you a powder,' said Cissie.

'Stop fussing,' said Henrietta, 'just run a bath for me in ten minutes, there's a good girl.'

'Yes, Miss 'Enrietta,' said Cissie, and she and Nell left. In the airy kitchen, she said, 'I don't think she's very well, wantin' just a sandwich for her dinner.'

'It's the Hon Cedric,' said Nell decisively, 'he's her trouble. She's in love, that's what. All that gallivantin' about comes from him goin' off to Paris. Ever since he's been gone there's been all these comings and goings and playing up. No wonder she's gettin' a headache.'

'Poor Miss 'Enrietta,' said Cissie.

'We'll have to make sure she eats properly this evening,' said Nell, 'we don't want her gettin' undernourished as well as a headache.'

CHAPTER TWENTY

The police had still made no arrest in connection with the murder of the docker, Dan Pearson, although they had been able to interview the two young men seen talking to the victim outside the dock gates on the evening of the crime. The interview had come about because the young men volunteered for it, arriving at the Whitechapel police station to say that their landlady, talking to them about the murder, had shown them the man's photograph in a newspaper. They were Russian architectural students enjoying a sabbatical in London. Among other things they wanted to sketch scenes in the docks, and on the evening in question had simply asked one of the dockers if he could help them get a pass that would enable them to spend a day inside the docks. He said to come with them to a pub, where they could talk about it while enjoying some beer. They went with him, they enjoyed the beer very much and the atmosphere of the English pub, and he talked to them about the London docks and told them to meet him at the gates tomorrow at eight in the morning, and he'd see that they got the pass. They showed the police the many sketches they had made of various London buildings. They returned to their lodgings at about eight-fifteen after saying goodbye to the docker, and by then the fog was very thick. Their landlady would vouch for the fact that they stayed in their lodgings for the rest of the evening, and the good lady did just that when the police called on her.

Joe, however, was puzzled that there was no mention in the newspapers of a man with a black beard. Through the press the police usually let the public know details of witnesses or suspects they required to interview. A bald announcement that two Russian architectural students had been cleared of involvement was hardly relevant when set against the fact that he'd given Scotland Yard information that pointed to Blackbeard being the central figure. No sense in chasing the unimportant when they should have been scouring London for that Russian thug.

Wait a minute. The students were Russian too. That letter. From Ivan and Igor, and written to Boris. Scotland Yard had a copy of it, the copy he had made and sent to them. Well, not a copy, a translation. It was fishy from start to finish, and it connected two obvious students to Blackbeard. But the police had let them go.

Joe could only assume that Scotland Yard did not want Blackbeard to know they had information on him, and that they were keeping their investigation quiet in case he bolted. Joe would have liked to know the man was under lock and key. Blackbeard was quite aware that he and Dolly could be key witnesses in the event of a murder trial. Well, Dolly was out of the way now. So she was, and it was damned quiet without her. The place was as dull as ditchwater.

'Would you like some tea, Mr Sharp?' asked Sir Hubert.

'Well, guv, that's kind of yer,' said Tubby, seating himself.

Someone tapped on the inner door and a female civil servant entered carrying a tray bearing a teapot, a cup and saucer, a small jug of milk and a small bowl of sugar.

'Another cup, please, Miss Verney,' said Sir Hubert.

'Very well, sir.' Miss Verney placed the tray on the desk. 'With saucer?'

'If it's no bother,' said Sir Hubert.

'It's no bother,' said Miss Verney, a serious-looking lady, 'only a reminder, sir, that in this department we are, by habit and necessity, particular about details.'

'By habit, Miss Verney, you are particular about everything.'

'I do my modest best,' said Miss Verney, her seriousness unmasked by a little smile as she went in search of another cup and saucer.

'Women,' said Tubby.

'What about them, Mr Sharp?' asked Sir Hubert.

'Handfuls, guv, handfuls, if you don't mind me sayin' so.'

'Not at all,' said Sir Hubert, 'perhaps you'd like to make that point to Miss Verney.'

The lady in question returned with the cup and saucer and placed them on the tray. She glanced at Tubby.

'Nice weather we're 'aving, Miss Verney, if you like April showers,' he said.

'Dear me, yes, Mr Sharp, I'm exceptionally fond of April showers,' said Miss Verney, and departed.

Sir Hubert, milking the cups, said, 'You failed that test, Mr Sharp.'

'Purposely, guv,' said Tubby. 'In my experience it ain't wise to provoke any female handful. Thank you kindly,' he said, as he received his tea.

'You're here to bring me up-to-date, I presume?' said Sir Hubert.

'I'm confirming, guv, that them two students lodgin' in Bell Lane still 'appen to be actin' as innocent as a pair of crafty crooks. With the extra men you provided, they're bein' watched and tailed from early mornin' to midnight. To me regret, they ain't puttin' a foot wrong, they're still inspectin' the sights and makin' their sketches. Not one contact 'ave they made. As to French Marcy, guv, it breaks me 'eart to tell yer I think she's slipped us. Not 'aving caught a whiff of 'er perfume these last few days, one of your extra men enquired after lodgings, by means of which 'e was able to get the landlady to inform 'im there

252

was only one lodger in residence at the moment, a gent by the name of Joe Foster, said to be late of the Army, as I advised you previous, and maybe a link between French Marcy and number one.'

'So we've lost the woman?' said Sir Hubert.

'Temp'rary, guv, temp'rary,' said Tubby. 'Could we just put it that she ain't presently visible?'

'That seems fair,' said Sir Hubert.

'Might I respectfully suggest we think about takin' them students in?' said Tubby, relishing his hot tea. 'With French Marcy 'aving slipped us, how are we goin' to look if number one's Bell Lane mates disappear up an imported foreign chimney? Smack in the eye that would be, guv. Might be advisable if we took 'em in while we still know where they are.'

'On what grounds?' asked Sir Hubert.

'On the grounds they're up to no ruddy good,' said Tubby.

'The advantage or disadvantage of detaining them is under constant consideration,' said Sir Hubert. 'At the moment, I'd prefer it if you could find the lady again. If you're right, if this man Foster is a link, he may well lead you to her.'

'True, guv, true, specially as me suspicions concernin' said gent won't go away.'

'Then shall I leave it to you to take the appropriate action, Mr Sharp?'

'Very good, guv, I'll now keep partic'lar tabs on Mr Joe Foster.'

'I'm sure you will,' said Sir Hubert, and Tubby came to his feet.

'Might I enquire after the 'ealth of your niece, Miss 'Enrietta Downes, the young lady I regard with admiration but caution, guv?'

'Her health is excellent, Mr Sharp. She'll rejoin the Bell Lane team on Monday.'

''Eaven preserve 'er, guv, I was 'oping you had 'er locked up safe and sound.'

'A vain hope,' said Sir Hubert.

'She ain't taken up embroidery?'

'Her aunt doesn't believe in young ladies taking up embroidery unless it's their dearest wish.'

'Told you, guv, they're handfuls, all of 'em,' said Tubby.

'Well, you and I know that, Mr Sharp, and it probably bothers us a little. Unfortunately, they know it too, and it doesn't bother them in the least.'

'Understood, guv, understood. Well, I'll be on me way now. I'm still comf'tably accommodated by the finances you advanced.'

'I ask only that you find the lady again, Mr Sharp,' said Sir Hubert.

'She's on me mind, guv, and so is Mr Joe Foster,' said Tubby.

The following morning, Joe was on his way to Charing Cross Road again.

Tubby was on his tail and noting the carpet-bag he was carrying.

Marcelle was about to depart from her rented apartment in Kensington to reconnoitre the Mall, down which King George V and Queen Mary and the royal procession would drive on the way to the coronation on 22 June.

Rokovssky was in Trafalgar Square.

'Ah, good morning,' he said, and Daisy, the flower girl, turned and found herself looking into the smiling blue eyes of a bearded man as dark as a gypsy. The beard and the smile both helped to disguise the brutal ruggedness of his strong-boned face. His Homburg hat was lifted, disclosing a wealth of black hair. With his morning suit he wore spats, and he also carried a malacca cane.

'Oh, 'ello, sir,' said Daisy. The gentleman had become her best customer in his kind generosity.

'And what do you have for me this morning?' asked Rokovssky.

'Oh, I got vi'lets, daffs an' tulips, sir,' said Daisy, showing him her laden basket.

'I see, yes, I see.' Rokovssky smiled again. 'But how am I to choose, when they are all as pretty as you are?'

'Buy some of each, sir?' suggested Daisy with a perky smile.

'Of course. That is good, very good. What is your name? I have seen you how many times? Seven? Or even eight? And you have not told me your name.'

'Well, you ain't asked me, sir. It's Daisy, Daisy Watts.'

'Daisy? So, you are a flower yourself.' Rokovssky was in excellent form. 'I will buy as you said, some of each.' He would throw them away later, as he had with all the flowers he had bought from her.

Daisy picked out a selection. An itinerant photographer, his camera complete with a developing agent and fixed to a tripod, saw his chance. He planted the tripod. The picture of a well-dressed customer and one of London's flower girls would surely make an irresistible souvenir photograph for the customer, especially if he happened to be a visitor. With the tripod firm, he focused the camera. The flower girl was ready to hand the selection over, the customer fishing for money. The photographer's head dived under the black cloth. Rokovssky, giving Daisy a florin, became aware of the camera.

'No!' he said sharply. He never allowed himself to be photographed.

Too late.

'Got yer, sir,' grinned the photographer, head reappearing. 'Good shot this'll be. Souvenir of Trafalgar Square. Be ready in a few minutes. Just a tanner, sir. Sixpence.'

Rokovssky's inclination was to smash the camera. But there were people around, too many of them. And not far away was a policeman, a policeman who was advancing with the measured tread common to the British constabulary. He was eyeing Rokovssky with interest.

'Give the photograph to the girl,' said the Russian, finding a sixpence. 'I am in a hurry.' He handed the sixpence over, nodded to Daisy and walked away at a fast pace. The constable trod leisurely on.

'Come on, then, Bill, let's 'ave the photo,' said Daisy.

'Couple of ticks, Daisy,' said the photographer, and waited for the print to develop in the little enamel tray of liquid. It was ready in a short while, a sepia photograph of the flower girl and her gentleman customer. It was an excellent likeness of Daisy and a highly recognizable one of Rokovssky.

'Well, bless me,' said Daisy, 'ain't yer taken a good one, Bill?'

'Worth a bob, that is, Daisy.'

'Don't come it,' said Daisy.

'There you are, George, that's the lot,' said Joe. He and George were in the back room of the bookshop. On the shop door was a notice. *'Back in ten minutes, closed until then.'*

'The complete works?' said George, studying the contents of the files that had come from Joe's carpet-bag.

'I burned some midnight oil,' said Joe.

'So what do we have, our own perfect conclusion to the Italian affairs of Byron, Shelley and their ladies?' asked George.

'I'll leave you to be the judge of that.'

'My dear fellow, I am, as always, brimming with confidence in you, and beg you'll accept a small advance of ten guineas against what I happily predict will be a small fortune. Allowing for necessary expenses, I shouldn't be surprised if we end up pocketing a little over two hundred pounds each. What d'you say to that, old chap?'

'That it's time we called it a day,' said Joe.

'Is that how you feel?' asked George.

'I feel that if we don't we'll come unstuck.'

'You're a man of commonsense, Joe, and I've always said you must be the one to decide. You don't think we should end our partnership with a great flourish, a Shakespearian one as I suggested?'

'We'd both be off our rockers if we tried that.'

George, examining some of the letters with unconcealed delight, said, 'But the temptation, old man.'

'Bloody frightening,' said Joe.

'You can resist it?'

'Easily. I want to buy a little house and settle down, George. I've applied to the Army for a job as a recruiting sergeant.'

'A recruiting sergeant?' George clutched his forehead. 'Never, my dear fellow, I won't hear of it. Don't you realize that with your talent you could inscribe manuscripts and make each a thing of beauty? That would earn you far more than a recruiting sergeant. There's also the copying of manuscripts for museums and the like. Allow me to put you in touch with such prospects.'

'Good of you, George, but I'd rather be put in touch with a landowner who could find me employment as a gamekeeper or who has a string of horses that I could help to look after.'

'Bless my soul,' said George, 'you've a hankering to be a country yokel?'

'I've a feeling I'd like to work in the fresh air,' said Joe.

'Damn me,' said George, 'I'm not sure that fresh air pays well, but I'll look into it for you. Fortunately, there are a few country squires who like good literature. It's a moot point, however, as to whether they see me as a tradesman or a gentleman. I can reach their ears, certainly, but will any of them favour me by finding a position for you? Horses, by Jove, yes, of course. You spent your Army years on horses. We'll see, Joe, we'll see.'

'You're not a gentleman, George, any more than I am,' said Joe. 'We're a couple of fly birds. But you're a good bloke, all the same, and I'm obliged to you for offering help. By the way, have you heard how Dolly's getting on at the Imperial?'

'What?' said George. 'You must know more about that than I do. She's still with you, isn't she?'

'What're you talking about?' asked Joe.

'All I know is that she didn't turn up. I dropped in to see my friend the manager on my way home last night. Just to ask after her, you know, and to find out if she was doing a good job for him. Alas, she ducked it, Joe. I don't think she favoured being a chambermaid. Haven't you seen her?'

Joe ground his teeth.

'That girl's had a relapse,' he said.

'A relapse?' said George. 'Good God, she's not a mental case, is she?'

'She will be when I get my hands on her again,' said Joe. 'I'll lock her up.'

Outside, Tubby was keeping himself to himself, and indulging in a reflective monologue.

'Something goin' on here, Tubby me lad. Mr Joe Foster, who knows French Marcy, arrives at this 'ere bookshop and what 'appens? Out comes a customer a minute later and up goes a notice sayin' the place is closed for ten minutes. What for, I wonder, eh? As the guv would say, what is the precise nature of Mr Foster's work and the precise reason for 'is private meetin' with a bookshop proprietor? In other words, is Mr Foster deep into skulduggery? 'Ave we got an Anglo-Russky plot? There's a plot all right, I'll lay to it. The guv suspects it, and I'm bettin' on it. I think I'll 'ave to talk to Mr Foster.'

The shop door opened then, the notice was removed, and out of the corner of his eye Tubby saw his latest suspect shaking hands with a portly gent. His carpet-bag was depending from his left hand. That could hold a decent-sized bomb, thought Tubby.

Joe began his walk to Trafalgar Square. He was thinking of Dolly. What on earth had got into her? Why hadn't she said she wasn't going after the chambermaid's job? She always had plenty to say for herself in the frankest way. Had she thought she could last out on what she had left of that ten pounds until she found some other job? She might well have thought she could do better for herself now that she didn't look like a ragbag. In fact, she might well have gone straight to Angus Dodds, seeing how attached to him she was. His family might even have taken her in on account of her new ladylike look. A ragbag, no. An attractive young lady, yes. The alternative was wandering again in search of lodgings and a job. Twenty to one that's where she was, with her young gent and his family. Where was it she said he lived? Rotherhithe, yes, next to Bermondsey.

Joe stopped to look at a shop window. He mused on its offerings. Then he retraced his steps for a short distance and addressed Tubby, who had come to a halt on the kerb and was looking as if he intended to cross the road.

'I keep seeing you,' said Joe.

A pained look wrinkled Tubby's round and pleasant face.

'You sure?' he said. It was a blow to his pride as a shadow.

'I'm bloody certain,' said Joe. 'You've been following me. What's your game?'

'I must be losin' me touch,' said Tubby. 'That's grievous to me, I can tell yer.'

'You were in Newington Butts the other day,' said Joe. 'Now you're here. So come on, what's your game, tosh?'

'Where'd you get that gammy leg of yours?' asked Tubby.

'Where'd you get that interfering conk of yours?' asked Joe.

'Army bloke, are yer? I'm Navy meself.'

'You're not now,' said Joe, 'you're just treading on my toes. Speak up, Fatty, or I'll tread on yours.'

'I don't regard meself as fat, just well-covered,' said Tubby. 'Tell yer what, let's walk, shall we? It makes the pavement look untidy, standin' about.'

'Suits me,' said Joe, and resumed his limping walk, Tubby beside him.

'Well now, Mr Joe Foster—'

'You know me, do you?' said Joe. Since bumping into Dolly in the fog, things had been happening. Odd things.

'I've 'eard of you, Mr Foster,' said Tubby, 'and I've also 'eard you're acquainted with a French lady, name of Marcelle Fayette.'

'Just who are you?' asked Joe.

'I can't tell yer the exact story of me life,' said Tubby, 'but I can tell yer me monicker's William Sharp and that I've got certain legal duties which make it proper for me to ask you personal questions, like who yer mum is, what yer father does, and who was that lady I saw yer with one night. That's a line in a well-known song, of course, but it gives yer the gen'ral idea.'

'Are you a copper?' asked Joe.

'Well, no, I ain't, Mr Foster. I could say I was, but I ain't. But you can believe I'm an approved up'older of the King's law.'

'D'you mean Parliament's?'

'I don't go much on Parliament,' said Tubby, 'but I'm for His Majesty. I'd be obliged if you'd answer a few questions, matey. It would save me 'aving to ask the coppers to run you in.'

'What's on your mind?' asked Joe. There was a lot on his own, including forgery. Had some special department of the law caught up with him? It wasn't unlikely, seeing this sharp-eyed bloke had been waiting outside George's bookshop for him. Had they both been found out?

'Well, Marcelle Fayette, she's on me mind,' said Tubby. The lady had not put in any appearance at Bell Lane since disappearing from the Butts. 'Now I ask yer first off, Mr Foster, where is she?'

'No idea,' said Joe.

'That ain't much of an answer,' said Tubby.

'It's all I can give you.'

Tubby looked at his man. Joe returned the look, and with interest. Tubby knew about people, especially those who had something to hide. And however much most of them tried to hide it, it showed as plain on their faces as a black eye. Mr Joe Foster didn't seem to show very much except curiosity.

'I'm inclined to believe yer, Mr Foster. Flew the coop, did she?'

'Hardly,' said Joe, 'she wasn't a bird in a cage. She simply left.'

'You knew the lady well, did yer, Mr Foster?'

'Hardly,' said Joe again. 'I met her for the first time a couple of weeks ago, when she applied to my landlady for lodgings.'

'That's a fact?'

'It's a fact,' said Joe.

'On the other hand,' said Tubby, 'did she apply by arrangement?'

'Not with my landlady, nor with me.'

'Straight up?' said Tubby.

'On the level,' said Joe.

'What did yer think of 'er?'

'Bit of a French handful,' said Joe, which struck a chord with Tubby, who grinned.

'Handful, eh?' he said. 'Ain't they all?'

'Some are, I suppose,' said Joe. Dolly was. Needed her bottom smacking.

'You took the lady out one evening, didn't yer, Mr Foster?'

'None of your business,' said Joe.

'Just a sociable outin', was it?' asked Tubby.

'Music hall, if you must know.'

'You're a mite short on 'elpful information, yer know.'

'Well, hard luck,' said Joe. 'Hold on a moment, I need some flowers for my landlady's daughters.' They had reached Trafalgar Square, and Daisy had seen him. She was waving. Joe went across and bought a dozen tulips from her, simply because he liked her. She was typical in every way of London's cheerful cockneys.

'Bless yer, sir,' she said.

'Bless you too, Daisy.'

'You're nice, you are, sir. Oh, I 'ad me photo took yesterday, with me other kind gentleman customer. Would yer like to see it?'

'Give us a butcher's,' said Joe, taking time off from being interrogated.

Daisy reached into the capacious pocket of her apron and brought out a stout envelope. From it she extracted the sepia print and showed it to Joe. He stared. Even without Dolly here to confirm it, he knew he was looking at a likeness of Blackbeard, just as he had known he'd been staring him in the face on the occasion when the man had followed Dolly into the London Road.

'Don't yer think it's a nice one of me?' asked Daisy with enthusiasm. Joe didn't reply. 'Sir? Don't yer like it?'

'Like it?' Joe came to. 'Peach of a photograph, Daisy. That's you right enough, best-looking flower girl in Trafalgar Square. And that's your gentleman, is it?'

'Oh, he ain't my gentleman,' said Daisy, 'just a kind customer that pays very gen'rous for me flowers.'

'What's his name?' asked Joe, still trying to adjust to the unexpected.

'Dunno 'is name,' said Daisy. ''E just comes an' buys reg'lar from me.'

'Well, I'll see you again,' said Joe. 'Hang on to the photograph, it's a first-class one of you.'

'Goodbye, sir, an' thanks.'

'I'm Joe,' he said, and returned to the man who called himself an approved upholder of the King's law, a strange title for a cockney bloke who looked a bit like Mr Pickwick.

'Tulips, I see,' said Tubby genially.

'Yes, four each for my landlady's three daughters,' said Joe.

'Ladies' man, are yer, Mr Foster?'

'Not so's anyone would notice,' said Joe.

'Are yer sure you can't put me in touch with French Marcy?'

'Who?'

'Mademoiselle Marcelle Fayette, your French friend,' said Tubby.

'Come off it,' said Joe. 'Look, what's all this about?' He was beginning to feel things weren't going in his favour, even if they didn't concern his dubious business relationship with George.

'Well, Joe,' said Tubby in matey fashion, 'I ain't at liberty to tell yer much except I'm duty-bound to 'ave a talk with 'er. What d'yer do for a livin', Joe? Don't mind if I call you Joe, do yer?'

'Can't say I mind all that much, but I could say that what I do for a living is my own affair.'

'Yes, you could say that,' said Tubby affably, 'except I'm askin' on behalf of law and order.'

'That's your story,' said Joe.

'Take my word for it,' said Tubby, 'then we'll get along like we was born to be mates. So what d'yer do for a livin'?'

'Odd jobs, anything that's going,' said Joe, 'including writing business letters for a friend of mine, the owner of the bookshop I've just visited.' He and George had an arrangement if questions were ever asked. George had several suitable letters in a drawer, stock letters offering certain customers lists of books available for sale.

'Good at writin', are you, then?' asked Tubby.

That was getting near the mark, thought Joe.

'Good enough for my friend to make use of me,' he said, 'although it's his opinion that typewritten letters are going to put an end to handwritten ones. At the moment, I'm existing partly on my savings, so I've recently applied to the Army for a job as a recruiting sergeant. I was a sergeant with the 2nd Dragoon Guards.'

'That lot, eh?' said Tubby. 'Well, good on yer, mate, even if I'm a Navy man meself. Would yer like to tell me why the bloke that runs the bookshop shuts it up when you call about the business letters you write?'

'Give over,' said Joe, 'he just likes a little privacy when going through my work, and I like a little privacy when I'm being paid for it. And it's only for ten minutes or so.'

'Only askin',' said Tubby. 'Anyway, next time you see Marcy Fayette, find out where she's livin' and let me know.'

'Don't make me laugh,' said Joe.

'Well, she might turn up for a bit more of the old music hall stuff,' said Tubby, eyeing the hustle and bustle of Trafalgar Square thoughtfully. 'Come an' see me. Seventeen Penton Place, Kennington. If I'm not in, leave a note. I'm keen on 'aving a talk with 'er.'

'That's your affair, not mine,' said Joe. 'I like to mind my own business. I can think of better things to do than poking my nose in where it's not wanted. No offence, of course.'

'None taken,' said Tubby. 'What's in yer carpet-bag, Joe?'

'Oh, a few million quid,' said Joe, 'I've just robbed the bookshop.'

Tubby chuckled.

'Then yer won't need that job as a recruitin' sergeant, will yer?' he said.

'I need my brains testing for going along with all your questions,' said Joe. 'If you must know, there's nothing in this bag. What there was were a number of letters I've written for my friend about available books, and I've just delivered them. Want to put your hooter in the bag?'

'No, take yer word for it,' said Tubby, 'and I'm pleased to 'ave met yer. Sergeant in the 2nd Dragoons, eh? You've soldiered right enough. So long, matey, don't forget me address if you run into French Marcy again.' And Tubby turned about and walked away. Not an unlikeable bloke, Mr Joe Foster, he thought, but still worth keeping an eye on. He might have only met French Marcy for the first time a couple of weeks ago, and he might not. If I don't lay me mitts on her soon, I'll lose me standing with the guv. So we'll have to keep our eyes on you, Joe, in the hope you'll lead us to that French female handful.

Joe had a thoughtful walk home. Life was mucking him about. Dolly had not only departed, she'd played him up as well. Blackbeard had become a kind of ugly Jack-in-the-box, and Marcelle had turned out to be a bit of a dubious element, a woman who had provoked the interest of the forces of law and order, if the word of that tubby gent was the gospel truth. Somehow, Joe thought it was. He also thought that having been mucked about by events he was entitled to a bit of peace and quiet. Instead, along had come the tubby bloke to ask him the kind of questions that made him feel he was suspected of being a law-breaking associate of Marcelle.

Yes, there was something fishy about Marcelle. He remembered again what she had said about Dolly. *Ah, the poor one you found in that very dreadful fog.* That had to mean she'd been in London at the time, yet she'd said the day she arrived at the Beavis house was the day she arrived from France. Yes, very fishy.

As for Daisy's photograph of herself and Blackbeard, that was something that ought to be sent to Scotland Yard.

What a life, he thought, and he bought himself a tasty pork pie from Merritt's cooked-meat shop near the Elephant and Castle, and ate it in his room with some pickle and a tomato while wondering about Dolly.

He was missing Dolly, who, for some reason, had virtually done a bunk.

CHAPTER TWENTY-ONE

'Concernin' our number one, guv,' said Tubby a few days later.

'The gentleman known as Boris?' said Sir Hubert. A letter that had come into his possession had given details of a man with a black beard who had been seen in company with a docker, Dan Pearson, on the night the latter was murdered. Also enclosed had been a letter, purported to be translated from Russian, that had given the names of four people. Boris the recipient, Ivan and Igor the signatories, and a woman called Alexandra Petrovna. Sir Hubert had not taken long to realize Ivan and Igor were the assumed names of the students Gregor Palovich and Peter Czernov. The woman Alexandra Petrovna was undoubtedly Marcelle Fayette, and Boris, of course, was the man with the black beard, the one to whom the letter had been carried by the docker who was subsequently murdered.

'Yes, 'e's our number one, guv,' said Tubby. 'Regret to report we've 'ad no luck. French Marcy hasn't led us to 'im, because we still 'aven't copped 'er, and them two students still keep leadin' us nowhere. Might I suggest bringing them in and allowin' me to break their legs to make 'em talk?'

'That could be powerfully persuasive, Mr Sharp, but a little uncivilized,' said Sir Hubert. 'Shall we continue being patient? Yes, I think so. Now, regarding Mr Joe Foster, whom you talked to a few days ago. He has indeed served with the 2nd Dragoon Guards, for eleven years and with distinction. However, that doesn't necessarily mean his association with Marcelle Fayette is innocent.'

267

'Quite agree, guv,' said Tubby. 'I still fancy 'e might be a go-between, in which case 'e could be usin' that bookshop as a kind of letter-box. Said shop and proprietor, name of Singleton, require lookin' into.'

'It's Singleton's Bookshop?' said Sir Hubert. 'No, I know the proprietor, and we can discount any possibility that he'd allow his premises to be used for clandestine purposes.'

'You got me there, guv, unless you mean dubious,' said Tubby.

'I do.'

'You're a customer of 'is?'

'I am.'

'Good enough, guv,' said Tubby, 'I note accordin' that Mr Singleton is to be classed as an innocent party.'

'You may further note, Mr Sharp, that Marcelle Fayette's description is now known to all members of this department.'

'Very good, guv. We need eyes all over the place. But it's me fond 'ope that mine'll spot 'er first on account of 'aving to make up for me grievous humiliation. I'm also layin' fond 'opes on 'aving Mr Joe Foster lead us to 'er.'

'Yes, that's still a possibility.'

'Before I go, guv, I confirm your young lady niece, Miss Downes, is standin' daytime watch at Bell Lane again.'

'She won't let us down,' said Sir Hubert.

'Well, with all due respect, guv, might I repeat she'd be a sight better off if you bought 'er some wool an' some knittin' patterns?'

'I doubt if she'd think so, Mr Sharp.'

'Just thought I'd mention it,' said Tubby.

'Quite,' said Sir Hubert.

'I think I'll trot off to Newington Butts now, guv.'

'Good luck, Mr Sharp.'

Tubby's journey was fruitless, however.

Joe was in Rotherhithe, close to the Surrey Docks. The residential area was a mixture of large old houses, compressed terraced dwellings and ageing slums. Families fought the poverty trap year in, year out. Unwashed and ragged kids, who should have been at school, were out on the streets playing truant in defiance of the certainty that they'd get their ears clipped or suffer a walloping when their dads found out. Cleaner and not so ragged kids under school age played in the better-looking streets, and here and there mums were seen whitening their doorsteps. Joe gave the slums a miss, feeling quite sure that Angus Dodds and his family weren't as far down the ladder as that.

In Albion Street, he made his opening enquiries.

'Morning, missus,' he said to a woman standing at her open front door, 'd'you happen to know of a family called Dodds?'

'What's that, mister? Dobbs?'

'Dodds.'

'You a copper?' asked the woman, a shawl around her shoulders.

'No, just a bloke,' said Joe.

'Coppers is aggravatin',' said the woman.

'So I've heard,' said Joe.

'So's my old man,' said the woman. 'Still, I can't say you look like that. A fam'ly name of Dodds, did yer say? Never 'eard of no Dodds round 'ere, but there's a Mrs 'Obbs at number ten. She's a young widder, and I know she'll be pleasured to see yer, she don't often get fellers like you callin'. Wait a bit, you ain't a tally man, are yer? There's more tally men creepin' up round 'ere than there's 'ot dinners.'

'No, I'm not a tally man, missus.'

'Well, I'm glad for yer, it ain't decent creepin' up on honest bodies that ain't been able to pay off what they've 'ad to 'ave on tick. You go an' see Mrs 'Obbs, she might be able to 'elp yer, an' she'll be downright 'appy to invite you in.'

'Don't think I've got time to be invited in,' said Joe, 'but thanks for mentioning it.'

He had similar conversations in other streets. Hard-working, hard-up housewives were only too willing to turn his enquiry into a chat and a gossip, and even if they didn't know where any Dodds family lived, most of them seemed to know where a hopeful widow hung out. Joe was a personable man, and since he liked cockneys he was always ready to lend an ear. One lady took a distinct fancy to him and kept off widows.

'Dodds?' she said. 'No, I can't say I know any Dodds, but me old man might be able to 'elp yer, 'im bein' a dustman. Well, 'e gets around streets I ain't never 'eard of meself. Would yer like to come in an' wait, 'e usually pops in for a bite at midday. I'll show yer me weddin' photo, if yer like, an' some I 'ad took on me 'oneymoon at Margate, when I was ridin' a donkey in me best goin'-away petticoat. Only you remind me of me 'usband's best man, who fancied me a bit.'

'Well, I like the look of ladies' petticoats, missus, believe me I do,' said Joe, 'especially going-away ones, but I'm a bit pressed for time.'

He managed to extricate himself from that kind of cockney friendliness without giving offence. He spent more than two hours making enquiries all over Rotherhithe, but no-one was able to point him at a young gent called Angus Dodds, or any Dodds. He called in at the town hall, but drew a blank there too. He could only think scatter-brained Dolly had been vaguely approximate in saying Rotherhithe. Well, if he couldn't find Angus, he was pretty sure he wasn't going to find her, either. It didn't do him much good, the feeling that she'd slipped out of his life.

Marcelle was lying low in Kensington. She had fully reconnoitred the killing ground, and she spent time each day studying newspapers for signs that the police were expecting to make an arrest in regard to Rokovssky's murder of a London docker. What a fool was the man who considered himself omnipotent. He had put the venture in danger by an act of bad-tempered foolishness. Joe Foster would never have committed such an idiotic murder.

Marcelle smiled into her mirror as the image of Joe entered her mind. Should she risk seeing him again? He was so diverting, and doing nothing was boring. Should she let him make love to her, knowing as she did that she had been ordered to kill him? Even though her role in the mission was the most responsible one, Rokovssky was the team's leader and she was under his orders.

Before the day of the assassination arrived, she had to collect the weapon from an armourer. Apart from that, there was nothing to do.

Except, perhaps, to see the man with a limp, the man who had once been a soldier and was now undoubtedly an agent of some kind.

Marcelle smiled again.

Rokovssky appeared again in Trafalgar Square. His thick body made a bruising advance on Daisy.

'Buy me sweet tulips, sir?' she smiled.

'Ah, more tulips, Daisy my flower?' said Rokovssky.

Daisy recognized his voice. She didn't recognize the man. All that was left of his face hair was a narrow black moustache. She stared. His prominent blue eyes were bright, his teeth moistly gleaming.

'Oh, it's you yerself, sir,' she said, 'you've been and lost yer beard.'

'True, true, I have been barbered this morning,' said the fanatical Tsarist. 'That is what you say, barbered?'

'Well, you've been to the barber's all right, sir,' said Daisy, 'and 'e's done an 'andsome job on yer, I must say. 'E's made yer look years younger.'

Rokovssky laughed. The sound came rumbling up from his chest like the beginnings of a benevolent avalanche.

'What, I am now young and handsome?' he said.

'Oh, you're a catch, you are, sir,' said Daisy, even if she thought Joe, her other kind customer, much more appealing to a girl. This man, without his beard, had a swarthy face that sort of missed its hairy covering. Joe had a brown healthy-looking face, and a lovely moustache. ''Ave yer come for some tulips, sir? Tulips is all I've got left in me basket.'

'I shall not go away without some. Ah, but the photograph, was it good or was it a fraud?'

'Oh, it's ever so good, sir. Look.' Daisy took out the brown envelope. She was so taken with the print that she'd been carrying it about with her to show Trafalgar Square friends and acquaintances. She'd shown it to a bobby, one who always treated her in a fatherly fashion, and he'd said something about Goldilocks and a black bear. Now she showed it to her kind customer. His teeth gleamed again as his mouth split in a smile.

'Ah, very good, Daisy, very good. The best of the flower girls of London, yes? Yes. I will have a copy made, so that there is a print for you and a print for me. I will have yours put in a frame and bring it to you in a day or two. Yes?'

'Oh, can you get a copy done, sir?'

'Of course. I am a magician, and can do many things. Look, watch the photograph.' The print was in his gloved right hand. His hand waved and danced, and the photograph disappeared.

'Crikey, me photo, where's it gone?' gasped Daisy.

'Is it here?' Rokovssky dipped his hand into her basket. 'Ah.' Out came his hand and the photograph with it. Daisy laughed.

'Oh, you're a magician all right, sir.'

'I agree.' Rokovssky slipped the photograph into his jacket pocket. 'Now, some tulips, Daisy, if you please.'

Miss Henrietta Downes, arriving at her apartment after a long day out, let herself in. But she could not escape the sharp ears of Cissie, who met her in the hall and followed her to her bedroom.

'Miss 'Enrietta, look at you, still wearin' those things you went out in this morning. All day in them, and they're hardly becomin'.'

Henrietta was dressed rather like a dowdy lady clerk, in a black skirt, black jacket, plain white blouse and a limp black bow tie. On her head was a crown-shaped hat that didn't really suit her.

'Cissie, you're not complaining again, are you?'

'Miss 'Enrietta, you know it's not my place to complain, I'm just sayin', that's all. But goin' out lookin' like an 'ard-up lady clerk, well, I just have to say something.'

'Now, Cissie, don't give me the horrors,' said Henrietta. 'My outfit is very suitable for the City.'

It was entirely suitable for her surveillance brief in Whitechapel.

'Oh, lor', you 'aven't been in the City all day, 'ave you, Miss 'Enrietta?'

'Cissie, you know very well that my aunt, Lady Amelia, doesn't approve of single girls living an idle life.' Her Aunt Amelia was a Lady by birth, being the daughter of an earl. 'I've been enquiring about a job in a bank.'

Cissie shuddered.

'Miss 'Enrietta, I hope you're jokin'. It just wouldn't become you, and how could Nell and me live it down if you took to bein' a bank clerk? I couldn't even tell her, she'd 'ave a fit and give notice.'

'Oh, well, you know what the saying is, Cissie,' said Henrietta, discarding her hat and jacket and throwing

273

them on the bed. 'Women must work and men must go out in their ships.'

'I never 'eard that sayin',' declared Cissie, picking up the jacket with an air of distaste. 'Did you throw this on purpose, Miss 'Enrietta? Did you want me to give it to our road-sweeper for his wife?'

'Certainly not. I can't go to work in a bank wearing a silk dress and an ermine coat. Really, Cissie, all this fuss.'

'Well, I just don't know what to say to Nell – oh, did you see in the newspaper that the Hon'rable Cedric's come back from Paris?'

'Who?' Henrietta was gazing out of a window. That's it, thought Cissie, all that pretending she's not interested. 'Oh, the fashionable gentleman, you mean, Cissie.' Henrietta turned.

'Yes, he is 'ighly popular, isn't he, Miss 'Enrietta? I'll go and get the paper, he's got a paragraph all to 'imself and a photo as well.'

Cissie went to fetch the newspaper.

'Our young lady's come in, has she?' asked Nell, busy preparing dinner. 'What's she been doin' all day in those funny clothes she went out in?'

'She's been in the City.'

'All day in the City? A young lady like her that's been a debutante?' said Nell. 'I hope she didn't meet anyone we know, like Lord Clifford who owns a bank. I'll come over faint if she did. Lady Amelia's given me enough turns in me time with 'er funny ways, I hope I don't get turned into a nervous wreck by Miss 'Enrietta.'

'She's thinking of workin' in a bank,' said Cissie in a rush, and hurried out with the newspaper to the sound of a crash. Cook had dropped a plate.

Henrietta read the paragraph and looked at the photograph. It showed Cedric at his handsomest, and wearing his famed smile. She gazed out of the window again.

Oh, Lord, I think I'm in love. How ghastly.

274

CHAPTER TWENTY-TWO

Rokovssky was as good as his word. He returned the photograph to Daisy in a decorative white metal frame. That is, he returned half of it, the sepia image of Daisy alone, neatly cut out to fit into the frame, an oval one. He did not make the mistake of buying a silver frame. Daisy would have thought that a suspiciously expensive present. Like most cockney girls she had her head screwed on right. There were the other kind, of course, the fast kind who liked to have rich gentlemen friends and knew what was expected of them in return for expensive presents. Daisy wasn't one of them. She was happy enough with the metal frame and what it did for her photograph. But what about the copy, had he made a copy of all the photograph, like he'd said he would? Rokovssky assured her he had, and that that too had been framed. He would take it with him when he went home. Daisy asked where his home was, and he said in France, although he did not say he was French. Daisy assumed he was, however, and asked him what Paris was like. Paris, he said, was a city in which all the flower girls were pretty, but not as pretty as she was. Daisy told him he was pulling her leg. No, no, he said, he had a wife and children, and never touched the legs of any girls. Daisy giggled; he bought some bright French mimosa from her and they parted on smiling terms.

Joe turned up the next day, chatted to her, bought some flowers from her, and then asked if he could have another look at the photograph. Daisy said it was now on her bedroom mantelpiece at home, in a frame, and explained what had happened. Joe made a light remark about it, but his thoughts were far from light. He came to the obvious conclusion, that Blackbeard did not like having his photograph taken. Daisy had said he didn't seem very keen at the time, but he liked the photograph when he saw it later.

'Well, he's got a soft spot for you, Daisy, he was bound to like it.'

''E's French, yer know,' said Daisy.

'Is he?' said Joe, who was certain he wasn't.

''E told me so, and 'e talks with a sort of French accent.'

'Well, watch out for the oo-la-la stuff, Daisy.'

'Oh, yer a joker, you are, sir.'

'I'm Joe. So long, Daisy.'

Joe wrote another anonymous letter to the Police Commissioner, Scotland Yard, saying that further to his previous letter, the man with the black beard was frequently in Trafalgar Square, and could almost certainly be picked up there. He didn't mention Daisy, he was sure the police would make life complicated for her if he did. Trafalgar Square was enough.

Scotland Yard could make neither head nor tail of this very brief letter from a person unknown.

Both Sir Hubert and Tubby were convinced that Marcelle Fayette was still the most likely person to lead them to the man called Boris, the bearded man who had been in company with the murdered docker on the night of the crime, a crime that was apparently baffling the police, according to the newspapers. Marcelle Fayette had to be found. Accordingly, a night watch on Bell Lane was maintained, and that included a watch on the upstairs back room of the house next to the students' lodgings. For this purpose, the rented room in the house in Toynbee Street was still being used. The landlord of the house next to the students' lodgings had informed Tubby that the upstairs rooms had been rented for six months by a lady who gave her name as Alexandra Smith and who paid the full amount in advance. Tubby was interested in the information. Alexandra Smith was the Alexandra Petrovna mentioned in the letter of course, and both those names belonged to French Marcy, of course. Crafty French female she was, thought Tubby, and no error.

Ex-Army Sergeant Joe Foster was also being kept under surveillance, although more in hope than conviction, and not every day.

Time was going by. Joe, restless with inactivity, was about to go out for a long walk when he heard the sound of the front door opening and closing. Too early for Linda and Ella to have come in from school. Footsteps sounded on the stairs, and a moment later someone knocked on his door. He opened it.

'Ah, there you are,' said Marcelle, her smile brilliant.

'God save Ireland, what do you want?' asked Joe.

'To talk to you, may I?' she said. She stepped into the room and he closed the door, regarding her suspiciously. Her eyes filled with amusement. 'Where is the poor creature you took in?' she asked.

'Can't say. No idea. She left some time ago, but not in the same hurry you did.'

'She left? She has gone somewhere special for you?'

'Somewhere special? For me?'

'Come, Joe, do you think me simple? I am sure she works for you.'

'At what?' asked Joe.

'How do I know, unless you tell me?' smiled Marcelle.

'Can't answer that. No idea what you're talking about. What are you up to yourself, you baggage?'

'Again I am a baggage? Joe, you are not a gentleman.'

'I know that.'

'But you're a very exciting man,' she said, 'and much more to my liking than many gentlemen.'

277

'Be your age, Marcelle, and stop trying to make a monkey out of me.'

'Be my age?' said Marcelle. 'What do you mean?'

'That you're a naughty girl,' said Joe, 'and up to something fishy. You didn't land in England the day you knocked on my landlady's door, or you wouldn't have known just how thick that fog was a few days before.'

Marcelle frowned. She had made a tiny slip there, and he had picked it up, as a man like him was bound to. To whom had he sold the contents of the letter his confederate had stolen from Rokovssky? And how had they known Rokovssky was expecting it? She could not ask. Above all else she was to avoid saying anything that would associate her with Rokovssky, an internationally known operative.

'I guessed, that is all,' she said. 'It is easy to guess about London fogs. Joe, I am disappointed in you. No-one speaks to me as you do. Most of the men I know would give all they had to make love to me.'

'Then most of the men you know must be gormless,' said Joe.

'Gormless?' said Marcelle, fascinated.

'Idiots,' said Joe.

'I shall strike you,' she said.

'I'll smack your bottom if you do.'

'I cannot believe my ears,' she said, but she laughed.

'Making love to a woman is all very nice—'

'Nice? Nice?'

'But it only takes about ten minutes, counting everything, and hardly worth any bloke beggaring himself.'

'Ah,' said Marcelle, 'you can never have made love to a real woman.'

'Just one or two baggages,' said Joe.

She laughed again.

'Would you like me to be a baggage to you, Joe? See, I've kept my promise, I've told no-one you are a forger.'

Joe was tempted to throw her out, but not at the risk of

having her inform on him. Some women would never rat on a bloke, but there were a few who would.

'If I were you, Marcelle, I'd keep my eyes open.'

'Why?' she asked.

'You never know who might be watching you.'

'Ah,' she murmured. He was suspicious of her. Perhaps he recognized in her something of the profession in which they both engaged. But he was giving her a gentlemanly warning. 'It is kind of you to say so, although I can't think what you mean. You may kiss me, if you wish, and then make love to me.'

'Is that necessary?' asked Joe.

'Necessary? Of course not. For you, it's a very special privilege.'

'Sounds as if it might be too much for me,' said Joe, 'and in any case, Ella and Linda will be home from school in a few minutes. One or both may come up.'

'You can lock your bedroom door, I think,' smiled Marcelle.

'I can, but I won't. Go on your way, Marcelle. Some odd characters have been patrolling around here lately.'

Another warning. Little alarm bells rang for Marcelle.

'Meet me at the Serpentine at three o'clock on Sunday,' she said.

'To be pushed in?' said Joe.

'No, no.' She shook her head at him. 'I shall have something important to tell you.'

'I think I'd be safer if I stayed at home and wasn't told anything,' said Joe.

'I am amazed,' said Marcelle.

'At what?'

'I am amazed that I like you. However, meet me as I have said, by the Serpentine at three o'clock on Sunday. *Au 'voir*, Joe.'

She left.

A man in a raincoat and cap followed her to the

Elephant and Castle, from where she took an omnibus to the Strand. He boarded it before it moved off. In the Strand, where he alighted after her, she waited until she was able to hire a cab at a moment when there were no others around. It left the man in a state of frustration. Even so, she asked the cabbie to take her only as far as Oxford Street. From there, she took another cab, to Kensington.

It was necessary then for the man to duly report to Tubby that he'd found and lost Marcelle Fayette.

Marcelle felt she knew how British Intelligence had found her. They'd been watching Joe, she was sure. It meant he *was* an agent for a foreign power. What an exciting man, the coolest and calmest one could hope to meet. It was not going to be possible for her to kill him. If it had to be done, then Rokovssky must do it himself.

Henrietta swept into Sir Hubert's office.

'Young lady, what are you doing here?' he asked. 'Shouldn't you be at Bell Lane?'

'Not at this time of the day. You know very well those students are always out from mid-morning, Uncle Hubert. They're out now, making sketches of the Albert Hall. One of them has just posted a letter, and I've rushed all the way here to tell you so.'

'A letter?' Sir Hubert quickened. 'Posted where?'

'In the pillar-box by the Albert Hall. The next collection is four o'clock. It's now ten to. Uncle Hubert, do something immediately, you will have to persuade the Post Office to let you have all of the collection, for we shan't know—'

Sir Hubert was leaving the office at speed.

The GPO was adamant in its refusal to hand over even a single letter, let alone a sackful. The request came from the Kensington police station. No, not a sackful, said the police, merely those from the Albert Hall box. That collection, said the GPO, was now quite certainly in a sack with other collections, and was being added to by stages. Then it has to be that particular sackful, said the police. Sorry, not without a warrant as specified in the General Post Office Act.

The warrant was obtained, the relevant sack of letters held back from sorting in a gesture of cooperation until the authorities concerned had traced the letter they wanted. The warrant allowed confiscation. It was brought by a senior police officer, who was accompanied by Sir Hubert and Henrietta. In a room set aside for the purpose, the mail sack was opened and the contents emptied out. Henrietta stared in dismay at the mountain of mail. She knew the letter in question had been posted in a white envelope of a small and common size. There were hundreds like that in the mountain. The superintendent of the sorting depot was present. He refused to allow any of the letters to be opened. The Act permitted such a thing only in times of war. And the warrant permitted only the confiscation of the letter in which the authorities were interested.

'Hopeless,' said Henrietta.

Sir Hubert spoke to the police officer. Taking a constable and Henrietta with him, the officer hurried off to the Albert Hall. The two young Russian students were still there, and Henrietta identified them. The police officer requested their help in a certain matter. Objecting not in the least, the students were taken to the sorting depot, where the police officer asked them to search the mail for a letter one of them had posted at about three-thirty.

'But why?'

'Please do it, sir.'

'Very well.'

Both students searched. It took ten minutes for them to find the letter. The police officer asked for it to be opened.

One of the students opened it and took out the enclosure. Sir Hubert requested to see it, and it was handed to him. It was a coupon cut out of a magazine, and a postal order was attached to it by a paper clip. The coupon had been filled in by Gregor Palovich of Bell Lane, Whitechapel. It asked for Model S508 to be sent to him by the advertisers, the Birmingham manufacturers of model railway engines. The postal order for seven shillings and sixpence covered cost of the model and postage and packing.

Henrietta would have died of mortification if she hadn't seen the funny side of it. Sir Hubert apologized like a gentleman to everyone, and assured the students it was a case of mistaken identity. They in turn assured him, in good English, that they were not offended. They smiled at Henrietta and left, carrying their portfolios. They returned to the Albert Hall, which they rather liked.

'Shall we post the other letter now?' asked Gregor Palovich.

'Yes, she is busy swallowing sour grapes now,' said Peter Czernov, 'and we shan't see her again until tomorrow.'

They laughed, and Gregor Palovich took a letter from the inside cover pouch of his portfolio and posted it. It was addressed to Marcelle Fayette of Gloucester Place, Kensington.

They had thumbed their noses at British authorities, and were hugely delighted at the diversion they were causing.

Henrietta, arriving home, walked straight through to the kitchen, taking her hat and coat off on the way. Nell and Cissie quivered as she sat down at the kitchen table, turning the chair sideways and sprawling her feet.

'Well, I just don't know,' said Nell.

'Miss 'Enrietta, you just don't look comfortable like that,' said Cissie, relieving her young mistress of her hat and coat.

'In the kitchen and all,' said Nell.

'I like your kitchen,' said Henrietta. 'Is there any tea? With a slice of cake?'

'Miss 'Enrietta, a cup of tea and a slice of cake in the kitchen was for when you were little,' said Nell. 'It don't become you now.'

'Oh, come on, Nell, be a sport,' said Henrietta.

'Put the kettle on, Cissie,' said Nell. The well-appointed kitchen had an up-to-date gas cooker encased in speckled porcelain and with four rings, a grill and a large oven. Cissie filled the kettle and put it on.

'Make a pot,' said Henrietta. 'Oh, and where's the cake? Is there any?'

'Bring the cake, Cissie,' said Nell.

Cissie brought it from the larder, on a decorative plate with a cover. She placed it on the table. Henrietta lifted the cover and disclosed what was left of a round fruit cake. She picked up a knife and cut herself a slice.

'Well, I don't know what's goin' on,' said Nell, 'I just don't.'

'Oh, I'm a little girl again,' said Henrietta, and bit into the cake.

'Miss 'Enrietta, you don't even 'ave a plate,' protested Cissie, and brought one.

'I don't want a plate, not now I've got cake,' said Henrietta. 'Who eats plates?'

'I don't know what the Hon'rable Cedric would say if he saw you now, Miss 'Enrietta,' said Cissie.

'He'd join me,' said Henrietta.

'He called this afternoon,' said Nell, 'and I must say he was surprised not to find you in again.'

'I'm clerking for my uncle,' said Henrietta. Sir Hubert had agreed she had better tell her servants something.

'You're doing what?' asked Nell.

'Yes, I'm a lady clerk in my uncle's employ, Nell.'

Nell sat heavily down. Cissie looked appalled.

'Miss 'Enrietta, you can't,' she said, 'we couldn't live it down.'

'It just don't bear thinking about,' said Nell faintly.

'Now don't fuss, you two,' said Henrietta. 'All play and no work doesn't do anything for a young lady. You don't want me to be useless, do you?'

'But, Miss 'Enrietta, young ladies of your standin' are supposed to be useless,' said Cissie, 'otherwise people like me and Nell wouldn't 'ave any jobs. Mind, I don't know if useless is the right word, but you know what I mean, Miss 'Enrietta.'

'Decorative, that's the word,' said Nell, still in shock.

'Yes, you were awf'lly dec'rative, Miss 'Enrietta, up to a few months ago,' said Cissie.

'Same thing,' said Henrietta, and cut herself another slice of cake.

'Same thing as what?' asked Nell, feeling the established order was falling apart.

'Useless,' said Henrietta. 'Is the kettle boiling, Cissie?'

'It's steamin',' said Cissie. 'Miss 'Enrietta, I don't like speakin' out of turn, but what would 'appen to the country if all young society ladies like you went out and did clerkin'?'

'Revolution, that's what would happen,' said Nell grimly, 'and I don't hold with revolutions; people get upset. We've all got our place in life. Kettle's boiling, Cissie.'

'I'll make it,' said Henrietta, jumping up. 'Where's the teapot and caddy?'

New shock rendered Nell and Cissie temporarily speechless. Cissie was the first to recover.

'I just don't know what's 'appening,' she gasped.

'I told you, it's revolution,' said Nell. 'Next thing you know, you and me will get our 'eads chopped off at the Tower for not being wanted. I'm sorry, Miss 'Enrietta, but it's not going to happen in my kitchen.'

Henrietta, whose working day had ended on a note of farce, was able to put it all behind her then. She shrieked with laughter. Nell and Cissie eyed her reproachfully.

'Oh, you sillies,' she said, 'I'm much too fond of you to send you to the Tower. But you don't really want me to be a useless decoration all my life, do you?'

'It's what you were born to, Miss 'Enrietta,' said Nell firmly, 'and I'd be failing in my duty if I let you make tea while I've still got breath in my body.' And she attended to the teapot herself, stiffly and proudly. Henrietta sat down again, a smile on her face.

'Are you really fond of us, Miss 'Enrietta?' asked Cissie.

'I treasure you both,' said Henrietta, 'even if you do fuss-fuss.' She received the cup of hot tea with a very sweet smile. 'Thank you, Nell. By the way, did the Hon Cedric leave a message when he called?'

'Yes, he asked us to tell you not to forget he's callin' to take you to the theatre at seven o'clock, with dinner afterwards,' said Cissie.

'Oh, hell, that means—'

'Miss 'Enrietta!' Nell shuddered under the impact of one more shock.

'Well, it is oh hell,' declared Henrietta, 'it means I've got to get dressed up.'

'Such language,' said Nell, shaking her head, and drank some reviving tea from her own cup.

'Which gown would you like me to lay out, Miss 'Enrietta?' asked Cissie.

'Oh, any old thing will do,' said Henrietta.

That collapsed her servants.

CHAPTER TWENTY-THREE

Marcelle received a letter the next day. It was the one the students had posted after the incident in the sorting depot. It was a singularly brief communication, informing her that her parasol was ready to be collected. It was not signed, and there was no address.

Joe, in response to a friendly letter from George, was in the bookshop, listening to the cheerful proprietor.

'How much?' he asked in astonishment.

'Three hundred and twenty pounds,' said George with a great deal of pleasure. They were in the back room of his shop. There were two customers in the shop itself, both of whom were merely browsing among the second-hand volumes at the moment.

'Each?' said Joe.

'One for me, one for you, two for me, two for you, and so on up to the stated amount, Joe old chap,' said George. 'And all expenses have been allowed for. The draft from our Italian contact arrived three days ago and I've since cashed it. My very good friend, here is your share.' He presented Joe with a stout brown envelope that was thick with banknotes.

'Saints alive,' said Joe.

'I agree,' said George. 'I'd go as far as to say Holy Mother Mary, what a heavenly finale.'

Joe smiled.

'Should a couple of crooks quote Mother Mary?' he asked.

'Crooks? Tut tut, Joe, that simply won't do.' George disappeared for a moment to check on the browsers.

Browsers came in different kinds. Some came for an hour's free reading, some came in the hope of finding a treasure, and a few came to buy a cheap tome and pinch an expensive one. George noted a third browser had arrived, told all three he'd be with them in a few minutes to attend to any requirements, and returned to Joe, taking up where he'd left off. 'Don't use painful language, old fellow. Don't you realize how happy we've made a large number of people? One can't speak of crooks without also referring to their unhappy victims. We have made no-one unhappy, and we have left a number of Italian collectors in rapture. Take what you've earned so well. With it you'll find a statement detailing all income and expenditure in respect of our Italian venture. Now, is there any change in your job prospects?'

'I've received a reply to my application for the job of a recruiting sergeant,' said Joe. 'It informs me my application is under consideration. With it was a form for me to fill in.'

'Well, since my return from Italy, I've passed your name to certain customers of mine and mentioned the kind of work you'd like to do,' said George.

'Much obliged,' said Joe, slipping the stout brown envelope into his inside pocket. 'Must say I appreciate what's come out of our partnership.'

'Friendship and mutual trust, they're the worthiest of our rewards,' said George. 'I hope we won't lose sight of each other. Meanwhile, if I hear of any manuscript work that would suit you, would you be interested?'

'Yes, must occupy myself with something until I'm fixed up with one job or another,' said Joe.

'Good man,' said George.

Joe smiled, shook hands and said so long.

The third browser followed him out of the shop and fell into step with him.

'Watcher, Joe,' said Tubby.

287

'Oh, it's you again,' said Joe, 'I had a feeling someone was breathing down my neck. What's on your mind today?'

'Just had a gainful business meetin' with Mr Singleton, 'ave yer, Joe?' asked Tubby.

'I need to earn something until a job comes along.'

'Ain't you after bein' a recruitin' sergeant?' asked Tubby affably.

'I'm under consideration,' said Joe, 'but that's not earning me anything.'

'I thought you might've come and seen me last night,' said Tubby.

'Why?' asked Joe, his limping walk as brisk as ever.

'Well, seein' French Marcy made a call on you yesterday afternoon, I thought you'd let me know. I 'ope you ain't an unreliable bloke.'

'Listen,' said Joe, 'I'm not in the market for doing your work for you. You asked me to come and see you if I saw Marcelle Fayette again, but I didn't say I would. I live among people who like to mind their own business, and I like to mind mine. It's not my fault that your business is to find out what everyone else's is.'

'Now, Joe, is that nice? Is it 'elpful? You've soldiered, matey, and as far as I'm concerned that makes you the kind of bloke I'd always be gratified to shake hands with. I ain't bothered how you earn yer livin', Joe, all I'm interested in is that you know French Marcy, which lady is what you might call 'ighly suspect to the forces of law and order. So I'll ask yer straight, are you up to something with her?'

'Yes,' said Joe.

'Mother O'Reilly,' said Tubby, 'I was hopin' I could put you down as an innocent party.'

Joe smiled. Summer sunshine patterned Charing Cross Road with light and shade, and women floated along in bright spring hats and long-skirted dresses.

'We're having an affair,' he said.

'Come again?' said Tubby.

'Should have said we're at the beginning of an affair.'

'You flannelling me?' said Tubby.

'Wish I was in a way,' said Joe. 'I don't go much on affairs, and at my age I'd rather get married. But I think Marcelle's hot-blooded, and I'm only human. The offer's there, though why the hell I should tell you about my private life, I don't know. Except that I suppose you'll worry it out of me. But it's a fact, she'd like me to make love to her.'

'Bust my bleedin' braces,' said Tubby, 'is that straight up?'

'Straight up,' said Joe.

'You and her? Well, now I come to consider it, sod me if I don't believe yer,' said Tubby. He put his pipe in his mouth, sucked it, took it out and pointed it at St Martin's-in-the-Fields. 'Lord bless yer, Joe, you could be a boon to us all.'

'Think so?' said Joe non-committally.

'Well, you'll be seein' a lot of her, won't yer?'

'Don't like the way you put that,' said Joe.

'Eh? Oh, see yer point, Joe.' Tubby was breezy. 'I meant you'll be seein' her frequent. Well, the first time you 'ave lovey-dovey with her in her own place, wherever it is, you let us know 'er address and I'll be yer best friend.'

'You mean you fell flat on your face yesterday?' said Joe. He saw Daisy outside the National Gallery. She was pinning a little posy to the buttonhole of a dapper man-about-town. She saw him and waved. He waved back, but gave her flowers a miss today. He had been taking flowers to Bessie Beavis and her daughters to the point where Nancy thought he had very fond feelings towards her.

'Would yer repeat that, Joe?' asked Tubby.

'Come on,' said Joe, 'you've had men looking out for

her in Newington Butts. There was a bloke yesterday, in a peaked cap and raincoat. Don't tell me that he lost her when she left.'

'You're paining me,' said Tubby. 'Yesterday was a grievous day for law and order, I tell yer, me old soldier.'

'Look,' said Joe, 'the first time Marcelle Fayette robs a bank or poisons an old lady, I'll do my best to help you cop her. Until then, leave me out of it, I've got nothing against her, she hasn't poisoned me. Get your bloodhounds to work, she's obviously in London somewhere.'

'When yer seein' her again, Joe?' asked Tubby. They were standing at the entrance to the Strand, Joe having come to a pointed stop.

'Give over,' he said.

'Well, you are seein' her again, ain't you?'

'Not if I find any of your men on my tail,' said Joe. 'I'll duck it, I'm against playing Judas Iscariot.'

'You're a disappointin' bloke, Joe,' said Tubby, 'but I can't say I don't admire that sentiment.'

'So long,' said Joe.

'See you again sometime, matey,' said Tubby, and watched as Joe set off on his walk, upright and soldierly, even if he did have a gammy knee. Well, I like the bugger, thought Tubby, but I've still got to find French Marcy, or me reputation as a bloodhound goes up the bleeding spout. Soldier Joe's the best bet, specially now she's partial to him. Right, so he's got eyes in the back of his head for me or young Rodney or any of the others, has he? Well, how about if I put a different tail on him, someone he don't know and won't suspect? That there lively young niece of the guv's, for instance. Miss Henrietta Downes, the female handful that won't take up knitting, that's the one. She ain't too experienced yet, but it's any port in a storm, as Admiral Nelson might say.

I'll have a word with the guv.

* * *

290

Sir Hubert said he'd think about it. Tubby said it wasn't that they'd got anything on ex-Sergeant Joe Foster, just that he was now a cert to lead them to Marcelle Fayette or whatever her real name was. Sir Hubert said his niece was intelligent enough, but a little headstrong and wayward, and he would need a day or two to decide. He'd give Tubby an answer after the weekend.

The shop close to St Paul's Cathedral sold hand-made gifts and ornamental household objects like brass or copper lamps, pretty candlesticks and very fine candelabra. The shop was owned by two middle-aged brothers, Turkish by birth and British by adoption. Both were gifted metallists and talented craftsmen. They were noted for turning out exquisite parasols to order, and could oblige customers whose requirements were highly individual.

Marcelle, entering the shop, waited to be served. It was a showroom of attractive wares, and she inspected them at her leisure. When the elder brother was able to attend to her, she said, 'I have heard from friends of mine that my parasol is ready.'

The Turkish shopkeeper did not ask for her name or any other details. He simply said, 'Please to come with me, madam.' He led her through the shop to the workroom. There he showed her the parasol and explained exactly how to make full use of it. It was a very expensive creation. Marcelle did not quibble, she paid the required sum. There was a long narrow cardboard box for it, but no, she would use it, she said, for the May day was lovely. She emerged into the sun with the parasol up, the material a delicate pink, the shaft white. The white was a glossy paint that hid what the shaft was made of, a finely toughened steel.

She wore a little smile. She had been assured that the only sound it would make was a tiny *phutt*.

* * *

At ten to seven that evening, Joe had finished tidying up after his supper and was about to take a constitutional walk and to drop in at a pub. Someone knocked on his door.

'Come in.'

The door opened and Dolly showed herself. Joe blinked.

'Hello, Joe, nice surprise, am I?' She stepped in, her smile bright and shameless. She was plainly dressed in a blouse and skirt and cheap straw hat, but no-one could have said she didn't look a cockney treat to a bloke's eye. In Joe's eyes, however, she was a bit suspect.

'What's brought you here?' he asked.

'What d'you mean?' said Dolly indignantly. 'That's a nice welcome, I don't think. I've come specially out of me way to see how you are. My, don't you still look proud and 'andsome? What about puttin' the kettle on so's we can 'ave a nice cup of tea together and one of our talks? You been keepin' all right, Joe? I don't 'ave any hard feelings about the way you chucked me out so's you could 'ave your bed back, I'm still ever so grateful at all you did for me. What d'you think about me looks now? Don't you think I'm improvin', that I don't look like I've come out of an orphanage any more?'

'What I think is unrepeatable,' said Joe.

'Here, I hope you're not 'aving one of your overbearin' Army moods,' said Dolly. 'Oh, come on, you're pleased to see me really, ain't you? I mean, we parted ever such good friends. I'll boil the kettle for you, if you like, and 'ave you got any biscuits or cake? I'm starvin'.'

'Serve you right,' said Joe, but he took the hob lid off and put the black iron kettle on. He stirred up the fire.

'Serve me right that I'm starvin'?' said Dolly. 'That's your 'ard heart comin' out, that is. Look, I'm not starvin' gen'rally, it's just that I've not 'ad any supper yet. Well, I've come straight from me work, I felt I ought to come and see you're all right. Friends ought to see a bit of each other now and again.'

'Fetch up,' said Joe, 'that was something you were against on account of Angus.'

'Well, I didn't want 'im gettin' jealous,' protested Dolly. 'It would 'ave upset me if he'd come round and broken your arm or something. Honest, I won't tell 'im about seein' you now.'

'I'm obliged,' said Joe drily, 'I don't fancy a broken arm or something.'

'No, well, it would be ever so painful, wouldn't it?' said Dolly.

'Might I ask if you've come straight here from your job at the Imperial Hotel?'

'Oh, I didn't get that one,' said Dolly blithely, 'but I didn't mind, I didn't really fancy being a chambermaid, and anyway I fell on me feet because Andy got me a job straightaway.'

'Andy?' Joe regarded her darkly. 'Don't you mean Angus?'

'What?' Dolly blinked. 'No, of course I don't mean Angus, I'm talkin' about his oldest brother, Andy. D'you know, Joe, he fancies me too, but I like Angus best. Anyway, Andy got me this job at a little fact'ry that makes wax fruit. You know, apples, bananas, cherries and everything. It's in Peckham, and I've got lodgings there too. I thought to meself this afternoon I'll go and see Joe, I bet he'll be ever so pleased I'm not a poor unfortunate girl any more. Of course, I still ain't much, I'll never get to marry a rich bloke.'

'Keep trying,' said Joe, 'you've got every chance of marrying an Indian rajah and all his diamonds.'

'Here, I don't want to marry no rajah,' said Dolly, 'what d'you think I am?'

'Don't know, can't say.'

'Oh, come on, stop bein' rotten,' said Dolly, 'you

'aven't said nothing nice to me yet or given me even a bit of a kiss. I'd 'ave thought you could 'ave managed a bit of a kiss and told me it was nice of me to come and see you.'

'I'm speechless,' said Joe, and the kettle began to steam.

'Speechless? That'll be the day,' said Dolly. 'Blow me, Sergeant Joe, the times you've given me what for, and me all 'elpless with me injured ankle. Still, I don't 'old it against you, ducky, I never 'ave and never will. I'll sit down, shall I?' She sat herself down in the armchair. 'Here, Angus is doin' ever so well at 'is job, he might get to be office manager at the fact'ry where he works. Mind you, I don't know I can call 'im me young man any more, he's not comin' to Peckham to see me as much as he did. Oh, I'd best tell the truth, Joe, he's given me up for another girl.'

'Hard luck,' said Joe, 'you'll have to make do with his brother Andy.'

'Well, I like that,' said Dolly, 'I didn't come and see you so's you could chuck me at someone's oldest brother. 'Ow would you like me to chuck you at Linda's oldest sister?'

'You tried that,' said Joe. The kettle was bubbling.

'Yes, but only out of the goodness of me kind 'eart,' said Dolly, 'and to save you from that French gypsy woman. Joe, don't you 'ave a biscuit or something to offer me?'

Silently, Joe took a plate from the larder. It contained a baker's currant bun. He brought it to the table with the butter dish. He sliced the bun in half and buttered both halves, Dolly watching him and making a face because he was ratty. He handed her the plate and bun.

'There you are,' he said.

'Oh, you're still kind really, Joe,' she said, and tackled the bun with healthy relish. She hadn't eaten since midday. The kettle boiled and Joe made a pot of tea. 'Look, what's up?' she asked.

'Where did you say Angus and his family lived?'

'Oh, near Peckham,' she said.

'I think you've been telling me fairy stories,' said Joe.

'Fairy stories? Me?'

'Yes, you.'

'Oh, all right,' said Dolly, finishing the bun, 'I didn't want to admit it, but when I went back to Angus—'

'Was that in Rotherhithe?' asked Joe.

'Yes, near Peckham, I told yer,' said Dolly.

'Watch your tongue,' said Joe, 'Rotherhithe isn't near Peckham.'

'Course it is,' said Dolly. 'Well, good as. Anyway, when I went back to Angus he'd gone off me, he'd got another girl, and I had to find that job meself. Still,' she said brightly, 'I didn't die of any broken 'eart, and I'm proud I didn't, that I stood up to me disappointment with me back straight and me chest out.'

'Say that again,' said Joe, pouring the tea.

'Yes, I've got you to thank for learnin' me to stand up straight,' said Dolly, 'and you don't 'ave to worry now about what Angus might come an' do to you if you'd like to take me out sometimes. Well, I know you fancy me a bit – you do, don't you, Joe? I don't mind that you do, and you ought to 'ave some girl to go out with, you don't want to turn into a sort of 'ermit. And I don't mind givin' you the pleasure of me company, it wouldn't 'ave to get serious.'

'That's a kind of small mercy, is it, that it wouldn't have to get serious?' said Joe, who was in an unusually indeterminate state. He didn't know whether to tan her bottom or kiss her into a yelling fit. 'Listen, you minx, you didn't even apply for that job at the Imperial.'

'Oh, you ain't ratty about that, are you?' said Dolly, sipping her tea. 'When I got there I thought oh, blimey, I just can't work in a posh place like that, specially as a chambermaid. I felt terrible embarrassed—'

'Pardon, did you say embarrassed?' asked Joe.

'Course I did, and I was, I'm a shy girl, I always 'ave been—'

'Jesus give me strength,' said Joe.

'Oh, don't you feel well, Joe, 'ave you got an 'eadache?'

'Yes, a large one,' said Joe.

'Oh, you poor thing, sit down for a bit,' said Dolly. 'Anyway, that posh 'otel made me so embarrassed I didn't even go in. Well, it was a blessin' in disguise that I didn't, or I wouldn't 'ave got this job makin' wax bananas, would I?'

'God help any sailors who get shipwrecked and find you in the lifeboat with them,' said Joe.

'You bein' funny?' said Dolly.

'Not much,' said Joe.

'Oh, go on with you,' said Dolly, 'I know you're pleased to see me, I don't know why you can't say so. What's goin' on downstairs?'

Noisy vibrations from the family kitchen were climbing upwards through the house.

'The usual,' said Joe, 'and they're probably on their afters now. It's date pudding this evening. Are you still hungry?'

'Oh, I don't want you to cook anything for me,' said Dolly.

'All right, I won't,' said Joe, 'I'll take you out—'

'There, you've spoken up at last,' said Dolly, 'you must fancy me to want to take me out. You don't 'ave to be shy about tellin' me, a man ought to speak 'is mind.'

'If I spoke my mind,' said Joe, 'you'd end up fried. Listen, I'm taking you out to buy you some fish and chips.'

'Fish an' chips? Oh, crikey,' said Dolly, 'I've never 'ad fish an' chips.'

'Never?'

'Well, they never give us any at the orphanage, nor didn't I get any when I was skivvyin', and after that I couldn't afford any.'

'You can get fish for tuppence and chips for a penny,' said Joe.

'Can yer really?' said Dolly, round-eyed. 'I was always too embarrassed by me poverty to go in and ask.'

'Beats me, all this embarrassment of yours,' said Joe. 'Come on, let's get you moving.'

As they went down the stairs, the house shook to yells, squeals and roars of laughter from the kitchen. Outside, the May evening was balmy. They crossed at the Junction and entered the New Kent Road, at which point Joe said it was strange the police still hadn't caught up with Blackbeard, especially as he'd sent them another letter.

'Another one?' said Dolly. 'The same as before?'

'No, I gave them a little more information,' said Joe, and told her about Daisy the flower girl, and how she'd had her photograph taken with Blackbeard, and then what Blackbeard had done with it.

'He took it and just brought 'er own photo back in a frame?' said Dolly.

'Right,' said Joe. 'Blackbeard's a bloke who obviously doesn't like being photographed. I wrote to the Police Commissioner, telling him to look out for Blackbeard in Trafalgar Square. He's a regular customer of Daisy's.'

'D'you mean he goes there a lot?'

'So Daisy says.'

'Here, what's all this Daisy lark?' asked Dolly. 'I just can't trust you, Joe Foster. First me, then that French gypsy woman, and now this Daisy. D'you go round fancying all the girls you meet?'

'Yes. Second nature in any bloke who doesn't want to finish up as a hermit. Keep to the point, scatterbrain. And the point is, why haven't the police picked Blackbeard up? Last time I spoke to Daisy, she said he was still a regular.'

'Well, you've done your duty, Joe, you've 'elped—'

'Halt,' said Joe.

'What?' said Dolly.

'Left turn. There you are, that's the door of the fish and chip shop.'

'Crikey, don't it smell lovely?' breathed Dolly.

'That's only the door. Wait till you get to the counter. Quick march.' Joe hustled her in. The aroma of frying fish and chips leapt to the ecstatic nose of the hungry Dolly. There were several customers at the white marble counter, which was long. At each end stood a vinegar bottle and a large metal salt canister peppered with holes. The proprietor and his wife were serving. On the wall behind the counter was a slate, on which were chalked the evening's options. Cod, plaice and rock salmon. Cod and rock salmon were tuppence, plaice threepence. Chips were a penny.

Several customers were at the counter, and the atmosphere related, as always, to the cockney love of fish and chips, considered highly nourishing and a treat for the gods. It was a well-known fact that kids attending Sunday School – if their mums and dads could get them there – regularly asked for the assurance that Jesus served fish and chips up in heaven. Woe betide any Sunday School teacher who misguidedly suggested that up in heaven there was only milk and honey. Indignant mums would come round and say to the teacher what d'you mean by telling our kids that heaven is all milk and honey, they hate milk and honey. Or something like that.

Dolly saw fish dipped into a large pan of creamy-white batter and lowered into the sizzling cooking fat. She saw hot golden chips scooped out from other bubbling fat and placed in a dry container. Her mouth watered. She felt fascinated and alive, really alive.

'What would you like, cod, plaice or rock salmon?' asked Joe. 'Cod's flaky.'

'Oh, I'll 'ave cod, then.'

'Rock salmon's meaty.'

'All right, rock salmon, then.'

'Plaice is a bit superior.'

'Oh, I don't want anything superior.' Dolly watched as a man was served with four helpings of cod and four helpings of chips, the whole lot wrapped up in several sheets of newspaper. He took the hot parcel to the near end of the counter, opened it up, sprinkled everything liberally with vinegar and then with salt, Dolly looking on with wide-open eyes. 'Can't he do that at 'ome?' she whispered.

'Don't let anyone in Walworth hear you talk like that,' said Joe, 'they'll think you've come from Mars.'

'Well, I'm only askin',' muttered Dolly, 'never 'aving had fish and chips.'

'That's no excuse, not for a cockney girl,' said Joe. 'It strikes me, Miss Smith, that you've been keeping the wrong kind of company. Don't you even know that if you put the salt and vinegar on at home, the fish and chips don't taste the same?'

'It's all right for you,' said Dolly, muttering again, 'you've been in the Army and everything, I've only been in an orphanage.'

'Don't start that again,' said Joe. The woman behind the counter looked up and asked him what his fancy was. That made Dolly giggle. 'Rock salmon and chips,' said Joe, 'and a separate helping of chips.'

Dolly saw the woman lift a freshly done portion of rock salmon from the frying vat. The batter was a lovely crisp golden-brown. On to newspaper the rock salmon went, and a helping of chips with it. Briskly, the woman wrapped the order up in three sheets of newspaper. She followed this by wrapping up one portion of chips. Joe said thanks and paid her fourpence.

'Pleasure, Sergeant Joe,' said the woman. 'Who you got with yer, yer real fancy?'

'Oh, just someone I found in a March fog,' said Joe, moving on.

'Bet me old man 'ere wouldn't 'alf like to find someone like 'er in a fog,' said the woman. 'Who's next?'

Dolly was on Joe's heels as he stopped at the end of the counter and opened up the packets.

'Bloomin' sauce,' she said, 'tellin' people you found me in the fog, like I was a pair of old boots. Oh, you're doin' it, you're puttin' salt and vinegar on. Joe, don't it smell good?'

'That's yours,' said Joe, handing her the re-wrapped fish and chips. 'And this is mine.'

'But you don't 'ave any fish.'

'I've had my supper, but I'll enjoy these chips. Come on.'

They left the shop, Dolly's parcel hot in her hand.

'Are we goin' 'ome to eat them, Joe?'

'Home?'

Dolly couldn't quite work out why she'd used that word.

'I mean to your lodgings.'

'Not as good if you put them on a plate,' said Joe. 'You eat them walking, out of the newspaper.'

'But we—' Dolly checked. She'd been going to point out they didn't have knives and forks. She left that unsaid. He'd only get sarky again. 'Oh, I was only thinking a soldierly bloke like you 'ad his dignity to up'old,' she said. 'I mean, I don't mind if you don't.'

He obviously didn't. He was already eating his chips, the packet open in his hand. With her handbag depending from her arm, Dolly opened up her own packet. Again the aroma made her mouth water, and she ate a hot chip. Rapture arrived in her mouth. Passing people looked and smiled as she and Joe walked towards the Old Kent Road. She ate chips, each one bliss to her appetite, each one lightly touched with salt and vinegar, and she dwelt on how she was going to eat the fish.

'The rock salmon all right?' asked Joe, who was

dwelling himself on the fact that she was a harum-scarum monkey who'd probably been getting up to all sorts of tricks during these last several weeks. He hoped she really did have a job, that she hadn't been pinching more wallets.

'I think I'll leave the fish till last,' she said.

'Can't do that. Not the way. Fish and chips are eaten together. Get your fingers working, Miss Smith.'

Oh, help. She was a novice, she was probably the only person in South London who'd never eaten fish and chips out of newspaper before. She made her attack, using her fingers, and the batter-covered fish fell apart. She tried some.

'Oh, Joe, ain't it good? Ain't it luscious? You must really fancy me to treat me to this and to be out walkin' with me.' Dolly ate another mouthful of hot rock salmon and batter. 'Imagine that woman sayin' I was your real fancy. Are you pleased I don't look like a starvin' orphanage girl any more? You could tell that woman could see I don't, I expect she thought I was doin' you proud to be out with you. I'm wearin' nice stockings too. D'you want to look at me ankle back at your lodgings? It's recovered ever so nice, no-one would ever think you nearly ruined it for me.'

Joe made a sound as if a chip had gone down the wrong way.

'You chokin', mister?' An approaching woman stopped as she put the question. Joe coughed. ''Ere, miss, 'e's chokin'.'

'Well, he shouldn't eat two chips at a time,' said Dolly. 'Wait till I get him 'ome, I'll learn him, eatin' two chips at a time on a public 'ighway.'

'I'm always 'aving to tell me old man that some men never grow up. 'Ere, them fish an' chips smell nice.'

'Yes, it's rock salmon,' said Dolly, 'would you like a taste?'

'Well, don't mind if I do,' said the interested party, and

helped herself to a generous lump. 'Lovely,' she said, and looked at Joe, then at Dolly again. ''E's stopped chokin',' she said.

'Yes, I'm dead now,' said Joe.

'There, told yer,' said the woman to Dolly, 'some of 'em never grow up.' And off she went, shaking her head about what a problem some men were.

'You all right now, Joe?' asked Dolly, through more luscious fish and chips. Joe didn't answer. He took her across the junction into Tower Bridge Road. 'Where we goin' now?'

'To Tower Bridge.'

'What for?'

'I'm going to chuck you off it.'

'Joe, you ain't 'alf funny sometimes. D'you want a bit of me rock salmon?'

'No, it's all yours. It's your last meal.'

Dolly chewed. Joe finished his chips. On either side of the road, old buildings rose in sombre acknowledgement of their age, and dusty windows blinked lazily in the fading evening sunlight.

'Joe, you ain't got the rats again, 'ave you?' said Dolly, the damp newspaper hanging slackly now on either side of her hand, her portion of fish and chips sizably reduced. 'I mean, talkin' about this being me last meal, as if you're goin' to hang me.'

'I'm not going to hang you, I'm going to chuck you off the bridge.'

'But, Joe, I can't swim.'

'Good, I was counting on that,' said Joe.

Dolly couldn't help herself. She shrieked with laughter. Joe muttered dark and dire things. But, of course, he didn't chuck her off the bridge when they got there. They stood on the pedestrian walk and looked down at the Thames and its gliding barges. Dolly was as perky as she'd ever been, Joe suspicious of what she'd been up to, but

302

getting nothing out of her except typical irrelevance.

On the way back he asked, 'What wages are you earning?'

'Oh, they pay me good wages,' she said.

'Does your landlady cook your food for you?'

'What a sauce, course she doesn't, I cook for meself. Just because I don't like peelin' potatoes and your fire set them kidneys and mushrooms alight one day, well, that doesn't mean I can't cook.'

'You can't cook,' said Joe.

'Stop being ratty,' said Dolly. 'Joe, ain't it nice being out together on a nice warm evening like this? Wasn't the fish and chips good? You do like being out with me, I can tell, only you keep purposely gettin' the rats because you don't want to show you're enjoying yourself. Still, I don't mind. Well, I don't seriously mind; you 'ave to put up with men being a bit funny, especially the ones who fancy you. I mean, it's compliment'ry really, so you can't get too cross with them. Help, wouldn't we get in a pickle if I got to fancy you, if we got to fancy each other?'

'God knows how we'd get out of that,' said Joe.

'Yes, we don't want that kind of problem, do we?' she said.

'It could give my head a bashing,' said Joe.

'What d'you mean? Joe, you ought to watch what you say sometimes, you don't make sense, and a bloke like you ought to make sense most times or you'll 'ave people lookin' at you. Mind, it don't make any difference to me, you'll always be me kind saviour even if you do sound barmy. I might not be very educated, but lots of people 'ave told me I'm very understandin'. I expect it'll be a help to you if I let you take me out again. I'll come on Sunday evening, if you like. I can't come in the afternoon, I'm goin' out with a feller who lives next door to me lodgings. 'Is sister and 'er young man are comin' too, so—' Dolly paused. Joe was muttering what she was sure were swear words. 'Joe, you don't need to get jealous.'

'Can't think why I should,' said Joe, 'not when there's nothing serious going on between us.'

'Crikey, no, we don't want to get serious, do we, it could spoil things,' said Dolly. 'I mean, suppose you fell in love with me now I'm nice-lookin', you wouldn't want that to 'appen when you could easy marry someone rich. I'm 'ardly nobody. Mind, I'm not saying it wouldn't be compliment'ry, because it would, you bein' such an 'andsome chap. Of course, if I was rich meself and well educated, that would be a lot better for you, you could fall in love with me a lot more easy then. Would you fancy me lots as a rich girl, Joe?'

'Can't afford to fancy anyone as much as that until I get a decent job,' said Joe.

'Here, don't get proud and 'aughty,' said Dolly, 'it don't suit you. Anyway, I'll come about six on Sunday evening, shall I? You could do Sunday tea for me, if you like, and then take me out for another nice walk, I won't mind.'

They stopped as they reached the Elephant and Castle, and Joe said, 'What can I say that you'll take any notice of? All right, come to Sunday tea, then.'

'Oh, ain't you kind, invitin' me?' said Dolly. 'It's been ever so nice 'aving you take me for a walk and treatin' me to me very first fish an' chips – oh, there's a tram – see you Sunday, Joe.' Away she went, running for a tram that was about to move off. She hitched her skirts and leapt aboard. She turned, waved to him and disappeared inside.

Where the hell does she think she's going? Joe asked himself the question in exasperation. The tram, rattling over the points, was heading for Blackfriars, not Peckham. Mad as a hatter, potty as a pancake. She'd given him no address, nor the name of the factory where she worked. All he'd had from her had been scatterbrained stuff. And now she'd charged aboard the wrong tram.

Or had she?

On Sunday he'd have to get some sense out of her, even if it meant tanning her bottom. Someone ought to tan it, or God knows how she'd finish up.

CHAPTER TWENTY-FOUR

Rokovssky was spending Sunday in enjoyable fashion, entertaining the erring wife of a hard-up insurance clerk at his lodgings in Grove Lane, Camberwell. His landlady, an elderly widow, was spending the day with her son and daughter-in-law in New Cross. The erring wife had met Rokovssky in a pub, and was the kind of woman who found his almost brutally rugged looks exciting. Even more exciting was his affluence. Her perennial lack of money made five-pound notes dazzling to her eyes. She contributed imaginatively to Rokovssky's Sunday enjoyment.

Henrietta's Sunday was utterly boring, although the boredom was mitigated at times when a wicked little desire for revenge made itself felt. Those Russian students had made a fool of her. All the same, it was deadly dull spending a lovely Sunday sitting at the window of the rented room of the house in Toynbee Street. Tubby had poured silver into the hand of the landlady, Mrs Bailey, weeks ago, silver that upped the rent and provided for the room to be used at any hour of the day and night by himself and any of his friends.

Sir Hubert, suspecting that Henrietta had become a familiar figure to the students, had made her take up a daytime watch from the rented room. That relieved her of the routine monotony of shadowing them on their daily wanderings around London, although she knew now that their wanderings were not as innocuous as implied in the letter that her uncle had received. It had been a bitter blow to her when, having seen one of them mail a further letter by the Albert Hall, she found herself fooled.

She had had to accept duty every alternate Sunday. Today she would be on watch until five o'clock. How boring. Nothing would happen. The woman would not come, of course. She would never show herself in daytime. She was the one named as Alexandra Petrovna in the letter, and she and the man called Boris were the people Sir Hubert really wanted. Henrietta had asked him again if she could team up with Tubby in his search for them, but he had repeated his objection to placing her in danger.

Sir Hubert, in fact, said virtually nothing to her about the man Boris and his female confederate. He knew it would place the bit between her teeth, especially as she seemed to have a burning interest in catching up with Boris.

At midday, Henrietta ate sandwiches prepared for her by an outraged Nell. Sandwiches? Sandwiches? On a Sunday? Well, Nell had said, if there's anything good that can come out of a young society lady eating sandwiches for her Sunday lunch, I'd like to hear it. I'll have a heart attack next, she said, which won't do me any good to start with. I just don't know what Sir Hubert's about, making you work at all, let alone on Sundays. Not every Sunday, said Henrietta, and if you don't stop fussing, Nell, I'll join forces with Lady Amelia in Advance Britannia. Only over my dead body, said Nell, that lot's worse than the suffragettes.

At five past three, Marcelle arrived at the Serpentine. Joe spotted her as she approached him, and recognized her walk before anything else. She was wearing a full veil, a jacket and skirt of Oxford blue, and a matching hat. So dark did the blue look against the white frocks of girls and the white hats of ladies, that her appearance was like that of a widow. She was carrying a folded parasol with her handbag.

'So, you came,' she said.

'I'm here, yes,' said Joe. 'Can't say I'm sure who you are behind that veil.'

'That is a greeting?' said Marcelle. 'How typical. Should you not bow and kiss my hand? I am, after all, fairly exceptional.'

'I'd gladly bow and kiss your hand if I happened to be fairly exceptional myself,' said Joe, 'but I'm just another bloke, and fairly ordinary.'

'I know you are not, and so do you. Come, Joe, stop playing games with me and let us walk about. I adore Hyde Park.'

They began to walk, to stroll. The sun was bright, the day warm. She opened up her parasol and let the slender shaft rest on her shoulder. The pastel pink covering lightly danced.

'You had something to tell me,' said Joe.

'Is that why you came, to listen to something I said I would tell you?' The veil had a little soft muffling effect on her voice.

'I'm curious to know what you're up to,' he said. 'I'll wager you're not teaching deportment at a drama school.'

'And I am sure forgery is not your only occupation,' said Marcelle.

'Gave it up weeks ago,' said Joe, 'and I'm looking for different work now.'

Marcelle took that with a pinch of salt, naturally.

She found Hyde Park both relaxing and stimulating. As a green oasis in the heart of London's brick and stone, it was always relaxing. As a playground of the people, it captured one's eyes. Girls in their Sunday frocks walked demurely with their parents, but cast inviting eyes at dashing young men, or were seen in giggling company with other girls. It made Joe think of Dolly having to spend her growing years in an orphanage, deprived of the pleasures of spending summer Sundays in a park.

Marcelle said, 'Perhaps I believe you, perhaps I believe

you need more time for your real work. That is so, yes?'

'Haven't got any real work yet,' said Joe. 'But I've hopes of rejoining the Army, on the recruiting side.'

'Recruiting?' Marcelle smiled again. That would be a cover for what the Army truly wanted him for. Intelligence work. They had probably approached him with an offer, and he was probably considering it. 'Come, Joe, I am not an idiot, I know too much about you.' What she didn't know, of course, was what she wanted to know, how he had discovered that Rokovssky was due to receive a letter. A thought struck her. Rokovssky had executed the man who brought the letter. For being an inquisitive and greedy idiot, he had said. Perhaps there was more to it than that. Perhaps Joe had known the man, and had known too that the idiot had met Rokovssky's student confederates by arrangement at the dock gates. And perhaps Rokovssky had found out that the idiot had betrayed him to Joe, who had used his own confederate to snatch Rokovssky's wallet. Rokovssky had said the fool handed the letter far too openly to him in the public house, enabling Joe's confederate to see it.

'What you know about me can only be what any of my friends know,' said Joe. 'Which is nothing out of the ordinary.'

'You collect information,' said Marcelle, 'and your confederate helps you.'

'I think you've got the wrong bloke,' said Joe.

'You think? Although it was of no interest to me or my country,' said Marcelle, watching three gleeful little girls sitting on one yelling small boy, 'there was a letter which I know was stolen by your confederate and passed to you. Yes?'

That told Joe something of significance. It told him that Marcelle either knew Blackbeard or knew of him. He thought about how she had applied to Mrs Beavis for lodgings shortly after the incident in the fog. Subsequently, she had searched his room and found the papers relating to his work for George. But that was not what she'd been looking for. It stood out a mile now that she'd been looking for the letter.

'You're a naughty girl,' he said.

'Excuse me?'

'And a silly one as well.'

'I do not like being called silly.'

'Can't help that, Marcelle. You're drivelling.'

'Drivelling? Drivelling? What is that?'

'Idiot talk,' said Joe. 'Drivel. I'd never met Dolly until I bumped into her in the fog. If you don't believe that, have a banana.'

She laughed. It escaped softly through her veil.

'Joe, you are very amusing, and I like you very much,' she said. Joe would have been amazed if he'd known he actually excited her. 'Come, I will take you to where I live and let you make love to me.'

'Sounds nice—'

'Nice? Nice? That again?'

'Yes, sounds very nice,' said Joe, 'but I'm not sure you won't murder me.'

Marcelle stiffened. Did he even know that, did he even know that she and Rokovssky had agreed he could not be allowed to live?

'Joe, how can you say such a thing, even in joke?'

'Just a passing comment,' said Joe.

'I am to believe that?'

'Why not? You're not going to murder me, are you?'

'You terrible man,' said Marcelle. 'Almost I have changed my mind about letting you love me, but no, we will go, and afterwards speak truthfully to each other, as lovers should.' She was quite sure that after he had enjoyed her beautiful body he would not deny her the truth about himself and that peasant girl who acted as his confederate.

310

'Can't be done, Marcelle,' said Joe. He knew that if she took him to where she was living, he'd have no option but to advise the tubby man of her address. He'd have to, simply because she knew about that Russian letter and therefore about Blackbeard. She was playing a game that was no game, but something dark and devious. She had to be, if she was involved with Blackbeard.

'Can't be done?' said Marcelle. 'What does that mean?'

'That I've arranged to see a friend later this afternoon,' said Joe.

'Ah, you are not only a terrible man, but a miserable one also,' said Marcelle. 'Yes, most miserable, to arrange to see a friend when you knew you were meeting me at three.'

'Only for the purpose of having you tell me something,' said Joe, 'and you've not told me much, except some rubbish about a letter.'

'Such insults you are giving me,' said Marcelle. 'Now I have every desire to murder you.'

'Sounds a bit drastic,' said Joe. 'Well, I'd better push off. You're a funny old lot, you women, but can't say I don't like you. Just watch what you're up to, that's all.'

'We shall meet again, Joe, and next time you will do what I want, you will see.'

'You're a baggage,' said Joe, and limped away.

Dolly arrived at fifteen minutes past six. Joe heard her tripping up the stairs in lively fashion, having let herself in by means of the latchcord. His living-room door was open and in she came.

'Hello, lovey, 'ow'd you do? Look, I'm in me best Sunday frock. Like it, do you?'

A white muslin dress with frilly neck and cuffs flowed over her body down to her ankle-boots, and a yellow straw hat adorned with cherries sat on her head. She looked a typically lively cockney girl in her Sunday best.

'Very nice,' said Joe, 'come in.'

'I am in,' said Dolly. 'Do I get a bit of a kiss?' She took her hat off and offered her cheek. Joe bent his head. What happened next he wasn't quite sure of, but somehow the kiss landed on her mouth, and her mouth was warm and sweet. Dolly quivered. Virtuously, she backed off. 'Oh, what a sauce,' she said, 'who said you could do that?'

'Accident,' said Joe, 'don't fuss.'

'Me fuss? Me? I never fussed since the day I was born, I'm not a girl who says a lot, anyway. Well, some of us are shy, y'know. Oh, don't the table look nice, Joe?'

The table was laid for tea over a white cloth. The plates and cutlery shone with cleanness, the cups and saucers sparkled. There was a plate of bread and butter, a cake, a bowl of shrimps and a bowl of winkles. The kettle was steaming on the hob, and the china teapot lay waiting on the table.

'Had a nice afternoon with your new feller?' said Joe.

'Beg your pardon?' said Dolly. 'Oh, Cuthbert, you mean, the bloke who lives next door to me lodgings.'

'Cuthbert?'

'D'you know, he fancies me already, and I've only been out with 'im this once,' said Dolly. 'I don't know what's come over me, havin' blokes fancy me; I suppose it's because I'm gettin' quite nice-lookin'. Here, and I don't know what came over you, kissin' me like that. What did come over you? I always thought you was a bit of a gent, not one for takin' advantage of an unfortunate girl.'

'Back to unfortunate again, are we?' said Joe.

Dolly looked at the mantelpiece clock and said, 'On me mouth as well, would you believe, I've never been more shocked. I just 'ope I don't 'ave to fight for me honour over tea. Who'd 'ave thought he'd 'ave turned out like this, and him an hon'rable sergeant in the Army once. You just can't tell with some people.'

'Sit down before you get your bottom smacked,' said Joe.

'Here, don't you try that,' said Dolly, and sat down quickly, as if in hasty protection of her bottom. 'Joe, you've got two lots of jam on the table as well, it all looks a lovely Sunday tea – cake too – here, what's them?'

'Winkles,' said Joe, and Dolly gazed at the shiny black shells containing fat meaty winkles.

'Crikey, I can't remember I ever 'ad winkles before,' she said, 'they didn't give us any at the orphanage. Of course, I've heard of them, and shrimps too. Actu'lly, I don't want to talk about me orphanage days any more, not now I look more ladylike. I don't think it does me any good, do you, to keep on mentioning them?'

'Quite right, leave them all behind you, Miss Smith.'

'Look, what's the idea, callin' me Miss Smith now?'

'Keeps things formal,' said Joe, 'and discourages me from taking more advantage of you. It beats me, by the way, that you've never had shrimps or winkles or fish and chips. You haven't been living properly. Well, now you're going to have a shrimp-and-winkle tea. Try the winkles first, there's a pin on your plate.'

Dolly picked up the long pin.

'What's it for?' she asked.

'I'll show you,' said Joe. He took a winkle, neatly flipped off its little protective cap with his pin, then used the pin to draw the winkle out. Dolly stared at it, blinked at it, and shuddered. Joe popped it into his mouth and ate it with a bite of bread and butter. Dolly almost turned pale.

'Oh, me gawd, you ate it,' she gasped.

'Nourishing,' said Joe. 'Try some.' He spilled a dozen on to her plate from the bowl.

'I couldn't,' said Dolly, 'I'll be sick, I never saw anything more 'orrible.'

'You'll get drummed out of Walworth – and Peckham too – if you talk like that about winkles,' said Joe, helping himself to a dozen. 'When the Beavises have them for Sunday tea, they make sandwiches of them.'

'Sandwiches?'

'Yes, a layer of winkles between two slices of bread and butter.'

'Oh, I'll turn green in a minute,' said Dolly. 'Joe, can't I just 'ave shrimps?'

'All right,' smiled Joe, 'put the winkles back and help yourself to a heap of shrimps.'

'Oh, bless yer,' said Dolly fervently, and exchanged the winkles for a handful of shrimps, which she peeled expertly and ate with bread and butter. Joe got on with his winkles. Dolly just couldn't look, she kept her eyes resolutely on her shrimps. The kettle boiled and Joe filled the teapot.

'What factory do you work at?' asked Joe.

'What fact'ry? Oh, the one in Peckham, like I told you. Yes, it's Parsons' Fancy Goods fact'ry, and Mr Parsons runs it 'imself. He's ever so pleased with me work, he said he'd give me a rise a bit later on. Could I 'ave some more shrimps?'

'Here,' said Joe, and emptied the bowl on to her plate.

'But now there's none for you,' said Dolly.

'You have the shrimps, I'll have the winkles,' said Joe, and poured the tea. Dolly went happily to work on the rest of the shrimps and on more bread and butter.

'Oh, I like Sunday tea, don't you, Joe? D'you want to take me out out for a walk after? I expect you do, and I expect your friends and neighbours will like seein' you walkin' out with me in me new Sunday best. I came here on a tram, y'know, and the conductor couldn't 'ave been more compliment'ry about me looks. I told him it was gracious of him to be so admirin' of just an ordinary fact'ry girl. Of course, he asked me if I was all dressed up to meet me best feller, and I said oh no, I'm just goin' to give the pleasure of me company to a kind sergeant I know. He said he'd never 'eard of a kind sergeant, he said he didn't know there were any. Oh, what a cheek, I said. I said I'll 'ave you know he's the kindest bloke ever. Mind, I didn't know then that you were goin' to jump on me and take advantage, I can't remember when I've been more shocked. Still, I'm not goin' to 'old it against you, Joe, I suppose you were a bit overcome at seein' how ladylike I was.'

'I'm overcome now,' said Joe.

'Oh, are you really, Joe? Are you overcome bad?'

'Don't know, can't say. Lost for words, in fact.'

'Crikey, that's a change,' said Dolly. 'Still, you ain't ratty, like you were the other night. Could I have some jam now?'

'Help yourself,' said Joe.

'You do look after a girl nice, Joe,' said Dolly, and ate her way through bread and jam, and then a large slice of cake from the baker's. When they were both on their third cups of tea, Linda came running up the stairs and put her head round the door. She smiled at Dolly.

'Oh, 'ello,' she said, 'Sergeant Joe told us you was comin' to 'ave tea wiv him. Crumbs, don't yer look nice? Don't she look nice, Sergeant Joe? Can me and Ella come up in a minute and bring our Snakes an' Ladders, like you promised? Can yer play Snakes an' Ladders, Dolly?'

'I'm hot stuff at that game,' said Dolly.

'Come up in fifteen minutes, Carrots, after we've cleared away,' said Joe.

'Oh, yer always a sport, Sergeant Joe,' said Linda, 'me and Ella loves yer, and I do specially.' She whisked away.

'Don't mind playing a Sunday evening game with them, do you, Dolly?' asked Joe.

'No, of course not.' Dolly eyed him a little pensively. 'D'you like it that those girls love you?'

'Just their way of getting round me,' said Joe.

'More like their way of lettin' you know how much girls

315

of their age enjoy having a man like you for a playmate,' said Dolly.

Joe, starting to clear the table, said, 'What happened after you boarded that tram the other night?'

'What tram? Oh, that one.'

'It wasn't going to Peckham.'

'Don't I know it,' said Dolly, getting up to help him. 'You should 'ave seen my face when I realized it was goin' the wrong way. I don't know what made me get on it, I suppose I must 'ave been a bit overcome at findin' out you'd got fond of me, even if it wasn't anything serious. Of course, when I got up to get off, the conductor wasn't 'alf peeved, he said I hadn't paid any fare, and I said no, why should I, when his tram was goin' the wrong way. He said trust a daft female to get on the wrong tram. I said don't you call me a female, nor a daft one, either. I said he was the daft one for not goin' to Peckham, like he should 'ave been. I'll wash up for you, Joe, shall I?'

'You'd better wash and dry,' said Joe, 'I'm about to pass out myself.'

'What d'you mean, what d'you want to pass out for?'

'No idea, except that it's probably the best thing for me at the moment.'

'Here, you're not overcome again, are you?' said Dolly.

Joe gave her a helpless grin and shook his head.

It was Snakes and Ladders a little later, the board on the table. Linda watched everyone else's moves with sharp and lively eyes.

'Sergeant Joe, look what you've done,' she exclaimed in delight, 'you've gone right up the longest ladder.'

'Not bad, that, for a bloke with a stiff knee,' said Joe.

'Is it 'urting yer tonight?' asked Ella. 'I'll kiss it better for yer, if yer like.'

'No, you won't, I will,' said Linda, 'I'm more friends

wiv Sergeant Joe than you are, and you don't save none of your spit for 'is shoes like I do.'

'No, but I kiss better,' said Ella.

'Ugh,' said Linda, 'you do gurgles when you kiss – oh, Sergeant Joe, look what Dolly's just done. She frew a four an' went five spaces so's she missed that snake.'

'Me?' said Dolly, her hair darkly defiant.

'I saw yer,' said Linda.

'I hate them snakes,' said Dolly.

'Can't help that, down you go,' said Joe, and Ella and Linda yelled with glee when they saw that Dolly had to descend to the bottom line.

'What a swizz,' said Dolly, 'I'm nearly in the dustbin.'

'Well, it does serve yer right really, Dolly,' said Linda.

'Yes, cheats never prosper,' said Ella.

Linda, taking her go, threw a five, moved her counter and said, 'Sergeant Joe says cheats get pimples all over.'

Dolly made a face. The game went on, everyone going up and down, up and down, until Ella won, much to Linda's disgust. They began another game, and Dolly, for the fun of it, cheated again. Linda and Ella yelled at her.

'She'll get pimples all over, Sergeant Joe!' cried Ella.

'There's always an option for girls,' said Joe, 'girls can be tickled all over.'

'Yes, tickles all over for Dolly!' yelled Linda in delight.

'Oh, me gawd,' gasped Dolly, 'I'll go barmy.'

'Shall we jump on 'er, Sergeant Joe?' asked Ella.

'All right, you and Linda go ahead,' said Joe, 'I'll find the feather duster and we'll start with her feet.'

'I'll scream the house down, you see!' yelled Dolly.

She was saved by the arrival of Mrs Beavis and a tray on which were mugs of cocoa for the girls, and tea for Dolly and Joe.

'What's goin' on up 'ere?' beamed the good-natured landlady.

'Oh, we was just goin' to tickle Dolly all over for cheatin',' said Linda.

'Well, don't make too much noise, love,' said Mrs Beavis. 'My, it's nice to see you again, Dolly, and don't yer look pretty? I expect you're a nice bit of company for Sergeant Joe on a Sunday evenin'. I was only sayin' to Connie Cousins yesterday, I wonder 'ow that nice young lady Dolly is gettin' on. I told 'er what an 'ard life you'd 'ad, and she said she could condole with yer, she was 'aving an 'ard life 'erself with that Archie of 'ers. She said 'e come 'ome last week with a silver candlestick, 'e said 'e'd found it lyin' about near Billingsgate. 'E'd better take it round to the police station, 'e said, and orf 'e went with it. Well, Connie follered 'im, and caught 'im takin' it straight to the pawnshop. So she took it orf 'im and 'it 'im with it. Best thing too, with an 'usband like Archie. Men like that never learn unless you 'it 'em with something 'ard. I 'ope you don't get yerself an 'usband like Archie, Dolly, specially as you look as if you could click for a really nice chap. Joe said you'd got yerself a job in Peckham. Me Charlie's got cousins in Peckham, name of Bartlett.' She went on non-stop. Joe smiled at the glazed look creeping up on Dolly.

By the time Mrs Beavis had passed on all the gossip she could think of, Dolly was numb and Linda and Ella were due for their beds. They said good night to Dolly and Joe, and left with their jolly mum. Dolly came to and picked up her hat.

'Well, I'd best be off meself now, Joe,' she said.

'I'll come on the tram with you,' said Joe.

'No, I'll be all right, I'm standin' on me own feet, remember,' said Dolly.

'I don't mind a ride to Peckham and back,' said Joe.

'Well, it's nice of you to offer to see me home,' said Dolly, 'but you mustn't feel obligated because you're fond of me.' She put her hat on, pushing the pin into her

318

auburn crown, which Joe thought very well-dressed. 'I'll come next Sunday, shall I? I'll come in the afternoon, as I expect you'd like to take me for a walk in a park. Well, until you've met someone rich, I honestly don't mind givin' you the pleasure of me company, Joe. Thanks for the Sunday tea, it was lovely, but you'd best not kiss me goodbye in case – well, in case—'

'In case I fall over myself,' said Joe.

'Still, if you insist,' said Dolly, and offered her cheek.

'Your hat's in the way,' said Joe. He took her hand, bowed low to hide the grin on his face, and kissed her fingertips.

'Oh, you did that ever so gallant,' said Dolly, 'you can be a real gent sometimes, Joe. When you meet a rich girl, she'll like you doin' that.'

'Seeing you've got rich girls on the brain, I'll start looking for one.'

'Yes, you ought to,' said Dolly, 'you don't want to leave it till you're gettin' on a bit. See you next Sunday, then.'

'So long, Dolly.'

After she'd gone he thought how very quiet things were again.

CHAPTER TWENTY-FIVE

Henrietta's apartment contained a newly installed telephone, and in response to a call from Sir Hubert early on Monday morning, she arrived at his office at nine-thirty. Tubby was already there.

'Good morning, Henrietta,' said Sir Hubert.

'Good morning, Uncle Hubert,' said Henrietta, 'and hello, Mr Sharp.'

'How'd yer do, Miss Downes,' said Tubby.

'Have you heard that those two students made a fool of me?' asked Henrietta.

'Deliberate, I reckon,' said Tubby, 'on account they've cottoned on to the fact that they're bein' tailed. It ain't advisable to be cottoned on to, yer know.'

'Don't look at me, Tubby,' said Henrietta, 'I'm faultless as a shadow.'

'You're comin' along, Miss Downes, comin' along,' said Tubby.

'How sweet,' said Henrietta.

'Concerning our number one suspect and Trafalgar Square,' said Sir Hubert.

'Happy news that was, guv, 'earing the perisher 'angs about there frequent,' said Tubby.

'I'm assured by my niece that the source of the information is unimpeachable,' said Sir Hubert.

'That's French for what, guv?'

'Much to be trusted,' said Sir Hubert.

'Well, good for yer niece, guv,' said Tubby.

'Thank you,' said Henrietta, 'and I'd like to point out that Trafalgar Square is where I should be, not Bell Lane. Those students are never going to lead us anywhere except round the mulberry bushes.'

''Ighly dangerous, lettin' you get too close to that cove, Miss Downes,' said Tubby. 'I'll look out for him, with young Rodney's 'elp.'

'Very well,' said Sir Hubert.

'That's a conspiracy,' said Henrietta, 'I'll turn bitter soon.'

'I asked you here, Henrietta,' said Sir Hubert, 'to let you know we're ready to move you from Bell Lane to Newington Butts.'

'That's the ticket, guv,' said Tubby approvingly.

'Newington Butts?' said Henrietta.

'I haven't bothered you with what's been happening there,' said Sir Hubert, 'I didn't want to distract you from concentrating on Bell Lane.' He meant, of course, that he hadn't wanted to give her the kind of information that would send her flying in all directions. Henrietta frequently gave the impression that she was perfectly capable of being in two places at once, or even more. She'd have asked for only a little help from Tubby, having taken to him. He knew the pursuits of her own kind were boring to her. She thought most of her friends lived fairly useless lives. As it was, she'd been up to something for quite a while now, something she was unusually evasive about. 'Let me inform you there's a gentleman residing in Newington Butts who knows the woman we're looking for and may be an associate of hers.'

'Pardon?' said Henrietta, looking spellbound.

'The woman is using the name Marcelle Fayette, but we're sure she's the Russian confederate of the man called Boris, the woman referred to in that letter as Alexandra Petrovna.'

Henrietta, drawing breath, said, 'Where *is* Newington Butts?'

'Walworth,' said Tubby, 'off the Elephant and Castle.'

'We'd very much like to have control of her movements,'

said Sir Hubert, 'and we can have that control if we can find out where she lives. And if Mr Sharp can sight Boris in Trafalgar Square, we'll have control of his too. I'm going to ask you to undertake surveillance at Newington Butts, since we feel there's an excellent chance that the gentleman there will lead you to Marcelle Fayette. Henrietta, are you following me?'

'Uncle Hubert, I'm all agog. Do we have the gentleman's name?'

'Joe Foster, ex-Army sergeant, twenty-nine years old,' said Tubby. 'A quite decent bloke in a gen'ral manner of speakin', but a bit deep, as you might say, considerin' 'e's got a fancy for Marcy Fayette and she's a bit partial to 'im. Which is why 'e's evens favourite for showing us the way to 'er doorstep.'

'He's got a fancy for her?' said Henrietta. 'How'd you know that?'

'I've 'ad the pleasure of a couple of chats with 'im,' said Tubby.

'How exciting,' said Henrietta.

'If I might say so, guv,' said Tubby, 'it ain't too professional of yer young lady niece to refer to strict law and order work as excitin'.'

'Say so, by all means, Mr Sharp,' said Sir Hubert.

'It's me respectful opinion, guv, that she'd be safer learnin' to play the violin.'

'That's not respectful,' said Henrietta, 'that's cheeky. And why is it you're not continuing to watch Joe Prosser yourself?'

'Foster,' said Tubby. 'Him bein' a bloke who wasn't born yesterday, 'e's been givin' me a hard time. Accordingly, as you're unfamiliar to 'im, the guv 'opes you'll remain unfamiliar, while at the same time not lettin' 'im out of yer sight. He won't be expectin' to be tailed by a young lady such as yerself.'

'He's lodging at number twenty-one,' said Sir Hubert.

322

'Very well,' said Henrietta.

'I can tell you he's a genuine ex-Army man,' said Sir Hubert.

'A tall bloke with dark brown hair, moustache and a limp,' said Tubby. 'I ain't sayin' 'e's definitely fishy, but 'e does 'ave an 'ighly suspect relationship with Marcy Fayette.'

'What a swine,' said Henrietta.

'We aren't positive he's in that category,' said Sir Hubert.

'Well, I am,' said Henrietta. 'Look, you both believe, don't you, that it's all to do with a plot to assassinate the Tsar of Russia when he comes over for the coronation of his cousin, King George.'

'Perhaps,' said Sir Hubert.

'It's no good being in two minds, Uncle Hubert,' said Henrietta. 'There's a plot, that's certain. When we've found Marcelle Fayette and the man Boris, have them arrested, with the two students, and shoot them. Then we can all enjoy the coronation. And if ex-Sergeant Joe Foster is in it with them, I'll shoot him myself.'

''Ighly practical suggestion, guv,' said Tubby.

'Quite,' said Sir Hubert.

'Then I can give me feet a rest and yer young lady niece can start knittin' socks and jerseys for the ragged poor,' said Tubby.

'An excellent idea,' said Sir Hubert.

'I'll fall out with you in a moment, Tubby,' said Henrietta.

'Beg to assure you, Miss Downes, that I've got your welfare at 'eart,' said Tubby.

'How kind,' said Henrietta.

'That's all for now,' said Sir Hubert, 'and perhaps you'll both proceed as suggested.'

Henrietta took a motor taxi back to her apartment.

Twenty minutes later she was ready to go out again. Cissie and Nell waylaid her in the hall and stared at her in horror. She was wearing clothes she kept in a locked trunk, an old grey dress, a black shawl, shabby ankle-boots and an utterly disreputable straw hat.

'Oh, I can't believe it,' gasped Cissie.

'I'll have a fit,' said Nell. 'Miss 'Enrietta, I've seen you in some disgraceful clothes just lately, but never in anything as common and disgraceful as them. Miss 'Enrietta, I've got to say it, I've got to tell you you look like something left be'ind by dustmen.'

'Oh, don't go on,' said Henrietta shirtily.

'It's no good you 'aving the rats,' said Nell firmly, 'you can't go out like that.'

'Miss 'Enrietta, you just can't,' said Cissie.

'Once and for all, I'm employed by my uncle,' said Henrietta. 'This week I have to sweep out his offices and scrub the floors. Do you expect me to do that in an Ascot outfit?'

Cissie tottered.

'Scrub floors?' she gasped.

'Oh, I never heard the like all the time I've been servin' the family,' said Nell faintly. 'Miss 'Enrietta, I shall inform Lady Amelia immediate.'

'Please yourself,' said Henrietta, and left.

'She's havin' a brainstorm,' said Nell.

'No, she's just got the rats about something,' said Cissie. 'It's the Hon Cedric, that's what it is. He's upset 'er by not proposin'.'

'If only she was a young girl again,' sighed Nell. 'I could do me proper duty then and lock her in till she came to her senses. But how can I do it now she's come of age?'

'She'd break the door down if you did do it,' said Cissie.

'I'll never believe Sir Hubert is makin' her scrub floors,' said Nell.

'No, I told yer, she's playin' up on account of the Hon Cedric,' said Cissie.

'Well, it's got to stop, or we'll never be able to 'old our heads up,' said Nell.

It didn't stop. Henrietta sallied forth every morning looking like an inmate of a workhouse, much to the increasing mortification of her devoted but circumspect servants. However, outgoing and unconventional Aunt Amelia descended on Nell and Cissie one afternoon, and with a reassuring flurry of gloves, gestures and words, left them in dizzy acceptance of the fact that they were not to worry about what was happening to Henrietta, although it did not change their fixed belief that their young mistress ought not to dress so disgracefully. What would people think? Let the blighters stew, said Aunt Amelia, and went off like a whirlwind to chair a meeting of Advance Britannia members.

Henrietta, of course, was keeping Joe under surveillance, and what a teeth-gritting duty that was. The bounder, whenever he appeared, looked, even at a distance, as if he had nothing on his conscience. Upright, square-shouldered, he looked as if he was just about to take command of a company of recruits and drill them until their feet were killing them. Yes, he'd known years in the Army, without a doubt, the swine. He kept her fretful, for he only ever went out to the shops or for a walk. But he did go up to Charing Cross Road late in the week, to call in at a bookshop. He walked all the way, punishing his lame leg. She followed him all the way. She refrained from making herself obvious, she did not enter the shop herself.

Joe had gone to the shop merely to have a chat with George and perhaps to buy a book or two. George was delighted to see him.

Henrietta wondered, of course, if he was meeting

Marcelle Fayette there. She risked a stroll past the shop and a casual glance in, but saw only a customer examining a book. He himself wasn't visible. So where was he, in a back room with the woman? And if so, was he plotting with her or making love to her? Either way, what a disgusting man, what a traitor. Horsewhipping was too good for him.

He emerged after twenty minutes. She saw him from the other side of the road. One might have expected him to look uneasy or furtive, but oh, no. He was hypocritically upright and – what? Smug, that was it, the bounder. Yes, smug. Pleased with himself, of course. She wondered if it would not be a good idea to wait. Yes, a very good idea. If Marcelle Fayette was in the shop, in a back room somewhere, she would have to come out eventually.

Henrietta waited. Joe disappeared.

She waited forty minutes, but in vain. Marcelle Fayette did not appear. Henrietta, fretful and frustrated, walked to Trafalgar Square. Spotting Tubby, acting on information received concerning the man Boris, she spoke to him.

'Yes, I'll grant yer that, it was a good idea to wait,' said Tubby, 'but Mr Joe Foster's what you might call a natural at leadin' law and order up the garden path.'

'What a swine,' said Henrietta through gritted teeth.

'Now, young lady, I don't 'old with gettin' personal. So 'e's led yer a bit of a dance all week, and 'e's disappointed yer that he wasn't enjoying lovey-dovey with Marcy Fayette, somewhere in that bookshop, but there's no call to start wantin' to bash 'is head in. He's a cool customer, and I'm admirin' of it.' Tubby's eyes were alert while he was talking. 'No good takin' it personal because he ain't doin' what you want him to do, or what's expected of 'im. But he'll do it one day soon enough, and maybe right under yer nose, or as good as.'

'He'll do what one day?' demanded Henrietta.

'Make love to Marcy.'

'Don't be disgusting,' said Henrietta.

Tubby, quizzing the scene in Trafalgar Square, said, 'I thought you said you thought that's what 'e might've been doin' in the bookshop with French Marcy.'

'French my foot, she's Russian, she has to be,' said Henrietta.

'She's a handful, I'm certain of that,' said Tubby.

'You haven't spotted Boris, obviously,' said Henrietta aloofly.

'Not yet,' said Tubby, 'just soldier Joe. Saw 'im buy some fancy blooms from the flower girl.' Tubby had seen other people buy from her during the course of the warm day, among them one well-dressed man in a morning suit and Homburg, a man without a beard. It didn't occur to him for a second that this was the number one suspect. 'Then what d'yer think he did?'

'Struck her down and robbed her of her takings?' said Henrietta.

'Now don't let yer frustrations send yer cock-eyed, Miss Downes,' said Tubby. ''Aving bought himself a bunch of flowers and 'ad a chat with the girl, over 'e came and handed me four of 'em. Told me to present 'em to me lady wife, with 'is compliments.'

'The blackguard,' hissed Henrietta. 'If my uncle hasn't enough evidence to arrest him and shoot him, I hope he'll at least have a good enough reason to horsewhip him.'

'Well, well,' said Tubby, 'and 'ere's me thinking you're a civilized young lady.'

'Really?' said Henrietta haughtily. 'Dear me, how simple you are.'

Tubby grinned as she left. Haughty she might be, but she looked, in her funny old clobber, as if she was a female down-and-out.

*　　*　　*

327

Cissie ran from her young mistress's bedroom into the kitchen later that day.

'Oh, I'll 'ave a fatal turn,' she breathed.

'Now what's happened?' asked Nell.

'Miss 'Enrietta's just smashed an ornament. I never seen her so fed-up.'

'Well, we'll just have to put up with it,' said Nell, 'Lady Amelia havin' instructed us not to worry about how she dresses and how she be'aves. Did she use any swear words when she broke the ornament?'

'Oh, I just couldn't repeat what she said,' gasped Cissie, 'it wasn't fit for nobody's ears.'

'Out with it,' said Nell. 'I've had enough shocks these last weeks to kill me off, so one more won't make much difference.'

'Oh, lor',' said Cissie. 'Well, I made so bold as to ask 'er if it was the Hon Cedric who was upsettin' her, and she said – oh, I 'ardly know how to tell you, but she said, "Bugger the Hon Cedric."'

In a hoarse voice, Nell said, 'Quick, pass me them smelling-salts.'

Henrietta's devoted servants were both having a bad time.

CHAPTER TWENTY-SIX

Little cotton-wool clouds sailed about in the sky. Dark parental clouds, having spent the morning scolding London with sheets of rain, had taken themselves off to give East Anglia a similar wet drubbing and left their fluffy white offspring behind. Sunlight was drying out Newington Butts as Dolly pulled on the latchcord of the Beavis house. The door opened and she stepped into the passage. She was immediately assailed by the aroma of Sunday dinner from the kitchen and by the familiar rumbustious sounds of the family going to work on their roast beef and Yorkshire pudding. It was twenty past two. Joe, she knew, always ate his Sunday dinner at about one-thirty. She climbed the stairs on quick feet. He was in his living-room, seated in the fireside armchair, his feet up on one of the table chairs, and he was reading his Sunday newspaper.

'Well, here I am, Joe, it's me.'

He looked at her over the top of his paper. Another new dress? Well, it seemed new, and its lemon colour shimmered in places like silk. Her white hat with its large brim was itself a picture, and she wore white gloves. He had to admit it, she looked ravishing.

'Top of the class, Private Smith, you're ready for promotion,' he said.

'Here, give over,' said Dolly, 'that's ancient 'istory, that Private Smith stuff.'

'Oh, I've fond memories of it,' said Joe.

'Like me improving looks, do you?' said Dolly.

'You're a treat,' said Joe. 'Never seen a factory girl quite like you.' He got up. He was wearing what looked like an ancient cricket shirt. Once white it was now an ivory yellow. He wore it with brown trousers.

'Goin' to take me to a park, are you?' said Dolly. 'I don't mind comin' with you, and I thought I'd better put something nice on, so that you could swank at being me escort. Mind, if I get the eye from a few fellers, don't be surprised.'

'I'll only be surprised if you don't,' said Joe, and put on a peaked brown cap.

'You're not comin' out not dressed proper, are you?' said Dolly.

'I'll carry my jacket over my arm,' said Joe, 'it's a warm afternoon. How about Battersea Park? They've got a tea room there.'

'You goin' to treat me to tea out? What a lovely bloke. Come on, then.'

'We'll take a tram through Kennington and Nine Elms Lane,' said Joe, which they did, Dolly chatting away about her respectable new life, and what a kind landlady she had, and how the nice feller next door was helping her to make lots of friends. Of course, he'd wanted to take her out this afternoon, but she'd had to say no on account of already having promised Joe she'd go out with him. The friendly young gent looked horribly disappointed.

'Definitely fancies you?' said Joe.

'I keep gettin' fellers fancying me,' said Dolly, 'it's nearly embarrassin'. 'Ave you been lookin' out for some posh girl for yourself? You know, someone rich?'

'Can't say I've had any luck so far,' said Joe, 'and can't say I haven't been looking. I'm looking every time I go out, and last night I looked under my bed.'

'Oh, you daft thing,' said Dolly, 'as if you'd find a rich girl under your bed. You don't think rich girls go about lookin' for beds to creep under, do you?'

'Don't they, then?' said Joe. 'Is it a fact that they don't? I was banking on finding one under my own bed, I'd have been halfway to the church. Had a good week at the wax-fruit factory?'

'Yes, I made over an 'undred bananas last week, and forty-two apples with rosy blushes. Mr Parsons, me boss, said rosy blushes on apples are the most popular. The fact'ry doesn't make green ones any more, Mr Parsons said they don't sell.' Dolly went chattily on about her work.

When they reached Battersea Park, the afternoon had become brilliantly summery. It was the first week in June, and preparations were being made by London's borough councils to show the flag on coronation day, 22 June. In Battersea Park some triumphal arches had been erected. Decorations would follow. The cockneys were out by the score. Families were enjoying the green grass, dried and warmed by the sun. Kids ran about. Park-keepers chased the scallywag element. Girls floated along in their full-skirted summer frocks, and hopeful young men tracked them.

'I'm curious about the fact that there hasn't been a single line in the papers about the police looking for a man with a black beard and a foreign accent,' said Joe.

'Yes, ain't it funny peculiar?' said Dolly. 'Here, I thought I saw that old gypsy woman when I reached the Elephant and Castle this afternoon.'

'What old gypsy woman?'

'Come off it,' said Dolly, 'that Fanny Bonbon who fancied you and made you take 'er to the National Gallery, then went off as if she was owing her rent. I wouldn't like to think you've been keepin' company with her.'

'I've seen her a couple of times,' said Joe.

'I could spit,' said Dolly. 'And you've got a cheek, askin' me out when you're all lovey-dovey with 'er.'

'Am I?' said Joe.

'You must be,' said Dolly crossly, 'goin' out with her every time my back's turned.'

'Hardly,' said Joe.

'Don't make excuses.'

'I'm not.'

'Well, it sounds as if you're goin' to.'

They passed flowerbeds lush with summer blooms.

'Look,' said Joe, jacket still over his arm, 'I'm not after her, if that's what you're on about. Frankly, I don't trust Marcelle Fayette.'

'Why not?'

'She's up to something,' said Joe. 'Usually, I like to mind my own business. Usually, I can't stand people who don't. But that lady's a case for investigation. Ruddy hell, she actually told me she knew I'd got hold of a certain letter, that I'm up to something myself and that you're my confederate. I've been turning a blind eye to her peculiar ways, but now I think I'd like to know where she lives.'

'Well, I'm blessed,' said Dolly, 'me your confederate? What at?'

'Pinching that letter, to start with,' said Joe. 'D'you realize what that means?'

'I just can't think,' said Dolly.

'It means she knows Blackbeard, or that she knows something about him. So if I found out where she lives, I'd probably have to forget about minding my own business and let the police know.'

'You'd do that, you'd tell the police about 'er?' said Dolly.

'Not the sort of thing I like doing,' said Joe, 'but yes, I'd think seriously about it.'

'Joe, d'you mean you don't really fancy her?'

'Come into my parlour, said the spider to the fly. That's Marcelle.'

'Oh, I'll forgive yer now,' said Dolly.

'What for?'

'For makin' me want to spit,' said Dolly. 'But if you go to the police, you'll 'ave to tell them what she's up to.'

'Shan't be able to,' said Joe, 'don't exactly know. But if

332

she knows about that letter and is something to do with whatever Blackbeard's up to, she's worth looking into.'

'Crikey, yes,' said Dolly. 'Here, Joe, if you do find out where she lives, I'll go to the police for you, if you like. I can see you don't like being an informer. Well, I don't mind doin' it, you've been a good bloke to me.'

'No, don't want to get you involved, Dolly.'

'Well, all right,' said Dolly. 'Look, is that the tea room?'

'Yes, come on,' said Joe.

They shared a pot of tea, currant buns and slices of fruit cake. Dolly said she was ever so pleased with him, not only for treating her to tea in a park, but also because he wasn't daft about that Marcelle Fayette any more. Joe said he couldn't recall that he'd ever been daft about her.

'Well, you acted daft,' said Dolly. 'When you goin' to see her again?'

'When she pops up again, I suppose,' said Joe, who had a sure feeling that she would. 'By the way, Dolly, what's your address?'

'What d'you want to know me address for?'

'Don't play about,' said Joe, 'where d'you live?'

'I'm movin' tomorrow,' said Dolly, cutting up her slice of cake.

'You're what?'

'Well, it's that feller next door, that Cuthbert,' said Dolly. 'He's gettin' ideas, he tried to – well, I just couldn't tell you what he tried.'

'You'd better,' said Joe, 'or I'll take you back to my lodgings and rattle your teeth.'

'Crikey,' said Dolly, 'are you gettin' that fond of me, Joe? Are you gettin' serious feelings? I'm ever so flattered and complimented.'

'How would you like a good hiding?' said Joe.

'What, on a Sunday?' said Dolly. 'Honest, Joe, don't you 'ave no reverence? Oh, all right, I'd better tell you

333

about the bloke next door, I suppose. He tried to undo me.'

'Undo you?'

'Yes, me blouse, where I keep me lovely bosom,' said Dolly. Joe choked on a mouthful of cake. 'Here, what's up with you, doin' all that coughin' like you did when you were eatin' chips. Oh, did I surprise you about me lovely bosom? Honest, that 'orrible Cuthbert, I nearly died. I didn't 'alf give 'im what for. I ain't staying next door to him no more; a friend of mine at me fact'ry knows where I can get new lodgings and she's takin' me there after work tomorrow. I'll be able to tell you where it is when I next come and see you, Joe. I'm glad you're a gent, I bet you wouldn't try to undo a girl.'

'Don't bank on it,' said Joe.

'Could I 'ave some more cake?' asked Dolly.

Joe laughed. He couldn't help himself. It made her smile.

They spent the afternoon in the park, and when they got back to the Elephant and Castle, Dolly took a tram to Peckham, saying she had to spend the evening getting ready for her move to new lodgings tomorrow. She'd come and see him again in the week, she said.

Joe felt she'd been standing him on his head again. But he'd stopped worrying about it. Dolly in all her moods was irresistible.

He went to Charing Cross Road the following day, to see George again. His cheerful friend had made a definite promise to speak to customers he had among the landed gentry.

'Your luck may be in, Joe old chap,' he said. 'Yes, indeed, I think you've got prospects. I mentioned you to a customer of mine, a gentleman of some distinction, with an estate in Surrey. Near Reigate. He seemed extremely interested in all I said about you. I sang your praises, naturally, and he assured me he'd consider the matter, particularly as you're ex-Army. I have other customers of distinction who'd baulk at taking on anyone who was ex-Army, private, sergeant or general, on the grounds that all military men have no brains. Fortunately, some gentlemen admire your kind, Joe. I do myself.'

'Well, you're a decent gentleman, George. What's the name of the landed gent who's got my future under consideration?'

'Sir Hubert Wilkins,' said George.

'Can't say I've heard of him.'

'Well, that might change. He's promised to let me know if he'd like to see you. He's a Government man, he lives in his town house during the week and spends his weekends at his country residence.'

'Does he run a stable?'

'He's got a string of nags, I believe,' said George, 'and several hundred acres. If anyone can provide you with an outdoor job, he can.'

'You're a good old bloke, George,' said Joe.

'Glad to be of help, Joe. It may come to something, and it may not, so take nothing for granted. Just live in hope. Excuse me now while I attend to my customers.'

On his way back, Joe stopped in Trafalgar Square to patronize his larky, friendly flower girl.

'Morning, Daisy.'

'Same to you, sir.' Daisy's smile sparkled. 'Buy me sweet roses?'

'Buy your smile as well,' said Joe. 'How's your other regular?'

'Me other kind gent? Oh, 'e's been around quite a bit, 'e's always buyin' from me. I bet 'e's got a fancy lady somewhere, don't you? Would yer like six roses, sir?'

'I'm Joe.'

'Would yer like six roses, Joe?' asked Daisy perkily.

335

'That'll do fine, Daisy,' said Joe, wondering why Blackbeard hadn't been picked up by the police if he'd been around quite a bit. Ruddy peculiar. Two letters to the Police Commissioner about Blackbeard and no results? Very odd. Was it because anonymous letters cut no ice with them?

Standing just inside the entrance to the National Gallery, Rodney Masters watched Joe talking to the flower girl. The flower girl laughed. Joe left, carrying his roses. Rodney continued his watching brief, but hopes were dwindling now. Neither he nor Tubby, in all their hours of surveillance in Trafalgar Square, had laid eyes on the number one suspect, a bearded man known as Boris. Or so they thought.

Marcelle had met Rokovssky again, at his insistence. The rendezvous was a suburban one, Streatham Common. They walked over the green grass. Rokovssky wanted to know if the man Joe Foster was still alive. If so, why?

'Why? Why?' Marcelle was suddenly short-tempered. 'Because I still need to know to whom he sold the contents of that letter.'

'Time is beginning to run away. The man is dangerous, and more so now that he has seen so much of you. Kill him the moment you no longer need him. Have you found out who his masters are?'

'No,' said Marcelle, 'and I have come to the conclusion he has no masters. That is because he is not a man to take orders. I cannot see him running around obeying directives from the French or the Germans or any other power. The information he collects is, I'm certain, placed on offer to anyone who will buy. He has no job, he is a free agent. And if he's to be killed, you—' Marcelle halted. Her ambitious and calculating soul was failing her. She had thought to tell Rokovssky that he must be the executioner.

336

The Russian Wolf would not hesitate. He would do the deed without turning a hair, the while marking her down as an agent who could show frailty. He would report so to Count Zhinsky, and her lover, who hid cold steel behind his façade of kindness, would change his mind about her worth. 'Yes, if the man is to be killed, you may rest assured I will see to it.'

'If? If? Give me no ifs,' said Rokovssky. 'See to it before we make our own kill. The means is now in your hands.'

'It is in my apartment at the moment.'

'You have used it?'

'I have practised with it,' she said, 'and a particular cushion is on the way to being ruined.'

'Perfect your aim,' said Rokovssky.

What arrogance, thought Marcelle. He thought himself cleverly playing the foil, along with Ivan and Igor; he thought how brilliant he had been in making her the instrument of destruction.

'Perfect my aim?' she said. 'But of course. I shall only be able to fire once. Circumstances will not allow me to reload.'

'Be sure it's tipped on the day of the kill,' said Rokovssky.

'I do not need lessons in procedure on such a day as that will be,' said Marcelle.

'There should be little risk,' said Rokovssky. 'The British are chasing shadows. That is good, very good.'

'And you have them chasing a man with a beard,' said Marcelle, 'which is not good, is it? There would have been no chase at all if you had not killed that man.'

'A fool, an idiot, with too long a nose and too greedy a hand. He assumed I would pay him a small fortune for delivering the letter when he realized how important it was to me. I will see you again, and let you know when and where.'

Joe thought about Dolly and the translated letter that evening. He thought about Dolly first, simply because he could not help himself. Damn the fact that he had no job yet. However, two might be in the offing. The Army might come up trumps by taking him on as a recruiting sergeant, and Sir Hubert Wilkins might be giving him very favourable consideration. Whoever he was, George seemed to think well of him. On the strength of one of these possibilities, Joe felt he should do what he wanted to do. Get Dolly into a corner, knock some sense into her, stop her chucking all that chit-chat into his ears, and ask her to marry him.

Yes, good idea. Do that, Joe.

Point is, though, could he rely on her to turn up again?

What a girl. Was she really making wax bananas?

As for that letter, there was only one thing to do about it. Go and talk to that tubby bloke called Sharp, who had some connection with law and order, and was a bit of a character.

'Hello, hello,' said Tubby, answering the front door in his shirt sleeves, 'if I ain't mistaken it's me old soldier friend, Joe Foster. I'm Navy meself—'

'We've had all that,' said Joe. 'It's not my fault you spent all those years being seasick.'

'Watch your lip, matey.' Tubby grinned.

'Can I come in?' asked Joe.

'Pleasure,' said Tubby, and took him into the parlour. Mrs Tubby called from the kitchen.

'Who's that?'

'Soldier friend of mine,' called Tubby.

'Soldier?'

'We can't all be lucky, old girl. I'll be back with yer after I've 'ad a chat with 'im.'

338

Tubby closed the door.

'Married life suit you?' said Joe.

'Don't know where I'd be without it,' said Tubby. 'What's on yer mind, Joe? French Marcy?'

'A bit more than that,' said Joe.

'Take a seat,' said Tubby. 'Fancy a glass of ale?'

'I won't say no.'

'Good on yer, matey,' said Tubby, and went back to the kitchen, where he had a few more cheerful words with his trouble-and-strife before returning with a bottle of Watney's pale ale and two glass tumblers. He twisted the rubber-banded stopper free and poured the ale. The foam rushed to the top of each glass. He handed one glass to Joe.

'Thanks,' said Joe, 'and good luck.'

They drank. Then Tubby took a chair opposite Joe and invited his confidence.

'Let's 'ave it, Joe, I'm all ears.'

Joe let him have it by recounting the incident on the night thick with fog, how he took the girl home to his lodgings and what followed over the course of a number of days, including the arrival of Marcelle Fayette, his sending of an informative letter to the Police Commissioner and his enclosure of a translation of the letter found in Blackbeard's wallet. The translation, he said, had been arranged by a friend of his. He told Tubby he had sent a further letter to Scotland Yard when he found out that Blackbeard often appeared in Trafalgar Square.

'How'd you find out?' asked Tubby, lively with interest.

'Never mind that,' said Joe, who was still determined not to have Daisy, the flower girl, harassed. 'Just take my word for it.'

Funny, thought Tubby. Young Henrietta Downes also found out about Russian Boris haunting Trafalgar Square, although neither he nor Rodney had laid eyes on the bloke. Further, that young lady had also kept the source of her information to herself.

'Let's get it straight, Joe. You had this ding-dong with a foreign bearded geezer and a bruiser in the fog, you took the girl 'ome with you on account of 'er damaged ankle, the bruiser got 'is throat cut later that night, and then a few nights after that the bearded cove broke into yer lodgings to get at the girl in regard to the letter that was in the wallet she nicked?'

'That's gospel,' said Joe.

'And 'e was followin' 'er on the mornin' she left yer lodgings?'

'Stake my life it was him,' said Joe.

'What did yer say 'er name was?'

'Dolly. Dolly Smith.'

'Orphanage girl, you said?' enquired Tubby.

'I did. She's had a hard life.'

'Ain't we all,' said Tubby. He mused. Joe's informative letter plus the translation had eventually arrived in Sir Hubert's mitts. His second letter was obviously still with Scotland Yard. 'Well, you've come up with a fair old story, Joe, which 'as knocked me sideways.'

'Yes, I'm out of nursery rhymes,' said Joe.

'Bloody joker you are,' grinned Tubby. 'Blowed if I don't like yer. Bet yer orphanage girl likes you as well. Real port in a storm, that's you, matey, to a girl that much down on 'er luck. You can see now, I 'ope, that we need to cop French Marcy and the bloke you call Blackbeard. Dirty work at the cross-roads is bein' planned, and no error. Now you get 'old of French Marcy, who ain't French but Russian, and find out where she lives, like I've requested before, and I'll look after locatin' Blackbeard in Trafalgar Square.' Neither he nor Joe knew that the beard had been shaved off, that he had actually seen the wanted man without realizing it.

'Hold on,' said Joe, 'I'm a simple bloke—'

'That you ain't, Joe.'

'I'm ruddy simple in accepting you're an arm of the law—'

'Which I am, matey, you got my word.'

'Are you attached to some branch of Scotland Yard?'

'I'm attached to a branch of the law, Joe.'

'All the same, I'm not,' said Joe, 'and I don't feel inclined to cop Marcelle Fayette. She's your pigeon. And look here, Scotland Yard must have passed my second letter to you or I wouldn't have seen you hanging around in Trafalgar Square. What's wrong with your eyes that you haven't spotted Blackbeard?'

Tubby, ignorant of the contents of the second letter until now, sucked his pipe.

''Ope I ain't gettin' to need glasses,' he said. 'I'll make sure me and me colleague take longer looks at people in Trafalgar Square.'

'Pleased to hear it,' said Joe, 'he cut that docker's throat, rely on it.'

'I'll be hauntin' Trafalgar Square meself, matey.'

'I know he's there regularly,' said Joe.

'I believe yer, Joe, I believe yer,' said Tubby. 'Look, all I'm askin' of yer is French Marcy's address. I ain't askin' for you to cop 'er and tie 'er up, just her address. You're law-abidin', ain't yer? You find out where she lives and then knock on me door again, eh?'

'Well, all right,' said Joe.

'Good on yer, soldier,' said Tubby. 'I'm appreciative you came and talked to me, 'ighly appreciative. Me friends call me Tubby, though I ain't sure why, seein' me old lady still thinks I'm a fine figure of a man.'

'Not much wrong with you that couldn't be put right by six weeks of foot drill and forced marches,' said Joe.

'Now then, Joe, you're talkin' to a Royal Navy petty officer, yer know.'

'Yes, slightly out of shape,' said Joe.

Tubby grinned and they shook hands. Five minutes after Joe had departed for his lodgings, Tubby left to call on Sir Hubert at his London residence, and to report that ex-Sergeant Joe Foster had turned out to be a bloke after his own heart.

CHAPTER TWENTY-SEVEN

Henrietta called on her uncle in his office the next morning to tell him that sooner or later Mr Joe Foster of Newington Butts was bound to notice her. She couldn't hang about there day after day without him becoming aware of her. Something had to be done about a change of the routine. She also wanted to know if Tubby or anyone else had sighted Russian Boris yet.

'Not yet, Henrietta. Sit down, my dear. I've something to tell you.' Sir Hubert eyed his niece with interest. 'In the first place, you can forget Newington Butts. In fact, you can take a holiday.'

'Pardon?' said Henrietta.

'Yes, why don't you go down to Reigate and enjoy yourself? Do some horse-riding. Invite a friend.'

'Cedric, for instance?' said Henrietta.

'Excellent,' said Sir Hubert.

'Nothing doing,' she said. 'It sounds too much like an underhanded way of getting rid of me. It won't work. I have my rights as a member of your department, you know.'

'What rights?'

'How do I know? They're all wrapped up in the small print of the department's regulations, I expect, and I don't read small print. I prefer to trust people. Besides, although I love your country house, I don't at the moment want to go there.'

'I've no underhand motives, Henrietta,' said Sir Hubert. 'I'm simply offering you a holiday. We no longer need to watch Mr Foster. He surprised us very pleasantly by calling on Mr Sharp last night with some extremely astonishing information.' Sir Hubert recounted details passed on to him by Tubby. Henrietta's face was a study in its infinite variety of expressions. 'Do you have any comments, Henrietta?'

'What?' said Henrietta.

'Do you have any comments?' asked Sir Hubert. 'In view of the fact that a few of the details have a familiar ring?'

'Pardon?' she said again.

'The evening when the fog was so thick and you—'

'Oh, that,' said Henrietta. In truth, her life was so complicated and mixed-up at the moment that she preferred to say nothing to anybody, but to work things out for herself. It was characteristic of her. 'Coincidences, Uncle Hubert, that's all.'

'Incredibly, the letter Mr Foster wrote to the Police Commissioner finished up in the department's mail addressed to me,' said Sir Hubert.

'How fortunate for the department,' said Henrietta, 'it meant that the police didn't blunder across our path. If Mr Foster made sure you received the letter and the translation, what a divinely helpful gentleman he is, isn't he?'

'Divinely?'

'What else?' said Henrietta, quite recovered from her confusion. 'We must give him his due. Having seen much of him recently, I can say what an honest and upright gentleman he looks. And he's recognized Marcelle Fayette for what she is, a low and scheming creature from darkest Russia. I'm touched, aren't you, Uncle Hubert, with the way he addressed himself to Tubby and came up with so much valuable information? It was a very honourable thing to do. We must regard him as a remarkable gentleman.'

'Honourable *and* remarkable?' said Sir Hubert.

'Please don't quibble,' said Henrietta.

'Perish the thought, young lady. By another coincidence, I had in mind an interview with the gentleman. Mr George Singleton, the bookseller in Charing Cross Road, is a close friend of his, and advised me that Mr Foster is seeking work in the country, either looking after horses or as a gamekeeper. According to Mr Singleton, he's a man of excellent character, something that's borne out by his Army record. I thought, at the time, that it would be intriguing to meet him in view of our – ah – other interest in him. Now I'm tempted to consider him as a replacement for Tom Jarvis, who'll be retiring in September.'

'Uncle Hubert?' said Henrietta, stiffening.

'Tom Jarvis, our groom, is retiring in September. I thought—'

'Certainly not,' said Henrietta. 'You can't turn Mr Foster into a groom. He'll smell of horses. Shame on you, Uncle Hubert, for even thinking of it, especially when you've just said what an honourable and remarkable gentleman he is.'

'I think it was you who said that.' Sir Hubert smiled. He was making deductions and drawing conclusions. 'If Mr Singleton advised me correctly, then Mr Foster himself favours working with horses. And why not, since he was once a dragoon?'

'That's no excuse, Uncle Hubert.'

'Dear me,' said Sir Hubert, drawing his hand across his mouth to hide a smile.

'I'm sorry,' said Henrietta, 'but Mr Foster must simply be down on his luck. He wouldn't be living in lodgings, otherwise. To ask to look after horses can only mean he's clutching at straws. How dreadful of you to think of taking advantage of him. With your influence, can't you get him a knighthood and five thousand pounds a year?'

Sir Hubert gaped.

'Henrietta, are my ears deceiving me?'

'Why, what have I said?' asked Henrietta.

'I think you mentioned a knighthood and five thousand pounds a year.'

'What's wrong with that?'

'It happens to be in the realms of fantasy,' said Sir Hubert.

'Now look here, Uncle Hubert, if we catch Marcelle Fayette and Boris Blackbeard, we'll owe it all to Mr Foster. Don't you dare make a smelly groom of him, or I *will* go down to your country house, but only to set it on fire.'

'Good God,' said Sir Hubert, 'all this in the interests of a man you've been watching but have never met?'

'One likes to be fair,' said Henrietta.

'Henrietta, I own to being uncertain about what has been happening to you lately. And neither am I sure about what you've been up to.'

'I think I shall go back home and lie down,' said Henrietta.

'Lie down?'

'Yes, you've given me a headache,' said Henrietta, and left.

She thought about Mr Joe Foster.

Oh, my God, I've got to tell him sometime.

He'll kill me.

He'll throw me off the top of Big Ben. Or Tower Bridge.

Tubby, spotting the Trafalgar Square flower girl, thought wake up, me lad, if she ain't a possible source of information, who is round here?

He spoke to Daisy. Daisy, liking his twinkling eyes and cheerful smile, was responsive. Tubby asked her if she'd ever noticed a bloke he was interested in, a foreign acquaintance of his. He described the gent, and in a breezy way that aroused neither alarm nor suspicion in Daisy.

Yes, she knew him, she said, he was a regular customer.

346

She didn't know his surname, but he had said to call him Alex, if she liked. Was that the name?

'That's it,' said Tubby, 'Alex Whatsisname, with a fine black beard and blue eyes, eh?'

'Oh, 'e don't 'ave a beard no more, 'e shaved it off,' said Daisy.

'Well, what d'yer know, I'll pull 'is leg about that,' said Tubby, and was so delighted with that useful piece of information that he bought a whole heap of flowers from her for Mrs Tubby. He knew now how to lay his eyes on Russian Boris when he next bought flowers from Daisy. Daisy didn't tell him she had an assignment with her generous regular. Well, he didn't ask, and her regular had said to keep to themselves what they were going to do. It was something to make the crowds laugh and clap.

'To be or not to be, Cissie, that's the question,' said Henrietta that evening.

'Not to be what, Miss 'Enrietta?' asked Cissie, fastening the hooks and eyes that ran down the back of her young mistress's evening gown.

'I'm glad you asked,' said Henrietta, regarding herself critically in the long mirror. 'The fact is, can I or can't I face up to a thousand slings and arrows?'

'I'm sure I don't know what that means,' said Cissie.

'Well, it means a thousand slings and arrows are going to hurt me all over,' said Henrietta.

'Yes, it do sound a bit 'urtful, Miss 'Enrietta,' said Cissie. 'Still, never mind, you're going to look lovely for the theatre tonight. Are you goin' with the Hon'rable Cedric, is he callin' for you?'

'Hope not, for his sake,' said Henrietta, touching her hair.

'What's he done, then?' asked Cissie.

'Nothing.'

'But you sound cross with 'im.'

'I'm not even thinking about him,' said Henrietta.

'What are you thinking about, then, Miss 'Enrietta?'

'Slings and arrows,' said Henrietta, and went off to the theatre later with two old school friends. It took her mind off problems she'd made for herself.

Joe received a letter from Marcelle the following morning. It bore no address. It invited him to meet her outside the Albert Hall tomorrow evening at eight o'clock and to tell his landlady he would be out all night. Do not fail me, she said, I have something really important to tell you this time.

Out all night? Joe had a good guess at what that meant. But where would it happen? In her own bedroom? And what was something really important? Action was required if she meant to take him to where she was living.

'Crumbs, I fink I'm in trouble, Sergeant Joe,' said young Linda in the evening.

'At your age, Private Carrots?' he said, putting his daily paper aside.

'It ain't me age,' said Linda, 'it's me spit, I don't 'ave much tonight, I fink it's all dryin' up. Crikey, Sergeant Joe, I might not be able to shine yer shoes any more.'

'Can't have that,' said Joe, 'drink some water.'

'All right,' said Linda, and took a glass to the tap in the landing loo. Joe returned to his paper. Linda came back with her tummy awash with water and her mouth wet with it. She produced some good spit then. 'Look, I've got lots now,' she said.

Joe didn't respond, he was glued to page four of the *Westminster Gazette*.

Mrs Beavis called from the foot of the stairs.

'Come on down now, Linda lovey, I'm just goin' to serve supper.'

'Won't be a minute, Mum,' called Linda, and gave

some final rubs to both shoes. 'There, I done 'em, Sergeant Joe, can I 'ave me penny now?'

'What?' Joe sounded a bit faraway.

'I finished yer shoes,' said Linda, 'can I 'ave me penny, please?'

Joe fished absently for a penny, found one and handed it to her. Linda said thanks, then went down. Entering the family kitchen she said Sergeant Joe had got a funny look.

'Well, why ain't yer laughin'?' asked Albert.

''Cos it ain't funny funny,' said Linda.

'Has 'e 'ad his supper yet?' asked Mrs Beavis.

'No, it's a stew, it's still cookin' on 'is stove,' said Linda.

'Well, I expect 'e's 'ungry,' said her mum, 'that can give anyone a funny look. I ought to 'ave taken 'im up some of me jam turnovers for 'is afternoon cup of tea. Sergeant Joe's a nice 'ealthy man, 'e's bound to get an 'ungry look if 'e don't eat anything of an afternoon. Still, 'e'll be all right when 'e's 'ad his stew. Come on, sit down, everyone, I've got a steak-and-kidney pie to serve.'

Dolly slipped into the house forty minutes later, closing the door quietly behind her. From the kitchen, tidal waves of sound were swamping the ground floor and rising upwards. She climbed the stairs to the landing. Joe's door was closed. She knocked, opened it and put her head in.

'Watcher, Joe, it's me again,' she said brightly.

Joe was sitting in his armchair, the uneaten pot of stew off the hob, the fire damped right down. He looked up, his expression wooden.

'Come in, Miss Henrietta Downes,' he said.

'Oh, Lord,' said Miss Henrietta Downes. She'd come because she couldn't keep away, and because she knew she'd got to tell him before the whole thing blew up in her face. But she was too late. He'd found out. She braced herself for a real storm of slings and arrows. 'Oh, blow and bother, I was going to tell you, really I was. How did you find out?'

'It's all there,' said Joe, indicating the newspaper lying open on the table. Henrietta advanced and looked. And made a face. There it was, a society story about the Hon Cedric, London's favourite bachelor, popular man-about-town and darling of the debs. And she had a mention as the young lady he was most often seen with. That wouldn't have mattered, it was the accompanying portrait photograph of herself that had given the game away. It was unmistakably herself.

'Honestly, Joe, these newspapers, don't they make you want to spit?' she said lightly, although her nerves were jangling. Joe had thunder written all over his brow. 'All right, hit me, then, shoot me at dawn, but I really am Dolly. Henrietta Dolly. And I really am an orphan, my parents died of cholera in India when I was six. My Aunt Amelia and Uncle Hubert took me over. They've been lovely to me, and Aunt Amelia, my word, she's a born eccentric. Wait till you meet her, she'll like you—'

'Don't go on,' said Joe.

'Oh, Lord, you're not going to be all cross and rotten, are you?'

'Can't see that that'll do me any good,' said Joe.

'Oh, that's a relief. Let's go out for a walk, shall we?'

'Listen, Miss Downes—'

'Miss Downes? Ugh to that,' said Dolly.

'You've had your fun,' said Joe. 'Now do me a favour and hoppit.'

'Me? Me, Joe?'

'Yes, you. Push off.'

'Not likely. Why should I?' Dolly meant to fight. 'I'm not a pair of old socks, you know. You can chuck me down the stairs, if you like, but I'll climb up again, even on two broken legs. Think of all I did for you while I was here. I tidied the place up for you—'

'You what?'

'Well, I would have if you hadn't kept dumping me on that bed. I swept the floors for you—'

'When?'

'Well, I'm sure I offered, and I peeled potatoes for you and cooked you a nice lunch once. Well, I would have if that disgusting frying-pan hadn't burst into flames. Honestly, I don't know why you're being so difficult. You haven't said one nice word to me.'

'Or given you a bit of a kiss?' said Joe.

'No, you haven't, you rotter. You're the stingiest man I know when it comes to giving a girl a kiss, and you haven't asked me to sit down.'

'I don't want you to sit down,' said Joe, 'I want you to vanish. Can't think what you got out of making a fool of me. Some peculiar kind of pleasure, I suppose.'

Dolly winced.

'I wish you hadn't said that, Joe. It hurt. I do have feelings, you know.'

'Pleased to hear it,' said Joe. 'But go home. It's all over, Dolly. I know it, you know it. So go home.'

'Just like that? You've got a hope. I didn't give you the best days of my life for nothing. And we had fun, you know we did. Oh, all right, I did play you up a bit, acting like a cockney girl—'

'An orphanage cockney girl.'

'Well, I am an orphan, I've just explained that. Yes, and how would you like to be one? It's jolly heart-rending when you're only six.'

Joe gave her a dark look. Dolly, hell-bent on not losing him, tried a smile. He saw only a minx who'd taken him in hook, line and sinker, and who'd been laughing at him most of the time. All that chat of hers, all that cockney stuff, put over with the ease of a born actress. Now she was trying to give him more chat, but as herself. What puzzled him was what she'd been doing on that foggy night, getting herself mixed up with Blackbeard and nicking his wallet in the guise of a down-at-heel cockney girl. Not that it mattered now. She wasn't his kind. She was a society girl, and probably rich enough to dress herself in silk, satin and mink. Hell, he'd gone to Annie at the pawnshop and bought those second-hand things for her. What a fool. And he'd have turned himself into a bigger one if he'd asked her to marry him.

'Give it up, Dolly,' he said. 'Go home, there's a good girl. There's no fun in it now, not for either of us. And you don't belong here, you know that.'

'Yes, I knew you'd say that,' said Dolly, 'and I'm not standing for it. Don't get superior with me, Joe Foster, I'm as good as you are. Just because you've been a dragoon and have seen the world doesn't mean you're better than I am. I could have been a dragoon myself, only I was born a woman.'

'First-class minx, you mean,' said Joe.

'I don't know how you can say a thing like that when you fancy me the way you do. I hope you're not going to cut off your nose to spite your face.'

'Give it up,' said Joe.

'Can I sit down and talk to you?'

'No,' said Joe, already sure he was being undermined. 'Be sensible and go away.'

'Blow that,' said Dolly, 'I don't care how much you hit me, I'm going to sit down and talk to you.' She seated herself and talked to him. She gave him her story.

At the time when they bumped into each other in the fog, she was working for her uncle, who himself worked for the Government. There were certain foreign people under suspicion, including two Russian students. Dressed as a poverty-stricken cockney girl, it was her responsibility to help keep an eye on their movements. That evening she'd seen them meet a docker outside the dock gates. The fog wasn't too thick at that time, and she'd followed them to a pub. The students went in, passing a letter to the docker before they entered. If they were aware they were under suspicion, they weren't aware of her on this occasion. The docker didn't go into the pub himself, and she followed him to the Embankment at Blackfriars, both of them riding on a bus. The docker walked over Blackfriars Bridge, with the fog beginning to thicken, and went into the first pub he came to. She took a careful look in, and saw him sitting by himself, drinking beer. He was there quite some time. When he finally left, the fog was a pea-souper, but she managed to stay behind him. At the Elephant and Castle, he entered another pub, the Rockingham. She followed him in this time, because she felt he'd only used the previous pub to pass an hour or so. It was there, in the Rockingham, that he met Blackbeard and where she got hold of the letter by snatching the wallet. She ran, she bumped into Joe, and he knew all about what happened after that. Because she was working for her uncle, she couldn't confide in Joe, the Government wouldn't let her, and it was then, in keeping up her pretence of being a cockney girl down on her luck, that all her troubles began.

'All *your* troubles?' said Joe.

'Yes, you kept bullying me, throwing me on the bed, giving me orders, smacking my bottom, making me peel potatoes—'

'No wonder you can't cook,' said Joe. 'I see why now, it's all done for you.'

'Joe, you're not going to be ratty with me all evening, are you?'

'No comment,' said Joe.

Dolly made another face, then went on with her story. At first, she'd only thought about getting away as soon as her ankle allowed her to. But she had to get hold of that letter. He had it, and the wallet. And things quickly began to go wrong. It was his fault they did. If he'd just been

353

ordinary, she wouldn't have got so interested in him. Most people were ordinary, why couldn't he have been? Oh, no, not him, he'd been in the dragoons and was superior to everyone else.

'Watch your tongue,' said Joe.

Dolly insisted it was true, that he should have been ordinary. But all that Army talk, all those orders, and all that Private Nobody stuff, she'd never come across a man like him before. Most of the men she knew were terribly boring and weedy.

The first time she did get out she went to see her uncle, who was in a frightful stew about her. She didn't want to tell him she was staying with a man in his lodgings and occupying his bed, and nor did she tell him she wanted to go back there. So she told him that in catching up with the docker and Blackbeard, she'd fallen over in the fog, hurt her ankle and knocked herself out. When she came to a kind family had taken her to their home in Walworth and looked after her until her memory came back. She said it had blanked out.

'Your uncle fell for that?' said Joe, beginning to experience familiar feelings of helplessness.

'My uncle has a kind heart,' said Dolly, 'which is more than I can say about some people I know.'

'Why didn't you tell him about me?'

'Well, I – oh, how do I know?'

'Of course you know,' said Joe. 'You're still playing about. You knew your uncle would have had you out of here there and then. He'd have had the sense to realize that that was the right thing to do. And it would have saved me—' Joe closed his mouth.

'What would it have saved you?' demanded Dolly.

'Never mind. Not relevant. Doesn't count. Is there more to come?'

'Of course there is,' said Dolly. 'I meant to tell you everything and I'm going to.' She told her uncle she was sure Blackbeard was living in Walworth, that she'd go back to the kind family and try to find Blackbeard from there. Her uncle fussed. But he let her go back to Walworth. First, however, she had to go to her dingy old apartment and speak to her servants.

'Servants, right,' said Joe, 'that's done it in for good. Hoppit.'

'Don't be rotten,' said Dolly, 'they're not actually my servants, they're my aunt's.' She told them she'd be away for a while, and they fussed too and got very cross with her. What with that and her sore ankle and Joe always getting ratty with her, it was a wonder she didn't jump into the river. Anyway, she went back to his lodgings, even if he didn't deserve her, and put herself out to be kind and loving because he'd really been good to her.

'Kind and loving?' said Joe. 'Did that cover all the orphanage carry-on and how you showed your legs for a penny a time?'

'Oh, wasn't that funny, Joe? But I had to act that way, there was Marcelle Fayette making eyes at you and getting my goat. Oh, Lord, I suppose you'll bite my head off now, because I have to tell you that when you wrote to the Police Commissioner and enclosed that translation, I didn't post it, I put it in another envelope and posted it to my uncle.'

'Hell's bells,' said Joe, 'it's actually getting worse.'

'Well, my uncle needed it, he needed to know about Blackbeard and exactly what he was up to, before the police got hold of him. I wish you'd stop giving me a magistrate's look, as if you're going to commit me to the Old Bailey. Why don't you think about the time when you gave me the push and sent me off to be a chambermaid? That ought to be weighing heavily on your conscience. How you could do that to someone you fancied and who'd given you a free look at her legs, I simply don't know – Joe?'

Joe was laughing. His hopes had crashed, but there she was, as irrepressible as ever, and no more lost for a word than she'd ever been. Dolly was a riot. He couldn't have her himself, but he envied the man who did get her. The way she'd made a fool of him had its funny side. At no time had he ever suspected she wasn't a saucy fun-loving cockney girl. He'd only been unsure of what she was up to at times.

'Don't say any more, Dolly. I can guess the rest.'

Oh, bless him, thought Dolly, she was going to be spared having to tell him she'd actually had him under surveillance.

'Joe, you have to believe I was going to confess tonight, you have to believe they really were the best days of my life. Don't you think, apart from Marcelle Fayette and Blackbeard, that it was lots of fun?'

'I think we can part friends, with no hard feelings,' said Joe.

'I hope that's a joke.'

'Commonsense.'

'I hope that's a joke too.'

'Different worlds, Dolly.'

'I see, it's that again, is it?' said Dolly. 'I'm not good enough for you. Well, I never thought you'd turn out to be a stuffed shirt. You want your head seeing to. I'll send a doctor round, with a mallet. Why aren't I good enough for you?'

'Don't stand the argument upside-down,' said Joe, 'and don't complicate it. You live in style. I live in lodgings, with no great prospects. I haven't even got a job. And that's it. No more need be said. Come on, I'll walk you to a bus or tram and shake hands with you.'

'Not on your life,' said Dolly. 'You're not a hairy old tramp, are you? Or a beery costermonger? Or an illiterate road-sweeper? You're a dragoon and you've had a life much more interesting than mine. And you care about

356

people. You cared about me. You're a gentleman, Joe Foster, and you're a man as well. If you think you can push me out of your life, you can think again. It's not going to happen.'

'It won't work, Dolly. By the way, do you know a man called Mr Sharp and known to his friends as Tubby?'

'Don't change the subject,' said Dolly evasively.

'I've a feeling you do know him, since he's interested in the same people you've been after. If so, tell him I'm meeting Marcelle Fayette outside the Albert Hall at eight tomorrow evening.'

'Joe? Joe, are you really doing that, are you really meeting her?'

'Tubby will know what to do,' said Joe.

'I suppose you think that's your goodbye message to me.'

'With no hard feelings, Dolly.'

'You'll be lucky,' said Dolly, 'all my feelings are up in arms. You wait. And further, Mr Foster, don't get too near Marcelle Fayette tomorrow night or she'll meet with a frightful accident. And so will you. Hell hath no fury and so on. I'm leaving now. I'll see myself out.'

Joe came to his feet. Dolly made for the door.

'Good luck, Dolly,' said Joe.

'You wait,' said Dolly again, and left. The door closed behind her. It opened again. Her hat and face appeared. 'It's going to be another Charge of the Light Brigade,' she said, and was gone.

There was just a chance that Russian Boris had mentioned his correct first name to Daisy the flower girl, Tubby had said to Sir Hubert. Sir Hubert agreed, and asked Miss Verney if she could possibly go through the Russian file and look for a gentleman whose first name was Alex.

'Sometimes, Sir Hubert,' said Miss Verney, 'one is confused by your kind habit of referring to every male

357

person as a gentleman. However, I will do my best.'

'Thank you, Miss Verney.'

Miss Verney came up with particulars on one Alexander Rokovssky. The particulars caused Tubby to whistle.

'Ruddy 'ell,' he said, 'what a bleeder.'

'I beg your pardon, Mr Sharp?' said Miss Verney.

'My 'umble apologies for me French language,' said Tubby, but that didn't alter the fact that if Russian Boris was Alexander Rokovssky, he and Sir Hubert were up against an assassin of proven ferocity.

CHAPTER TWENTY-EIGHT

Henrietta went straight to her uncle's town house. He was in his study, poring over papers relating to arrangements for the coronation procession. The great day was not far away.

'Henrietta? What brings you here?'

'Marcelle Fayette,' said Henrietta. 'You must let Tubby know that Mr Joe Foster is meeting her outside the Albert Hall at eight o'clock tomorrow evening.'

Sir Hubert rose from his chair.

'How do you know this?'

'I've just come from Mr Foster himself. What a fine upright gentleman he is. He volunteered the information. I shall go with Tubby, of course.'

'Henrietta—'

'I insist. Tubby and I will track the creature down to her lair. Uncle Hubert, are you sure you can't arrange a knighthood for Joe?'

'Joe?'

'Mr Foster. Such a great help to the cause of law and order, and I'd quite like being Lady Foster.'

'Young lady, what exactly are you saying?'

'That I'm going to marry Mr Foster, even if it's the last thing I do.'

'Good God,' said Sir Hubert.

'I'm pleased you approve. You'll like him, Uncle Hubert. Mind you, ducky, he's being a bit of a stick-in-the-mud. He has some stuffy idea that I'm not good enough for him. He seems to think that as an ex-sergeant of the 2nd Dragoons, only an exceptional woman deserves his favours. He probably has Cleopatra or Helen of Troy in mind. I should have mentioned it and let him know they're both dead. Uncle Hubert, you think I'm good enough for a dragoon, don't you?'

'At this precise moment, Henrietta, I'm incapable of thinking at all. But am I to understand you know Mr Foster well enough to consider marrying him?'

'Yes, of course,' said Henrietta. 'It may take a month or two to make him see he has no option. It's a long story, how I came to meet him and to know him, and I'll tell you one day. I'm glad I have your blessing, and I'll leave you to your papers now.'

'Wait,' said Sir Hubert. 'What exactly does he do for a living?'

'Oh, nothing very much. He's a gentleman.'

'Of independent means?'

'No, just down on his luck. We shall have to live in the country and keep chickens. I must fly now. Don't forget to send a message to Tubby.'

'Henrietta, this is altogether ridiculous.'

'Not really,' she said.

'Keeping chickens is the height of absurdity.'

'No, it isn't. I like chickens,' said Henrietta.

June was blowing hot and cold. The morning had been quite chilly, the afternoon blustery. By evening, a warm south-west wind had taken over. A piece of torn newspaper, overlooked by the street cleaners, skittered about the concourse fronting the main entrance to the Albert Hall. Joe was walking about. It was five to eight and he was waiting for Marcelle. But it was Dolly he had on his mind. Henrietta Dolly.

From a standing motor taxi in Albert Court, Tubby and Henrietta watched him.

'Tubby, old thing, what do you think of Joe Foster?'

'Well, I'm Navy meself, Miss Downes—'

'Dear me, I'd never have guessed,' said Henrietta, eyes

following Joe's every movement. He knew they were there. He was walking up and down. She noted his limp, the limp he was trying to get the better of.

'But I like the bloke,' said Tubby. 'Man after me own 'eart. He's pulling our chestnuts out of the fire. I'd buy 'im a pint any time.'

'Bless you,' said Henrietta.

'Eh?' said Tubby.

'Bless you.'

They watched and waited, the taxi clock ticking away. At seven minutes past eight, Tubby said, ''Ope French Marcy 'asn't got wind of us. I've 'ad some grievous disappointments lately. If I get another one tonight, I'll resign on the grounds that I ain't up to the job any more.'

'Cheer up, she'll come,' said Henrietta. 'She's after Joe, the hussy.'

Marcelle appeared a minute later, when she seemed to Joe to suddenly materialize before him in a lightweight blue mackintosh and a matching pull-on hat.

'Ah, you have come,' she said.

'I'm here, yes,' said Joe. 'So are you.'

'But of course, my handsome friend.'

'Don't like to say so, but you're late.'

'Late? Late? In my little note to you, I said eight o'clock, yes?' Marcelle shook a finger at him. Young couples strolled about, the men in boaters, the girls summery. 'Come, Joe, it is a lady's privilege not to be early.'

'Can't make up my mind if that could be called a privilege or not,' said Joe.

Marcelle laughed. Softly. Clouds, buffeted by the wind, galloped through the sky.

'Joe, you are very different,' she said.

'Different?'

'From all the others.'

'What others?' he asked.

'Men I have known.'

'That's not my fault. Accident of nature.'

'Silly man, it is not a fault, it is very appealing.'

'Don't see myself like that,' said Joe, 'don't see any man like that. Just women. Now, what's important about what you have to tell me?'

'Your life is important, isn't it?' Her eyes flickered. 'Go away for the next six days. Go anywhere, do not stay in your lodgings.'

'My lodgings aren't safe?'

'No. And you, you are not safe, either.'

In his direct way, Joe said, 'I fancy you're talking about a man called Boris.'

Evasively, she said, 'Who is Boris? Do I know such a man? I only know you must go away. For six days.' Since she knew she could not do what Rokovssky had said she must do, she knew he would do it himself. 'Believe me, you must go.'

Joe felt then that in warning him she had earned a reprieve for herself.

'Marcelle, you need to be warned too. Have to tell you that tomorrow you must pack your bags and go home. Catch a boat train. They're after you.'

'Who?' she asked quickly.

'The same forces of law and order who've been following me around because they know I know you. Whatever you're up to, Marcelle, forget it.'

Marcelle bit her lip. 'Joe,' she said, 'you are saying your people know where I live?'

'They don't know yet,' said Joe, 'but they're closing in.' He knew Tubby and Henrietta Dolly were in that standing taxi some eighty yards away. 'Best thing you can do now is to go your way, while I go mine.'

'Ah,' she said, 'you and I are two of a kind, yes? I always knew we were. That is right?'

'Can't say we're two of a kind, Marcelle, only that you'd

362

be better off on a boat train than anywhere in London. Don't see that they can stop you going home if you haven't been naughty yet.'

'We are not to make love, to spend the night together in my apartment?'

One thing Joe was certain of. He couldn't make love to a woman whom he'd already betrayed. He could only give her the right kind of reason to take herself off while her hands were still clean.

'Run for it, Marcelle, I don't think the time's right for bedding you.'

She sighed.

'Come to St Petersburg one day,' she said. 'Ask for me at the Winter Palace. Ask for Alexandra Petrovna.'

She went then, she glided away, towards Prince Consort Road. The taxi moved. Joe left, knowing now she was the Alexandra Petrovna mentioned in the letter.

Taking morning tea to her young mistress the next morning, Cissie saw she was sitting up in her bed, hands to her hair, fingers making ringlets of strands. And she was humming a song.

'Miss 'Enrietta, you 'appy this morning?'

'I'm unscathed, Cissie.'

'What's unscathed?'

'Unpunctured,' murmured Henrietta.

'Miss 'Enrietta, that don't sound very nice.'

'It feels nice. There were no slings and arrows.'

'I don't know what you mean,' said Cissie.

'It means he loves me.'

'Who, the Hon Cedric, Miss 'Enrietta?'

'Ugh,' said Henrietta, and closed the conversation.

'Got 'im, guv,' said Tubby at midday.

'A splendid turn of the tide,' said Sir Hubert.

'You could say so, guv. Nabbed French Marcy's

363

address last night, spotted Boris this morning. Buyin' a bokey from the flower girl. 'E's lost 'is beard all right. Crafty geezer, that one. Lives in Albany Road, Walworth. Goes under the name of Boris Kirsch. I've got two men on the job of keepin' tabs, and young Rodney and Saunders are watching French Marcy. I'm relievin' one of the Walworth men in an hour. I ain't very partial to losin' Boris. You advisin' Scotland Yard, guv?'

'I'll advise them when we finally pick him up, Mr Sharp.'

'Thought yer might do that,' said Tubby. 'Thought yer might agree 'e's our teddy bear.'

Tubby was in Walworth when Rodney Masters called on Sir Hubert to report that Marcelle Fayette had departed bag and baggage from her apartment and taken the boat train from Victoria. Sir Hubert requested him to repeat that. Rodney Masters obliged, adding a rider to the effect that it looked like their pigeon had got the wind up and had flown the coop.

'Kindly do me the favour of calling on Mr Foster of Newington Butts,' said Sir Hubert. 'If you find him in, ask the gentleman to oblige me by coming to see me immediately.'

Joe was in, having just returned from seeing George Singleton. George expressed only mild surprise when Joe asked if he could lodge him for six days. He murmured something about deep waters, then offered Joe the use of a room above his shop or the guest room at his home in Maida Vale. Joe elected for the room above the shop. He thanked George and said he'd be back later, with a few belongings. He might have elected to stay in his lodgings and give himself a face-to-face confrontation with the man he knew as Boris, but he suspected Boris was far likelier to come at his back.

He accompanied Rodney Masters to Sir Hubert's office,

and there the gentleman who worked for the Government took an interested look at the gentleman whom Henrietta had said she was going to marry. He dismissed Rodney Masters to a waiting room, then addressed Joe.

'Mr Foster, I'm pleased to meet you. I'm Sir Hubert Wilkins.'

Joe, working things out, said, 'Have to ask you, sir, are you in charge of the bloodhounds?'

'I'm in charge of the department, Mr Foster. Please sit down.'

Seating himself, Joe said, 'Have to ask another question, Sir Hubert. Does your department employ a certain female bloodhound?' Sir Hubert Wilkins, he suspected, was the uncle whom Dolly had mentioned.

'I'll come to my niece in a moment,' said Sir Hubert. 'First, allow me to thank you for the help you've given us, particularly as that help has enabled us to find the two people with whom we're most concerned. However, the lady, Marcelle Fayette, is no longer at her apartment. Since you saw her last night, and spoke to her for several minutes, would you know why she has gone and where she's going?'

'Well, damn my boots,' said Joe. 'Have you lost her already?'

'Not altogether, Mr Foster,' said Sir Hubert, making a study of his man. 'She's on a boat train.'

'Sensible,' said Joe.

'Pardon?'

'Wasn't sure if she'd take my advice,' said Joe. 'I've heard more than once that most women don't think much of advice from men. However, I suggested to Marcelle Fayette that if she was up to something, then she'd be better off if she forgot it and went home. I think she lives in St Petersburg, since she mentioned she'd be there if I cared to call. That, I suppose, is where she's going to now.'

'Mr Foster, you told her in effect to vacate these shores?'

'Best thing for her under the circumstances,' said Joe.

'I see.' Sir Hubert showed a faint smile. 'All the same, we should have liked to have found out what it was she was up to.'

'How would you have done that, sir?'

'By means various, Mr Foster, or by catching her in the act.'

'Well, she's saved you the bother,' said Joe.

'It relieves us of some pressures,' said Sir Hubert. 'We can concentrate on the man called Boris now. Thank you for giving Marcelle Fayette sound advice, and for letting us know where and when you were going to meet her. Now, my niece, Henrietta Downes. Am I dealing with an indeterminate state of affairs?'

'Can't answer that question, Sir Hubert,' said Joe. 'Don't understand it.'

'I'm not too sure of things myself, alas. However, let me ask you a simpler question. Do you have it in mind to marry Henrietta?'

'Can't see myself doing that,' said Joe. 'I'm not up to it. Can't offer her anything. A few hundred pounds in the bank, that's all I own. It's enough to buy a cottage in the country and keep me for a bit while I cast around for something to do, like looking after cows or horses. Frankly, Sir Hubert, you know and I know that it can't be done, marriage between self and Dolly.'

'Dolly?'

'Henrietta Dolly. Won't work. Different people, different backgrounds.' A name suddenly entered Joe's mind, a name mentioned by George. Sir Hubert Wilkins. None other than this man. 'Have to ask you, sir, did Mr George Singleton, a friend of mine, speak to you about me?'

'Indeed he did, Mr Foster.'

'Oblige me by forgetting it,' said Joe.

366

'Very well, Mr Foster,' said Sir Hubert, 'and thank you again for all your help and for persuading Marcelle Fayette to pack her bags and leave. You spoke of advice. May I give you a little?'

'Why not?' said Joe.

'Watch out for Henrietta. I don't think you're going to get off as lightly as you seem to think you are.'

'I'll manage,' said Joe.

Sir Hubert smiled.

Joe made himself comfortable in the room above the bookshop. Mrs Beavis wasn't sure exactly what he was up to in absenting himself for six days from his lodgings, but accepted his explanation that he was simply going to spend the time with an old friend. He did not want a murderous fracas to take place in the house of his cheerful and lovable landlady.

He helped George in the shop from time to time. He was far more at home among books than among paintings of fat and fleshy women. He bought flowers twice from Daisy and put them in a vase in the shop window, much to George's amusement. He went back to his lodgings one day, just to see if there was any communication from the Army Recruitment Centre. There wasn't.

The coronation was only two days away when he strolled down to Trafalgar Square one morning. Royal personages from Europe had descended on London, which was colourful with flags and bunting. The German Emperor and the Tsar of Russia were among the arrivals. So was King Ferdinand of Bulgaria.

Daisy was nowhere to be seen. Another flower girl had taken her place.

'Hello, where's Daisy?' asked Joe who, when he wasn't helping George was out and about, since every activity took his mind off Henrietta Dolly.

'Oh, Daisy's gone to Buckingham Palace with 'er

friend. She's let me 'ave 'er pitch today. She's taken a whole basket of flowers with 'er.'

'Who's her friend, then?' asked Joe.

'Oh, 'er best regular, a kind bloke, even if 'e is a foreigner. She 'ad 'er photo taken with 'im once.'

A little alarm bell rang for Joe. What was drawing Russian Boris to Buckingham Palace today, along with Daisy and a whole basket of flowers? The coronation procession was still two days away, so what was he up to? A look at the Palace through the railings? Never. Joe wondered if he should worry about it. Tubby and his team would surely be dogging Blackbeard's every footstep.

Wait – a royal unveiling of the Queen Victoria Memorial, directly outside the Palace! Visiting monarchs would be present, particularly those related to Queen Victoria.

'Here's sixpence,' he said, giving the coin to the flower girl.

'But you ain't bought no flowers, mister.'

'Never mind, treat yourself,' he said, and was away, limping fast. He went up to the Palace by way of The Mall, threading a course through sauntering crowds. He reached Queen's Gardens, the site of the Memorial. Spacious, it was immediately outside the Palace, and was encircled by people in depth, the June sun beaming down on them. The circle was broken at the gates of the Palace, from which led a hugely long strip of plush red carpet. Policemen at intervals stood with their backs to the human surround. The silken canopy that covered the Memorial shone with light and dancing ripples. Dignitaries of a proud and haughty kind were in position and waiting. Union Jacks fluttered in the crowds.

Joe edged and elbowed his way around the assembled onlookers, searching for Daisy and the man who was her most regular customer.

''Ere, who yer pushin'?' demanded an indignant young lady, lifting angry eyes to Joe.

'Sorry,' said Joe, 'I'm trying to find my friends.'

'Oh, all right,' she said. 'Here, if yer don't find 'em, I'll be a new friend to yer.'

'In that case, I'll report back,' said Joe, and went on looking. He was motivated by an urgency that wouldn't go away. Quite suddenly, his quarry leapt to his eyes, and so did Daisy, not because of her best hat and summer frock, but because of her basket of flowers. There he was, next to her, without his beard and in a handsome Homburg hat and morning suit, his strong-boned face wreathed in smiles as he talked to Daisy. They were at the front and directly opposite him, his view of them slightly obscured by hats. He used his height to get a better view, and that brought Tubby to his eye, and Dolly too, by all that was holy. She was on Tubby's left, and on her own left was another man. Joe felt sure all three were a team, and they were right behind Daisy and the Russian.

It was yesterday that Tubby, during another cheerful and friendly chat with Daisy, had found out she was going to see the unveiling of the Memorial with her regular patron, that he had asked her to accompany him and to bring a basket full of flowers. The flowers were for throwing. That was what her kind regular wanted, he said everyone in his country threw flowers at royalty on public occasions. And he was paying for all of them. Wasn't that nice of him? Mind, he didn't want anyone knowing, and he'd only just gone.

Tubby knew he'd only just gone. Young Rodney and another man were on his tail, each keeping a separate distance.

Now, waiting for King George and Queen Mary to appear, with a number of royal visitors, she was saying, 'Oh, lor', I still feel a bit shy about throwing them.'

'I shall throw some with you,' said Rokovssky, 'we shall throw them together. It is my way of helping to celebrate a tribute to your great Queen Victoria.'

A black hat moved, blotting out Joe's view. It was worn by a lady dressed completely in black, and with a black veil. Her hair too was black, raven black. She was at the front, opposite Daisy and the Russian. Joe stared fixedly at the back of her neck. Lightly, she brought up a folded pink parasol and touched her shoulder with it. Her head moved and Joe saw Daisy and the Russian again. Beardless Blackbeard touched his hat.

God Almighty, thought Joe, that's Marcelle, in widow's weeds. They were totally camouflaging her. She's fooled Tubby, she's fooled them all, and me as well. She caught the boat train, but not the boat. What a woman. She had just signalled to Russian Boris, and he'd acknowledged it.

Joe began to push into the crowd.

'Oh, no yer don't,' growled a man, 'you'll get the sharp end of me bleedin' elbow you try shovin' me.'

A band in the forecourt of the Palace rolled its drums, and buglers sounded a fanfare. The crowd buzzed.

'They're coming out, they're coming out!'

They came on foot, King George and Queen Mary, and they were followed by their family, the popular Prince of Wales among them and receiving cheers of delight. The German Kaiser and the Tsar of Russia appeared. Addicted to military uniforms and medals, the Kaiser was a figure of martial brilliance today. Tsar Nicholas was also uniformed, but in more modest fashion.

Tubby, Henrietta and Rodney Masters, behind their quarry, were watching his every movement. They had no idea that almost immediately opposite them the woman in sombre black widow's weeds was Marcelle Fayette, and they spared not a glance for her. It was occurring to Tubby now that Russian Boris was aiming to fox everyone, that he meant to disturb the peace here in a deadly way, at the unveiling of the Memorial, and not during the coronation procession. The crafty bleeder. What did he have in mind? There was no bomb on his person, his morning suit fitted him like a glove. But this was just the kind of occasion that fired a certain kind of Russian into throwing bombs. Put a king or emperor within chucking distance, and bang. Well, if he didn't have a bomb cooking somewhere on his person, how about a revolver?

Watch him, Tubby me lad, even if he is acting like a bloke full of the joys of spring.

Joe was hemmed in. The noise of the cheering crowds were drowning all other voices. He was watching Marcelle like a hawk. There were scores of parasols up, but hers was folded, he could just glimpse its handle, held in her right hand, which was ungloved. Amid the sound of the massed audience welcoming the foot procession from the Palace, her hand moved and he lost all sight of the parasol.

Royal feet trod the red carpet, and King George and Queen Mary came to a halt close to the shrouded Memorial. Behind them, the distinguished princes and crowned heads also halted. Someone began to make a speech, the crowds falling respectfully silent. Joe edged farther forward, but was still having trouble with resentful people. Marcelle, he thought, was showing no interest in the speechmaker or in King George. She was, in fact, interested only in the German Kaiser, head of the formidable German Army. That he would launch his great fighting force into war eventually was a conviction in the minds of the Russian Army High Command. Russia had a huge supply of men, but every division was poorly equipped. Nor was the Russian economy in great shape. They could not afford a war, least of all against Germany. Count Zhinsky, head of Russian Intelligence, had been asked by certain generals to contrive the collapse of Germany's aggressive intentions by assassinating the man whose pen would sign a declaration of war. The German Kaiser. Zhinsky contacted Rokovssky, and Rokovssky, with Zhinsky's approval, formulated a plan in which his

371

selected confederate, Marcelle Fayette, would deal the death blow.

The speech over, King George stepped forward, pulled on a cord and the silk covering fell away in huge soft folds to reveal the Memorial. The crowds were a cheering mass again, for the Memorial was a triumph of design, the sculpted figure of Queen Victoria seated in majesty.

'Now,' said Rokovssky to Daisy with a happy and encouraging smile. 'Now.'

Daisy began to pluck flowers from her basket and to throw them in the air. And Rokovssky joined in. Colourful blooms sailed up and fell lightly down. The crowds roared approval, the royal personages deigned to glance and to smile. The unveiling had been diverting, the throwing of flowers was differently so, drawing a thousand eyes. Marcelle held her parasol with her ungloved right hand tight around the steel shaft, her gloved left hand around the folded silk halfway up, the handle resting against her stomach. Practice had made perfect. The protruding tip of the shaft was directed at the Kaiser, and the shaft was loaded with a steel dart dipped in poison. Her right thumb sought the button that was flush with the shaft. Joe, his alarm bell suddenly ringing loudly, simply because of how intense was her concentration on the Kaiser, pushed himself roughly forward, much to the anger of people thrust aside. Marcelle's body hid her parasol from him. No-one was looking at her, everyone was cheering or shouting or laughing as flowers from a girl's basket sailed into the bright sunshine from her hand and the hand of the man beside her. A policeman, turning, was not sure if this should be allowed, and Henrietta was hissing words into Tubby's ear.

'Tubby! Her basket! What's under the flowers?'

She didn't need to say more. Tubby launched himself between the Russian and the flower girl. He seized the basket. It aroused a commotion, and the commotion was a further diversion. Joe saw Marcelle glance down. Then her head lifted again and he saw her perceptibly steady herself. He barged brutally forward, knocking people aside, and he laid a jerking hand on her right arm just as she pressed the button. The tiny firing bolt shot forward through the hollow shaft of the parasol, and the dart flew, a thin sliver of steel, seen for a split second only by Joe. It did not matter where it struck the Kaiser. Anywhere on his body would do. But her aim had been wrecked by Joe's brutal hand, and the poisoned dart buried itself in the thick red carpet at the German Kaiser's booted foot, without him being in the least aware of it.

Marcelle expelled hissing breath, turned her head and looked into Joe's fiercely disapproving eyes. Her expression of fury and frustration changed. She smiled.

'*Bonjour*, Joe darling, how nice to see you,' she said.

Henrietta, across the way, had the basket and what were left of the flowers. There were only flowers. No bomb. Tubby and Rodney Masters were holding on to Rokovssky. He was making no fuss and offering no resistance. He merely smiled in enquiring fashion. After all, what had he done? Nothing, except help a flower girl throw some blooms. And what did he have on him? Nothing, except an innocuous wallet.

Daisy stood bewildered, not understanding that her kind gent had made use of her.

Tubby still didn't believe their man had come to the unveiling just to throw flowers. But he had his orders in the event of having to lay hands on the Russian, and he considered he had had to do so in the end. Bring him in, the guv'nor had said.

'Well now, Mr Boris Kirsch or whoever you are, would yer like to come along with me and me friend Rodney Masters?'

'Who are you?' asked Rokovssky.

'Representatives of 'Is Majesty's law and order.'

King George and Queen Mary were at this moment returning to the Palace, their family and their royal guests following, all to new cheers from the crowds.

'Why should I come with you?' asked Rokovssky in his thick guttural voice.

'Oh, just on account of a murder enquiry,' said Tubby. 'Scotland Yard's lookin' forward to 'aving you help them. Don't mind, do yer? No, I thought you wouldn't.'

Henrietta was setting Daisy's mind at rest, and Joe was engaged with Marcelle. The crowds were breaking up, most people wanting to take a closer look at the Memorial. Policemen were shepherding them into a queue.

'Why didn't you board a boat?' asked Joe.

'I changed my mind,' said Marcelle calmly. 'But how did you know I was here, and why did you put such a rough hand on me?'

'I didn't know you were here. I found you by accident while looking for your friend Boris, who's shaved his beard off, and I put a hand on you to save you being hanged.'

'Heavens, why should I be hanged?' smiled Marcelle. 'What have I done?'

'We'll see, won't we, when someone takes a look at your parasol,' said Joe.

Marcelle shrugged. She had missed, she had failed. One would have to try again, if Count Zhinsky insisted.

'Joe, you are very tiresome,' she said.

'And you're a fool of a woman,' said Joe, and jerked the parasol from her hand.

A tide of people broke around them and swamped them in a surge towards the Memorial. Marcelle seemed to be sucked away from him. Hundreds more people, streaming into Queen's Gardens from The Mall, added quantity to confusion. Marcelle disappeared. Joe made no effort to look for her. It was up to the Government man and his team, it was their work to find her, if they wanted to.

There was a huge cheerful mill of people in this spacious circle that was now dominated by the Memorial. Tubby, Dolly and Russian Boris had all disappeared. So had Daisy.

Joe went back to the bookshop.

Tubby, Rodney Masters and Dolly, accompanied by a uniformed policeman, took Alexander Rokovssky to Sir Hubert before handing him over to Scotland Yard.

That evening, Joe went to Kennington to see Tubby again, to tell him of the incident concerning Marcelle Fayette, and to hand him the parasol.

'Wicked number she is, Joe,' said Tubby, pouring beer for both of them. 'Saucy too, blow me if she ain't. Didn't get on the boat, eh? See it all now. Boris gets every eye on 'im and young Daisy and them flowers, leavin' Marcy to aim this 'ere fancy umbrella at poor old Kaiser Bill, who ain't very poor. A dart, you said?'

'Sure of it,' said Joe, 'and I think it hit the red carpet.'

'All rolled up now, that is, I'd say. But we'll 'ave a look at it. 'Ow about that, Joe, eh? Needle in a red carpet a mile long. Talk about 'aystacks. Well, good on yer, matey, 'ere's to yer. Scotland Yard's got their murder suspect, and I wouldn't mind betting that French Marcy caught another boat train this afternoon. Point is, me friend, did she catch the boat this time? We'll find out. Oh, the police are 'olding two Russian students on account of them bein' witnesses to the movements of that unfortunate docker on the evening 'e was murdered. 'E was the bloke that carried the letter to Russian Boris that turned out to be Alexander Rokovssky, a geezer with a very nasty record for doin' people in, and them students, of course, were the ones who 'anded the letter over for carryin'. 'Ave a fag, Joe.'

'Thanks, Tubby.'

'Pity you was never a naval bloke.'

CHAPTER TWENTY-NINE

A suitcase stood in the hall. Cissie, seeing it, at once went to question her young mistress. Henrietta was standing in front of her dressing-table, putting on a new straw boater.

'Miss 'Enrietta, there's a suitcase in the hall,' said Cissie.

'Is there? Oh, yes, it's mine. I've packed a few things.'

'But what for?'

'I'm going away for a day or two. Well, it might be a little longer.'

'Miss 'Enrietta, you went away for a bit a while ago, and no-one knew where you were till you come back with a bandaged ankle.'

'Now don't fuss,' said Henrietta.

'Miss 'Enrietta, Nell and me ought to know where you'll be. If 'Er Ladyship, your aunt, calls—'

'She won't. I've spoken to her. She's a kindred spirit.'

'But what about if the Hon Cedric calls?'

'He won't, either. I've given him the push.'

'Oh, lor', Miss 'Enrietta, you sure you're well?'

'Fit as a fiddle, Cissie.'

Mrs Bessie Beavis, back from her afternoon shopping, put three pounds of pork sausages on a plate and placed them in the larder. She was going to make a huge sausage toad-in-the-hole for supper tonight, with new potatoes, green peas and fried onions. She'd best shell the peas now, get that job over with and then go across the road to have a cup of tea with Connie Cousins, who'd be bound to have something new to tell her about that fly husband of hers.

A knock on her front door sent her to answer it.

'Well, I never,' she said when she saw who it was.

'Hello, Bessie,' said Dolly – Henrietta Dolly – and smiled. A suitcase stood on the doorstep beside her. ''Ow's the fam'ly?'

'They ain't no trouble, love,' beamed Mrs Beavis. 'And you didn't need to knock, you could of just come in by the latchcord, you bein' a friend.'

'I thought I'd better knock,' said Dolly, 'seeing I've sort of arrived official, like.'

'Official?'

'Sort of. What I mean is I've come to ask if I can rent your upstairs front. I wasn't too keen on me Peckham lodgings. I'm all right for money, I'm a bit well off just now, so I can pay in advance.'

'Come in, come in,' said Mrs Beavis, her beam expansive. She was sure Sergeant Joe would like having Dolly back. He hadn't been his usual self just lately. 'Come on, love.' Dolly picked up her suitcase and followed the landlady into the kitchen. 'Well, it'll be nice 'aving you for a lodger, Dolly, you can 'ave the upstairs front with pleasure. Funny thing, I was askin' Sergeant Joe if 'e knew 'ow you was keepin', and 'e said there'd never be anything wrong with you that a smacked bottom wouldn't cure, and I said fancy sayin' a thing like that about a nice young lady like you. 'E said 'e wouldn't 'ave said it if 'e 'adn't 'ad an 'eadache, so I knew 'e was only jokin'. Mind, 'e 'asn't said a lot of jokes lately, 'e's been mutterin' a lot, which 'e never used to, 'e's nearly always spoke up very clear. My, ain't yer lookin' well, Dolly? In the pink, as Charlie would say. And I never seen you more nice or more respectable.'

Dolly was dressed in a bright new boater, a plain but crisp-looking white blouse, and a trim flannel skirt of silver-grey.

'Yes, I'm goin' to be a lady clerk,' she said, stretching

377

the truth a fair bit. 'Not just yet, mind, but soon. Is Joe in?'

Joe had been back in his lodgings a week. The coronation of the King and Queen had taken place eight days ago. The nation had enjoyed a day's holiday in celebration, with London, the capital of the Empire, rejoicing in the pomp and pageantry of the occasion, which had been all of happy and glorious. Not that Alexander Rokovssky thought much of it or saw anything of it. He had been charged with the murder of one Dan Pearson, a docker. And, as Dolly knew, Marcelle Fayette had completely disappeared.

'Oh, Joe went down in the country this mornin',' said Mrs Beavis, ''e told me 'e was goin' to see a country gent that might give 'im a job lookin' after cows.'

'Cows?' Dolly quivered, not with shock but with trying not to laugh.

'That's what 'e said, love.'

'He's got a hundred ways of bein' funny,' said Dolly.

''E didn't look funny,' said Mrs Beavis, ''e looked serious.'

'Serious about cows?' said Dolly. 'He's barmy. D'you think he's had a sort of shock, that it's sent 'im off his head?'

'Take a lot to send Sergeant Joe off 'is 'ead,' said Mrs Beavis. 'Mind, 'e did say that where there's cows there's bound to be a dairymaid. 'E said 'e could fancy marryin' a dairymaid.'

'He's got a hope,' said Dolly under her breath.

'What was that, love?'

'Him and a dairymaid, he's gone barmy all right,' said Dolly. 'When's he gettin' back?'

'Later today. If 'e don't fall off the train, 'e said.' Mrs Beavis laughed. 'You can go up and get yerself settled in, love. Turn the bedclothes down, it'll air the sheets. They're quite clean, mind, but just want a bit of airin'.

378

Then come down and we'll 'ave a nice cup of tea together. I was goin' across to Connie Cousins, but I'll go tomorrer instead.'

'Oh, I could do with a nice cup of tea,' said Dolly.

'I'll cut you a nice slice of me coconut cake as well, just to 'elp you keep body an' soul together, I always say it don't do to get faint from lack of nourishment at this time of the day.'

At twenty to five, Linda heard Sergeant Joe enter the house. All the family could recognize the sound of his limping walk over the linoleum-covered floor of the passage. Linda darted from the kitchen and followed him up the stairs.

'Sergeant Joe, Sergeant Joe,' she called excitedly, and followed him into his living-room. Joe had visited a Sussex landowner. George, through a third party, had heard that the gentleman was looking for a man of character to take charge of his newly acquired string of hunters. So Joe took a train to Sussex. The landowner, larger than life and addicted to oaths, had put him to a number of tests, then told him to come down again in a week, by which time he would have interviewed other applicants. Joe said a letter would do, whether it was yes or no. The landowner said he'd never written a bloody letter in his life, except to his mother. Didn't believe in letters, preferred talking man to man, never mind if he was dealing with a digger of ditches or the King himself. The estate steward told Joe not to be put off by the old boy's manner, and that if he'd been asked to come down again it was because he'd made a favourable impression.

'What's up, Private Carrots?' asked Joe, who had a soft spot for Linda.

Linda closed the door.

'Crikey, what d'you fink, Sergeant Joe, Dolly's come back.'

'She's what?'

'Yes, Mum told Ella and me when we come 'ome from school a bit ago. She said Dolly's rentin' the front room that the French lady 'ad for a little while. Yes, and Mum said if we 'ave any more lodgers we might get a bit rich, then we could all 'ave two weeks 'oliday at Margate instead of only one. Are yer glad about Dolly? Mum said she expected you would be.'

'I'll kill her,' said Joe.

'What, me mum?' gasped Linda.

'No, slip of the tongue, Carrots.'

'Is Dolly what me mum calls a good woman, one that makes a nice wife, Sergeant Joe?'

'Well, you could say your mum's a good woman herself, that you're a good girl, Ella's good for bouncing about, and Nancy's good for a second helping of afters. I won't tell you what Dolly is.'

'Oh, do yer fink she's romantic?' asked Linda.

'What I think about Dolly I couldn't even write down,' said Joe. 'Is she in that room now?'

'No, Mum said she went out shoppin', to get some food for 'er supper, and that she was lookin' ever so nice and respectable.'

'Nice and respectable? Is that a fact, Carrots? Well, we'd all better start praying.'

Linda giggled.

'Oh, yer do say funny fings sometimes, Sergeant Joe.'

'Dead serious that was, Private Carrots,' said Joe.

They heard someone come in then. They heard the front door open and close. Footsteps sounded along the passage and up the stairs. They were quick and confident footsteps.

Henrietta Dolly, reaching the landing, turned and walked to her room. She entered, closing the door behind her.

'She's come back from 'er shoppin',' said Linda.

'Well, I think I'll go and have a word with her before the roof falls off the house,' said Joe.

'Crikey,' breathed Linda, 'our roof can't fall off, can it?'

'Not without the help of an earthquake,' said Joe. 'Right, I'll go and talk to Dolly now.'

'Yes, she's nice, ain't she?' said Linda. 'Can I come up after I've 'ad me supper?'

'Yes, my shoes need a shine,' said Joe, 'they've been down in the country.'

Linda giggled again and went downstairs. Joe, wondering of course what Sir Hubert Wilkins' niece was up to now, knocked on her door.

'Who's that?'

'The hangman. Come out, you minx.'

The door opened and Dolly showed herself in her snowy white blouse and grey skirt. Her hair looked magnificent. Joe gritted his teeth at the weakening effect she had on him.

'Who's that shoutin'?' she asked. 'Oh, it's you, Joe. Pleased to see me, are yer?'

'How would you like to be skinned alive?' asked Joe.

'Well, that's charmin', that is, I don't think,' said Dolly.

'Don't talk, don't say a word. Just pack your bags and get out of here.'

'Blessed cheek,' said Dolly. 'I'm lodgin' here official, I'll 'ave you know. I've paid me first week's rent in advance, and I ain't bein' ordered about by you, Joe Foster. I'm stayin' till you've come to your senses.'

Joe could hardly believe his ears. She was playing a female cockney again to the life, and she was telling him she was going to stay here and drive him to drink. Well, as good as. And she already had him on the rack.

'Listen,' he said, 'stop talking like someone you're not.'

'Now 'ow can I be someone I'm not?' she said. 'I'm gettin' worried about you, Joe Foster, there's a rumour you're goin' off your 'ead. Me landlady, Bessie Beavis, was talkin' to me earlier, and I couldn't 'ardly believe it when she said you were thinkin' of gettin' a job lookin' after cows. I bet all the dragoons would fall off their 'orses if they 'eard you'd gone as barmy as that. I'd invite you in so we could talk about it, only this is me bedroom and I don't invite men in. It ain't respectable, and I'm busy, anyway.'

'If you don't stop sounding like Nellie Wallace, I'll strangle you,' said Joe.

'Oh, got the rats again, 'ave we?' said Dolly. 'I don't know, I never met any man who gets the rats more than you do, you ought to see a doctor about it. Well, I can't stand 'ere talkin' all day. I've got to start cookin' me supper.'

'You can't cook, you can't even peel a potato.'

'Well, I'm makin' a start, ain't I?' said Dolly.

'What for?'

'Well, you don't want a wife who can't cook, do you?' said Dolly, and made to close the door. Joe put his foot in the way. 'Here, d'you mind not doin' that?'

'I'll give you half an hour to pack your bags and go back to where you belong,' said Joe.

'If you don't take your foot out of me door in five ticks,' said Dolly, 'I'll kick your bad leg.'

'Jesus hold me up,' said Joe, 'what exactly are you playing at?'

'I'm just livin' next to you,' said Dolly.

'Why?'

'Because you fancy me, and because I'm as good as you are, Joe Foster.'

'You've got half an hour,' said Joe. 'If you're not on your way by then, I'll dump you, bag and baggage, on the doorstep.' He went back to his room. Dolly smiled. She liked a battle of words, more especially with Joe. She knocked on his door five minutes later, opened it and put her head in.

'Joe, be a sport, lend us a match to light me gas ring with, would yer? I forgot to buy some when I went shoppin'.' Silently, Joe took a box of matches from his mantelpiece and handed it to her. 'Ta, love,' she said, 'you're still a kind bloke really.' She disappeared, only to immediately reappear. 'Joe, I just thought. You don't want to look after cows, it's daft, and you'll get all mucky. Couldn't you and me keep chickens? I like chickens.'

Joe went for her. Dolly pulled the door shut and fled. That left Joe prowling about his room and fighting his feelings. He looked in his larder, wondering what to have for his supper after his long day out, but found he wasn't in the mood to prepare anything.

Hell, there she was again, knocking on the door and putting her head in.

'Joe?'

'Now what?'

'Look, I know what you're trying to do, I tried it too, I went away and tried to tell myself it wouldn't work, but I couldn't stay away. I'm not rich, if that's what you think, I just get an allowance from my uncle. In any case, you're not marrying any fat dairymaid, I can tell you that, and I'd like to know why you're too stuck-up to ask me.'

'Get out of here,' said Joe.

'Oh, all right, be stuck-up, then.'

That didn't help his feelings, either. Dolly was Dolly, and there'd never be another like her. But there were all these damned buts. How to make a decision? Do it the Army way. Lie in wait, and let the nature of the opposition's next attack govern his reactions.

Somehow, Joe knew it would depend entirely on what she said. He had no idea what might come next from that versatile tongue of hers, but he knew for sure that it would decide him.

It came, of course, the next attack. The knock at the door and Dolly showing her face and a winning smile.

'Joe?'

'Yes?'

'Joe, could yer be a love, could yer come and 'elp me peel me potatoes?'

THE END

ON MOTHER BROWN'S DOORSTEP

To Wendy and Jeffery

THE INCIDENT

It was in December, 1924, when a ward sister in a London hospital noticed that the door of a drugs cupboard had been neatly forced open. A large bottle of chloroform, new and unused, with its glass stopper still sealed, was missing. She reported the matter immediately to the matron. The police were called in to investigate the theft. They talked to all members of the staff and to walking patients. They made enquiries among out-patients, and checked up on visitors known to have entered the hospital on the day in question. They wondered, of course, why the thief should want chloroform. It brought them eventually to the reasonable assumption that the person was an outsider, a clever crook who had done his homework and had lifted the chloroform with the intention of using it to put prospective victims to sleep.

That theory looked remarkably like fact when, a month later in January, 1925, a Lewisham jeweller entered a police station in what appeared to be a state of inebriation. He reported having been chloroformed by a heavily masked man who came into his shop just as he was about to close up. When he recovered consciousness some time later, his takings for the day were missing. The thief left no fingerprints and had not yet been traced.

Among other things occupying the attention of the police in 1925 was the usual list of missing persons. The list included three young girls. Ivy Connor of Bermondsey had disappeared in February, Mary Wallace of Rotherhithe in October, and Amy Charles of the Old Kent

Road in December. Their disappearances had been investigated without success and their case files were still open.

CHAPTER ONE

The March day was brilliant, the air crisp, the sun sharpening the sooty chimneys and rooftops of Walworth. Fog might arrive overnight and blanket London tomorrow, but today the weather made people feel cheerful and lively. It was 1926, the year of the Bright Young Things, with flappers showing their legs in short skirts, smoking cigarettes in long holders, and being jawed at by the law for the wildness of their ways. Some responded by flinging their arms around upbraiding bobbies and kissing them. The law and the Church and Mother Grundy were collectively shocked, of course.

In Walworth's East Street market, some women shoppers were wearing their best hats to celebrate the arrival of the sun. William Edward Brown, in the khaki uniform of the East Surreys, took in the old familiar scene with a sense of nostalgia. He could not count the number of times he had ducked and dived under stalls as a boy, looking for discarded fruit such as specked apples or slightly pulpy oranges. His family had been bitterly hard-up during the post-war years, but his mum had never lost her smile and his dad had never let go of hope.

William was known as Will. He had kicked against being called Willy and fought street kids who had tried to label him so. Entering the Army as a drummer boy at the age of fifteen in 1921, he sailed with his East Surrey battalion for service in India in 1922, and during the next four years he had come to know that India, with its teeming cities, its many religions, its cultural variations and its extraordinary mixture of peoples, was something he'd need a lifetime to understand. But he hadn't done so badly; he'd got along with the Indian regiments of the British Army. Indian soldiers served with pride and distinction alongside the British, particularly in the flare-ups on the North-West Frontier.

Will reached the rank of full corporal when he was only nineteen, having distinguished himself in a bloody battle against the Pathans. Subsequently, however, something went wrong with his chest. He had moments when he found it difficult to breathe. His commanding officer ordered him to go sick, and he finished up in hospital in Poona. Conditions were better there, the air was finer and not laden with sultry heat. But as soon as he was discharged and rejoined the battalion in Delhi, his chest began to complain again. He was invalided home and given three months leave, during the course of which he was to attend a London chest hospital once a week. He'd been home just over two weeks, had visited the hospital twice and heard the worrying word asthma mentioned, although oddly enough smoky old Walworth seemed to be doing him good. He hadn't had one attack since arriving home.

He was enjoying his reunion with old Walworth and with his family, getting to know brother Freddy and sisters Sally and Susie all over again. Well, everyone was five years older. The whole family had gone barmy when he walked in on them with three months leave in the bag. His sisters fell on him, and Susie went all moist-eyed because he would be able to attend her wedding three weeks from now. The man in question was Sammy Adams, reputed to be Southwark's most well-known businessman. Will had felt immediate pride in Susie. At twenty-one she'd grown into a picture postcard beauty. Besides which, she was a typical flapper in her 1926 outfits. She took him as soon as she could to meet Sammy and all the Adams family, showing him off as her soldier brother, which went down well with Boots, Sammy's eldest brother. Boots had fought with the West Kents in France and Flanders during the Great War. He asked Will what the pay was like now. Lousy, said Will, but the grub's free. Same old tight-fisted Army Paymaster, said Boots, and what are the socks like? I think I've been wearing your leftovers, said Will. Boots asked if they'd got darned toes. Darned heels as well, said Will. Yes, they're mine, said Boots.

Susie was as happy as a lark about everything, and head over heels as well.

'Ain't I a lucky girl, Will?' she said in the old way.

'Not as lucky as Sammy,' said Will.

'But I wasn't anybody when I first met Sammy.'

'Well, you're somebody now,' said Will, 'and Sammy knows it. You hold on to that, Susie, you need to be on top with a bloke like him.'

'I am on top,' laughed Susie.

'Are you?'

'All the time,' said Susie. 'Mind, Sammy doesn't know it.'

Will didn't think his parents had changed much. His mum was still plump and placid, his dad still wiry and cheerful, and making light of the gammy leg he'd brought out of the trenches. He thought the Army had done a lot for Will, and said so. Done me brown, said Will. At which his mum said she'd never seen anyone more brown, then asked exactly what it was he'd got to go to the hospital for each week. Just to check up on the nurses, said Will. Well, I never heard the likes of that before, said his mum, coming all the way home from India to see if the hospital nurses are behaving themselves. That can't be right, she said. I expect Will's got a bit of India in his system, said

393

Mr Brown, and the hospital's got to get it out of him. There's funny things that can get into a soldier in India. Still, there must be nice things as well, said fourteen-year-old Sally, because they've made our Will all brown and handsome. I bet the girls will all go potty about him. I'd like some of that, said Will.

After his second visit to the hospital, Will let his family know that all he'd got was a little touch of asthma. Freddy asked what asthma was. Will said something like a cold on the chest.

'That's a blessin',' said Mrs Brown, 'I thought it might be one of them Chinese diseases like gangrene.'

'Mum, 'ow can you catch a Chinese disease in India?' asked Sally.

'What's gangrene?' asked Freddy.

'Nasty,' said Mr Brown.

'I think I'll buy you some thick woolly vests while you're 'ome, Will,' said Mrs Brown. 'They'll keep your chest warm.'

'Make it itch as well,' said Will.

'What's gangrene?' asked Freddy.

'It's what you get if your leg falls off and the doctors don't put the right kind of ointment on it,' said Susie.

'I ain't fallin' for that,' said Freddy. 'I mean what's the use of puttin' ointment on a leg that's fell off? I ain't daft, yer know, Susie.'

'Not much,' said Sally.

'And only now and again,' said Susie.

'There y'ar, Will,' said Freddy, 'you can see what I 'ave to put up with from me skin-and-blisters. They'll give me a complaint one day, and I'll 'ave to come to the hospital with you.'

'Good idea, Freddy,' said Will, 'you can help me check up on the nurses.'

'Cor, I fancy that,' said Freddy.

Will, his thoughts on his family, came out of the market and entered King and Queen Street. Kids just out of school were racing towards East Street. It was a thing with some Walworth kids to go to the market on their way home from school, and to do some scrumping for apples under the fruit stalls.

Walking to Browning Street, he saw a woman approaching, shopping bag in her hand and her best Sunday hat on.

''Ello, soldier, ain't another war on, is there?'

'Not here,' said Will.

'Thank gawd for that, I ain't got over the last one yet.'

'Never mind,' said Will, 'your titfer's in the pink.'

'Me 'at?' said the woman. 'What's wrong with it?'

'Looks like spring,' said Will. 'I like it.'

'Fancy me, do yer, soldier?' twinkled the woman.

'Yes, I'll pop round on Sunday,' said Will.

'Me old man'll chop yer legs orf.'

'So he should,' said Will, 'that's what husbands are for.'

The woman laughed and went on. Will continued towards Browning Street. A boy wheeling a home-made pushcart at a run caught him up and passed him. Round the corner came a girl. The pushcart collided with her, and down she went with an involuntary yell.

'Oh, crikey,' gasped the boy, a lad about nine.

'Hard luck,' said Will to the girl, and stooped to help her up. Winded, she turned on her back and gazed up at him. She saw the tanned face of a soldier under a peaked cap, and concerned eyes. Will saw a young lady with bobbed jet-black hair clasped by a knitted blue hat with a bobble. Her frock was rucked, her black lisle stockings showing to her knees. Her grey eyes looked cross. 'Are you hurt?' he asked.

'Did you knock me over?'

'Not me,' said Will.

'Me pushcart done it,' said the boy.

'You were lookin' at me,' said the girl to Will in an accusing way. She sat up. She winced and rubbed her right knee. She winced again. 'Now look what's 'appened, I've hurt me knee.'

'Sorry about that,' said Will. 'Let's try getting you up.'

'What, on one leg?' she said spiritedly. 'I'll look daft.'

'Oh, 'elp,' said the boy, 'you ain't broke yer leg, 'ave yer?'

'I'd better not have,' said the girl, touching her knee gingerly, 'or me dad'll push both your faces in.'

A woman came across from the other side of the street. She looked like one of Walworth's numerous motherly bodies.

''Ere, young man,' she said to Will, 'what's that gel doin' on the pavement?'

'She's bumped her knee,' said Will.

'Excuse me, if you don't mind,' said the girl, 'it was the other way about.'

'Is it 'urting?' asked the motherly body.

'Oh, no,' said the girl, 'it's just swellin' up, missus, that's all.' She was cross. She ought to be home by now, getting tea for her brother and sisters.

Looking at Will, the motherly body said, 'She can't just sit there on the pavement.'

'I know,' said Will, 'but she's against standing on one leg.'

The girl looked as if she didn't think that very funny. Another woman hurried up.

396

'What's 'appened?' she asked. Happenings were meat and drink to Walworth's motherly bodies.

'Me pushcart accidental 'it the girl's knee,' said the boy, who wanted to get home himself for a bit of tea.

'Oh, ain't that a shame? Oh, yer poor dear,' said the second motherly body to the girl, 'that's just what 'appened to me niece Ivy, she done 'er knee in two days before 'er weddin' and 'ad to walk up the aisle on crutches. Is it painful, ducky?'

'Oh, no,' said the fed-up girl, 'it's only cripplin' me.'

'That's what it done to me niece,' said the second motherly body. 'What's 'er soldier friend doin' about it?' she asked the first woman.

'Well, 'e'll 'ave to do something,' said the first woman.

'He's not my soldier friend,' said the girl.

'Couldn't you carry 'er to 'er home?' suggested the second woman to Will.

That was out as far as Will was concerned. He'd been advised to avoid that kind of exertion, and he certainly didn't fancy having an attack before he got the girl home. He'd be no help at all to her then. All the same, he couldn't walk away.

'Where'd you live?' he asked her.

'Blackwood Street,' she said. Blackwood Street was off the market.

'All right,' he said, making up his mind that he'd got to give it a go, 'up you come and I'll carry you.'

The girl, taking in his lean manly look, didn't fancy him carrying her at all, not at her age.

'I ain't bein' carried,' she said. 'I'll lose all me dignity, I'll get catcalled by the street kids. I'm seventeen, I am.'

'Better to be carried than to stay here gettin' trodden on,' said Will, who felt it would all have had its funny side if the girl's knee hadn't been so obviously painful.

'Excuse me,' said the girl, whose dignity was already suffering, 'but I'm not bein' carried. I'll 'ave to hop on one leg.'

'Yes, you got to get 'ome somehow, ducky,' said the second woman. 'Me sister fell over down Petticoat Lane one Sunday, an' got trod on till she was nearly ill, and it didn't do 'er back no good, either.'

''Ere,' said the boy, 'can't yer put 'er in me cart, mister, an' push 'er home? I'll come with yer so's I can take me pushcart off yer. I'll be late for me tea an' get a clip, but it won't 'urt. Me mum don't believe in knockin' me 'ead orf. There y'ar, mister, wheel 'er home in me cart.'

Bright idea that, thought Will, it solves everything.

'Right, up you come, Daisy Bell,' he said. He stooped again, and the girl gasped and grabbed at the hem of her frock as he lifted her.

'Oh, I won't – you're not to – me in a pushcart at my age? I won't – oh, me legs, I don't believe it!'

Resistance was all too late then. Will lowered her into the pushcart bottom first. It was a solid wooden crate on bicycle wheels. Her knees were up, her legs showing.

'There we are,' said Will.

'Yes, she fits in quite comfy,' said the first motherly body.

'You'll be all right now, love,' said the second, 'the soldier'll get you 'ome. 'E seems a decent chap.'

'Decent?' gasped the girl. 'Look what he's done to me, put me in this cart with me legs showin' – I'll die in a minute.'

'Off we go,' said Will. He turned with the cart and proceeded to retrace his steps, the cart running easily over the pavement, the boy following. 'What's your name?' he asked the flushed and outraged young lady.

'Oh, you 'ooligan,' she breathed, 'I don't give me name to 'ooligans that've put me in a kid's cart. Well, it's Annie Ford, if you must know, and I hate yer.'

'I'm Will Brown. Nice to meet you, Annie. Sorry about your knee, but with luck, it'll only be bruised.'

'Never mind me knee, what about me dignity?' said Annie, dreading street kids. Sure enough some appeared. They goggled at her. A fat one sang out.

'Where did yer get that gel, oh, yer lucky feller,
If I get tuppence from me mum, would yer like to sell 'er?'

'Oh, I'll kill him,' gasped Annie. 'Oh, look at people lookin', they'll think I'm only ten years old.'

'You look like a young lady from here,' said Will, pushing the cart on towards the Lane. The East Street market was known as the Lane.

'Oh, don't mind me,' said Annie bitterly, 'just keep lookin'. I like bein' in a pushcart with me knees up and me legs showin', don't I?'

'I'm not lookin', said Will.

Annie, who was facing him, gritted her teeth. People were looking and gawping, of course. Oh, the shame of it, at her age. It was worse when they reached the market, where Will turned left. She was sure everyone in Walworth was there.

'Oi, Tommy Atkins,' said some grinning middle-aged man, 'did yer buy them goods off a stall?'

'Yes, five bob the lot,' said Will, and Annie fumed.

'Five bob?' said the interested party. 'You should've 'ad 'er wrapped up in fancy paper for that, an' tied with ribbon as well.'

Will grinned and pushed on, crossing the street.

'Did you hear that, did you hear what 'e said?' demanded Annie.

'I expect you'd look nice in ribbon,' said Will, trying to cheer her up.

'Oh, you saucy devil, you didn't ought to be a soldier, you ought to be locked up till you can treat a girl proper.'

'How's your knee?' asked Will, the boy still behind him.

'Oh, thanks for askin',' said Annie.

A passing woman said, 'Givin' yer sister a ride, are yer, soldier?'

'Not so's you'd notice,' said Will, 'she's just a new friend of mine, and we're getting to know each other.'

'I wouldn't be his sister or his friend, not if he gave me a sackful of diamonds,' fumed Annie. 'He's a demon, he is.'

'Cheer up,' said Will and pushed on.

'Look, I don't want you to think I'm not grateful,' said Annie, 'but how would you like to be wheeled 'ome in a pushcart?'

'Won't be long now,' said Will.

'Oh, blessed agony,' breathed Annie. He had turned into Blackwood Street. 'I know what's goin' to 'appen now, all the kids are goin' to look.'

Kids were there all right. They stopped their street games to stare. Recognizing Annie, they came running up.

'Crikey, look at you, Annie!'

'What's the soldier wheelin' yer in that cart for?'

'Is that yer knees showin'?'

A girl darted from an open door and came to a halt in front of the pushcart. She addressed Will indignantly.

''Ere, that's our sister you've got in there, mister.'

'She hurt her knee,' said Will, 'so I've given her a ride home.'

'Crikey, me an' Charlie wondered why she was late,' said fourteen-year-old Nellie Ford. ''Ave yer really 'urt yer knee, Annie?'

'Yes, and me pride as well,' said Annie.

'You kids, push off,' said Nellie, like Annie in her looks.

'Can't we see 'er knee?' asked a small girl. 'I never seen an 'urt knee except me own. I seen a bunion, me mum's got one—'

'Push off,' said Nellie. The kids backed off for about a yard.

'Right,' said Will, 'I'll carry Annie indoors. You lead the way,' he said to Nellie. 'Up you come again, Daisy Bell.'

'She ain't Daisy Bell, she's Annie,' said Nellie.

'Well, she'd look just like Daisy Bell if she had a boater and a bicycle,' said Will. He lifted Annie. She clutched the hem of her frock. 'Thanks for the loan of your pushcart, young tosh,' he said to the boy, who at once made off with it before foreign street kids could get their hands on it.

'This way, mister,' said Nellie, and Will followed, Annie up in his arms, legs dangling, frock rucked.

'Crikey, Annie,' called a precocious boy, 'I think yer knickers is showin'.'

Annie gave a tight little scream as Will carried her indoors.

CHAPTER TWO

The Ford family, renting their house in Blackwood Street for twelve bob a week, consisted of Mr Harold Ford, a forty-two-year-old ganger on the LSER, his three daughters Annie, Nellie and Cassie, and his son Charlie. His wife, unfortunately, had developed pneumonia during the last year of the war. It proved fatal, as pneumonia nearly always did. She lay in the South London cemetery now, under green turf and a headstone. The vicar of St John's Church had approved the wording.

'RUTH ANNIE FORD. Born 1888, died 1918. Wife of Harold Stanley Ford and mother of Annie, Nellie, Charlie and Cassie. OUR MUM.'

Annie was her dad's right hand now. She had any amount of spirit and as much bossiness as was necessary to get the better of twelve-year-old Charlie. She wasn't averse to chasing him with the brush and pan. The back of the brush was good for whacking his bottom, and the pan good for giving his head a thump. Charlie complained she'd knock it off one day. She told him he wouldn't miss it.

'Course I would,' said Charlie, 'I couldn't even walk about without me loaf of bread, nor see where I was goin', neither.'

'Dear oh lor',' said Annie, 'what a shame.'

Not that affection wasn't there. Annie had a characteristically warm cockney heart under her scolding exterior, and was very fond of her family, especially her dad. But someone had to keep them in order, her dad as well.

Sometimes on Sundays she'd make them all go to church with her.

'You too, Dad,' she'd say.

'Well, Annie, I was thinkin' about mendin' the chair that's—'

'No, you weren't. Go and put your Sunday suit on. And you, Charlie – here, where you off to, Cassie? Come back here. Sit on 'er, Nellie, till we're ready. Charlie, you goin' to put your suit on, or do I 'ave to belt you one?'

Charlie, strong-willed, was a holy terror who needed belting occasionally. Annie made do with thumping him and applying her own will, which was just as strong as Charlie's. So whenever she said they'd all got to go to church with her, Charlie went too. Annie could fashion hurtful beds of nails for defaulters.

Her dad gave her a hand with meals at weekends, but he was always home too late to be a help on weekdays. Still, he never failed to do full justice to what she set before him. Everyone had to wash their hands before they sat down to a meal. Annie was nearly ten when her mum died and could remember how particular she'd been about clean hands at meal times. She remembered lots of things about her lively pretty mum, nice things, and Annie meant never to let her down. She could never quite understand why the Lord had taken her when she was only thirty. Nellie asked a question on those lines once, and their dad said he supposed the Lord often took the ones He liked best while they were still young. Nellie said she didn't want the Lord not to like her, but she didn't want to be liked so much that she'd have to go to an early grave. Wouldn't it be better if the Lord took people like Mrs Potter? She's not young, said Charlie, she's ninety and she's got whiskers. Still, age before beauty, said Nellie. Not when it's got whiskers on, said Charlie. You Charlie, said

Annie, don't you talk like that about kind old ladies.

Annie could sort Charlie out fairly well most times. Ten-year-old Cassie was a different problem. She was a dreamy girl with a vivid imagination that took her into the realms of never-never land far too often. A neighbour would stop Annie and say something like what's all this I hear about your family being invited to tea at Windsor Castle next Sunday afternoon? Or, Annie love, I can't hardly believe your dad swam the Channel last week, there wasn't nothing about it in the papers. Or even, fancy your Charlie saving a girl from drowning in the Serpentine last week and being given a gold medal by the King.

It could all be traced back to Cassie, and Cassie would get a talking-to.

'Now, you Cassie, you've been tellin' stories again.'

'Me, Annie?'

'Yes, you. I saw Alice Miller down the Lane. What d'you mean by tellin' 'er Dad's goin' to get a job at Buckingham Palace?'

The Royal Family and much of what was associated with it featured prominently in Cassie's inventive mind.

'Annie, I only said Dad might. Well, 'e might one day. The King and Queen 'ave to 'ave men doin' jobs there, they couldn't do them themselves, they 'ave to sit on their throne mostly. I bet Dad could do a good job at Buckingham Palace.'

'Cassie, you little 'orror, the best job Dad could do would be to stop you tellin' all these fancy stories about us. You even told Mrs Woodley last week that Dad used to be a sea captain. If you keep on like this, you'll never go to 'eaven.'

'Well, I don't want to go yet, Annie, honest, not before Mrs Potter.'

If Charlie could be thumped for being a bit of a

tearaway, there wasn't much that could be done about Cassie and her imagination, except hope that she'd grow out of it. All their dad did about it was to cough a bit. Annie told him he could cough as much as he liked, but none of it would cure Cassie. No, but it's a help to me, said her dad. What sort of help? It stops me falling about, said her dad.

Cassie, Nellie and Charlie were all attending school. Annie had a job from ten until four with a grocer near the Elephant and Castle. The grocer, Mr Urcott, was a really kind bloke, he let her work those hours so that she could see to the family in the mornings and get home in time to make a pot of tea and do some bread and marge for herself and her brother and sisters. Supper came later.

Banging her knee against that pushcart meant she had failed them today. It also meant she'd arrived home in a mortifying way for a girl her age, even if she knew she couldn't have got there by herself on one leg. She'd never live that pushcart down. Neighbours would ask if she really had been wheeled home in it by a soldier.

Will sat her down on the edge of the kitchen table. With its solid legs and square deal top, it was the kind of table seen in most Walworth kitchens, and the kitchen itself, with its oven range and its window facing the back yard, was like a thousand others. The range fire was alight, burning very slowly, the coals covered by a pinky-white ash. China filled the dresser shelves and cups hung from hooks. Will thought the kitchen had a homely look similar to his mother's. He didn't think Annie and her family were too hard-up. Her sister's gymslip and white blouse had quite a new look, and the blue frock she herself was wearing was quite pretty.

'What yer doin' that for, sittin' Annie on the table?' asked Nellie, intrigued at having a soldier in the house.

'I'm taking care of her knee,' said Will, and stood back to regard Annie, who at once brushed at the skirt of her short frock and covered her knees. Crumbs, thought Nellie, what's our Annie gone all shy for?

Annie stared accusingly at Will.

'I don't know why you keep lookin' at me,' she said. 'I never met anyone who does more lookin' than you. I might not 'ave bumped into that pushcart if you hadn't been lookin' then.'

'We've had all that,' said Will, smiling. Crikey, thought Nellie, ain't he handsome? 'Where's your mum?' asked Will.

'She died when we was young,' said Nellie.

'Oh, sorry,' said Will, who couldn't imagine what it must be like for a family to have no mum. His own mum had always been there, placid, affectionate and un-critical.

'But we got a nice dad,' said Nellie.

'That's a consolation,' said Will. 'About the knee, Annie—'

'Never mind me knee,' said Annie, 'you're not gettin' a look at that too.'

'Pity,' said Will, 'I like knees. Well, girls' knees. Anyway, Annie, from what I've seen of yours, I'd say you've just bruised the right one. If it's a bit stiff, put some liniment on it.'

'Yes, all right,' said Annie, 'and thanks ever so much, I'll try and forget how you dumped me in that pushcart. Nellie, where's Cassie and Charlie?'

'Charlie's next door,' said Nellie. 'Pam Nicholls sauced him over the wall, so 'e jumped over it so's 'e could chase 'er into 'er kitchen and smack 'er up-an'-downer.'

'I'll kill the little 'ooligan,' fumed Annie.

'What's her up-and-downer?' asked Will.

''Er bottom,' said Nellie, giggling.

'Jamaica Rum?' said Will, grinning.

'Charlie calls it up-an'-downer, I don't know where 'e got it from,' said Nellie.

'Wait till I get my hands on him,' said Annie.

'Oh, it's all right, Annie,' said Nellie, 'Pam likes it. That's why she sauced him. Oh, an' Cassie's gone to look for Tabby. Tabby's our cat,' she said to Will. ''E's always goin' off an' gettin' lost. Annie says she'll drown 'im one day.'

'Nellie, have you all had a bit of tea?' asked Annie, her knee feeling stiff.

'Yes, I did some bread an' marge,' said Nellie. 'an' Charlie made a pot of tea. 'E only took 'alf an hour. Annie, could yer do with a cup yerself?'

'Yes, I could,' said Annie, 'but you're not to make it, you'll 'ave another accident with the kettle.'

'I upset the kettle once, when it was boilin',' said Nellie to Will. 'Not over meself, thank goodness, over the gas stove. Annie won't let me go near one now. Would you like a cup of tea yerself now, mister? I'll try an' get Charlie in.'

'I'll make it,' said Will, 'I've got plenty of time.' He was making a leisurely thing of his leave, as he'd been advised to. 'Annie ought to rest her knee on her bed, of course. Come on, Annie, I'll carry you up.' He could manage that, he thought.

'Oh, no you don't,' said Annie. 'I don't let soldiers I 'ardly know carry me up to me bed. Nellie can help me up the stairs when I've had that cup of tea. You really goin' to make it?'

'Where's the kettle?' asked Will. 'There it is.' It was on the hob, and he transferred it to the top of the gas oven in the scullery. He searched for a match.

In the kitchen, Nellie whispered, 'Oh, ain't he 'and-some, Annie? Fancy you findin' a nice soldier like 'im.'

Since Annie knew that her dignity had taken a hiding, she said loudly, 'Well, I won't say he wasn't helpful, nor that he 'asn't got a kind heart somewhere, but dumpin' me in that pushcart with 'undreds of people about, I wonder I didn't die of bein' looked at. I expect some soldiers – what's that I can hear?'

'It's 'im,' whispered Nellie, ''e's laughin'.'

'Well, he would, wouldn't he?' said Annie, even more loudly. 'He was laughin' all the time he was wheelin' me home. Some soldiers would have covered my legs up, but not 'im, oh, no. He let all the street kids have a look.'

'Yes, and Eddie Marsh said 'e saw yer knickers,' said Nellie.

'Oh, you Nellie, wasn't it bad enough havin' that little 'ooligan speak the word without you speakin' it as well?' fumed Annie.

'It's all right,' said Will from the kitchen, 'I didn't see them myself.'

'Oh,' breathed Annie, 'I'll spit in a minute.'

'Annie, you shouldn't spit,' said Nellie, 'Dad wouldn't like you to.'

'Got a teapot in there?' called Will. 'And some tea?'

Nellie took the teapot and caddy out to him.

'You goin' to stay and keep an eye on our Annie till our dad gets 'ome?' she asked, putting the question in the belief it was a sister's natural duty to help an older one enjoy a romance. Annie mostly turned her nose up at young men. She said she was too busy to go walking out with any of them, and that she liked her family best, anyway. Nellie knew she was wild with this soldier for putting her in a pushcart, but she wasn't actually turning her nose up at him. If she had been, she'd have spoken

408

very politely to him, thanked him for bringing her home, and asked her, Nellie, to show him out. Instead, she was giving him what for and not making any move to get off the table and hop to a chair. It was like she was waiting for him to carry her up to her room, even though she'd said he wasn't to. And Nellie thought her knee hadn't suffered a mortal injury, she was hardly taking any notice of it. 'I don't mind if you stay,' said Nellie, as Will stirred the pot, 'only me an' Charlie can't do much with her at times, specially if she's a bit upset, poor woman, an' needs someone to see she rests 'er knee.'

There was a muffled little yell from Annie.

'You Nellie, I'm listening to you!'

'Poor what, Nellie?' asked Will, grinning.

'Yes, poor woman,' said Nellie. 'Mind, she's ever so nice really, and our dad says she's pretty too. So does 'Arold Seymour down the street, 'e's potty about 'er, but 'e's got ginger 'air and Annie 'ates ginger 'air. D'you think she's pretty?'

'You Nellie!' yelled Annie. 'I'll smother you!'

'There, you can see she's upset,' said Nellie.

'Poor woman,' said Will, waiting for the tea to draw.

'I heard that!' cried Annie, who had never felt more put upon since she'd become a young lady. 'I'm not a poor woman!'

'We'll be with you in a moment,' called Will.

'What's yer name?' asked Nellie.

'Will Brown, from Caulfield Place.'

'That's a nice name. What's them stripes on yer sleeve for?'

'To show I'm a corporal and can order people about,' said Will.

'Crikey, can yer really? You goin' to order Annie about?'

'What'll happen if I do?'

'Oh, she'll think you're ever so manly,' said Nellie.

Annie could hardly believe what she was listening to. That Nellie, talking as if butter wouldn't melt in her mouth.

'Here we are,' said Will, bringing the teapot in. 'How about some cups and saucers, Nellie, and some milk and sugar?'

Nellie supplied the requirements.

'I'm still sittin' here like a lemon, you know,' said Annie.

'All right, let's try a chair,' said Will, and lifted her and sat her on one. Annie was a slender girl of five feet seven. She was proud of her legs and happy about her bosom, which was happy about itself. Well, it was firm and didn't joggle about like some other girls' bosoms did, especially if they didn't wear decent stays. Any bosom that didn't joggle felt happy about itself.

'I'm not goin' upstairs,' she said, 'there's the vegetables to do.'

'I'll help Nellie do them,' said Will, pouring the tea, 'I've got to do something to make up for puttin' you in the pushcart.'

'Well, it's kind of you,' said Annie, 'but I'm sure you've got to be on your way soon.'

'Time's my own until six,' said Will.

'We'd best let 'im help, Annie,' said Nellie. ''E's a corporal and can order people about, can't you, Will?'

'On top of that I'm bossy as well,' said Will.

'Don't I know it,' said Annie darkly.

Well, bless me, thought Nellie, two bossy people together, what a lark. And where's our Cassie got to, that's what I'd like to know. Wandering about in a dream, I shouldn't wonder, and looking for the cat.

CHAPTER THREE

'A sailor suit?' said eleven-year-old Freddy Brown in horror.

'A nice sailor suit would look lovely for Susie's weddin',' said Mrs Brown, his affable mother.

'Not on me it wouldn't,' said Freddy. 'I ain't goin' to wear no sailor suit, not for Susie's weddin' nor anyone else's. I'll fall down dead. You wouldn't like that, I bet, me fallin' down dead in the church.'

'But, Freddy love—'

'I'm eleven, I'll 'ave you know,' said Freddy, 'I ain't six.'

'Still, you'd look ever so sweet in a sailor suit,' said Sally, his fourteen-year-old sister. They were just home from school. They lived in Caulfield Place, off Browning Street, Walworth. Easter was approaching, so were the school holidays and so was their sister Susie's wedding. It was a time of excitement for the Brown family, and for the whole street. A cockney wedding wasn't the sort of event that concerned only the bride and her family. Everyone wanted to know everything about it, and Mr Brown kept saying to Mrs Brown that the way things were going the bridegroom would finish up finding himself married to every female in Caulfield Place. And Mrs Brown kept saying of course he wouldn't, he'd get charged with multiplied bigamy if he did.

'No sailor suit, if yer don't mind,' said Freddy resolutely.

'Perhaps Freddy wants to be a bridesmaid, Mum, and wear a pink frock,' said Sally.

'Here, leave off,' said Freddy, eating a slice of cake to keep the wolf from the door until supper.

'Well, all right, love,' said Mrs Brown, a natural peacemaker, 'perhaps a nice dark grey suit, then, that you could wear afterwards for Sundays.'

'With long trousers,' said Freddy.

'Long trousers at your age?' said Sally.

'I've made up me mind I ain't wearing shorts at Susie's weddin',' said Freddy, 'they ain't important enough.'

'Oh, I don't know about long trousers,' said Mrs Brown, cutting away surplus greenery from a firm cauliflower. 'You are only eleven, Freddy.'

'All right,' said Freddy, 'I won't wear no trousers at all, just me shirt, waistcoat an' jacket.'

'Oh, yer rotten 'orror,' said Sally, 'I'm not goin' in that church if you're not wearin' any trousers.'

'Can't 'elp it,' said Freddy, 'me mind's made up, I'm not wearin' no trousers unless they're long ones.'

'Well, listen to 'im,' said Sally, 'just wait till Dad comes in, I bet 'e'll make you sing a different tune.'

'I bet 'e won't,' said Freddy, 'I bet Dad wouldn't wear no trousers, either, if Mum tried to put 'im in shorts for Susie's weddin'.'

'Dad's a man, you soppy date,' said Sally, 'you're only a boy.'

'Can't 'elp that,' said Freddy, 'me mind's made up.'

'Now, Freddy love, stop actin' up,' said Mrs Brown.

'Crikey, what a life,' said Freddy. 'Me mate Daisy's moved and me mum won't let me wear long trousers. I 'ope this kind of bad luck ain't goin' to last me all year.'

'I'll speak sympathetic to your dad,' said Mrs Brown placatingly, 'but as for Daisy, she and her fam'ly couldn't help 'aving to move, love.'

Young Daisy Cook had been Freddy's best street pal. She and her family had moved because their house had a rather unhappy history. A grisly murder had taken place there twelve years ago, in 1914.

Freddy, eyeing his sister, took on a puzzled expression.

'What's 'appening to Sally?' he asked. His young sister, who had fair curly hair and hazel eyes, was getting pretty. And something else. Crikey, she'd stopped growing short, she was shooting up. He'd been taller than her, even though three years younger. Now she was suddenly above him. All in a few months. 'Here, what're you wearin', sis?'

'Me?' said Sally, her blue school gymslip short. 1926 was the year of exceptionally short hemlines. Legs were in. Or legs had come out, according to how one thought about the fashion. 'What d'you mean, what'm I wearin'?'

'Whose legs you wearin'?' asked Freddy.

'Not yours,' said Sally, 'or Susie's.'

'Look at 'er, Mum,' said Freddy, 'she's standin' on some kind of stilts.'

'Oh, I see what you mean,' said Mrs Brown, and smiled proudly at Sally. 'Yes, she's goin' to be as tall as our Susie.'

'Something's goin' on,' said Freddy. 'Come on, you Sally, let's 'ave a proper look at them legs of yours, I don't want me friends sayin' you're walkin' on someone else's.'

'Keep off,' said Sally. Freddy, as larky as any Walworth boy, sped around the kitchen table to get at her. Sally yelled and rushed.

'Mum, stop 'im!'

'Now, Freddy, leave Sally be, there's a good boy,' said Mrs Brown placidly. In all her forty-three years, nothing had ever seriously ruffled her, except the possibility, during the war, that her husband Jim might not survive his terrible life in the trenches.

'Mum!' shrieked Sally, as Freddy kept after her.

'Freddy, stop teasin' her,' said Mrs Brown.

'Someone's got to see whose legs she's wearin',' said Freddy, but gave up when Sally put herself behind their plump mother.

'Oh, yer daft ha'porth,' said Sally, 'how can anyone be wearin' someone else's legs?'

'Yes, it beats me,' said Freddy, 'unless you bought a pair of long wooden ones down the market. I dunno what I'm goin' to do if me mates find out one of me sisters is walkin' about on wooden legs.'

'Now you're talkin' silly, love,' said Mrs Brown, going into the scullery to peel potatoes at the sink, 'our Sally's got nice natural legs.'

'Yes, but 'ave yer seen what's been 'appening to them lately?' asked Freddy.

'Sally's growin' up,' said Mrs Brown.

'I remember Susie growin' up once,' said Freddy.

'Now how could anyone remember Susie only growin' up once?' asked Sally.

'Well, I was only little at the time,' said Freddy.

'You're potty,' said Sally. 'Mum, don't you think it's lovely our Will bein' 'ome for the weddin'? Susie nearly cried when she saw 'im.'

'It beats me, girls nearly cryin' when they're 'appy,' said Freddy. 'Mind you, Mum, I dunno that me brother's all that well.'

'He's just got a bit of a chest,' said Sally.

'He'll be all right now he's home and not 'aving to suffer all that terrible heat,' said Mrs Brown.

''Ope so,' said Freddy. 'Well, I think I'll go an' see if Ernie Flint'll lend me 'is bike on Sunday, so's I can cycle to Brockwell Park.'

'I'll come with you as far as Cotham Street,' said Sally,

'then I'll go an' see Mavis.' Mavis Richards was a close friend. They shared the giggly little secrets of schoolgirls.

'I don't know I want you ridin' bikes, Freddy,' said Mrs Brown, 'not with Susie's weddin' next month, you might fall off and hit your head on the road.'

'With an 'ead like's he's got, I bet Dad would get a bill for road repairs,' said Sally.

'Our Sally's nearly a comic sometimes,' said Freddy.

'Bless 'er,' said Mrs Brown.

'And 'er wooden legs,' said Freddy.

Out he went with his sister. Sally was bare-headed, Freddy wearing a blue cap. From the open door of a house shot the figure of a neighbour, Mr Higgins. He was a tram conductor whose duties sometimes brought him home early, sometimes late. After him came a rolling-pin. It struck him between his shoulder blades. Down he went. Following the rolling-pin came Mrs Higgins. Mr Higgins was thin and bony, Mrs Higgins was buxom. Freddy and Sally could tell she was riled. She had a wealth of dark brown hair, the pins were loose and it was all over her head and face.

'Get up,' she said to her fallen husband, and she retrieved the rolling-pin.

'What for?' asked Mr Higgins, feeling safer on the pavement.

'So's I can give yer another one,' said Mrs Higgins. 'I don't like 'itting you when yer on the ground.'

'I can't get up,' said Mr Higgins, 'I'm wounded, and me leg's broke as well.'

'I'll give you wounded,' said Mrs Higgins. 'Look at 'im,' she said to Sally and Freddy, 'would yer believe 'im capable of it?'

'Capable of what, Mrs Higgins?' asked Sally.

'Kissin' and cuddlin' 'is lady passengers, that's what.'

415

'Is he supposed to?' asked Freddy.

'Is 'e what?'

'Well, I only asked,' said Freddy.

''E's forbidden,' said Mrs Higgins, 'but 'e done it. Stay where you are,' she said to her husband, giving him a rap on his head with the rolling-pin. 'Mrs Blake saw it all this mornin', at the market tram stop. Me own 'usband, would yer believe, and in front of everyone in Walworth.'

'Now would I do that?' said Mr Higgins, his conductor's uniform dusty from the pavement. 'I'd lose me job.'

'That's what I've been tellin' yer,' said Mrs Higgins, 'and don't answer me back in front of Sally an' Freddy, they'll think I don't get no respect from you. Mrs Blake told me that when she saw it 'appen, she near dropped dead with shock.'

'Pity she bleedin' didn't,' muttered Mr Higgins.

'What's that? What's that you said?'

'I said I think me leg's bleedin'.'

'Shall I get 'im a bandage an' some ointment, Mrs Higgins?' asked Sally.

''E don't want a bandage, not yet 'e don't,' said Mrs Higgins. 'I'll give 'im what for when I get 'im back indoors. 'E'll need a doctor then, not a bandage. To think after all these years I'm burdened with the shame of what 'e's done today, and in public too.'

'Look, me pet,' said Mr Higgins, 'I just 'elped a lady off me tram with 'er foldin' pram and baby. Yus, and a shoppin' bag as well. She 'appened to be overcome with gratitude, I suppose—'

'She what?' said Mrs Higgins threateningly.

'She was overcome with gratitude, Mrs Higgins,' said Freddy. 'I mean, that's what Mr Higgins just said.'

'Well, what else would've made 'er give me a kiss?' said Mr Higgins. 'I asks yer, me love, what else? I didn't kiss

416

'er meself, nor cuddle 'er, it's against the regulations.'

'You're answerin' me back again,' said Mrs Higgins.

Along came Mr Ponsonby, a lodger in a house farther down the Place. An eccentric, he was fifty years old, his lean body clad in a black frock coat, black drainpipe trousers, and a grey waistcoat. He also wore a bowler hat, a red bow tie and elastic-sided boots. And he carried a rolled umbrella. At first glance he seemed a dapper man, but a closer inspection revealed crumbs on his waistcoat, wrinkles in his bow tie and a dent in his bowler. And his boots were dusty. On the other hand, his smooth unlined face had a very neat look, as if nature had taken pains to put each feature tidily in place. Sometimes his expression was querulous, and sometimes that of a kind and gentle man. He could often be heard talking to himself. 'Dear me, dear me, what a day, what a day.' That sort of thing.

Up he came in dainty pigeon-toed fashion and looked down at Mr Higgins.

'Mr Higgins? Dear me, what's this all about?' His voice had a piping lilt.

'I ain't sittin' 'ere of me own accord, yer know,' grumbled Mr Higgins.

'No, of course not, of course not,' said Mr Ponsonby.

''E fell over,' said Sally.

'Ah, who is this I see?' enquired Mr Ponsonby, and peered at Sally. He smiled. 'Ah, yes, a young lady.'

'She ain't a young lady, she's me sister,' said Freddy.

'Now now, Freddy,' said Mrs Higgins, 'course she's a young lady, anyone can see that. My, ain't yer growin' up nice, Sally? Yer goin' to rival Susie in a year or two. What're you doin'?' she demanded of her husband.

'I was thinkin' of gettin' up,' said Mr Higgins.

'I'll knock yer block off,' said Mrs Higgins, 'I ain't finished with you yet.'

'Come now, Mrs Higgins, have a peppermint drop,' said Mr Ponsonby, and produced a paper bag from his pocket. He always had peppermint drops somewhere on his person, and offered them generously to all and sundry. The street kids knew this, and sometimes ran after him, asking for one, and he always obliged. He sucked them regularly himself, and breathed peppermint fumes.

'Don't mind if I do, I need something,' said Mrs Higgins. As she helped herself from the bag, Mr Higgins came to his feet and disappeared indoors. It didn't fool Mrs Higgins.

'Gotcher!' she cried. 'I'll learn yer!' And she went bouncing in after him.

'Tck, tck,' said Mr Ponsonby and peered at Sally again. 'Ah, yes, Sally, our pretty young lady. Have a peppermint drop.'

'Oh, thanks,' said Sally, and took one. In return, she gave Mr Ponsonby a happy little smile. Life was doing her proud at the moment. Not only was she going to be a bridesmaid in three weeks time, she had also started to grow again after a gloomy year of thinking she was going to end up as a real tich of a girl. She was positive she could actually feel her legs getting longer every week. Not every day, of course. Every week. With fashions so short, and flappers showing their knees, no girl who had just had her fourteenth birthday wanted to have legs that hardly went anywhere. It was bliss that she'd shot up inches in just a few months. Mind, she still had to wear dreary old black lisle stockings for school, but Susie had recently bought her imitation silk ones for Sundays. They made her lengthening legs feel ever so posh. Susie, her sister, though, wore real silk nearly all the time. Well, she had ever such a good job, of course, as personal assistant to her fiancé, Sammy Adams, who was boss of Adams Fashions and other enterprises. Sally could hardly believe he was going to be her brother-in-law. When she left school at the end of the present term, perhaps she could get a job in one of his shops.

Mr Ponsonby blinked in the sunshine of her smile.

'Charming, charming,' he said. 'Well, good afternoon, good afternoon, I must get to my lodgings.' He put the bag of peppermints away, then turned and began to retrace his steps. Freddy and Sally went after him.

'Excuse me, Mr Ponsonby,' said Sally, 'you're goin' the wrong way.'

'No, no,' he said, stopping, 'I'm going to my lodgings, I have things to do.'

'Yes, but you're still pointin' the wrong way,' said Freddy.

Mr Ponsonby blinked again.

'Dear me, so I am, so I am,' he said.

'It's back there,' said Sally, 'in Mrs Mason's 'ouse.'

'Thank you, thank you, how kind. My, you are a pretty girl. Have you had a peppermint drop?'

'Yes, thanks,' said Sally.

'One can't be too careful.' Mr Ponsonby regarded brother and sister cautiously. 'One is never sure who has had one and who hasn't. Dear me, what a day, good afternoon.' And off he went to his lodgings, the point of his umbrella clicking on the pavement. He stopped to inspect a chalked hopscotch design. 'Bless my soul, what's that doing there? Never mind, never mind.' He hastened on.

'Ain't 'e funny?' said Freddy.

'You didn't get a peppermint drop,' said Sally, as they turned into Browning Street.

'Nor I didn't,' said Freddy. 'I'll take two next time 'e offers, 'e won't mind.'

419

'Bet he won't even notice,' said Sally. 'Don't he talk posh, though? Mum says 'e's prob'bly come down in the world.'

'Yes, 'e prob'bly 'ad a wife that took to drink an' drove 'im to ruin,' said Freddy. 'Still, 'e don't go around cryin' about it.'

'No, but he blows 'is nose sometimes,' said Sally.

'What's that got to do with it?'

'Well, lots of people blow their noses to 'ide they're cryin',' said Sally.

'Susie blew her nose a little bit when our William came 'ome,' said Freddy.

'There you are, then,' said Sally. She parted from him at Cotham Street, where her school friend lived. Freddy stopped for a moment to watch her. He grinned. She was walking as perky as anything in her short school gymslip. Showing off, just because her legs were getting longer. But he couldn't help grinning, he was fond of Sally, the cheeky one of the family.

He called after her in the fashion of a street urchin.

'Oi, darling, 'ow's yer farver's tadpoles?'

Sally turned, saw him grinning, put a thumb to her nose and then went on. A man coming the other way took notice of her. Tall and muscular, his eyes were dark and hollow beneath the peak of his flat cap, as if he didn't sleep very well, and his black serge overcoat was unbuttoned, his watch chain showing. Sally bridled because he was staring at her all the time during his approach. She didn't like his eyes one little bit, nor their fixed stare. And he was coming straight at her, as if he was going to knock her down and walk over her. Sally had to dodge aside, and as he passed her his body seemed to bruise the very air.

''Ere, d'you mind?' she said with spirit, but he just kept going, nor did he look back. Ugh, I don't like his kind, thought Sally, I like the ones that Susie likes. Sammy Adams, and his brothers, Boots and Tommy. Why wasn't there another brother, a younger one? One for her?

She laughed to herself then and went on to her friend's house.

Freddy, on his way to Ernie Flint's home in Rodney Place, approached a factory. Well, it had been a factory once, but had caught fire some years ago. It had all caved in except for a section at one end that used to house offices and store-rooms. A high wooden fence had been erected around the devastated property, but kids could squeeze in because the double wooden gates had been busted open one time, and the repair job had been makeshift. When kids did get in, they played around over piles of bricks and rubble. They couldn't, however, get into the section still standing. The door was padlocked and all windows heavily boarded up.

Passing the sagging gates, Freddy was brought to a stop by a girl's voice.

''Ere, you boy, come 'ere.'

He went back to the gates and saw a face visible through the gap.

'What's up?' he asked.

'I've lost Tabby,' she said.

'Who's Tabby?'

'It's our cat, of course. Can you come through 'ere and 'elp me find 'im?'

'Well, I'm on me way to—'

'You'd better come and 'elp or me dad'll wallop yer. I don't like lookin' by meself, not in 'ere.'

'All right, I suppose I'm not specially busy,' said Freddy, and squeezed his way through the gap. The girl, ten years old, looked him up and down as if she needed to be convinced he was capable of finding a lost cat. Well-brushed raven hair hung down her back. The black elastic of a straw boater was around her neck, the boater itself resting at the back of her head. Her face was a bit dusty, her gymslip likewise, but Freddy could see she had round brown eyes that were like Daisy Cook's. 'What's yer name?' he asked.

'Cassie Ford. What's yours?'

'Freddy Brown. Me fam'ly lives in Caulfield Place.'

'Oh, I know Caulfield Place,' she said, 'ragged kids live there.'

''Ere, mind yer tongue,' said Freddy, 'I ain't a ragged kid.'

'Well, all right,' said Cassie graciously, 'but what about me cat? Could yer start lookin' for it? Then me dad won't wallop yer. 'E's good at wallopin' boys. He give one to the boy next door last week, and it nearly done 'im in. When the boy's dad came round about it, Dad gave 'im one too.'

Crikey, what a crackpot, thought Freddy. Still, all girls were a bit potty. Not that he minded. He liked girls, and you had to accept they were off their chumps most times.

'All right,' he said, 'but you sure your cat's in 'ere?'

'Yes, a girl told me she'd seen 'im go in. Only I don't like bein' in 'ere alone.'

Freddy looked around. Mounds of bricks, mortar and rubble littered the place, the bright sunshine picking out all kinds of colours. Over on the right was the still standing section. It looked a bit desolate, even in the crisp daylight.

'All right, you stay 'ere, Cassie, and I'll go lookin'.'

'No, I'll come with yer,' said Cassie. 'I don't want to be alone when one of them skeletons comes up out of the ground.'

'Eh?' said Freddy.

'Yes, didn't you know that if you're alone in 'ere a skeleton comes up and rattles its bones at you?' said Cassie.

'Well, I'm blowed,' said Freddy solemnly, 'is that a fact?'

'Fancy you not knowin' that,' said Cassie.

'Well, like me dad says, you live an' learn. Come on, then, and if we do see a skeleton rattlin' its bones, I'll chuck all these bricks at it.' Freddy started walking and looking. 'What did yer say yer cat's name was?'

'Tabby,' she said, close on his heels. ''E's always gettin' lost.'

'You'd be better off with a canary,' said Freddy.

'I don't want a canary, I want our cat,' said Cassie, and she followed Freddy around the large area of collapsed walls and roofs, around the mounds capped with brick dust, and they both kept callng the cat's name. In and out of the gaps they went. 'Tabby, Tabby, come 'ere, will you!' called Cassie in exasperation.

'I'll chuck some stones about,' said Freddy. 'If 'e's around, that'll make 'im show 'imself.'

'Don't you throw stones at our cat, you might 'it 'im,' said Cassie indignantly.

'I dunno it wouldn't serve 'im right if 'e's always losin' himself,' said Freddy. 'And if you ask me, I don't think 'e's in 'ere.'

They reached the still intact section.

'Oh, lor',' breathed Cassie, ''e couldn't be in there, could 'e?'

'Don't see 'ow he could be,' said Freddy, 'it's all boarded up. Mind, we could go an' see if the door's open.'

'I ain't goin' in there meself,' said Cassie, 'it's 'aunted. Me dad's Aunt Tilda lived in an 'aunted house once, and it turned all 'er hair white, and me dad 'ad to go an' see what was 'aunting it, and it turned all 'is hair white too, and when 'e was only twenty.'

'Rotten 'ard luck, that was, Cassie.'

'Yes, our milkman said it made our dad old before 'is time.'

'Did 'e find a ghost?' asked Freddy.

''E never said, I expect it was too 'orrible to talk about.' Cassie eyed the boarded windows apprehensively. 'We'd best go,' she said.

'Wait a tick, let's 'ave a look,' said Freddy, and made a beeline for the padlocked door. He'd noticed something. It was the padlock, it was hanging loose. The thick steel staple hadn't been pushed in. He removed the padlock, released the metal bar and pushed the door. It swung open. ''Ere we are, Cassie,' he called, 'we can get in.'

'Oh, don't,' begged Cassie, 'you might get struck down or ate up.'

'But someone's been in,' said Freddy, 'and yer cat might've followed. I'll take a quick look, I won't give anyone time to eat me up.'

'You goin' in all by yerself?' Cassie was awe-struck. 'Can't you just put yer 'ead in and call Tabby? Oh, suppose 'e's trapped in there an' can't get out?'

'I expect all 'is hair's turnin' white, like yer dad's,' said Freddy. 'Still, I'll give 'im a shout.' He put his head in and bawled the cat's name. Nothing came of that, except the echoes of his voice, which ran hollowly about. 'Some cat,' he said, 'turned invisible, prob'ly. I'll 'ave a look, Cassie, might as well.'

'Oh, lor',' breathed Cassie. All the kids who lived close by said the place was haunted at night. Cassie thought it could be haunted by day as well, and the kids weren't too sure because none of them came and played around the brick hills any more.

'You stay there,' said Freddy, and went in, seeing how worried she was about her daft cat. He entered a wide passage with doors on either side. The dusty floor was marked, proving someone had been in. The light from the open front door showed up the marks. Perhaps a night watchman came on duty sometimes. Or perhaps the owner came and took a look at the place now and again. He opened each door in turn, but saw only empty dusty store-rooms. They all said a silent hello to him in the gloom of boarded-up windows. No cat appeared. There were stairs at the end of the passage. They creaked as he climbed them. He stopped when he reached the landing, he had a sudden odd feeling of being sort of cut off from the humming life of Walworth. It was even gloomier up here, and very silent. But despite the gloom he glimpsed a large spider scuttling along the foot of a wall between doors. It made no sound. Well, spiders didn't, they were always silent. Bluebottles weren't, nor bees, nor birds. And monkeys, talk about chattering, they could beat the band at the Zoo. But spiders, they'd invented silence, they had.

He stood still for a little while. He wasn't a boy who suffered from nerves, but he had to admit it felt a bit creepy up here. Still, he'd better see if the cat had got trapped in any of the rooms. He moved along the landing, and the floorboards creaked under his feet, breaking the silence. He supposed everything was as dry as dust. He reached to open the first door, then held back as a plaintive little miaow came to his ears. That was the sound of a cat all right. He opened the door. Another empty room and no cat. I don't know that Cassie would like that, she'd say he'd just heard the ghostly miaow of a cat that had died up here.

'Come on, Tabby, is it you or not?' he called. That brought a second miaow, and it pointed him at the next door. He opened it. All gloom again, but the room wasn't bare and empty. He made out a table, a chair, and a truckle bed with rumpled blankets. On the table was a candle in a holder, and something else. He squinted. It was a sealed and labelled tin of corned beef. He heard a little movement then, and out from under the blankets leapt a cat. It darted past him and whisked through the door, a streaking bundle of tabby fur. Moments later he distinctly heard a glad yell from Cassie. His nose began to twitch, to pick up all kinds of smells. Cat smells, he supposed, mixed with others. The others probably had something to do with a watchman spending nights up here now and again. That was the reason for the bed, blankets and corned beef. And the reason why the padlock hadn't been pushed home was probably because the bloke had been all bleary and careless the last time he'd left the place.

Freddy closed the door and shut the smells in, but as he went down the stairs he thought some of them were following him. He heard Cassie calling.

'Freddy, come on out, I've got Tabby, and you ain't fell down a hole, 'ave yer?'

He walked through the passage and emerged into the late afternoon light. Talk about the joys of fresh air and sunshine, especially as there'd been a lot of fog about up to a week ago. It was nearly like summer now. Well, spring, anyway. He pulled the door to, slipped in the padlock and fastened it with a click. He turned. The cat was in the girl's arms, doing some daft purring.

'Good idea if you got that cat chained up,' he said.

'Oh, yer cruel thing,' said Cassie. 'But fancy Tabby gettin' in there.'

'Well, I did say 'e might've followed someone in, there's a room upstairs that looks like it's used by a night watchman, except I dunno what 'e's got to watch.'

426

'More like a ghost, I bet,' said Cassie. 'Wasn't you brave, goin' in by yerself? Me dad's brave too, 'e saved an 'orse once from drowning in the sea.'

'How'd it get in the sea?'

'It fell off a ship,' said Cassie, cuddling her cat.

'You sure?' said Freddy. 'I never 'eard of no 'orse fallin' off a ship before.'

'It slipped,' said Cassie. 'Or something,' she added after a moment's reflection. 'It was when me dad was a sea captain, and 'e 'ad to jump in and rescue the poor thing, it couldn't swim. They give me dad a medal.'

'Who did?' asked Freddy, walking back to the gates with her.

'I can't remember. Well, yes, it was the Horse Savin' Society, I think. Yes, that was it. Mind, that was before 'e took to drink.' Cassie sighed and her cat purred.

'That's funny,' said Freddy, 'I was only sayin' to me sister Sally earlier that a neighbour of ours prob'bly 'ad a wife that took to drink an' brought 'im to ruin. 'As yer dad brought yer mum to ruin?'

'No, me mum died when I was little,' said Cassie.

'Well, I'm sorry for yer about that, Cassie.'

'It's all right, I 'elp me dad as much as I can,' she said.

They rounded the final heaps of rubble and reached the gates, on the insides of which kids had chalked anti-social messages.

'I hate Eddie Banks.'

'I hate his bruvver.'

'Loopy Lily Jarvis luvs Billy Palmer.'

'What, him? She's loopy all right.'

'Elsie Nunn's got a fat bum.'

'Cissy Dawes don't wear no drawers.'

'YES I DO!!!'

'Don't read them, they're rude,' said Cassie.

'Come on,' said Freddy, and they squeezed their way out, the cat staying happily in Cassie's arms. 'Where d'you live?'

'Blackwood Street,' said Cassie.

'That's not far from us,' said Freddy. 'Well, I might see you around, Cassie, if I don't see yer cat first.'

'We used to live in a mansion in Dulwich,' said Cassie. 'That was when me dad worked at Buckingham Palace, servin' the King an' Queen. 'E used to take them their 'ot cocoa at night.'

'You sure?' said Freddy, hiding a grin.

'Course I'm sure,' said Cassie, 'they liked 'ot cocoa. Well, goodbye, Freddy, thanks for findin' Tabby.'

'So long,' said Freddy. She went one way cuddling her cat, and he went the other. Well, he thought, there's some girls a bit barmy, some a bit dozy, and some real crackpots. Still, as his dad always said, blokes had got to live with that.

He found Ernie Flint at home and asked about the loan of his bike. Ernie said not likely, his bike wasn't for lending, specially not on a Sunday. Get a bike of your own, he said. Me dad can't afford it, said Freddy. Bet your sister can, said Ernie, the one that's getting married. Girls about to get married can be a real soft touch, you could ask some of them for fifty bob easy and they wouldn't even remember giving it to you, they're at their soppiest when they're getting married.

'I dunno that Susie's soppy,' said Freddy.

'Bound to be,' said Ernie. 'You could ask 'er for a fiver, seein' what a good job she's got, and if she ain't soppy enough to give yer as much as that, tell 'er you'll just take 'alf that amount. You can buy a decent bike for fifty bob.'

'Crikey, I knew you'd got a bike, Ernie,' said Freddy, 'I didn't know you'd got brains as well.'

''Ow would yer like a punch in the eye?' said Ernie.

'I don't think I'll stay for that,' said Freddy, 'it might spoil me supper.'

He went back home, whistling with optimist cheerfulness as he thought about touching Susie for the price of a bike. Of course, he wasn't sure if her feelings about getting married really were soppy. She didn't act soppy, not Susie, but she did go about sometimes looking as if she'd lost a penny and found ten quid. But she never went off to work wearing odd stockings or forgetting to put her hat on or what day it was. That would have been a sign that she really was soppy about her engagement to Sammy. Still, she was up in the clouds sometimes. Promising, that was, thought Freddy.

CHAPTER FOUR

Will was ready to leave. It was after six, the best of the bright March day was over, the sun was deserting the Western sky, and sharp twilight was waiting in the wings. The chimneys and rooftops of Walworth were growing a sombre colour. Will had helped Nellie prepare the vegetables and to put them on, and a dissected plump rabbit was stewing. It had all been sending Annie mad, not being able to look after things herself on account of her stiff knee. She felt like a back number.

Will had met ten-year-old Cassie. Her hair was long, not bobbed, and she had dreamy eyes and an even dreamier smile. But she looked breathless when she heard about how Annie had come to meet this soldier. She obviously thought it the most romantic meeting ever, and Annie had a ghastly feeling she was going to say so. She prevented that by demanding to know where she'd been, and Cassie said she'd had to go and find Tabby and that a boy had helped her. What boy? Oh, said Cassie, he was the son of a lion tamer who'd just come back from darkest Africa to look after the Trafalgar Square lions for the King. They're not real lions, you silly, said Nellie, they're statue lions. Yes, he's got to keep them polished, said Cassie. I'm going to write about it in my diary, she said, and about Annie meeting a royal guardsman. He's not a royal guardsman, said Nellie. No, but he could be, said Cassie, and went up to confide her imaginings to her diary.

Will also met Charlie, a boy with a shock of untidy hair

and socks down to his ankles. Charlie thought Will had done a good job bringing Annie home after she'd hurt her knee. He brought her in a pushcart, said Nellie wickedly, and Annie gritted her teeth because Charlie, being what he was, made a lot of that.

'Cor, in a pushcart,' he said, 'our Annie and all. Bloomin' 'eroic, that was. I bet even Tarzan couldn't 'ave got 'er in a pushcart. I'm 'eartbroke I missed it. 'Ere, could yer put 'er in it again, Will? Yer don't mind me callin' yer Will, do yer? I ain't met no-one 'eroic before. Could yer put Annie in the pushcart again so's I could see it with me own mince pies?'

'Oh, you little 'ooligan,' said Annie, 'if I didn't have a stiff knee I'd boil you in the copper.'

'And besides, we don't 'ave a pushcart,' said Nellie.

'And besides, if I tried it,' said Will, 'she'd boil me as well. If she didn't have a stiff knee.'

'That's it, everyone laugh,' said Annie bitterly.

When Will was ready to go, he offered to carry her upstairs so that she could rest her knee and have her dad bring her supper up to her later.

'Well, all right,' said Annie, 'I suppose it's best – oh, mind me frock!' Will had lifted her. He carried her out of the kitchen, and she went on about her frock much as she had before. Charlie, following on with Nellie, couldn't think why Annie was having problems.

'What's she fussin' about, Nellie?' he asked. 'I can't see nothink wrong with 'er frock.'

'It's not 'er frock,' whispered Nellie, 'it's just that she ain't never met an 'andsome soldier before.' She darted, squeezing ahead of Will on the landing to open the door of the back bedroom, which was Annie's. 'In 'ere, Will,' she said, 'our Annie sleeps in this room.'

'Right, let's do the delivery job,' said Will. He carried

Annie in and placed her on her bed. She tugged at the hem of her frock. 'All right?' said Will.

Just the hint of a smile showed on her face.

'Thanks ever so much, honest,' she said.

'Don't mention it,' said Will, and it happened then. It came suddenly, the tightness in his chest, the sensation of constriction and the shortness of breath. He'd be coughing and wheezing in a few moments, an embarrassment to everyone. 'Got to go now. Good luck, Annie, you too, Nellie and Charlie.'

They all stared at him as he walked straight out.

'Crikey, 'e's gone,' said Nellie.

'Nellie, run down and make sure he knows I'm grateful really,' said Annie, 'tell 'im thank you again.'

Nellie dashed out, ran down the stairs and caught Will at the front door. He'd picked up his peaked cap from the kitchen.

'Annie said she's ever so grateful really, an' wants to thank you ever so much,' said Nellie.

'Pleasure,' said Will, wheezing now.

'Oh, 'ave yer got a cold?' asked Nellie.

'Sort of,' said Will huskily, and left, pulling the door to behind him. Nellie went back upstairs.

''E's got a sort of cold,' she said.

''E didn't look as if 'e had,' said Charlie. 'Blimey, what an 'eroic bloke, gettin' you in a pushcart, Annie.'

'If you mention that once more, Charlie, your life won't be worth livin', d'you hear?' said Annie.

'Yes, an' what did you do to Pam Nicholls?' asked Nellie.

'Well, I did 'ave a go at tryin' to push 'er foot into 'er mouth—'

'You what?' yelled Annie.

'But 'er mum come in then an' give me a thick ear,' said

Charlie, rubbing his left one. 'That Pam, she told 'er mum to give me another one. Just wait till I get 'er alone, I'll push both 'er feet into 'er mouth.'

'Nellie, get the chopper and hit your brother with it,' said Annie.

'Yes, in a minute, Annie,' said Nellie. 'I wonder if Will's comin' back sometime?'

'Of course not,' said Annie. 'What would 'e want to come back for?'

'Well, 'e might want to see if your knee's all right,' said Nellie.

'More like 'e'd want to give Annie another ride in a pushcart,' said Charlie.

'Oh, you wait, you 'eathen,' breathed Annie, 'as soon as me knee's better I'm goin' to hit you with the chopper meself, and don't think I won't. Didn't I tell you not to mention pushcarts again?'

'I only said what Will might do if 'e comes round again,' said Charlie.

'I don't know why you and Nellie call him Will,' said Annie.

'It's 'is name,' said Nellie.

'You shouldn't be familiar when you've only just met 'im,' said Annie. 'Look, both of you go down and make sure the supper's cookin' properly. Don't let anything burn, and mind how you handle the saucepans, Nellie.'

'All right,' said Nellie, and down she went with Charlie. Nellie descended quietly. Charlie's descent created a minor earthquake. Annie lay looking at the ceiling. She thought about being wheeled home in that pushcart. Her at her age, and him as good as laughing all over his face.

I might as well die and not have any supper.

No, I won't, I'll have some supper and die later.

*   *   *

433

Outside, Will leaned against the railings. He tried to let his body relax, he tried to keep still, but he wheezed like an old man with bronchitis, and a periodical cough racked his chest. He supposed he'd brought it on himself by carrying Annie upstairs. But just doing that had brought on the attack? He could see what was going to happen if his condition didn't improve. He'd be invalided out of the Army at the ripe old age of twenty.

The attack began to ease a little after ten minutes. He watched the street kids. He heard the faint sounds of Walworth traffic. Trams, omnibuses, horse-drawn vehicles. Not like Indian traffic. Bullocks provided horse-power out there. But not cows. Cows were sacred. If one sat down in a crowded city street, it could cause prolonged congestion. Well, if it wouldn't move, no-one tried to make it, so it stayed there.

As to the heat, it sapped a bloke's energy unless you ate lots of curry. He couldn't count the number of times he and other East Surrey men had longed for the April showers of home, and for things like the smell of eggs and bacon, the taste of fish and chips, the savoury flavour of hot faggots and pease pudding, and the creaminess of a rice pudding with a golden-brown skin just out of the oven.

Come to that, even street kids could be missed. Look at these, he thought, ruddy monkeys, the lot of them. Walworth kids never changed. This bunch were no different from those of his own generation. All generations scrapped, argued, broke windows, kicked tin cans and got their ears clipped by their dads. But they all grew up cheerfully and optimistically, with exceptions. That counted, cheerfulness and optimism.

It took over fifteen minutes before his breathing became normal, and a few more minutes before he decided to go on his way.

'What's that about our Annie?' asked Mr Harold Ford, a railway ganger of five feet ten and rugged all over. Just home from his work, his jacket was off. He always took it off the moment he entered the kitchen. His waistcoat was an old leather one, his shirt of thick striped flannel, and his trousers were of hard-wearing corduroy. There was a scarf around his neck and a belt around his trousers. He had a little round bald patch to his black hair that had inspired Cassie into asking him if he was going to be a monk later on. He said he liked the thought but didn't think he'd ever be holy enough.

'Yes, our Annie's upstairs, Dad,' said Nellie, and told him how her sister had bumped her knee and been brought home by a nice soldier. In a pushcart.

'What's that?' asked the Gaffer. Everyone called him that on account of his ruggedness. It made him look like a man who was in charge. 'Did you say a pushcart, Nellie?'

'Well, the soldier said it was the best way to bring 'er.'

'Oh, me old Adam, a pushcart?' said the Gaffer, trying to hide a grin. 'Where'd the soldier come from?'

''E didn't say,' said Nellie, 'except 'e did tell me 'is fam'ly live in Caulfield Place and 'e's 'ome on leave.'

'I think 'e comes from Windsor Castle,' said Cassie, 'I think 'e guards the King and Queen there.'

'Who said?' asked Charlie.

'Well, it's only what I think,' said Cassie, 'and only the way 'e looks.'

'Now 'ow can anyone look like Windsor Castle?' asked Charlie.

'You kids work it out,' said the Gaffer, whose ruggedness actually hid a heart made of marshmallow, 'while I go up an' see Annie.'

Up he went. He found Annie's knee was just a bit stiff

and bruised. Be all right in a day or so, he said. Annie wasn't too concerned with that, apart from thinking she might have to hop to work tomorrow. She still had indignity on her mind. So she regaled her dad with an account of the purgatory she'd suffered being wheeled home in a boy's pushcart with thousands of people all having a look at her.

'Thousands?' said the Gaffer.

'Yes, and all grinnin',' said Annie, 'and me with me knees nearly up to me chin.'

'Gawd save the starvin' poor,' said the Gaffer in a strangled voice, and suddenly wasn't there any more.

'Dad, where've you gone?' yelled Annie. She heard him out on the landing. He sounded as if he was choking to death. 'Oh, I don't believe it, you're out there laughin'! Call yourself me dad? You ought to be ashamed, laughin' like that, and don't think I can't 'ear you, because I can. What about the indignity I suffered, me a young lady near to eighteen.'

The Gaffer reappeared, his face red. He was coughing now. From her bed, Annie eyed him in outrage. He cleared his throat, rubbed his mouth, and made an attempt to come to terms with her feelings.

'Did yer say with yer knees up to yer chin, Annie?' he asked.

'You heard,' said Annie. 'Me, your eldest daughter.'

'Well, I ain't 'aving me best gel upset like that,' he said. 'I'll learn the bloke, Annie, soldier or not. I'll find out where 'e lives in Caulfield Place. It ain't far, I'll get 'im, and when I do I'll break 'is legs.'

'You'll what?' gasped Annie, sitting up.

'Break 'is legs, both of 'em.'

'Dad—'

'Don't you worry, Annie, I'll give 'im what 'e's asked

for, dumpin' you in a pushcart with yer knees up to yer chin, I'll make 'im wish 'e'd never been born.'

'Don't you dare,' gasped Annie, 'I'll never forgive you.'

'All right, Annie, just one leg.'

'Dad, you can't! It ain't Christian.'

'Ah,' said the Gaffer.

'Nor gentlemanly,' said Annie.

'Well, I'll grant yer that, Annie, breakin' legs ain't too gentlemanly.'

'Besides,' said Annie.

'Besides what?' asked her dad.

'Ain't it funny really, when you think about it?'

Charlie, Nellie and Cassie came running up the stairs to see what all the noise was about. Their dad was roaring with laughter, and Annie was giggling like a girl who'd forgotten she was a young lady of dignity.

CHAPTER FIVE

The evening had become cold and frosty, but Mrs Brown's kitchen was warm and cosy, the range fire glowing, and a supper of hot shepherd's pie was on the table, the potato crust patterned with crisp brown ridges. The house was old, going well back into the Victorian era, but its foundations and walls were solid and enduring. All members of the Brown family were present, and like the Adams family who had preceded them as tenants, they were never short of something to say. They were at it now, in response to what Will had said about a young lady who'd hurt her knee.

'Come again, Will?' said Mr Brown, a wiry old survivor of the trenches.

'Yes, say it again, Will,' said Susie.

'Yes, you'd best, love,' advised Mrs Brown, 'it sounded a bit funny.'

'It wasn't to her,' said Will. 'I decided I'd better not carry her, me in my condition, so I sat her in the pushcart and wheeled her home.'

'Crikey, you didn't, Will, did yer?' said Sally.

'How old was she?' asked Susie.

'She let me know several times she was seventeen and that I was mucking up her dignity,' said Will, 'but I had to get her home somehow.'

Susie laughed, and her engagement ring, a diamond solitaire, winked in the gaslight.

'Some palaver,' grinned Mr Brown.

'Wish I'd seen it,' said Freddy, 'only I went to Ernie

438

Flint's to see if I could 'ave a loan of 'is bike, not 'aving one of me own.'

Nobody took any notice of that. Will's way of getting a seventeen-year-old girl home was grabbing all the attention.

'I don't know I'd like bein' wheeled 'ome in a pushcart, and I'm only fourteen,' said Sally.

'Oh, but it must've been a nice ride for her with her knee hurtin',' said Mrs Brown proudly. She found it easy to be proud of almost anything her sons and daughters did, short of knocking a policeman's helmet off. She was against anything showing disrespect for the law.

'But the young lady didn't think it was nice, Will?' said Susie, twenty-one, and generally regarded as a corker, even by small boys still vague about why girls were different. And the vicar wouldn't tell them, except to say the ways of the Lord were wondrous.

'Yes, come on, what did she say?' asked Sally.

'Quite a lot,' said Will. Susie, sitting next to him, gave him a look. If Sally and Freddy were close, so were Susie and Will. She saw his little grin and how brown he was. The Army had done something for Will, made a man of him at twenty, and a good-looking one, with an air of self-confidence. An NCO's air of self-confidence. Susie could easily imagine a girl of seventeen dying of embarrassment at having him wheel her home in a boy's pushcart.

'What's a lot?' she asked.

'Well, most of it meant how much better off she'd have been if she'd never met me,' said Will.

'What a funny girl,' said Mrs Brown.

''Ere, listen, I met a funny one meself when I was on me way to Ernie Flint's,' said Freddy. 'Mind, I could've cycled there if I'd 'ad me own bike—'

'What's the young lady's name, Will?' asked Mr Brown.

439

'Talk to yerself,' muttered Freddy.

'Eat your supper up, love,' said Mrs Brown.

'Come on, Will, what's 'er name?' asked Sally.

'Annie Ford,' said Will.

''Ere, listen, I met a girl name of Ford,' said Freddy, 'it was the funny one, it was when I was on me way to—'

'Where's she live?' asked Sally.

'I dunno where she lives,' said Freddy, 'but I betcher she's got 'er own bike. If I 'ad me own—'

'I'm talkin' to Will, you blessed boy,' said Sally.

'Yes, where's the young lady live, Will?' asked Mrs Brown, beginning to think there might have been love at first sight if the young lady happened to have been pretty.

'Blackwood Street,' said Will. 'She's got a dad, two sisters and a hooligan brother.'

'So 'ave I,' said Sally, 'he's sittin' next to me. Is the young lady's brother purgat'ry to 'er?'

'Probably,' said Will. 'I was simply told about him by her sister Nellie. Anyway, they've all got each other but no mum. She died some years ago.'

'That's a shame,' said Mrs Brown.

'I don't know any Fords at our school,' said Sally.

'Sammy knows a Mr Ben Ford, a big fat man,' said Susie, and smiled reminiscently, knowing that Sammy's elder brother Boots had twice sorted out Fatty's troublesome bully boys.

Freddy, noting Susie's smile, thought this was a good time to try again.

''Ere, Susie, I like Sammy,' he said, 'I don't wonder you're romantic about 'im, seein' 'e's goin' to marry yer. 'As he got a bike? I ain't got one meself—'

'I wonder if Annie Ford and her fam'ly could be relations of Mr Ben Ford?' mused Susie. 'I hope not. Well, you'll have to take her some flowers, Will.'

'Eh?' said Will, and eyed Susie in suspicion. She smiled sweetly. Stone my brainbox, he thought, the way the female mind works. They were all the same, sisters, mothers, aunts, cousins and anyone else with a bosom. 'Watch what you're sayin', sis.'

Sally caught Susie's eye. Sally winked. Susie smiled again.

'But you should, Will,' she said, 'shouldn't he, Dad?'

'What?' Mr Brown exercised a cautious note on behalf of his eldest son. He knew about female minds himself. Well, you had to know a bit when you were married or you could wake up one morning and find your Sunday watch and chain had been pawned behind your back.

'Dad, just think,' said Susie, 'that poor young lady of seventeen bein' pushed home by Will in that home-made cart. Think of her feelings. I'd have died ten times over myself. Will's got to make it up to her.'

'Yes, course you 'ave, Will,' said Sally.

'Listen,' said Will, 'if I show up on her doorstep again, she'll chuck a brick at me. My face can't afford to stop a brick, it's the only one I've got.'

'Mrs Parks down in Charleston Street chucked a brick at Mr Parks once,' said Sally. 'It knocked all 'is teeth out, and 'e can only eat porridge now, and rice puddin'.'

'I don't suppose anyone 'ere could buy me a bike, could they?' suggested Freddy.

'I've been thinkin',' said Mrs Brown.

'Bless yer, mum,' said Freddy, 'I—'

'Not you, love,' said Mrs Brown, 'I was meanin' our Will. I think it might be nice if he did take the young lady some flowers now she's an invalid and don't have no mum. I expect she'd like some flowers.'

'Talk to yerself,' muttered Freddy again, 'that's it, talk to yerself.'

441

'What's up with Freddy?' asked Mrs Brown. ''E keeps talkin' to 'is supper.'

'Oh, don't mind me,' said Freddy, 'I ain't 'ardly 'ere.'

'Daffodils are nice,' said Susie, 'they're in the market now.'

'Yes, daffs 'ave just come out,' said Sally.

'I've got a special likin' for daffs,' said Mrs Brown, 'they were the first flowers your dad give me. Mind, he wasn't your dad then, of course, we'd only just met. Flowers always come first, Sally.'

'Then what?' said Sally.

'Us,' said Susie.

'Oh, a weddin' first, love,' said Mrs Brown placidly. 'Flowers, then an engagement, then a weddin', and then blessings.'

'What, us? We're blessings?' said Sally. 'Crikey, d'you mean Freddy as well? I don't call 'im a blessin'.'

'I ain't been blessed with no bike, I know that,' muttered Freddy.

'Daffodils, they'll do, Will,' said Susie.

'I'm not listening,' said Will, accepting seconds of shepherd's pie from his mum.

'I'll get them for yer, Will,' said Sally, 'on me way 'ome from school tomorrow. They're only sixpence a dozen down the market.'

'I've gone all deaf,' said Will.

'Sixpence and a penny for goin',' said Sally, 'I don't mind doin' a nice errand like that.'

'If I 'ad a penny for ev'ry errand I've done,' said Freddy, 'I bet I'd be able to buy me own bike.'

'Why am I bein' pushed?' asked Will.

'Because it's the nice thing to do, lovey,' said Susie, 'and you don't have to stay long enough for her to throw a brick at you. Is she pretty?'

'I'm barmy,' said Will, 'so's any bloke daft enough to mention a girl to a family full of females.'

'Excuse me, lovey, but we're half and half,' said Susie. 'Bet you two bob Annie Ford is pretty.'

'Will, would yer like to give me the sixpence now?' said Sally. 'And the penny for doin' the errand?'

Determinedly, Freddy tried yet again.

'If I 'ad a penny for—'

'Daffodils suit pretty girls,' said Mrs Brown, and Freddy's determination went to pot then.

'Biggest mistake I ever made, opening my mouth about Annie Ford,' said Will. 'In front of anyone in trousers, that wouldn't have mattered, but in front of anyone in bloomers—'

''Ere, d'you mind?' said Sally. 'I get enough of that from Freddy, 'e don't 'ave any respect for unmention-ables.'

'I don't 'ave no bike, either,' said Freddy. 'Mind, it's a relief someone's noticed I'm alive, I can't tell yer what a blessin' that is. Now if I could just say—'

'Will, you still haven't told us if Annie is pretty,' said Susie.

'That's done it, that 'as,' said Freddy, 'I might as well go an' sort meself out a plot in the cemet'ry.'

'No, don't leave the table yet, love,' said Mrs Brown, 'there's syrup puddin' for afters.'

'Oh, all right,' said Freddy gloomily, 'I'll stay for that, a bloke can drown 'imself easier when 'e's got a full stomach.'

'Sit up, Freddy love,' said Mrs Brown, and brought the syrup pudding to the table.

'Susie, Will still 'asn't told us if Annie Ford's pretty,' said Sally.

'I didn't notice,' said Will.

443

'That's it, Sally, she's seventeen and pretty,' said Susie.

'Well, we hope so,' said Mrs Brown, serving the pudding.

'What're you up to, you hope so?' asked Will.

'I'm only sayin', Will love,' said Mrs Brown.

'Fancy our Will only just 'ome from India an' findin' someone seventeen an' pretty,' said Sally.

'Fancy findin' your syrup puddin' down your gymslip?' said Will.

'Funny thing, yer know,' said Mr Brown, 'I found yer mum when I was about Will's age.'

'Why, was she lost, then?' asked Freddy bitterly.

'Lost?' said his dad.

'I only asked,' said Freddy. 'Look, I dunno I can eat all this syrup puddin'. Still, I will. If it kills me, no-one'll notice, and it'll save me 'aving to drown meself.'

'Yes, eat it up, love,' said Mrs Brown fondly, 'syrup pudding's good for a growin' boy.'

'D'you want to tell us any more about Annie, Will?' asked Susie.

'Right, monkey, I'll come clean,' said Will, going on the attack, 'I only noticed her legs.'

'You shocker,' said Susie, putting aside any suggestion that she liked to see Sammy looking at her own legs.

'Not my fault,' said Will, 'they kept staring me in the face.'

'You listening to that, Mum?' asked Sally.

'Well, I must say you and Susie's both got ever such nice legs, lovey,' said Mrs Brown, equability undisturbed.

'Wooden ones, that's what Sally's got,' muttered Freddy.

'I didn't know that,' said Mr Brown.

'Well, 'ow could she get inches taller in a few months unless she's wearin' wooden ones bought off a market stall?' said Freddy.

'I don't think you can buy wooden ones off a stall, Freddy,' said Mrs Brown. 'You have to go somewhere special for wooden ones.'

'I bet she bought special ones from Mr Greenberg,' said Freddy, 'you can get anything from 'im. I bet if you looked, you'd see 'is sold label on Sally's.'

'Sounds a good bet, Freddy,' said Will. 'Let's all take a look after supper.'

'I'll scream for me mum,' said Sally, 'and I won't get the daffs for yer, not even if you give me tuppence for goin'.'

''Ere, listen,' said Freddy with reborn determination, 'if I'd 'ad tuppence for ev'ry errand I've done, I'd 'ave 'ad me own bike years ago. Mind, if Susie feels—'

'What's that blessed boy talkin' about?' asked Sally.

'I expect 'e'd like some more syrup puddin',' said Mrs Brown.

Bitterness uppermost again, Freddy decided to have his own back by dropping a bombshell. He addressed his mum. Loudly.

'I suppose Susie knows I ain't wearin' no trousers at 'er weddin'?'

'What?' said Susie.

'Nor I ain't,' said Freddy, 'I already informed Mum, an' she knows me mind's made up.'

'I'm dreamin',' said Susie.

'And I ain't wearin' no sailor suit, either, not at my age I ain't,' said Freddy. 'Just a scarf an' shirt. I just 'ope the day won't be windy. If it is, well, I'll just 'ave to grin an' bear it.'

Sally shrieked. Mr Brown hid his face in what was left of his helping of syrup pudding. Well, nearly. Will laughed his head off. Susie's face was a study.

Mrs Brown said, 'Bless us, Freddy, I don't know you

ought to 'ave said a thing like that. It don't sound a bit nice.'

'Can't 'elp that, Mum,' said Freddy firmly, 'I told yer, me mind's made up.'

'Well, take precautions if it's windy, Freddy,' said Will, 'wear a long shirt.'

'I've only got me short ones,' said Freddy.

Sally had hysterics and fell off her chair. Mr Brown choked on his pudding this time. Mrs Brown giggled like a girl. Susie held herself in check. She waited until the supper table had stopped rattling before she made herself heard.

'So your mind's made up, is it, Freddy Brown? Well, so's mine. You're goin' to wear a suit.'

'No, I ain't,' said Freddy, 'not unless it's got long trousers. I ain't wearing short ones, not at your weddin', Susie, and it ain't my fault if I ain't got long shirts.'

'Wear one of Dad's,' said Will.

Sally had more hysterics, on the floor.

'Listen, my lad,' said Susie, 'it's goin' to be a boy's suit or nothing.'

'I ain't wearin' nothing,' said Freddy, 'it ain't decent.'

'I mean you won't be there,' said Susie.

'Susie, I got to be there,' said Freddy, 'your weddin' is special to me.'

Susie smiled.

'Really special?' she said.

'Special special,' said Freddy.

'There's a good boy,' said Susie. 'Dad, buy him a suit with long trousers. You can get one at Gamages.'

'I'm ready to fork out, Susie,' said Mr Brown, who knew one thing for sure. Sammy Adams, important businessman and a decent bloke though he was, was getting a lovely, warm and generous girl on his wedding

446

day, the kind a duke wouldn't say no to.

'There, that's settled,' said Mrs Brown happily.

'Mind, Susie, if I 'ad a bike as well, I could cycle to the church and do weddin' errands for yer,' said Freddy.

'Sally, get up off the floor, there's a love,' said Mrs Brown, 'you been down there long enough.'

'Talk to yerself,' muttered Freddy.

Later, Susie spoke to her dad.

'Dad, Sammy said he'd like to see you first thing in the morning.'

'What about?' asked Mr Brown, who was employed by Sammy as a full-time odd-job man.

'He didn't say.' Actually, Sammy had said he didn't think his future dad-in-law ought to be seen doing odd-jobbing around the offices and the Olney Road scrap metal yard. He'd have to talk to him, he'd said.

'Right you are, Susie, I'll go an' see 'im first thing in the morning.'

'Good old Dad,' said Susie, and then got Will on his own. Will at once said she'd got a look in her eye. 'Oh, I only want to ask if you've been all right today,' she said.

'Is this a crafty way of bringing up that girl again?'

'No, we were only pullin' your leg, love. I was wonderin' about your chest, that's all.' It was difficult for the family to believe Will had a serious complaint when he looked so healthy. If the doctors had talked about consumption, well, that really would have been serious. It was something Walworth people dreaded. 'You didn't get an attack through helpin' that girl, did you?'

Will thought about it and decided not to worry her.

'No, left me as fit as a fiddle, Susie.'

'That's good,' she said, 'only Boots mentioned that asthma can be a bit of an unsociable headache.'

'Well, I could do without it, and that's a fact,' said Will. His little grin showed. 'Specially at my age,' he added.

'That's right,' said Susie, 'so look after yourself. You don't know how pleased I am you're home for my weddin'.'

'I think you like the idea of marryin' Sammy,' said Will.

'Love it,' said Susie, 'even if we do have ups and downs.'

'Mum and Dad have had a few, I suppose.'

'Every married couple have some,' said Susie, 'but Mum's always been able to sort hers out with Dad.'

'Who's goin' to sort out those you have with Sammy?'

'Me,' said Susie, 'it'll never do to let Sammy be on top.'

'Never?' smiled Will.

'What? Oh, you,' laughed Susie, but turned just a little pink. Susie may have been twenty-one and adult, but she was still a virgin.

CHAPTER SIX

Mr Sammy Adams, managing director of Adams Enterprises, Adams Fashions and Adams Scrap Metal, had a handsome office above his established shop on the Denmark Hill side of Camberwell Green. Its old-style furniture was handsome, especially his large desk that sat on part of the square brown carpet.

Mr Brown knocked.

'Come in,' said Sammy, a tall young man in his twenty-fourth year and the energetic engine of the business.

Mr Brown entered.

'You wanted to see me, guv?' he said. It was a bit of an awkward relationship in a way, with his elder daughter Susie engaged to his young boss, and he'd settled for calling him guv. He'd tried Mister Sammy and Mister Adams, but come the engagement and he'd fixed on guv. Sammy didn't mind. Most of his employees called him Mister Sammy, distinguishing him from his eldest brother Boots, general manager of the business, whom they called Mister Adams. Sammy questioned whether this was right or not, seeing he'd founded the business. Boots said it was right all right, he was the eldest of the family and Sammy was still a lad. Ruddy rhubarb, said Sammy, did I hear you say that? It's a question of respect for my old age, said Boots. Sometimes, said Sammy, I ain't sure you're believable.

He looked up from his desk.

'Hello, Jim,' he said. That was how he'd always

addressed his hard-working and loyal odd-job man. 'Take a pew.'

'Nice of yer, guv,' said Mr Brown and sat down, not without thinking that it meant something serious was about to happen.

'How's the fam'ly?' asked Sammy, blue eyes showing, as always, something of his inner energy.

It's serious all right, thought Mr Brown.

'Fine,' he said. 'Well, except we can't 'ardly believe Will's got a touch of asthma.'

'Yes, perishin' hard luck,' said Sammy, 'and highly incredulous as well. But he'll beat it. Young man like him,' he added, speaking from the position of being as old as nearly twenty-four. 'I've been thinkin', Jim.'

'You do a lot of that,' said Mr Brown, frankly admiring.

'Well, if I don't,' said Sammy, 'me competitors'll start walkin' all over me, and gettin' walked over can hurt considerable. Jim, it's like this. You're Susie's dad, which for a start ought to earn you several medals. Now you can appreciate I don't want you as me dad-in-law mendin' our shop doors and keepin' our Olney Road scrap yard consistently tidied up.'

'You can give it to me straight, Sammy.' Mr Brown spoke as the future dad-in-law. 'You don't reckon it's right me workin' for yer.'

'You can chuck that notion out of the top window right now,' said Sammy. 'It's not good business, sackin' anyone who earns his wages as well as you do. But it won't look right, keepin' you doin' odd jobs here and at the scrap yard. Now, I'm about to acquire a new scrap yard in Bermondsey, Jim. You know all about scrap metal from bein' efficiently acquainted with the Olney Road yard. So I'm puttin' you in charge of the new yard in Bermondsey. You're startin' next Monday. You'll get a yard manager's wage, of course. Is that proposition agreeable to you?'

Jim was gaping.

'Sammy—'

'Good,' said Sammy briskly, 'I like a man who makes up his mind quick.'

'I tell yer straight, you just flabbergasted my mind,' said Mr Brown, 'but that ain't goin' to stop me askin' if I can shake yer hand.' They shook hands across the desk.

'That's it, then, Jim,' said Sammy, 'I'm off out now.'

''Alf a tick,' said Mr Brown, 'you givin' me this job because you think I can do it, or because—'

'You're gettin' it because I've got trust in yer, Jim.'

'Well,' said Mr Brown, 'I'll say this much, young guv, if there's any bloke good enough for Susie, it's you.'

'As the manager of one of me scrap yards, you can call me Sammy in or out of business hours. Right, good on yer, Jim. Don't forget the weddin', you're givin' Susie away.'

'It'll be me special pleasure,' said Mr Brown.

Will Brown had been mentally toughened by his years of hard soldiering, but he still had a soft spot for his family, particularly his parents. His mother was just about the most easy-going woman alive. They'd known desperate poverty when the family lived in Peabody Buildings in Brandon Street, but his mum had never had a cross word for any of them, especially not for his dad, who had come out of the trenches with a gammy leg and no job until Sammy Adams had taken him on. Dad with his optimism and Mum with her ability to always make the best of things, had kept the family going even when hunger stalked and clothes were things of darns and patches.

So, being the son of his warm-hearted parents, Will arrived on the doorstep of Annie's home at half-past four

451

on the day after she'd suffered what she obviously felt was multiplied misfortune. Will knew he'd laughed, that he'd made her want to spit. So he was carrying a bunch of daffodils, wrapped all over. It would be asking for catcalls from street kids for a grown-up bloke, especially a soldier, to be seen carrying a bunch of flowers. He was still wearing his uniform. None of his old clothes fitted him, since he'd only been fifteen when he joined up as a drummer boy, and he hadn't yet bothered to shop for new stuff. But he had ordered a grey suit for Susie's wedding.

Nellie answered his knock. With Cassie and Charlie, she was home from their school in Trafalgar Street.

'Oh, 'ello,' she said, 'it's you.'

'I see it's you too, Nellie,' said Will, 'I thought I'd come and see how the patient is.'

'Our Annie? Oh, she went to work this mornin', at Urcott's the grocers, but Mr Urcott let 'er come 'ome at two o'clock. She was limpin' a bit. She's in the kitchen, she's just been chuckin' things at Charlie because 'e said she wasn't as bossy as when she was lyin' down. And she chucked the tea cosy at me because I said one of the street kids asked if she was goin' to 'ave another ride in a pushcart. Would yer please come in?'

'She's not goin' to chuck something at me, is she?' said Will, stepping in.

'Oh, it won't actu'lly 'urt,' said Nellie, closing the door. 'We're 'aving some bread an' marge an' cups of tea—'

'Nellie, who's that?' The voice of the young mistress of the house rang out loud and clear from the kitchen.

'It's yer soldier friend,' called Nellie.

'It's what?'

'It's 'im, Annie, 'e's come to see how you are.'

There was a short silence, then Annie called, 'Has he got that pushcart with him?'

452

'No, course 'e 'asn't, have yer, Will?' said Nellie.

'Well, is he laughin', then?' demanded Annie.

Nellie looked at Will. He tucked his grin away.

'No, 'e's not laughin', Annie.'

'He'd better not be. He can come in, then.'

Nellie led the way to the kitchen. Cassie and Charlie were sitting at the table, eating bread and marge and drinking tea. Annie was standing with her back to the range. On one leg. Her hand was on the back of a chair, supporting herself. She looked attractively slender in a jumper dress of dark green. The style was a bit out of fashion, particularly as it was waisted, but Annie had bought it half-price at a sale and it suited her. She'd shortened it to knee-length, and that was fashionable at least. Well, these days it was death to a girl not to look a bit fashionable.

'Good afternoon,' she said.

'Same to you,' said Will, inspecting her one standing leg.

'D'you mind tellin' me what you're lookin' at?' asked Annie, with Cassie and Charlie keeping the peace for the moment. She'd told them to.

'I'm lookin' for your other leg,' said Will.

'I'm restin' it,' said Annie.

'Yes, but where is it, upstairs on your bed?' asked Will.

'No, it's at the doctor's,' said Annie, and Cassie burped a giggle she'd tried to suppress. Charlie grinned.

'What's it doin' at the doctor's?' asked Will. 'Havin' an operation?'

Nellie spluttered.

'Annie, you've got it behind you,' she said.

Annie lowered it, and Will saw both legs then. Annie's eyes danced, and she laughed.

'Caught you there,' she said.

'Feelin' better, are we?' said Will.

'She was 'aving you on, Will,' said Charlie, 'she said she'd give me an' Cassie what for if we let on.'

'Well, it's my turn to laugh today,' said Annie.

Charlie said how's your father to Will, and then told Annie he'd got to go out and bash Georgie Simmonds. He owed him one on his conk. Annie told him to stay where he was or she'd tie him up. Cassie asked Will if he'd just come from guarding the Tower of London. Will said no, that was a job for the Beefeaters.

''Ere, 'ave yer fired yer rifle a lot?' asked Charlie.

'Now and again,' said Will.

'Christmas,' breathed Charlie, ''ow many blokes 'ave yer shot dead?'

'I hit an Indian elephant once,' said Will.

'Crikey,' said Cassie, 'did it fall down?'

'No, it hit me back,' said Will.

'Oh, did it squash yer flat?' asked Cassie in awe.

''Fraid so,' said Will, 'but I'm gradually fillin' out.'

Nellie let out a yell of laughter. Annie smiled.

'Would you like a cup of tea?' she asked.

'Thanks,' said Will.

Nellie brought a cup and saucer.

'What's in yer parcel?' asked Cassie of Will.

'Cassie, don't be nosy,' said Annie, pouring the tea.

'But it might be the Crown Jewels,' said Nellie, ''e might be mindin' them.'

'Cor, talk about bein' up the pole,' said Charlie.

'You can sit down,' said Annie to Will, 'if you'd be so kind.'

'Yes, Annie's honoured you've come and asked after 'er,' said Nellie.

'Let's see,' said Will, 'who's got a vase?'

'Oh, the Queen's got lots,' said Cassie.

'Well, can you ask her to lend us one?' said Will, unwrapping the daffodils and offering them to Annie. The golden blooms were a bright splash of colour against her dress. Annie stared.

'Oh,' she said.

'Just to make up for dumpin' you in the pushcart,' said Will.

'They're for me?' she gasped.

'They just need a vase and some water,' said Will, and Annie took the bunch and blinked at them. Will thought she looked very appealing in her surprise and uncertainty.

'Oh, ain't they lovely?' said Nellie, and dashed to the parlour. She came back with a tall vase and half-filled it with water from the scullery tap. She put the vase on the mantelpiece and took the long-stemmed daffodils from Annie, who for once looked as if she didn't quite know where she was. Nellie placed the blooms in the vase and spread them out. 'Look, Annie, ain't they a picture?'

'Yes, they're lovely,' said Annie, feeling all funny. Funny nice, of course.

Noting that Annie, vigorous in chastising him for some of his antics, didn't seem all there, Charlie said, 'I ain't keen on flowers meself, I think I'll go an' bash a hole in a wall with Georgie Simmonds' 'ead.' And he vanished before Annie knew he was even on his feet.

Will, drinking his tea, said, 'You girls managin'? Is there anything I can do? Old soldiers like me can be useful.'

'Old?' Annie came out of not being quite herself. 'Old?' she said. 'How can you be old?'

'The Army puts years on blokes.'

'Well, it's not put any on you,' said Annie.

'Don't you believe it,' said Will, 'I'm nearly a hundred in a way.'

455

'What way?' asked Annie.

'Mrs Potter's nearly an 'undred,' said Cassie.

'There you are, then,' said Will, 'some people do get to be that old.'

'You're not makin' sense,' said Annie.

'Anyway,' said Will, 'you're managin' to limp around and get on with things? No help needed?'

'Thanks ever so much, but no, I'm managin' fine,' said Annie, and took a little rest then by sitting down in the fireside chair. Her short dress let her knees show. Will looked. Annie pulled on her dress and covered her knees. 'Excuse me,' she said haughtily.

'Just havin' a look at your bruised knee,' said Will. 'Well, nice to know it's improvin'. I'll get movin' now. So long, girls.' Tabby the cat darted in then, made straight for Annie and leapt on to her lap. Annie gave a little yell and her knees showed again. Will grinned. 'I'm not lookin',' he said, 'I'm off.'

Nellie went after him to see him out.

'Thanks ever so much for comin' to see our Annie,' she said.

'Pleasure,' said Will. 'Tell her I'll send a pair of trousers round.'

'Trousers?' said Nellie. 'What for?'

'She'll know,' said Will, and went off laughing.

Nellie, returning to the kitchen, said, 'Will's funny, ain't 'e?'

'What d'you mean?' asked Annie.

''E said 'e'd send you a pair of trousers. 'E said you'd know why.'

'He said what?'

'A pair of trousers,' giggled Nellie, ''e said 'e'd send them round.'

Annie quivered all over.

'Are you laughin', Nellie?' she asked.

'Me?' said Nellie.

'I'm not,' said Cassie.

'I bet he is,' said Annie, 'I bet he went off laughin'. Did he?'

'Well, 'e wasn't actu'lly cryin',' said Nellie. 'Ain't 'e nice, though, Annie? It's a shame 'e didn't stay a bit.'

'I expect 'e's gone to Windsor Castle to make some lemonade for the Queen,' said Cassie. 'She likes lemonade. Annie, what's 'e goin' to send you trousers for?'

'Never you mind,' said Annie. 'Just wait till – Nellie, did he say he was comin' back again?'

'No, not direckly,' said Nellie, ''e only said about the trousers.'

'I bet he'll be laughin' all the way home,' said Annie. 'I – oh, blow, look at the daffs.' She was shocked at herself.

'Yes, 'e must like yer,' said Nellie, scenting romance, 'you ain't ever 'ad anyone bring you flowers before. Oh, if 'e don't come again, though, p'raps it's because 'e's finished 'is leave and is goin' back to the Army.'

Annie gritted her teeth. What must he think of her? She hadn't thanked him for them, not properly she hadn't. She'd been so astonished she'd hardly said anything. Oh, blow and bother.

'Where was it he said he lived?' she asked.

'Caulfield Place,' said Nellie, 'it's only down in Browning Street.'

'I'll 'ave to—' Annie stopped. No, she'd have to go in person, so that she could thank him properly, she couldn't just send a note. She'd be very nice about it, then she'd feel she could give him an earful about sending trousers round. She knew what he'd meant by that, even if her sisters didn't. And he'd better not laugh at her again. A young lady her age ought to be treated seriously.

CHAPTER SEVEN

'Sammy darling?' purred Miss Susie Brown, private secretary, personal assistant and exclusive fiancée to the managing director of Adams Enterprises Ltd.

Sammy, just back from a visit to his East End garments factory, looked up at her from his handsome old desk.

'Yes, what is it, Miss Brown?' he asked in strict businesslike fashion.

'Pardon?' said Susie.

'If you could hurry it up, Miss Brown?'

'I'll give you Miss Brown,' said Susie threateningly. Sammy had days when he tried to re-establish an authority she'd managed to knock sideways.

'Me principles relatin' to business hours—'

'Oh, yes, highly formal,' said Susie.

'Bless you, Miss Brown,' said Sammy, the youngest of his mother's three engaging sons. She'd brought them all up to count their blessings, and Susie happened to be top of his personal list. He thought the world of her and her status as his fiancée, even if he did sometimes wonder what had hit him. Her blue eyes mostly, which on a sunny day could sparkle like sapphires. In a stylish navy-blue costume that set off her fairness, not even a French count with arched eyebrows and a haughtifying family tree could have said she wasn't a stunner. She was all her own work too, allowing for the original contribution made by her mum and dad. She'd done it all on her own, she'd pulled herself up from being just another shabby and hungry-looking Walworth girl and turned herself into a May

Queen. Lovely figure too, and very high-class legs. Meritorious, it was, all the Adams female women owning high-class legs. Lizzy, his sister, to start with, Tommy's wife Vi and Boots's wife Emily, though Emily was getting a bit thin lately. In a few weeks, Susie's legs would join the high-class collection. Lovely girl, Susie. Sammy Adams, his mother had said, I never thought you'd have enough sense in your money-box head to ask Susie to marry you, I thought you had hardly any real sense at all. Actually, his feelings for Susie were such that he often didn't know whether he was upside-down or back to front. In a rash moment, he'd mentioned that to Boots. He should have known better, because Boots of course said well, Sammy, I'd say upside-down, since we all know Susie's been standing you on your loaf of bread for years.

Susie, viewing him lovingly, said, 'Sammy, you darling.'

'You want something,' said Sammy, feeling he was going to have to raid his wallet. He'd do it too. He was in the hopeless and helpless position of never being able to say no to her.

'You're a lovely bloke,' said Susie.

'This is goin' to cost me,' said Sammy.

'It's goin' to earn you a smacker,' said Susie. 'Sammy, you've given my dad a new job managin' our new scrap metal yard.'

'Think nothing of it,' said Sammy.

'I think everything of it,' said Susie, 'and you too.'

'Very good, Miss Brown, if that's all we'll now get on with our work.'

'It's not all,' said Susie, and came round the desk to bend over him.

'Miss Brown, not in the office—' Too late. Susie delivered a warm and loving smacker. Sammy yielded a

459

principle or two and made an advance of his own. Inside the jacket of her costume, Susie quivered and straightened up.

'What's that doin' there?' she asked, and took his hand out.

'It's mindin' its own business, I'd say,' observed Sammy reasonably. 'Well, what's mine is yours, Susie, and what's yours is mine.'

'Not yet it isn't, and certainly not in the office,' said Susie. 'You're always breakin' your own rules, Mister Sammy Adams.'

'I don't recollect—'

'I do.'

'You sure, Susie?'

'Mmm, lovely,' said Susie, 'but kindly stop helpin' yourself to what's not yours till the weddin' certificate's signed. And even then, wait till we leave the church. I don't want you committin' unlawful sacrilege.'

'In front of the vicar? Perish the thought,' said Sammy, 'he's been my vicar man and boy, and I don't want to get struck by his lightning on me one and only weddin' day. It might be fatal. Fine thing that would be, gettin' married and goin' to me own funeral on the same day. All me old friends and neighbours would talk. Well, that's definitely all, Miss Brown, now let's get on with things.'

Susie laughed. There was no-one quite like Sammy, the driving force behind Adams Enterprises and its associate companies.

'Sammy love, you're sweet for what you did for my dad.'

'Well, I can't have me dad-in-law sweepin' floors, not when he's up to runnin' a scrap yard.'

'You're still a sweetie,' said Susie. 'Oh, there's something else.'

'If it's not business, I'm not listening,' said Sammy.

'Yes, you are. Sammy, we're goin' to have a horse and cart for our weddin'.'

'A whatter?' said Sammy, who had work to do, including reading every word of a contract relating to Adams Fashions.

'A pony and cart, actually.'

'I was under the official impression that me best man Boots is arrangin' to drive us from the church to the weddin' breakfast in our motorcar.' Sammy was the owner of a motorcar. He wore the approved peaked cap and goggles when driving it, which had made Susie tell him he looked as if he was about to enter a race at Brooklands. Sammy said he quite fancied that. Susie said she'd blow the car up if he got serious.

'Yes, I know about that arrangement, Sammy, but I've just been speakin' to Mr Greenberg. He's with Boots, they're talkin' about Mr Greenberg supplying our new upstairs offices with furniture. Sammy, you didn't tell me that both your brothers and your sister Lizzy all had Mr Greenberg's pony and cart for their weddings. I want that too, it's a fam'ly tradition now, and Mr Greenberg's goin' to be really upset if we don't ask him to do the honours.'

'Well, Susie—'

'I don't want any flannel.'

'I'm not in the habit—'

'Yes, you are, but like your mum says, you're a nice boy really.'

'That was fifteen years ago. I now happen to be—'

'Yes, you're lovely, Sammy. I'll ask Mr Greenberg to come and see you.'

'What's the use?' mused Sammy as Susie disappeared. 'I can't even answer her back now. I'm done for, I'm already gettin' careless about me overheads – here, hold on, what's

461

this, a hundred per cent disclaimer clause in the event of delivery failing to be made on the due date? That's not friendly, Harriet, nor Christian.' Harriet de Vere was the chief buyer for Coates, a West End store with branches all over the South of England, and the contract was between Coates and Adams Fashions. 'That's not up for signin', Harriet me female alligator, that's up for discussion.'

Susie reappeared, in company with Mr Eli Greenberg, who had known Sammy as a boy and had long been his most obliging business friend. He was also a family friend. A family friend who doubled as an obliging business friend was priceless. Mr Greenberg advanced with his mittened hands lifted in a gesture of expansive pleasure. He wore an old round black hat and a dark grey overcoat with capacious inner and outer pockets. His grey-flecked black beard split in a happy smile and his white teeth moistly beamed.

'Sammy, my poy, vhat a pleasure, ain't it? You and Susie in a state of expectant marriage, vhat a joy to my heart, and vhat a fair princess, ain't she?'

'Hello, Eli, old cock.' Sammy stood up and shook Mr Greenberg's hand. 'Mind, I'm up to me ears.'

'Vhen veren't you up to your ears, Sammy? Up to your ears has cost me time and money, but who minds starvin' vhen it's in the name of friendship? The vedding, a blessing, ain't it?'

'I'm not denyin' it,' said Sammy, 'and I'm refrainin' from mentioning what it's going' to do to me wallet. I'm notin' your kind sentiments, Eli, and am takin' the opportunity to say Susie and self would be obliged if you'd do us the favour of transportin' us from the church to St John's Institute in your pony and cart.'

Mr Greenberg beamed again.

'Vhy, Sammy, vhat a pleasure, vhat a privilege. Already

I am invited to the veddin', now I am to cart you and Susie. Vell, don't I remember doin' the selfsame for Lizzy and Boots and Tommy? Vhat a privilege indeed, my young friend.' Mr Greenberg took out his large red handkerchief and blew his nose. 'You'll ask vhat vill I charge you. Not a penny, Sammy, not even a farthing. It vill all be for friendship and Susie's blue eyes.'

'You're a love, Mr Greenberg,' said Susie.

'Ah, vhat a fine turn Sammy has come to, Susie. Business is business, vun can't say it ain't, but vhere vould it lead a man to if he vas married to it and not to a young lady like you?'

'To my dad's chopper,' said Susie.

'Ah, such a joke, Susie.'

'It's no joke,' said Susie, and Mr Greenberg's deep chuckle rolled up from his broad chest and gurgled in his throat.

'Vell, I must be on my vay now,' he said, 'I have had the pleasure of obligin' Boots regardin' handsome furniture at a price that vill take the shirt off my back, and now I have to oblige a handsome lady.'

'If I had the time and wasn't church-goin', I'd oblige her meself,' said Sammy.

'Over my dead body,' said Susie, and Mr Greenberg departed still chuckling.

The moment the door closed behind him, Sammy said, 'This contract, Susie, is a pain in me posterior. There's a delivery clause in it which could make us walk the plank with nowhere to go but down. And the pirate captain is Harriet.'

'Miss de Vere of Coates?' said Susie.

'Selfsame,' said Sammy.

'Well, kindly let her know that you're mine, Sammy, not hers, and that you're not to be made to walk the plank so that she can rescue you from drowning, dry you out and get you into something comfy in her flat. Or I'll push her face in.'

'Don't like the sound of that, Harriet with her face pushed in,' said Sammy. 'It might be considerably detrimental to Adams Fashions. Further, Susie, my mother, bein' fond of you, wouldn't like to hear you talkin' in an unladylike manner. I'll deal with Harriet, I'll phone her and arrange to see her tomorrow afternoon.'

'Sammy darling, don't be silly,' said Susie. 'Tomorrow's Saturday.'

'Yes, I'll see her in the afternoon,' said Sammy.

'You won't,' said Susie.

'Did I hear you right, Miss Brown?'

'Yes, Mister Sammy Adams, you did. Tomorrow afternoon is when we're going out to buy the rest of our furniture.'

'Ah,' said Sammy. He had acquired a handsome house in Denmark Hill, and Susie, excited by all it meant, had been leading exultant charges into furniture emporia to help him spend his money. He'd had to tell her that each charge was causing him personal ruination. Susie, who knew him through and through by now, noted with affection that he accepted ruination manfully.

'You promised,' she said.

'Well, Susie, a promise is a promise,' he said. 'Is this one goin' to cause me serious injury?'

'Oh, it won't be fatal,' said Susie.

Boots came in then. Long-limbed, grey-eyed and twenty-nine, he was the man who held everything together. He had the gift of easy communication and a very whimsical side. Women always looked twice at him, and most of the office girls had crushes on him. His left eye, almost sightless, sometimes seemed a little lazy. He'd been blinded on the Somme. An operation had cured his right eye, but the left one was fairly useless.

'Still at it, Susie?' he smiled.

'I'm a slave to his nibs,' said Susie. 'This is his nibs.'

'His nibs would like to do some work,' said Sammy.

'Sammy, have you seen the contract I left on your desk?' asked Boots.

'I've seen enough to know we're not goin' to sign it,' said Sammy.

'The delivery clause?' said Boots.

'You spotted that too?' said Sammy.

'Can't let it stand, Sammy. Not as it is. Harriet de Vere is trying it on. What they'll do if delivery is late, of course, will be to accept the stuff at a reduced price. We'll lose our profit, they'll increase theirs.'

'You happen,' said Sammy, 'to be speakin' to the managin' director of Adams Enterprises, which is me, a highly sharp business bloke already arrangin' to smack Harriet de Vere's posterior.'

'She'll like that,' said Boots, 'lay it on like a man, Sammy, and she'll see a new clause is written in.'

'I'm hearin' things,' said Susie.

'Startling, perhaps,' said Boots, 'but glad you like that kind of action, Susie.'

'I'm glad too,' said Susie, 'glad you're jokin'.'

Boots winked, lazily, using his left eye, then asked how her brother Will was.

'Oh, he always looks fine,' she said, 'but if he's really asthmatic, he'll have to leave the Army, won't he?'

'Probably,' said Boots, 'and he'll have to fight for a disability pension. The Army's bound to say his condition wasn't brought about by soldiering. But they gave him a medical in the first place and must have passed him A1 for service or they wouldn't have taken him on. So he's got a case. If it comes to a fight with the Ministry of Bowler Hats, Susie, I'll pitch in with him.'

'Oh, that's so good of you, Boots,' said Susie. She knew he'd committed his help, that as a soldier of the trenches he'd stand with Will if necessary. She felt Will might need a pension if he had to leave the Army, because jobs were as scarce as ever and his asthma might limit him in what he could do.

'Work on Harriet, Sammy,' said Boots, and returned to his office.

'Sometimes,' said Sammy, 'I'm not sure if it's Boots who's teachin' me to suck lemons or if it's me heavenly Father.'

'Yes, he is heavenly, isn't he?' said Susie a little wickedly. 'Doreen says she can't sleep at night for thinkin' about him.'

Doreen was the general office maid-of-all-work, although she had an office boy to help her now.

'Well,' growled Sammy, 'you tell Doreen that if I catch her bringing her bed to the office to get some daytime kip, she'll get dropped on her head.'

'Oh, dear me,' said Susie, 'I'm not sure even that will cure her.'

'Well, oh dear me for nothing,' said Sammy, 'then I'll have to get your dad to chop her up, won't I? Now can we do some work, Miss Brown?'

'Yes, very good, Mister Sammy.'

A house damaged by fire in Rockingham Street, by the Elephant and Castle, was being demolished. The last of its walls collapsed under an iron pounding and amid spurting clouds of dust. Ten minutes later, the little gang of labourers packed up for the day. Henry Brannigan put on his long black serge overcoat, straightened his cap, and set

466

off for his lodgings. He did not button the coat and it flapped as he walked. Tall and muscular, he might also have been handsome, but his face had lost flesh and his eyes were hollow. He lived with his sister and her husband in Stead Street, off Brandon Street. They'd given him a room after the death of his wife seven months ago.

A seemingly dour and introspective man, he did not mix well with people, but his sister, a lazy woman, did not mind having him as long as he paid his rent and didn't make work for her. He had no children, was set in his ways at forty-five and didn't intrude on either her or her husband.

He had a very obsessive habit when walking the pavements. He measured his strides to avoid treading on the lines that divided the paving stones. People who got in his way or stood in his way made his blood boil, for they could cause him to deviate and put him in danger of treading on a line. And if that happened, it ruined the whole day for him and it also meant bad luck.

He made a square turn into Larcom Street from the Walworth Road. Two approaching women blocked his path and intense irritation seized him. He did not check, however, he barged straight on, bruising his way between them. One woman staggered.

''Ere, you brute, what d'you think you're doin' of?' shouted the other woman.

'Time you learned to keep out of me bleedin' way.'

'Time you learned some manners!'

He went striding on. He crossed the street, walked past St John's Church and entered the paved path that led into Charleston Street. There he encountered a very lean man in a black frock coat. He carried a rolled brolly. One man or the other needed to step aside. Mr Ponsonby would have done so without argument, but Henry

467

Brannigan, rageful at this new obstacle, came straight on with the obvious intention of compelling him to shift himself. Offended, Mr Ponsonby came to a dramatic halt and Henry Brannigan was brought up short by the rigid point of the umbrella. It actually dug into his stomach.

'Sir?' said Mr Ponsonby querulously.

'Get out of my way.' Henry Brannigan struck the umbrella aside. That did him no good, for the point returned at speed and dug him in the chest.

'Manners, sir, manners,' said Mr Ponsonby.

'You bleedin' interferin' ponce,' said Henry Brannigan, and looked down at his feet. They were no more than half an inch from a line. He quivered, it was a hair's-breadth escape. If he'd trodden on it, it would have meant worrying about his immediate future and the advisability of changing or cancelling any plans he'd made. He didn't like doing that, but it didn't pay not to. Bad luck came along otherwise. As he'd told a coroner seven months ago, he'd trodden on a line coming home from work on a Saturday, and on the Sunday he'd taken his wife on a planned day trip to Brighton, not wanting to disappoint her by cancelling it. In the train, she'd got up to look out of the window, the door swung open and she fell out and killed herself. That was the worst bit of luck he'd ever brought on himself for treading on a line, and that only happened because some fool of a woman had been in his way. The coroner had the gall to make some very peculiar remarks about it, damn him.

He looked at the geezer with the umbrella.

'Well, sir, well?' said Mr Ponsonby impatiently.

'Lucky for you I ain't standin' on a line,' said Henry Brannigan. He did a measured sidestep and went on his way.

'Dear me, what an unpleasant fellow,' said Mr Ponsonby, and resumed his pigeon-toed walk.

Freddy Brown was on his way home. He'd been with Ernie Flint, his school mate, and Mrs Flint had given them both a cup of tea and a rockcake, just to keep them going until their suppers. Freddy thought his rockcake lived up to its name. Like eating a brick, it was, and tasted like one too. Must have been two weeks old. His mum's rockcakes weren't like that. Well, his mum knew and the whole family knew, that rockcakes were best eaten on the day they came out of the oven, and certainly not later than the day after.

Ernie had eaten his own rockcake as if he liked bricks. Freddy was going off Ernie a bit as a mate. He wouldn't lend his bike even for five minutes. If his old mate Daisy had had a bike, she'd have lent it every day.

Well, I'm blowed, he thought, there's that girl crackpot. He was in Brandon Street and Cassie Ford was coming towards him. Grinning kids were catcalling her. And no wonder. She was leading her cat on a long piece of string that was tied to a ribbon around its neck. The cat was padding along on the lead as if it thought it was a dog.

'Watcher,' said Freddy, 'what's that you got with you on a piece of string?'

'Oh, it's you,' said Cassie from under her boater. 'What d'yer mean, what's that on a piece of string?'

'Ain't a pony, is it?' said Freddy.

'Course it ain't,' said Cassie scornfully, 'it's me cat.'

'You sure?' said Freddy.

'Course I am. Anyway, we don't keep ponies no more. We used to when we lived in the country, and we 'ad trained 'orses too.'

'Trained 'orses?' said Freddy.

'It was when our dad used to run a circus,' said Cassie. 'We 'ad elephants as well. Dad used to be an elephant tamer.'

'Was that before he used to be captain of a ship?' asked Freddy.

'No, after,' said Cassie. 'You've got crumbs down yer jersey.'

'Oh, just rockcake crumbs,' said Freddy. ''Ere, you got a sister called Annie?'

'Oh, she's the one that's a maid to the Prince of Wales,' said Cassie. 'She irons 'is best shirts.'

'Me bruvver Will met 'er last week,' said Freddy.

'Oh, is 'e yer brother? Ain't 'e good-lookin'?'

'Yes, so am I,' said Freddy, 'it's in the fam'ly, yer know.'

Henry Brannigan turned into Brandon Street then, and could hardly believe the cursed nature of the day. Two kids and a bleeding cat, and even a long piece of string, all in his way. First those two women in Larcom Street, then that ponce with the umbrella, and now these two kids and a cat on a string. He had to stop. At once the cat started to use his left leg as a rubbing post. He lifted his foot and kicked at the creature.

''Ere, don't you kick my cat,' cried Cassie. He glared at her. Freddy squared his shoulders. 'I'll tell my dad of you,' said Cassie. Kids, thought Henry Brannigan, bleeding kids. They all want doing away with.

'Get it out of my way or I'll squash it flat,' he said.

'Mister, you ain't nice,' said Freddy. 'You touch Cassie's cat and I'll whistle up all the kids in the street.'

'Get out of it before I knock yer brains out.' Henry Brannigan swept the boy and girl aside and strode away, drawing a hissing breath as he almost trod on a line. Cassie and Freddy stared after him.

'Well, I don't want to meet 'im again,' said Freddy.

'I expect 'e lives in an underground cave somewhere,' said Cassie, 'with witches and ev'rything.'

''Ere, d'you want to be my mate?' asked Freddy.

'I don't mind,' said Cassie.

'All right, come on, I'll walk yer 'ome,' said Freddy.

'Our first 'ome used to 'ave a drawbridge,' said Cassie, leading her cat.

'And a moat as well?'

'Annie fell in it once and nearly drowneded,' said Cassie. 'It was lucky the Prince of Wales come along an' saved 'er, because she 'ad to go to a ball in the evening.'

What a crackpot, thought Freddy.

CHAPTER EIGHT

On Sunday morning, Annie announced everyone was to go to church. Her late and adorable mum had liked her family to do a bit of church-going, about once a month. Annie always felt she had to follow the example.

Charlie, of course, shot out of the kitchen like an arrow from a bow, except that arrows never had socks down.

'You Charlie!' yelled Annie. 'Come back here!'

But the front door was already closing.

'I'll go after him,' said the Gaffer, and off he went too. 'Meet you in church, Annie, if I can catch 'im,' he called.

'Dad, come back here! Dad, d'you hear me?'

But the front door opened and closed again, and the Gaffer took off for the Sunday morning market at a smart pace. He might catch up with Charlie there and he might not. But he could rely on catching up with a half-pint when the pubs opened. He'd done his stint of helping prepare the Sunday vegetables.

'Well,' said Cassie, more sure than dreamy for once, 'Dad an' Charlie won't go to 'eaven if they keep dodgin' church.' She thought for a bit. 'P'raps they don't know there's free ice cream up in 'eaven.'

'Who said there was?' asked Nellie, putting a heap of potato peelings in a sheet of newspaper and wrapping them up for the yard dustbin.

'A lord did,' said Cassie.

'What lord?' asked Nellie.

'I dunno 'is name,' said Cassie, 'but 'e come out of 'is castle one day and said so. Everyone 'eard him.'

472

'I didn't,' said Nellie. ''Ere, take these out to the dustbin.'

'Yes, all right,' said Cassie, accepting the packet.

'Then take your aprons off,' said Annie, 'and we'll go to church.'

'What, now?' said Nellie. 'It's not 'alf-past ten yet.'

'Oh, so it isn't,' said Annie, looking surprised. 'Well, never mind, I'll let you two off, as Dad and Charlie 'ave dodged it. But I'll make sure we all go next Sunday, we don't want Mum turning in her grave. You keep an eye on the roast, Nellie, only don't try takin' it out of the oven, I don't want to find it's been on the scullery floor when I come back.' She took her apron off.

'Annie, you don't 'alf look nice in yer best frock,' said Cassie, holding the now soggy packet to her chest.

'It's Sunday,' said Annie.

'It's your bestest Sunday one,' said Cassie. Annie's bestest was a turquoise crepe de chine, paid for by her dad on the occasion of her seventeenth birthday. To her sisters it looked as expensively posh as real silk.

'Annie, you do look swell,' said Nellie.

'Is your soldier goin' to church with you?' said Cassie.

'Who?' said Annie.

'The soldier that's guardin' Windsor Castle,' said Cassie.

'Cassie, if you don't stop makin' things up,' said Annie, 'the cat'll get your tongue and you'll 'ave to do without it.'

'Oh, lor', will I?' said Cassie, not too happy about the prospect. But her irrepressible imagination chased the thought away, and she asked if the soldiers guarding Windsor Castle were given free ice cream in the summer.

'No, course not,' said Nellie, 'they've all got to wait till they get to 'eaven, the same as ev'rybody else. And if you cuddle them potato peelings much longer, they'll start comin' out of your ears.'

473

'I'll just go and put my mac on,' said Annie, 'then I'm off to church.'

'But it's still early,' said Nellie.

'Oh, I don't mind bein' early,' said Annie.

Susie was having an absorbing morning in partnership with her dad. They were working out table arrangements for the sit-down wedding breakfast at St John's Institute. Williamson's the caterers were looking after everything relating to food and drink. Mr Brown and Susie were taking care of protocol. Mr Brown had made a pencil sketch, and Susie had a list of everyone who would be there. They were sitting at the parlour table, keeping out of Mrs Brown's way in the kitchen. Susie said both families and their closest relatives had better be at the top line of tables. She counted and said that would amount to thirty grown-ups and children.

'Seems to me the Browns and Adams are a bit prolific,' said Mr Brown.

The front door knocker sounded.

'That can't be Sammy yet,' said Susie. Sammy was due to pick her up at noon and drive her to his mother's home for Sunday dinner there. The time now was twenty to eleven. Answering the door, she found herself looking at a dark-haired young lady with wide grey eyes framed by sooty lashes, and wearing a light mackintosh and a round rain hat. The day was showery.

'Hello,' said Susie.

'Oh, hello,' said Annie. Thinking that wasn't quite enough, she added, 'How'd you do?'

'I can't complain, and I'm not,' smiled Susie. Lord, thought Annie, who's she? She's stunning. 'Are you lookin' for someone?' asked Susie.

'Oh, I'm just callin',' said Annie, who had asked at

474

the first house where the Brown family lived.

'So I see,' said Susie, smiling again. Neighbours were passing by, going early to church. She took a more thoughtful look at the girl. Age? Yes, seventeen, she'd bet on it. Hurt knee? No, that wasn't obvious. All the same, she might be the girl. 'I suppose you're not askin' to see my brother Will, are you?'

Help, thought Annie, is this his sister? I think I've seen her about. She's really posh.

Susie looked a Sunday dream in a tailored spring costume made by Lilian Hyams, designer for Adams Fashions.

'Is your brother a soldier?' asked Annie.

'That's him,' said Susie. What had Will been up to, saying he hadn't noticed if the girl was pretty or not? She was all of that. And if anyone deserved her, Will did. He needs a helping hand. 'I think you're Annie Ford. Come in, we've heard all about you. Will's wandering around the Sunday market with Sally and Freddy, my sister and younger brother. Come on in, Annie.'

'Oh, I only called to thank him,' said Annie.

'Come in. Will won't be long.' Susie took the girl into the parlour. 'Meet my dad. Dad, look who's here.

Mr Brown looked. He liked what he saw.

'I don't think I've 'ad the pleasure,' he said.

'Well, you have now,' said Susie, 'this young lady is Annie Ford.'

'Pleased to meet yer, Annie,' said Mr Brown, rising and shaking her hand. 'But to me sorrow, I still can't say I know yer.'

'Of course you know her, Dad,' said Susie, 'Annie's the young lady who hurt her knee and—' She paused, she smiled. 'And was helped home by Will.'

'Well, I'm blowed, so you're her,' said Mr Brown with

a huge grin that gave Annie a sinking feeling.

'Oh, he didn't tell you how he helped me home, did 'e?' she asked.

'Well,' said Mr Brown, and let it go at that.

'Did he?' asked Annie of Susie.

'I'm Susie. Is your knee better, Annie?'

'Oh, he did tell you.' Annie gritted her teeth. 'It's not fair, I suppose everyone in Walworth knows now that he wheeled me home in a pushcart. Can you believe it? I'm seventeen, goin' on for eighteen, and I expect even when I'm ninety there'll be people talkin' about how I stopped the traffic.'

'Will never mentioned the traffic,' said Susie, trying to keep her face straight.

'No, but you know what I mean,' said Annie. 'Oh, wait till I see your brother. It's not that he doesn't 'ave some nice ways – well, I've come to thank him for the flowers he brought me, and it's upset me dignity again to find he told everyone about me in a pushcart.'

'Flowers?' said Mr Brown.

'Daffodils?' said Susie.

'Yes, they were lovely, a whole bunch,' said Annie, 'only I didn't thank 'im properly. I was a bit overcome.'

'I like bein' overcome by flowers myself,' said Susie.

'I'll overcome yer mum tomorrow, Susie,' said Mr Brown, 'I'll buy 'er some daffs on me way 'ome from work, seein' it'll be me first day in charge at the new yard. Now don't fret about that pushcart incident, Annie, I can tell yer Susie 'ad many a ride in one when she was young.'

'Excuse me, Mr Brown,' said Annie, 'it wasn't when she was seventeen, was it, and with 'er legs showin'?'

Mr Brown, who could put a cheerful face on most things bar an earthquake, said, 'Well, it's not all bad news,

Annie. I mean, there ain't too many girls that could stop the traffic in a pushcart.'

'Yes, cheer up,' said Susie, 'Will was only tryin' to get you home the best way he could.'

'Yes, but tellin' everybody,' said Annie. She glanced at Mr Brown. Mr Brown tried to look as if he thought a ride in a pushcart for a seventeen-year-old girl happened ten times a day in Walworth. Annie glanced at Susie. Susie looked reassuring. 'Oh, well,' said Annie, 'I'll just have to do my best to live it down. I don't suppose it'll take more than fifty years. I'd better go now or I'll be late for church. Will you tell your brother I called to thank him properly for the flowers?'

'We'll tell him,' said Susie.

'Mind you,' said Annie, 'it's only fair to say that if I do meet 'im again, I'll have to give him a talkin'-to for tellin' everyone about my indignity.'

'Oh, yes, do give him that kind of talkin'-to,' said Susie. 'We girls shouldn't suffer indignities in silence, or we'll never get the better of men, will we?'

Annie looked at her. Susie smiled. Annie saw a kindred spirit.

'Is he goin' back to the Army soon?'

'No, he's got a long leave, three months,' said Susie.

'Then I might 'ave a chance of givin' him a talkin'-to,' said Annie, and laughed. 'Well, it's been nice meetin' you both,' she said, and Susie saw her out. The church bell was ringing.

Mrs Brown appeared in the passage.

'Who was that, Susie?'

'Annie Ford.'

'What, the girl Will met? What did she want?'

'To thank Will for a bunch of daffs he bought her,' said Susie.

'Well, bless me,' said Mrs Brown, 'he did take her some, then. Wasn't that nice of him?'

'I think he bowled her over.'

'What was she like?' asked Mrs Brown.

'Just right for Will,' said Susie.

'Well, dearie me,' said Mrs Brown, 'd'you think Will might start askin' her out?'

'Well, Mum, while we don't want to keep on about the pushcart, the fact is Will owes her something for puttin' her in it,' said Susie, 'and he knows it. The daffs were only part-payment.'

Monday morning saw Mr Brown at the Bermondsey scrap metal yard. The double wooden gates were in good order, and so was the brick wall surrounding the yard. The rest was a mess. That included the large lock-up wooden shed. Sammy had said it'll be a tidying-up job for the first week, Jim. The shed's close to falling down, so there'll be a couple of men to help it on its way. They'll knock it down and prepare the site for a new shed that'll arrive in sections on Tuesday. You'll have a mountain of timber from the old shed to get rid of.

Granted, Sammy, Mr Brown had said. It could be burned in the yard, but that would be wasteful. Sammy said the natives of Bermondsey didn't like wastefulness, it would upset them. Right, said Mr Brown, I'll put a notice up on the gates, inviting them to come and help themselves to firewood. That'll get rid of it unwastefully. Sammy, who liked a bit of imaginative wordage, said you sound like one of my family already, Jim. Sort out what stock there is with Eddie Mason, your assistant, and let me have written details when they're ready. If any prospective customers look in, let them have a ten per cent discount on all standing stock to encourage them to clear us out. At present, the standing stock makes the place look like a junk yard. I'll pop in and see how you're doing from time to time.

Mr Brown knew Sammy was being typically himself. It didn't matter how much he was involved with all the big happenings, he still kept himself interested in everything else.

The large old shed was coming down. The men had the tarred roof off and had smashed it up. Now the boarded walls were being hammered, split and torn out. Huge heaps of timber were building up for the benefit of the poverty-stricken people of the immediate neighbourhood, who were always in need of fuel for their fires. Mr Brown had put the notice up on the outside of the gates, inviting people to come and collect free firewood at four in the afternoon. That would allow mums to send their kids as soon as they came home from school, and the kids would arrive with eager arms, large sacks, empty prams and home-made pushcarts. And it would keep everyone away until all the dismantling work had been done.

It was towards midday when the two men began to attack the floorboards, using long crowbars to lever the planks free from joists, which were set in a thick layer of gravel. At noon, Mr Brown sent his assistant, Eddie Mason, off to the pub for a beer and a sandwich. At about fifteen minutes past twelve, there was a sudden halt on the part of the workmen. Mr Brown, busy sorting out what there was in the way of brass, copper, lead and iron among the heaps of scrap, turned at the sudden silence. One workman, looking as if his face was drained of blood, said in a hoarse voice, 'Guv'nor, I think you'd better come an' take a look, an' then fetch the police.'

Mr Brown crossed the yard and looked at what the men had uncovered. An old soldier of the trenches, he'd seen death and he'd seen bodies that had lain unburied for days, but he too suffered a draining of blood at what he saw now.

Uniformed police and CID men had been and eventually gone, and the decomposing body of a girl had been taken away. Mr Brown felt sick. Some of the repercussions were going to land in Sammy's lap. The police had said nothing was to be touched for the time being, everything was to be left just as it was. Meanwhile, they had the job of trying to identify the dead girl.

Sammy being out for the day, Mr Brown went to the Camberwell offices to see Boots, the general manager. His wife Emily was with him. She was his shorthand-typist and worked from nine-thirty until three-thirty. She was just about to go. She was a lively and energetic woman of twenty-seven, but very thin. To Mr Brown she seemed a little thinner each time he saw her, as if her inner energy devoured all the goodness of her food before it had any chance to do something for her body. But she owned magnificent auburn hair and big green eyes, and it was in her eyes that all her energy seemed to show.

'Hello, Jim,' she said, 'thought you were at your new job in Bermondsey.'

'Well, I was,' said Mr Brown, feeling he didn't want to land Boots's wife with unpleasant news just when she was about to go home to spend time with her little son. It was the kind of news a man didn't like giving a woman. 'But I 'it a snag, which I ought to talk to Sammy about, only I just remembered 'e's up in London Town somewhere.'

'Kensington, among other places,' said Boots.

'Well, you can talk to Boots about it,' said Emily. 'Sammy's good at verbalisin', Boots is good at listening. I'm off to see young Tim.' Tim, her son, was four and a half years old. 'So long, lovey,' she said to Boots, and gave him a warm kiss. 'So long, Jim.' Off she went, her step quick, as it always was, much as if she was continually trying to beat the passage of time.

'Now, what's the trouble, Jim?' asked Boots.

'Nasty,' said Mr Brown.

'How nasty?' asked Boots.

Susie's dad recounted how the body of a girl had come to light. He had gone for the police, and they'd summoned a police doctor, who was of the opinion that the body had lain in the gravel under the shed floorboards for over a year. The doctor also said it would have been more decomposed than it was if it had been lying in earth.

'Hell,' said Boots, 'that's not a very good start, Jim.'

'Told yer it was nasty, Boots,' said Mr Brown. He got on well with Boots, who rarely turned a hair at setbacks. Sammy could be dramatic.

'Poor young girl,' said Boots. He supposed it was murder, and he disliked murder even more than most people. He'd been close to a grisly one in his teens, close enough for it to have been only a few doors away. He had memories of that which he would never forget. 'Think of her moments of terror, Jim.'

'Murder, that's what it was,' said Mr Brown, 'and 'anging's too good for the bugger who did it. The police 'ave made me shut down the yard for the time bein', and they've got the spare key for the gate padlock. The point is, what's it goin' to do to the business?'

'It needn't do anything,' said Boots. 'It's bloody unpleasant, but it's the previous owners who'll have to cope with the real worries. We've only just taken it over. Let's see, who were the previous owners?'

'Collier and Son,' said Mr Brown. 'I told the police.'

'D'you know when they stopped doing any real

business, Jim? Sammy said the place was pretty run-down.'

'I only know Sammy said on Friday that they hadn't done any business for gawd knows how long,' said Mr Brown. 'It seemed they was just 'anging on to the site. I suppose what you're on about, is that someone 'ad use of the place, and use of the shed, if you can call it use when you do a young girl in an' bury 'er there. An' he 'ad to 'ave that use without anyone gettin' suspicious the day after.'

'Such as noticing certain floorboards had been removed and replaced,' said Boots. 'Yes, you'd notice a thing like that, I'd say. Well, all right, Jim, it's not your worry, nor mine, nor Sammy's. The headache belongs to Collier and Son. We've just got a nasty taste in our mouths. Why don't you push off home and get Mrs Brown to make you a large pot of tea? You look whacked.'

'No, I'd rather do a bit,' said Mr Brown, 'I'll clean the shop windows.'

'I don't think Sammy would recommend that,' said Boots.

'I'd like to do something,' said Mr Brown. Boots's phone rang, and Susie's dad slipped out. He supposed Boots was right, that Sammy wouldn't want him to clean windows, not now he was a yard manager and only a few weeks away from being Sammy's dad-in-law. So he went to the firm's scrap yard in Olney Road, which was always busy, and where he could do some useful work for an hour or so before going home. Doing something would take that body off his mind.

Emily had decided to walk home, thinking it would be a lot more healthy for her than sitting in a bus when she'd been sitting at her typewriter most of the day. She walked briskly along Denmark Hill, liking the attractive look of

482

its trees, houses and gardens. She'd never been able to do anything slowly, anyway. But she did get a bit tired more quickly these days. The doctor said she was anaemic, that she should eat more, especially lightly cooked liver. Actually, she didn't seem to want a lot of food, and a large plateful put her off. She thought it might be a good idea to go and see her old general practitioner, Dr McManus of Walworth, and get a second opinion.

She didn't want to get ill, that was certain. If she became a sort of invalid and couldn't be a proper wife to Boots, that woman Polly Simms, a teacher at Rosie's school, would be all over him, showing him how healthy she was herself. Emily knew Polly had had her eye on Boots for ages, and of course being upper class, she wouldn't think anything of trying to pinch someone else's husband. She wanted to pinch Boots all right, Emily was sure of that.

I'll fight that to me last drop of breath, she thought, I'll fight it even if I have to eat pounds of nearly raw liver every day. I'm not going to let any woman get her hands on Boots. I know we've got a good marriage, even if we have had one or two ups and downs. I just wish I'd given him more children, I know he'd have liked four, like Lizzy and Ned have. Oh, lor', could it have been me hidden anaemia that worked against me? It's only come out these last few months. I'll get to be a bag of bones soon instead of a wife.

Boots and Sammy had been so good, giving Susie's dad a job as a scrap yard manager. Sammy had mentioned the idea to Boots, and Boots of course had said well, as he's Susie's dad, yes, you could treat him as one of the family instead of a window cleaner. That was it really with Sammy and Boots and all the Adams. They made you one of the family if your connections were close enough. The family was what they lived for. It all came from their mum, Chinese Lady. The family was everything to her. Strangely, she could be much more critical of her sons than her daughters-in-law. But she was a cockney mum, and most cockney mums knew boys needed their ears boxing far more than girls did. Telling them off now that they were all grown up was a sort of substitute for boxing their ears.

Emily smiled as she let herself into the house. Tim, her lively four-year-old son, came running into the hall. Not feeling too tired after her walk, she hugged him, lifted him and kissed him smackingly.

'Is that you, Em'ly?' called Chinese Lady from somewhere.

'Yes, it's me, I'm home, Mum,' called Emily.

Home. That was the best word ever.

Annie had gone to her work in a thinking frame of mind. She kept asking herself if the present of that bunch of daffs had meant more than a nice gesture, if it meant Will Brown would come round and see her again. She'd had boys give her the eye when she was younger. Lately her dad had said it was time she had a young man. She wouldn't object if Will Brown asked to take her out, except she'd let him know she didn't want him laughing at her and treating her as if she was more of a joke than a young lady.

Her place of work, the grocer's shop in the New Kent Road, was large and always had a lovely grocery smell. The open sacks that lined the floor against the front of the counter gave off the aroma of currants, sultanas, raisins, rice, sugar, prunes and other items. Mr Urcott, in his spotless white apron, presided at the dairy counter, and had a miraculous way of shaping chunks of butter or

484

margarine into neat oblongs and expertly wrapping them in grease-proof paper. He was a funny old bloke. Well, he was over fifty, had thinning hair and spectacles that always perched halfway down his nose. But he was really kind, he had a smile for all his customers and even for ragged kids who came to ask did he have a pound of broken biscuits for tuppence? If he said no, one of them was sure to say he'd break up a pound of whole ones, if Mr Urcott would like.

He kept his shop clean, and he kept two large cats, which padded around silently at night in search of any mice foolish enough to be drawn out by the smell of cheese.

The shop had been open for an hour when Annie arrived at her prescribed time of ten o'clock. Mr Urcott greeted her with a smile and a comment over the head of a little old lady customer.

'Well, here you are, Annie. Did you hop all the way?'

'No, I treated meself to a tram ride this mornin', Mr Urcott.'

'Best way too,' said the little old lady, who was wearing a granny bonnet. 'I 'opped all the way up our street once when I was a girl, and me drawers fell down. You don't want that to 'appen at your age, Annie, it'll upset yer dignity. So don't do no 'opping.'

'You can be sure I won't, Mrs Gurney,' said Annie.

'It's what comes of tapes wearin' out,' said the little old lady, not a bit concerned that Mr Urcott was listening. 'My granddaughter says elastic's best, but I don't trust elastic meself. Yes, now I'll 'ave two ounces of yer New Zealand butter, Mr Urcott, I can afford that this week. I don't know I can afford elastic, even if I trusted it.' She prattled away.

'Hello, Annie.' That greeting came from Mr Urcott's

other assistant, Miss Banks, a single lady in her thirties and a niece of the grocer. She was kind too, but more brisk than Mr Urcott. She looked after the opposite counter, and Annie helped her there. Annie also kept the shop looking tidy, and attended to all orders that required anything from the open sacks to be packeted up in twists of brown paper after being weighed. The shop was busy most days, its prices being competitive, its atmosphere laden with the appeal of a good grocery establishment that had well-stocked shelves, shining marble counters and cheerful staff. Striving, hard-up housewives knew they could get good value and a little gossip as well, if they wanted it.

Mr Urcott had three customers at his counter, and Miss Banks had four. Annie, donning her white apron, began to help. There was a lull after all the customers had been served, and Mr Urcott took the opportunity to ask Annie if her knee was quite better.

'Yes, thanks, Mr Urcott, it's only a bit twingey now,' she said.

'Twingey? Well,' said Mr Urcott, smiling benevolently at her over the top of his spectacles, 'if it gets hurtful twingey, Annie, you can sit down on one of the customers' chairs.' There were two chairs, one at each counter, mainly for the benefit of old ladies.

'Oh, I won't 'ave to do that,' said Annie.

The day passed pleasantly for her, she liked the work and her wages of ten bob a week were quite generous. Lots of factory girls only earned seven and six for doing a fifty-hour week. At a quarter to four, close to her finishing time, Annie was rearranging a shelf. Mr Urcott and Miss Banks each had a customer. Annie jumped as someone addressed her back.

'Afternoon, miss, and a pound of turnips, if yer please.'

She turned. Oh, help, it was him, and with a straight

face. But he wasn't in uniform, he was wearing standard Walworth casual clothes, trousers, jersey and jacket, and a brown cap. What was it he'd asked for? Turnips?

'That's daft,' she whispered, 'we don't sell turnips.'

'You sure?' said Will. Nellie had told him where her sister worked.

'Course I'm sure. We're not a greengrocer's.'

Will looked as if he might dispute that. Just for the fun of it. He'd returned an hour ago from his weekly visit to the hospital, where he'd been told his condition shouldn't be considered alarming, that he might merely be allergic to the Indian climate. So I might, he'd said, but what about the attack I had, exerting myself a little? Oh, that can be expected, but we still feel your condition is only temporary. Come and see us once a fortnight now, instead of once a week.

'All right, miss, no turnips, then,' he said, 'so I'll have four pounds of potatoes. Can you put them in a bag?'

'I'll hit you,' breathed Annie.

'What for?'

'You know what for. Comin' in here and playin' about.'

'No good askin' for some spring onions, I suppose, or a cauliflower?'

'How would you like a kick in the leg?' whispered Annie.

'Not much,' said Will. 'All right, how about a tin of Peak Frean's mixed biscuits for me mum?'

'Serious?' said Annie.

'Well, I don't think me mum fancies funny ones,' said Will.

'You'll come to a sad end, you will,' said Annie. With Miss Banks having served her customer, Annie became brisk. 'A tin of Peak Frean's mixed, you said, sir?'

'Thank you, miss, yes,' said Will 'and I'll have a bag of coal as well.'

'We don't sell coal, sir,' said Annie, 'you'll 'ave to go down a coal-mine for that.' She fetched the tin of biscuits. 'Anything else, sir?'

'Yes,' murmured Will, 'I'll wait for you outside, I heard you finish at four.'

'Pardon?' said Annie.

'Yes, not a bad afternoon outside,' said Will. 'Can I have one of your penny carrier bags for the biscuits?'

Annie put the tin into a carrier bag and Will paid, Annie eyeing him with the suspicion of a young lady who felt he might just have a pushcart waiting for her outside the shop.

'Good afternoon, sir, thank you for your custom,' she said.

'Pleasure,' said Will, 'pity about no turnips, though.' He departed, his face still straight, which made Annie sure he was laughing at her. And she was sure he wouldn't be outside the shop when she left.

But he was.

'You're here,' she said.

'Walk you home?' said Will, eyeing her in approval. She looked quite the young lady in a short skirt, red jumper and buttoned-up jacket.

'D'you mind tellin' me what you're lookin' at?' asked Annie.

'Just you,' smiled Will.

'Well, I just don't know,' said Annie, 'you're always lookin'. I never met any feller who did more lookin' than you. You could get both eyes blacked one day. And how did you know where I worked?'

'Nellie told me.'

'That's all very well,' said Annie, 'but what d'you

488

mean by comin' into the shop and 'aving me on?'

'I wanted a tin of biscuits,' said Will.

'You asked for turnips. And coal.'

'I forget myself sometimes,' said Will, and Annie laughed.

'You're daft,' she said.

'Now and again, I suppose,' said Will. 'D'you want to take a tram down to East Street?'

'What, under me arm or in a carrier bag?' asked Annie, having some of her own back.

'No sauce,' said Will.

'You can talk, you've got more sauce than all the street kids,' said Annie. 'And I'm walkin' home, thanks.'

'I was thinkin' of your knee,' said Will.

'How kind,' said Annie. She was still suspicious of him. 'You can walk with me, if you like, I always go home by the Walworth Road.' She liked the Walworth Road with its shops, its trams and buses, its people and its handsome town hall.

They walked to the Elephant and Castle.

'I was told you called at our house yesterday,' said Will.

'Yes, I wanted to thank you properly for the flowers,' said Annie. 'I'm sorry I didn't thank you properly at the time – oh, wait a minute, when you left you told Nellie you'd send a pair of trousers round for me, and you went off laughin' about it.'

'Did I?'

'I bet you did,' said Annie, as they turned into the Walworth Road. 'And what were the trousers for, might I ask?'

'To stop you worryin',' said Will.

'What about? Just tell me, go on. I didn't 'ave any worries at all until I bumped into that pushcart because you were lookin' at me.'

'Yes, it's all this lookin',' said Will, 'and I thought you could use a pair of trousers to cover your legs and knees up when I'm around.'

'Oh, I never heard anything so barmy,' said Annie. 'You're laughin' at me again. Anyway, how would you like to be a grown-up girl with her knees in the air in a pushcart?'

'You're not still worried about that, are you, Annie?' said Will.

'I'll never get over it,' said Annie, 'and I never thought you'd be rotten enough to tell your fam'ly about it, specially that nice sister and dad of yours. I bet it won't be long before everyone in London knows.'

'Only if it gets in the newspapers,' said Will.

'Newspapers?' Annie nearly fainted in public.

'They'll send reporters round to see you, and they'll take photographs.'

'Photographs of me?' gasped Annie in horror.

'In the pushcart,' said Will.

'D'you want me to die? I'm not bein' sat in any pushcart again, I can tell you, I'll—' Annie stopped and gave him a searching look. 'Oh, you rotten ha'porth, you're havin' me on again.'

'No, it could get serious,' said Will, 'they might drag me in and take photographs of me pushin' the cart with you in it and your knees up in the air. Strike a light, Annie, if the Army saw it, they'd throw me to the lions.'

'They wouldn't, would they?' Annie gave him another searching glance. Will tried to look worried but brave. It didn't work. 'Oh, you lunatic,' said Annie, 'you're doin' it again, laughin' at me. And you a soldier too, a corporal. Where's your uniform?'

'In my wardrobe,' said Will. 'I bought some civvies this mornin'.'

'Your sister said you were on three months leave, I've never 'eard of any soldier havin' that amount of leave before.'

'It's for good behaviour,' said Will, 'for bein' respectful to officers, nice to old ladies and kind to girls.'

'I'm not simple, I'll 'ave you know,' said Annie. 'Did you get three months leave as a reward for doin' something brave?'

'No, just for doin' three years duty in India.'

'India? Oh, no wonder you look so brown. What's it like there?'

'Hot, mostly,' said Will, and talked to her about that teeming continent. When they reached Caulfield Place down Browning Street, they stopped.

'Here's where you live,' she said. 'I'd best get a move on now and give Charlie and Nellie and Cassie a bit of tea.'

'How many young men come knockin' at your door?' asked Will.

'Hundreds,' said Annie.

'As many as that? Well, I suppose there's no point askin' if I can take you out when you've got—'

'Of course I 'aven't,' said Annie.

'All right,' said Will, 'how about a row on the Serpentine next Sunday afternoon, if the weather's fine?'

'You askin' serious?'

'Yes, d'you mind?' said Will.

'No, I like bein' asked out,' said Annie.

'Good,' said Will, 'I'll call for you at half-past two next Sunday.' He thought he could manage a gentle row on the Serpentine. There was no real exertion in that. He wouldn't be entering a boat race. 'That suit you?'

'A row round the Serpentine sounds nice,' said Annie.

'Don't fall out of the boat,' said Will.

'You'd better make sure I don't, or I'll pull you in with me.'

'I'm hopin' for a fine afternoon, not a wet one,' said Will.

Annie laughed, and they parted, Will strolling down Caulfield Place and Annie hurrying along to King and Queen Street, a little smile on her face.

CHAPTER NINE

Monday having been washday, the Brown family expected the usual supper of cold meat with mounds of piping hot bubble-and-squeak. But because it was Mr Brown's first day as manager of the new scrap yard, Mrs Brown put herself out to do grilled pork chops. However tasty bubble-and-squeak was, the cold meat just wasn't good enough for celebrating a proud day like this. Mrs Brown's scullery had been full of steam from the copper for hours, and the yard line was still laden with laundry. The scullery was still full of the smell of washing, but the door from the kitchen was shut tight to keep the smell from interfering with the aroma of the supper. Mr Brown had decided to say nothing about the grisly find at the yard. He didn't think he needed to upset his family, especially with Susie's wedding in the offing. In any case, it was nothing to do with Sammy's ownership of the yard. Any headaches belonged to the previous owners, Collier and Son. With luck, when it got into the papers, Adams Enterprises wouldn't even be mentioned. Boots was a godsend in cases like this, he'd know how to talk to the police and to any newspaper reporters if they asked questions.

Enjoying his supper, he came up with the opinion that his trouble-and-strife was worth her weight in roast beef. Susie said you mean pork chops, Dad. Sally said no, he meant gold. Same thing, said Mr Brown, seeing I'm talking about the roast beef of old England.

'Now, Jim,' said Mrs Brown, 'I don't want to be stood up pound for pound against roast beef.'

''Ow much roast beef would it be, then?' asked Sally.

'With any luck, a few 'undredweight,' said Mr Brown.

'Me a few 'undredweight?' said Mrs Brown, whose motherliness was constant and unvarying. 'Dad, you're askin' for a clip, makin' out I'm like the Fat Woman of Peckham.'

'I think it's the Fat Boy of Peckham,' said Will.

'Well, I'm not him, either,' said Mrs Brown.

'You're a nice comfy lady, Mum', said Susie, 'and worth all the pork chops in the Tower of London.'

''Ow many they got there, then?' asked Freddy.

'Millions,' said Susie.

''Ow'd they get millions?'

'Well, they order ninety every week for the Beefeaters,' said Will, 'but the Beefeaters won't eat them, they only like beef chops.'

'I never 'eard of beef chops,' said Sally.

'Well, you wouldn't, would you?' said Will. 'The Beefeaters grab them all.'

'Mum, if I 'ave to listen to any more jokes like that, I'll leave 'ome,' said Sally.

'Oh, don't do that, lovey,' said Mrs Brown, 'just finish your pork chop.'

'I 'eard a joke once,' said Freddy, holding his chop and biting at what was left of the pork. 'There was this absent-minded bloke, yer see, an' when 'e got to 'is work one day someone told 'im 'e was wearin' odd socks. "No, they ain't odd," he said, "I got another pair at 'ome just like these."'

Sally giggled. Mrs Brown smiled fondly. Susie smiled. Will grinned.

Mr Brown said, 'An' then what, Freddy?'

'Joke over,' said Freddy. 'Wake up, Dad. 'Ere, do all the fam'ly get presents at the weddin'? I wouldn't mind a bike meself.'

'Blessed boy,' said Sally, 'what's 'e talkin' about?'

'It's only the 'appy couple that get presents, Freddy,' said Mr Brown.

'I dunno what Susie's gettin' any for,' said Freddy, 'not when she's goin' to get all Sammy's worldly goods. Crikey, she'll get 'is motorcar as well, and I ain't even got a bike.'

'I'll buy you a bike, Freddy,' said Susie.

Freddy nearly swallowed his chop bone.

'Now, son, you can't eat that bone,' said Mr Brown.

'Did our Susie say something?' asked Freddy, slightly hoarse.

'She said she'll buy you a bike,' smiled Will.

'Crikey,' said Freddy, 'ain't our Susie lovely, Will? I bet there ain't many bruvvers that 'ave got a sister like her. I bet Ernie Flint's sister could eat broken glass. Susie, did yer really say you'd buy me a bike?'

'I have bought it, lovey,' said Susie. At Sammy's request, she had placed an order with Mr Greenberg and Mr Greenberg had said what a pleasure to see you, Susie, and what a pleasure to buy up certain textiles at certain warehouses for Sammy at ten per cent commission. Two and a half, said Susie. Susie, Susie, said Mr Greenberg, and sat down under the stress of a sudden heart attack. Seven and a half, he said faintly. Susie smiled, and Mr Greenberg recovered slightly. Four, said Susie. Mr Greenberg had a relapse. Susie fanned him. Six, he said hoarsely. Five, said Susie. Susie, Susie, you'll be my death, he said. But five is twice as much as two and a half, and you don't want to ruin us, do you, Mr Greenberg? Mr Greenberg settled for five and forgave Susie because of her blue eyes. Susie saw some bicycles among a mountain of stuff in his yard. She examined them. She found two very good ones and offered to take them both off Mr Greenberg's hands. On my life,

Susie, said Mr Greenberg, ain't it a pleasure at twelve and six each? Bless you, Mr Greenberg, said Susie. Eh? said Mr Greenberg. Thanks, said Susie. Mr Greenberg said did I hear a quid for the pair? No, I'm happy with twenty-five bob, said Susie. Done at a guinea, Susie, said Mr Greenberg. Susie laughed. She was happy to pay up. Earning twelve pounds a month, which few young women of her age did, her savings made her relatively affluent, and she had insisted on helping her dad with the wedding expenses.

'Susie, you really bought me a bike?' asked Freddy, blissfully agape.

'Mr Greenberg's deliverin' it tomorrow,' said Susie, 'with one for Sally as well. A lady's bike, and both nearly as good as new, with bells.'

'Oh, Susie,' breathed Sally in rapture.

'Bless you, Susie love,' said Mrs Brown.

'Seconded,' said Will, and Mr Brown looked affectionately proud of his one and only elder daughter. Sally jumped up and gave Susie a hug and a kiss. Freddy said he'd do all Susie's wedding errands for her, and what's more, he said, I won't come to the church in me shirt tails, I'll wear me new suit.

'What a blessin',' said Sally, 'we're all honoured, ain't we, Dad?'

''Ighly,' said Mr Brown.

'I'll wear me bicycle clips as well,' said Freddy.

'Not in the church, lovey,' said Mrs Brown.

'Well, all right,' said Freddy generously. 'Susie, we goin' to 'ave "Knees Up, Mother Brown" in the Institute?'

'Sammy says you can't have a Walworth weddin' without a knees-up,' smiled Susie.

'That you can't,' said Mr Brown.

'It occurs to me,' said Freddy, 'was—'

'Crikey, listen to 'im,' said Sally, 'fancy anything occurrin' to 'im.'

'Yes, was "Knees Up, Mother Brown" wrote for our mum, Dad?' asked Freddy.

'Funny you should ask that, Freddy,' said Mr Brown. 'It was the Sunday our Susie was christened, and we 'ad a bit of a do afterwards. Me and yer mum did a lively dance, and a bloke in a posh suit and a bow tie come up as yer mum was showin' 'er knees. 'E complimented 'er and asked me would I mind if 'e wrote a song in 'er honour, and what was 'er name. Seein' she'd become a mother, I said you can call 'er Mother Brown. 'E said 'e was much obliged, then went an' sat in a corner and wrote the song there an' then. Then 'e played it on the joanner. "Knees Up, Mother Brown", that's what it was, and everyone did a dance to it, and ever since everyone in Walworth's danced to it.'

'Dad, you scream,' said Susie, 'you just made all that up.'

'You ask yer mum,' said Mr Brown.

'Well, I do remember some saucy bloke comin' up and sayin' he liked me knees,' said Mrs Brown, 'but I don't remember him writin' a song about them. Well, I boxed 'is ears.'

Susie laughed. She listened as her dad talked about how he felt he'd had one over the eight when he first met their mum. She was that pretty he was sorry none of them had been there at the time. Freddy tried to puzzle that out while his dad went on to say that for the first time in his life he'd felt inebriated without a single drop of what you fancy having passed his lips. Susie listened to Sally pulling his leg, and to her mum announcing that Will had treated her to a lovely tin of biscuits after getting back from the hospital. It was a relief, she said, that the doctors had told him his asthma might only be temporary, and that they'd given him some special tablets to take, specially if it got temporarily chronic.

'Aspro, I reckon,' said Mr Brown, 'they give yer that for everything.'

'Yes, Henry the Eighth's wives were given a couple each after he had their heads chopped off,' said Will. 'but it didn't cure their headache.'

Susie laughed again. Will could be really funny, and he was letting his sense of humour make light of his condition. The evening sunshine was going, but its light was still lingering on the grimy rooftops of Walworth and touching the kitchen. It was a lovely old kitchen to Susie. She could rarely sit at the table in the evenings without thinking of the previous tenants, the Adams family. Sammy and his sister and brothers had all grown up here. She often felt that she and her family were an extension of the Adams. Sammy said life was all about families, that loyalties began with the family, and that if you didn't have loyalties you didn't have anything worthwhile to hang on to when you started slipping. She and Sammy would have a family. Two boys and two girls. That is, Sammy had said would she mind doing him the honour four times and come up with two of each. Susie said would he mind giving her a little help, since she didn't think she could manage everything by herself. Sammy asked if she'd write down exactly what he had to do, as he was dead ignorant about that sort of thing. So am I, said Susie, but we can practise together. What, now, in your parlour? said Sammy. No, when we're married, said Susie, so leave my legs alone. Now? said Sammy. Well, not exactly now, said Susie, not immediately.

It was definitely cold meat and bubble-and-squeak for

Gaffer Ford and his family. Annie had had to see to the washing, which Nellie and Charlie had collected from a bagwash on their way home from school. It had all needed to be sorted out and hung on the yard lines. Still, the bubble-and-squeak, crisply browned, was a treat any Monday.

Gaffer Ford thought of something.

'Seen any more of the soldier bloke that wheeled your knees 'ome in a pushcart, Annie?' he asked.

'You done it now, Dad,' said Nellie.

'Done what?' said the Gaffer.

'You're not to say that word,' said Nellie.

'No-one ain't,' said Charlie, 'and I got orders to bash any of the street kids that talk about it.'

'No, you ain't,' said Nellie. 'Annie didn't give you no orders to do any bashin'. You just said you would, it's yer 'ooliganism that makes yer want to go around bashin' people.'

'Charlie,' said the Gaffer, 'I 'ope I ain't goin' to have to take me belt to yer one day, which I've been recommended to by certain neighbours. Anyway, what word ain't I to say?'

'Pushcart,' piped up Cassie.

'Cor, she's said it,' groaned Charlie.

'Cassie, you know Annie's forbid it,' said Nellie.

'Yes, I don't want it ever mentioned again,' said Annie, 'not by any of you – Dad, is that you laughin'?'

'Bless yer, Annie, not me,' said the Gaffer.

'It's bad enough him always laughin' – no, never mind that,' said Annie, 'just get on with your suppers.'

'Who's 'im?' asked the Gaffer.

'Pardon?' said Annie.

'The one that's always laughin',' said the Gaffer, who knew the answer.

'Betcher it's 'er soldier,' said Charlie.

'If you must know,' said Annie, 'he came into the shop to buy a tin of biscuits for 'is mum, and I just happened to serve him.'

'Then what?' asked the Gaffer.

'What d'you mean, then what?' asked Annie.

'Did 'e come on 'orseback?' asked Cassie.

''Ow could 'e come on 'orseback for a tin of biscuits?' asked Charlie. ''Orses ain't allowed in grocers' shops.'

'Small 'orses are,' said Cassie.

'Cassie,' said Annie, 'stop givin' your meat to that cat.'

'It's only the bits of fat,' said Cassie.

'Did yer soldier 'ave a chat with yer, Annie?' asked the Gaffer.

'Well, he did walk down the Walworth Road with me on me way home,' said Annie, 'when I spoke to him about makin' a joke of what I suffered.'

'Cor, I bet 'is ears 'urt,' said Charlie.

'The Queen went down the Walworth Road once,' said Cassie dreamily.

'What for?' asked Nellie.

'Well, she 'ad some shoppin' to do,' said Cassie.

'What shoppin'?' asked Charlie.

'Oh, jellied eels an' pie an' mash, I think,' said Cassie. 'Yes, it was that, I remember now, they don't 'ave any in Windsor Castle, only liver an' bacon an' fairy cakes with pink icing. And plums an' custard,' she added, after a brief but thoughtful pause.

'Cassie,' said Annie, hiding a smile, 'I just don't know what we can do with you and all your fancies.'

'We could turn 'er upside-down an' shake 'em out of 'er,' said Charlie.

'No, we couldn't,' said the Gaffer, 'not our Cassie, she's one of me sweet'earts.'

'We could turn Charlie upside-down and make an 'ole in the floor with 'is big 'ead,' said Nellie.

'Yes, time we 'ad some 'oles knocked in the floor,' said the Gaffer. 'Anyway, so yer soldier walked you 'ome, Annie, did 'e?'

'Yes, and he asked me to go for a row on the Serpentine with 'im next Sunday, if it's fine,' said Annie.

'Annie, did yer say yes?' asked Nellie.

'I 'ad to be gracious and forgivin',' said Annie. 'You can't be church-goin' and not forgivin'.'

'You'll look nice in yer best Sunday frock, Annie, while you're standin' on yer dignity in a rowin'-boat,' said the Gaffer. 'I couldn't be more pleased for yer.'

'Ain't it nice, Annie's soldier bein' romantic about 'er?' said Nellie.

'Romantic's daft,' said Charlie.

'Annie, I'll come as well, if yer like,' said Cassie, 'there might be a circus with lion tamers in the park.'

'Cassie, you can't go, you silly,' said Nellie.

'I could take Tabby,' said Cassie, ''e's really a circus cat.'

'First I've 'eard of it,' said Charlie.

'Well, 'e can do circus tricks,' said Cassie, 'like puttin' 'is tail up in the air an' standin' on one leg.'

'I never seen 'im standin' on one leg,' said Nellie.

''E did it once, I saw 'im,' said Cassie.

'Then what 'appened?' asked the Gaffer.

'Well, 'e fell over,' said Cassie dolefully.

The family yelled with laughter. Cassie couldn't think why.

'You're a real scream, you are, Cassie,' said Nellie.

'She's our little coughdrop,' said the Gaffer.

'Who wants some marmalade tart?' asked Annie. They all wanted a slice of one she had made on Saturday evening.

'Can I 'ave mine 'ot?' asked Charlie. Annie said yes, put it in the fire for a minute. The family yelled with laughter again, and the Gaffer was certain of one thing then.

And that was that a man's kids were the best thing in his life when he'd lost his wife.

Mr Brown was at the Bermondsey yard again on Tuesday morning. Not that there was anything he could do. The police had said don't touch. He sent his assistant off to the Olney Road yard, which was busy and could use a bit of help. The police had appeared early. They were going to take away the boards that had lain above the corpse and give them a minute examination. Mr Brown asked why, and was astonished to hear them talk about fingerprints. Fingerprints on floorboards that had been walked on ever since that poor girl had been buried there? On the underside, said the police. It's smooth planking.

Mr Brown asked if the girl had been identified. The police said they were working on it, using a list of missing persons. Did they know how old the girl had been? Not yet. The pathologist would come up with that information pretty soon. Had they got any helpful information from Collier and Son? The reply made Mr Brown infer that Collier and Son had let their business go to the dogs on account of too much time spent in pubs. The father and his son had had no employees at this yard, they worked the business themselves. On and off. And mostly off during the last eighteen months. Mr Brown drew another inference, that the CID were investigating father and son. He asked if he could get rid of the stacks of timber. He'd taken down the notice on the gates after the body had been uncovered yesterday. The police said they'd be obliged if he left everything just as it was. Finally, he asked if they wanted to speak to Mr Sammy Adams, managing director

502

of the firm that had bought the yard and the business just a week or so ago. The police said they had no plans to at the moment.

That was something, thought Mr Brown.

One of the closed double gates was pushed open and Boots entered the yard, raincoat over his arm. The day was showery.

'Morning, Jim,' he said, and introduced himself to the police. He spoke to them and received from them the same kind of information they'd given to Mr Brown, no more and no less. Mr Brown couldn't help noting how easily he conducted himself. He never seemed to let people bother him, whoever they were and however awkward they could get. Mr Brown knew him for a man to whom the fact of being alive in God's world was far more important than the attitudes of people. People seemed to amuse him, and he nearly always looked as if a hint of amusement was lurking in his eyes, even his almost blind one. He might not be amused at the moment. He wasn't. You could see that, you could see a steely light, and Mr Brown knew he was thinking of the man who had murdered that poor young girl and buried her body under a scrap yard shed.

Mr Brown knew his background, that he was the eldest of his redoubtable mother's four children, that he'd been born and bred in cockney Walworth, won a place in a grammar school, made himself temporarily famous as the most important defence witness at an Old Bailey murder trial and soldiered in the trenches of France and Flanders before being blinded on the Somme. He'd married the girl next door while he was still blind, and now he was the general manager of his brother Sammy's business. Mr Brown thought that for all its complications, Boots did the job standing on his head. Unlike Sammy, however, he did not seem ambitious. He seemed a contented man, although his wife, Emily, once said there was a lot more to him than met the eye. His adopted daughter Rosie adored him. And, according to what Mr Brown had heard from Sammy in an unguarded moment, so did Miss Polly Simms, daughter of General Sir Henry Simms. Miss Simms had been an ambulance driver during the war, and although she had never met Boots while in France, Sammy said she complained bitterly that Emily had pinched Boots while her back was turned. But keep it dark, Jim, said Sammy, or there'll be ructions and my dear old Ma will start boxing ears all round. Not that Boots can't handle the situation. He's a family man.

The police, ready to depart, requested that Mr Brown and Mr Adams leave with them. They locked the gates and went on their way, the relevant floorboards wrapped in an old sheet. Boots took a stroll with Mr Brown.

'Good of yer to come,' said Mr Brown.

'Just wanted you to know it's not your problem or your worry,' said Boots, 'and that the scrap yard in Kennington is short of a manager. He's off sick. Would you care to take over, Jim?'

'That'll suit me, Boots.'

'I need to get back to the office,' said Boots.

'I'll push off to Kennington,' said Mr Brown. 'By the way, I've kept all this to meself.'

'So have I,' said Boots.

'I didn't want me fam'ly to know, specially Susie.'

'Everybody'll know soon, of course,' said Boots, 'but the papers might not mention it's now an Adams yard.'

'Well, with the weddin' comin' up, yer know, Boots.'

'We're all looking forward to it, Jim.'

'Special special it's goin' to be for Susie.'

'And a revelation to Sammy, I'd say,' said Boots, and the lurking hint of amusement turned into a smile.

* * *

The midday editions of the evening papers came up with the news of the discovery of a girl's body in a scrap yard in Bermondsey. The possibility that she'd been murdered was hinted at. Mr Brown felt certain the police had no doubts. The pathologist's report was expected today, and the papers informed their readers that the police were trying to establish the girl's identity by checking their lists of missing persons.

'Ah, good afternoon, Mrs Brown,' smiled Mr Greenberg as the good lady opened the door to him. 'And vhat a pleasant day, ain't it?'

'Oh, I suppose a nice drop of rain is doin' someone some good,' said Mrs Brown in her agreeable way. No disillusioned male could ever have said Mrs Brown was a contrary female. ''Ave you brought the bikes, Mr Greenberg?'

Mr Greenberg's small pony and cart stood outside the house. The well-known rag-and-bone man also had a horse and cart.

'Vell, how could I let Susie down? Vhat a happy young lady she is, ain't it? Might I bring the bikes in, Mrs Brown?'

'I'd be ever so obliged,' said Mrs Brown proudly. Some neighbours were on their doorsteps, watching through the light shower of rain. It could make any woman proud to have neighbours witnessing two bikes going into her house. 'And I'm that glad you're deliverin' now, as Sally and Freddy will be home from school in half an hour.'

'I vill bring them in at vunce, von't I?' beamed Mr Greenberg.

'And stay for a cup of tea,' said Mrs Brown.

'Vell, time ain't alvays money,' said Mr Greenberg, his

505

beard curling happily, 'and ain't this a house and a home of fond memories for me? Vhy, ain't it the only house that's known the Adams and Browns, all of vhich are my friends? I vill bring in the bikes and drink tea vith you vith great pleasure.'

'Leave them in the passage,' said Mrs Brown, and bustled back to her kitchen to put the kettle on.

Mr Greenberg unloaded the bikes one at a time and placed them in the passage. He returned to his cart to put the nosebag on his pony. He looked around for a moment. The shower of rain ceased its patter, the clouds broke and the sun came out, creating a rainbow over Walworth. Ah, such a country with its rain, its rainbows and its good people, thought Mr Greenberg. His love for his adopted country surfaced, and he took out his large red handkerchief and blew his nose. He thought of the trodden muddy streets of Russian villages, and the perils of being Jewish whenever a patrol of Russian police or Cossacks rode in. The tsars and their knout-wielding Cossacks had gone, and the Bolsheviks and their commissars had Russia now. They were no better than the tsars. Who would want to go back and live under them? Who would ever exchange a life with the people of London for a life under the Bolsheviks? There were a few people, ah, yes, who would never smile on a Jew, but did he not have a thousand friends who would laugh with him and crack jokes with him?

How busy he had been almost from the day he and his parents and his sisters had stepped ashore and taken their first steps over the soil of England. He had been fifteen then and was now just fifty. In all that time he had been too busy to find a wife. And now, when grey was peppering his hair and his beard, a woman had entered his house in the Old Kent Road. A woman of thirty-six, a widow, Hannah Borovich, who had three children, all boys.

'Mr Greenberg, shame on you,' she had said.

'Vhat? Vhat? You enter my house and address me in Russian, not even in Yiddish?'

'We are Russian,' she said.

'I spit on Russia.'

'Tck, tck,' said the handsome widow. 'It is time you were married, time you became a father.'

'To whom should I be married?'

'To myself. You are a good man, Eli Greenberg, and a kind one. I will take you for my husband and give my sons what they need, a father. Go to Rabbi Goldstein and tell him so.'

What could a man do with such a woman who had three sons all with dark liquid eyes and crisp curly black hair? Should he take a wife at his age and her three sons too? She was poor and was concerned for them.

What could a man do except think about it?

Mr Greenberg smiled, raised his round black hat to Mrs Brown's neighbours who were still on their doorsteps, then entered the house to drink tea with Susie's affable mother.

CHAPTER TEN

One could have said that Sally and Freddy came out of school in leaps and bounds, such was their rushing eagerness to get home and see if their bikes had come. School friends laughed and shouted at them.

'Go it, Freddy, old Nick's behind yer!'

'Leg it, Sally!'

That Sally and her growing legs, thought Freddy, it just ain't right. His sister was yards ahead of him and running fit to lick him to their door. Exuberant Sally ran on. Appalled at being beaten by a girl, and his sister at that, Freddy charged after her. Up through Walcorde Avenue they flew, Freddy gaining. Sally turned into Browning Street.

''Ere, you Sally!'

'Slowcoach!' called Sally.

Freddy belted after her and they were almost together as they turned into Caulfield Place. And there they almost sent Mr Ponsonby flying.

'Oh, 'elp,' panted Freddy.

'Oh, sorry, Mr Ponsonby,' said Sally. They stopped.

Mr Ponsonby, regaining his balance, straightened his bowler hat and peered at them.

'Dear me, what a day,' he said, 'what high spirits. Who are you?'

'I'm Sally, 'e's Freddy.'

'Ah, yes, Sally Brown. Charming, charming, such a sweet girl. And Freddy, yes, such a firework, my word, yes. Dear me, where are you going?'

508

''Ome,' said Freddy, 'to see if our bikes 'ave come.'

'Bikes?' said Mr Ponsonby, looking puzzled. 'Ah, bicycles, of course. Have a peppermint.' He produced the bag, opened it and proffered it. Sally and Freddy each took a peppermint while their feet fidgeted.

'Thanks ever so, Mr Ponsonby,' said Sally.

'Not at all, Sally, not at all. My, you're a pretty girl.'

'She's got special wooden legs,' said Freddy.

'He's barmy,' said Sally, and Mr Ponsonby peered at her legs.

'Dear me, dear me, well, I never,' he said, 'how very charming.'

'She just 'ad ordin'ry short legs before,' said Freddy. 'Well, we got to go now, Mr Ponsonby – crikey, look, Sally, that's Mr Greenberg's cart outside our front door – come on.'

Off they ran. Mr Ponsonby turned to watch them, a kind smile putting a crease in his tidy-looking face.

'Dear me, what a very nice photograph I could take,' he said, and helped himself to a peppermint. 'But one is so busy, so busy. I must get on. Now, where am I going? Ah, yes.' He turned about and twinkled off, rolled umbrella lightly tapping the pavement.

Having paid their joyous respects to the beaming Mr Greenberg, and gobbled up cake with their cups of tea, Sally and Freddy took up rapturous ownership of their bikes. Off went Sally to ride round and see her friend Mavis. Boys whistled at her legs.

'Soppy 'a'porths,' said Sally and cycled on.

Freddy just went careering around the back streets, having promised his mum and Mr Greenberg too not to tussle with trams and buses in the Walworth Road. Trams always come off best, said his mum. And Mr Greenberg said bikes were valuable as business goods, but boys were valuable to their families.

Pedalling from Rodney Road into Orb Street, Freddy spotted Cassie. She was meandering along and singing to herself. With a tyre-hissing swerve, Freddy crossed to her side of the street and stopped.

'Watcher, Cassie.'

'Oh, 'ello,' said Cassie.

'Like me bike, do yer?' said Freddy.

'Crikey, is it yourn?' breathed Cassie in awe.

'Not 'alf,' said Freddy, 'it's a present from me eldest sister. She's wealthy, yer know. Well, she is a bit.'

'Oh, does she wear furs?' asked Cassie. 'I 'ad an aunt once who wore furs. An' jewels. An' she 'ad 'er own carriage with four white 'orses. Only she fell on 'ard times and 'ad to go an' do the laundry for a wicked uncle.'

'Rotten 'ard luck,' said Freddy. 'Did it turn 'er hair white?'

'Oh, no, she 'ad lovely gold 'air,' said Cassie, 'and 'er wicked uncle tried to cut it off. 'E chased 'er all round the laundry room. Only 'e couldn't see where she was in all the steam, and 'e fell in the great big laundry tub.'

'Did 'e? You sure 'e did, Cassie?'

'Oh, yes, and it boiled 'im all over,' said Cassie.

'Did it drown 'im as well?' asked Freddy.

'Oh, no, 'is servants got 'im out,' said Cassie.

'And hung 'im on the line?'

'I think they 'ad to,' said Cassie, 'he was all soppin' wet. Still, me aunt did say he was sort of different after that. Is it really yer own bike?'

'Yes, like a ride?' said Freddy. 'You can sit on the carrier be'ind me.'

'Oh, could I?' Cassie was aglow with pleasure.

510

'Yes, come on,' said Freddy, and held the bike steady. Cassie perched herself astride the wire carrier.

'Oh,' she said.

'What's up?'

'It's all wiry,' she said, ''ave yer got a little cushion I could put in me knickers?'

'I dunno, you girls don't 'alf 'ave soft bums,' said Freddy. 'I suppose us blokes ought to carry cushions around, only we don't. Never mind, Cassie, use this.' He took his soft cap off and handed it to her. Cassie unperched herself and with no more than two or three facile movements she lodged the cap in the seat of her knickers. Then she frowned.

'It's all lumpy,' she said.

'Look, Cassie, as me mate you ain't supposed to complain,' said Freddy. 'Me old mate Daisy never complained not once.'

'I ain't complainin',' said Cassie, 'I'm just sayin', that's all. I'm just sayin' it's a bit lumpy.'

'Well, try it,' said Freddy, and Cassie perched herself astride the carrier again. ''Ow's that?' he asked.

'Oh, it don't feel 'alf so lumpy now,' said Cassie.

A boy came up.

'What's she doin' on yer bike?' he asked.

'Sittin',' said Freddy.

'You ain't supposed to give girls bike rides. Get 'er orf, and I'll ride.'

'She's me mate, Alfie Gibbons, and you ain't,' said Freddy.

'Bleedin' cissy,' said young Alfie Gibbons.

''Ere, Cassie, 'old me bike while I roll me sleeves up,' said Freddy.

'Oh, you goin' to 'ave a duel?' asked Cassie in excitement.

511

'No, I ain't, I'm just goin' to flatten 'is 'ooter,' said Freddy, who had a lot of his mum's equability but couldn't stand being called a cissy.

'Ain't you got a sword?' asked Cassie, off her perch and holding the bike. 'Me dad 'ad lots of swords once and 'ad lots of duels. 'E 'ad one once with a French duke. On 'Ampstead 'Eath. Dad cut 'is 'ead off.'

'Cor blimey,' said Alfie Gibbons, 'she's yer mate? She's as daft as old Ma Simmonds, who ain't got no teef, eiver.'

'Right, put yer dooks up,' said Freddy, sleeves rolled up and muscles flexed. Cassie's eyes grew big. It was the first time a boy had threatened to fight a duel on her behalf. Street kids were approaching, sensing an up-and-downer.

'I just remembered, I got to do some errands for me mum,' said Alfie Gibbons, and made tracks for his home in Stead Street.

Freddy rolled his sleeves down and Cassie said, 'Oh, 'e didn't give you a chance to bash 'im.'

'Still, it saved 'im goin' 'ome with a flat 'ooter,' said Freddy. 'Come on, let's 'ave our ride.'

Once again Cassie perched herself astride the carrier, Freddy's soft cap cushioning her bottom, and away they went. It was Cassie's very first bike ride and she pictured herself being carried away on a white horse by King Arthur, the horse galloping and six wicked uncles chasing after them.

Around the back streets Freddy cycled, but could hardly believe his ears when Cassie, coming out of her dreams, suddenly said, 'I'm 'ungry'. They had just passed the shop in Rodney Road that sold boiled sheep's heads for sixpence, or half a one for fourpence.

'Well, if yer don't mind, Cassie, I ain't stoppin' to buy yer any sheep's 'ead.'

'Ugh, I don't want no sheep's 'ead,' said Cassie, 'I was just sayin' I'm 'ungry, that's all.'

'Could yer wait till next time I see yer?' said Freddy, turning into Charleston Street. 'Then if I got a bit of pocket money on me I'll buy yer a toffee-apple.'

'Oh, I like toffee-apples,' said Cassie, legs swinging, hands holding on to Freddy. At the end of Charleston Street, he let the bike bump gently up on to the pavement and rode along the path separating St John's Church from the vicarage. This time he could hardly believe his eyes. It was that big bloke again, the one with a flapping overcoat and hollow staring eyes. He was striding straight towards them.

Henry Brannigan hissed with rage. A bloody bicycle and two bloody kids riding on it. Those kids, the ones who'd been in his way before. Look at that girl, she had her legs stuck out, curse her. She was bad luck, if any kid was. But he refused to stop, he came barging on, keeping to the measured stride that ensured he trod on no lines.

Freddy wavered and veered. The man, glaring, brushed the bike as he bruised his way by. The machine fell over, and Cassie and Freddy toppled and sprawled.

'Oh, yer rotten great elephant!' yelled Freddy.

'Bloody bikes, bloody kids, ridin' on pavements, I'll 'ave the rozzers on the pair of yer,' said Henry Brannigan in a growling roar, and strode on.

'I bet me bruvver Will 'ud kick 'is teeth all the way down 'is throat,' said Freddy. 'You 'urt, Cassie?' He helped her up.

'I don't like 'im,' said Cassie, brushing herself down, 'I bet 'e's someone's wicked uncle, I bet 'e tramples people to death under 'is 'orses, I bet 'e rides six 'orses at once.'

'Yes, but are you all right?' asked Freddy.

'Yes, course I am, I just fell over, that's all. Me sister Annie fell over last week and 'urt 'er knee.'

'That was when me bruvver Will met 'er,' said Freddy, examining his bike for dents.

'Yes, 'e looked at 'er, an' that was what made 'er fall over, she said.'

'Don't be daft, Cassie, 'ow could anyone fall over just by bein' looked at?'

'Well, she could see 'e was a lion tamer,' said Cassie, 'that was what done it.'

''E ain't a lion tamer, 'e's a soldier,' said Freddy.

'Yes, ain't 'e 'andsome?' said Cassie. 'I expect 'e'll get a job one day servin' the King an' Queen with their Sunday teas. They always 'ave strawberry jam with their Sunday teas, did yer know that, Freddy?'

'I suppose I know it now,' grinned Freddy.

'Can we do more ridin'?' asked Cassie.

'D'you like me bike, then?'

'Not 'alf,' said Cassie, 'an' yer cap's ever such an 'elp.'

'All right, we'll do more ridin' till our suppers,' said Freddy. 'Lucky there ain't no dents in me bike.'

'Your cap's got all creased, lovey,' said Mrs Brown when Freddy returned home alive and unscratched.

Freddy, taking his cap off, gave it a critical look, then banged it about on his knee.

'Yes, well, it's been in Cassie's bloomers,' he said.

'It's what?' said Will.

'It's what?' yelled Susie.

'Oh, dear,' said Mrs Brown.

'That blessed boy, you can't believe 'im, can yer?' said Sally.

'Bein' 'is dad, I want to believe 'im, but I ain't sure I 'eard 'im right,' said Mr Brown.

'I dunno what yer all fallin' about for,' said Freddy.

'Cassie rode on me carrier an' used me cap for a cushion, and it ain't my fault girls 'ave got soft bums.'

Sally had a fit, Susie shrieked with laughter, Will grinned all over, Mr Brown rolled his eyes and Mrs Brown said, 'It's best to say bottoms, Freddy love, specially in company. Now let's all sit down and 'ave supper.'

'Wait a tick,' said Will, 'I'd like to know who stuffed your cap down Cassie's whatsits, Freddy. Was it you, or did Cassie manage it herself?'

'Oh, don't,' gasped Sally, 'I'll fall ill.'

''Ere, can you see me doin' a thing like that?' protested Freddy.

'Not without usin' my imagination,' said Susie.

'Cassie did it 'erself,' said Freddy.

'Well, I suppose some part of the fam'ly honour's been saved,' said Will.

'I'm still goin' to be ill,' said Sally.

'It's a corkin' bike, Susie,' said Freddy, 'I really like yer for it.'

'Me too for mine,' said Sally.

'Well, if we could all sit down now?' said Mrs Brown, and they all took their places at the table for rabbit stew, highly succulent and flavoursome.

Mr Brown had brought an evening paper in and was sitting on it. It contained the news that the dead girl had been strangled, that the scrap yard in which her body had been found used to be owned by Collier and Son of Bermondsey and was now the property of Adams Enterprises of Camberwell. The pathologist had given her age as twelve at the time of death. This had enabled the police to narrow the field in respect of missing persons, and the police were interviewing a Bermondsey family whose daughter had disappeared thirteen months ago. They were also making enquiries in other directions.

They were, in fact, giving beery Mr Collier and his equally beery son a hard time.

Susie asked her dad how he was getting on in Bermondsey.

'Well, we're 'eld up a bit on account of 'aving to sort a lot of things out before we can start doin' any business,' he said.

'You'll do it, Dad,' said Susie, 'you're a good old sorter-out. Sally, don't forget that on Saturday afternoon you're comin' with me to our Brixton shop for a fittin'. We're meetin' Sammy's nieces Rosie and Annabelle there.'

The fittings were for Susie's bridal gown and the bridesmaids' dresses.

'Oh, I wouldn't forget that, Susie,' said Sally. 'I could cycle there on me new bike, if yer like.'

'No, you couldn't, lovey,' said Mrs Brown, 'we can't have you cyclin' in all that traffic.'

'I don't mind takin' 'er, Mum,' said Freddy, 'she can ride on me carrier, like Cassie did.'

'With a decent cushion down her whatsits,' said Will.

Hysterics ran around the table, but stopped when they reached Mrs Brown, who said, 'No, Freddy love, you're not ridin' any bike to Brixton, either.'

'There's a murder been done down Bermondsey way,' said Mrs Queenie Watts, who lived with her husband in Brandon Street and had her brother, Henry Brannigan, as a lodger. She was reading her husband's evening paper.

'There'll be a nasty one done 'ere in a minute,' said Stan Watts from the scullery. He was regarding the sink. It was full of washing-up. 'There's two days' dirty dishes out 'ere.'

'Oh, I ain't been feelin' up to things recent,' said Mrs Watts, hairpins loose and a button looking as if it was

516

about to desert her blouse. 'I think I'm gettin' an 'eart condition. 'Ave yer read about this pore young girl that's got done in?'

'I've read it all right,' said Mr Watts, 'and I'll be readin' tomorrer about you bein' done in yerself.'

'That ain't a very nice joke,' said Mrs Watts.

'It ain't a joke.'

'Nor's me 'eart condition, I can feel it gettin' chronic. Now come in 'ere, Stan, an' pour yerself a glass of beer. I'll 'ave one too, it'll cheer me up a bit. I don't like readin' about murders.'

'One thing,' said Mr Watts, 'you won't get the miseries readin' about your own, you won't be doin' no more readin'.'

'Strangled she was, pore girl,' said Mrs Watts.

'So will you be, Queenie, if I keep comin' 'ome to this kind of mess,' said Mr Watts.

'Only twelve she was, did yer read that?' said Mrs Watts.

'Well, you're nearly fifty, but that won't save yer,' said Mr Watts. Resignedly, he filled the kettle and put it on a gas ring, knowing he'd got to do the washing-up himself. If his wife was lazy, she was still good-natured and always managed to give him a decent supper. Hearing footsteps on the stairs, he said, ''Enry's on 'is way out, Queenie. 'E's always goin' out, that brother of yourn.' The front door opened and closed.

'Well, 'e don't do no 'arm,' said Mrs Watts, 'and I expect 'e can enjoy a bit of company in a pub.'

'Not 'im,' said Mr Watts, ''e don't need company.'

'Course 'e does, Stan, 'e's still a grievin' widower and 'e knows 'e can get cheered up in a pub.'

'Always found 'im a funny bloke meself,' said Mr Watts, 'and it didn't do 'im much good losin' 'is wife

Matilda like that. Ruddy 'orrible that was, fallin' out of a train. Poor old Matty.'

'Don't talk about it,' said Mrs Watts, and let a shudder squirm its way through her stout and indolent body.

Lines at night didn't count if they couldn't be seen. It was only when they showed up under the light of shop windows or street lamps that they offered their challenge. It was then that Henry Brannigan had to step carefully. He sometimes had horrible dreams, dreams in which he trod on a pavement line and then had bad luck rushing at him in the shape of howling red-eyed wolves. In the nightmarish dreams he ran like a madman, the animals at his back, and every dream always finished with him running until he fell off the edge of the world into a black void. His plummeting fall jerked him awake and brought him out of his nightmare.

He went out frequently at night to escape the solitude of his room. He liked walking, he liked to use his long vigorous stride to eat up the pavements, knowing the lines that couldn't be seen didn't matter.

It was damned dark tonight, with no moon and the starry sky blanketed by heavy clouds. The patches of light at intervals caused him to watch for the visible lines. Approaching a pub that cast faint light, he knew a few lines would show up. A man appeared, coming towards him. Henry Brannigan judged they would meet in the faint light. Damnation. It was always a challenge to him not to falter or check, so he kept going, eyes searching for the lines he knew would be visible, even if only faintly. The approaching man had a stride as determined as his own. Curse him. Calamity loomed. Then the pub door opened and a woman in a large hat and a long coat came out. It caused the approaching man to change step and to

518

leave the pavement. It got him out of Henry Brannigan's way at a moment when lines appeared and he needed to lengthen his stride. He was able to do so freely, and a sigh of relief escaped him.

''Ere, 'alf a mo', dearie.' The woman was at his back, and his feet were in darkness again. He stopped. He owed her a favour, although she didn't know it. He turned. The faint light reached out to make her face visible. She was handsome after a fashion, but she was tarted up with paint and powder.

'What d'you want?' he asked.

'Make me an offer, lovey.'

He realized what she was, but he still owed her a favour. It wasn't often that someone's action was helpful. Usually it was the other way about. He parted his unbuttoned coat, thrust a hand into his pocket and drew out a silver coin, half a crown.

'Here,' he said, and gave it to her. Her hand closed over it, and its weight and its feel told her its value. She had had a blank evening, and no-one had even bought her a drink. She liked a drink, just one. She knew that a lot of drink didn't help a woman's looks, and she needed her looks. At thirty-eight she had to take care of them.

'Kind of yer, lovey,' she said, smiling up into his dark face, 'but can yer make it five bob? I've got a nice flat and you can stay till midnight, if yer like.'

'I don't go with women,' said Henry Brannigan, who would already have gone on his way if he hadn't felt that fate required him to be friendly as well as grateful. 'Out of respect for me late wife.'

'Oh, yer poor man, but what did yer give me this 'alf-crown for, then?' asked Madge Simpson, who'd been on the game for five years and knew how to keep an eye open for the coppers.

Henry Brannigan wasn't going to explain. People were bleeding idiots. None of them understood. That coroner hadn't understood. What a man had to do, he had to do.

'You 'ard-up?' he said to the woman.

'Who ain't?' said Madge Simpson.

'Well, keep the 'alf-crown.'

'You don't want nothing for it, lovey?'

'Nothing.'

'Yer a gent,' said Madge. 'Mind, I ain't fond of takin' something for nothing, I ain't come down to plain beggin' yet. 'Ere, come 'ome with me, anyway, an' keep me company for a bit. I'll make us a pot of tea and a sandwich, it's one of them evenings when customers don't seem in the mood.'

'I'm pleased to 'ave met yer, lady,' said Henry Brannigan, 'but I don't go in for keepin' company. Good night to yer.' And he went on his way. He entered the Walworth Road, which was full of lighted shop windows and street lamps. The pavements were bathed in light. His feet knew the Walworth Road paving stones well, he adjusted his stride to them.

''Ere, be matey.'

The woman had caught him up and was walking beside him, taking quick steps to keep up with him.

''Oppit, lady,' said Henry Brannigan, the familiar scowl appearing on his face.

'Don't be like that, lovey,' she said, and did a little one-two with her feet.

'What made you do that?' he asked, keeping relentlessly to his measured stride.

'I don't like treadin' on the lines,' she said, 'it's bad luck.'

'What?' Henry Brannigan could hardly believe his ears.

'Last time I trod a bit careless on a line, a customer did

520

it on me. Pulled 'is trousers on quick an' went off without payin', the swine,' said Madge. 'Not all me customers are gents, I can tell yer. 'Ere, I live in Amelia Street, it's just across the road. You can come an' spend 'alf an hour with me, can't yer? I can do with a bit of company – 'elp, I nearly 'it that crack. Cracks count as lines to me. Don't think I'm barmy, I ain't, I'm just superstitious. I don't walk under ladders, neither.' She stopped. 'Come on, share a pot of tea with me, I like yer, and I won't pester yer or ask to see yer wallet.'

'I'll do that, lady, I'll share a pot of tea with yer,' said Henry Brannigan, hiding the excitement of discovery. This woman felt the same way as he did about lines? 'Yes, I'll come with yer.'

'That's more like it,' said Madge, a good-natured woman, even if she was a fallen one. A fancy large-brimmed hat crowned her head, and her waisted coat owned a glossy collar of fox fur. She'd bought both items for a song down Petticoat Lane, and they gave her quite a posh look. But she didn't charge posh prices, her going rate was five bob. 'Come on, then, but don't tread on the tramlines.' She laughed.

'Tramlines count,' he said as they stepped off the kerb.

'What?' she asked.

'I'm careful meself about treadin' on lines.'

'Well, I never, are yer really?' said Madge. They crossed the road and she laughed again as they both took care not to tread on the tramlines. They reached the pavement. The road was darker on this side.

'We can walk easy now,' he said. 'Lines don't count, of course, if you can't see 'em.'

'That's right,' said Madge, entering Amelia Street with him. 'My, fancy you bein' superstitious as well, lovey. Ain't it a funny old world? Me lodgings ain't far down 'ere, except they're on the other side. Come on.' She took him across the street and to the house in which she lodged. She fished her key out of her handbag, slipped it into the lock and opened the door. A glowing gas mantle illuminated the passage. Lace curtains framed the approach to the stairs. 'This way,' she said, 'me dear old landlady don't mind me bringing gents 'ome. She 'ad gentlemen friends 'erself when she was a chorus girl up West.' Henry Brannigan closed the door and followed her up the stairs to the back room, where a slow-burning coal fire offered a warm cosiness. She took a box of matches from the mantelpiece, struck a match and applied the flame to a gas mantle. The onset of light drove away black shadows, and the room took on an inviting look. A rug of brown wool covered the linoleum in front of the hearth fender. Two leather-upholstered armchairs seemed slightly at odds with a kitchen dresser, but only in a friendly way. 'This is me livin' room,' said Madge. 'Me bedroom's on the landing, but we won't be usin' that, will we?'

'I ain't felt the need since me wife died,' said Henry Brannigan.

'All right, lovey, I ain't goin' to push yer. Take yer coat off, and yer titfer, and I'll put the kettle on.'

He took his hat and coat off and hung them on the door peg. She looked at him. His features were gaunt, his eyes dark and hollow, but he had the kind of strong-boned face that would have been handsome if there'd been more flesh to it. His black hair was well-brushed, his working clothes coarse and hard-wearing.

'Givin' me the once-over, are yer?' he said.

'Well, I like to see what I bring into me livin' room, ducky,' said Madge, and filled a tin kettle with water from a pitcher. She put the kettle on a gas ring. 'In me bedroom, well, I just shut me eyes. A gel can't be too

522

choosy when it's what you might call a matter of business. Come on, sit down.'

But Henry Brannigan remained on his feet, placing himself with his back to the fire and eyeing her in undisguised curiosity. Madge removed her hat and coat, and his dark eyes flickered, for she wore a white high-necked lace blouse with a lace front and a red flared skirt saucily short. It was knee-length, and the frilled hem of a white petticoat peeped and flirted above legs in lace-up boots and black stockings. Her hair was auburn, her mouth generously touched with lipstick and her face heavily powdered. She was a good five feet eight and still handsome. She'd been kept by a man for ten years, from the age of twenty-three. She'd have preferred marriage, but he had a wife. When she was thirty-three, he stopped visiting her. He had always visited twice a week, on Tuesday and Friday afternoons. When he failed to appear, she waited for an explanatory letter. It never came, and she had no idea where he lived. He had always kept that from her. She thought he must be either ill or dead, but was unable to find out. She felt bitter about it. With his disappearance, her allowance stopped. She thought about getting a job, but it was 1921, and any job was hard to come by. She took herself up West one evening and met a young RAF pilot. She was willing, he was eager. He took her to a small hotel in Kensington and she slept with him. When she woke up in the morning, he'd gone, leaving her three pounds on the bedside table. Truthfully, she hadn't thought about money. She simply owned a very healthy body and it was a bit starved. She put the three pounds in her purse and left the hotel, the manager giving her a funny look on her way out. Blow you, she thought.

She started looking for a job, a decent one. She didn't fancy factory work, not a bit, and not after ten years of being kept in comfortable style. She tried her luck in some West End clubs, thinking a job as a dining-room waitress might suit her. That proved unsuccessful. She had no family. She was the only child of a Bermondsey docker and his better half, and they were dead. But she met a very nice gent by one of the clubs, and he gave her a whole five quid for spending the night with him. It enabled her to set herself up in cheap lodgings. And that was the start of her real fall from grace. She'd come down in the world since then, a long way down, and had finished up here while plying for trade in Walworth pubs. She had to keep her eye open for the rozzers. She hadn't ever been run in. A girl got her name in the papers when that happened.

'You're on the game, of course,' said Henry Brannigan.

'Well, how'd yer guess, lovey?' she smiled. She quite liked him. She felt he was a bit withdrawn, but he looked a girl in the eye and spoke frankly. Well, everyone on the game was always a girl. 'Like me workin' outfit, do yer?'

'Suits yer,' he said, 'you've got fine legs. Bit too much powder, though.'

'Eh?' said Madge.

'Tone it down, you don't want to look as if you fell in a flour bag. A bit less powder and not so much paint, an' yer'll look more like a lady than a pro. Men fancy ladies.'

'Saucy devil,' said Madge, but laughed. 'Like a sandwich, would yer?'

'A biscuit would do for me.'

'Sure?'

'Biscuit and a cup of tea, I don't need more.'

'Suits me too,' said Madge, and he watched her as she brought out a tin of biscuits from the dresser cupboard and prepared to make the tea. She chatted while she waited for the kettle to boil. He made responsive comments. He was absorbed, even fascinated. What a find, a woman who shared his feeling that to tread on lines was bad luck. Kids played at it on their way home from school, giving yells if they failed, and pushing at each other to try to bring about failure. But it was a serious business when you were an adult, and sod kids who got in your way. He couldn't remember the last time he'd consorted with a woman apart from his wife. And his wife had gone now.

Madge made the tea, let it stand for a minute or so, then filled two cups with the steaming golden liquid. God's gift a cup of hot tea was, and nor was it unpleasing to have a man keeping her company, a man who wasn't here to go to bed with her. She got him to sit down in front of the fire, and she sat down herself, in the other armchair, each of them with a cup of tea and a biscuit. He was a strong-looking figure even seated. She was a woman who had an affinity with men, and so she sat, of course, with her legs and knees unveiled and the lacy hem of her white petticoat showing.

''Ow long you been watchin' lines?' he asked.

'Five years,' she said, 'ever since a bloke either died on me or walked out on me. Something got to me, something about bad luck an' good luck, and I'm superstitious up to the top of me corsets now.'

'Lines, I reckon, are put in yer way to test yer will power,' said Henry Brannigan, crunching biscuit with strong teeth. 'I ain't sayin' it applies to everyone, just to some of us. You're kind of kindred, lady.'

'Kind of tarty, yer mean,' said Madge.

'Not to me,' he said, 'except for yer paint an' powder, but that can easy be washed off. It ain't tarty to ask me up 'ere to share a pot of tea with yer, and to sit me in front of yer fire. That's human kindness.'

'What's yer name?' asked Madge.

He wasn't keen on offering his name to all and sundry, not since the inquest, when the newspapers had shouted it out.

''Ave I asked you for your name, lady?'

'No, but I'd like to know yours, seein' you just said something very nice to me,' said Madge.

'I'm Henry.'

'Just Henry?' Madge smiled. 'All right, good enough, Henry. And I'm Madge. I'll be thinkin' of you when I'm next walkin' the pavement an' dodgin' the lines.'

'That's it, you watch them lines.'

'Mind, I only do it sometimes. You can't be doin' it all the time, only when the mood takes yer.'

'You should do it all the time. Once you start, you're on the wheel of fortune, take it from me.'

'Oh, it don't count if you ain't botherin',' said Madge, and Henry Brannigan shook his head dubiously. 'More tea? Let's give you a refill.' She took his cup and saucer, got up and took the cosy off the teapot. She refilled his cup and her own. He thanked her in a sober way, looking at her in her white blouse and short saucy skirt. She sat down again, and he eyed her legs quite openly. She didn't mind. She liked a man to be frankly appreciative.

'What got you on the game?' he asked.

'Me legs?' she said jokingly.

'I shouldn't think so,' he said.

'Well, I'll tell yer, Henry, seein' yer keepin' me friendly company,' she said, and told him how she had been a comfortably kept woman for ten years before her lover just disappeared from her life. She recounted what happened after that. 'Well, I didn't fancy slavin' in a fact'ry. It spoils yer for fact'ry work, bein' kept by a gen'rous bloke who's fond of yer as well. Mind, I sometimes wish it 'adn't

526

spoiled me that much, I might 'ave got used to a job and ended up a respectable workin' woman, or even got married.'

Henry Brannigan thought for a moment, then said, 'I'll keep you.'

'What?' said Madge.

'A woman like you, and kind of kindred,' he said, 'you shouldn't be on the game. I'll make you an allowance. I've got savings, and the insurance money paid to me on the death of me wife, and I've also got me wages of two pound ten a week.'

'What?' said Madge again, staring at him. 'Listen, Henry, you've only just met me, and I ain't takin' that proposition as serious.'

'I'm offerin' serious,' he said. 'It'll keep you out of pubs, it'll keep you off the game, which'll turn you into an old 'aybag sooner than yer think if you don't give it up. You look an 'andsome woman to me. That day you picked up a West End gent and 'e paid yer for services rendered, I'd say that was a day when you trod on a line after startin' the fateful business of avoidin' them. That time with the clubman put you on the game, an' that was bad luck, I tell yer. It's bad luck for any woman the day she goes on the game. Now you get yerself a flat, say at twelve bob a week.'

'Twelve bob would get any woman an 'andsome flat,' said Madge, wondering if he really was serious.

'Well, like I said, Madge, you're 'andsome yerself,' said Henry Brannigan. 'I'll take care of the rent an' the cost of keepin' yerself in decent comfort.'

'As yer mistress?' said Madge.

'I ain't askin' for that, but I'll come to keep yer company frequent.'

'But you'll want yer pleasure, won't yer?'

527

'Just yer company,' he said, 'I'm short of company that suits me.'

''Old on, ducky,' said Madge, 'there's a ruddy catch somewhere. You'll keep me and only ask for me company now and again? Don't yer fancy me, then?'

'I ain't partial to usin' a woman like that,' he said, 'I'm more partial to sharin' 'er fireside, or doin' a bit of walkin' with 'er when the summer evenings come. We can beat the lines together.'

'Sounds nice,' said Madge, 'but not much of a bargain for you.'

'You look for a flat tomorrer,' he said, 'and I'll meet yer outside the town 'all at eight in the evenin'. Are yer willin'?'

'Henry, you're cheatin' yerself,' she said.

'Are yer willin'?'

'More like dreamin',' said Madge. 'No, of course I'm willin', but it's goin' to cost yer, Henry, for just me company. Rent an' keep cost more than a bag of 'ot chestnuts.'

'Just one thing,' he said. 'No more customers. You got that, lady?'

'That was included when I said I was willin'. I don't go in for cheatin' a man.'

'It don't pay a woman, cheatin',' said Henry Brannigan, and the ghost of a smile came and went.

CHAPTER ELEVEN

Sammy, who had left for Manchester on Monday evening without returning to the office, was back on Wednesday afternoon. In Manchester he'd been talking to mill owners. His new contract with Coates meant he couldn't take the slightest risk in respect of fabric deliveries.

Susie, hearing him enter his office, immediately went to see him.

'Ah, good afternoon, Miss Brown,' he said, hanging up his hat and coat.

'Ah to you too,' said Susie, and walked up to him, lifted her face and pursed her lips.

'Not in office time, Miss Brown,' said Sammy.

A kick arrived on his left shin.

'Take that,' said Susie. There had been other times in her prolonged and electric relationship with Sammy when she'd had to deliver kicks.

'You did that with your eyes shut,' said Sammy, and kissed her.

'That's better,' said Susie.

'Not bad at all,' said Sammy, 'but I think we'll have to stop meetin' like this in office hours.' But another kiss arrived, a lovely one to Susie. He had a man's fine firm lips, and didn't believe in pecking a girl.

'Now you're takin' advantage,' she said.

'Well, Susie, while I'm not purportin'—'

'While you're not what?'

'While I'm not purportin' to imply the Manchester girls don't have fashionable legs and female bosoms, the fact is what you've got, Susie, is high-class and adorable all over. Mind, I haven't been all over yet—'

'Sammy!'

'So I'm speakin' blindly, you might say, but not without bein' confident and optimistic. Accordingly, when we keep meetin' like this I can't help takin' advantage – hold on, is me declaration of confidence amusin' you, Miss Brown?'

Susie, laughing, said, 'Sammy, I love it. More, please.'

'Later, Miss Brown, later. Did you see Eli?'

'I did, and he's goin' to put his nose into every suitable warehouse. Sammy, exactly why do you want him to buy up our kind of materials?'

'Well,' said Sammy, 'Harriet—'

'Miss de Vere.'

'The selfsame, Susie. Our summer fashions are sellin' like hot faggots in her branches—'

'Cakes. Hot cakes.'

'Same thing, Susie, except hot faggots are tastier and more nourishing,' said Sammy. 'Now, on account of that, Miss de Vere, who is actually a widow name of Mrs Bird, persuaded her directors to give us a huge contract for autumn and winter designs.'

'I know that,' said Susie.

'Well, I'm glad you do, Susie, it does me heart good to know your brainbox is tickin', because we've got to make sure we don't fall flat on our faces when it comes to delivery. I acquired promises in Manchester regardin' delivery of fabrics, and before I went there I had a specialized talk with Harriet—'

'Miss de Vere,' said Susie. Before becoming engaged to Sammy, she'd felt somewhat threatened by his attachment to his old girlfriend, Rachel Goodman. So she'd discouraged the development of anything but a strictly business relationship between Sammy and Harriet de Vere. Harriet

had found Sammy mesmerizing. However, she had subsequently met Boots and found him fascinating. Even so,
Susie was taking no chances. The horrendous casualties of
the Great War had resulted in a shortage of eligible men
and a worrying surplus of women.

'The obligin' lady—'

'I don't like that word,' said Susie.

'Let's say she was reasonable, then,' said Sammy.
'She'll have the delivery date altered to give us two extra
weeks. All the same, promises from the mills don't always
work out, which is why we want Eli Greenberg to nose out
our kind of materials in certain London warehouses and to
buy them for us.'

'But if the Lancashire mills come up with deliveries in
good time,' said Susie, 'we'll be stuck with all the fabrics
Mr Greenberg buys on our behalf.'

'Ah well,' said Sammy.

'Mister Sammy Adams, kindly explain what ah well
means,' demanded Susie.

'Yes, you've got it, Susie.'

'I haven't got it,' said Susie.

'Well, it could mean some of our competitors will be
dyin' of wantin' what we happen to have,' said Sammy.

'Sammy, that's not fair.'

'Eh?' said Sammy.

'You'll have cornered the market,' said Susie. 'It's not
nice.'

'Pardon?' said Sammy.

'It's not decent,' said Susie.

'Am I hearin' you correct, Miss Brown, or is there
something wrong with me listenin' equipment?'

'If I thought I'd helped you starve our competitors, I
just couldn't look the vicar in the eye on our weddin' day,'
said Susie.

'I'm glad you've got principles, Susie,' said Sammy, 'I've got some meself. Would I let our Shoreditch competitors starve for want of fabrics?'

'I hope you've still got some Christian goodness,' said Susie. 'And I've just thought, they'd be getting all they wanted from the mills. Except, of course, some firms do order from the London wholesalers.'

'Well, if our competitors couldn't get what they wanted from the mills, I'd sell them what they wanted from our stocks,' said Sammy.

'There's a good boy,' said Susie.

'At a fair price, of course.'

'Sammy?'

'One of me strictest business principles, Susie, is never to let me charitable inclinations interfere with the profits.'

'You're wicked,' said Susie.

'Well, we've got to live, Susie.'

'Yes, ruination's very upsetting,' said Susie. 'By the way Boots wants to see you.'

'If he's been enquirin' after me, you can let him know I'm here,' said Sammy.

'I don't think it was an enquiry,' said Susie.

'Watch what you're goin' to say next.'

'Oh, he just said tell Junior to come and see me as soon as he gets back from Manchester – Sammy, don't you dare!'

Sammy was after her. Susie fled back to her office. Sammy, grinning, went to see Boots. On the way he looked in on Emily, busy typing in her own little office. Its privacy related to the fact that she was the wife of a director.

'Hello, Em. Everything all right with you?' Sammy thought she was getting much too thin.

Emily's smile was overbright, so were her big green eyes.

'Hello, Sammy love. I'm fine. I think me lord and master's been askin' after you.'

'It's my serious opinion that Boots has been the fam'ly's lord and master since he first put on long trousers,' said Sammy.

'It's his posh education,' said Emily.

'I'm now goin' to sort him out,' said Sammy, and departed for his brother's office, where he informed Boots he was against being given messages by his personal assistant that made him sound like the office boy.

'Is that a fact?' said Boots.

'I hear someone's been referrin' to me as Junior,' said Sammy.

'First I've heard of it,' said Boots, and Sammy cottoned on.

'That Susie,' he said, grinning again. 'Wait till she's Mrs Sammy Adams.'

'We're all waiting for that,' said Boots. 'How did you get on in Manchester?'

'Manchester was what you call promisin',' said Sammy, 'but I'm buyin' in from London wholesalers in case the promisin' bit gets rheumatism. Before I took me train to Manchester, I had to talk serious to Harriet about that delivery clause.'

'You mean you floored her,' said Boots.

'Well, she fell about a bit,' said Sammy, 'but the delivery date's goin' to be put back two weeks. Now can I ask what you wanted to see me about?'

'The Bermondsey scrap yard's been temporarily shut down, Sammy.'

'It's what?'

'That's just between you, me and Susie's dad at the

moment,' said Boots, and went on to recount how a young girl's body had been found in the gravel under the shed floor. He'd been keeping in touch with the police, and an hour ago they'd informed him over the phone that the girl's identity had been established. She was the daughter of a Bermondsey couple, officially listed as missing from home thirteen months ago. Her name was Ivy Connor and she'd been twelve years old at the time. The pathologist had diagnosed strangulation.

'Jesus,' breathed Sammy, 'a twelve-year-old girl? The sod who did that to her ought to be put in an empty room with her father for an hour before they hang him.'

'I feel the same,' said Boots. 'Her name and the pathologist's report will be in today's evening papers. So far, Susie doesn't know the body was discovered in our scrap yard, and Jim's said nothing to her or any of his family. Further, he's kept the relevant page of their daily paper to himself. He doesn't want Susie upset with the wedding not far away, and she won't necessarily find out it concerns our Bermondsey yard unless the papers mention the firm's name again. On the other hand, there'll be an inquest, of course, and I don't doubt Jim will be called on to confirm he was present when the body was discovered. He and his assistant are working at the Kennington yard at the moment. How much d'you know about the previous owners of the Bermondsey yard, Collier and Son?'

'Couple of boozers,' said Sammy.

'I think the police are investigating them.'

'Waste of time,' said Sammy. 'Old man Collier and his son Walter as boozers are harmless except to their business. Listen, I think Susie'll have to be told.'

'I thought you might think that,' said Boots, 'but left it to you to decide.'

'The staff don't know?' said Sammy.

'Some do, those who read the newspaper accounts,' said Boots, 'but they're keeping quiet.'

'I'll tell Susie,' said Sammy, and did so at once. It was a shock to her, but she was her dad's daughter, she had his brand of resilience and was concerned more for him than for any shadow it cast over the wedding. She was concerned because the yard had been shut down just when he'd been appointed manager and because he'd had to see the body.

'I feel sick, Sammy. That poor young girl.'

'I share your feeling, Susie, and don't think I don't.'

Susie spoke to her dad that evening. She'd bought an evening paper on her way home. The details were all there, all relating to the grisly conclusion that the girl had been murdered and her body hidden in gravel under a shed in a scrap metal yard in Bermondsey. Reported missing from her home thirteen months ago, her murder was now commanding a full investigation by the police. There was no mention of Adams Enterprises as the present owners of the yard, but the report did state that the owners at the time of the murder were Collier and Son. It also stated that two men were helping the police with their enquiries.

Susie agreed with her dad not to discuss the matter with the rest of the family.

'You've come, then,' said Henry Brannigan in the evening twilight. The woman had got to the town hall before him.

'You didn't think I'd play you up, did yer, Henry?' asked Madge.

He looked at her. Her face was only lightly powdered, her lips not quite so richly carmine. She was wearing a smaller hat and a less fancy coat. She looked very respectable, in fact. She had a little smile on her face.

'Did yer tread on any lines gettin' 'ere?' he asked.

'Not one,' said Madge, 'I wasn't goin' to risk a bit of bad luck poppin' up and knockin' me off me feet. It can injure a girl. I must say you're lookin' a gent this evenin', Henry.'

He wore no coat. He was dressed in a serviceable blue suit that fitted him well, with a collar and tie and a trilby hat. His eyes looked deepset in his gaunt face. He was middle-aged, but his body was straight and without a paunch. She was willing to bet he was as strong as a horse, and that he was good in bed.

'You're lookin' presentable yerself,' he said, 'but don't think I didn't like what you wore last night, except for yer paint an' powder.'

'Oh, yer fancied me saucy skirt, lovey?' said Madge, smiling. 'You should've said, I'd 'ave worn it again tonight.'

'Good company you were,' said Henry Brannigan. ''Ave yer found a flat?'

'I found a really nice one in the New Kent Road, above that little paper shop,' said Madge. 'It's got its own door an' stairs at the side of the shop, and it's two nice rooms and a kitchen, it's all self-contained at ten an' six a week. You'll be able to visit when yer like, with yer own door key. I'll cook supper for yer sometimes, if you fancy that. D'yer want to come an' see it? Only I said I'd take it, it's fully-furnished and I gave the newsagent five bob as a deposit on the first week's rent. I couldn't afford to give 'im the lot in case you – well, you know.'

'In case I didn't turn up.'

'Well, a girl can't trust every man she meets, even if she does like 'im,' said Madge.

'We'll go an' see it,' said Henry Brannigan. 'I know that shop, we'll cut through Wansey Street. Watch the lines, it ain't dark yet, an' seein' we're after settin' you up in the flat, let's keep bad luck away from its door or we'll risk it catchin' fire the day you move in.'

'Yer a thoughtful man about me superstitiousness, Henry,' she said, and they began their walk, partners in their belief that it was unlucky to tread on lines, although Madge only practised this belief when the mood took her. They went down Wansey Street and made for Balfour Street, which would bring them into the New Kent Road. Dusk fell and the lines between paving stones began to be lost to the eye. Treading on them didn't count then. They passed the sagging gates of the destroyed factory. Madge made a comment. 'They ought to build a new one,' she said, 'an' give the people round 'ere a bit of work. I did 'ear a new one might be goin' up.'

'You 'eard that, did yer?' Henry Brannigan gave it some thought. 'Well, you ladies usually manage to 'ear more than men do.'

'Henry, you got a nice way of makin' a lady of me.'

'A woman like you, you've got the makings of bein' a lady, that's me honest opinion. I 'eard meself that this place is a kids' playground, which keeps 'em off the streets an' gettin' in people's way. Watch that lighted bit of pavement comin' up, the lines'll be showin'.'

Madge did a little one-two step at the right moment, and Henry Brannigan couldn't help being highly approving of her.

He liked the flat. It was very nicely furnished, the bedroom neat, the living room cosy and the kitchen just right. It had new wallpaper and an almost new gas oven.

'Yer really like it?' said Madge.

'Be a pleasure for me to keep yer comfortably resident 'ere, Madge. I'll give yer thirty bob a week to pay for yer rent and yer livin' expenses.'

'Thirty bob?'

'It'll keep yer respectable, an' now and again I might treat yer to some new togs. That fair, is it?'

'It's all that to me,' said Madge, 'but I still can't see what you get out of it.'

'I like yer, I like yer company, and I like bein' able to talk to yer,' he said. 'I'll pay you the allowance monthly. Here.' He took out his wallet and extracted six pound notes. Madge reckoned he had twenty of them in the wallet. It didn't give her ideas. If she'd become a tart, she'd never been a sly or calculating one. Henry represented the turn of the tide, a turn that was highly welcome to her at her age. 'That's yer first month's,' he said, and handed her the banknotes. 'I'll come an' see yer Tuesday an' Thursday evenings, and I'll take you out Saturday evenings an' Sunday afternoons. I know yer'll play fair with me.'

'You sure you know?' said Madge.

'I'm bettin' on yer.'

'I'm short of flour and bakin' powder,' said Mrs Brown the next morning. Her husband and Susie had gone to work, and Sally and Freddy to school, but Will was still around and thinking of going to the public library to borrow a couple of books. 'And I need some bakin' eggs as well.'

'What's bakin' eggs?' asked Will.

'Cracked ones that come half price. I'll have to go out, I can't start me bakin' till I do.'

'Well, I'm goin' to the library, Mum,' said Will, 'I'll get the stuff you want.'

'Oh, would you?' Mrs Brown spoke fondly. 'I'm a bit busy, love, I'd be grateful. I'd like two pounds of self-raisin' flour, a tin of bakin' powder, four cracked eggs

538

that's not too cracked, and two pounds of caster sugar.'

'Right,' said Will, a little grin on his face as he decided which shop he'd patronize. 'Special reference to four cracked eggs not too cracked, eh, Ma?'

'If you would, love,' said Mrs Brown. 'You can take me shoppin' bag.'

'D'you mind if I don't?' said Will. 'I'm a bloke, not a mum.'

'Oh, you don't want to take no notice of what people might say,' said the affable Mrs Brown, 'and you'll have to carry the shoppin' in something.'

'I'll work it out,' said Will, who was keeping active but without putting himself under stress. He'd had a couple of mild evening attacks, that was all.

There were customers in the shop, and Mr Urcott, Miss Banks and Annie were all busy. Will, entering, hid himself behind a large lady whose voluminous apparel doubled her size. Her hat was a further help. Not until Annie finished serving her did Will become visible. It was like a Houdini trick to Annie. One moment there was only a large lady at the counter, the next moment Will materialized. With a grin on his face, of course. Still, he had a nice face, a sort of country face because it looked brown and healthy. A girl could put up with a grin on that kind of face. But he's going to sauce me, she thought, and prepared herself for verbal battle.

'Can I help you, sir?' she asked.

'Any cauliflowers, miss?' enquired Will.

'No, nor any coal, either, nor any soldiers' sauce, except yours.'

'What a funny shop,' said Will. 'Never mind, I'll try for two pounds of self-raisin' flour, two pounds of caster sugar, a tin of bakin' powder and four cracked eggs not too cracked.'

'I hope you're serious,' said Annie, bobbed hair smooth, neat and shining, grey eyes daring him to be joking.

'Mrs Brown is,' said Will.

'Mrs Brown?'

'My mother. She wants to do some bakin'. Go to a good grocer's, she said, where they serve you with a smile and don't give you any lip.'

'Any lip? You can talk,' said Annie. 'Are you really shoppin' for your mum?'

'It's me pleasure,' said Will.

'Nice you've got some good points, like bringing a girl flowers and doin' your mum's shoppin',' said Annie, and served him. The flour, sugar and baking powder were placed on the counter, and then she found four very acceptable cracked eggs for him. Brightly she asked, 'Have you brought your shoppin' bag, sir?'

A female customer spoke up. Like most cockney women, she wasn't given to reticence.

'Oh, is yer wife laid up, young man? If I was laid up, I don't know that my old man would let 'imself be seen with a shoppin' bag. I admire yer for not mindin'.'

'You don't seem to have it with you, sir,' said Annie, tongue in cheek.

'No, I left it on a tram with me handbag,' said Will. Customers laughed. 'Use this, miss.' He brought a folded brown paper carrier bag out of his pocket, the one he had bought previously from Annie. 'I'll give you shoppin' bag,' he murmured.

Annie placed his purchases in the carrier. The eggs, which she'd put into a brown paper bag, she rested carefully on top.

'There you are, sir, thank you for your custom – oh, and

you can get a nice strong straw shoppin' bag for sixpence down the market.'

'You can get carpet beaters too,' said Will.

'What for?' smiled Annie.

'Smackin' saucy bottoms,' murmured Will, and departed, leaving Annie not quite sure who'd won the battle. Still, it had been nice seeing him. She hoped he hadn't forgotten about Sunday, only he hadn't mentioned it.

'Mum, 'ave yer got a cushion I could borrer?' asked Freddy a few minutes after he arrived home from school.

'What d'you want a cushion for, lovey?'

'For Cassie.'

'Cassie?'

'Yes, that girl who's me new mate,' said Freddy. 'I'm takin' 'er for a ride on me bike again. She's outside.'

'Well, bring 'er in,' said Mrs Brown, 'you don't have to keep your friends on the doorstep.'

'Yes, go on, bring 'er in,' said Sally, 'me and mum would like to see where you put the cushion.'

'Bless us,' said Mrs Brown, 'don't you go puttin' no cushion where you shouldn't, Freddy, not like you did with your cap.'

'I didn't do it, Cassie did,' said Freddy, and went to the kitchen door. 'Cassie, come in,' he called, and Cassie entered the passage and came through to the kitchen.

'Oh, 'ello,' she said.

'You've got a sister called Annie,' said Sally.

'Yes, our Will's friendly with her,' smiled Mrs Brown.

'Are you Freddy's mum?' asked Cassie.

'Yes, I have that pleasure,' said Mrs Brown.

'We don't 'ave a mum,' said Cassie, 'she died. But we've got a nice dad that builds railway engines. 'E saved a lady from being eaten by lions once.'

'My, did he do that?' said Mrs Brown.

'Yes, it was when 'e was in darkest Africa,' said Cassie. ''E was a famous explorer, 'e was explorin' a jungle and 'e saw this lady. She was all tattered an' torn. Well, 'er clothes were. 'Er ball gown was nearly ruined by the lions' claws. They were runnin' after 'er.'

'Why was she wearin' a ball gown in a jungle?' asked Sally.

'She was goin' to a ball with an African prince,' said Cassie, 'only the lions ate 'im.'

Sally rolled her eyes. Mrs Brown smiled.

'My goodness, Cassie,' she said, 'why did they want to eat the lady as well?'

'Dad didn't say.' Cassie did a bit of thinking. 'Oh, yes, I remember now, it was for afters. Lions like afters.'

''Ere, Cassie,' said Freddy, who'd heard a lot like this before, 'd'yer want a slice of cake?'

'Yes, please, I'm not 'aving none at 'ome,' said Cassie, 'I told Annie I was 'aving a ride on your bike.'

'Here we are, love,' said Mrs Brown and cut slices for all three of them.

'Cassie, you 'aven't told us how your dad actu'lly saved the lady,' said Sally.

'Don't worry,' said Freddy, 'she won't forget to tell yer.'

'Yes, me dad got down from the elephant 'e was ridin',' said Cassie, eating cake, 'and 'e swept the lady up into 'is arms. Her hat fell off, but she didn't mind.'

'Fancy wearin' an 'at with a ball gown,' said Sally.

'Well, it was rainin' a bit,' said Cassie, rarely at a loss. 'Me dad said you should 'ave 'eard the lions, they didn't 'alf roar, 'e said.' Cassie ate more cake. ''E climbed up on his elephant with the lady an' they galloped off.'

'Crikey, you sure, Cassie?' queried Sally. 'I mean,

gallopin' elephants, I never 'eard of elephants gallopin' before.'

Cassie did some more thinking. She plucked at her fertile imagination.

'Well, it was galumpin' actu'lly,' she said. 'Elephants do a lot of galumpin' in darkest Africa. After me dad 'ad saved the lady, she wanted to marry 'im, but 'e was too busy at the time, so she gave 'im a lock of 'er golden 'air instead. And I think she sent 'im a Christmas card once, with robins on it.' She smiled at Freddy's mum. 'That was ever such nice cake, Mrs Brown. 'Ave yer got a cushion I could use for the bike ride, please?'

'Get one from the sofa, Freddy,' said Mrs Brown. 'Cassie, you mind you put it on the carrier, not anywhere else.'

'Yes, I can't put it in me things,' said Cassie, 'a cushion's too big. Our Aunt Eileen 'ad to kneel on a church cushion once, but it did 'er back in an' she 'ad to be lifted out of the pew by a fire engine. She was ever so blushin'. Well the 'Ouse of Lords was there, it was in St Paul's Cathedral.'

Sally had one of her hysterical fits. Mrs Brown just smiled placidly.

'Come on, Cassie,' said Freddy, wearing a huge grin, 'let's get the cushion.'

He and Cassie were outside a minute later with the bike. Sally brought hers out too. Cassie was placing the cushion on Freddy's carrier when Mr Ponsonby appeared.

'Well, dear me, dear me,' he said, 'what's all this on the pavement?'

'It's our feet, Mr Ponsonby,' said Sally.

'And our bikes,' said Freddy.

Mr Ponsonby peered and murmured.

'Good gracious, and a cushion too,' he said.

'Yes, it's for Cassie to ride on,' said Freddy. 'This is Cassie, she's me new mate.'

'Good afternoon,' said Mr Ponsonby, and raised his bowler hat.

''Ello,' said Cassie, 'you give me a peppermint once.'

'So I did, so I did. Did I?' Mr Ponsonby puzzled over it. 'What a charming girl. Ah, yes, and Sally too. You must all have a peppermint now. Dear me, what am I thinking of not to have offered them?' He produced the bag, and Sally, Cassie and Freddy took one each. 'Where is my camera? Bless me, two such pretty girls and I've forgotten my camera. Stay there and I shall bring it. Good afternoon, good afternoon.' Off he went, his pigeon-toed walk making him look as if he was twinkling over the pavement.

'Come on, 'e won't come back,' said Freddy. 'On yer get, Cassie, and I'll ride yer round the 'ouses. You can come, if yer like, Sally, I see you got yer wooden legs on.'

'Oh, she ain't got wooden ones really, 'as she?' said Cassie, sitting astride the cushion.

'Well, she used to 'ave ord'nary short ones,' said Freddy, 'so she went an' bought wooden ones down the market.'

'Golly, they look real,' said Cassie.

'You're both daft,' said Sally, and away she went on her bike. Freddy went whooping after her with his delighted passenger.

Henry Brannigan, on arrival home from work, put his head round the kitchen door. His sister was preparing supper for herself and her husband. Her crumpled blouse could have done with some ironing, and her hair could have done with some hairpins.

''Ere y'ar, Queenie.'

'What's this?' asked Queenie Watts.

'Box of choc'lates,' said her brother. 'I appreciate you fixin' me up with lodgings.'

Mrs Watts, taking the box out of its bag, gazed at it in bliss.

'Well, ain't you a love?' she said. 'And you ain't no trouble, 'Enry; I'm pleased to 'ave yer after all yer troubles. 'Ere, is that a new coat yer wearin'? It looks really nice on yer.'

'I reckoned it was time I 'ad a new one.'

'Listen, what d'yer go out a lot for of an evenin'?' asked Mrs Watts. 'You found yerself someone you like? Only you never come an' talk about yerself.'

'I 'appen to 'ave got over me troubles, Queenie.'

'That's good, 'Enry. Yer still a fine strong man, except yer don't always look as if yer put enough food into yerself, and yer don't go in for talkin' much. You could be welcome company for someone like a widder woman if yer talked a bit more.'

'It's been me troubles and me bad luck,' said Henry Brannigan, 'and all them street kids gettin' in a man's way.'

'Gettin' in yer way?'

'Specially some. Still, can't be 'elped.'

'Well, there's got to be kids, 'Enry.' Mrs Watts helped herself to a cream chocolate. 'It wouldn't be no life for anyone if there wasn't no kids. Mine are off me 'ands, of course, but I'm 'oping for some grandkids some day.'

'You could do with some 'airpins first, Queenie, if yer don't mind me sayin' so.'

'I don't know where all me 'airpins get to,' said Mrs Watts, and ate another chocolate.

'You could look a bit 'andsome if you took more time with yerself.'

'It's me back, yer know, 'Enry, it catches me something chronic, but the choc'lates'll cheer me up. Yer a good sort, an' don't you let street kids worry yer.'

'Young devils some of them are,' said Henry Brannigan, and went up to his room.

CHAPTER TWELVE

The following afternoon, Sammy's mother entered his office. She was known to her family as Chinese Lady on account of her almond eyes and the fact that she had once taken in washing. She was in her fiftieth year, a slim woman of upright carriage and firm bosom. As she had once said to Boots, she didn't believe in letting anything become unfirm. Not that she'd been referring to her bosom. Never would she have mentioned it to any of her sons. She regarded bosoms as unmentionable, in fact. No, she'd been talking about women who let themselves go. Go where? asked Boots. Chinese Lady simply gave him a look. She'd been giving her eldest son those kind of looks ever since his schooldays, when he'd learned to use his tongue in a way she found highly suspicious.

She appeared in Sammy's office wearing a brown velvet toque hat and a beige-coloured raincoat. She looked sprightly. Boots was there as well as Sammy.

'Hello, who's this lady?' asked Sammy. 'Hold on, is that you, Ma?'

'I don't know how many times I've told you not to call me Ma,' said Chinese Lady. 'I don't mind any of us bein' poor, but I didn't bring any of you up to be common.'

'Who's poor?' asked Boots.

'You know what I mean,' said Chinese Lady, who always stuck to her guns however much her sons tried to confuse her. 'I don't want people tellin' me that Sammy's grown up common, specially now he's in business. Mind, it's not the sort of business I'd of expected of any of you, ladies' clothes and things I won't mention. I can't bring meself to even look in that shop window of yours downstairs. When I think of you, Boots, lettin' my youngest put things like that in the windows of all 'is shops, I wonder you sometimes don't feel uncomf'table.'

'I suppose I'm blasé about it,' said Boots.

'Don't you use them French words of yours to me,' said Chinese Lady, 'you know I don't hold with them, nor with them fast French females you learned them from durin' the war. Still, you come out of the war without gettin' your head blown off, so I won't go on at you about lettin' Sammy get a bit unrespectable in his business. I just hope he won't end up leadin' his whole fam'ly astray. Lizzy was only sayin' the other day that it's embarrassin' havin' all her brothers workin' in ladies' unmentionables.'

'I work in a suit myself,' said Boots.

'I do too,' said Sammy, 'you got my word for it, me old love.'

'Don't be familiar,' said Chinese Lady, 'you know what I mean. It's just not decent, designing things for female persons.' She was on her favourite hobby-horse, and Boots and Sammy knew it. 'I don't mind frocks and skirts and suchlike, but things, well, I can't hardly bear thinking about it.'

'I suppose I'm blasé about it myself,' repeated Boots. 'Well, I was taken into ladies' underwear by Emily at an early age. In Gamages.'

'I don't know how you can talk so disreputable,' said Chinese Lady, 'and usin' vulgar French words again as well.'

'You're a good old girl,' said Boots.

'And might I point out we don't design ladies' unmentionables ourselves?' said Sammy. 'We acquire them from manufacturers.'

'Kindly don't argue,' said Chinese Lady firmly, 'I don't like any of my children to be argufyin'.'

'Children? Who said that?' asked Sammy of the pile of work on his desk. He knew it was no good telling Chinese Lady he was up to his ears. 'Anyway, Ma, to what do we owe the pleasure of your visit and your omelette?'

'Omelette?' said Chinese Lady. 'What omelette?'

'I think he means homily,' said Boots.

'And what's that, might I ask? Another French word? If you must know why I'm here, I just happened to be passing.'

'Passing, yes, I see,' said Boots.

'Yes, I thought I'd better pop in and see what you're gettin' up to,' said Chinese Lady, who made a habit of that. She was, of course, proud of her sons' accomplishments, but was never going to encourage them to get above themselves. She was always saying to her daughter Lizzy that they were good boys really, except that Sammy didn't go to church as often as he ought to. Lizzy was of the opinion that Sammy was a live wire who'd only go to church regularly if he could sell the vicar a new organ, that Boots was a danger to well-behaved housewives and Tommy as honest as the day was long.

'Well, we won't keep you, Ma,' said Sammy, who'd been talking to Boots about the murder investigation. It seemed from today's papers that old man Collier and his son had been cleared.

'Also,' said Chinese Lady, 'I happen to be meetin' Rosie here from her school. I'm buyin' her a special little something for always helpin' me to wind me knittin' wool. Where's Susie?'

'I think she's workin',' said Sammy, 'it's what she's here for.'

That went over Chinese Lady's head.

'Perhaps I'll have a cup of tea with her in her office while I'm waitin',' she said.

'What's she sayin' now, Boots?' asked Sammy helplessly.

'She wants you to put the office kettle on,' said Boots, as Chinese Lady advanced on Susie's office door. At the door she turned, frowning.

'I've just remembered,' she said, 'I've been readin' about a murder done in a Bermondsey scrap metal yard. Boots, I hope it wasn't an Adams yard.'

'Well, old lady,' said Boots at his most reassuring, 'you can take it from me that we didn't own any yard in Bermondsey until a couple of weeks ago.'

'I don't know I hold with you and Sammy bein' in the scrap metal business at all,' she said soberly. 'There's a lot of shifty people in that sort of trade. It's no wonder there's been a murder.'

'Now don't give our yards a bad name, Ma,' said Sammy, 'we don't go in for anything shifty.'

'I should hope not,' said Chinese Lady. 'That poor girl,' she said, shaking her head. 'Still, I won't keep on at you about your business, I don't believe in bein' interferin', and I'm sure you both do your best. There's some mothers that have got worse sons, a lot worse. You're good boys most of the time. Well, I'll see Susie now.' She knocked.

'Come in,' called Susie, and Chinese Lady entered. Boots and Sammy heard Susie exclaim. 'Oh, what a nice surprise, Mrs Finch.' Finch was the name of Chinese Lady's second husband, presently abroad on Government business.

Sammy grinned. Boots smiled. Chinese Lady would get her cup of tea. Susie thought the world of her future mother-in-law.

'What a character,' said Sammy.

'Yes, not too many like her,' said Boots, 'she keeps putting us in ladies' unmentionables.'

Twenty minutes later an open sports car pulled up outside the shop. In it were Rosie, Boots's adopted daughter, and Rosie's favourite teacher, Miss Polly Simms. Rosie, nearly eleven, was fair-haired, blue-eyed and enchantingly vivacious. Polly, an ex-ambulance driver of the Great War, was twenty-nine, her rich chestnut hair styled in a Colleen Moore bob, her vivid good looks accentuated by her large and expressive grey eyes. Her sense of humour was irrepressible, although there was often a brittle note to it, a legacy of her years among the men of France and Flanders. She regarded all surviving Tommies as old comrades. Her special regard for Boots, a survivor himself, was of an incurable kind, and it caused her a great deal of heart-burning.

'I expect Daddy's got his nose to the grindstone,' said Rosie. She never thought about Boots as her adoptive father, simply as her one and only daddy. No-one, except perhaps Polly, quite knew just how much Rosie loved him.

'Frightful, if he finishes up with no nose,' said Polly.

'Oh, he'd just say that that would save him having to blow it when he got a cold,' said Rosie, and a little giggle arrived.

'Yes, he would say that, wouldn't he?' smiled Polly, a cloche hat cuddling her head.

'Nana says he's airy-fairy.'

'Is airy-fairy good or bad?' asked Polly.

'Well,' said Rosie, 'Nana's always saying it wouldn't have happened if she'd boxed his ears more often when he was younger.'

'Yes, I've heard her talking to him,' said Polly. She

spent most Tuesday and Thursday evenings at the house which Boots and his family shared with his mother and stepfather. She was coaching and cramming Rosie for a scholarship exam next January.

'I'd better go up and meet Nana now,' said Rosie. 'I'll say hello to Daddy first.'

'Yes, do him a favour, lift his nose off the grindstone for a few minutes,' said Polly.

'Whose nose?' asked Boots, and they looked up. There he was standing beside the car, a smile lurking.

'Oh, hello, Daddy, where did you spring from?' asked Rosie.

'I saw the pair of you from my window,' said Boots.

'You actually left your grindstone to come down and say hello?' asked Polly.

'What a blessing,' said Rosie. 'We don't want you to wear your nose away, Daddy.'

'Well, if I do I'll have a wooden one fixed,' said Boots, 'and the grindstone can have a go at that.'

Rosie laughed.

'We thought you'd say something like that, didn't we, Miss Simms?' said Rosie. 'Is Nana up there, Daddy?'

'Yes, she's waiting for you in Susie's office,' said Boots, and Rosie scrambled out of the car, said goodbye to Polly and ran into the shop. 'Thanks for giving her a lift, Polly.'

'My pleasure,' said Polly, 'the girl's adorable. So am I.' She looked up at him from the car. She couldn't help herself, she loved everything about him, his looks, his masculinity, his whimsical self and his lazy, almost blind left eye, which she always wanted to kiss. 'Well, say something.'

'Yes, all right, you're adorable, Polly. Can't stop, though, must get back to my desk.'

'Stinker. Look, couldn't we dash off to Paris together for a little while? Say for a year?'

'Sounds exciting,' said Boots, 'and French.'

'Do you mean I excite you?' asked Polly.

'Frequently,' said Boots.

'Well, then?'

'Well what?'

'You can manage a little adultery, can't you?' said Polly. A tram clanged by. People went by. The driver of a horse and cart whistled at Polly. She was oblivious of all the hustle and bustle of Camberwell Green, and didn't even hear the whistle.

'Polly, do you want to wreck my marriage?' asked Boots.

'Yes.'

'You don't mean that,' said Boots, who had had this kind of conversation with her before.

'Oh, come on, old love,' said Polly, 'meet me somewhere at midnight. Is it fair, is it even decent, for Emily to have all of you all the time?'

'I'll have to pass on that one,' said Boots.

'I hope you've heard that hell hath no fury,' said Polly. 'I've lived like a virgin ever since I met you, and I'm getting fed-up waiting for you to take me to bed. I'm going to sleep with the next man I meet, even if he's hairy all over.'

'Don't do that, Polly.'

'Bloody hell,' breathed Polly, 'why shouldn't I?'

'I'll break your leg if you do,' said Boots.

'You'll what?' Polly stared at him. He actually looked as if he meant it.

'Sorry, my mistake,' said Boots, 'it's none of my business. See you at the house this evening.' He went back to his office through the shop, leaving Polly almost giddy.

Suffering pangs of love, she thought, he cares, he actually cares.

Chinese Lady's special little gift to Rosie was a silver locket. She had already paid the Camberwell jeweller a deposit on it. She paid the balance and it became Rosie's. She could place heart-shaped cut-outs from family snapshots inside it, one of Emily and one of Boots. Rosie was rapturous. She did the cut-outs as soon as she got home, and fitted them into the locket. One was a head and shoulders of Boots, the other of Emily and herself, their heads close together. Then, when she closed the locket, she and Emily were both kissing her daddy. Rosie felt blissful about that.

Henry Brannigan spent the evening with Madge in her new flat. He arrived with a bunch of flowers for her, which touched her considerably. But she still felt confused and uncertain, she still felt there must be a catch in the arrangement. She knew men well, of course. There weren't many who would give on a generous scale to a woman and ask for nothing in return. Henry had said company was enough for him. He didn't seem to quite realize exactly what he was doing for her. First and foremost he was relieving her of the wretched necessity of going out at night to pick up men in pubs. For three nights now she hadn't had to do that. The pleasure of keeping her body to herself surprised her.

She asked him where he lived. He told her.

'You've just got one room in yer sister's place?' she said. She had the fire alight and they were sitting in front of it. She wore the short skirt and teasing petticoat he had said he liked. 'Henry, that's daft, you livin' in one room when you could easy afford a flat. Does yer sister cook for you of an evenin'?'

'No, I always eat a good meal midday,' he said.

'But you 'ave to 'ave something of an evenin',' said Madge.

'Well, I frequently pick up fried fish when I'm out walkin'.'

'You shouldn't 'ave to do that,' said Madge. 'I'll do a light supper for both of us every evenin'.'

'I wouldn't want to ask that of yer,' said Henry Brannigan.

'You 'aven't asked,' said Madge, 'I've offered. You come 'ere at seven every evenin' and we'll eat supper together. You like company, you said—'

'I like your company.'

'Well, I like company meself.'

'You're a good woman,' he said.

'I was once, I ain't able to call meself that now.'

'Perhaps you ain't been all that respectable, but that don't mean you're not a good woman.'

'Well, it's downright kind of you to say so, Henry.' Madge eyed his gaunt look. ''Ave you been sufferin' on account of losin' yer wife?'

'It's been on me mind,' he said.

'Still, you're lookin' a bit better since I first met yer,' said Madge. His eyes weren't so dark and brooding. He looked more satisfied with life. 'Didn't you 'ave any children?'

'No, no children,' he said. 'Nor you, of course.'

'No, nor me,' she said. 'Missed out on that, didn't I?'

'Now don't let it worry you,' he said. 'What you didn't 'ave an' what me an' Matilda didn't 'ave won't be missed. There's too many perishin' kids, anyway. They get under yer feet ten at a time in some places.'

'Henry, you can't blame kids for bein' born,' said Madge, 'and it would please me to 'ear you talk less uncharitable about them.'

'What's this? Givin' me orders, are yer, lady?'

'As if I would,' said Madge.

'Only jokin',' he said. 'Now, 'ow about a walk and pickin' up some fish an' chips?'

'You don't 'ave to break me arm, not over fish an' chips,' she said. 'I'll be pleasured to walk to the shop with yer, Henry.'

'We'll watch the lines, eh?'

'Henry, we don't 'ave to do that all the time, only when we're in the mood. I'll 'ave to take yer mind off doin' it all the time, or you'll get too serious about it.'

'We'll see,' he said.

'I'll put me 'at an' coat on,' said Madge.

They enjoyed a nice companionable walk down to the shop, and she went along with his wish for them not to tread on visible lines.

The inquest on the young Bermondsey girl was held on Friday. Boots attended, with Mr Brown. It was merely a question of the parents confirming what day it was when their daughter went out for a walk and never returned, and of Mr Brown confirming how the body was found. That, together with the post-mortem report, proved enough to bring in a verdict of murder by a person or persons unknown.

The Saturday newspapers published details of the inquest. Mr Brown, whose name was mentioned, collared the family's newspaper when it plopped on to the mat and took it to work with him. He did not bring it home with him. Saturday, anyway, wasn't a day when too many people sat down with their dailies.

Mrs Mason did mention the matter to her lodger, Mr Ponsonby, on his way out of the house, however.

'What, what?' he said.

'The pore gel, Mr Ponsonby, down Bermondsey way. Murdered, she was. It says so in the paper.'

'Dear goodness, what are we coming to, Mrs Mason?'

'Found in a scrap yard, 'er body was, by some workmen an' the yard manager. 'Orrible. I 'ope they catch the brute that done it.'

'What a day, what a day,' sighed Mr Ponsonby. 'What can be done to such people?'

'Hang 'em,' said Mrs Mason.

'Yes, indeed. Ah, now I've forgotten where I'm going.'

'Down the market,' said Mrs Mason.

'Ah, so I am, so I am.' Mr Ponsonby beamed at his landlady. 'Thank you.'

'Don't forget to come back,' said Mrs Mason.

It was mid-afternoon, and Mr Ponsonby, having found his way to the East Street market, was about to inspect the rosy apples on a fruit stall when he came face to face with the unpleasant person whose path he'd crossed some days ago. Certainly, he was dressed more acceptably, in a trilby hat and suit that looked new, but Mr Ponsonby recognized him immediately with his dark eyes and dark features. And, as before, they were in each other's way. Mr Ponsonby at once brought up his rolled umbrella to hold the fellow off.

Henry Brannigan stared at him.

'What's up with you?' he asked.

'Mind your manners, sir, I shall not give way,' said Mr Ponsonby.

'Eh?' Henry Brannigan gave the silly old sod a surprised look before realizing there was something familiar about him. His memory placed him among the many people with

557

whom he'd had pavement confrontations. And that led him to recognition. 'Oh, it's you, you barmy old bugger,' he said.

'Stand off,' said Mr Ponsonby.

''Ello, 'ello, 'ello,' said the stallholder, 'you gents set for a ding-dong, are yer? Well, don't get in the way of me customers or me bananas.'

Henry Brannigan, his life much less bedevilled by fantasies since finding a woman who was a kindred spirit, pushed the brolly aside quite good-temperedly.

'No 'ard feelings, mate,' he said. 'It's only on pavements that I don't like people gettin' in me way.' He made a little detour, brushing Mr Ponsonby's shoulder unaggressively as he went by him.

'What an ugly fellow,' murmured Mr Ponsonby to his umbrella. 'Ought to be hanged, ought to be hanged. I must tell Mrs Mason. Now, what was I doing?'

CHAPTER THIRTEEN

'Well, just look at our Annie,' said Charlie.

Sunday dinner was over and everything tidied up. The Gaffer was ready to relax with *The People*, and Charlie, Nellie and Cassie were thinking of going to Ruskin Park, Cassie in the hope that the Prince of Wales would be there, when she could ask him if he'd mind giving her father a job guarding Buckingham Palace on a horse. As for Annie, she'd just come down from her bedroom in a pure white cotton dress with a scalloped hem that lightly danced around her knees. With it she wore a long string of beads and a round straw hat that sat on the back of her head like a crisp yellow halo. The dress, the beads and imitation silk stockings turned her into a fashionable flapper.

'That's our Annie?' said the Gaffer.

'Ain't she something, Dad?' said Nellie. 'Crikey, look at yer frock, Annie, I never saw that one before.'

'Oh, I've had it ages,' said Annie. She'd bought it yesterday, in fact, at Hurlocks by the Elephant and Castle during her short midday break. Twenty-four hours could be called ages by any girl not wanting to be accused of dolling herself up on account of a certain young man. 'Mind, it's the first time I've worn it. D'you like it, Dad?'

'Looks a treat, Annie,' said the Gaffer. 'Must've cost a packet, though.'

'Oh, a bit out of me savings,' said Annie.

'Well,' said the Gaffer solemnly, 'if you'd 'ad a bit more savings you could 'ave 'ad a bit more frock. I recollect there was an uncomfortable occasion when you were 'ighly embarrassed by the shortness of one of yer other frocks.'

'Dad, I told you never to mention that again,' said Annie. 'Didn't I tell you?'

'So yer did, Annie.'

'Well, I don't want to 'ave to tell you again, Dad, nor anyone else in this fam'ly. D'you all hear me?'

'Yes, Annie,' said Nellie.

'You Charlie,' said Annie, 'what're you grinnin' at?'

'Me?' said Charlie.

'Yes, you.'

A knock on the front door made Nellie dart.

'I'll answer it,' she said.

'I bet it's 'im,' said Charlie.

Nellie, finding Will on the doorstep, brought him through to the kitchen. The day being surprisingly balmy, he wore an open-necked cricket shirt, blue jacket, flannel trousers and no hat or cap. He said hello to everyone and took the opportunity to meet Annie's father and to shake hands with him.

'So you're the bloke,' said the Gaffer, taking a naturally long look at the young man who had wheeled Annie home in a pushcart.

'The bloke who what?' smiled Will.

'Who—'

'Dad, Annie said you're not to say,' warned Nellie.

'Oh, about the pushcart?' said Will.

'Oh, 'e's been an' said it,' breathed Cassie.

'Askin' for a wallop from Annie, that is,' said Charlie.

'Where is she?' asked Will.

'Mister, she's just there,' said Cassie.

'Strike me pink,' said Will, casting an eye over Annie in her pristine white, 'that's Annie? I thought it was someone's bridesmaid.'

'No, that's our Annie,' said the Gaffer.

'Don't take no notice of 'im, Dad,' said Annie, 'he's always talkin' daft. I don't know what 'is mum 'as done to deserve a son like him. Nor do I know what I'm doin' to be goin' out with him.'

'Might I have the pleasure of takin' her to Hyde Park, Mr Ford?' asked Will.

'You're welcome, Will,' said the Gaffer, smiling.

'I'll see he gets 'ome all right, Dad,' said Annie. 'I don't want 'is mum to worry about 'im. I expect she worries a lot about him bein' barmy. I'll 'old his hand for 'im when 'e gets off the bus.'

Will grinned. So did the Gaffer.

'Like the Army, do yer, Will?' he asked.

'On and off,' said Will.

'Well, we won't keep yer,' said the Gaffer, 'off yer go with Sergeant-Major Annie.'

'Oh, you just wait till I get back, Dad,' said Annie.

'Crumbs,' breathed Cassie, 'is Annie goin' to wallop our dad, Nellie?'

'Not till she gets back,' said Nellie, giggling. She and Cassie went to the front door to see the couple depart. They watched them walking up the street, Annie's light dress fluttering, her legs shining.

'Don't they look nice?' said Cassie. 'I expect they might meet Lord Percy in the park.'

'Who's Lord Percy?' asked Nellie.

'I don't know, I just read 'is name somewhere,' said Cassie dreamily.

The rowing-boat moved in a slow jerking fashion over the sunlit waters of the Serpentine. Will was exerting himself economically on the oars. Other boats skimmed or floundered according to skill or lack of it. Annie was in charge of the rudder. It was her first time in a rowing-boat, and

561

there was water, water everywhere, plus the challenge of steering. She liked a challenge, however. Will had explained how to use the ropes, and she took up her fearsome responsibility with resolution. So far, they'd only collided with one boat after narrowly missing another, which she thought their fault, anyway, not hers.

Will was enjoying the outing, the March day was really warm, the Serpentine a pond-like playground. Laughter, yells and recriminations were constant on all sides.

'You Cissie, you'll drown us in a minute.'

''Erbert, stop splashin' me, d'you 'ear?'

'Blimey O'Reilly, some mothers do 'ave 'em, Alice, but fancy yours 'aving one like you.'

'Fancy yours not chuckin' you back under the gooseberry bush, Danny.'

Will liked Annie as a spectacle of early spring. Her self-confidence tickled him. She was sure other boats were at fault when a bump looked likely. She sat upright, hands holding the rudder ropes, her eyes alight. Will, pulling gently on the oars, smiled at her.

'Excuse me,' said Annie, 'but would you mind lookin' where we're goin'?'

'Annie, you're the one who has to look where we're goin',' he said. 'I can only look at where we're comin' from.'

'You sure that's where you're lookin'?' asked Annie, all too aware her legs were right in front of his eyes. 'I suppose you haven't got lookingitis, have you?'

'Is it my fault you're only wearin' half a dress?' grinned Will.

'Listen,' said Annie, 'this dress is highly fashionable.'

'Highly? Shortish, I'd say.'

'Still, I'm pleasured you like it – here, watch yourselves,

you two!' Annie raised an indignant voice to a boat bearing down on them. Will turned his head.

'Pull with your right hand, Annie,' he said.

Annie pulled. The boats collided. Her legs went up in the air.

''Ere, mate,' said a young gent in a Hackney accent, 'would yer mind tellin' yer lidy driver to watch what she's a-doin' of?'

'How's your own driver?' asked Will, keeping the boat steady with his oars.

'Glad you asked, mate,' said the young gent, pulling with one oar and pushing with the other. 'She's keen, I tell yer that. Yer keen, ain't yer, Clara?' he said to his girlfriend, who was pretty, plump and fairly sporty.

'Well, a girl can only get drowned once,' she said, and the young gent eyed Annie, who was right way up again, but considerably put out.

'Like to swop drivers, mate?' he asked Will.

'What's he mean, swop drivers?' demanded Annie.

'He means he fancies you,' said Will. 'How about you?' he asked the plump and sporty girl. 'D'you feel like swoppin'?'

'Well, you look all right,' she said, 'but can I trust yer? I can't trust Nobby; 'e squeezes me in all the places I didn't know I 'ad.'

'I don't know if Annie would go for that,' said Will, with the boats paddling around each other.

Annie, hardly able to believe what she was hearing, said, 'I certainly wouldn't. What d'you think I am?'

'You look a bit of all right from where I'm sittin',' said the young Hackney gent.

'You'll be sittin' in the Serpentine in a minute,' said Annie. 'You're common, and clumsy as well. You shouldn't be allowed in a boat. Will Brown, kindly start rowin'.'

'So long,' said Will to the matey couple, and rowed away.

'What d'you mean talkin' about that fat girl and me swoppin'?' asked Annie.

'Just passin' the time of day with them,' said Will.

'Did you bump into them on purpose just to get my legs up in the air?'

'I'll be frank,' said Will, rowing without pushing himself. 'I like a bit of a treat. You don't get to see too many legs in India. Cows' legs, yes, but they're not much of a treat, except to bulls, I suppose. By the way, the bump happened because you pulled on the left rope, not the right. Where're you takin' us now?' He turned his head again, then pulled hard on his left oar to avoid another collision. Annie tugged on a rope. By the grace of God it was the correct one, and they floated by the oncoming boat. But Will's sudden muscular pull brought on a familiar warning. He gritted his teeth. Of all things he didn't want an attack to turn him into a wheezing old man in front of a healthy young girl. Sod it, he thought, I'm going to be a sorry case for the rest of my life if I can't even row a slow boat round the Serpentine. He eased on the oars, paddling with them, waiting for an attack to follow the warning. Much to his relief, his breathing remained normal. He paddled on, towards the boat park.

Annie asked if they were going in. Will said they might as well, their time was nearly up and he fancied a little walk to the refreshment rooms. Would she like some tea? Annie's response was happily in the affirmative.

The tea rooms, always well patronized on fine Sundays, were crowded, but they found a table, and Will ordered a pot of tea, buttered fruit buns and slices of fruit cake. Annie enjoyed the occasion tremendously, and told Will he was being really nice to her. Will said so why had she

564

poured him only a half-cup of tea? Annie said it wasn't good manners to have full cups in places like this.

'Blow good manners,' said Will.

'You've got to have good manners in public,' said Annie, who always remembered that although her lively mum enjoyed a laugh and a joke, she wouldn't stand for any misbehaviour, especially in public.

'You think a couple of mouthfuls of tea add up to good manners, you dotty girl?' said Will.

Annie made a decision there and then. She decided, definitely, that her dad was right, that it was time she had a young man, and that the only one she'd like to have was Will. Accordingly, she had to stop letting him confuse her, and take him in hand, just as if he was her young man.

'I hope you're not goin' to make a scene at your age, Will Brown,' she said amid the chatter and clatter of the tea rooms. 'I'm sure your mum wouldn't like you makin' a scene when you're takin' a young lady out. You can have more tea when you've finished that – oh, and would you like me to butter your bun for you?'

'Would you repeat that?' asked Will.

'Yes, I'll do it for you,' said Annie. It was, to her, a quite natural way of taking him in hand, of letting him see that as his young lady she didn't mind doing things for him. Will watched in amusement as she took his bun, sliced it in half, buttered both halves and gave it back to him. 'There, you can eat it now,' she said. 'Imagine, real butter and all. Will, don't you think you ought to take your elbow off the table in a place like this?'

'Here, half a mo',' said Will, 'are you tryin' to be a mother to me?'

'Course not, you silly,' said Annie, 'how could I be your mother at my age?'

'I've still got a funny feelin' you're tryin' it on,' said Will.

'Eat your bun,' said Annie. 'Isn't it nice in 'ere, Will?'

'Yes, Mother, very nice,' said Will.

Annie smiled. She enjoyed every moment of the tea, and was kind and gracious to her young man, letting him see she didn't act like a common person in public. Will, of course, had a terrible time trying not to laugh. He had a feeling, in any case, that a full-blooded laugh wouldn't do his chest any good. Little danger signals kept hovering.

Annie lingered over the tea because of her enjoyment. She made Will tell her about his family, all of them, and in return she told him any amount of things about her sisters, her brother and her dad, including what an imagination Cassie had and what a kind and homely man her dad was.

The waitress arrived with the bill.

'Everything all right, sir?' she asked.

'Yes, thanks, we'll come again, me and Mother,' said Will.

'Who?' asked the waitress, glancing at Annie.

'Don't take any notice,' said Annie, 'my young man's a bit funny at times.'

'So's my young lady,' said Will, and Annie experienced little tingles of pleasure. She watched him as he paid the bill, giving the waitress a tip, and she thought oh, he's really nice, I don't mind now how much he looks at me in my highly fashionable frocks. When they left she was very gracious in her thanks.

'It was a lovely tea,' she said, 'and you behaved really nice.'

'I had to,' said Will. 'Mother was watching me.'

Annie laughed, then said he'd still got room for improvement.

Will, strolling through the park with her on their way to

566

the bus stop, said he'd do his best. Annie said she hoped he would, as she didn't want to walk out with any young man who had as much sauce as he did. Mind you, she said, I expect there's some young men a lot worse. That sounds as if there's hope for me, said Will. Oh, I think you've got the makings, said Annie graciously.

They enjoyed a very companionable bus ride home, with Annie's shining knees showing, and both knees didn't mind him looking. When they reached her doorstep, she was surprised and disappointed that he wouldn't come in. He'd trot off to his own home, he said. Annie wondered if he'd kiss her, but he didn't, nor did he say a word about seeing her again, and that left her very miffed. Will, however, had symptoms to fight, and they reached their inevitable peak the moment he opened his front door. He took himself straight up to his bedroom, and there his attack took its coughing, crippling hold of him. His mum came up.

'Will, we can hear you coughin' all over the house,' she said in concern.

'Give us – a minute – be all right – in a minute.'

'Can't I do something, lovey?'

Will couldn't reply, he was trying to suck in air. He'd taken one of the prescribed tablets and could only wait for it to work. He made a gesture, and Mrs Brown did the sensible thing. She left him to his privacy. As she went downstairs she thought, I hope it's not consumption, I just hope it's not, I'll have something to say to the Army if they've helped to give him consumption. No wonder he's gone up to his room instead of coming to tell us about his girl Annie.

Will was thinking, I'm a hopeless case, and that's a fact. I'm going to be as useful to myself or anyone else as a saucepan with a ruddy great hole in it.

Freddy had had a mixed-up afternoon himself. Calling on his new mate, Cassie, he found she was just about to go to Ruskin Park with Charlie and Nellie. He offered to take her on his bike. His mum had said he could do that as long as he didn't use the main road, where young boys on bikes could make tram drivers have fifty fits and give bus drivers nightmares. So he'd promised to get to the park through the back streets, which was easy.

'Oh, yes, I'll come with you, Freddy,' said Cassie.

''Elp yerself to 'er company, Freddy,' said the Gaffer, looking forward to putting his feet up with his Sunday paper.

''Ere,' said Charlie to Freddy, 'you don't go out with girls, do yer?'

'No, just me mates,' said Freddy.

'What yer goin' out with me sister for, then?' asked Charlie, puzzled but not aggressive.

'She's me new mate,' said Freddy.

'But she's a girl,' said Charlie.

'Well, that ain't 'er fault,' said Freddy, 'she was born like it. Me mum was born a girl. Course, she's a woman now.'

'Blimey,' said Charlie, 'you sure you ain't feelin' unwell?'

'You Charlie,' said Nellie, 'leave Freddy be. 'E can 'ave Cassie for 'is mate if 'e wants.'

'Well, I ain't complainin' about it, am I?' said Charlie. 'I'm just askin' 'im if 'e's all there.'

'Freddy looks all there to me,' said the Gaffer.

'Well, I ain't been taken' away yet, Mr Ford,' said Freddy. 'You ready, Cassie?'

'I'll just get me cat,' said Cassie.

'Not likely,' said Freddy, 'we ain't takin' that barmy cat

568

up the park with us. I don't mind yer takin' a cushion, but not yer cat.'

'All right, I'll just get me 'at,' said Cassie, and left the kitchen.

'I wish yer luck, Freddy, yer'll need it,' said Charlie, and went off to the park with Nellie, Nellie hoping to get off and Charlie hoping to find a few boys who needed bashing.

Freddy went out to mind his bike. Cassie appeared at the open front door and chucked a cushion at him to put on the carrier. Vanishing again, she reappeared with Tabby in her arms.

'Now look 'ere, Cassie—'

''E wants to come,' said Cassie. 'I asked 'im.'

''E's a talkin' cat now, is 'e?' said Freddy. 'Listen, as me mate you're supposed to do what I tell yer.'

'Me dad never said so. Freddy, Tabby wants to come, and I've got 'is string.'

'Oh, all right,' said Freddy, who had some of his mum's good nature, 'but I ain't 'aving 'im sit on me 'andlebars, you'll 'ave to 'old him.'

'Yes, I'll 'old him to me bosom,' said Cassie, whose imagination embraced a multitude of fancies. Getting astride the cushioned carrier with Tabby clasped to her, she added, 'Did yer know they could only tell the Sleepin' Beauty was actu'ally still alive because 'er bosom was 'eaving?'

'Oh, gawd,' said Freddy, but away he went, round to Portland Street and on to Wells Way. He cut through Church Road and other back streets to reach Champion Park, almost opposite the entrance to Ruskin Park. Cassie hummed a song all the way, and Tabby purred at her bosom. Or rather, her bosom-to-be.

At the park-keepers' hut just inside the entrance, Freddy asked if they'd mind his bike.

'Come again, me young lord?' said a park-keeper, smart in his brown uniform and brown bowler.

'Yes, could yer mind me bike, please, if I leave it 'ere? Only I can't take it round the park, it says so on the notice.'

'Well, me lord, what it also says on that there notice is that it ain't incumbent on me to mind bikes.'

'I ain't never seen that on the notice,' said Freddy.

'You sure you ain't?' said the park-keeper.

'Honest,' said Freddy.

'Well, blow me braces,' said the park-keeper, 'then I suppose I'll 'ave to think about mindin' it – here, wait a bit, what's that girl doin'?'

'Oh, she's just putting 'er cat on a piece of string so's she can walk 'im round the park,' said Freddy.

'Gawd love us,' said the park-keeper, 'mindin' bikes, cats on pieces of string, I'm hearin' things. I'll be hearin' an elephant on a yard of elastic next. Might I refer yer young lordship to the notice again?'

'Mister, I dunno it says anything about elephants,' said Freddy.

'No cats or dogs, that's what it says – here, where's she goin'?'

Cassie was away, walking, the cat following on its string lead.

'I'll go after 'er, mister, an' tell 'er,' said Freddy.

'You do that, me lord, and quick,' said the park-keeper, 'because if she runs into me superintendent, he'll drown the cat and 'er as well. And he'll sell yer bike in aid of the starvin' poor, of which I'm one.'

Freddy grinned. The park-keeper winked. Freddy ran in chase of Cassie. He caught her up. People were staring at the girl with a cat in tow. Boys were cackling and offering comments.

'What yer got there, a walkin' canary?'

''Ere, Lulu, yer bein' follered.'

'Does yer muvver know yer out?'

'Listen, Cassie, no cats nor dogs,' said Freddy. 'Nor elephants. We'll 'ave to take Tabby back and ask the park-keeper to mind it. 'E's mindin' me bike, so I expect 'e'll mind yer cat as well.'

'Tabby don't like bein' minded by park-keepers,' said Cassie.

'Well, if yer don't take 'im back—'

'Freddy, d'you think we might meet a lord or something? I just saw a lady lookin' like a Spanish senrika that was once captured by an 'andsome pirate that was really the Prince of Wales.'

'What's a Spanish senrika?' asked Freddy.

'Oh, an 'igh-born lady,' said Cassie. 'She was ever so upset at bein' captured because she was supposed to be meetin' an 'igh-born duke that was in love with 'er.'

'Well, I'm sorry about 'er 'ard luck,' said Freddy, 'but we've got to take yer cat back, and besides, everyone's lookin'. Cassie, I've got to tell yer, Tabby looks barmy on a piece of string.'

'No, 'e don't,' said Cassie, taking absolutely no notice of looks, stares, comments and giggles. 'Of course, the Spanish senrika didn't mind when she found it was the Prince of Wales who'd captured 'er. If we see 'im in the park, I'm goin' to ask 'im if me dad can guard Buckingham Palace on an 'orse for him.'

''Adn't you better ask 'im first 'ow he got on with the Spanish senrika?' said Freddy, trying a bit of sarcasm. 'Now look 'ere, Cassie, I never 'ad any trouble with me other mate, Daisy Cook—'

'Mummy, mummy,' cried a little girl, 'look, she's got a cat.'

571

'Well, she shouldn't 'ave,' said the maternal parent, 'it's not allowed, so come 'ere, I don't want you 'aving anything to do with what's not allowed.'

'There, yer see, Cassie?' said Freddy. 'There'll be a bloomin' riot in a minute.'

'Course there won't,' said Cassie, 'it's Sunday. The King don't allow riots on Sundays. Me dad told me so.'

Tabby's head suddenly slipped the string. The animal whisked in front of Cassie and ran into the path of a handsome lady in a flowery dress and a hat shaped like a pudding basin. Without hesitating, it sprang upwards into her arms, much to her startled astonishment. It purred blissfully.

Cassie stopped. Freddy stopped. Beside the handsome lady was a man who looked strong enough to squash Tabby with one blow. He also looked as if he was prepared to do just that.

'Ruddy blind 'ow'djerdo's,' he said 'now it's kids with climbin' cats in the park, would yer believe.'

Cassie and Freddy stared and blinked. It was actually him again, the man who'd knocked them off the bike some days ago. It's like bloomin' doom, thought Freddy.

'Oh, 'elp,' he breathed.

'It's all right, Henry,' said Madge. Henry was taking her for an enjoyable saunter round the park, and she was going to give him Sunday tea at the flat later.

Henry Brannigan inspected the boy and girl, laying his dark eyes first on Freddy, then on Cassie. Little glints appeared, glints of recognition.

'What's the idea?' he said. 'In me way again, are yer? Lucky for you this ain't a pavement.' The park paths were surfaced with tarmac.

'Henry, what're you goin' on at them for?' asked Madge, handing the cat back to Cassie.

572

They're haunting me, these two kids, that's what they're doing, thought Henry Brannigan.

'Cats ain't allowed in parks, nor dogs,' he said.

'Nor's elephants,' said Freddy, 'the park-keeper down by the gate just told me so.'

The handsome lady laughed at that, and even the man looked as if he had a bit of a grin on his face.

'We're sorry our cat jumped on yer, missus,' said Cassie nervously.

'That's all right, I like cats,' said Madge.

'Yes, all right, but just watch it, yer young perishers,' said Henry Brannigan, and resumed his saunter with Madge.

'Freddy, that was 'im,' whispered Cassie, cuddling Tabby.

'Don't I know it,' said Freddy, 'except 'e 'ad a Sunday suit on. Listen, what d'yer mean by sayin' it's our cat? It's yours. I wouldn't want a barmy cat like that, I'd sooner 'ave an 'eadache. I – oh, crikey, Cassie, there's a park-keeper comin'. Come on, bunk down 'ere.'

They did a quick bunk down a path that took them past the public conveniences. They met Nellie, who'd found a school friend, and together they'd found four boys who fancied having a lark with them. Nellie and her friend Pam didn't go in for larks, so the boys were settling for saucy chat and the girls were settling for giggles. Nellie wanted nothing to do with Cassie, not while she had her daft cat with her, so that left Freddy still in charge of her. He perforce had to keep her out of trouble. It almost wore him out. His old mate Daisy Cook hadn't ever been a trial to him. Nor had she ever talked about her dad being an executioner at the Tower of London. Cassie was insistent that that was what *her* dad had been.

'Yes, 'e 'ad to execute people that run off with the

Crown Jewels,' she said. 'The King put 'im in charge of them.'

'I bet that was a worry to 'im', said Freddy, 'I bet it didn't do 'is white 'air any good. Still, it must've got better, I noticed it's not white any more.'

'Yes, it made a recov'ry,' said Cassie.

Freddy took her home then, while he still had the strength to ride his bike. The park-keeper who had minded it for him turned a blind eye on Cassie's cat as she sneaked through the gate with it.

CHAPTER FOURTEEN

'It ain't what I'd like, guv,' said Bert Roper, the man who looked after the maintenance and the security of the factory Sammy was renting in Islington until his new one was built in Shoreditch. Bert and his wife Gertie, supervisor of the sixty machinists, were in the factory office with Sammy and his brother Tommy, the manager. All three sons of Chinese Lady had something to offer the kind of world she believed in. They had manliness and a liking for hard work. Chinese Lady was proud of what they'd achieved, but never said so. They'd only get above themselves, and that was another thing she believed in, a man not getting above himself. She'd often had to tell Boots he knew too much for his own good. Still, he had very distinguished looks. And Sammy with his blue eyes that always looked as if he had an electric motor behind them, was sort of arresting. As for Tommy, well, he was as handsome as his late father, Daniel Adams, and that was saying something.

At this moment, Tommy and Sammy were up against the prospects of a strike in the manufacturing side of the rag trade. All the trade union workers were threatening to come out, whether they could afford to or not, and few could. But bosses were trying to make a case for cutting wages, which were already sinfully low. Even non-union workers in some of the sweatshops were thinking of supporting the strike. Trade union agents were haranguing them. They'd been at the seamstresses in Sammy's factory.

'It's 'ard on Bert, yer see, Mister Sammy,' said Gertie, ''im 'aving been a docker an' still 'aving dockers for 'is mates. And it ain't too easy for me an' the girls.'

'I'm takin' your point, Gertie,' said Sammy. 'What you and Bert are sayin' is that he's goin' to come out.'

'I ain't said that yet, guv,' said Bert. He and Gertie were as loyal to Sammy as any two workers could have been, and even a bit more. Bert had given up his docker's card to look after the factory, and he knew it was as steady and well-paid a job as any East End man could have wished. 'We all know this fact'ry ain't a union shop, so I don't 'ave any legal standin' if I come out on strike, which would mean you'd 'ave the right to sack me. But I'm a union man at 'eart, and you're the only bloke I'd work for without a union card. In me 'eart, guv, I'm wantin' to support the strikers.'

'And not wantin' yer mates to turn their backs on yer,' said Gertie.

'I can 'andle me own discussions, Gertie,' said Bert.

'Not without me you can't, said Gertie. 'I'm yer wife, for better or worse. If you've got problems, they're my problems too. Mister Sammy, Bert's an upset man about all this.'

'So am I,' said Sammy, thinking of the new contract. 'I don't know anything more upsettin' than ruination.'

'Bert's got to make a gesture,' said Tommy, 'against low wages being cut to starvation level. And the girls are bein' got at. The local union officials want them to sign on and come out.'

'I've told them officials,' said Gertie, 'I've told 'em a dozen times that if they can look after us better than you do, Mister Sammy, then we might sign on. A good boss is better than a union card, I told 'em. You've got a lot of appreciative girls, an' they ain't goin' to change you for a union that'll be orderin' them to walk out on you every time some seamstresses somewhere else 'ave a complaint about their bleedin' boss – if yer'll excuse me French, Mister Sammy.'

'Well, Gertie old girl,' said Sammy, 'I'm not partial, as you know, to havin' you and your hands bein' called out on strike on account of trouble in some other workshop. Nor am I in favour of everyone in Adams Fashions bein' in an upset state, as Bert is.'

'We're goin' to be more upset when the strikers stop delivery vans gettin' through,' said Tommy. 'Wait a tick, though, we've got loads of materials comin' in from all over.'

'Which I duly advised you would,' said Sammy.

'You clever old cock,' said Tommy, 'did you get advance warnin' that a strike was on the cards?'

'I don't recollect I did,' said Sammy, who had had other reasons for getting Susie to go to work on Mr Greenberg while he'd been in Manchester. 'However, Eli's comin' up with the goods, is he?'

'We're up to the ceiling with stocks,' said Tommy. 'Quality varied, but all in our ranges. Bert's goin' to arrange the hire of a small warehouse in Canonbury Road to take the overflow. He knows the geezer who owns the place, so he'll give 'im a friendly goin'-over regardin' the rent.'

'My compliments,' said Sammy. 'Right, then, with considerable feeling I've got to admit Bert has his back to the wall, and Gertie and the girls likewise. So what I propose is that when the time comes, if it does, we'll run a banner outside the fact'ry. What'll be on it, you'll ask.'

'Yes, I'll ask,' said Tommy.

Sammy quoted what he had in mind.

'ADAMS FASHIONS SUPPORT THE STARVING

577

FAMILIES OF THE STRIKING WORKERS WITH
DONATIONS FROM STAFF AND EMPLOYERS –
DROP YOUR OWN DONATIONS IN THE
BUCKET.'

'Bloody 'ell,' said Bert.

'Watch yer language,' said Gertie.

'Yer a bleedin' genius, guv,' said Bert.

'Hold on,' said Tommy, 'I'm not approvin' donations
my girls can't afford, Sammy.' Tommy, in daily touch
with his staff of seamstresses, knew just how hard-up most
of them were, and how much they relied on the weekly
bonuses they were paid on the understanding such
payments weren't made known outside the factory.
Sammy knew the girls generally, Tommy knew them
individually, and Tommy had the softest heart of Chinese
Lady's three sons.

'If I might continue?' said Sammy.

'Keep it simple,' said Tommy.

'My proposition,' said Sammy, who wasn't partial to
words of one syllable, 'is that everyone donates half their
wages while the strike's on, and that this sacrifice is
gen'rally made known. It can also be communicated to the
local paper. I'll donate the same amount, which'll be
the sum total of all the staff donations.'

'Strike a light,' breathed Bert.

'Good of your pocket, Sammy,' said Tommy, 'but
nothing doin' as far as the girls are concerned. They can't
afford anything like 'alf of their wages.'

'I've got to say it's a bit more than I thought you 'ad in
mind, guv,' said Bert.

'Fortunately,' said Sammy, 'I can inform you the firm's
in the financial position of bein' able to reimburse
everyone, so long as it's kept under yer titfers, which if it
isn't might blow a ruddy great hole in the look of things.

You've got to be seen makin' the sacrifice. Kindly inform the machinists of same, Gertie.'

'Bless yer kind 'eart, Mister Sammy, yer the best boss goin', and yer smart as well,' said Gertie. 'We don't come out, we stay at work to 'elp support the strikers' fam'lies? We got yer. And 'oo's goin' to be able to say that that ain't better than a non-union shop goin' on strike, specially as you're donatin' too, out of yer pocket. Bert's right, Mister Sammy, yer a bleedin' genius, and 'im an' me couldn't 'ave put it nicer if we tried. Excusin' me French again.'

'Clever, I grant yer,' smiled Tommy.

'Bert still bein' in an embarrassin' position, however,' said Sammy, 'he'll stand outside the fact'ry to take charge of the collectin' bucket, or it'll get half-inched. Might I suggest, Bert, that to anyone who drops a coin in you say, "The starvin' fam'lies of the strikers cordially thank you, mate." Or missus, as the case may be. Now, you'll look as if you've come out, but if we need you to do a piece of work, I'd like to ask you to do it and to send Gertie out to keep an eye on the bucket. And if you could arrange for security to be kept goin', I'd appreciate it.'

'You'll need a bit of security, guv,' said Bert, 'because there'll be some geezers that'll think about firin' the fact'ry on account of it not bein' on strike.'

'Can I take it you've got no more worries?' asked Sammy.

'I'll settle for your wheeze, guv,' said Bert. 'Like you pointed out, it'll look as if I'm on strike, anyway, which I will be most of the time, an' besides, I'm thinkin' donations'll be more of an 'elp than closin' the fact'ry down.'

'Right,' said Sammy, 'and would you like to make it your business to see that all the donations land up where they're intended to?'

'With the strikers' fam'lies,' said Tommy.

'Be a pleasure,' said Bert.

'I know you're our boss, Mister Sammy,' said Gertie, 'but yer one of us and always will be. So's Mister Tommy.'

'We happen, Gertie, to have been born one of you,' said Sammy.

'Two of you,' said Tommy.

'Back to work, Gertie,' said Bert.

'Back to me girls,' said Gertie, 'and if what I tell 'em don't make 'em sing, me name ain't Mrs Gertrude Amy Roper.'

Left alone with his brother, Tommy said, 'Business wearin' you out, Sammy?'

'Business, sunshine, is what perks a bloke up,' said Sammy.

'Business,' said Tommy, 'is what 'ands you the perks.'

'Unfortunately,' said Sammy, 'you can't always dodge the contrary hand of fate.'

'You've got verbal tonsilitis, d'you know that, sonny?' said Tommy.

'Caught it from Boots and his educative infection,' said Sammy. 'I was sayin', I think, that fate's got provokin' ways of pokin' a finger in your eye.'

'You get problems, you mean,' said Tommy. 'So do the rest of us.'

'In my case,' said Sammy, 'I'm havin' to hope St John's Church stays upright next Saturday week. I don't want it fallin' down just as Susie's promisin' to love, honour and obey. Come to that, can I rely on her to obey yours truly?'

'I hope I can rely on her to poke a provokin' finger in your eye occasionally,' said Tommy, studying a batch of delivery notes from Mr Greenberg's warehouse contacts. It looked to him as if Sammy was cornering the stocks held by London wholesalers.

580

'I ain't appreciative of that kind of comment,' said Sammy. 'I'll remind you that as managin' director of Adams Enterprises, I've got problems other blokes never hear of.'

'Well, keep 'em close to yer chest,' said Tommy, 'because if your best friends get to hear they'll want some of them. I'd say what you'd say yourself, that most of the problems you've got are 'ighly desirable.'

'I can't hang about here any longer,' said Sammy, lodging some invoices in his business attaché case for Boots's attention back in Camberwell. 'All I've got time for is to inform you that you and Boots both come up with jokes that don't make me laugh. Give me love to Vi. I'm partial to Vi. Her jokes are funnier than yours. So long, Tommy.'

'Wait a bit – all this material Mr Greenberg's buyin' on our behalf – it's more than we need as a reserve—'

'Precautionary, Tommy, precautionary,' said Sammy. It wasn't a rag trade strike he really had in mind but rumours of a General Strike.

On his return journey to Camberwell, he made a detour that took him to the Bermondsey scrap yard. He brought his car to a stop outside the gates. They were barred and locked, the yard deserted, by order of the police. It could be they were going to keep it that way until they'd solved the murder. The place, of course, was now an object of morbid curiosity among the locals. Open, it would have attracted swarms of them. Sammy thought about the unfortunate young girl. It made him grit his teeth. Hanging was too good for any man who could strangle an innocent. It was hard luck on Susie's dad, the discovery of the body and the closing down of the yard, but that was nothing compared to the brutal ending of a young life. He could imagine the murderer having the run of the yard.

Old Collier and his son had often neglected it for days on end. But at least the investigation had moved away from the place and away from Adams Enterprises.

Why had he come here when he couldn't really spare the time? In the hope, of course, that he'd find the police there with the news that they'd laid their hands on the bloke responsible. A young girl. It could have been Rosie, Boots's adopted daughter, or Annabelle, Lizzy and Ned's girl, given different circumstances. Or Susie's lively young sister, Sally.

Sammy drove away, wishing the police luck in their investigations.

Scotland Yard had taken them over, and were conducting enquiries not only in respect of the murder but also in respect of two other missing girls. There was the possibility that the initial disappearance of all three girls was linked to a common factor. They were examining the missing persons file on thirteen-year-old Mary Wallace of Rotherhithe, who had disappeared in October, 1925, and twelve-year-old Amy Charles of the Old Kent Road, lost to her family in December. The parents of both girls were still making regular calls at their local police stations to ask if searches were continuing. Scotland Yard began to interview the parents, the neighbours and friends of the missing girls, as well as combing Bermondsey for any kind of information that might help to connect the dead girl, Ivy Connor, to a suspect.

'Annie me pet,' said the Gaffer over supper that evening, 'did we 'ear from you as to when soldier Will is doin' 'imself the honour of walkin' you out again in a rowin'-boat?'

'Doin' what?' asked Annie.

'Dad, yer silly,' said Nellie, ''ow can anyone walk Annie out in a rowin'-boat?'

582

'Well, yer know what I mean,' said the Gaffer. 'Is 'e callin' for yer again on Sunday, Annie?' He asked the question naturally, for he was quite sure Will appreciated his nice-looking daughter and had made some arrangements to see her again.

'I'm sure I don't know,' said Annie, feeling very put out that Will had made no arrangements at all. If he turned out to be a chronically casual type, she'd show him the door quick when he did happen to call, or if he did. Except that she hoped he wasn't like that, she really did.

'Well, I'm blowed,' said the Gaffer, and wished he hadn't asked.

'Oh, I bet 'e'll be on the doorstep soon,' said Nellie.

' 'E might be at Buckingham Palace,' said Cassie.

'She's orf,' said Charlie, rolling his eyes.

'Well, 'e might,' insisted Cassie. 'The King might be makin' 'im a lord.'

'A dustman, more like,' said Charlie.

'Course not,' said Cassie scornfully, ' 'e don't 'ave a dustman's smell. 'E's a soldier. And 'andsome,' she added, after one of her brief thoughtful moments. 'I expect the Queen fancies 'im a bit.'

'Well, I 'ope she don't, Cassie,' said the Gaffer, 'because if she does, the King might chop 'is 'ead off.'

'Cor, I'd like to be there,' said Charlie, 'I ain't never seen a bloke 'aving 'is loaf chopped orf.'

'Ain't you an 'orrible boy?' said Nellie.

'Funny you should say that,' said Charlie, chewing on a chop, 'one of me teachers calls me 'Orrible 'Arry. I told 'er me name's Charlie, but she went an' said I was still an 'Orrible 'Arry.'

'Well, Charlie, if you don't mend yer ways,' said the Gaffer, homely face stiff and stern for once, 'I'll mend 'em for yer. You won't like it, me lad, you can be sure you won't, but it'll 'appen.'

Charlie went a bit red. Nellie, who didn't like uncomfortable family moments, said brightly, 'Annie, you never told us if Will liked yer new white Sunday frock.'

'What there was of it,' said the Gaffer, returning to his normal good-humoured self.

'I heard that, Dad,' said Annie.

'There, see what comes of talkin' out loud, Cassie?' said the Gaffer.

'Mrs Bell's parrot talks out loud,' said Cassie.

'Yes,' said Charlie, never subdued for long, 'it says things like 'ello, cock, and 'ow's yer farver?'

'It spoke to me once,' said Nellie.

'What did it say?' asked Cassie.

'"Who's a naughty girl, then?"' Nellie giggled.

'Cheeky old bird,' said the Gaffer.

'They got 'undreds of talkin' parrots in Windsor Castle,' said Cassie, 'an' goldfish as well.'

'Cassie, you're goin' cuckoo,' said Nellie.

'Yes, they got them as well,' said Cassie, 'the Queen likes cuckoos.'

'She'd like you, then,' said Nellie.

'Yes, I might be 'er maid one day,' said Cassie.

'Bless yer, Cassie,' said the Gaffer.

'Yes, bless her,' said Annie, fond of her dreamy, imaginative young sister.

'I went out with Freddy on Sunday,' said Cassie.

'We know yer did, an' with yer barmy cat,' said Charlie.

'Well, I'm Freddy's mate,' said Cassie, ''e told me so.'

'Wait till 'e finds out what's 'it 'im,' said Charlie.

The talk among the Brown family was mostly about the forthcoming wedding. Susie was having three bridesmaids, her sister Sally and two of Sammy's nieces, Rosie and Annabelle. The conversation was a trial to Freddy. He did his best to make it more interesting.

'That Cassie Ford,' he said, 'I dunno I ever 'ad a mate as scatty as her. Did I tell yer—'

'Susie, I do think cerise pink for the bridesmaids' dresses is lovely for a weddin',' said Mrs Brown.

'Wouldn't do for a funeral, though,' said Mr Brown, 'so it's lucky you only 'ave bridesmaids at weddings.'

'Funny ha-ha,' said Susie.

'I ain't wearin' pink meself,' said Freddy, 'just me new suit.' He'd been fitted out with a ready-made grey suit at Gamages. 'Did I tell anyone that when I took Cassie up the park on Sunday, she brought 'er cat and I 'ad to—'

'I do hope it'll be a fine day,' said Mrs Brown, 'I wouldn't want to go to Susie's weddin' under an umbrella; it wouldn't seem right.'

'Better than bein' rained on, Ma,' said Will, victim of two asthma attacks during the day.

'You could get Freddy to 'old the umbrella,' said Sally, 'then you could walk into the church all dry an' digni-fied.'

'Good idea,' said Mr Brown, 'we'll make Freddy official umbrella-'older.'

'I dunno I ought to 'ave a mate that takes 'er cat to a park,' said Freddy. 'Daisy Cook never—'

'Eat your supper up, love,' said Mrs Brown.

'Dad, you made up your mind yet about what kind of 'at you're goin' to wear?' asked Sally.

'Well, I've been offered the loan of a top 'at by an undertaker friend,' said Mr Brown.

'Bless us, Jim,' said Mrs Brown, 'I don't know it'll be right to wear any undertaker's hat.'

'Dad, it's out,' said Susie.

'I think I'll go for a bike ride up to Scotland,' said Freddy.

'Yes, all right, love, when you've 'ad your afters,' said his fond mum.

'What's the use?' muttered Freddy.

'Keep tryin', pal,' said Will, 'it got you your bike.'

Freddy's problem came knocking on his door after school the following day.

'Can I come on yer bike, Freddy? I've been 'ome and 'ad some tea an' cake, and Annie said you can ride me round a bit but not make me late for me supper.'

Freddy said how kind of her, then asked Cassie if she'd brought the cat. Cassie, long hair slightly awry and boater sitting on the back of her neck as usual, said no. Tabby, she said, had gone out with another cat.

'He's what?' said Freddy.

'Yes, 'e likes goin' out with another cat,' said Cassie. 'She's a lady cat. Well, I think she is.'

'I suppose 'e takes 'er to the pictures,' said Freddy.

'Yes, she likes the pictures,' said Cassie, 'specially Mary Pickford. Can we go on yer bike?'

'All right, you're still me mate, I suppose,' said Freddy. 'I was goin' round to see Ernie Flint, but I'll give yer another go.'

'Oh, does Ernie Flint go up in balloons?' asked Cassie.

'No, 'e just blows them up at Christmastimes,' said Freddy, and brought his bike out.

'Me dad went up in a balloon once,' said Cassie.

'I bet 'e's been down in a submarine as well.'

'Yes, 'e was a submarine captain once, I think it was in the war,' said Cassie. 'Freddy, you 'aven't brought a cushion.'

'Well, 'ard luck on yer bum,' said Freddy.

586

'I got to 'ave a cushion,' said Cassie,

'Oh, all right,' said Freddy, and went back to get one. Mr Ponsonby, who had been watching from the gate of his lodgings, came twinkling up to Cassie. He smiled down at her.

'My word, how pretty,' he said. 'Dear me, what a charming girl. Do I know you?'

'Yes, I'm Cassie. You give me a peppermint sometimes.'

'Well, everyone must have a peppermint,' said Mr Ponsonby. Out came Freddy with a cushion. 'Ah, Freddy, is this your pretty friend? Has she had her photograph taken?'

'No, but me sister Annie 'as,' said Cassie, 'it was when she was with the Prince of Wales in Hyde Park.'

'Dear gracious me, how delightful,' said Mr Ponsonby. 'Did you hear that, Freddy? This pretty girl's sister photographed in Hyde Park with the Prince of Wales.'

'Yes, can't 'ardly believe it, can yer?' said Freddy. 'I expect she 'ad tea with 'im as well.'

'Yes, they 'ad a whole pint of winkles with bread an' butter an' strawb'ry jam,' said Cassie. 'Well, I think they did.'

'Dear me, dear me,' said Mr Ponsonby, smiling gently, 'photographs are so nice to have. Come and see me about it. Goodbye now.'

Back he went to his lodgings murmuring to himself.

''E forgot to offer us any peppermints,' said Freddy.

'I've 'ad lots from 'im,' said Cassie.

''Undreds, I suppose,' said Freddy.

'Yes, I think so,' said Cassie.

'Come on, I'll 'ave to put up with you bein' scatty,' said Freddy, and away they went for a ride round the houses.

★　　★　　★

Mrs Mason, going up to her lodger's room, found him sitting in the window chair at a little table. He was beaming at a photograph on the table.

'Excuse me, Mr Ponsonby—'

'Come in, come in, Mrs Mason,' he said.

Mrs Mason, already with her head round the door, brought all of herself in. She had to admit he was an ideal lodger, he kept his room very tidy, made no fuss and grumbled about nothing. Whatever possessions he had, he kept them tidily locked away in his cupboard.

'I don't like 'aving to ask,' she said, 'but it's this week's rent, yer see. You don't 'appen to 'ave paid me yet.'

'Heavens, how remiss of me. Do forgive me.' Mr Ponsonby brought his wallet out from his inside jacket pocket. 'Let me see, how much is it?'

'Just five bob, Mr Ponsonby.'

Mr Ponsonby took a ten-shilling note from his wallet and handed it to her with a smile.

'There, that's for two weeks, then,' he said. 'Dear me, what a day, I must apologize for my forgetfulness.'

'That's all right,' said his good landlady, 'you don't forget very often. Who's the photo of, if I might ask?'

'Pardon?' Mr Ponsonby peered at her. 'Ah, yes,' he smiled, 'a niece of mine, young Clementine.'

'Oh, like the one in the song,' said Mrs Mason, and looked at it as he showed it to her in a proudly beaming way. He was a bit eccentric, so she said, 'Yes, what a nice girl.'

'Charming, charming,' said Mr Ponsonby.

What a funny old codger, thought Mrs Mason as she made her way downstairs to her kitchen. The girl in the photo had had her eyes shut.

'How's your young lady, Will?' asked Susie. She was in

the parlour with him. She was doing some embroidery and he was playing records on the gramophone bought from Sammy's East Street stall five years ago.

'Very healthy,' said Will.

'Why'd you say that?'

'Why not? It's true.'

'I think what you're really talkin' about is your health, not hers,' said Susie.

'Well, mine's a problem, hers isn't.'

'You old silly, you shouldn't talk like that,' said Susie. 'I thought she was very sweet. When are you goin' to take her to a cinema?'

'Suppose I had an attack watchin' Pearl White bein' tied to a railway line?' said Will wryly.

'Change the record, love,' said Susie. 'Put on "Happy Days Are Here Again".'

CHAPTER FIFTEEN

Annie, hurrying home after her day's work, turned into Browning Street from the Walworth Road and almost bumped into Will, who was on his way to see Dr McManus.

Startled, she still managed to say, 'Watch out, mind my knee.'

'Hello, Annie.'

'Hello yourself,' said Annie. ''Ave you been laid up?' It was a whole three days since Sunday and the Serpentine. And the weather was cold. She thought Will looked manly in a new overcoat, and as brown as ever. The sun of India had burned the brown into his face. But she thought he was a little bit drawn. Will had had three attacks during the day.

'Laid up?' he said.

'Well, I 'aven't seen you for ages, have I?' said Annie, then wished she hadn't said that because he really did look a bit drawn. 'No, I mean, 'aven't you been well?'

'A bit of a cold on me chest,' said Will. 'Let's see, d'you fancy the pictures tomorrow evening? There's a Tom Mix film on.'

'Honest?' said Annie.

'That's what my sister Sally told me.'

'No, I mean, you're invitin' me honest?'

'Lovaduck, Annie Ford, is there another way of invitin' you, then?' said Will, showing his amiable grin.

'I'll have you know me dad told me some young men have got crafty ways of invitin' young ladies,' said Annie, 'but I'll let him know my young man invited me honest.'

'I'll call for you at half-seven,' said Will, 'and you'll find out how honest I am in the back row of the Golden Domes.'

'I'll scream for the manager,' said Annie happily.

'That won't help you,' said Will, 'he's my uncle. See you tomorrow, then, Annie?'

'Yes, I'll risk it,' she said, 'but I think I'll bring a 'atpin.'

Will laughed. Annie couldn't help herself. She fell in love.

Susie mentioned to Boots the next day that her mum and dad had had a letter from Polly Simms. Polly was one of the many wedding guests. But she wasn't coming, after all, said Susie, she'd written to apologize for crying off, but she was having to go abroad as soon as the schools broke up for the Easter holidays at the end of this week.

'That's news to me,' said Boots without changing expression.

'Yes, she gives Rosie extra lessons at your house two evenings a week, doesn't she?' said Susie. 'I can't think why she didn't tell you. It's a pity she won't be with us, she's such good fun. I wonder what she's goin' abroad for?'

'Fun, I suppose,' said Boots.

He took time off from the office in the afternoon, and was at the school at twenty to four. Classes finished at four. Polly, called from her class by the headmaster, went to the teachers' room where Boots was waiting for her. Dressed in professional fashion, in a pale grey blouse and a dark grey skirt, she nevertheless managed to look as vivaciously appealing as always, her Colleen Moore bob curving to points that lightly kissed her cheeks.

591

'Hello, old thing,' she said, and her brittle smile arrived. Boots, standing with his back to the fireplace, his hat off and his overcoat unbuttoned, regarded her frowningly. 'Oh, dear,' she said, 'am I in the doghouse?'

'Why are you having to go abroad?' he asked.

'Who told you I was?'

'Susie. You wrote to her parents.'

'Well, one must do the right thing sometimes,' said Polly.

'Why are you having to go abroad?' asked Boots again.

'To get away from you,' said Polly. 'Darling, I love you dearly, but you give me nothing. You care for me, but you give me nothing. I'm expected to live with that kind of frustration? It's killing me. At home, I get on stepmama's nerves, I get on my father's nerves, and I get on my own nerves. If you care for me but won't love me, what's the point of my life here? There's my teaching, but that's not enough. I have to get away, and far enough to know you're not just around the corner. So I'm going to Kenya to stay with family friends out there, and to find a less frustrating life for myself. I'm leaving by boat this Saturday. The school breaks up on Friday.'

'Why haven't you told me anything of this?' asked Boots.

'I'm telling you now, aren't I, old thing? I was intending to let you know tonight, when giving Rosie her last cramming lesson. Look, old dear, I admit I've had my passage booked for some time, but gave myself the option of cancelling it in the hope you'd still become my lover. But you're too much of a family man, so I'm chucking you to give myself the chance of a new life by getting you out of my system. I'll never be able to do that while I stay here, using Rosie to find out what you're doing and even what you're saying. I must give Rosie up. I shan't bother either of you any more.' There was just a touch of bitterness to that remark. She had tried, God knows she had, but she accepted now that he was never going to be unfaithful to Emily.

'Bother us?' Boots looked disappointed in her. 'That's not up to your usual standard, Polly. You can't really believe you've ever bothered Rosie, and certainly not me. Your friendship and affection have always been special to me.'

'Affection?' Polly drew a deep breath of exasperation. 'Is that what you think it is, affection? God, if it was only that, I'd be laughing, not running away.'

'Must you run?'

'Yes, I must.'

Boots let out a little sigh. He was a more sophisticated man than either of his brothers, but he was as much his mother's son as Tommy or Sammy. He believed marriage really was for better or worse, unless a wife or husband was totally impossible to live with. Emily was far from that. To make Polly his mistress would be to destroy all three of them in the long run.

'I'm going to miss you badly, Polly,' he said.

Polly regarded him in melancholy. She had known thousands of Tommies in France and Flanders during her years as an ambulance driver. Of them all, Boots was the finest, a man without airs and graces, a man with a whimsical tolerance of clowns and idiots, a man born in the heart of cockney Walworth who had come out of it simply as a man.

'Let me ask you for the last time,' she said, 'will you be my lover?'

'Polly—'

'No, you won't, will you?' The bitterness surfaced then.

'Well, damn you, ducky, for giving me nothing. I wish I'd never met you.'

She turned on her heel, a swift and willowy figure. She left. It was a gesture of finality. Boots stood there. Was it for the best? What a cliché. It did nothing for his emotions. He turned his hat in his hands and listened to the sounds of the school, a place of the young, the active and irrepressible young.

The door opened.

'Daddy?'

He looked at her, his Rosie, nearly eleven and already heart-breakingly pretty, her fair hair black-ribboned, her blue eyes a little sad.

'Hello, kitten.'

'Miss Simms said you were here. I've just finished classes. Daddy, Miss Simms – she's leaving us.'

'Yes, I know.'

'She said goodbye to me, and asked if you'd mind if she didn't come this evening.'

'Well, it's a blow, Rosie, but for a long time now she's been convinced you'll walk that scholarship exam next January.'

'But I'm sad, Daddy, aren't you?'

'People come and go, Rosie, friends come and go, it's all part of life.'

But he was sad, Rosie knew he was. Every gesture of his, every mood and, at times, every word, registered with her. He was the man who had given her a home and the warmth and security of family life. He loved her. More than anything else, that counted with her.

'I shan't ever come and go, Daddy.'

'You will, you know, later on.'

'No, I'm never going to leave you, never.'

And Rosie meant it.

Will, setting off to pick up Annie, was in a cheerful frame of mind. Dr McManus had been more open than the Army doctors, and was quite willing to offer a second opinion, while pointing out he was a general practitioner, not a specialist. He could say, however, that the cause of an attack was the swelling of the lining membrane of the minor bronchial tubes, but how this came about couldn't be generally determined. It might be because a patient was allergic to something like a feather pillow, but on others it might have no effect whatever. Certain foods such as eggs or strawberries could bring about the spasm that caused the swelling that caused the attack. Some sufferers were affected by living in a city or town, others by living in the country. How long had Will been home from India? About four weeks. And how many attacks had he had in that time? About eight or nine. That's two a week. That's not bad at all, said Dr McManus.

'Except that I've had most of them during the last ten days,' said Will.

'Which makes you think it's catching up on you?'

'It makes me think I've got asthma,' said Will, and Dr McManus smiled.

'Well, you have, Will,' he said. He'd conducted an examination and asked questions. 'Let's see, you were fairly free from attacks up to the last ten days. Have you been eating food generally different from what you had during your first two weeks home?'

'Not really,' said Will. 'Plain, but well-cooked and pretty nourishin'.'

'Let's look at your activities, then. What's been different about your activities over the last ten days?'

'Nothing,' said Will, 'I've been taking things easily gen'rally.'

'Was your condition worse in Indian towns and cities, than in open country?'

'No, definitely not,' said Will.

'Are you sure that over the last ten days your life hasn't seen a little difference?'

'Are you talkin' about excitement?' asked Will.

'Good question,' said Dr McManus.

'D'you mean I could be affected by the excitement of winnin' a bet on a horse race or landin' a job at five quid a week?'

'Stimulation of an asthmatic condition can be caused by a variety of agencies, Will, external or internal. It can be caused by the air you breathe, if the air contains an irritating factor, or an infection of the nose or throat. Or simply by the infectious nature of simple excitement. Have you had a winning bet lately?'

'No, nothing like that,' said Will. His little grin appeared. 'But I met a girl about a fortnight ago.'

'What kind of a girl?'

'Lively,' said Will. 'Stands up for herself and answers me back. Name of Annie Ford. Would you know her?'

'Yes,' said Dr McManus, 'if she lives in Blackwood Street with her family.'

'That's her,' said Will.

'And you've been seeing her?'

'Frequently,' said Will.

'Well, that's a change in your pattern of life, isn't it?' said the doctor.

'Hell's bells, I meet a girl and that affects my asthma?'

'Would you say, as a young man, that you find her exciting?'

'She's a saucebox,' said Will.

'Yes, an engaging girl.'

'I had an idea,' said Will, 'that physical exertion, such

as rowing a boat on the Serpentine, caused attacks.'

'That and a difference in your routine might have done it. Look, next time you have an attack, make a note afterwards of exactly what you were doing at the time, what your last meal consisted of, if you'd been sneezing or not, and whether you were in or out of doors. Then come and see me again.'

'I'll do that, doctor, and thanks.'

Annie found him in top form on the way to the cinema, and was sure he might be a candidate for a thick ear if he secured seats in the back row. But she was spared having to set about him, for he bought sixpenny seats halfway up the stalls.

'Lucky for you you changed your mind,' she whispered.

'Lucky for you, you mean,' he whispered back.

'Young men ought to be respectful to their young ladies.'

'And young ladies ought to say sir to their young men.'

'Yes, sir, three bags full, sir.' Annie was happy. She liked being with him and sitting close to him in the cinema, their shoulders touching. She really felt like his young lady. They enjoyed the programme. A Mack Sennett comedy featuring the Keystone Cops preceded the Tom Mix film. It made the audience roar. In the big film, Tom Mix was his usual breezy self. His cowboy and Indian films often had an amusing side, and he could sometimes give the impression he was taking the mickey out of the Wild West. Will bought ice creams before the film started, and Annie said he was getting to be quite a nice feller.

They went home on a tram, Will relieved he'd had no attack all day. He thought about what Dr McManus had said. Did it excite him to have met Annie and to take her out? Well, he had to admit she wasn't exactly unexciting, and her legs were a treat to his eye.

597

'You're a bit quiet,' she said.

'I'm thinking would it help to be a cowboy?'

'What sort of 'elp do you need, then?'

'All those wide open spaces must be good for most people. And I might leave the Army.'

'Honest?' said Annie. 'Oh, that's good.'

'What's good about it?'

Well, I'd like it, thought Annie, I'd like to have him just a few streets away from me all the time.

'What's makin' you think about leavin'?' she asked.

'Cowboys and Indians, I suppose,' said Will. The tram was running smoothly, the traffic light at this time of night, and he liked the feel of Annie close beside him, thigh, hip and shoulder. Steady, mate, he thought, don't get excited, you might be allergic to excitement; your doctor said so. 'Is that good?'

'Is what good?' asked Annie.

'Leavin' the Army for the wide open spaces, joinin' the cowboys and Indians,' said Will. 'Didn't you say it was?'

'Oh, you daft thing,' said Annie, 'there's wide open spaces down near Brighton in Sussex. Dad took us there once, on the train. Besides, cowboys and Indians ride 'orses. You can't ride 'orses, can you?'

'Not without fallin' off,' said Will, 'but I can ride a bike.'

Annie laughed. Other passengers glanced at her. They saw a girl in happiness. Will saw a girl bright and alive, her hip and thigh communicating feminine warmth to his. His body, vigorous and healthy despite his asthmatic condition, stirred reactively. Steady, he told himself again.

They alighted at East Street.

Feeling peckish, Will said, 'Fancy some fish and chips, Annie?'

'Oh, who wouldn't?' said Annie, liking the offer

because it was just the kind of treat a girl could expect from a young man when she was his young lady.

So they walked along the Walworth Road to the fish and chip shop near Manor Place, where Will bought two helpings of rock salmon and chips. They put salt and vinegar on, and spent a happy time eating them out of the newspaper wrapping on their way back to East Street. Annie deposited the newspaper in the wire basket fixed to the lamp-post on the corner of the street, and then Will walked her home.

In the doorway of the Ford house, the cold night darkly enclosed them. Annie looked up at him. Her face seemed misty.

'Will, thanks ever so much for a lovely evenin',' she said a little throatily.

Will kissed her. He couldn't help himself. Blissfully, Annie received the kiss, her first romantic one. Oh, help, swoony. Her mouth clung to his, and she pressed close. Ruddy fire and hell, thought Will, as warning signals arrived. Kissing a girl was doing it to his tubes? He released her.

'Bless you, Annie,' he said.

'Oh, bless you too,' she said, breathless and rapturous. 'You'll come in, won't you, and see Dad and 'ave a cup of tea?'

Will's chest was tightening, but he felt it would be like giving her a slap in the face if he said no.

'A cup of tea sounds just what the doctor ordered,' he said. Annie opened the door and they entered, she in a quick way, he moving carefully, nursing his condition.

The Gaffer was up, the rest of his children in bed. He greeted Will with cockney heartiness, and Annie put the kettle on. Then she set about making some corned beef sandwiches with pickle for her dad.

'Good film, Will?' enquired the Gaffer, sitting at the table with him.

'Tom Mix? You bet,' said Will.

'Will was sayin' on the tram that he might leave the Army and go and be a cowboy,' said Annie, bobbed hair dancing a little as she sliced bread.

'Ruddy good idea,' said the Gaffer. 'Let's all push off an' get away from bosses in top 'ats an' gold watch-chains. Let's all be cowboys.'

'Me as well?' said Annie, a little glow on her face.

'I like the picture,' said Will.

'What picture?' asked Annie, spreading margarine on the slices.

'I reckon 'e means you on a cowboy's 'orse in yer 'ighly fashionable frock, Annie,' grinned the Gaffer.

'Dad, you're gettin' as bad as Will, and if you don't leave off I'll make you stand in a corner.'

'Gawd 'elp us,' said the Gaffer.

'Sounds fierce,' said Will. The tightness was easing.

'Yes, I'm the boss in this kitchen,' said Annie, and made the tea and the sandwiches. Then she sat down with Will and her dad. Her dad tucked into the sandwiches and they drank the hot tea. Will mentioned that Susie was getting married at St John's Church next Saturday week. Annie, at once intrigued, wanted to know who the bridegroom was. Will said Sammy Adams, and that he'd once run a glass and china stall down the market, where he'd first met Susie.

'Oh, I know 'im,' said Annie. 'I mean, I saw him lots there. He's a real lively feller, and good-lookin' too. I bet he's never put a girl in a—' She stopped. The Gaffer coughed.

'In a pushcart?' said Will.

'Blimey, yer done it now, Will,' said the Gaffer, 'that's a word that's forbidden in this 'ouse.'

600

'What do I do now, then, duck under the table?' said Will.

'What's he doin', where's he gone?' asked Annie, as his head and shoulders disappeared. She shrieked, knowing that under the table she was all legs. Will's head re-emerged.

'Dropped me teaspoon,' he said.

'I bet,' said Annie. 'I don't know how you can just sit there grinnin', Dad.'

'Well, a bloke can't 'elp droppin' 'is teaspoon,' said the Gaffer, frankly tickled by what was developing between his lovable daughter and her likeable soldier. He knew Annie far too well not to realize she was in high spirits and uncommonly happy. She'd had a tough time since the death of her mum, and she'd taken on all kinds of responsibilities while doing a job as well. It hadn't got her down, even though she'd never had much time to spare for herself or for boys. Now, when she was in her eighteenth year, it looked as if she'd got a young man. It was making her come alive. Well, Will was a bit of all right, and he'd got a nice sense of humour.

Will, remembering that a wedding guest had cried off, someone called Polly Simms, said, 'Like to come, Annie?'

'Come where?' she asked.

'To Susie's weddin'.'

'Me?' said Annie, eyes opening wide.

'There's room for you. There'll be dancin' at the Institute in the evenin'.'

'But your parents must've done all the arrangement,' said Annie, 'they couldn't take an extra guest now, could they?'

'Not extra big and fat ones, no,' said Will, 'but you're not big and fat. We could fit you in nicely.'

Annie went warm with pleasure, then made a face.

'Oh, I couldn't, Saturdays are Mr Urcott's busiest days, I couldn't ask 'im for the afternoon off.'

'Well, come to the Institute when you've finished work,' said Will.

'Oh, I'd love to,' said Annie.

'Good,' said Will, 'and now I think I'd better push off. Good night, Mr Ford.'

'Best of luck, Will,' said the Gaffer.

Annie saw Will to the front door.

'Thanks for the tea,' he said.

'It's been a lovely evenin',' said Annie, wondering if he was going to kiss her again. 'Oh, and thanks ever so much for the weddin' invite.'

'Wear your high fashion knockout,' said Will. 'Like to go to Ruskin Park on Sunday afternoon?'

'You're gettin' quite nicer all the time,' she said.

'Hope I can keep it up,' said Will, and went off with a smile, but without kissing her.

I'll have to go and see Dr McManus again, he thought, and ask him if kissing a girl is fatal to me asthma.

CHAPTER SIXTEEN

At the sound of the front door closing the following evening, Mrs Queenie Watts said to her husband, ''Enry's out ev'ry evenin' now reg'lar as clockwork.'

'Doin' 'im good,' said Stan Watts, 'makin' 'im more human. 'Ere, what's this out 'ere on top of the copper?'

'Oh, just some of 'is shirts,' said Queenie, 'I offered to put 'em in me Monday wash, if I'm up to doin' it.'

'But 'e uses the laundry, don't 'e?' called Stan from the scullery.

'Yes, but I offered. I 'ad a weak moment, I forgot about me chronic back.'

'What's 'e use three shirts in a week for?' asked Stan. 'They're bleedin' best shirts, look at 'em.'

'I can't see from 'ere,' said Queenie, lumpily lazing in a fireside chair, 'but I take yer word for it.'

''Ere, yer know what three best shirts in a week mean, don't yer?' said Stan. ''E's got a fancy woman, that's what's takin' 'im out reg'lar ev'ry evenin' about the same time. 'Ere, wait a bit, there's a bloodstain on the cuff of one shirt, Queenie. I 'ope that don't mean 'e's cut 'is fancy woman's throat.'

'Oh, yer daft lummox, Stan. You don't suppose, do yer, that 'e cut 'er throat last night and 'as gone back tonight to bury 'er somewhere? 'E just 'appened to nick 'is wrist when 'e got back 'ere last night, 'e told me so, and 'e showed it to me. It's only a small nick.'

'Well, 'e's got some woman all right,' said Stan, 'dressin' smart like 'e does an' goin' out so reg'lar in 'is new overcoat. And 'e don't look these days as if the rozzers are 'unting 'im down.'

''E couldn't help lookin' like that,' said Queenie. 'It was Matty fallin' out of that train that did it to 'im. 'E's gettin' over it at last.'

'And 'e's got a fancy piece that's 'elping 'im,' said Stan.

'Time 'e 'ad a little bit of what 'e fancies,' said Queenie indulgently.

After a nice homely supper of fresh haddock and poached eggs with Madge, Henry Brannigan took her for a walk along the Walworth Road. He, as usual, measured his strides whenever they reached a patch of light. Madge, as usual, fitted in with him, even though she was cheerfully disposed this evening to ignore the superstitions. Henry, however, was very set in the way he observed all the rules, and she didn't like to go against him.

'That one near caught the both of us,' he said, as they came out of the light cast by a shop window. Some shop windows always showed light, but most had their shutters up.

'Still, we both beat it,' said Madge.

'Well, good for both of us, eh? Like a drink? Say a port an' lemon?'

'That's nice of you, Henry. I don't know I ever met a man more gen'rous than you, nor more kind.'

'I ain't ever sure meself that dibs do a bloke much good by bein' kept in 'is pocket,' said Henry Brannigan. 'Dibs, yer might say, is there to be spent when there's something worthwhile to spend 'em on. A good woman's worthwhile, Madge, and it ain't nothing to do with bein' gen'rous. And I don't know I'd call meself kind, I'm more rough and ready, like.'

'A rough diamond, then, that's you,' said Madge, full-bodied and hearty, and surprising herself in her liking for taking walks with this strange and earthy man. The night was fine, the inky sky studded with a million tiny stars, the day clouds of early April swept from the heavens by a wind that had come and gone.

They crossed the road when they reached East Street, darkly empty of stalls. The tramlines, straight and true, faintly glimmered. They stepped over them, Madge doing so with a little laugh as they made for the pub on the corner of Penrose Street. The lamp above its door illuminated the paving stones. Madge, just a little bit careless then, trod on a line. Henry Brannigan emitted a sharp hissing breath.

'Shouldn't 'ave done that, Madge,' he said.

'Oh, it don't really count, Henry,' she said. 'I'm not in a superstitious mood tonight, I'm 'appy bein' out with yer.'

'All the same, I don't like it,' he said. 'Just take care tomorrer in case bad luck comes runnin' after yer.'

'I'll do that, Henry, I'll take care,' she said, sorry that she'd upset him.

'Good,' he said, and took her into the pub. It gave them a warm if fuggy welcome, the clay pipes of elderly cockneys issuing smoke. The place was fairly full, lively customers enjoying old ale at fourpence a pint from the barrel. A table, unoccupied, offered itself. 'You sit there, Madge, and I'll order up yer port an' lemon.'

He was a real gent, she thought, in the way he treated her, especially as a lot of people would just see her as an old pro. Still, she was off the game now. She sat down while he took himself to the crowded bar. Her handsomely mature looks drew the eyes of some men. She knew this pub, of course, she knew all the pubs and their noisy cockney atmosphere and their sawdust floors. Walworth men and women liked their pubs.

A man, catching sight of her, gave her a second look, then elbowed his way out of a group of men and women. He shifted his cap a little until its soft peak was at a perky angle and walked across to Madge.

'Watcher, Daisy gel, ain't seen yer around lately,' he said, and winked at her.

Oh, blow it, thought Madge, he's been a customer of mine, I suppose. Daisy was the name she'd always used. She could rarely remember any of their faces, not generally she couldn't, and she'd hoped none of them would remember hers now that she wasn't tarted up.

'Beg yer pardon?' she said.

'Are yer booked, love?' The man wasn't at all bad-looking. He was about thirty, with a fine pair of shoulders and a scarf around his brawny neck. A faint sexual surge disturbed her healthy body. That was often the trouble. She *was* healthy. She liked men, except the pathetic kind who'd never been able to look her in the eye. Henry looked her in the eye like a real man should. She frankly fancied Henry. He was middle-aged but as strong as a horse, she could tell that.

'You after something, mister?' she said distantly.

'You offerin', Daisy? 'Ow about a bit of what I've 'ad before, eh? Bleedin' fine woman, you are, and 'ere's me 'ard-earned silver in advance.' His hand dipped into his pocket and came out with two half-crowns, which he placed on the table in front of her. Madge felt sick, then angry. 'Meet yer outside in twenty minutes, say?' The man gave her another wink.

A glass of port and lemon appeared. A hand set it down beside the heavy silver coins. That was followed by a pint glass of old ale, and Henry Brannigan, having rid himself of both glasses, addressed himself to the intruding third party.

'The lady's with me,' he said.

'Well, don't be greedy, tosh,' said the third party, 'I'm paid-up an' booked.'

Henry Brannigan drew a long breath. It seemed to expand him and to lengthen him. He picked up the half-crowns and dropped them into the third party's jacket pocket.

'Do yerself a favour, mate, an' bugger off,' he said.

'Watch yer north-and-south, cully, I ain't yer private doormat.'

'Would you be invitin' me outside?' asked Henry Brannigan.

'You want it, you'll get it.'

'Right.' Henry Brannigan glanced at Madge. 'Won't be a tick,' he said.

'Henry—'

'Look after me pint,' he said, and went outside with the man. No-one took any notice. Amid all the boisterous noise, the brief dialogue had gone unheard except by Madge. She sat stiffly, biting her lip. But she didn't have long to wait. Henry was back within a couple of minutes. He didn't look ruffled, and he didn't look heated. He sat down and picked up his glass of ale.

'Oh, me gawd, what've yer done to 'im?' breathed Madge.

'Hit 'im,' said Henry Brannigan. ''E won't be comin' back. I 'ope that'll show yer, Madge, that it don't do to challenge them fates.'

'What d'yer mean?' she asked.

'Trod on a line outside, didn't yer?' he said. 'An' bad luck didn't take any time to catch up with yer, did it? You're off the game now, so I'd say you count it as bad luck to get an offer from a bloke when you're livin' respectable, don't yer?'

'So 'elp me, I don't want to go back on the game,' breathed Madge, 'nor 'ave anyone makin' an offer.'

'There y'ar, then, lady, don't risk it. Don't ask for bad luck to come runnin' after yer. It chased after yer when you trod on that line, and caught up quick with yer. I ain't partial to 'aving you accosted, not now you're keepin' yer bed to yerself. Well, the fates 'ave taught you yer lesson. Now 'ere's good 'ealth an' good luck to yer, Madge.'

Madge, a shaky little smile on her face, said, 'Bless yer, Henry, and 'ere's good luck to you too.'

They drank to each other, with Madge thinking he's right, you can't shut superstitions up in a cupboard whenever you feel like it, you've got to keep them out in the open all the time and pay respect to them.

Susie entered Sammy's office on Saturday morning the moment she heard him come in.

'Mister Sammy,' she said, consulting her watch, 'you're late.'

'Did I hear you say something, Miss Brown?'

'You did. It's nearly eleven, and I wasn't aware you had any appointments this mornin'. Lilian Hyams phoned and said to tell you all the autumn and winter designs are now finished in respect of suggested alterations by Miss de Vere. And Tommy phoned to say the hire of another warehouse has been arranged. And there's a letter from Shuttleworth Mills about their new cotton fabrics that wants answerin'. Eleven o'clock in the mornin' won't do, Mister Sammy, unless you've got a good excuse.'

'I'll come after you in a minute,' said Sammy.

'Yes, please – no, I mean no – not in office time. Just kindly explain why you're late, and if it's because you've been up to see Miss de Vere, I won't invite you to my weddin'.'

'Sometimes,' said Sammy, 'I get a painful feelin' I'd be better off deaf, you saucebox. I'd give you the sack if it wasn't for the fact that I'd miss your legs walkin' in and out of me office. What's kept me, you want to know? Well, I'm able to inform you, Miss Brown, that I've been to the Bermondsey Borough Council and offered them the scrap yard as a buildin' site, at the price we paid for the business, so that they could put up a block of municipal flats.'

'You want to sell that yard?' asked Susie.

'Well, I know your dad could get back to it in time, Susie, but there's always goin' to be some geezers nosin' about to get a look at where that girl's body was found. It's what's called morbid curiosity. You remember, don't you, a woman called Mrs Chivers, who was murdered a few doors away from where you're livin' now?'

'Yes, everyone in Walworth knew about that,' said Susie. 'Your fam'ly told me the full story. Boots was a witness at the trial of Elsie Chivers, the daughter, and so was your mum.'

'Boots got her off,' said Sammy. 'Our respected Ma said he gave his evidence like the Lord of creation, and juries take notice of the Lord of creation.'

'I can imagine,' said Susie. 'It must've been awful, a woman accused of murderin' her own mother. Em'ly said she wouldn't have hurt a fly. Yes, I can imagine Boots bein' impressive. He's got such an air, don't you think so?' Susie smiled teasingly. 'We all adore him, of course. Doreen says he makes her bosom rise and fall.'

'Might I remind you that I've told you before I won't have any adorin' on these premises, it interferes with business. Nor don't I want to see any bosoms risin' and fallin'. Tell Doreen a decent corset will solve her breathin' problems. Let's see, where was I? Yes, the point is, Susie, after the trial geezers from newspapers haunted the street for weeks. When they'd given up, along came the Nosey Parkers to look at the house and to ask questions. They kept comin'. Morbid curiosity, don't yer see, a bit of wordage Boots acquainted me with. It's goin' to be like that at Bermondsey, partic'larly if the police find the murderer and hang him. I don't want your dad to have to put up with staring eyeballs and queer questions. So I made the Council an offer of the yard, which they're considerin', and after that I made an offer for Rodgers and Company's scrap yard off the Old Kent Road. Which old man Rodgers accepted on the spot. That's the yard for your dad, Susie.'

'Sammy, oh, you lovely feller,' said Susie.

'Sound as a bell, your dad is,' said Sammy.

'Sammy, I'm goin' to be your best and only wife ever.'

'I'll try not to mind the expense,' said Sammy.

'I'll try not to as well,' said Susie. 'Tommy said he thinks you're usin' Mr Greenberg to corner all the textiles held by London wholesalers. I told him I was grievously afraid you are.'

'Well, we might get lucky,' said Sammy.

'It's just not fair,' said Susie.

'So you said before, Susie, but it's rattlin' good business. Now, kindly inform Ronnie to mount his bike and ride off to our Brixton shop with this box. They're expectin' it.'

The cardboard box, white, was on Sammy's desk.

'What's in it?' asked Susie.

'Silver-white bridal stockings,' said Sammy.

'Silver-white? Oh, let me see,' said Susie.

'You've already got your weddin' stockings, haven't you?'

'Yes, white, but not silver-white.' Susie picked up the box and sped into her office with it, closing the door behind her. Sammy grinned. Susie's legs in silver-white. Even a high-class reputable businessman could hardly wait.

When Ronnie, the office boy for two months, rode off to Brixton with the box, one pair of stockings was missing, a note from Susie in its place.

Sammy, having heard from Susie that Polly Simms wouldn't be at the wedding, after all, because she had to go abroad, felt a bit sorrowful about it. He liked Polly, the whole family did. She might be upper class, but could mix with all kinds. They'd miss her, the family, but it was just as well she was going abroad. She was a lot too fond of Boots, and Chinese Lady would raise the roof if Boots let it get out of hand.

Yes, just as well she was leaving.

A business acquaintance, a Covent Garden wholesale florist, popped in to see Sammy at twenty minutes past eleven. Susie had left at eleven – she had a hundred things to do, all in respect of the wedding. Josh Walker, who had gravitated from a flower stall in the East Street market to Covent Garden, owed Sammy a small favour. It was one of Sammy's profitable principles, to contrive for business friends or acquaintances to owe him favours.

'Well, 'ow's yerself, Sammy? In the pink, I see. Bloomin', as yer might say.'

'I might, if I didn't have headaches, Josh,' said Sammy.

'Oh, we all got those, Sammy. I'm just on me way to Peckham, so I thought I'd just look in on yer and 'and yer something for your fiancée, seein' yer doin' the honours with 'er next Saturday.' Josh Walker placed a long cardboard box on Sammy's desk. Sammy lifted the lid and saw at least a dozen bunches of magnificent King Alfred daffodils.

'Josh, I'm overcome,' he said.

'Pleasure. Good luck, mate. I can tell yer, marriage don't actu'lly kill yer.'

'Is that a fact?' said Sammy. 'Well, it suits me, one of me main business ambitions is to stay alive.'

'I admire an ambition like that,' said Josh Walker, and shook hands and departed, a large grin on his face.

Sammy, left with a plethora of superb blooms, decided this was ladies' day. He called Doreen in, gave her three dozen and told her to share them out among the girls.

'Mister Sammy, oh, ain't you an angel?' said Doreen.

'Glad you mentioned that,' said Sammy, 'in me modesty I sometimes forget it.' He took another four dozen blooms through Susie's office to Emily's little sanctum. She was at her typewriter. She worked from ten to twelve on Saturdays, the rest of the staff from nine to twelve-thirty.

'Sammy?' she said, gazing huge-eyed at the King Alfreds. Sammy winced a little at her thinness. His affection for Emily, who'd been a godsend to the family when they lived in Walworth, was deep-rooted. 'Sammy, what're all those daffodils doin' against your waistcoat?'

'Nothing useful,' said Sammy. 'Josh Walker's just handed me a box of them. Here's some for you. There you are, Em. Look a lot better against your bodice than my waistcoat.'

'Sammy, all these?' Emily, always demonstrative, positively sparkled. 'I'll stand them in a vase in the hall, where everyone can enjoy them. And you can give us a kiss for bein' a lovely bloke.'

'Cost you tuppence,' said Sammy.

'Oh, still chargin', are you?' smiled Emily, cuddling the blooms. 'All right, let's go mad, give us fourpennyworth.'

Sammy gave her two smackers, one on her cheek and one on her good-looking mouth. 'Here, that's not a brother-in-law's kiss.'

'Just a tuppenny one,' said Sammy. 'All right, Em, are you?' He hadn't the heart to refer directly to her thin look.

'Me?' said Emily, who hated what was happening to her, and only talked about it with Boots and Chinese Lady. Chinese Lady was doing her best to stuff her with lightly cooked liver and almost raw red meat. 'Me?'

'I like to ask after the health of me close relatives,' said Sammy.

'Well, this one's fine, Sammy love.'

'Tower of strength, you are, Em, as our shorthand-typist and a close relative.'

'Well, bless yer cotton socks for sayin' so, Sammy, and you're not so bad yourself. We're all lookin' forward to the weddin', and me and Boots are prayin' marriage won't ruin you.'

'Kind of you, Em. You had a wartime weddin', so did Lizzy. If mine's as good as yours was, I'll face up to the consequent ruination.'

'Same old Sammy,' said Emily.

'Good on yer, love,' said Sammy. On his way back to his office, he said, 'By the way, you owe me fourpence. Pay me later.' Emily laughed.

Sammy then called Ronnie in, the office boy having just got back from Brixton. Sammy had finally given in to demands from the general office staff for a runabout lad, and sixteen-year-old Ronnie Jarvis of Camberwell, looking for a job and eager for anything, had been taken on two months ago. Sammy already had his eye on the lad. He was willing, adaptable and good-natured. He stuck stamps on letters as readily as he helped Mitch, the firm's van driver, to load and unload. And he assisted in the shop below whenever he was asked to. Sammy liked anyone who liked work.

'Right, Ronnie, got your bike at the ready still, have you?'

'At your service, Mister Sammy, sir,' said Ronnie, slim, lanky and pleasant-looking. Sammy approved the fact that he didn't sport a quiff or put brilliantine on his hair.

'Good. Saddle up, then, me lad, and kindly deliver this box to Miss Brown. I've scribbled her address on the lid. Mind you hand it in with my compliments, and don't damage the contents or you and your bike will be hanged upside-down, which will hurt considerable.'

'Mister Sammy, I can frankly tell yer I don't like bein' hurt considerable.'

'Highly sensible,' said Sammy. 'Kindly get movin', and when you've made the delivery you can go home, which you'll be entitled to if it takes you up twelve-thirty. Here's a tanner for doin' this special delivery.'

'Well, thanks, sir,' said Ronnie, 'and I'd like to say I'm pleasured to be included with the staff at your weddin', seein' I've only been workin' here for two months.'

'Can't leave any of you out,' said Sammy, 'or there'd be ructions. Off you go.'

Ronnie had contributed to the staff collection for a wedding present, and the money had been used to buy Susie and Sammy a chiming clock.

Off went the whistling office boy to Caulfield Place, Walworth, the box strapped securely to the carrier. A knock on the door of the Browns' house was answered by Sally. She blinked at the caller.

'Hello,' he said, the cardboard box balanced on his hands.

'Hello yerself,' said Sally, looking pretty nice in a Saturday frock.

Ronnie, who hadn't worked in the offices for two months without taking educational note of the verbal attributes of Boots and Sammy, said, 'Am I addressin' a lady member of the Brown fam'ly?'

'You 'ave that honour,' said Sally, deciding he was putting it on.

'Might I 'ave the further honour of speakin' with Miss Susie Brown?' asked Ronnie, deciding he wasn't in any hurry.

'Alas,' said Sally, who'd never yet played second fiddle to a boy's chat.

'What?' said Ronnie.

'Alas.'

'Alas what?'

'Miss Susie Brown, my sister, don't 'appen to be in,' said Sally, 'she's gone shoppin' from 'er work.'

'Oh, well,' said Ronnie, 'p'raps I might have another further honour.'

'You're comin' it a bit with all these honours, ain't you?' said Sally.

'Could I enquire your name?'

'What for?'

'I think I like you,' said Ronnie.

'That's nothing,' said Sally, 'ev'ryone likes me, even me brother Freddy. What's that box you're 'olding?'

'Special deliv'ry to Miss Susie Brown, with the compliments of Mister Sammy Adams. I'm 'is assistant.'

'No, you're not,' said Sally, 'that's Susie.'

'Yes, I'm his junior assistant,' said Ronnie. 'Shall I come in and wait? I don't mind havin' a chat with you in your parlour.'

'I'm thrilled,' said Sally, 'but alas.'

'Alas what?' asked Ronnie, grinning.

'Alas, I'm just goin' to have poached eggs on Welsh

Rabbit with me fam'ly,' said Sally. 'You honestly on the firm's staff?'

'I have that honour,' said Ronnie.

'You're not comin' to the weddin', are you, with all the staff?'

'I have that further honour,' said Ronnie.

'You're a sad case, you are,' said Sally, 'you talk like someone's butler.'

'Funny thing, I was once—'

'Well, never mind, you're a junior assistant now,' said Sally. 'You can give the box to me.'

'Pleasure. I'm Ronnie Jarvis, by the way. Who did you say you were?'

'I didn't. Well, all right, I'm Sally Brown.'

'Pleased to meet yer, Sally. D'you go out with fellers?'

'No, course I don't, I'm still only fourteen.'

'I used to be fourteen,' said Ronnie. 'You soon grow out of it. Here.' He placed the box in her arms. 'I might come and sit in your parlour with you sometimes, and bring my mouth organ.'

''Elp, I can 'ardly wait,' said Sally.

'Me neither,' said Ronnie, and rode off whistling. Sally giggled and took the box to her mum, who lifted the lid and saw it was full of daffodils. She was so overcome by Sammy's flowery gift to Susie that she hardly heard anything of what Sally said about the boy who'd brought them. So Sally had to say most of it twice.

Coming to, Mrs Brown said, 'Oh, was he a nice boy, then?'

'Well, 'e was honoured at just standin' on our doorstep,' said Sally.

'Why, is our doorstep special, then?' asked Freddy.

'No, but he probably thinks Sally is,' said Will.

616

'Our Sally's only fourteen, she's only just left school,' said Mrs Brown.

'Oh, you soon grow out of only bein' fourteen,' said Sally.

CHAPTER SEVENTEEN

On Sunday afternoon, Annie and Will took to the winding paths of Ruskin Park along with other people, of whom there were plenty. The weather had warmed up. A fine Sunday always brought the cockneys of Camberwell and Walworth to the park, as well as better-off people from the neighbourhood of Denmark Hill. Annie had been able to put on her second best Sunday dress and to wear it without a coat. Will said it was nearly as highly fashionable as her white one. Annie said she was keeping that for his sister's wedding, that she'd be able to get to St John's Institute by a quarter to five. Was there really going to be dancing in the evening? Yes, to a three-piece band, said Will, and 'Knees Up, Mother Brown' would be performed.

'Crikey,' said Annie, 'will the vicar be there?'

'Yes, just for the knees-up,' said Will, sauntering beside her.

'I bet,' said Annie. 'Anyway, I'm not goin' to do any knees-up in me highly fashionable dress, not with you lookin'.'

'And the vicar,' said Will.

Annie bubbled with laughter. The exciting little undercurrents of being in love exhilarated her, but she kept her head, she didn't make the mistake of falling all over him in a manner of speaking. Of course, if he fell all over her – in a manner of speaking – she wouldn't mind that. She asked if he'd thought any more about leaving the Army. Will, who felt the Army's medical experts would make the decision for him, one way or another, said yes, he'd

618

thought more about it, and that he'd make up his mind before his leave was up. Annie said she supposed it was sensible for him to take his time. It didn't occur to her to ask him how long he'd signed up for simply because she didn't know enough about the conditions imposed on a man when he entered the Army. Will said as soon as he'd made the decision she'd be the first to know outside his family.

'Me?' said Annie.

'Well, you're—' Will checked. Better not to say because she was his young lady. If he was going to suffer asthma all his life, he didn't think he could ask a girl to suffer it with him. Suppose, for instance, it took hold of him every time he made love to her? That wouldn't make any wife rapturous, she'd think she'd married a wheezing old man. Mind, he'd only had one attack these last few days, and that was when he woke up on the morning after taking her to see Tom Mix. So he'd attended Dr McManus's morning surgery. Dr McManus wanted to know exactly what had preceded the attack. Will said eight hours good kip. Dr McManus asked if he had feather pillows. Will said the Army doctors in London had mentioned feather pillows, but there'd been none in India, and in any case, this was the first time he'd had an attack while still in bed. Dr McManus wanted to know what was the last food he'd eaten the night before. Will said fried fish and chips. Might have been the frying fat, said the doctor, you might be allergic to its acidity. Will asked if he might also be allergic to being close to a girl, and he mentioned his evening out with Annie, their closeness in the tram and their extreme closeness when he kissed her.

'Are we talking about physical excitement, Will?' asked Dr McManus.

'You did mention that,' said Will, and the doctor said he

supposed the Army medical specialists had mentioned a hundred and one possible elements. Will said they'd mentioned over-exertion as something to avoid, but hadn't said a word about physical excitement. Ruddy hell, doctor, he said, if he couldn't even kiss a girl without his bronchial tubes taking a hiding, what was the point of marrying one? Dr McManus said thousands of asthmatic men and women were married. Yes, said Will, but perhaps they can all do what comes naturally without wheezing and coughing over it.

'Well, do those two things again,' said Dr McManus.

'What two things?'

'Kissing your young lady and eating fried fish and chips. But not on the same day. Let's see if one or the other affects you. If not, then do what you did before, enjoy them near to each other.'

'Sounds barmy,' said Will.

'It might well be,' smiled Dr McManus. 'Do you carry your tablets about with you?'

'I do now,' said Will.

'You should.'

So there it was, then. It wouldn't do at this stage to give Annie any impression that he was courting her. It wouldn't be fair to her. Annie deserved a bloke who was a hundred per cent fit.

'Come on,' she said, 'what's on your mind?'

'Oh, just the Army,' he said, 'and if I'm goin' to be in or out of it.'

Annie wondered if his relationship with her had been anything to do with his idea about giving up the Army. She hoped he would.

They stopped by the tennis courts, all of which were being used.

'Let's sit and watch for a bit,' she said. There was a

bench vacant and they seated themselves. On another bench were a strong-looking man and a handsome woman. They were watching a tall man in a white cricket shirt and light grey flannels playing against a young and deliciously pretty girl in a white dress. Will recognized the players. The man, whom his family called Boots, was Sammy's eldest brother. The girl, Rosie, was Boots's daughter. Will had come to know them when Susie took him to meet the Adams family.

They were playing a typical father-and-daughter game, Boots teasing Rosie by making her chase from side to side, using his racquet in a lazy-looking way but making the ball fly over the net. Rosie, utterly involved, ran and scampered, the skirt of her short dress flying, her legs in white socks. She did more than chase after the ball, she yelled.

'Daddy, you stinker!'

But she was heart and soul into the fun of it, as she always was when any kind of game was just between her and Boots and she had him all to herself. All her affinity with him surfaced then.

Will thought the watching man and woman were very taken with her. Well, she wasn't bad at tennis. She had energy, enthusiasm and a good eye for a ball. Her enthusiasm was infectious. She screamed when Boots put a short one over, but she flew to get at it and just managed to plop it back. It left Boots stranded. She jumped up and down in her joy.

'Isn't she a young sport?' said Annie. 'I wish I could play tennis, it looks fun.'

'If I could play meself,' said Will, 'I'd teach you. Mind you, Annie, I've played football for the battalion. Like me to teach you that?'

'It's always been me dearest wish to play football, I don't think,' said Annie, sitting close to him because she liked being close, and Will began trying to puzzle out why the natural pleasure of the contact set off the little stirring sensations that threatened to sensitize his bronchial tubes, as they had the other evening.

Rosie yelled again.

'Daddy, I'll stick pins in you!'

'Play up, Rosie.'

'Will, what a lovely girl,' said Annie.

'She's Rosie Adams,' said Will, 'and that's her dad, Sammy's eldest brother.'

'Crikey, d'you know them?' asked Annie.

'Yes, I met all the Adams fam'ly, through Susie,' said Will.

''Ave they all turned posh, then, the Adams?'

'Not posh, no,' said Will. 'They used to live in the house we live in now. They bettered themselves when they left.'

'I don't blame them,' said Annie. 'I wish me dad had a chance to better 'imself, I bet he'd take it with both 'ands. Still, he's not down in the dumps about it, nor me. Nor you, are you, Will? I mean, well, I think we're betterin' ourselves just sittin' in the park and watchin' the tennis, don't you?'

'Are we?' asked Will, trying to ignore vibrations.

'Well, if we were sittin' on a doorstep in the Old Kent Road, we'd be more lower than better, wouldn't we?'

'More lower than better, yes, see what you mean,' said Will, who thought the strong-looking man on the other bench was concentrating a very fixed pair of mince pies on the scampering Rosie.

'It's nice we agree,' said Annie. 'I thought, when I first met you, I thought what an 'orror, I bet his parents despair of 'im. I don't know how you've managed to be such an improvin' feller; it must be the improved company

622

you've been keepin'. 'Ave you been goin' out to look at cathedrals with our vicar? He's ever so improvin', and nice as well.'

Will grinned. He watched Rosie serving, he watched her dance on quick feet as she waited for the return. He thought about Sally. Sally had quick feet and enthusiasms. He could just see her dancing about on a tennis court if she'd been given the chance to learn the game.

On the other bench, Madge said, 'Don't you wish she was yours, Henry?'

'What?' said Henry Brannigan.

'I mean don't you wish she was your daughter? She's a bit young for you otherwise.'

'I'm lookin', that's all,' he said.

'You ought to 'ave 'ad kids, Henry,' she said, 'then you wouldn't be such a lonely man. Come on, let's go back to the flat and I'll do us a nice Sunday tea, which I'd like to do, seein' 'ow good you're bein' to me.'

He had increased her allowance to two pounds a week because she was giving him suppers and Sunday dinner. She didn't think he'd only want food and company for ever. Well, when he wanted what was good for any real man, she'd be very willing.

Will and Annie left a few minutes later, Will deciding not to intrude on Boots and Rosie by making his presence known to them. Annie said he was going to have Sunday tea with her and her family, wasn't he? Will, who had kept the vibrations at bay simply by listening to Annie and watching the tennis, said he'd be pleasured.

'Pleasured?' said Annie. 'I 'ope you don't have larks in mind.'

'What larks?'

'Well, I don't know exactly how improved you are,' said Annie, 'you might not be improved all that much.'

'I think I've got larks comin' on,' said Will.

Annie's laughter gurgled.

I'll have to watch he doesn't put his head under the table again, she thought.

She experienced little vibrations then, but they weren't quite as alarming to her as Will's were to him.

'Me mum says you can stay to Sunday tea, Cassie,' said Freddy, who'd managed to resist her demands to be taken up the park again with her barmy cat. He'd persuaded her to ride around all the back streets instead, although she'd made his ears ache with her complaints that they wouldn't get to see the Prince of Wales or soldiers on horseback or the lady of a hundred and one nights. Freddy had had to ask the lady of what? Cassie, who naturally did a lot of reading, said there was a book about her and that she told stories to a sheikh on a white horse every night. Freddy said if he spent every night sitting on a white horse, he was as crackers as she was. Cassie complained he wasn't listening properly. Freddy said he was, that was why his ears were aching, and that anyone who told stories for a hundred and one nights was going a bit short of sleep. Cassie said well, she thought it was a hundred and one, and that she told her stories while she was wearing a big red ruby in her tummy button. Blimey, said Freddy, no wonder the sheikh couldn't get off his horse, with a big red ruby staring at him. Cassie complained he wasn't paying attention, and Freddy said he couldn't pay attention and ride his bike as well. Anyway, when they finally got home, Mrs Brown said Cassie could have Sunday tea with them, if she liked.

'Please, what yer got for tea?' asked Cassie.

'Boiled eggs, bread an' butter, salmon and shrimp paste, raspb'ry jam and cake,' smiled Mrs Brown.

'Crumbs, I'd like that,' said Cassie, 'but I'd best go 'ome first an' tell me dad I'm 'aving tea here.'

'I'll ride yer there,' said Freddy. A mate was a mate, even if she was scatty.

'No, I'll do a bit of walkin',' said Cassie, 'I don't think me bottom wants to sit on yer bike any more today.'

'Freddy, didn't you give her a cushion to sit on?' asked Mrs Brown.

'Course I did,' said Freddy, 'she gives me a rollickin' if I don't.'

'Yes, but I've gone all numb,' said Cassie.

'Cor,' said Freddy in glee, 'Cassie's got a numb bum.'

'Now, Freddy, you didn't ought to say that in front of Cassie,' said Mrs Brown.

'Oh, the Little Princess 'ad one of them,' said Cassie, 'when she sat on six velvet cushions that 'ad an 'ard pea under them. Well, I won't be long, I'll just go an' tell me dad.' Off she went, leaving Freddy grinning and Mrs Brown smiling. Will, Susie and Sally were all out, and Mr Brown was in the parlour, his feet up.

Along the pavement twinkled Mr Ponsonby, beaming at the sight of Cassie turning into Caulfield Place, her cat in her arms.

'Well, well, what a day, what a peaceful day,' he said, stopping.

'Yes, it's Sunday,' said Cassie.

'Sunday? Dear me, are you Cassie?'

'Yes, I'm goin' to 'ave tea with Freddy Brown,' said Cassie. She thought. 'I'm 'is mate. This is Tabby, me cat.'

'Charming, what a delightful picture,' said Mr Ponsonby happily. 'Have you had your photograph taken?'

'No,' said Cassie. 'Could yer take one, please, of me an' Tabby?'

'What a charming idea,' said Mr Ponsonby. 'I must find my camera. Dear me, where did I put it? Never mind, we must meet again, Sally—'

'I'm Cassie.'

'Why, yes, how pretty. Have a peppermint, Cassie.' Out came the paper bag. Cassie took one of the sweets. Tabby shifted about.

'Thanks ever so, I'll save it till after tea,' she said. 'Oh, could I 'ave one for Freddy?'

'Of course, of course, everyone must have a peppermint,' said Mr Ponsonby, and Cassie took one for her mate. Mr Ponsonby went pigeon-toed on his way, talking happily to himself. There were prospects, prospects.

Cassie arrived at the Browns' house with her cat. Freddy groaned.

'But 'e wanted to come,' said Cassie, ''e told me so. Well, 'e likes salmon an' shrimp paste.'

'An' boiled eggs?' said Freddy.

'No, just salmon an' shrimp paste,' said Cassie, 'as long as it's Kennedy's.'

In the parlour, Mr Brown shuffled his Sunday paper, turning again to a report on the Bermondsey murder. There was a reproduction of a Brownie snapshot of the unfortunate girl, and an artist's impression of the two missing girls. The Bermondsey scrap yard was mentioned more than once, and Collier and Son also featured. But not Adams Enterprises. All the same, Mr Brown neatly ripped out the relevant page, folded it and put it into his pocket.

Mr Brown was an old-fashioned guardian of his family's peace of mind. Susie, of course, knew the yard was the one he'd been promoted to manage, but none of the others did. More peaceful to keep it like that.

On the other hand, if the police caught the bloke, he

might have to appear at the trial as a witness to the discovery of the body. Then all the neighbours would be coming round to ask questions of his dear old Dutch and to say fancy your Jim finding that poor girl under his shed at work. Oh, well, thought Susie's cheerful dad, I'll look after that worry when it arrives, like old Noah said about the flood.

When Will finally said good night to Annie at her front door, he was in two minds about kissing her. Blimey, he thought, what a load of old turnips that was, any bloke being in two minds about kissing a girl like Annie. All the same.

'Well, Annie, it's been—'

'Lovely,' said Annie, and he wasn't given a chance then to do more shilly-shallying, because Annie wasn't in two minds herself. She kissed him. Well, of course, that did it for Will and he kissed her back, doing what came naturally instead of mucking about like a bloke who didn't know his knee from his elbow. Annie went wobbly with bliss and wondered what was happening to her legs. It felt as if they were going for a walk without her, leaving her with no support. So she hung on to Will. Ruddy marvels, thought Will, kissing her again, we're bosom to bosom and I like hers better than mine. Vibrations chased about, but nothing happened to his minor bronchial tubes. He felt A1 and in good order, and he also felt Annie was definitely just what the doctor ordered for Easter. So he kissed her some more. 'Help,' she said, coming out of a final kiss.

'Yes, I feel like a lie-down meself,' said Will. 'I'll go and collapse on me charpoy.'

'Your what?' said Annie faintly.

'Me Hindustani bed,' said Will. 'Good night, Annie, see you sometime durin' the week.'

'Good night, Will.' She closed the door when he'd gone. She felt breathless from being well and truly kissed. Oh, lor', me legs, they've run off somewhere.

It caught Will forty minutes later, the sensitization of his tubes. The time was twenty to eleven and he was just about to undress for bed in the room he shared with Freddy. Freddy was sound asleep and everyone else had retired. Knowing his coughing and wheezing would wake his young brother, Will just had time to get down to the kitchen before he began to fight for breath. He swallowed a tablet with difficulty, and then his coughing was racking him. He hoped his noisiness wouldn't disturb his parents, who occupied the downstairs bedroom between the kitchen and the parlour.

Mrs Brown lay awake listening to him and sighing for him. It was cruel, what life had done to her son, a young man only twenty. Poor Will. She wanted to get up to see if there was anything she could do for him, but she knew there wasn't, and she knew too that Will would rather be left alone.

It went on for what seemed like ages. It was for ten minutes, actually, but it left Will drained. You're bloody hopeless, mate, he told himself. It was a while before he took himself upstairs again.

Mrs Brown heard him go up.

CHAPTER EIGHTEEN

Susie had spent Sunday with her three closest girl friends, Evie Kent, Cora Bargett and Marjorie Willet, because it was her last Sunday as a single young lady. Accordingly, her friends weren't really sure if it was a Sunday of lamentation or celebration. They didn't put it quite like that, of course. If they had, they'd have thought they'd swallowed a dictionary. They'd never found the need to, not as Sammy had when establishing himself as a businessman who wasn't going to be out-talked.

As far as Evie was concerned it was more like poor old Susie, you're done for now. Cora suggested Susie could still be saved if someone came up with a just cause. Evie wanted to know what kind of just cause. Cora said some knowing bloke might be able to stand up in the church and yell bigamy on account of the bridegroom already having six wives. Evie said crikey, yes, that could save Susie. Marj said Susie might not want to be saved, that she didn't look as if she did. Susie said don't mind me, just keep talking. Evie asked her if she wanted to be saved. Only from you lot, said Susie.

Cora said Susie was bound to have worries. Have you got worries, Susie? Marj asked the question. Course she has, said Cora, she's got the terrible worry of being jumped on on her wedding night. Evie said you ain't half getting common, Cora. Come on, girls, let's clap hands and sing 'Here Comes The Bride', said Marj. Evie said what, on Clapham Common? You bet, said Cora, and let's do a knees-up as well. All right, said Marj, but let's all have a drop more port first.

Susie put a stop to that idea. A girls' picnic with port wine and lemon on Clapham Common was all right, but not a knees-up. Still, they all had a riotous hen party and tea out as well.

Susie went into Sammy's office first thing on Monday morning, presented herself to him as a very personable private secretary, said she was pleased to see him and gave him a kiss.

'I liked that, Miss Brown, and I won't say I didn't, but what was it for?'

'You,' said Susie.

'I naturally hope so, Miss Brown,' said Sammy, 'I'm against it bein' for anyone else.'

'It's for that great box of daffodils, Sammy darling.'

'A small token of me feelings, Susie, on account of you bein' invaluable in the office and highly desirable on your mum's parlour sofa. That's when your mum's not actu'lly there, of course.'

'Lucky for you she's not,' said Susie, 'she'd be shocked at the way you interfere with my bosom. Still, I love you for the daffodils, the house is full of them, except that Cassie's cat ate one at teatime yesterday, I'm told.'

'Who's Cassie?' asked Sammy.

'Freddy's young lady mate,' said Susie.

'Good on Freddy,' said Sammy. 'Did you enjoy a lively hen party?'

'Well, we had a port wine picnic and a knees-up,' said Susie.

'Where?'

'On Clapham Common.'

'Here, hold me up, I'm fallin' over,' said Sammy. 'A

knees-up on Clapham Common and you nearly me better half?'

'Oh, the knees-up was only nearly too,' smiled Susie. 'By the way, Boots says there's a mountain of post.'

'Right, see what our share is all about, Miss Brown, and let's get down to some work.'

'Yes, very good, Mister Sammy.'

Sammy popped into Boots's office later and asked him how Emily was. Boots said she was in her office. Sammy said he knew that. The point was, why was she getting so thin? Anaemia, said Boots briefly. You can be fat and still have anaemia, said Sammy. I know, said Boots, and you can be thin too. She needs lots of liver and exercise, said Sammy. I know, said Boots. I don't like to see her looking skinny, said Sammy. Nor do I, said Boots. Thought I'd ask about her, said Sammy. Yes, thanks, said Boots.

Just after twelve, Mrs Rachel Goodman knocked on Susie's outer door and entered.

'Good morning, Susie,' she said.

'Oh, good mornin', Mrs Goodman,' said Susie. If there was one woman she'd really been jealous of, it was Rachel Goodman, a dark and lustrous beauty who, in Sammy's younger days, had been his one and only girlfriend. According to Boots, she paid Sammy a penny to kiss her, and Sammy had acquired a small fortune in pennies from her. During his growing years, Sammy refused to kiss or be kissed unless he was given a penny. Susie suspected Rachel still had a soft spot for Sammy. Further, she really was a beautiful woman, a cockney Jewess whose father had given her an excellent education and helped her acquire a flair for always looking superbly dressed. Today she was wearing a light spring coat over a silk dress of lilac blue, and a dark blue cloche hat.

For her part, Rachel was careful not to go straight to Sammy's office. She had always done so before Susie became engaged to him. Nowadays she announced herself to Susie first, much though it went against the grain. As a girl she had adored Sammy, her gentile boy friend who not only took her roller-skating but also to his home to enjoy a Christian Sunday tea with his family. As a woman she still hankered after being close to him. Her husband, Benjamin Goodman, was a course bookie and coming up in the world. Horse-racing did not interest her in the least. Clothes did, and so did the rag trade. She was a shareholder in Adams Fashions Ltd and on the board of directors with Sammy, Boots, Tommy and their sister Lizzy. It was her way of being part of Sammy's life.

'Is Sammy in?' she asked.

'Is he expecting you?' asked Susie, and the fair and lovely clashed with the dark and lustrous. The dark and lustrous smiled.

'My life, Susie, must he be expecting me?'

'Oh, it's a sort of informal call?' said Sammy's extremely personable private secretary.

'Yes and no,' said Rachel, who liked Susie, as everyone did. She would simply have preferred Sammy to remain a bachelor. 'He's aware there might be a strike in the rag trade?'

'He's growlin' about it, but keepin' his end up,' said Susie.

'I've something to discuss with him.'

'I'll tell him you're here, Mrs Goodman,' said Susie. She got up, opened the door to Sammy's office and said, 'Mrs Goodman's here and would like to see you.'

'Well, I never,' said Sammy, 'ask her to step in.'

'There, you can go in, Mrs Goodman,' said Susie.

'Thank you, Susie,' said Rachel, her smile winning. She

was not a mean-minded woman, she was generous and warm-hearted. 'Good luck on Saturday, have a wonderful wedding. Sammy's a lucky man.'

'How kind,' said Susie, 'thank you.'

Rachel went in and Susie closed the door, although she would have liked to leave it open.

Sammy came to his feet. Rachel flowed towards him with soft little rustles of silk.

'Bless me soul, Rachel,' he said, 'ain't you a sight for me sore eyes?'

'Well, bless you, Sammy love, for saying so.'

'I'm up to me ears, but sit down. To what do I owe the pleasure of havin' you decorate my office?'

'You're my business interests, sweetie,' said Rachel. She parted her coat, delicately hitched her dress and sat down. Long legs gleamed in fine silk stockings.

Predictably, of course, Sammy said, 'Pardon me, but ain't that slightly out of order for a married female person?'

'Slightly,' agreed Rachel, 'but no more than you deserve, Sammy, having always been complimentary about my remarkable female legs. I'm coming to your wedding, of course, but I'll be a little mournful. You understand?'

'It won't make any difference to me respectable affections for you,' said Sammy. 'You bein' a well-behaved married woman and me bein' the reverent son of Chinese Lady, me affections have always been respectable, which if they weren't would make Susie hit me with her dad's chopper. I think she keeps it in her handbag. Choppers are injurious, Rachel.'

'Same old Sammy,' murmured Rachel. 'I should want a different one? Never. Now, what's going to happen to Adams Fashions if there's a strike that'll be injurious to our new contract with Coates?'

'I'm in touch with the mills and I've taken certain steps

633

concernin' buildin' up stocks,' said Sammy and put her fully in the picture. He included details of how he was going to keep the factory working.

'Ain't you a clever boy, Sammy, ain't you a love?' said Rachel, reverting to her Jewish cockney style. 'My life, what a bright boy. Oh, and my daddy says that to help you get married with two smiles on your face, he's arranged with the third party for you to sign the lease on the Oxford Street shop on Friday, the day before you go to the altar.'

'I'm touched, Rachel. Ain't you and Isaac me lifelong friends?'

'And ain't it mutual, Sammy love? Take me to lunch now, will you, while you're still a bachelor?'

'Did I catch that?' asked Sammy.

'Just a drink and a kosher sandwich, Sammy, for old times sake,' murmured Rachel, voice and eyes velvety. 'Last lunch, lovey, last time. I promise. Unless we accidentally run into each other in town.'

'I'll have to consult with me personal assistant who, bein' me personal fiancée as well, might say no and also beat me brains out.' Sammy found Susie up to her elbows in correspondence. 'Ah, Miss Brown, would you kindly note I'm about to depart on a business lunch? I'll be out for forty minutes or so.'

'Who with, if I might ask?' said Susie. 'I don't happen to have recorded any business lunch in your diary.'

'Just an oversight, I forgive yer,' said Sammy.

'Might I ask if it's with a certain married woman?'

'A member of the board of Adams Fashions,' said Sammy. Susie gave him a look. Sammy fell into her blue eyes. He coughed to clear his throat. 'Well, now I remember, she does happen to be related in marriage to her better half.'

Susie laughed. Sammy wriggling was so funny.

'It's the last time, Sammy, you hear?' she said.

'Which I've agreed on with the selfsame board member.'

'Your old flame,' said Susie.

'In a way, Susie, in a way.'

'Tell her her light's gone out,' said Susie.

'No worries, Susie.'

'I know.' Susie smiled. 'Run along, Sammy.'

'Do what? I'm hearin' things again,' said Sammy, departing.

'Well, lovey?' said Rachel.

'That Susie, what a performance,' said Sammy. 'I sometimes wonder who invented female women. Well, let's pop across to the pub, Mrs Goodman.'

'Lovely,' said Rachel, 'I want to talk to you about your old friend Eli Greenberg.'

Over lunch and sitting close to Sammy in the well-appointed saloon bar, Rachel dwelt on the present misfortunes of Mr Greenberg. He was, she said, a harassed gent. A certain lady had him in her liquid sights. Sammy asked if that meant her mince pies were floating in gin. Rachel said the lady was a respectable widow with three growing sons and had never touched a drop in her life. Mrs Hannah Borovich, that was her name.

'Russian, like Eli?' said Sammy.

'You've got it, Sammy,' said Rachel, a laugh in her eyes. The lady, she said, had made up her mind she needed a new father for her sons and had decided Mr Greenberg would fit the bill and also make her a fine husband. What, Eli Greenberg? Quite so, Sammy, said Rachel, and pointed out that Mr Greenberg, when dressed up on the Jewish Sabbath, was a handsome man. Sammy said he had to admit that when the well-known rag-and-bone man attended Chinese Lady's wedding to her second husband,

635

he looked highly presentable. Mrs Borovich, said Rachel, was prepared to devote herself to making him look presentable every day of the week. Dear Mr Greenberg was now beginning to panic, and was looking for hiding-places.

'He needs your help, Sammy.'

'What, to get out of the country?'

'No, to be saved from becoming a husband and father in one go.'

'Can't he just say no?'

'Mrs Borovich is deaf to negatives.'

'Well, poor old Eli and hard luck as well,' said Sammy.

'What help are you offering?'

'Who can help any bloke who's up against a deaf woman?'

'He's not up against her, Sammy love, she won't allow that until they're married. Mr Greenberg needs your brains. Think of something.'

'Any use offering him the loan of Susie's chopper? Well, her dad's chopper.'

'There'll be blood, Sammy. No blood, if you don't mind.'

'I'm beat,' said Sammy, but took time off to do some thinking. Rachel watched him with a little sigh in her eyes. Sammy, perking up, said, 'This deaf Mrs Boggervich—'

'Borovich, Sammy.'

'Just as you like, Rachel me affectionate friend. Point is, just how respectable is she?'

'Highly,' smiled Rachel.

'Good on yer,' said Sammy, and suggested that the only way to put off a female woman who was rigid with respectability and deaf to negatives was to personally assault her and interfere with her bosom as well.

Rachel almost choked on a mouthful of kosher beef sandwich with mustard.

'Sammy, Sammy, I'm to tell dear Mr Greenberg that?' she said, laughter choking her as well.

'With the compliments of me brains,' said Sammy.

'Never, Sammy, never. Mr Greenberg will collapse at the idea.'

'Not if he's desperate. He'll give it desperate thought. It could be all over in a couple of ticks. Chuck her on to his sofa, grab all he can of her, undo her buttons—'

'Sammy, you're killing me.'

'Hope not, Rachel, I've got fond memories of you as a roller-skater. Now, as soon as Mrs Boggervich realizes Eli is treadin' all over her widow's respectability, she'll jump out of his window and run a mile.'

'Oh, my God,' breathed Rachel, 'you're my one and only Punch and Judy, and with knobs on. Chuck the lady on to his sofa, grab her all over, undo her buttons—'

'That's just a few loose details, Rachel. Eli's got sense enough to tighten them up and to make the lady feel he's a ruddy wolf, never mind how respectable he looks on his Sabbath.'

'Sammy, I'm going to miss you as a bachelor,' said Rachel, and put her hand on his knee and squeezed it.

'Is that a personal assault?' said Sammy.

'Why couldn't you have assaulted me a bit when I was your girl?'

'What, at my age?' said Sammy.

The schools having broken up for the Easter holidays, there were kids everywhere, swarms of them. Henry Brannigan, a ganger working for contractors that specialized in demolishing buildings and clearing sites, reckoned there wasn't a pavement in London free of kids. Some of them were here, watching him and his mates clearing the site of what was left of a demolished builders' yard and sheds in Peckham. To one side was a huge fire they were feeding with wrecked timber.

''Ere, mister, can we 'ave some of that wood?' asked a boy.

'No, yer can't, so shove off, all of yer,' he growled.

'Go on, mister, be a sport.'

''Oppit, yer standin' in people's way,' he said. They were doing just that, the whole lot of them, filling the pavement just outside the barrier of ropes. Passing people had to push a way through the kids or step into the road. You could never tell about people. Some could be the kind that didn't like going under ladders or stepping on lines. These loitering kids could make life difficult for all kinds. Henry Brannigan had sympathy for kindred spirits, and life had done him a good turn for once by having him meet Madge. A bloke could talk to a woman like that, knowing she understood. She didn't mind kids herself, she didn't even mind them getting in her way.

'Mister, there's some nice bits of wood over there.' The voice was persistent.

'If you lot don't push off—' Henry Brannigan growled himself to a stop. 'Bloody 'ell, all right.' Madge wouldn't like him handing out clouts and thick ears instead of timber that was only going to finish up on the fire. ''Ere y'ar, then.' His workmates looked on in surprise as he got rid of a whole heap of timber by distributing it among the eager kids. Boys and girls all scrambled for it. Sacks materialized. Gawd blimey, he thought, look at that, the young bleeders have brought sacks. He chucked wood over the ropes at them. They scattered in retreat from a deluge of timber. Back they came when he'd finished showering the pavement. They loaded their sacks. Shafts of wood protruded.

638

'Ta, mister, yer a real sport.'

'Me mum'll like this lot.'

'Can we come back for some more, mister?'

'Well, all right. Now 'oppit.'

They hopped it. Away they went, dragging the heavily laden sacks along behind them. He stared at them. Look at what they were doing now, turning themselves into a sack-pulling procession, crowding the pavement with their feet as well as their sacks, and getting in everybody's way. There ought to be a law against awkward kids.

He spoke to Madge about it when they were walking that evening. Madge just said she thought he'd been kind.

'You like kids really, yer know,' she said, 'or you wouldn't 'ave 'anded out all that wood.'

'I don't like 'em gettin' in me way.'

'But they don't mean no 'arm,' said Madge. 'Well, they don't know about our superstitions.'

'Granted, Madge, but it don't do to treat fate light, I can tell yer,' he said, and they adjusted their walk as they entered the light of a street lamp. A running boy nearly cost Henry Brannigan dear. He almost stepped on a line that was plainly visible. The boy dashed by. A girl appeared. She was running too, and shouting as well.

'You Billy, come back 'ere! I'll wallop yer if you don't!' Up she came and ran straight between the man and the woman, who stopped. Henry Brannigan checked and drew a breath of relief.

'Nigh on done it in, both of us,' he said. 'Kids. Didn't I tell yer?'

'Wasn't the girl a goer, though?' said Madge, as they walked on and left the light behind them. 'Wish I 'ad one like 'er. Henry, can we go in a pub?'

'Well, you like a pub, Madge, even if you ain't much of a drinker.'

'Well, I ain't ever taken to mother's ruin,' said Madge, 'and I ain't likely to, but yes, I do like a pub and can make a glass last me a long time.'

He took her to one in the New Kent Road, where no-one recognized her or made her an offer. She wanted to stand treat, although she said it would be out of his money. He said it was always a gent's privilege to pay. He bought her the drink she liked, port and lemon, and himself an ale, and in the smoky, cosy atmosphere of the pub she told him she'd been to an orphanage near Norwood today, with the woman from next door. She'd already made friends with her, and she went with her to do a bit of voluntary work, because the place was crowded out with orphans and they were short of staff. There was a girl, nine years old.

'A girl, eh?' said Henry Brannigan brusquely.

'She's dyin' for a proper 'ome,' said Madge. 'I expect they all are, poor kids, but this one, well, she touched me 'eart. Would yer mind if I asked if I could 'ave her? I'd like to look after her, I could put another bed in the bedroom. I mean, now I'm livin' a decent life—'

'They'd ask yer for references, they'd ask if you was married.'

'Oh, gawd,' said Madge.

'No girls, anyway,' said Henry Brannigan.

'Don't yer like girls?'

'I'd be glad if yer'd drop the notion.'

'Well, all right, I will for a bit,' said Madge, 'but I know you've got a soft 'eart, and I'll ask yer again later on. You might be able to 'elp me get over any problems about references or not bein' married. You 'ave got a soft 'eart or you wouldn't be doin' for me what you are doin', settin' me up in that nice flat, givin' me an allowance an' not askin' for nothing. Yes, I'll ask yer again, Henry.'

'I 'ope you won't,' he said.

Scotland Yard had been busy. They'd established from available evidence and new enquiries that the murdered girl and the two missing girls had all disappeared during daylight hours on separate Saturday afternoons. They'd further established that not one person had seen any of them in company with a man. Enquiries concerning the possibility that someone might have witnessed an act of abduction came to nothing. But there was the reasonable assumption that Saturday afternoons suggested a pattern of acts by one man, a man whose job kept him off the streets during the day until his working week finished at Saturday midday.

The girls had disappeared in circumstances that had attracted no notice. Abduction would surely have been noticed in one case out of three.

Scotland Yard decided all three girls had known the man.

'Ton of Brooke Bond tea,' said a well-known voice on Tuesday morning, and Annie looked up from the till. Will had done it on her again, hiding himself behind a customer and then popping up.

'I think you're familiar to me,' she said.

'Hope not,' said Will, 'me mum and the Army both brought me up not to be familiar to young ladies.'

Annie glanced around. Mr Urcott and Miss Banks both had customers.

'It didn't feel like that at me front door on Sunday night,' she whispered.

'Didn't feel like what?'

641

'As if you didn't go in for bein' familiar.'

'Must have forgotten me manners,' said Will. 'What about the Brooke Bond?'

'How much did you ask for?'

'Quarter-pound packet,' said Will, 'plus a pound of dried apricots, a tin of mustard powder and a pound packet of salt.'

'Yes, sir, thank you, sir,' said Annie, liking the look of him very much. She served him. 'Anything else, sir?'

'Well,' said Will, who felt he ought to step aside in favour of some bloke who could offer Annie health and virility instead of a wheezing chest, 'I've decided I'd better stay in the Army. There's too much unemployment knockin' around in Southwark and Lambeth.'

'Oh,' said Annie wishing he hadn't chosen to tell her here in the shop. At home she could have talked to him about it.

Will, knowing the Army was more likely to discharge him than to let him stay on, could have told Annie so and given her the reason. But he preferred not to present himself as a semi-invalid. It was a case of a young man trying to step aside in what he thought was the way a decent bloke should.

'I'll probably be rejoinin' my battalion in India when my leave's up,' he said. The battalion, actually, was due to be posted home in a few months, when its spell of duty in India would be at an end.

Annie felt a painful blow had been struck.

'Rotten old Army,' she said bravely. Two new customers came in. 'Look,' she said, 'I'll speak to my dad. He might know if you could get a job on the railways.'

'Well, thanks, Annie,' said Will. 'How much for the groceries?'

Annie told him, he paid up, put the items into his

carrier bag, said he'd see her at the wedding dance on Saturday, gave her a smile and left. Annie felt then that some old dark blind had been drawn over her sunshine.

'Lookin' forward to dancing at the weddin', Annie?' said the Gaffer over a supper of fried mackerel that evening.

'If I get there,' said Annie, and the Gaffer glanced at her. She wasn't too lively this evening.

'But it's only down Larcom Street,' said Nellie.

'I ain't keen on dancin' meself,' said Charlie.

'Lucky you ain't been invited, then,' said Nellie.

'Nor me,' said Cassie, 'I ain't been invited, either.'

'Well, you'd only want to take the cat wiv yer,' said Charlie.

'Yes, 'e likes weddings,' said Cassie, ''e'd like to go to Lord Percy's weddin'.'

'Cassie, who's this Lord Percy you keep talkin' about lately?' asked Nellie.

'I read about 'im,' said Cassie, ''e lives in a castle with four 'undred servants.'

''Ow many?' asked the Gaffer.

'Yes, and 'e's got ten motorcars and an 'undred black 'orses an' carriages. 'E's goin' to marry a princess.'

'What princess?' asked Nellie.

'I didn't read which one it was,' said Cassie. 'Here, Tabby.' She fed a piece of mackerel to the cat, a large piece.

'Cassie, you just fed 'alf yer supper to Tabby,' said the Gaffer.

'Well, 'e likes fish,' said Cassie, 'an' besides, 'e's courtin'.'

''E's what?' said Nellie.

'It's Mrs Boddy's lady cat,' said Cassie, ''e's been out nearly all day with 'er, and it's made 'im 'ungry.'

643

'Why?' asked Charlie.

''Ow do I know?' said Cassie. 'I know some things, I don't know ev'rything. Annie, does courtin' make ladies blush?'

'Don't ask me, I'm not bein' courted,' said Annie.

'Oh, ain't Will courtin' yer?' asked Nellie.

'He's married to the Army,' said Annie. No, blow that, she thought, putting aside depression, I'm not going to let him get away with it. Just wait till Saturday and I see him in the Institute. I'm going to stand up for my rights. I've got rights after being kissed till I couldn't hardly stand up. 'Cassie, I suppose you read it somewhere, did you, that courtin' makes ladies blush?'

'Yes, it was in a story, it said that when the 'andsome explorer kissed Lady Penelope on 'er marble staircase, it made 'er blush all over.'

'Well, I'm blowed,' said the Gaffer, 'a kiss on 'er marble staircase, was it? I don't ever remember I kissed any lady meself except on 'er dewy lips.'

'Dewy lips?' Nellie giggled. 'Where'd you get that from, Dad?'

'Well, I do a bit of readin' meself,' said the Gaffer.

'Cassie, 'ow'd yer know Lady Whatsername blushed all over?' asked Nellie.

'Wasn't she wearin' nothink?' asked Charlie.

'Course she was,' said Cassie, 'she was wearin' a ruby velvet gown.'

'So 'ow'd yer know she blushed all over?' asked Charlie.

'It said so. It said – oh, 'elp,' sighed Cassie, looking down at the cat.

'What's up?' asked the Gaffer.

'I think Tabby's just done a wee-wee on the kitchen floor,' said Cassie.

CHAPTER NINETEEN

The horse and cart crossed the junction at Camberwell Green, entered Denmark Hill and pulled up outside the public house that was opposite the shop and offices of Adams Enterprises. Mr Greenberg climbed down, put a nosebag on his horse and crossed the road like a man so careless of his life and limb that a tram driver gave him a full clang of his bell. It was doubtful if Mr Greenberg heard it.

He arrived in Sammy's office with his hat off, his red handkerchief mopping his distracted brow.

'Hello, Eli, what's brought you?' asked Sammy.

'Sammy, Sammy, you have ruined me.'

'First I've heard of it,' said Sammy. 'Are you speakin' of bankruptcy?'

'Vorse, Sammy, vorse, ain't it?'

'Is it?'

'Vasn't it only yesterday I vas hale and hearty and a free man? A poor man, Sammy, but a free one. Today I am ill and in chains.'

'Well, I'm up to me ears in work meself, Eli, but sit down and get it all off your chest. I've got a feelin' you're referring to a highly personal matter concernin' your private life.'

Mr Greenberg, sighing, sat down and began to recount the sad story of his highly personal and private downfall. In the belief that Sammy's advice, passed to him by Rachel Goodman, would relieve him of the pressing attentions of the widow, Mrs Hannah Borovich, he received her into his

645

house last night in his shirt, braces and trousers, which itself startled the lady, she being a woman of propriety. Forthwith, as advised, Mr Greenberg laid hands on her like a man of no propriety at all and bore her to the sofa. There, he did what he could to assault her respectable bosom in a way that would convince her to regard him as the daughters of Abraham regarded Lucifer. Calamity occurred. Mrs Borovich flung her arms around him, kissed him and declared herself his willing woman. She further declared that afterwards she would go with him at once to Rabbi Goldstein for the marriage contract to be arranged. Mr Greenberg, aghast, began to struggle. Alas, Mrs Borovich declared herself already fully compromised, for her blouse and corset were gaping, which Mr Greenberg swore to Sammy wasn't his doing.

Sammy roared with laughter. Mr Greenberg eyed him in sorrow.

'Ve are not amused, Sammy.'

'She cooked your goose for you, Eli.'

'Vhat a schemin' voman, ain't it?' groaned Mr Greenberg.

'Do you good, old cock,' said Sammy, 'seein' Rachel informed me she's a handsome lady. You saw the rabbi?'

'Vhat else could I do, Sammy? Vhat else vould she let me do? Didn't she herself take me there vithout vunce lettin' go of me, and didn't Rabbi Goldstein greet me vith a hundred smiles and shake my hand?'

Sammy said it was a lesson to both of them, that it didn't matter what kind of a straightforward plan a man thought up, any female woman could put her foot through it and set about turning him upside-down. He himself had been stood on his head by a certain young woman on frequent occasions, despite him being a self-made man of considerable brains. Which proved one thing for certain.

'Vhat thing?' asked Mr Greenberg.

'Blokes never learn, Eli, not even you and me,' said Sammy. 'I ought to have remembered that when I put my wheeze to Rachel to pass to you. Now I know why she laughed. She knew what was goin' to happen, that Mrs Boggervich was goin' to turn you upside-down. Well, I'll resign meself to your weddin', Eli, and hope you'll invite me and Susie.'

'Ah, the veddin',' said Mr Greenberg, and groaned again. 'A vife and three growing sons to be my responsibility? The expense, Sammy, the expense.'

'I feel for you, don't think I don't,' said Sammy. 'Ruination has already hit all me own pockets. Still, a handsome woman, think of the compensations. And she can cook, I suppose?'

'Sammy, I should think of food vhen my stomach don't have any heart left?'

'Look on the bright side,' said Sammy.

'But a vife and three sons, Sammy.'

'Congratulations,' said Sammy. 'There's a bottle in me sideboard there. Kindly take a nip with me on account of the blessings.'

'Vell, Sammy, a nip at a sad time like this is a velcome sign of friendship, ain't it?'

'Cassie, you ain't bringing that cat,' said Freddy. His mum had made some sandwiches for him and Cassie, and supplied an apple each as well. They were going to eat them in Kennington Park.

''E's got to come,' said Cassie, ''e keeps goin' off with Mrs Boddy's lady cat. 'E'll go off with 'er for good one day. She wants 'im to marry 'er.'

'Oh, he's said so, 'as 'e?' said Freddy.

'Yes, 'e tells me ev'rything,' said Cassie.

'Well, ask 'im to tell yer if 'e minds stayin' behind,' said Freddy. 'They won't let 'im in the park.'

'I'll look after him, love,' said Mrs Brown.

'Oh, all right,' said Cassie.

'I went up the park earlier,' said Freddy. 'They said they'd mind me bike when we get there, Cassie, but they said they didn't want yer cat around, that they'd got orders to chop its 'ead off if yer bring it. So yer'd better let me mum mind it.'

'Yes, I said all right. 'E likes fish best, Mrs Brown.'

'I'll find him something,' said Mrs Brown.

Off the boy and girl went, Cassie riding astride a cushion and swinging her legs. Going along Manor Place, she said, 'Me sister Annie's been invited to the weddin'.'

'Yes, but me bruvver Will says she can't get there till about five,' said Freddy.

'I ain't been invited,' said Cassie.

'Well, you can come with 'er, if you like,' said Freddy. 'I expect me mum'll let yer.' Up Doddington Grove they went, Freddy ringing his bell at kids. 'Do yer do dancin'?'

'Course I do,' said Cassie, dreaming of kings in scarlet and queens in diamonds. 'Is there goin' to be photographs?'

'Susie won't 'alf get vexed if there ain't.'

'I'm 'aving me photo took,' said Cassie.

'Who by?' asked Freddy, totally resigned to having a scatty mate.

'Mr Po's'by,' said Cassie.

'Is 'e goin' to charge yer?' asked Freddy, skirting a slow-moving corporation water-cart.

'Course not,' said Cassie. ''E likes me, 'e gives me peppermints.'

'Fancy that,' said Freddy. ''Ere, if you come with yer sister on Saturday, don't expect me to dance with yer.'

'I'll kick yer if you don't,' said Cassie.

When they reached the park, a keeper obligingly took care of the bike, and Cassie took care of Freddy. That is, she made him go where she went and she made him carry the shopping bag in which were the wrapped sandwiches and the apples. She also told him to get her a bunch of daffodils. There were beds of them. Freddy said not on your life, his mum didn't allow him to nick daffodils and his dad would give him a talking-to. Cassie said he didn't have to nick them, just help himself when the park-keepers weren't looking. The Queen helped herself to lots of daffodils at Windsor Castle, and the King never told her it was nicking. Freddy said as he didn't happen to be the Queen, he wasn't going to help himself. Cassie said he couldn't be the Queen, anyway, he wasn't a lady.

'Thank gawd for that,' said Freddy. Still, even if she was scatty, she wasn't such a bad mate, because when it came to eating the sandwiches she let him have two and a half while she only had one and a half. And when he'd eaten his apple, she let him have two bites out of hers, and she also let him have the core, which he crunched to juicy destruction.

A mate like that was quite valuable to a bloke.

'Here's all the letters, Boots,' said Emily that afternoon, and placed the tray on his desk. 'I'm off now to buy the fam'ly's Easter eggs.'

He looked up at her, into her green eyes. She was all green eyes and thin face.

'Good for you, Em. Sure you're not overdoing things?'

'I'm fine. And you know me, if I've got nothing to do except sit and twiddle me thumbs, I'm not fit to live with. Behave yourself now, see you at home later.' Emily kissed him, warmly and affectionately. It left him in a reflective mood, signing the letters without taking too much notice of their contents.

'I did yer room out today, 'Enry,' said Mrs Queenie Watts, intercepting her brother as he entered the house in the evening.

'What for?' asked Henry Brannigan.

'Well, you've been in a nice and 'elpful mood lately,' she said, 'and yer lookin' lots better.'

'You don't need to do me room out, Queenie,' he said, sure she hadn't done very much to any of the others. His own room was private to him, anyway.

'I'd of done yer cupboard out, given it a bit of a tidyin',' she said, 'only yer keep it locked, I notice.'

'I've got personal things in it, mementoes, like.'

'Oh, about yer poor Matty, of course. Still, I thought I'd give yer room a nice clean-up, and I put a bit of polish on the furniture.' Actually, she'd just given everything a flick with her feather duster while nosing around to see if there was anything that would point to him having found a woman.

'Good of yer, Queenie, but I can manage.'

'Well, it's pleasin' yer not so sorrerful about things,' said Queenie. 'You sure you ain't found someone that's givin' you a bit of a lift?'

'I've made a few friends lately.'

'Well, I'm glad to 'ear it,' she said, and let him go up to his room. She wondered if there was any money in that cupboard. He got a decent wage and he'd collected from an insurance company when his wife fell out of that train and went to her death, poor woman. Queenie felt she wouldn't mind a bit of a loan that would pay for her and Stan to have a week in Margate.

* * *

650

Scotland Yard men were in dogged pursuance of the conviction that the man they were after had been known to the murdered girl and the two still missing. For the two still missing, they had the gravest concern, and at the moment were conducting exhaustive enquiries in and around the respective areas in which the three girls had lived.

Good Friday being a holiday, Susie had a word with Sammy at four o'clock on Thursday afternoon. First, might she leave now to go to certain shops before they closed?

'You might, Miss Brown, except—'

'Thank you, Sammy.' Second, might she point out that when they next met it would be at the altar?'

'What altar?'

'Yes, I hope I remember which one too. Sammy, I just want to say thanks for everything, for givin' me a chance and believin' in me when I had my first job on your market stall, and for – oh, you know.'

'What, Susie?'

'For lovin' me and askin' me. I like it, don't you, Sammy?'

'Marryin' each other?' said Sammy.

'Yes, it's such a nice idea,' smiled Susie, 'and don't forget to promise to love, honour and obey.'

'Me? Me do what?'

'Yes, it'll be best that way,' said Susie. 'I'll speak to the vicar.'

'You Susie—'

'There's a good boy. See you Saturday, love.' Susie kissed him and departed, leaving Sammy floored. She looked in on Boots.

'Going?' said Boots, seeing she had her hat on.

'Yes, to do some quick shoppin',' said Susie. 'Boots, thanks ever so.'

'What for?'

'For bein' on my side all the time.'

'Orders from above,' said Boots. 'Years ago.'

'Your mum?'

'Yes. Make sure, she said, that your disreputable brother Sammy puts a ring on Susie's finger now she's growing ladylike.'

'I bet you said that, not your mum.'

'Same thing. Good luck, Susie.'

'Em'ly's all right?'

'Fine.'

'It's rotten about her anaemia. Oh, I've got to fly. 'Bye, Boots.'

Not until ten past five did Sammy remember something he'd forgotten. He wasn't surprised his brains were failing him. The wedding was only two fateful days away. He opened the top drawer of his desk. It contained four small packages wrapped in white decorative paper. One bore Susie's name, and the others were for the three brides-maids, Sally, Rosie and Annabelle. He took out the packets for Susie and Sally, and called Ronnie in. Ronnie arrived briskly at his desk.

'Got your bike, Ronnie?'

'You bet, sir.'

'Good,' said Sammy. Ronnie could deliver to Susie and Sally, and Boots would take care of the packets for Rosie and Annabelle. He himself would be working late. Well, it was Good Friday tomorrow, the wedding on Saturday and then the honeymoon. 'I recollect, Ronnie, that you did me a favour last week. You can do me another. Same house. Kindly hand in these packets, and make sure you don't lose either of 'em. You've heard about bein' buried alive, have you?'

'That I have, Mister Sammy, and I don't fancy havin' it 'appen to me,' said Ronnie.

'Well, it will if these don't get safely delivered. Buzz off in immediate fashion and then go home.'

'Right, sir,' said Ronnie. He looked at the names on the packets, and a little grin showed. Off he went, riding his bike at speed along the Walworth Road.

It was Freddy who came to the door this time.

'Hello,' said Ronnie, 'how's your father?'

'I'd ask 'im,' said Freddy, 'only 'e ain't 'ome from work yet.'

'Might I see Miss Sally Brown?'

Freddy turned and shouted.

'Sally, there's a bloke wants to see yer!'

Sally came to the door and Freddy left them to it.

'I know you,' she said.

'Am I addressin' Miss Sally Brown?' asked Ronnie.

'Don't start that again,' said Sally, 'or I'll call me mum to 'elp you put a sock in it.'

'Would you like me to come in an' meet her?' asked Ronnie.

'You can meet 'er at the weddin', if you're really comin',' said Sally, 'and you can 'ave a dance with 'er.' She saw the two small packets in his hand. Presents had been arriving at intervals. 'You sure you should've asked for me? I mean, are those for Susie? She's not in yet.'

'It says Miss Sally Brown on this packet, and I'm deliverin' it with the compliments of Mr Sammy Adams.'

'Honest? It's for me?'

'He asked me to safeguard it with me life or I'd get buried alive.'

'Well, I believe that,' said Sally. She took the packet

and saw her name on it. 'You sure 'e hasn't made a mistake?'

'Workin' as I do with Mr Sammy Adams, I can tell you he doesn't go in for makin' mistakes,' said Ronnie.

'Well, thanks for bringing this,' said Sally. He gave her the packet for Susie. 'An' for this one as well.'

'Don't mention it,' said Ronnie, 'a pleasure, yer know.'

'I don't want to keep you,' said Sally.

'All right, I'll buzz off now, shall I?'

'Yes, we're sort of busy,' said Sally, wondering what Sammy had sent her, but willing to wait a bit before opening it.

'Yes, you've got the weddin',' said Ronnie, 'so I won't come in.'

'No, all right,' said Sally.

'So long, then.'

'So long,' said Sally.

'See you at the weddin',' said Ronnie.

'You'll see my dad as well, so don't try to get off with me.'

'Why not?'

''E'll bash your face in,' said Sally.

'I still like you,' grinned Ronnie, and went off whistling again.

Sally opened her packet and disclosed her bridesmaid's present, a lovely chased silver bracelet. With it was a note from Sammy.

'*To Sally, my new sister. Lots of love, Sally love. Sammy.*'

Susie's bridal present was a gold bracelet, suitably engraved. Susie, on receipt of it, wondered if she could ask the lovely man to give Sally a job in one of the firm's shops.

Annie was preparing for battle. Not of a noisy kind or of

the kind where blood would flow. Nor of the kind that would spoil the wedding celebrations. The battlefield would be a quiet corner in the Institute. Will wouldn't finish up actually wounded, but he might have a headache as well as an earache. She'd let him know she wasn't going to be kissed like he'd kissed her and then be expected to listen to him more or less saying that the most she could look forward to was a picture postcard from somewhere in India. Just you wait, Will Brown.

Will was preparing to enjoy the wedding as much as he could, without having any idea of what was going to hit him. Aside from that, Dr McManus had asked him this morning if Annie used scent. Scent? Yes, you could be allergic to scent. That could have brought on your attack after you left her on Sunday night. I don't think Annie uses scent, said Will, but Susie does. Not every scent need affect you, said Dr McManus. I'm a case for the dustbin if any scent at all affects me, said Will.

The evening being sunny, Boots and Emily took a walk. Tim and Rosie went with them, except that Rosie took Tim by the hand and made him walk with her in advance of their parents.

'What you doing this for?' asked Tim.

'So that Mum and Dad can have lovey-dovey Easter talk,' said Rosie.

'What, about choc'late Easter eggs?' asked Tim hopefully.

'Crikey, what a clever boy,' said Rosie, 'fancy guessing right.' She was sure, however, that Boots was going to talk to Emily about her being too thin.

Emily was saying, 'Boots, I'm goin' to see Dr McManus. Dr Thompson said I could if I want, he said a second opinion might help.'

'Good idea,' said Boots.

'I don't want to end up as a collection of walkin' bones,' said Emily.

'You'd rattle,' said Boots lightly. It was one way of bringing a smile to her face, making little jokes. She didn't like anyone being a wet blanket about her condition. Wet blankets had never been a great favourite with Emily.

She was smiling as she said, 'Stop tryin' to make me laugh, I might come apart.'

'Not you, Em, you'll always soldier on.'

'Bless yer,' said Emily. 'Look at our Rosie, she's always so nice with Tim. Aren't we lucky, all of us havin' each other? Is Polly Simms goin' to write to you?'

'Hello, where did that question come from?' asked Boots.

'From all me suspicions that she's only gone to darkest Africa so's she can play hard to get,' said Emily.

'Silly girl,' said Boots.

'Who, me?'

'Yes, you,' said Boots, and put an arm around her waist.

Rosie, glancing back, smiled.

'There, I told you,' she said to Tim, who was trying out a hop, skip and jump way of getting along. 'They're having lovey-dovey.'

'I like choc'late Easter eggs better,' said four-year-old Tim.

656

CHAPTER TWENTY

There was no day off on Good Friday for some workers, including Henry Brannigan. And of all the cursed luck, he trod on a line on his way to work. Coming out of a baker's shop, where he'd bought a couple of hot cross buns to eat with his can of mid-morning tea, he stepped aside for two women. If things hadn't changed a bit for him, he'd have stood his ground or barged his way between them. But his companionship with Madge had been making him act like a gent. He'd been stepping aside, although always with an eye for the lines. This time he did it without taking heed. He actually had a careless moment. Immediately, he knew a line was under the sole of his boot. He knew it. He looked down. Curse it, there it was, his right boot on a line. He had to start watching out for bad luck from then on.

The works manager arrived on the site at twenty to twelve. He spent ten minutes inspecting progress, then demoted the foreman on the spot. He cast his eyes around, then spoke.

'Brannigan, come here.'

This is it, thought Henry Brannigan, the bleeding bad luck's caught up with me already, and I'm going to lose a well-paid job. And that means giving Madge the push from the flat.

'What's the trouble, guv?' he asked.

'The gang's not pulling its weight, that's the trouble, Brannigan,' said the works manager. 'Your bloody fore-man's useless.'

'Maybe he is,' said Henry Brannigan, 'but I ain't.'

'I grant that. How'd you get on with the rest of the men?'

'I don't spend time socializin' with any of 'em, I've got me work to do.'

'Right. You're the foreman at ten more bob a week. But you'll be out on your neck if you don't get the right amount of work out of them. That clear?'

'That's clear, guv.' Henry Brannigan gave no indication of how astounded he was.

'Right. Inform your gang and get 'em working. That includes Duffy, who's just lost the foreman's job.'

Henry Brannigan got the men working and the ex-foreman too, the while wondering if fateful bad luck was going to come chasing after good luck. Bad luck could arrive in the form of a pickaxe being accidentally dropped on his head by one of the men.

Madge spent the day helping at the orphanage with her friend, taking with her six pounds of bull's-eyes, which she had made up into little packets of five sweets each. She was allowed to give them out to the girls and boys, and was able to talk to the nine-year-old girl, Lucy Peters, who had taken her fancy. Lucy was pathetically eager to have a family adopt her. It did happen from time to time, one child or another being given a home, and they were nearly always the younger children.

'Where's that scatty girl got to?' grumbled Freddy, and went out to the gate to have another look for her. Will had taken Sally and Susie for a tram ride all the way to Purley, to help calm the nerves of tomorrow's bride and bridesmaid. But we've got things to do, Susie had said. No, you haven't, said Will, everything's organized, and the pair of you are only trying to find something that isn't. So at two o'clock, the three of them left, by which time young Cassie was late. She'd said she'd come round at a quarter to two and go to Ruskin Park again on his bike. She'd bring Tabby, she said. You won't, said Freddy. Cassie said perhaps his mum would mind him again then. Mum and Dad's going for a walk, said Freddy. Oh, I'll bring his piece of string, said Cassie, and they can take him with them. Freddy ordered her to leave the daft cat at home. Oh, all right, I'll see, said Cassie.

It was now a quarter to three, and Freddy was by himself, his mum and dad out on their walk. So he rode round to Cassie's house in Blackwood Street, although he knew he might miss her if she was on her way, because she could wander dreamily in all directions before arriving in Caulfield Place.

There was no answer. Mr Ford had taken Annie, Nellie and Charlie for a bus ride to Hyde Park, the day being warm and fine, the April breeze quite balmy. Freddy started to ride around the back streets in a search for his wandering mate. He rode everywhere he could think of, stopping once or twice to ask kids if they'd seen Cassie Ford. Who's she? He described her. No, we ain't seen her. He kept going back home during his tour of the streets, but there was no Cassie, and his parents were still out. They were actually in the house of neighbours in Browning Street, having been invited in for a cup of tea and a bit of a chat.

By half-past four, Freddy was frankly a worried lad. Cassie wasn't so daft as to lose herself. He rode again to Blackwood Street, but she wasn't at home, nor was anyone else. He asked a girl if she'd seen Cassie Ford.

'Yes, I seen 'er come out of 'er house ages ago,' said the girl.

'D'yer know what time it was?' asked Freddy.

'Well, I might if I 'ad a watch, but I ain't. It was just ages ago.'

That really worried Freddy. Again he searched around, and again he went back home. Nobody was there. So he rode to Rodney Road police station and told the desk sergeant all about Cassie and how she was missing.

'If you're havin' us on, me lad, you're for it,' said the desk sergeant.

'Course I ain't 'aving you on,' said Freddy. 'She was comin' round to our 'ouse at quarter to two, an' look at yer clock, it's gone five.'

'Where's her fam'ly?'

'I dunno,' said Freddy, 'except they ain't in.'

'Well, she's probably with them.'

'No, she ain't,' said Freddy, 'if she'd gone with them she'd 'ave come an' told me first. She's me mate.'

'What's her name again?'

'Cassie Ford.'

'And her fam'ly live where?'

'Ten Blackwood Street,' said Freddy. He described Cassie and gave her age.

The police sergeant alerted himself then. Missing girls. Scotland Yard.

'Right, Freddy Brown, you're a bright lad, after all. We'll get someone round to her house immediate.'

'But there's no-one there.'

'There might be now, Freddy, and we'd like to talk to her fam'ly. They might know where she went if she didn't go with them.'

'But she was comin' to see me, I told yer,' said Freddy.

'She might have changed her mind. Now don't you worry, we'll see to it. You keep searchin', like you have been and come and tell us if you find her. Will you do that?'

'All right,' said Freddy.

'Good lad.'

Freddy rode back home. A taxi passed him as he turned into Caulfield Place. He was in hope that Cassie would be at his gate. She wasn't, but the taxi pulled up outside it. Freddy rode up. Out stepped a man he knew, a man he liked. It was Sammy's eldest brother, Boots. His daughter Rosie followed him out of the taxi. Father and daughter were both laden with gift parcels.

'Hello, Freddy,' said Boots, and asked the cabbie to wait.

'I got yer, guv,' said the cabbie, and kept his clock ticking.

'Hello, Freddy,' said Rosie. They'd met once. They were going to be loosely related. 'We come bearing gifts, don't we, Daddy?'

'Wedding gifts from various members of the family,' said Boots.

'Ev'ryone's out except me,' said Freddy.

'Well, we'll load them on to you,' said Boots.

Freddy led the way into the house, and Boots and Rosie placed the gifts on the parlour table. The parlour was awash with wedding presents.

'Mister Adams—' Freddy hesitated.

'What's up, Freddy?' Boots liked the boy.

'It's Cassie.'

'Who's Cassie?'

Freddy rushed into words. Boots eyed him searchingly. Rosie looked concerned.

'If you've been to the police, Freddy,' said Boots, 'how can I help?'

'I dunno, Mister Adams, honest I don't,' said Freddy,

661

'except I think – well, I think – Mister Adams, I dunno what I think.' What he actually thought was that Boots was the kind of bloke he needed at the moment.

'Daddy, you've got to help look,' said Rosie, 'we can't just leave Freddy here on his own. He's Susie's brother. Well, Aunt Susie's, I suppose. I mean my aunt from tomorrow. Daddy, buck up.'

'Come on, Freddy, we'll use the taxi,' said Boots, 'we'll eat up the streets with that.'

'Yes, come on, Freddy,' said Rosie, 'let's all buck up.'

Thirty minutes later, they were still riding around in the taxi. They'd been first to Cassie's house, where there was still no-one home. Boots thought that just as well in one way, for the hope was that Cassie could be found before her family were sent into a state of alarm. He had his mind on the murdered girl and the missing girls. And he didn't doubt that Cassie was somewhere in this area, whether she was lost or someone had her.

He asked the cabbie to head for the police station. Once there, he spoke to the desk sergeant, who said he had men out searching, men who were making regular calls at Blackwood Street. Boots asked to use the phone. He had a quiet authority. He phoned home. Chinese Lady answered. He explained what he was doing and that he and Rosie would be late back. Chinese Lady said she didn't mind what time he and Rosie got back, that Emily wouldn't mind either, as long as he found the girl.

'You got a tickin' meter, guv,' said the cabbie, as he re-entered the taxi.

'Never mind that,' said Boots.

'I'm with yer all the way,' said the cabbie, who knew what the search was all about now. 'Let's get goin', eh?'

They set off again, the cabbie pulling up whenever

required to, so that Boots or Freddy could get out and ask the relevant questions of people. They widened the search, then headed back towards Browning Street. Freddy shouted.

'It's 'er cat! Look! Mister Adams, look!'

Tabby was whisking away down the shabby street, the street in which sagging timber gates guarded the entrance to a destroyed factory.

'Pull up,' said Boots.

The taxi came to a stop outside the gates.

'Mister Adams, the cat, it came out through the gates!' shouted Freddy. 'I saw it!'

Tabby was disappearing fast. A moment later the street was deserted except for the taxi. The derelict ruin of the factory brooded in the evening light of Good Friday, a day given over to religious rites. Boots alighted, followed by Freddy and Rosie.

'Mister Adams, there's a place in there where Cassie might be, honest there is,' said Freddy, and told Boots of the time he'd been here with her, looking for her cat, and how he'd found it in what was left of the factory. He said there was a room that looked as if it was sometimes used by a night watchman. It had a bed, a table and cupboards.

'Right, Freddy, we'll go in,' said Boots.

'I'll come with yer, guv,' said the cabbie. He switched off his meter and climbed out.

'All right, troops,' said Boots, 'it's the first lead we've had, so let's see what we can make of it. Perhaps Cassie got herself locked in.'

Freddy thought what a great bloke he was, and as calm as you like. He'd been a sergeant in the war. Freddy reckoned he ought to have been a general.

Boots squeezed his way through the gap in the gates and brought Rosie through after him. Freddy and the cabbie followed. Boots saw the standing section. It looked gaunt and forlorn. He led the way around the mounds of brick and rubble. Feet made crunching noises. They reached the barred and padlocked door. Boarded windows stared blankly. Freddy shouted.

'Cassie? Cassie? You there, Cassie?' He banged on the door with his fist. They listened. There was no response, not a single sound. Boots examined the padlock and the stout metal bar.

'Anything in your taxi that might help?' he asked the cabbie.

'I reckon there is,' said the cabbie, and returned to his taxi at speed.

'Daddy, could she be in there?' asked Rosie, hopeful but uncertain.

'We'll see, kitten,' said Boots, thinking that if the girl was inside or had been, then she hadn't got in by herself. The padlock was evidence of that. Apart from his set mouth, he hid his feelings, which were all to do with a murdered and buried girl, and what might have happened to Freddy's young friend, Cassie.

The cabbie returned with a wrench. Boots took it and used it to savage the bar and burst it from its timber bed. That allowed him to open the door. Silent gloom seemed to actually stare at him.

'It's upstairs, the room,' said Freddy. Boots went in. He turned.

'Rosie, stay there,' he said.

'But, Daddy—'

'Stay.'

'Yes, all right,' said Rosie. She wasn't afraid, not while he was present, but there was no way she would go against him.

'I'll stay with 'er, guv,' said the cabbie, 'you just holler if you need me.' But he knew, as Boots knew, that the only person who could possibly be inside this standing section was a girl who had been locked in. A girl who might or might not be alive.

'Come on, Freddy,' said Boots. The lad plainly was not going to stand and wait himself. Boots, however, did not let him lead the way. If there was only a body to be discovered, he was not going to let Freddy see it. He walked through the passage, stopping to open doors on either side.

'No, it's up the stairs, Mister Adams,' breathed Freddy.

'It's as well to take a look down here first,' said Boots. Reaching the wooden stairs in the gloom, he began to climb them, Freddy behind him. The stairs did not creak, but the landing did, just a little. Boots halted, the silence a lonely and discouraging one.

'It's that door,' said Freddy pointing.

'Right, Freddy, guard the other doors.'

'Guard 'em?' Freddy wanted to rush into that certain room. Boots wasn't going to let him.

'Just in case,' he said. He advanced, turned the handle of the door in question and quietly opened it. And there she was, a girl, a young girl, on a truckle bed, untidy blankets beneath her. She was seemingly asleep. Freddy deserted his post. He had to look. He appeared at the open door as Boots entered the room. He gave a yelp of joyful relief.

'That's 'er, Mister Adams, that's Cassie!'

'Stay there, Freddy.' Boots moved to the bed. The girl, was she asleep or dead? He went down on one knee and gently turned her head. He looked down into her face. Cassie sighed, but her eyes remained closed. Well, praise be to God, thought Boots, and the steel inside him became less cold and rigid. Freddy appeared beside him.

''Elp, she's asleep,' he said.

Boots caught a faint odour then. It pervaded the air around the bed.

Chloroform.

He thought then that there were other smells as well. He came to his feet.

'We won't wake her, Freddy. Let her come to by herself.'

'But we ought to wake 'er, Mister Adams, an' find out 'ow she got 'ere,' said Freddy.

'Well, I'll carry her down, Freddy. The open air will help to wake her.' Boots stooped and lifted Cassie up into his arms. 'Right, here we go.'

Freddy, following him out of the room, said, 'Mister Adams, I told yer I didn't know how you could 'elp, but I think I just knew you could.'

'No, you did it, Freddy old chap,' said Boots, carrying Cassie down the stairs. 'You spotted her cat. It meant nothing to me. It meant everything to you.'

'But I wouldn't 'ave spotted it if I 'adn't been with you,' said Freddy. 'Mister Adams, I can't think why Cassie's asleep and ain't wakin' up.'

'She'll come to in the fresh air,' said Boots, and Cassie sighed again as he brought her out into the light.

Rosie stared and the cabbie looked a happy man.

'Good on yer, guv,' he said, 'good on yer, me lad.'

'Yes, we got 'er,' said Freddy, 'but she's asleep.'

'Maybe that's just as well, poor little kid,' said the cabbie, catching Boots's eye. Boots gave a little nod.

'We still need your taxi,' he said.

'It's all yours, guv, all night, if yer want it.'

Rosie, her eyes shining, said, 'Bless you, Daddy.'

'Bless Freddy,' said Boots, holding Cassie close to his chest. He spoke to the cabbie again. 'Will you take Cassie home? Her family must be back by now, and if the police have seen them, they'll be worried sick. Freddy and Rosie will go with you. Then will you let the police know and ask them if they can get a doctor to Cassie? I think she'll need a sedative.' He hoped that was all she would need.

'Ain't you comin', guv?'

'No, I'm going to wait,' said Boots.

'But what for?' asked Freddy.

'Because whoever locked her in will be coming back,' said Boots, 'and he might arrive before the police get here. Come on.' He carried Cassie to the gates. The cabbie exerted himself and widened the gap, allowing Boots to get through with the girl. Then he took off his jacket and Boots let him place it around Cassie. Freddy and Rosie climbed into the taxi, and Boots leaned in to settle the unconscious girl between his daughter and Susie's young brother. They held her. Her head lolled and a little sighing murmur escaped her. 'Take care of her.'

'You bet,' said Freddy, 'she's me mate.'

'Daddy, you watch out,' said Rosie, not liking the thought of him coming up against some horrible man.

'I'll meet you at Cassie's home,' said Boots, and watched as the taxi moved off. Then he went back to that room. The faint smell of chloroform still lingered. On the table was an oil lamp, a box of matches and a white paper bag. He picked it up. It was empty, with a peppermint smell. He examined cupboards, of which there were two. One was empty. In the other was a large plate camera, a wooden tripod, a box of photographic plates and a T-shaped flash contraption.

He was conscious of smells. He thought again of young Ivy Connor, murdered, then buried under the floorboards of a shed. In the gloom, he inspected the bare wooden floor of this dolorous room. None of the boards seemed to have been disturbed. He went downstairs. About to examine the rooms, he checked as a sound reached his ears. It was faint but perceptible. He knew what it was. Feet moving over ground littered with chips of mortar and brick. He took himself quickly to the only entrance into the place. The door, its metal bar wrenched free, was closed. He had closed it himself. He waited behind it. The sounds of a moving man were closer. They stopped. He heard a strangely petulant exclamation. He pulled the door open.

Mr Ponsonby stared at him.

'You bugger,' said Boots.

A rolled umbrella was instantly levelled at him, and from its point a six-inch shining blade leapt and clicked into place.

'Interfering busybody!' hissed Mr Ponsonby, and made a lightning-like thrust. But he had picked the wrong man. Boots had prepared himself for a murderous reaction. If Mr Ponsonby was quick, he was quicker. He knocked the umbrella aside before the blade reached his chest, and with his left fist he hit the man savagely on his right jaw. Mr Ponsonby fell stunned. Boots reached, picked up the umbrella, and with the man flat on his back, he bent over him and slipped his left hand into the capacious inner pocket of his frock coat. He drew out a bottle with a glass stopper. He put the umbrella under his arm and pulled the stopper free. He sniffed.

Chloroform.

He replaced the stopper and stowed the bottle in his jacket pocket. The man stirred. Boot stood over him and placed the blade of the umbrella against his chest. Then he waited for the police to arrive.

CHAPTER TWENTY-ONE

Cassie came to, on her bed. Her eyes opened and she blinked. A man with a kind face smiled down at her.

'There's a good girl,' he said.

Cassie made a face.

'I feel a bit sick,' she said.

'I expect you do.' Dr Sadler had examined her. She'd suffered nothing worse than chloroform, although probably two or three applications, and some fright, no doubt. He went to the door, opened it and said, 'You can come in now, but don't smother her.' The family swarmed in. An inspector and a sergeant of the CID looked enquiringly at Dr Sadler. 'Not yet,' he said, 'give her another five minutes.'

'Right,' said Detective-Inspector Grant of Scotland Yard. They'd got the man. The cabbie had driven police from Rodney Road to the factory site, and Mr Gerald Francis Ponsonby was now under lock and key, awaiting interrogation.

'Cassie, Cassie love,' breathed Annie, appalled for her young sister.

'Safe and sound now, Cassie,' said the shaken Gaffer, sitting on the edge of the bed and taking her hand.

Cassie looked dreamy.

'I feel a bit sick,' she murmured.

''Ere, what 'appened to yer?' asked Charlie, and Cassie stared vaguely at him.

'Charlie, leave 'er be,' said Nellie, who'd shed a few tears.

'She'll tell us in a bit,' said Annie. They'd all had distracted minds from the moment the police told them Cassie had been missing for hours, and that a search was being made. Dr Sadler, having mixed a sedative, allowed Annie to give it to the girl. Cassie sat up, her dad's arm around her, and drank the sedative in the dreamy hope it would stop making her feel sick.

'That's a good girl,' said Dr Sadler again.

Cassie blinked and looked around. The Gaffer let her lie back.

''E said 'e was goin' to take a photo of me,' she murmured.

'What?' said the Gaffer, having a hard job to keep his blood off the boil.

'Who said that, Cassie?' asked Annie.

'Mister Po's'by,' said Cassie.

''Oo's 'e?' asked Charlie.

''E gives me peppermints,' said Cassie.

Annie looked at her dad, and her dad looked tight-faced and grim.

'I think the police can talk to her now,' said Dr Sadler, and called the CID officers in. Freddy had gone home to acquaint his own family of events, and Rosie had been taken by the cabbie to rejoin her father. Boots was at Rodney Road police station, making a long statement. He had phoned home again and this time had spoken to Emily.

Inspector Grant, exercising a kind paternal approach, was able to get quite a coherent story from the relaxing Cassie. On her way to Freddy's house she had met Mr Ponsonby, who had promised to take a photograph of her. He said what a busy day he was having, but if she would like to be photographed now, he could spare the time. Cassie asked him if he was going to do it in his lodgings.

He said oh, no, in his studio. Cassie, who had her cat with her, said she couldn't spare a lot of time herself, because she was going to Freddy's house. Mr Ponsonby said it would hardly take any time at all, and Cassie asked if he could take the photo with her holding Tabby. Mr Ponsonby said yes, come with me.

She went with him. It seemed a bit of a long way and she kept saying she'd be late meeting Freddy. Then they came to that place where there'd been a fire and where it was haunted, and she said she didn't want to go in there. Mr Ponsonby said no, of course not, have a peppermint. He always had peppermints. Tabby jumped out of her arms then and ran into that place through a gap in the gates, and she asked Mr Ponsonby to get him for her. He said he would, but have a peppermint first, and he offered her the bag. There was only one in it, and as she put her hand in the bag, something was pushed against her face, and she couldn't remember any more, except she did dream it happened again.

Dr Sadler thought it must have happened several times, considering how long she was in the place. The man had been playing with the girl's life, before absenting himself. And why had he absented himself? The CID officers knew he'd been caught coming back, with the bottle of chloroform still on his person, but were anxious to get the girl's story before fully interrogating the man.

'Cassie,' said Inspector Grant, 'thank you very much, you're a brave young lady.'

'I don't feel so sick now,' said Cassie. She thought. 'Fancy 'im puttin' that bit of stuff over me face, I don't like 'im any more. Does Freddy know?'

'Freddy 'elped to find you, lovey,' said the Gaffer.

'Well,' said Cassie dreamily, 'I'm 'is mate, 'e told me so.'

The CID officers left then and returned to Rodney Road police station. The cabbie was still there, so were Boots and Rosie. And so was a uniformed constable, with the news that two bodies had been discovered under the floorboards of a room below the one containing the truckle bed and a camera. Two other constables were still at the place. The bodies were of young females, but had not been touched. Inspector Grant received the news in the grimly painful fashion of a police officer who hated what it meant. However, he allowed Boots to go, thanking him for all he had done.

'I suppose you'll find all other evidence you need at his lodgings,' said Boots.

'I'm damn' sure we will, Mr Adams. Thanks again.'

Boots joined Rosie and the cabbie, and they left the station.

'Can I drive you 'ome, guv?' asked the cabbie.

'You've had a long day,' said Boots.

'So 'ave you, guv, so 'as your Rosie here. Mind, we've done some chattin', ain't we, Rosie?'

'Oh, I'm very well-versed at chatting,' said Rosie, 'I caught it ages ago from Daddy and my Uncle Sammy. But mustn't he be an awful man, the one who took Cassie?'

'Worse than that, Rosie,' said the cabbie.

'Look,' said Boots, 'I know it's asking one more favour, but could you stop at Freddy's house on the way, just for five minutes?'

'Don't mention it, guv. 'Op in, you an' Rosie.'

While Rosie talked to the rest of the Brown family in the kitchen, Boots talked with Mr Brown in the parlour. He gave him the full story. Mr Brown looked sick at the ugliness of mankind.

'So there it is, Jim,' said Boots, 'the police have nailed

the son of Satan. There's no point now in keeping it from the family. They already know what Freddy's told them. Now you can tell them the rest, to save them having to find out from the newspapers tomorrow. And at least, it's all cleared up.'

'Not the best piece of news, though, for a weddin' day,' said Mr Brown.

'It won't spoil this wedding,' said Boots, 'it's special. Sammy, the engine driver, has met his match. Get Rosie for me, would you, Jim? We need to be on our way now.'

Jim fetched the girl. Susie appeared too.

'Bless you and Freddy, Boots,' she said.

'It's been Freddy's day,' said Boots. 'It's yours tomorrow, Susie. By the way, here's something I almost forgot.' He took an item wrapped in tissue paper from the inside pocket of his jacket. 'Emily said she'd arranged to let you have something borrowed to go with something blue.'

Susie unwrapped the tissue, disclosing a pink garter.

'Lovely,' she said, 'thank Em'ly, won't you?'

'Pretty, that is,' said Mr Brown.

'Well, we'll all expect to see how it looks on Susie,' said Boots.

'Daddy, you're cheeky,' said Rosie. Boots gave her a wink and they said goodbye and left. The cabbie drove them to their home in Red Post Hill. Rosie said farewell to him, then dashed in to give Emily, Chinese Lady and Chinese Lady's husband a first-hand account of the happenings.

'What's the damage?' asked Boots of the cabbie. 'All of it.'

'Listen, guv, what kind of a bloke would I be to make a charge?'

'Fairly daft not to, I'd say. It's your living.'

'Look, I tell yer what. You place five bob in me mitt an' we'll call that fair an' square, eh?'

Boots placed five shillings in his hand, and added a pound note.

'That's the least I can do,' he said.

'Don't want it, guv. It's been—'

'There's a wedding in our family tomorrow,' said Boots, 'so have a drink on us.'

'Guv, it's been a privilege meetin' you and yer daughter. You got a sweet girl there. Any time you need a taxi from East Dulwich, I 'ope I'll be the one to oblige yer. Gus Allbury, that's me.'

'Many thanks, Gus. Couldn't have done without you today. Good night.' Boots shook hands with the cabbie, watched the taxi depart, stood for a moment thinking of young Cassie and how close she'd been to death, then turned on his heel and entered the house. There he was greeted by Emily, who wrapped her arms around him.

Charlie answered a knock on the door. Will was on the step.

'Oh, 'ello,' said Charlie.

Annie, coming down the stairs, checked for a moment.

'I thought I'd come and see how Cassie is,' said Will.

Annie came quickly down to the passage and to the door.

'Oh, it's nice you thought of us,' she said, 'and Cassie specially. Come in. She's sleepin' now. She's all right, she won't ever remember much because that evil man chloroformed her. Will, come on in, we're just makin' a pot of tea and you'll 'ave a cup, won't you?'

Will joined the family for a cup of tea around the kitchen table, and everyone talked at once. The Gaffer said next time he took his children out, he'd take them all and leave no-one behind. Only Cassie had been keen on being with Freddy. Couple of real mates, they were, he said, and while he was saying it, Annie was talking about how kind the doctor had been, Nellie was going on about the police being ever so nice, and Charlie was muttering that a certain bloke ought to have his head bashed in. The Gaffer said if it hadn't been for Freddy keeping on and on in his search for Cassie, she might not have been found. Will said Freddy was now a hero, even to his sister Sally. But he said nothing about the news that Boots had brought concerning the discovery of the bodies of two young girls. The shock of Cassie's abduction was enough for them to cope with tonight. Tomorrow would be soon enough for them to learn about all that was grisly.

Annie felt deep relief at the doctor's assurance Cassie hadn't been harmed in any way, even though she'd obviously been kept unconscious for hours. She also felt very glad that Will had called. He stayed quite a while, and helped to cheer things up no end. She decided he was really a very nice young man, not a bit loud or brash, and not at all a cocky corporal. He was a lot quieter in his manner than she imagined most soldiers were, but he had a nice sense of humour.

She saw him to the front door when he left.

'Thanks ever so much for comin',' she said.

'Well, I couldn't not pop round to see how everyone was,' said Will, and did what he'd told himself he shouldn't do. He kissed her, and at the same time tried to detect if she wore scent. He didn't think so.

'That's done it,' said Annie, when he released her lips.

'Done what?' asked Will.

'You're goin' to get talked to tomorrow,' said Annie.

'Seriously?' said Will.

'Well, it's not goin' to make you laugh, I can tell you that,' said Annie.

Under interrogation, Mr Ponsonby was querulous and petulant, but patchily informative. One of the first things Inspector Graves found out was that the reason why the man had absented himself related to his need to develop his plates. He needed to know if the photographs were satisfactory, or if he needed to take them again.

'So you kept her alive, did you, in case of that?' said the inspector.

'Of course, of course. What is the use of photographs of someone who is dead?'

He had developed the plates quickly, in his lodgings, shutting out the light by drawing the thick curtains he himself had installed. The photographs were very good. Charming, in fact, charming. Such a pretty face, and such pretty legs. Inspector Grant felt an urge to throttle him. Ponsonby, of course, had drawn back the unconscious girl's clothes. The CID officer controlled himself, and by asking questions in a sympathetic and understanding way, or so it seemed, he finally induced a full confession.

Mr Ponsonby had always thought young girls enchanting because of their purity. But it was difficult to photograph them in the way he wanted to, not without them getting upset and threatening to tell their parents. So he stole a bottle of chloroform from a hospital where he had once worked as assistant to the lady almoner. He used a chloroform pad to effect a robbery at a jeweller's shop, and to delude the hospital authorities and the police into thinking that was why he had taken the bottle. He did not like the police, he said, they were interfering busybodies, disturbing to a gentleman like him.

It was a pity, of course, but it had been necessary to let the girls ascend early to heaven after photographing them.

'How many girls?' asked the inspector in a conversational way.

'Only a few,' said Mr Ponsonby. 'Dear me, it's been terribly difficult arranging to photograph any girl. One can't be too careful, parents are unfriendly people. One simply has to win a girl's confidence before inviting her to sit for me.'

Sit for him? You nasty old sod, thought Inspector Grant.

'You gave them peppermints, Mr Ponsonby?'

'Ah, everyone had to have a peppermint.'

'From out of a bag like this?' said the inspector, producing the white bag Boots had found. It smelled of peppermint.

'Of course, yes. Dear me, dear me.' Mr Ponsonby was very petulant. 'How silly of me to leave it there.' He rubbed his bruised jaw. 'I wish to complain about the interfering busybody who struck me.'

'Complaint noted,' said the inspector. 'How many girls, how many did you say?'

'A few, just a few. Three.' Mr Ponsonby explained how he had come to know them and subsequently invited them to be photographed. The first was in Bermondsey, where he used a scrap yard's shed. No-one else seemed to be using it, and he had a key that opened the gates. He had found it one day, it had been left in the lock. The girl had been so pure, so delightful, with the prettiest legs. Unfortunately, she recovered very quickly from the second dose of chloroform and he had had to quieten her.

'Strangulation is very quietening,' said Inspector Grant.

'I trust that is not a criticism,' said Mr Ponsonby in some irritation. 'It was quick and merciful, yes, indeed.' He went on to say he had been just as quick and merciful with two other girls, after finding a most convenient place

677

in which to photograph them. After finding it, he had picked the padlock and replaced it with another. Yes, he agreed with the inspector's suggestion that he had buried the girls under floorboards. It was convenient to do so, and a kindness to the girls. One simply could not leave them lying about.

'You have the photographs in your lodgings?' said Inspector Grant.

'Of course, of course, where else? One must have the pleasure of looking at them.' He hoped he would be allowed to keep them, together with those he had taken of the charming girl Cassie. He could think of nothing more to add, and therefore would like to be allowed to go home to his lodgings.

'I note your request, Mr Ponsonby. After developing the plates at your lodgings, you returned to the factory to help the girl Cassie ascend early to heaven?'

'Much the best thing,' said Mr Ponsonby. 'Really, I can't see why you need to ask. It's late, and I must get back to my lodgings.'

'We'll see you do. We'll go with you, and perhaps you'll show us these photographs,' said the inspector.

'Oh, very well,' said Mr Ponsonby in new irritation. 'What a day, what a day.'

As the CID officers suspected, most of the photographs showed the terribly unfortunate girls unconscious and with their clothes drawn back. Much to his sense of outrage, Mr Ponsonby was arrested for murder.

Cassie slept soundly.

678

CHAPTER TWENTY-TWO

Annie woke up, looked sleepily at the little tin alarm clock, found it was only five past six, turned over, thought about Cassie, murmured in dreamy relief, thought about Will, wondered about him, and drifted back into sleep.

Cassie's cat woke up, sprang on to the bed she shared with Nellie, curled itself up close to the hump of her warm body and purred itself to sleep again, perhaps to dream about Mrs Boddy's lady cat.

The Gaffer woke up and got up. He was on an early shift this morning, but would finish at twelve. He looked in on Cassie. Sleeping like an angel next to Nellie. Should he stay home, just in case she woke up with upset feelings? Yes, he would. Only right. Then Annie could go off to her job without worrying. It was his place to stay home, not Annie's. Annie was looking forward to going to that wedding dance this evening. She was fond of Will, the Gaffer knew that. He'd asked her yesterday morning exactly what she thought of Will as a bloke. Well, Annie had said, he's my kind of bloke in most ways, he just wants talking to, that's all. Talking to about what? I'm giving it deep thought, said Annie.

A little later, Will woke up, thought about the fact that he hadn't had an attack after kissing Annie last night and wondered if he should take another look at himself.

Susie woke to the dawning of a sunny Easter Saturday and to the necessity of being at the hairdresser's with Sally by nine o'clock. And to saying love, honour and obey. She smiled.

Sammy woke to the dawning of married life, and to the probability that it was going to ruin his pocket. But he had a singular feeling that his pocket didn't seem to care.

Freddy woke and thought about Cassie. Crikey, it was hardly believable what had happened. He'd cycle round after breakfast to see her and to tell her she could come to the wedding breakfast. His mum had said so, and that there was a place at the tables for her because Miss Simms had dropped out. If he'd cycled round yesterday, instead of letting her walk round to him, that old geezer Mr Ponsonby wouldn't have made off with her. But she'd insisted she'd come round to him. Freddy guessed why now. She'd had her barmy cat with her, she'd have arrived at his house with it and he wouldn't have been able to do anything about it. A bloke's mate didn't ought to be a problem to him. He couldn't thump her, seeing she was a girl. Still, he could talk to her, although he had a feeling it would be like talking to the empty air. Crikey, it was Susie's wedding day today.

Mrs Brown woke to see her husband bringing a morning cup of tea to her, bless him.

Mr Greenberg, waking, thought about the privilege of carting Susie and Sammy to their Christian wedding breakfast. That reminded him his own wedding was in the offing. Should a free man take to his heels or dwell on the compensation available? The widow Hannah Borovich was splendidly handsome and also an excellent cook. But would her three growing sons eat him out of house and home? Life was a torment to a man when he had to consider taking to his heels or fulfilling the marriage contract. Ah, me, thought Mr Greenberg. He arose, washed himself, put on some old clothes, ate a simple breakfast and then went to the Old Kent Road stables to brush down his pony and polish the little cart.

680

Chinese Lady woke up beside her husband, Edwin Finch, recently returned from what she thought of as the Frenchified Continent, where he'd spent some months on Government business. It was nice, having him beside her again. It was what God had ordered for a woman, having a providing husband beside her. She meant ordained, of course. She smiled. It was Sammy's wedding day. That Sammy, with his sauce, it was time he found there was more to life than making money. Susie was just right for him, she'd become as ladylike as Lizzy had, and she had enough sense to see to it that Sammy turned into a responsible husband, father and provider. That was what any real man was born to be. God's orders were very strict.

Will received an official letter that morning. It informed him that as he was medically unfit for further service, he was to receive his discharge papers at the termination of his three months leave, together with back pay due to him. There was a formal acknowledgement of his past services to the Army, but no mention of a disablement pension. The family said what a rotten lot the Army high-ups were, and Sally said she hoped their roof would fall in on them and disable them all. Mrs Brown said well, let's look on the bright side, Will doesn't have to go to India any more, nor get fired at. It's dangerous, getting fired at, said Mr Brown. Yes, I just told you so, said Mrs Brown. You'll be all right, Will, she said, it's good news really, specially on Susie's wedding day. She said nothing about Mr Ponsonby, nor did any of them.

As soon as he'd had his breakfast, Freddy cycled round to Blackwood Street. There he found Cassie in the pink, the pet of her family.

''Ello, Freddy, where you been?' she asked.

'Well, I like that,' said Freddy, 'I ain't been anywhere

except in me bed an' then 'aving me breakfast.' He looked at her father. 'Is she all right, Mr Ford?'

'Right as rain,' said the Gaffer.

'She's our sunshine girl this mornin',' said Annie.

'That Mister Po's'by,' said Cassie, ''e put something over me face, Freddy, and I don't remember any more.'

Freddy could have said a lot about Mr Ponsonby. His dad had passed on the news given to him by Boots, but his mum had told him not to say anything in front of Cassie. Mr Ford and Annie weren't saying anything themselves, although Freddy knew it was all in the newspapers this morning. Well, it was in Dad's paper, and had caused his mum to say she hoped the guests wouldn't all talk about it at the wedding. It was a blessing that Mr Ponsonby's name hadn't been mentioned, she said, or the whole neighbourhood would be coming round to stare at the Mason house, where he'd been lodging. The paper just said a man was being held in custody. It was another blessing too that Cassie's name wasn't in the paper either, and that the police were working to identify the two dead girls.

The Gaffer's morning paper had sensational headlines. He'd shown the paper to Annie, and they were keeping it to themselves for the time being.

As it was, Cassie seemed herself. Her only complaint was that she'd felt sick when she woke up. She was happy to tell Freddy that her cat had come back, and that she thought Mrs Boddy's lady cat might have gone and fetched him home. Freddy said he wouldn't be surprised. He also said Cassie could come to the wedding breakfast, his mum had told him to invite her. Cassie nearly fell over in her delight. Annie, due to go to work for the day, told her dad to make sure Cassie was dressed in her Sunday best, and that Nellie could see to it that Cassie's hair looked nice, with a clean ribbon. Freddy said he'd come

682

and fetch her, otherwise she might go wandering off and end up at Peckham Rye. Cassie said Queen Alice went to Peckham Rye once. Nellie asked who Queen Alice was. Cassie said she'd never met her, she'd just read about her, and that she went to Peckham Rye to meet a magician. She wanted him to cast a spell on a wicked witch and make her disappear, only when she got to Peckham Rye, he wasn't there. Charlie asked what had happened to him. Cassie said he'd already cast his spell, only it had gone wrong and he'd made himself disappear and no-one ever saw him again.

Cassie was back to normal.

She was so much herself that she asked Freddy if she could bring Tabby to the wedding. Annie said no, Cassie love, you just can't take a cat to a wedding.

'But 'e likes weddings,' said Cassie.

'Still, leave 'im at home, me pet,' said the Gaffer, 'and 'e might 'ave a weddin' of his own, with Mrs Boddy's lady cat.'

Cassie giggled. Annie began to get ready to go to work, and Freddy, after telling Cassie he'd come for her at a quarter to twelve, went back home to do any wedding errands that were necessary.

Just after eleven, Boots answered the phone.

'Is that Mr Adams?'

'Speaking,' said Boots.

'Inspector Grant here, Mr Adams. Sorry to interrupt, I know you've a wedding on today, but I thought I ought to speak to you.' Inspector Grant sounded as if his nerves had just taken a hammering.

'What about?' asked Boots.

'The fact is, Ponsonby's slipped us.'

'What? I'm to believe you've been as careless as that?'

'Bloody inexcusable. He got out through the lavatory window at the station an hour ago. I'm there now. If you could see the size of the window you'd wonder how anyone could have managed it. But he did, the slippery bugger. We're looking for him, of course, and not sparing the manpower, but he's a peculiar character and I don't like the thought of what he might get up to.'

'You're not asking me to join the search, are you?'

'No, no, not at all, Mr Adams. But he doesn't like you, he doesn't like the fact that you interfered, to start with.'

'He calls that interference, does he?' said Boots.

'Intolerable interference, Mr Adams, those were his words. Nor does he like you for knocking him out and handing him over to us. He's got a vindictive streak, and I've a nasty feeling it'll be aimed at you. Or your daughter. Unless we can find him first.'

'Thanks very much for that slice of cheerful news,' said Boots. 'Does he know I've got a daughter?'

'When we brought him to the station yesterday evening, Mr Adams, your daughter was waiting with the taxi driver. You were with us. Your daughter greeted you.'

'Well, damn that for what it means,' said Boots.

'Mr Adams, we'll do our very best to round the man up, and I'll let you know immediately we do. I'll have someone contact you at the wedding, if necessary. Meanwhile, can I ask you to take great care of yourself and your daughter? Ponsonby doesn't look dangerous, but you and I know he is.'

'If I were him,' said Boots, 'I'd be running for my life, not thinking about having my own back. But as I'm not him, I'll watch out. Thanks for letting me know, Inspector.'

'I'm bloody sick,' said Inspector Grant, and rang off.

Boots steeled himself to face the day.

The ceremony was for twelve o'clock. At ten minutes to, St John's Church was full to overflowing for the wedding of two people who, having been born and bred in Walworth, had risen from poverty to become, respectively, an affluent young lady and a highly reputable businessman. Susie Brown was just about the poshest young lady to be seen in Walworth, and Sammy Adams, well, what a bright spark he'd always been. But they never turned their noses up at any of their old friends and neighbours.

Mrs Brown in a spring coat and a new toque hat, sat with Will and Freddy in the front pew on the left side of the aisle. Cassie, in her best Sunday dress and a little round straw hat, sat as a special treat between Will and Freddy.

In the front pew on the right sat Sammy and Boots, the best man. Boots, with Ponsonby on his mind, had brought Rosie to the church along with himself and Sammy. He'd been able to calm Sammy's nerves by telling him to think of how to cut the overheads on the new contract with Coates. Good idea, said Sammy, your dad's quite bright sometimes, Rosie. I know, said Rosie, I live an awful trying life trying to get the better of him.

Behind Sammy and Boots sat Chinese Lady, her husband Mr Finch, Emily and Emily's four-year-old son Tim. Also present were brown-eyed, glossy-haired Lizzy, her husband Ned Somers and three of their children, Bobby, Emma and Edward. Their eldest, Annabelle, was a bridesmaid, along with Rosie and Sally. Then there were Tommy and his wife Vi. Their daughter Alice, eleven months old, was in the care of neighbours, and Vi was just over four months pregnant with her second child. Next to them were Vi's parents, known to the family as Aunt

Victoria and Uncle Tom. Aunt Victoria was inclined to find fault, though not as much as she used to, and Uncle Tom, bluff and equable, was inclined to turn a deaf ear.

Chinese Lady, Emily, Lizzy, Vi and yes, even Aunt Victoria, were all wearing new outfits purchased at Sammy's Brixton shop at such an horrendous family discount that he said he'd never lost that much profit in all his life. You're breaking my heart, said Lizzy. I feel for you, said Sammy, but that kind of thing can undermine the firm's financial foundations and ruin the whole family. Emily said there would have been no fun in the transactions if Sammy hadn't mentioned something about the discount ruining him. He thanked her for her kind words. Aunt Victoria said she wasn't sure that she couldn't have done better at *Bon Marché* of Brixton. Uncle Tom said only at twice the cost, so Aunt Victoria changed the subject. Chinese Lady told Sammy he'd got a cheek to let his shop manageress charge her at all. Me, your own mother, she said, you're heading for purgatory, my lad. I suppose I'll have to start up a new kind of business when I get there, Ma, said Sammy. Don't call me Ma, said Chinese Lady, it's common, and I didn't bring you up to be common. However, Vi was so delighted with her outfit and the huge discount that she gave Sammy tuppence, which entitled her to give him two smacking kisses. Sammy was so touched he gave her a penny back.

At five minutes to twelve, with the church waiting for the arrival of the bride, Boots got up and walked along the side aisle to the open doors. The three bridesmaids were there, with the vicar. In their cerise pink, all three girls looked enchanting. Sally, suffering a crush on Boots, blushed as he smiled at her.

'Daddy, it can't be all over,' said Rosie, 'Aunt Susie hasn't arrived yet.'

'I'll tell your Uncle Sammy that,' said Boots, and spoke a few words to the vicar while looking around. He'd noticed a policeman outside the church, a uniformed constable. He was still there. A few people were at the gates, waiting to see the bride. Boots felt the constable was a safeguard for Rosie, and rejoined Sammy.

Mrs Rachel Goodman sat in a pew with Mr Greenberg, and neither felt out of place in this Christian church simply because they did not feel out of place with a family of gentiles whom they had known for years and had come to love. Rachel wore a midnight blue costume and hat, as close to black as she could get in letting Sammy see she was in mourning for the imminent loss of his bachelor status. Mr Greenberg, in handsome grey, looked a figure of solemn and august maturity. A nephew of his had charge of the pony and cart for the duration of the service.

Rachel wondered why Polly Simms wasn't present. She knew she'd been invited. She also knew the brittle and amusing Polly was incurably attached to Boots. They'd both served in the war, and they had a shared experience of its horrors. But Polly would never get Boots. Rachel knew the family so well she was absolutely certain none of Chinese Lady's diverting sons would indulge in an affair. And Boots had fine steel beneath his easy-going exterior. Was Polly not going to attend the wedding because she could no longer stand being on the outside of the family?

The church was buzzing, not only in anticipation of the bride, but because of newspaper headlines. A man was being held in custody over the murder of a young girl in Bermondsey and two right here in Walworth. Horrible. Still, Mrs Brown didn't look too upset about it.

Susie was punctual. She had made up her mind not to be late for her wedding. At two minutes past twelve, the organist turned his head. Sammy and Boots came to their

687

feet, and the whole church rose as the Wedding March began to peal out. The vicar, the Reverend Edwards, a rosy-faced and gentle man of God, entered in the van of the bridal procession. Susie was on her dad's arm, and her dad, gammy leg and all, looked as if the Queen of Sheba couldn't have made a better bride than his Susie. Her gown of white silk was soft, shimmering and flowing, her little circular headdress of white silk roses supporting a full veil. Slowly she floated, Sally behind her, Rosie and Annabelle following, all bridesmaids holding little bouquets, circlets of pink silk roses adorning their heads. Sammy, Boots and Ned had covered the expense of outfitting the bridesmaids.

Mr Greenberg, turning his head, beamed at Susie. Rachel emitted a little sigh. Emily, watching the advance, thought of her own wedding, a wartime one, when Boots was still blind and she had had to be his guide and his mainstay. They had had a good marriage, hadn't they? She hoped so, even if she was in doubt of herself sometimes. Needing reassurance, she received it from him, and unfailing affection too, to help her through her illness.

Mr Brown brought Susie to her bridegroom and relinquished her, not without a little throaty swallow.

Sammy whispered to the bridal veil.

'Is that you in there, Susie?'

'It's me, Sammy.'

'Bless you, then.'

'Bless you too, Sammy.'

Boots smiled. Sammy and Susie were always going to be a star turn together.

The ceremony over, the photographer posed the principals and their retinue outside the church and in the bright sunshine. Susie had her veil over her head, her eyes a bright sparkling blue, her bouquet colourful against the white of her gown. Sammy's smile was that of a businessman who had just signed the most valuable contract of his life, never mind the crippling overheads. The forecourt was crowded with people, and there were others outside the church gates.

Henry Brannigan, on his way home from his Saturday morning's work, checked his measured stride and took a look at the scene on the forecourt. He saw scores of people in their glad rags, and a shimmering bride with a lovely laughing face. A ruddy wedding. Still, they weren't in his way. He eyed the newly-weds on the church steps and listened to the shouted remarks of amateur comics. He took in the enchantment of the young bridesmaids. He gave them their due, they were sweet-looking right enough, but he'd bet they took their turns every day to get in people's way. All kids did. Still, he had to admit girl kids could look like angels as bridesmaids. They didn't always grow up like angels. One or two did. Come to think of it, Madge wasn't far short of being an angel of cheerfulness. Good company, she was, not moody, like his wife had been at times.

Look at the kids there. Little terrors they probably were, but look at them now with their clean faces. Madge was keen on kids. She hadn't given herself much of a chance to have any.

He walked away, his mood thoughtful. Ruddy hell, he was treading on lines. He adjusted his step. Too late now, though. He'd have to watch out for bad luck. Wait a tick, no bad luck had caught up with him after he'd trodden on that line outside a baker's shop the other day. Far from it. Not only had he been made foreman, but this morning the works manager had told him he'd already proved himself and the job was his for good. On top of that, when he was up a ladder an hour later to gauge the best way for the gang to tackle a dismantling piece of work, one of the sods had kicked the ladder from under him. Accidental, of course, you bet it wasn't. He might have broken his neck, but he didn't even bruise himself in the fall. If that wasn't a large slice of good luck, what was? He'd spoken to the ganger, he'd delivered himself of a few choice words, and he knew it wouldn't happen again.

Life had turned round for him. He reckoned that was all due to Madge. His lucky charm, that's what she was.

Henry Brannigan began to tread on lines with careless abandon.

The photographs had been taken, and Mr Greenberg, having received permission from the vicar, drove his sleek pony and polished cart into the forecourt. The guests made way for him and he pulled up outside the church doors. Lifting his hat, he beamed down at Susie.

'Vhy, ain't it Mrs Sammy Adams, I presume?' he said.

'Hello, Mr Greenberg,' smiled Susie.

'Might I have the pleasure of cartin' you and Sammy off to the place of reception? My vord, Susie, vhat a pleasure, ain't it?'

'Oh, it's a handsome offer, Mr Greenberg,' said Susie.

Boots, his hand on Rosie's shoulder, watched as Sammy helped his bride up into the cart. Sammy looked at Emily, all huge green eyes that seemed a little moist. Leaving aside Chinese Lady, Emily was first among the wives. Boots was the first of the brothers, and Sammy and Tommy acknowledged he had always worn his seniority with distinction. That made Emily the first lady of the family, again leaving aside Chinese Lady.

'Emily, up you come too,' said Sammy, 'and Boots, and the bridesmaids.'

'In the cart?' cried Rosie. 'Oh, spiffing! Come on, Annabelle!'

Boots lifted the two girls, one after the other. Sally moved forward.

'Might I lend you a hand, Miss Sally Brown?'

Sally turned, and there was Ronnie from the Camberwell offices, all togged up in his best suit and wearing an admiring grin.

'Oh, it's you,' she said.

'What a peach,' said Ronnie, 'I can't wait to shake a leg with you later.'

'Not if I see you comin',' said Sally, and then she was up in the cart too. So was Emily, and so was Boots.

'Full cartload, Eli,' said Sammy, 'so don't gallop. There's no hurry.'

'Vhy, that there ain't, Sammy,' said Mr Greenberg, 'so I'm cartin' you all the vay round, through the Valvorth Road and down Browning Street, and so on, ain't it?'

'Blessed saints,' said Rosie, 'what a palaver, ain't it?'

They were all perched on the narrow side seats, Sammy and Susie, Boots and Emily, and the three bridesmaids, much to the uproarious delight of the guests.

'It's a lovely weddin', Jim,' said Mrs Brown to Mr Brown.

'Our Susie, eh?' said Mr Brown. 'Ain't you proud of her, Bessie?'

'That I am, Jim.'

'Sammy's got himself a lovely wife in Susie,' said Vi to Tommy.

'I've had one for a few years meself,' said Tommy.

'That's funny,' said Vi, 'I've had a nice husband a few years meself.'

'Good on yer, Vi.'

'Good on you too, Tommy.'

'Who's goin' to be on top out of those two?' asked Lizzy of husband Ned.

'Well,' said Ned, 'if Sammy does what comes naturally—'

'I didn't mean that, Ned Somers,' said Lizzy. 'Honestly, your mind, if I don't straighten it out I won't be able to take you anywhere.'

'Not even to church?' said Ned.

'You're not goin' to dodge that,' said Lizzy. 'There, they're off.'

Mr Greenberg drove the pony and cart out through the gates, turning left for the Walworth Road, and after the cart went the younger guests who, of course, began to sing.

'*My old man said follow the van . . .*'

Susie waved her bouquet at everyone the cart passed in Larcom Street. Emily remembered her own wedding, her own ride in the cart with Boots and others. She slipped her arm through his.

'We did this,' she said. It had been nearly ten years ago.

'So we did,' said Boots, leaving alone the fact that he'd been blind at the time. He watched the street. He wondered if Ponsonby knew of the wedding. The man knew his name. Inspector Grant had mentioned it in the man's presence. Ponsonby had lodged only a few doors away from the Browns and would have known, as everyone in the street did, that Susie was engaged to Sammy Adams. The man was clever enough to make the right assumptions and to ask questions that would turn assumptions into fact. He'd have to ask those questions of people in the neighbourhood. He was on the loose, unless the police had caught up with him again. Boots was willing to take his chances with the man, but in no way was he going to leave Rosie at risk. Tim at the moment was with

692

his cousin Bobby, Lizzy and Ned looking after him. But Boots felt that if Inspector Grant was right, Ponsonby would be after Rosie or himself, or just Rosie. The vicious lunatic had a fixation on young girls.

'Boots, it's a lovely day,' said Emily.

'Specially arranged by Sammy, Em.'

'Well, it's gladsome, don't you think?'

'I'd say so, Em.'

Rosie, utterly delighted with everything, with her place in the cart, with waving to people in the Walworth Road and with the singing young people following the cart, whispered, 'Mummy, are you and Daddy having happy talk?'

'Well, it's a weddin' day,' said Emily. 'Oh, lor', I forgot about Tim. Who's lookin' after him?'

'Aunt Lizzy and Uncle Ned,' said Rosie.

The bridal cart nearly stopped the traffic, especially when the young people began to sing to the bride.

'If you knew Susie like I know Susie, oh, oh, oh what a girl . . .'

Boots noticed then that the uniformed constable was following.

Inspector Grant was obviously convinced that Ponsonby would make an attempt to strike.

CHAPTER TWENTY-THREE

St John's Church Institute was by no means unattractive, with its stage at one end and a gallery at the other. Cloakrooms were accessible on either side of the stage, as were kitchen amenities. The local Boy Scout Troop used the hall, made their Friday evening cocoa there and sang camping songs around the piano on the stage.

Today, the two families and their guests sat down to the wedding breakfast at large trestle tables covered in white cloths and placed together to form an open-ended rectangle. The top tables were occupied by the bride and groom, their families and two friends who were rather special, Rachel and Mr Greenberg. Sammy and Susie had both agreed that to have put them elsewhere would have put them among strangers for the most part. Rachel was touched, Mr Greenberg beaming. There was kosher food for them.

There were over seventy guests and the caterers served an excellent meal. Susie, looking around and taking everything in, remembered the years of desperate poverty, when the best her dad could do for his family was a cheap flat in Peabody Buildings in Brandon Street, and she never seemed to have any frock that hadn't already outlived its time. The occasional rat poked about around the dustbins of Brandon Street yards, and the numerous cats enjoyed active nights hunting mice. She would never forget the day when, in her sixteenth year, Sammy gave her a job helping to run his market stall. She'd been a shabby and hungry-eyed waif at the time. The memory made her put a hand on Sammy's knee and squeeze it.

'Hello, who's doin' that?' he asked.

'Me,' said Susie.

'I hope it's not goin' to cost me,' said Sammy.

'Say a tanner, Sammy.'

'Make it a tiddler, Susie.'

'Fourpence,' said Susie, laughing. Sammy gave her two pennies. 'That's only tuppence,' she said.

'I'll have to owe you the rest, Mrs Adams,' said Sammy, 'it's been a ruinous week.'

'Uncle Sammy, what're you doing?' asked Annabelle.

'No idea,' said Sammy, 'it's been like that for a year, Annabelle.'

'You're funny, Uncle Sammy.'

'Point is,' said Sammy, 'will I recover?'

It was like that all around the hall, and the breakfast turned into an exhilarating affair, riotous with laughter. There was beer for the rousing cockney element, such as old friends and neighbours like Mr and Mrs Blake, Mr and Mrs Higgins, and Mr and Mrs Pullen, as well as Sammy's factory friends Gertie and Bert. There were soft drinks for the children and wine for those adults who fancied it. Ned, who now had a very good job with a wine merchant of Great Tower Street, had supplied the wine.

Susie caught Will's eye. She framed words.

'All right, lovey?'

'Fine.'

Will was actually finding himself in a waiting mood. Not for an event, nor the speeches. It was Annie. Everyone seemed to have someone. Sally, unattached, seemed to have a pleasant-looking boy sending her pencilled notes by the hand of one of the caterers' waitresses, and each one had her giggling. Will kept thinking about Annie, lively, spirited and always giving as good as she got. But she wouldn't be here until about a quarter to five. He felt it was going to be a long wait. But what was the point of thinking about her? Here he was, chucked out of the Army on account of his asthma and having to look for a job that would be kind to him. He was no sort of a catch for a girl like Annie, or for any girl. Ruddy great balls of fire, he thought, I'm a mess, I'll probably have an attack as soon as she arrives. Blow that for a lark.

Boots felt Rosie was safe for the time being, except that there was something lurking in the back of his mind, something that he couldn't get hold of. What was it? The atmosphere of revelry was interfering with concentrated thought, and it prolonged the breakfast. But when it was finally over, Susie's dad was the first to make a speech. It was in honour of the guests.

On his feet, he began by saying, 'I don't want none of you to worry, because I'm not goin' to get you to listen to more than you want to 'ear.'

'Good speech, Jim!'

'Short an' sweet, old mate.'

'Give 'im a cheer.'

'No, give 'im a beer.'

Rosie made herself heard with the aplomb of a girl already self-assured.

'Don't take any notice, Mr Brown, we're all ears,' she said. 'At least, I am and so's my Uncle Sammy.'

'Thank you kindly, Rosie,' said Mr Brown. 'Anyway, I've only got a few words to mention, which is that me and my wife, Mrs Bessie Brown, who's wearin' a new titfer, wish to thank all of you for bein' here in honour of our daughter Susie and 'er new better 'alf.'

'What's she done with 'er old one, then?'

'Got 'im under the table, has she, Jim?'

'If you don't all keep quiet,' said Freddy, 'me dad won't make 'is speech.'

''Ooray!'

''Ooray twice!'

'Where was I?' asked Mr Brown.

'In honour of Susie and Sammy,' said Boots.

'Thank you kindly, Boots,' said Mr Brown. 'Yes, me an' Bessie thank you all for bein' with us today an' for all your good wishes, and we 'ope everyone 'as a fine time without falling over, which some guests did when we got married ourselves. Is that the lot, Bessie?'

'Yes, it's our pleasure, Jim,' said the smiling Mrs Brown.

'Well, then, me an' Bessie drink yer very good 'ealth,' said Mr Brown.

'Same to you, Jim!'

'Same to you, Bessie!'

Boots was on his feet a few minutes later, with Rosie looking ready to giggle, Chinese Lady looking suspicious of the lurking smile on his face, and her husband Mr Finch looking as if his eldest stepson was going to be worth listening to.

'Ladies—'

'Where? What ladies?' asked a wag.

'Ladies and gentlemen—'

'What's he talkin' about?'

'You mean who's he talkin' about.'

'They're after you, Daddy,' said Rosie.

'Let's have it, Boots,' said Ned.

'I'll fire the next clever gent out of a cannon,' said Boots.

'Now, Boots, we don't want any aggravatin' talk,' said Chinese Lady, 'not on Sammy and Susie's weddin' day.'

'Duly noted, old girl,' said Boots. 'Now, ladies and

gentlemen, family life that begins with marriage needs to be blessed with good plumbing, and the first principle of good plumbing is all to do with frost-proof pipes. Frost-proofing can be achieved in several ways, all of which are described in Stopcock and Company's plumbing manual.'

'What's that only oldest son of mine talkin' about, Edwin?' asked Chinese Lady of her husband.

'Plumbing,' said Mr Finch. 'Good plumbing is dear to the hearts of all of us.'

'Not at a weddin' it's not,' said Chinese Lady.

'I expect you all want to know how to deal with a burst pipe,' said Boots. 'You first find out where all the water's coming from.'

'Is that a fact?' asked Tommy.

'It's news to me,' said Sammy.

'It's useful information for newly-weds,' said Boots, and went on to say that his mother, bless her cotton socks, had twice been a newly-wed and twice endowed with worldly goods, including good plumbing.

'Is it me who's goin' barmy, or is it Boots?' asked Mr Higgins.

'I knew it,' said Chinese Lady, 'I knew that son of mine would go off his 'ead one day, I always said he would, but I never thought it would happen at his brother's weddin'.'

'Sounds all right to me, Mrs Finch,' said Will, 'and I know for a fact that Susie's expectin' Sammy to endow her with good plumbin'.'

'Plumbing's serious,' said Sammy.

'Especially if you can get ten per cent discount,' said Susie.

Guests rolled about, and the bridesmaids were all in fits.

698

'In addition to good plumbing,' said Boots, 'newly-weds need an efficient mangle.'

'Of vhich I have a stock at five bob each,' said Mr Greenberg, 'and no charge for delivery.'

'Good on yer, Eli!'

'Ve are all friends,' beamed Mr Greenberg.

'Efficient mangles are a must,' said Boots, 'and so are ladies' undergarments. Particularly for brides.'

'Daddy!' shrieked Rosie.

'Stop him, someone,' begged Susie.

'Hit him, you mean,' said Lizzy.

'While I can't speak as a gentleman,' said Boots, 'I can say, as a common or garden bloke, that brides not only go for good plumbing and efficient mangles, they've also got a thing about reliable elastic.'

'Sammy, stop him!' cried Susie.

'Why, what's he said?' asked Sammy.

'Keep goin', Boots,' said Will, hoping that laughing moments wouldn't affect his tubes.

Rachel thought, I should miss this? Not likely. What a family.

Boots touched on the subject of bridal trousseaux. He said he hadn't seen Susie's trousseau, but he had it on good authority from her sister Sally that it wisely contained some winter warmers.

'I can't hardly believe what I'm hearin',' said Chinese Lady.

'Nor me,' said Sally, close to hysterics.

'It's the winter weather,' said Boots. If Sammy was rarely lost for hitting English on its head, Boots was never lost for whimsical or deceptive patter. And he was talking as much to divert himself as the guests. Something was still worrying him, something he felt he'd forgotten or overlooked. He caught Rosie's eye, and Rosie waited in

699

delight for his next piece of nonsense. 'You'll all be interested to know that Susie's bottom drawer is as good as she hopes Sammy's plumbing will be.'

'Never mind the plumbin',' said Sammy, 'just give me a list of me fancy expectations.'

'Well,' said Boots, 'how'd you like the sound of four ladies' woolly vests down to the knees, two red flannel petticoats and one plumbers' spanner for giving you a headache?'

'That's out for a start,' said Sammy. 'I don't like headaches except as a matter of business.'

'I never heard anything more deplorable in all me life,' said Chinese Lady, 'and I can't take kindly to you laughin' about it, Edwin.'

'Believe me, Maisie, I'm not laughing,' said Mr Finch, 'I'm crying.'

'So am I,' said Susie.

'Don't see why,' said Will, 'I like the sound of four woolly vests down to your knees, sis.'

'I'll kill Boots,' said Susie.

'You've done it now, Daddy,' said Rosie.

'Regarding the happy couple,' said Boots, 'I've known Sammy all his life, and it's my considered opinion that if there were two more like him, the rest of us would be walking backwards.'

'Granted,' said Sammy.

'Seconded,' said Tommy.

'Thirded,' said Lizzy.

'I've known Susie since she was sixteen,' said Boots. 'Sammy runs on electricity, Susie runs on sunshine. If you put two people like Susie and Sammy together, they'll never have a freeze-up, even if their plumbing is a major disaster.'

'Is that son of mine makin' sense?' asked Chinese Lady.

'Now and again,' said Mr Finch.

'Sammy fell on his head when he first met Susie,' said Boots, 'and he's still not right way up. Long may Susie keep him like that, it's one way of emptying his pockets. Ladies and gentlemen, I give you the bride and groom and a long-lasting marriage.'

'Well done, Boots,' said Mr Finch, and everyone came to their feet to toast the happy couple. After which, Rosie whispered to Boots that she was sure his mum was going to box his ears.

'Never a dull moment in this family, kitten,' he said.

'Mummy's still laughing,' said Rosie, 'I think she's getting better, don't you?'

'Thumbs up to that, Rosie.'

Sammy's speech was appreciated by one and all. He admitted Susie had floored him, and that she answered him back as well, but it hadn't been painful all the time, and he was hoping to make a recovery. He further admitted he had had to hand Susie all his worldly goods on account of the vicar listening, and he could only hope she'd let him have enough back to take care of his overheads. He thanked Mrs Brown for having had Susie as a result of a twinkle in Mr Brown's eye, and he thanked them both for making sure that Susie hadn't run off with a floor-walker, as that would have upset him no end. He hoped that as his wife she'd cure herself of answering him back. He thanked everyone for their presents, and he thanked his mother for bringing him up to be virtuous, charitable and a bit of all right in the business world. Modesty prevented him saying more than that. He complimented Mr Finch on becoming his stepfather, and he complimented the bridesmaids on looking highly adorable. He proposed a toast to them, and he himself toasted his bride.

'Good luck, Susie!'

'Good on yer, Sammy!'

'Bless you both,' said Mrs Brown happily.

There was an interval before the three-piece band arrived and dancing began. Ladies took themselves off to their cloakroom and Boots took himself into the street. The uniformed constable was patrolling about. Boots asked him if he was acting under instructions. The constable said yes, that his orders were to make sure that Ponsonby, the wanted man, did not enter the Institute or intrude on the wedding celebrations in any way. A colleague was just round the corner in Brandon Street to check on people entering Larcom Street. There was a third man near the vicarage and church, watching people coming up from Charleston Street or from the Walworth Road. In addition, there were scores of men combing the whole area.

'Thanks,' said Boots, 'I'll have cups of tea and some wedding cake sent out to you and your colleague in a while.'

'Kind of you, Mr Adams, we'll appreciate that. Good luck, sir.'

He and Rosie needed that, did they? If so, how much? Ponsonby, obviously, was still at large. He went back into the hall. Everyone, of course, knew about the murders and a man who'd been charged by the police. What they didn't know was that the slippery bugger had escaped custody. Well, there was no point in telling them, no point in introducing an ugly note. It was Susie's big day. Let it stay like that.

There was a queue tailing back from the ladies' cloakroom beyond the stage, and the caterers were busy setting out cups and saucers and making huge pots of tea. The cake was waiting to be cut. Susie and Sammy were circulating in dutiful and sociable fashion, talking to as many guests as possible. Boots looked instinctively for Rosie. Young Tim was his pal, Rosie his sweetheart. He sometimes had to be careful not to show more attention to the girl than the boy, and Rosie herself took care to see that Tim was never pushed into the background.

Will came up, a smile on his face. Boots liked Will, he liked the whole of the Brown family, very much a reminder of his own when they were living in Caulfield Place.

'How's it goin', Boots?' asked Will.

'It's going well for Susie,' said Boots. 'Have you seen Rosie?'

'She's over there, with Freddy, Cassie and your niece Annabelle. Sally's gone into hidin'. There's a young bloke from your offices tryin' to turn her into his girlfriend.'

Sally appeared then, a young vision in pink.

'Who's this?' asked Boots.

'Boots, it's me,' said Sally.

'Well, don't go home too early,' said Boots, 'not before I've had a dance with you.'

Sally turned a thrilled pink that almost matched her cerise dress. Boots was her hero after what he'd done for Cassie yesterday. Will recognized her then as a girl with a crush.

'Oh, I'll be ever so pleasured,' she said. 'Boots, 'as Will told you the Army's goin' to discharge 'im?'

'Is that a fact, Will?' asked Boots.

'Had an official letter this mornin',' said Will.

'With an offer of a pension?' asked Boots, glancing across the hall at Rosie.

'Not a word,' said Will.

'Well, we'll go to work on it together,' said Boots. 'I'll come and see you sometime next week.'

'Oh, ain't you nice?' said Sally.

'The Ministry of Pensions won't think so,' said Boots.

'Blow them,' said Sally.

'I won't say five bob a week wouldn't be useful,' said Will.

'We'll start by getting you to ask for two quid,' said Boots.

'Two quid?' said Sally, blinking.

'Will won't get it,' said Boots, 'but it'll send the Ministry into a panic. That'll give Will a chance to settle for twelve and six, or ten bob at the worst.'

'I'm not proud,' said Will.

'Nor am I,' said Boots, 'it alters the shape of your face.'

Sally laughed. Boots had a quiet word with a waitress about tea for the policemen.

The tables had all been folded and stowed away, except for two covered with cups and saucers. The hot tea was ready and the wedding cake was cut amid the sounds of revelry. Boots went across to Emily, who had just taken young Tim in hand and was trying to show him how to dance the Boston Two-Step. Boots collected a cup of tea on the way and gave it to Emily.

'Lovely,' she said, 'just what I need.'

'Sit down and drink it,' said Boots. The chairs now lined the walls.

'But I've already been sittin' for ages,' said Emily.

'Well, good for you,' said Boots, 'now do some more. I'll see to Tim. Come on, young 'un, let's go out to the yard and see if we can have five minutes football before the band arrives.'

'Crikey, could we, Dad?' asked Tim, plainly preferring that to the Boston Two-Step.

'Did I hear someone mention football?' asked Emily.

'Yes, Dad did,' said Tim.

'Not likely you're not,' said Emily, 'not in your suit, me lad, nor your dad in his. I don't know, goin' out to a yard to kick a ball about when there's a weddin' on. Your grandma will have a fit. So will I. That dad of yours wants talkin' to sometimes.'

'No football, then,' said Boots, 'just a look at the fresh air. It's getting a little warm in here.'

'Well, lovey, if it's fresh, bring some back 'ere,' said Emily.

'I'll find a paper bag,' said Boots, and took Tim around the stage and through the kitchen to the back door, which opened on to an alley used as a yard for dustbins. He wanted to check the door, to find out if the caterers were keeping it locked. They weren't. They were using the dustbins. But just beyond the entrance to the alley, he glimpsed a constable. So there he was, the colleague of the man on duty outside the Institute. Inspector Grant was taking seriously his feeling that before Ponsonby attempted to slip off to wider pastures he meant to revenge himself for being handed over to the police in that factory wasteland. With other police officers swarming elsewhere, Ponsonby must be feeling squeezed, wherever he was.

'Look, there's a bobby, Dad,' said Tim, 'I'll go and ask him the time.'

'What for, young feller-me-lad?'

'Dad, you always ask a bobby the time,' said four-year-old Tim.

'No, you don't,' said Boots, catching hold of his energetic young son before he had a chance to slip the parental leash. 'Up you come.' He picked the boy up and slung him over his shoulder. Tim yelled with delight as Boots carried him back into the hall. Chinese Lady intercepted father and son, a cup of tea in her hand, her hat a wedding triumph.

'So there you are,' she said.

'Hello, old lady,' said Boots, eyes picking out Rosie.

'What's that boy doin' over your shoulder, might I ask?'

'What boy?' asked Boots.

'Me!' yelled Tim.

'What's he doin' up in the air?' demanded Chinese Lady.

'Search me,' said Boots, and his mother put on her severe look.

'I don't know what I'm goin' to tell people about that speech of yours,' she said. 'It's a mystery to me where you got that tongue of yours from.'

'It's a mystery to me too,' said Boots, 'so we're both in the same boat. Well, you do the rowing, old lady, while I keep a lookout for the old man of the sea.'

'What old man of the sea?' asked Chinese Lady suspiciously.

'The one with all the answers,' said Boots.

Chinese Lady's firm mouth twitched.

'Put that boy down,' she said.

'Down you come, Tim,' said Boots, and set the lad on his feet. 'Go and get yourself a cup of tea and a slice of cake. Then I'll show you how to turn cartwheels for your grandma.'

'Crikey, yes,' said Tim, going at a run.

'Lovely wedding, old girl,' said Boots.

'It was,' said Chinese Lady, 'till you started talkin' about Susie's bottom drawer. I was never more embarrassed for any of my sons. Sammy's bad enough, but at least he 'asn't got any of those Frenchified ways you picked up in France.'

'Well, that's something to be thankful for,' said Boots. The three-piece band had arrived, a little surprised to have been closely inspected by a policeman. They were now up on the stage and getting ready for their part in the proceedings. As soon as everyone had had a cup of tea and a piece of wedding cake, the caterers would finish clearing the hall.

'I can't for the life of me think why Edwin don't disapprove of that tongue of yours,' said Chinese Lady, who wouldn't have allowed him to, in any case.

'Never mind, live in hope,' said Boots. He glimpsed a movement in the gallery. 'Just a moment.' He walked to the far end, climbed the stairs and came upon Freddy and Cassie. 'Hello, what's happening up here?' he asked.

Cassie regarded him in dreamy adoration, having been told he was the man who had helped Freddy bring her home.

''Ello,' she said shyly. 'Me an' Freddy's lookin' for Queen Mary's best 'at.'

'Well, she's lookin',' said Freddy, 'I'm just bein' wore out.'

'Yes, Queen Mary come up 'ere once,' said Cassie, 'and lost 'er best 'at. I read it somewhere. It's got green feathers. Mister, 'ave you met Queen Mary and 'ad Sunday tea with 'er?'

'Not lately,' smiled Boots.

'There, I told yer, Freddy,' said Cassie. 'I told yer 'e was bound to 'ave met Queen Mary.'

'Yer'll 'ave to excuse 'er, Mister Adams,' said Freddy, 'she can't 'elp bein' scatty.'

'I ain't scatty, am I, mister?' said Cassie.

'I like scatty girls,' said Boots. 'We're all a bit that way. In fact, the whole world's barmy, Cassie.' He ruffled the girl's hair. 'Enjoy yourselves. Hope you find Queenie's hat.'

The band struck up then. The tables were all out of the way, the hall clear. The dancing began.

And Annie arrived.

CHAPTER TWENTY-FOUR

Annie entered the Institute at five minutes to five. Crikey, she thought, it must be an important wedding to have a policeman on duty outside. Actually, there'd been quite a few about. Had she bought an evening paper on her way home from work she'd have known why. They were head-lining the escape of the man held in custody. His name was revealed and his description, together with the warning that he was dangerous.

The atmosphere of revelry reached Annie at once. The guests were dancing to the music of a three-piece band, and the hall was a picture of colour and movement. Girls were all dolled up, and all the women looked wedding-worthy. Annie noticed some very smart ladies and some posh-looking men. She supposed Sammy Adams had friends all over because of his business. Young men looked frisky, and the middle-aged women looked kind of mellow, as if beer and port had been flowing. The band were playing 'Miss Annabelle Lee', and the dancers were doing a quick-step. It all looked lively and exciting, and there wasn't a gloomy face anywhere. The bride herself was dancing, her white gown swirling and floating, and she was laughing up into the face of a very interesting-looking man. Combing the vague recollections she had of seeing Sammy Adams at his market stall, Annie felt sure she was seeing him now. There were chairs along the side walls, but not many people were using them at the moment. Most were dancing. Annie looked around for a sight of Will. Not seeing him, she slipped into the cloakroom to take off her hat and her light raincoat, and to unnecessarily tidy up her face.

She emerged in her highly fashionable loose-waisted white dress, her stockinged legs gleaming. The first person she saw was Cassie, who was in argument with Freddy. Freddy was in a new grey suit with long trousers, but still looked very much a boy.

'Hello, you two,' she said, 'what's up?'

'I just don't believe it, but it 'appened,' said Freddy. 'Cassie's barmy cat 'as invited itself.'

'D'you mean it came in 'ere?' asked Annie.

'Well, Tabby likes weddings,' said Cassie. 'I keep tellin' Freddy, but 'e keeps not listenin'.'

'Crikey, Annie, don't yer look posh?' said Freddy.

'Do I, Freddy?'

'I bet Will's goin' to fall over when 'e spots yer,' said Freddy.

'Annie, Tabby's gone in the men's cloakroom,' complained Cassie, 'an' Freddy won't go an' get 'im.'

'Beats me 'ow it got here,' said Freddy, 'but I ain't fetchin' it. D'you know what she wants to do? Take it round in a dance.'

'Well, Tabby likes dancing,' said Cassie. ''E used to dance as Dick Whittington's cat in a pantomime.'

'Bloomin' Muvver O'Grady,' breathed Freddy, 'she ain't real.'

The dance came to an end. Annie watched couples leaving the floor. There was no sign of Will with a partner.

'Hello.'

Annie turned, and there he was, smiling and looking a fine young man in his new grey suit, bought for the wedding.

'Hello, Will.'

'You're lookin' highly fashionable again, Annie,' he

said, thinking her just about the nicest girl a bloke could hope to walk out with.

'I don't like the way you say highly,' said Annie, 'you're as bad as me dad.'

'Well, it's not our fault you look good enough to eat,' said Will. 'Come on, come and meet the bride and groom and lots of other people.' He took her to that part of the hall where the Brown and Adams families were sociably grouped. He introduced her first to Susie and Sammy. Susie, recognizing her and wanting her to be a bright light in Will's life, greeted her like an old friend. Sammy, who had been told about her and what had happened yesterday to her sister Cassie, shook hands warmly with her. She was immediately conscious of electric energy.

'What a pleasure,' he said. 'Are you the girl my new brother-in-law Will found in a pushcart?'

'Sammy!' Susie shook a finger at him.

'Oh, I can't believe it,' said Annie, looking at Will. 'You've done it on me again.'

'Not me,' said Will. Susie was the guilty party, actually. She thought the incident the funniest thing ever, although she was aware Annie didn't.

'I'd give five bob to see Susie in a pushcart,' said Sammy. 'Unfortunately, I can't afford it at the moment.'

'Sammy, go and stand in a corner,' said Susie.

'Who said that?' asked Sammy, and Will, grinning, introduced Annie to his mum. She'd already met his dad. Mrs Brown was that taken with the girl she almost gave her a motherly cuddle. Mr Brown said hello again, Annie, glad you could come, but watch some of the fellers here, they'll be after you. Annie met Chinese Lady, introduced to her as Mrs Finch, and her husband Mr Finch, ever such a distinguished-looking man. She also met Boots and Emily, Lizzy and Ned, Tommy and Vi. Then there was a

710

quite beautiful woman whom Boots introduced as Rachel, a friend of the family, and a dark-bearded fatherly-looking man with whom all Walworth was acquainted, Mr Greenberg. Annie, knowing Boots was the man who had been such a great help to Freddy in finding Cassie, discovered him to be distinguished-looking himself, but with a very easy-going air. His wife Emily had marvellous auburn hair and magnificent green eyes, but was awfully thin. Then there were two people called Aunt Victoria and Uncle Tom, and several children. Lord, thought Annie, why am I meeting all these people if I'm just someone who's only going to get a picture postcard from India, and perhaps not even that?

Guests were dancing again, and most of the people she had just met melted away to take the floor. Annie waited for Will to ask her. Instead, he began chatting to Sammy's mother. Annie ground her teeth. Tommy came up.

'Now we've met and me wife Vi's havin' a sit-down,' he said, 'might I have the pleasure? I'm Tommy, in case you've already forgotten.'

'I'm Annie, if you've forgotten,' she said.

'Which I haven't,' said Tommy, and so she danced with him, but she was wild with Will.

Boots was taking Aunt Victoria round. Emily had said he ought to, for the sake of family relations. Aunt Victoria was saying that she was very complimented. Boots said well, you can still shake a fine leg for a woman of forty. Aunt Victoria, well past forty, felt so pleasured by this further compliment that she overlooked his mention of her limb. It was a lovely wedding party, she said, and she didn't want to complain, but she thought the caterers' port was a little vinegary, that it was very inconvenient that in the ladies' cloakroom one of the cubicles was out of order, that she was sure Mr Higgins was getting drunk on all the beer he was ordering free from the waitresses, and that some of the children seemed a little rowdy. Well, I'm like you, Aunt Victoria, said Boots, I don't want to complain, either, and I'm glad you agree we shouldn't. Well, I was just mentioning one or two things, that's all, she said. Boots smiled, and Aunt Victoria went girlishly giddy in his arms.

The dance over, Annie looked for Will, a fierce light in her eyes. He'd gone missing, the coward. She intercepted Susie.

'Susie, could I ask you, doesn't Will dance?'

Susie looked at her and saw vexation. She realized Will had said nothing about his condition to this very attractive girl. Susie felt she knew why. All the same, Annie should be told, it was only fair. They stood together in the middle of the hall. Waitresses appeared with trays of beer, port and soft drinks. Spirits in the church hall weren't allowed.

'Annie, Will's got asthma. That's why he's home from India, and why he's havin' to leave the Army. He received a letter today, telling him they were goin' to discharge him. He hasn't told you, obviously. He gets attacks, sometimes not for a day or so, sometimes three a day. He probably thinks he'll have an attack if he dances, and he's a bit fed-up with himself.'

'He's got asthma?' said Annie. She felt very upset. 'Oh, that's not like consumption, is it?'

'No, of course not,' said Susie, still softly brilliant in her wedding gown. She and Sammy weren't going on their honeymoon to Devon until tomorrow. They were spending their wedding night in their new home. Susie was having nervously excited moments about it, and Sammy was wondering if Susie was going to wear a black silk nightdress. 'It's just that it makes Will feel he's only half a man some days.'

'Oh, where is 'e?' said Annie. 'Fancy not tellin' me. If I

712

can put up with bein' dumped in a pushcart and havin' him tell everyone about it, he can put up with tellin' me about his asthma.'

'Well, good for you, Annie,' said Susie. 'Look, there he is, up in the gallery, watchin' us.'

The band struck up again as Annie made for the gallery stairs. It didn't take her long to corner Will and to speak her mind. She didn't make the mistake of being sad and pitying, although she did feel sad.

'Will, you silly, you ought to be ashamed,' she said, 'takin' me out, kissin' me till I didn't know where me legs were, and not tellin' me you've got a bit of a chest complaint. Lots of men 'ave got chest complaints, but they don't go round deceivin' girls.'

'Deceivin'?' said Will.

'Well, it is deceivin', isn't it, not confidin' in a girl who's your young lady?'

'I thought it was best if—'

'As if I care you've got a funny chest—'

'You haven't. Yours is—'

'Don't be cheeky. I want to know all about the attacks you 'ave. Will Brown, look me in the eye when I'm talkin' to you.'

'Annie, I've even been chucked out of the Army.'

'Thank goodness for that,' said Annie. 'I don't want my young man in any Army, anyway. And you're still not lookin' at me.'

'Can't,' said Will.

'Why can't you? What's wrong with me?'

'If I look at you, I'll kiss you.'

'Well, that's nice. I like you sayin' things like that. Let's sit down in the corner over there.'

'Annie, if I get an attack, you won't like what it does to me.'

713

'Well, come and sit and talk to me,' said Annie, 'about what makes you have attacks. We don't 'ave to dance, just sit together.'

Will gave in. Annie put her arms around him and kissed him. Nothing chronically disastrous happened, even though Annie was wearing a little scent. Well, when a girl had made up her mind to be someone's young lady, a little scent was a great help.

The band played on, and on, contributing to the revelry infectiously and exhilaratingly, especially after each member had been served with a pint glass of the free beer. Old-fashioned dances alternated with lively modern fox-trots, and young people nearly fell over themselves in their delighted dash on to the floor to perform the Charleston. Sammy's office girls rushed with young men. Into the fray went Lizzy, Vi, Emily and Susie with their husbands. In went Rosie and Annabelle to dance it with each other. In went Cassie, dragging an appalled Freddy with her.

Chinese Lady could hardly believe her eyes. Those short frocks, and Sammy's office girls all wearing pink garters, the delight of flappers. She knew where they came from. Sammy's ladies' shops. That disreputable young man was heading for purgatory all right. And look at Boots, her only oldest, he was performing with three partners now, Emily, Rosie and Annabelle. And that Tommy, going it with Vi. As for Lizzy, well, there she was with Ned, and Ned performing as if he didn't have an artificial leg. Well, thought Chinese Lady, if I don't have something to say to all of them, my name's not Mrs Maisie Finch.

'I never saw anything so shockin',' she said to her husband.

'Wait until they're performing "Mother Brown",' said

Mr Finch, well-versed in this cockney ritual, known as a knees-up.

'Oh, that's different,' said Chinese Lady.

Emily emerged exhausted at the finish of the Charleston, and Boots made her sit down. Ned came up, and advised Boots a bloke wanted to see him, he was waiting at the door.

'I'll get Emily a port, Boots, while you go and see the bloke.'

Boots found a detective-sergeant waiting for him.

'Sorry to disturb you, Mr Adams, but Inspector Grant asked me, as I was comin' this way, to drop in on you.'

'You've copped Ponsonby?' said Boots.

The CID sergeant said no, not yet. What he wanted to say was that they'd traced a call made by Ponsonby on a shop in King and Queen Street, near the market. He'd made the call not long after his escape from the Rodney Road police station. He'd bought a toy periscope.

'A what?' said Boots.

A toy periscope, said the CID man, made of cardboard with two small mirrors and sold to kids for tuppence. Boots asked where Ponsonby had got the money from. Wasn't it standard practice for the police to empty a suspect's pockets? Yes, and that had been done, said the sergeant, but in making enquiries in the market, they'd discovered Ponsonby had sold his silk-lined waistcoat to a second-hand clothes stall for threepence. Incidentally, they'd also found a stack of money in a cupboard in his lodgings, which was believed to relate to a robbery. Anyway, the point was, Inspector Grant was convinced Ponsonby was still somewhere in this area, and he wanted Mr Adams to take great care, especially when the wedding celebrations were over and he left with his family to go home. There would be police around, and if Mr Adams didn't mind, they'd like to give him an escort to his home.

Bloody hell, thought Boots, how the devil can I tell Emily and Rosie that there's a maniac after my blood, and how the devil could Ponsonby have really worked out that I'm here with them? And what the hell did he want a periscope for?

'Look, Sergeant,' he said, 'Ponsonby could have been sharp enough to find my address from the telephone directory. Can you ask Inspector Grant to check the area around our house?'

'Good idea, sir,' said the CID sergeant, 'I'll get that message to him. He's not far away. Sorry if I've worried you as well as disturbed you, but Inspector Grant doesn't like the bugger or what he's capable of gettin' up to.'

'Tell him I share his feelings,' said Boots, and the sergeant left. Boots rejoined the party. He saw Rosie and Annabelle talking to Chinese Lady. Sally, in retreat from Ronnie Jarvis, who had managed to collar her for the Charleston, begged Boots to save her from more of the office boy's larks.

'I think you're playing hard to get, Sally,' he said. A waltz had just begun. 'Is this our dance?'

'Oh, crikey, could we?' breathed Sally in hero-worship, and Boots took her into the waltz. Sally was swoony all the way, but plucked up enough courage to ask him if he thought Sammy would give her a job in one of his shops. Boots said as an apprentice shop assistant? Oh, lor', would he, d'you think? The advantage is all yours, Sally, you're one of the family now, said Boots. 'Oh, bless yer, Boots,' said Sally, and swooned on.

Will had managed a cautious dance with Annie, she bright-eyed now that she knew exactly where she stood, and that she had made him understand where he stood himself. They were walking out. Officially.

The atmosphere was rousingly festive. Cockneys didn't believe in enjoying themselves quietly. Ain't there goin' to be a knees-up? Later. What about a knees-up? Later.

Sammy, noting Will and Annie sitting together and looking as if they were already thinking of good plumbing, efficient mangles and bottom drawers, decided he couldn't let Susie's likeable brother suffer unemployment as well as asthma. He told Susie he'd find him a job that wouldn't crucify his chest. Susie hugged him and let his own chest introduce itself pleasurably to her bodice.

'Lord love yer, Mrs Adams,' he said, 'not here if you don't mind. Later.'

'Love you, Sammy.'

Rosie spoke to Emily.

'You all right, Mummy?'

'Fine, Rosie love.'

'I expect you're getting a bit tired.'

'I'm not goin' to be too tired for the knees-up,' smiled Emily.

'We're really going to have one?' said Rosie.

'There'll be a riot if we don't,' said Emily.

Boots appeared.

'Rosie,' he said, 'I don't think I've had the pleasure yet. How about it, kitten?'

'Well, I think I'm disengaged, Daddy, yes, I think I am,' said Rosie. 'You can have the pleasure.'

'Come on, then,' said Boots and they went flying into the Boston Two-Step, Rosie in sheer exhilaration. Cassie couldn't get Freddy to participate, so she made him go and look for her cat. She did some more looking herself, and tried the ladies' cloakroom. No-one was there. She looked and she called. Tabby didn't miaow or show himself, it was just ever so quiet in the cloakroom, the door of one cubicle locked and chalked 'OUT OF

717

ORDER'. She didn't like it being so quiet and she ran out.

It was not Cassie Mr Ponsonby was waiting for, however.

It was Rosie.

Rosie, coming off the floor with Boots, said, 'I'll tell Miss Simms that just everyone was here this evening, Daddy – oh, silly me, I can't. She's gone to darkest Africa. I'm sorry, aren't you? I think she liked you lots. Never mind, I'll tell all my school friends just everyone was here.'

'From all the noise we're making, I should think everyone knows already that just everyone's here, Rosie. We might—' Boots stopped. It hit him then, the point he'd overlooked. Everyone included Ponsonby. Boots recalled the scene in the police station, when there was the necessity of making a statement. Quite close was the handcuffed Ponsonby, who knew by then whose daughter Rosie was. Boots had said, 'Let's get it all over with now, Inspector, I'm attending a wedding here, at St John's Church tomorrow, with my family.' It was a wedding Ponsonby knew about, and he probably knew too that the reception was taking place at the Institute. And at that point he also knew the man who had knocked him out would be there with his family. He had seen Rosie, he had heard her. *Hello, Daddy.*

It was after nine-thirty now, and Ponsonby was somewhere close, Boots was absolutely certain of that now. He told Rosie to get hold of Tim, and for the two of them to give Emily a little company until he got back. He was just going to the cloakroom. Rosie looked at him. The hall was alive with laughter and uproarious jokes, with young people awaiting the next dance.

'Daddy, something's worrying you,' said Rosie.

'Oh, just the thought of doing the knees-up,' said Boots.

'Daddy, I'm not silly, you know,' said Rosie. His worries were her worries, his pains her pains.

'Nor am I, I know when I need to go to the cloakroom,' said Boots. 'Collect Tim, Rosie, and go and sit with Mummy, there's a sweet girl.'

'Yes, all right, Daddy,' said Rosie and went looking for Tim. The band struck up for the next dance. Rachel intercepted Boots as he crossed the hall.

'Boots, may I?' she said, her smile affectionate.

'In two ticks, Rachel, promise,' he said, and off he went to check the back door again. It was still not locked, the caterers were still using the dustbins. They were on duty until ten-thirty. But this time, there was a policeman on duty in the alley itself. In the darkness, Boots made him out. A street lamp beyond the alley cast a faint light over the entrance. It would pick out anyone entering.

Boots returned. Rachel was waiting. Rosie was watching, and she watched the person she loved best in all the world dance a fox-trot with the most beautiful woman in the hall. Rachel was purring.

'Lovely,' she murmured.

'I am?' said Boots.

'God, I hope not,' said Rachel. 'Not you or Sammy or Tommy. I like you all for being men, not pretty ones.'

'Bless your proud bosom, Rachel,' said Boots, thinking, thinking.

Will suddenly came to his feet.

'What's up?' asked Annie.

'Something's hittin' me tubes,' said Will. 'Give us a few minutes, Annie.'

'Yes, all right, Will,' she said, and watched as he made his way to the cloakroom, where he entered a cubicle, locked it and stood with his back against the door. He drew in breath. The danger signals fluttered and weakened. He sighed with relief, but guessed he'd have an attack by the time he got home, if not before.

Boots came off the floor with Rachel, and they both sat with Emily to let Rosie and Tim join Lizzy's children. Susie appeared in a swirl of white.

'Knees-up after the next dance,' she said, 'everyone in.'

'I should be worried?' said Rachel. 'Susie, I can't wait.'

'I've got a wooden leg,' said Boots.

'No excuses,' said Susie, and delivered the order next to Chinese Lady, Mr Finch, Mr and Mrs Brown, and Mr Greenberg.

'Well, I don't mind any company doin' a knees-up,' said Chinese Lady, 'but I'm not sure—'

'No excuses, Mum,' said Susie, now a daughter-in-law.

'Well, my goodness, Susie, at my age and all.'

'No excuses, Maisie,' said Mr Finch, who had come back from Germany with definite worries of his own, all concerning the political ambitions of a man called Adolf Hitler.

'Ve are all friends,' beamed Mr Greenberg, 'and vhat is a knees-up for if not for friends, ain't it?'

Guests swarmed again as the band struck up 'On Mother Kelly's Doorstep'.

'Come on, Boots, let's you, me, Timmy and Rosie all do this together,' said Emily.

They collected Tim, and Boots called Rosie.

'Yes, in a minute, Daddy,' said Rosie, coming up, 'but I've got to shake hands with the water board first.' That was a family thing. Spending a penny was called going to shake hands with the water board. Rosie dashed off. Boots, taking hold of Tim's hand and Emily's hand, was hit by a shaft of light.

Ponsonby. The ladies' cloakroom. Two cubicles, one out of order. The curate, knowing a large wedding party was using the Institute today, would have moved heaven and earth to ensure there was no inconvenience of that kind. Plumbing, for God's sake.

'Just a moment, Em,' he said, and was away, skirting the dancers. Then he ran to the ladies' cloakroom. He opened the door without knocking. Rosie was there, waiting. She turned, her mouth opened. Boots put a finger to his lips, then beckoned, urgently. Rosie came out into the passage.

'Daddy, what *are* you doing?' she whispered.

Boots, pulling the door to, said, 'Rosie, I think there's a man in the other cubicle.'

'Ugh,' said Rosie.

'Do you remember the man you saw at the police station last night? He escaped.'

'Oh, blessed saints,' breathed Rosie. 'He's in there?'

The door opened and Mrs Higgins emerged.

''Ello, 'ello, what's all this 'ere?' she said.

Rosie pulled the door to again.

'We're thinking up larks, Mrs Higgins, Daddy and me.'

'Oh, I'm all for larks, Rosie, specially with Boots.'

'You're wanted at the moment by Mr Higgins for "Mother Kelly's Doorstep",' said Boots.

'Oh, I ain't missin' that,' said Mrs Higgins. 'I'll 'ave me larks later, Boots.' Away she went, pink and hearty with beer.

'Rosie,' said Boots, 'we don't want any fuss, do we? We don't want the party spoiled, do we?'

'Daddy, are you sure that man's in there? Oh, is that what you've been worrying about?'

'Listen, kitten, go through the back door. You'll find

721

there's a policeman out there. Ask him to come through to this cloakroom and to bring his colleague with him.'

'Oh, Lord,' breathed Rosie. 'I do want to shake hands, though.'

'All right, kitten. Speak to your Uncle Ned. I don't think he'll be dancing this one. Ask him to take you to the men's cloakroom, and then you can speak to the policeman. Uncle Ned will want to know what it's all about. Tell him to come and see me.'

'Good idea, Daddy, ever such a good idea,' said Rosie, and dashed to find Lizzy's husband.

Boots remained where he was, outside the door of the ladies' cloakroom. While the dance was on, the ladies would stay away, he hoped. He thought about Ponsonby. It would have been the easiest thing in the world for him to have slipped into the Institute this morning, while the caterers had the place opened up. And then to print 'OUT OF ORDER' in chalk on a cubicle door before locking himself in. He'd been prepared to stay there all day, waiting and hoping. Which meant it was Rosie he was after. A young girl. But how would he have known of her entry?

The toy periscope!

Boots knew that the wall dividing the two men's cubicles did not reach the ceiling. There was a foot-high gap. Exactly how disgusting could a sadistic man get?

Ned arrived.

'What's up, Boots?'

Boots told him. Ned took the details in with a soft whistle.

'Is the cubicle the one against the outside wall?' he asked. 'If so, and if it's like the men's, there'll be a window. A small one, but probably no smaller than the one he climbed through in the police station. The moment he suspects something, he'll be after worming his way out. That'll land him in the alley. Leave the alley to me, Boots. You stay here.'

Ned met two constables on his way through to the back door. He nodded to them. Rosie was beside the first policeman, looking a little pent-up.

'No worries, Rosie, all under control,' said Ned reassuringly and carried on to the alley. Rosie led the policemen to the cloakroom, where Boots stood with his back to the door. They could hear the band and the sounds of dancers filling the hall with rousing revelry.

Boots explained briefly but concisely to the uniformed men.

'Right, got you, sir,' said one constable, 'he might be in there or he might not.'

'He's in there,' said Boots. 'I'll prove it. Rosie love, go and talk to Annabelle.'

'Must I?' said Rosie.

'Off you go, kitten.'

Rosie went, but hardly knew how she was going to keep quiet about what was happening.

Boots opened the door of the cloakroom. The cubicles were on the left, facing him, a row of clothes pegs on the right. The policemen watched from the doorway. He opened the door of the vacant cubicle in noisy fashion, then stood back a little and kept his eyes on the top of the dividing wall. The gap was wide enough for a man as slim as Ponsonby to worm through, to fall headlong on to his victim, or, if no-one else was in the cloakroom, to catch her when she left the cubicle. He heard the faintest of sounds, and the next moment the square open head of a cardboard periscope appeared. It angled, and Boots knew its mirror could pick up a vision of head and shoulders, the head and shoulders of anyone using the seat. That would be enough. Ponsonby had waited all this time, certain of course that Rosie would be in his sights eventually. The mirror picked up nothing now. It turned, stayed still for a brief second and then vanished. Boots gestured to the policemen, then turned the handle of the door marked 'OUT OF ORDER'. It was locked, of course. The two policemen were in. There was the noise of a window frame vibrating. Facing each other, shoulders pointing at the cubicle door, the policeman hit it together, and with all the force they could muster. The door crashed open at a moment when the band and the dancers reached the noisy crescendo of the finale.

Ponsonby was standing on the closed lavatory seat, his socked feet on tiptoe, his head already through the window, eyes staring down at the shadowy figure of Ned, who had a dustbin lid in his hand. Ponsonby's elastic-sided boots, tied together, were hanging around his neck. The policemen hauled him down, pinned him and handcuffed him.

'Ruffians, ruffians!' hissed Mr Ponsonby. 'What a day, what a terrible day.'

Boots saw the intended instrument of Rosie's death, a shiny new leather bootlace. It was wound around the man's left wrist, one end loose and dangling.

Dear God, his Rosie.

The policemen took the demented man out through the back door, much to the gaping astonishment of a caterers' assistant.

'Boots dear, I don't want to complain,' said Aunt Victoria ten minutes later. The wedding party was resting on its laurels, using an interval to gather itself for the last number of the evening and waitresses bringing the last orders for the free drinks. Boots, Rosie and Ned alone knew what had taken place in the out-of-sight ladies' cloakroom.

'Complain? I'm sure you don't, Aunt Victoria,' said Boots, Rosie beside him.

'Well, not at Sammy's wedding, Boots dear,' said Aunt Victoria, 'but would you believe, someone's gone and smashed in that door that was out of order.'

'Yes, I think other people are talking about it,' said Boots. 'I put it down as the act of some desperate woman. Good idea for none of us to complain, Aunt Victoria. It'll only embarrass the woman, whoever she was.'

A hand squeezed his, and he looked down into the moistly shining eyes of Rosie.

She swallowed, then said, 'I think everyone's getting ready for the knees-up, Daddy.'

'Not before time,' said Boots.

In the flat above the shop in the New Kent Road, Henry Brannigan cleared his throat.

'It's been a real 'omely evenin' with yer, Madge,' he said.

'You've been very welcome, Henry,' said Madge. 'You're 'omely yerself, and I know you've got a soft 'eart under that waistcoat of yours.'

'I've been thinkin'.' He cleared his throat again. 'Yer a warm woman, Madge, and yer fond of kids. You'd like to 'ave that orphanage girl for yer own, but you can't because you ain't married. Well, Madge, I'll marry yer if yer'll 'ave me, and give yer a real 'ome where we can bring the girl up decent an' proper.'

Madge stared at him.

'Henry, you mean that, you'll marry me? After what I've been?'

'It ain't what you've been, Madge, it's what you are. But

I reckon we'd better leave Walworth an' make our 'ome in Peckham, say.'

'Henry, you can put a ring on me finger any time you like,' said Madge, 'and I won't let yer down, ever. And you can stay the night, if you want.'

'Your kind offer is appreciated, Madge, but I 'ope it won't offend yer if I say no. I'm a bit of what they call conservatyve, and I like doin' things proper. I'll wait till we're married, if that's all right with you.'

'Well, I'd just like to get married quick, Henry.'

'Real quick, Madge?'

'I'm a woman, Henry, and you're a man.'

The centre of the hall was clear, the band at the ready on the stage. Pianist, accordion-player and drummer all had grins on their faces. Susie and Sammy advanced amid loud and encouraging cheers. Sammy looked electric with anticipation. Susie, still in soft shimmering white, smiled.

'Ready, Sammy?'

'Ready, Susie.'

'Here we go, then,' said Susie, and hitched her gown and underskirt. Her silvery stockings flashed.

The band launched itself into the music everyone had been waiting for, and Susie and Sammy began to set the example for all to follow. The whole company provided the vocal accompaniment.

'Knees up, Mother Brown, knees up, Mother Brown,
Under the table you must go,
Ee-i-ee-i-addy-oh!
If I catch you bending, I'll saw your legs right off!
Don't get the breeze up,
Just get your knees up!
Knees up, Mother Brown!'

Up went Susie's knees, one after the other, and up went

Sammy's. Into the heart of the cockney ritual came their families, friends and neighbours. In came Will and Annie, Will willing to chance it, his young lady willing to be with him through thick and thin, to help him lay the ogre of asthma. In came Freddy and Cassie, Sally and Ronnie. In came Lizzy and Ned, Annabelle, Bobby, Emma and toddler Edward. In came Mr Finch, bringing Chinese Lady with him. In came Boots, Emily, Rosie and Tim, followed by Tommy, Vi, Aunt Victoria and Uncle Tom. In came Gertie and Bert and all the old friends and neighbours of Caulfield Place. Rachel and Mr Greenberg entered the lists, so did the office girls and, of course, Mr Brown with his beaming old Dutch, Mother Brown herself.

'*Knees up, Mother Brown, knees up, Mother Brown . . .*'

Skirts and dresses whisked and flew, the floor vibrated and frisky quips alternated with shrieks of laughter.

'Mind me eye, Susie.'

'I know where both your eyes are, Sammy Adams.'

'*Under the table you must go,*
Ee-i-ee-i-addy-oh!'

'Get 'em up, Annie.'

'What, higher, Will Brown?'

'Gawd save us, Annie, no higher, or I'll have an attack – a heart attack.'

'*If I catch you bending, I'll saw your legs right off!*'

''Ere, watch it, Cassie, yer nearly showin' yer knickers.'

'Freddy, did yer know Queen Mary wears royal blue ones? And you better find me cat after this, or me dad'll wallop yer.'

'*Don't get the breeze up, just get your knees up!*'

'My life, Rachel, vhat's all this?'

'Me remarkable legs, Eli. Get yours up, old love, it's Mother Brown's night.'

727

'*Knees up, Mother Brown!*'

'Get 'em up, Vi.'

'Not likely, Tommy Adams, there's two of me.'

'*Just get your knees up, knees up, Mother Brown!*'

'What's happened to your knees, Maisie? Where are they?'

'Where they should be, Edwin Finch, hidin' under me skirt.'

'*Under the table you must go, ee-i-ee-i-addy-oh!*'

'Steady as you go, Em.'

'I'll last out, Boots, you see if I don't.'

It went on and on, towards the time that heralded the finish of the celebrations, half-past ten. Faces shone and legs kicked. Susie was flushed, blue eyes entranced. Sammy was grinning all over. Boots was watching Emily, whose nervous energy showed in the sparkling glitter of her eyes. But it went from her, suddenly, just as the final notes were played, and there was a look of dismay on her face as she sagged. Boots was beside her at once, one arm around her, a strong arm. She looked up at him, her eyes dizzy.

'Thanks, lovey,' she said huskily, 'but I lasted out, didn't I? Hold me, Boots, it's been a lovely fam'ly weddin'.'

Aunt Victoria's voice was heard.

'I don't want to complain, but who let that mangy-lookin' cat in?'

A month later, Polly Simms, standing on the verandah of a rambling bungalow in Kenya, looked out over the brick-red earth and wondered why love would not go away.

THE END